[HAVE MERCY]

Have Mercy

G.P. Sandefjord

Cover art by GPS
Published by House of Jyze
ISBN 978-1-7376850-0-5
Library of Congress CIP Pending
www.HouseOfJyze.com

Poetry, letters, and other writings attributed in
this work to Valerie Mailloux Bando appear by
permission of their actual author, who wishes to
remain anonymous.

To R.M.T.

So it was not meant to be?

...to be overpowered by the deep love of another for oneself is the greatest victory possible in human relations, even if outwardly it seems like defeat. This, unfortunately, is difficult to consciously accept.

-- Bruno Bettelheim

Part One

[Shacking Up With Valerie]

Wednesday 1

St. Mary's Square. Splendid day. Hot. Before coming here I held hands in a "Human Chain to Protest the War" on Montgomery Street. An unexpected dividend: one of the protesters passing out armbands was a stunningly foxy Emp employee I've never seen before. Valerie Bando: small, black-haired, blue-miniskirted, sort of Mayan looking, I'd say, with voluptuous lips and honey-colored skin and an outasight body: extension 708 (as she kindly informed me in a delicious French accent, not Mayan -- as if I'd recognize Mayan -- when I asked for a way to get in touch with her again). I'll call tomorrow, with the excuse that I want to talk about the letter she told me she sent to "the Roach."

The second-biggest surprise of the day so far came when Nadine, sitting with me for twenty-five minutes in the dungeon during lunch hour and never taking off her shades despite my pleas that she do so, revealed why our balling last night was so confusing. In short, she's woefully inexperienced and ignorant about such matters. Imagine what she'll be like in the sack when she learns! I've happily agreed to tutor her on this at no extra charge. She told me she's rarely touched a male sexual part and never sucked one. "My momma would say it's bad," she laughed. She's never even tried positions other than the basic two (of which her being on top is not one). And last Friday with me was the first time she'd ever been "eaten." "What do you do with all the come?" she asked. "Swallow it?" (Yes, "come" was her word for her own sexual fluids.)

She also wanted to know whether it would be possible for Byron to determine she'd been getting it on with someone else.

"Not too likely -- unless you tell him."

"That's one thing I'm certainly not going to do!"

Her apparent lack of guilt or regret regarding the
Byron predicament -- and I'll note here she still
doesn't know his release date -- is infectious.

Last night we prowled North Beach boutiques, dined
at Tivoli, and saw "The Strawberry Statement" (in which
my very own presumptive ex, who by the way is still
going by Ciara Sandefjord, supposedly gets about three
seconds of screen time; but if that's true, I missed
her). And we talked a lot. Byron, I must say, sounds
more and more like a first-rate con man in another sense
of the term "con." Nadine admits now that not only did
he commandeer all her savings but he even had her
walking the streets for him -- and his wife's sister was
doing the same. (The acid test came when he wanted
Nadine to go down on "a filthy old man" for a paltry
five bucks, and she said no.) Oh yes, and Byron's
sister stole most of Nadine's clothes. Nadine put up
with all this out of fascination, fear, "my need to be
dominated" (as she explicitly said), and, perhaps, love.
Byron must be a wizard with words. Or with something.

What a trip, riding to work with Nadine at my back
on the 90 this morning, she leaning left as I leaned
right and vice versa during our swoop through Golden
Gate Park. At coffee, still wearing yesterday's
clothes, she looked a little rumpled and very, very
funky (though this didn't prevent other women from
looking good too).

And Jang? Still not a word from her.
Consequently, I'd say, my idea of writing a short daily
paragraph or two for her has run seriously aground. I
do have a manila envelope in my bag containing several
early installments, but will I ever mail it? I'm
starting to think maybe not.

Thursday 2

Whew. Hot. Again. From today's perch in St.

[Shacking Up with Valerie]

Mary's Square I can't see the Equitable time/temp
flasher, but I'm sure it must read at least eighty-five.
Maybe ninety.

    Moments ago an urge arose to squeeze out a few
sentences about the park itself, but when life's going
really well, jotting down particulars on that uncommon
condition must come first (it's a law of journalism of
the personal type). What brought me to the park today,
for example, wasn't its verdant splendor (however rigged
it may seem with the parking garage "parked" right
beneath it), but the chance of running into Valerie
Bando here. I missed her, though, because lunch with
Nadine at the Owl'N Pussycat took longer than expected,
and then before hitting the park I checked out all three
foot entrances to the Emp mausoleum for stacks of the
Imp, curious to see how my articles looked in print.
But the bundles hadn't arrived yet.

    I noticed a slight aberration in Nadine's walk
today. She attributed it to the huge vegetarian meal we
downed last night -- and more seriously to her pussy
rash which she thinks was aggravated by our balling
Friday night on her living-room floor.

    -- But it's too hot to go on. Sweat glues my
wrists to these pages and stings as it drips down from
my brows into my eyes.
                      *   *

    This is better. Lolling now in a red canvas camp
chair in the shade of an old gnarly tree in Emp's
central plaza. "In the Shade of an Old Gnarly Tree" --
I like it! This is the place where the noontime rock
concert was to be held back before Lee Krause, in fear
of the mad Emp bomber, canceled it. This is also the
stillness at the center of the clattering storm: the
typewriters, the keypunch machines, the Dupe presses.
At the moment no one else is out here except me.
Occasionally someone cuts through on the way from the
Pine Street wing to the California Street wing or vice
versa, and I flash a rueful smile and shrug, as if to
say I don't know how I rated this cushy job either.
Soon the three o'clock bell will ring and I'll take

[Have Mercy]

Nadine her bottle of Sprite.

*   *

Khaki, Nadine's boss, a gray, unsmiling battlewagon
of an ex-military woman with just the right first name,
keeps a whistle on a string around her neck and when
it's time for "her" girls to take a break she blows it.
That's just how she is. So it came as no surprise today
when, after Nadine got back a few minutes late from
lunch for the second day in a row, Khaki told her to
tell me she "doesn't rub elbows with the big wheels and
not have any obligations" -- like me supposedly.
Actually Nadine, as a supervisor, has a lot more
official authority than I do. But as the head honcho's
speechwriter I do have more clout, yeah. I could say,
"Mr. Roach, sir, fire that Khaki, she's a tyrant," and
he would pick up the phone and do it. (Oh sure.)

Brother Rob arrived yesterday after hitching up
from "that hellhole" Phoenix. He seems to have survived
unscathed his trip across the western two-thirds of the
country via Route 66, which understandably had Mother
"frightened to death" for him. The only concession he
made was to pin his hair up beneath his hat while on the
road in certain ultra-reactionary areas resembling those
in "Easy Rider." -- And he's wowed by the view at 1616.
This morning he was already up and gazing out at it when
I emerged from my room. "It's so white!" he cried.
"It's like a Mediterranean city at sunrise!" Not that
he's ever seen a Mediterranean city except in photos or
on TV or in the movies -- as he'd be the first to admit
-- but the coastal mountains, the Marin ocean shoreline,
the bridge, the park, the little Inner Sunset village
down below with the twin church steeples poking up, the
big hill looming so majestically above 1616 -- "You
chose well, Glen! Nice goin'!"

Jud North, as a gesture of thanks for our
hospitality, invited all of us to dinner last night at
Joy, the new vegetarian restaurant out near Ocean Beach.
Eight strong we piled into the L.C., and I felt like the
group's honorary house father. Dinner lasted from seven
until well after ten owing to the restaurant's

"informality." The food, praise be, was edible. I had
miso fried rice, apple juice (super-thick and chunky,
as if it had just been stomped out by bare feet with
lots of space between the toes), and a mysterious
dessert called Banana Zap. Sister Barb's "true hippie"
friend Clay, who's been staying with us sporadically of
late (and with her in her bed even more sporadically) --
Clay, I say, restored our spirits whenever they waned:
his offbeat wit was never sharper. He also led group
yoga exercises and formed us into a kind of vespers ring
around the table to ward off ever deepening hunger pangs
as the hours rolled by.

And I should note this: owning a new vehicle poses
certain problems I hadn't anticipated. Shortly before
noon Rob called wondering whether he and his Gatewood
friend Don, who arrived in town by bus from L.A. late
last night (they had split up on the road in New Mexico;
now they'll both be crashing in our living room for a
couple of weeks before Don moves on to Portland) -- Rob,
I say, was wondering whether they could use the L.C. for
a jaunt to the beach. I postponed making a policy
decision by telling him I'd rather not have anyone drive
it until I can confer in depth with that person,
preferably while taking it out for a test spin. It's
scarcely broken in, after all, and I already know it has
some idiosyncrasies which must be respected. Whether
I'll want to make it "free wheels" as others have made
their real estate "free land" in our hang-loose era is a
ticklish question. -- And besides, the N Judah line
that runs east-west two blocks down the hill from the
house goes straight to the very beach Rob and Don were
interested in. Rob hadn't realized this.

*

Nadine just came by again. With Roy taking the day
off and Jerry working upstairs in Sales Promo this
afternoon and the dungeon door closed, we warily played
with each other behind the high cabinets and machinery-
cluttered A-V table like lust-crazed teenagers in the
den after the fossils have gone to bed. She had just
dropped a "red." She let me know it's possible Byron's

9

release will come tomorrow or even tonight. She talks
about it freely, but if our growing attachment threatens
her feeling for him, she shows little sign of it. Maybe
this is because she knows that if she did, I'd have to
give her up. But I doubt it.

An intriguing night ahead: dinner with my new
acquaintance Valerie from the "Human Chain" (ostensibly
to talk about the letter she wrote to Roach on behalf of
the Emp Peace Committee) and then "The Tempest" with Pam
Wineberry, who called last night saying she had an extra
ticket available. She teaches acting at ACT and knows
Ciara and has heard about me from her -- "only good
things," she swears. She's an extroverted, loud,
"brassy" drama type probably in her late thirties who's
helping Jerry with "M for M." ---

Friday 3
     Such a gorgeous morning. Boots and shirt off, I
bask on the sundeck at 1616 glorying in another wild and
wondrous night. The morning Chronicle is heaped in a
pile on the gravel at my side. Chopper sniffs at a
grapevine skeleton that looks something like a 3-D
diagram of a human lung (I bought the grapes in a moment
of elation this morning when for the first time I
spotted the Aztec thunderbird, logo for Chavez's union,
on a box in the Ninth & Kirkham Market).
     Emp's closed today, I should note, because
tomorrow's the Fourth. Hallelujah! I mean, huzzah for
the Empire! May it soon crack itself up for good! (And
I mean "crack up" in both senses if not more.)
     A moment ago I caught a glimpse, oblique, through
the window behind me, of sister Barb in her blue
nightgown rising wraithlike from bed (earlier while she
was in the bathroom I snuck a small bunch of grapes and
a plum over to her pillow in the "yellow room"). Also,
about sixty degrees farther to the left, the hands and
forearms of the retired man who lives next door, name of
O'Connor, gripping the Chronicle as his TV flickers, can
be seen through his dining-room window a story and a

10

half down; the rest of him is not visible.

Now Rob pokes his head out the sundeck door. "It's not very often you see clouds like this in the summer, is it?" He still has that strong meteorological streak but it's been refashioned at one end of the spectrum into a love of poetry and at the other into interest in another kind of weatherman. (Yeah, those clouds -- high, ragged, like scuffed snow -- are rare at this time of year, I tell him. But then I have to admit I'm not really all that sure.)

It's already so warm my "man things" (Nadine's lingo) droop heavily and damply because I'm sans underwear and my crotch itches inside the thick wool navy bells owing to last night's sexual dousings -- so I'll go rinse them off and change into some shorts and come right back.

*

Now the mowers have started up and our faucets just gurgle thirstily in the bathroom and kitchen when you try to turn them on -- spouting no water at all -- because so many people higher up the hill are watering their lawns in this unusual early-summer heat wave, and therefore no genital rinse-off is possible for me or anyone else down here lacking bottled water or a rain barrel. Meanwhile I discover I'm more than a little lead-lidded and loggy from lack of sleep.

So, last night. Something of a miracle I'd say. In less than a day I met and slept with and fell hard for the joltingly sexy nineteen-year-old French-Eurasian Valerie Bando (nee Mailloux) (rhymes with "bayou").

So flabbergasted was I by everything about her and then by her readiness to sleep with me so soon, and the way she showed it, and also by the presence of another person, small but not insignificant, in the bedroom with us, that I was rendered impotent for a good part of the night. It was the first time a woman has ever told me while balling, "You should try to relax a little." Thankfully she turned out to be very understanding and patient.

First dinner at Tommy's Joynt on Geary near the

Unitarian Church. We chowed down on buffalo burgers
and talked mostly politics and basic get-acquainted
stuff. Very quickly she had me fumbling and stuttering
like a schoolboy, and doubly so after she doffed her
shades for the first time (she'd also been wearing them
in the "Human Chain") to reveal riveting dark sultry and
impossibly beautiful Asian-looking eyes. Then a few
hours later I was astonished when I called her from a
bar near ACT, after seeing "The Tempest" with Pam, to
learn whether she'd be leaving town for the weekend (as
she'd said at dinner she might); and now she confirmed
she would be, yes, unfortunately, and very early in the
morning, but to compensate she invited me to come over
immediately. Pam, I'm pleased to say, was understanding
about my sudden urgent need to depart (and one of her
ACT friends we were sitting with kindly volunteered to
give her a lift home).

    So alluring was this Valerie when I arrived that I
became extremely cautious: I didn't want to say or do
anything to mess things up. ---
*

    (Chaos reigns on the sundeck! So never mind the
chronological tale. Scattershot notes instead.)
    ** She's such a knockout. (Did I not already
say?) At work she wears her hair parted in the middle
and rolled into a tight bun at the back of her head ("I
want people to be able to identify with me"), but when
released at home it cascades thick and jet-black almost
to her waist. And her body. Oh lord. A dancer or
gymnast's body (she's had considerable training in both)
but with very fine breasts ("from my father," she
chuckles, "like the nose"). And narrow hips and an
irresistibly perky little tilted-up super-firm ass.
Legs so strong and shapely, right there, all the way to
the ground. And her face...hail that perfect oval
shape, those impressive high cheekbones and fleshy full
and wide lips to go with the hawklike "Mayan" nose and
the electrifying eyes. Mesmerize me O Valerie! Or just
lay it out like this: ravishing "erotic exotic" this
girl. It's a fact too, not just aesthetics, since she's

12

three-fourths French and one-fourth Chinese and also
still a girl for real (in some ways) at nineteen. And
small, no more than five-two. Skin smooth and close to
flawless and warm mmm smells so good and it turns out --
ha -- only slightly more honey color than my own. She
likes to tan! In jeans or a mini (all that I've seen
her in), oh my goodness. Naked? Have mercy! (And she
has serious slightly off-white bikini shadows.)

    ** Her family. Intriguing -- fantastic even. Her
grandfather was a high-ranking official in French
colonial "Indochine" (as she calls Indochina) and her
father's a lawyer/journalist widely known for his
writings in France who also was in the French foreign
service. "He was a draft-dodger back then. He went to
Indochine during World War II and to France when the
Indochine war broke out. He met my mother at a dance
hall in Saigon. For my whole life that war has been
raging inside me!" She has two brothers, one married
and living in S.F. (he's three years older, just like me
and Barb) and one on the U.S. East Coast, and a half-
brother and half-sister residing in other countries.
Valerie herself was conceived in Saigon, born in Orleans
(Joan of Arc turf), lived in palaces "with lots of black
servants" during her father's foreign-service postings
in Senegal and Ivory Coast when she was between three
and five, then returned to Orleans where she attended a
very good boarding school, or maybe more than one, until
she was fourteen.

    ** Her parents divorced when she was six or seven.
"It was very, very nasty, more nasty than I can tell
you or even can bear to think about." Within a year her
mother was forced out of France and split to California,
married an older Chinese man for his papers, opened a
restaurant in a small town called Holton outside
Sacramento. At fourteen Valerie joined her mother in
Holton, supposedly to study English for a year before
returning to France.

    ** But she never did return. Instead she married
Jim Bando, a Sacramentan and a mongrel white dude, much
the same ethnic mix as me but quite a bit shorter and

just two years my junior. At the time he was a college
dropout and a drifter trying to stay one step ahead of
the draft, working for the local phone company and doing
lots of drugs. They eloped on her sixteenth birthday
(she was pregnant at the time) (she did say both of her
parents "always encouraged me to be independent") and
they moved to San Francisco, which she liked because it
reminded her of Paris. Jim found a new job as a
computer programmer and took to peddling coke on the
side to pay for his own increasingly heavy drug trip;
Valerie attended Galileo High School in North Beach,
dropped out to give birth, mothered their son Danny and
did the housewife thing for a while, got her GED,
attended City College for a semester (missed becoming a
possible student of mine there by one year), dropped out
"because it was even worse than Holton High School."
And: some two years after the fact Jim admitted he'd
gotten her pregnant intentionally as a way to avoid the
draft, which is to say: their story is somewhat like
mine with Ciara (except in our case Ciara faked the
pregnancy, among other differences) -- and both nuptial
stories went down at right about the same time.
     ** V&J's marriage "was a disaster from the start"
and by the time she turned nineteen this past April it
had fallen apart (it was her idea that they divorce) and
in fact they're still going through the process now,
with the end only a few weeks away if all goes well.
"He's schizo," she says, "but I didn't see it at first.
He kept it well hidden." Almost every night for three
years they had "sauvage" arguments "that everybody on
the block could hear" and several times he suggested she
ought to kill herself -- once even handed her his gun to
do it with (he packs heat to protect himself during drug
deals) (shades of Byron!). He also liked to threaten
her with knives he stashed in various places, including
in the headboard of the bed where she and I were
sleeping last night. And: he's hot-tempered ("even
worse than me," says Valerie) and since the separation
he's tried to break into their Dolores Street apartment
twice, "but not in the past few weeks."

[Shacking Up with Valerie]

(At seven this morning he called as I lay in what
had been their marriage bed. "He's checking up on me
again," she groaned. Her tone as she talked with him in
another room about divorce and lawyers and childcare and
the like was distant, cold, wary, and wearily
exasperated, and yet her fetching accent -- surprise! --
was always the same.)

    ** Valerie's politics? Militant liberal-left,
antiwar, humanist, social-democratic, radical --
somewhere in there. On this score, as on so many
others, we seem to have few disagreements. She puts in
enormous amounts of time working as a volunteer for the
Downtown Peace Coalition. She also writes for the Emp
Imp; in fact, she and I, although unknown to each other,
were the two main contributors to this week's non-issue
(publication's been postponed until next week). (Was
this liaison of ours meant to be or what?)

    And: she's a member of a local women's-lib group.
The cause is righteous, says she, but the particular
group she's in is largely a waste of time. "Men need to
be liberated too," she declared. "These women don't see
the bigger picture." (At Tommy's Joynt she made a point
of picking up our tray and carrying it to the table.
Therefore this morning I made up the bed. She seemed
surprised. Then she added a few finishing touches,
finding my effort less than wholly up to snuff.)

    ** Okay, culture. From her elite early education
she clearly knows a lot, but right now she feels
politics are more important than reupping in college.
She smokes weed "socially" (much like me, sounds like)
and isn't at all into harder stuff. Nor does she go for
the natural-food or back-to-the-country trips. She
didn't know about the upcoming Hare Krishna parade which
everyone's gaga about at New Age in the Inner Sunset.
When I filled her in on it, her faintly acid reply was
something like, "A lot of people will enjoy that."

    And she writes poetry -- "I just jot down what I'm
feeling, I'm not critical about what comes out" -- loves
to sketch and paint and decorate interiors and cook and
make clothes. She's obviously lavished a great deal of

15

[Have Mercy]

loving care on her apartment: rich drapes, color
collages and paintings, intricate mobiles -- all of them
her own creations. But she's done little reading since
she left school. "I just don't have time for it." (Her
estimate of what she learned from her two years of high
school in the U.S.: "Zero. Less than zero.")

Here's a poem she gave me, written on the spot in
under a minute (shades of Lisa!):
>   purple passions
>   red compassions
>   happiness is
>   a small green corner by
>   just one cloud in the blue high
>   one friend is all you need
>   someone with whom
>   sharing
>   understanding
>   will signify
>   always rising
>   enlightening....

That "happiness is" cliche, she said herself later, was
a "misstep but it helped open a new path." Parallel
placement of "passions" and "compassions" does it for me
all by itself. And I like the odd ending.

** And: she's got energy to burn. Jumpin'
Jehoshaphat! Throws herself into whatever she does,
whether it be passing out leaflets, pushing a door open,
or shifting over a few inches in bed. On her gymnastics
team in high school, both in France and here, she
practiced "twice as long as everyone else and twice as
hard too. That's how I like to do it."

** Seems to be a good mother: conscientious but
not too strict. She changed Danny's diapers, fed him,
taught him new words, played with him -- all while
chatting breezily with me. I like! Shows no sign of
excessive dependency on him. (And no coy babytalk.
Didn't object at all to his seeing me naked in bed with
his mother. Neither did our balling in front of him
appear to trouble her -- but it did trouble me, I'll
admit, even though at all times we were either in the

16

dark or under the covers or both.)

    ** In bed...well, here it's hard to say. With Danny raising a ruckus about two feet away every time I moved just slightly or emitted an "Ooh yeah like that" I wasn't in the best frame of mind for balling, even though we did little else -- if extended foreplay counts as balling -- between two and six a.m. (she got no sleep at all and then went off for the weekend). She didn't hesitate to touch me, suck me, fuck me. It's too early to tell about orgasms. She likes to be held, likes to snuggle, doesn't like kissing as much as I'd like her to like it (but those fabulous lips, how can I resist?).

    ** She intimated there are other men in her life and they've been causing her problems. Mentioned that in her experience most men like talking about commitments more than actually making them. "Isn't this much bet-tare?" she cooed when we moved past the retrograde makeout stage in the living room and got all our clothes off and ourselves into bed in the bedroom. That retro stage on the couch ended quickly, by the way, when she said after a few minutes of exploratory kisses, "why don't I just take this off," referring to the soft red V-necked sweater above her jeans, revealing when she did so nothing but bare skin underneath.

    ** Some language difficulties. She often talks fast and intense, sometimes in machine-gun bursts, and in that same accent, of course, and with strange word order at times and the occasional untranslated French word. (She always carries a well-thumbed two-way French/English dictionary in her purse "but I hate to let anyone see me using it.") All night we were asking each other to repeat things. (She also mutters and mumbles at least as much as I do.)

    ** Once I asked her what she was thinking about. "I'm trying to identify my feelings for you," she said with a frown. Her only direct compliment all night was to say, "You're very pleasant" (pleasingly pronounced French style: 'pleez-AHNT'). Another time she remarked upon how "strange" I was and added a moment later: "I think you're a new kind of American man for me."

[Have Mercy]

   ** My feelings for her? Easy! I'm a believer!
Hesitations here and there of course, but most can be
put down to her age; to the long-running marital battles
and the recent and ongoing, and now crescendoing, run-up
to divorce; to her lingering antipathy to some aspects
of American culture (e.g., "excessive cheeriness,"
sloppiness, funk). She can be extremely intense and
serious: it's not always easy to get her to laugh. She
sometimes talks quite nervously, with quick, uncertain
smiles. She admits she finds it hard to trust men.
Occasionally her eyes and brow cloud over and it becomes
obvious her mind is drifting. "Many things are
bothering me," she acknowledged. Just what she meant by
this she didn't say (nor did I press her to -- yet).
   ** In a nutshell: she looks to be up there in
Jang's class. They're a lot alike in a number of ways.
In size, body configuration (other than breasts),
vitality (energy level and physicality), intelligence,
strong arts interest -- in all these respects and many
others they could almost be sisters. And: Valerie
clearly has some qualities Jang lacks: candor, for
instance, directness, political involvement, an up-to-
date worldview -- those just for starters.
   (And I'll note here Jang's making it a whole lot
easier for me to get interested in other women. If she
were writing me loving letters, things might be much
different. -- Or would they? I guess I don't really
know. But I do know I've stumbled upon a true contender
in Valerie (she dislikes "Val"). And to think that for
the past six months this woman -- teenybopper! -- has
been working on my floor of the Emp Life building in the
other wing! But I'm sure I never saw her before,
because if I had I would've gone after her in a blink.)
   (The only words I have from Jang so far, by the
way, came in just yesterday and I didn't see them until
this morning.
      After the sweating hours, resting under
      the trees. Do you play basketball and
      swim in the evenings? Healthy? Blue
      ocean, blue sky. Love. Jang.

This on a lame "Surfing at Waikiki" postcard.)
     ** So -- Valerie. On the outside of her hallway
entrance door she's hung a large poster showing upraised
index and middle fingers split into a V-sign
superimposed on a peace sign -- exactly the same image I
have in decal form on the L.C. and the 90. She says she
put the poster up for three reasons: her antiwar stance
is one, to be sure, but also the "V" is for victory in
gaining her separation from Jim and at the same time it
stands for -- Valerie! I really liked the proud and
mischievous spirit with which she told me this.
     ** And regarding the Emp Imp, oddly enough one of
the V-girl's contributions to the previous issue dealt
with a matter which happened to be in dispute between
Barb and me at the time. To wit: is it wrong to give
someone who's romantically interested in you "false"
hope? Not at all, her short free-form poem declares,
for the simple reason that in such circumstances there's
no such thing as "false" hope. If you can give someone
romantic hope you give them a rare gift. What that
person makes of it is up to him or her. And I can
paraphrase the poem with some confidence now because I
clipped it at the time and looked at it again this
morning. (I had intended to show it to Barb but never
did -- probably because she'd just scoff at it anyway.)
                    *   *
     (Five hours later, sunburned, living room.)
     How things can change in a day! Valerie has so
bedazzled me I've lost all interest in calling Nadine.
Lovely doe-eyed Nadine (but you have to work very hard
to see the actual eyes behind the big white-framed near-
opaque shades she always wears, indoors or out).
     And other things have happened:
     ** Denise called around noon -- she wanted to talk
with Barb, not me. And she did just that, for an hour
or more. (She's the one the "false hope" dispute was
about. Barb thought I encouraged her when I knew things
couldn't possibly work out between us, but that's simply
not true. To me there always seemed to be a chance for
us -- a good chance -- until after a couple of months

19

there suddenly didn't. And that's when things ended.)
Denise also invited Barb and Rob and Don to go swimming
with her this afternoon in Sausalito, but then an hour
later she called back to renege on the deal -- and to
announce she'd met Richard Brautigan at lunch and
accepted a date with him for tomorrow.

    ** The first dent has mysteriously appeared on the
L.C., left rear panel. I know I shouldn't mind -- dents
on cars like scars on people just prove the bearer has
been around -- but it turns out I do mind. -- Or I did.
Now it suddenly seems I don't anymore. Do I? At least
not as much as I thought I did at first.

    ** Pam Wineberry's a gas. We got mildly zonked in
the L.C. last night on the way downtown and then rather
more righteously zonked while parked outside ACT. After
the play she began dropping blatant hints about her
availability and sang the praises of stoned sex. So say
she's a raunchy gas. But Valerie intervened.

         *   *

    So tired. My plan for tonight is to read until I
fall asleep. If Nadine calls, as she said she might --
depending on her parents' plans and Byron's status --
I'll probably put off seeing her until tomorrow.

    I have a hunch Valerie (who's in Tahoe right now
with her mother and her S.F. brother and some others --
a hunch that Valerie will be the one. No, that's
ridiculous. There's something very important I don't
know. Does she have a talent for loving? Jang has it
in abundance, and I mean both emotionally and sexually
-- not to mention emotionally-sexually. No doubt
that's a major reason why I've stuck by her for almost
six years now -- though off and on, true -- and despite
her nearly continuous display of some of the quirkiest
behavior ever observed on this hyper-quirky planet.

         *

    And there's this. I'm really ticked at Barb.
Earlier I had told Rob that starting in August I'd be
asking him to pay a small portion of the rent. Now Barb
has objected on his behalf without even checking with
him first. She insists I'm expecting too much and I

20

ought to pony up the full rent for August myself. She's willing to help Rob as much as she can, given her scanty income from jewelry making; but "since you have all that money saved up" she feels I should be Rob's major support. After all these months of her living mostly off my subsidy, she feels Rob should be able to do the same. What gargantuan gall!

I may carry the whole load for August anyway, and even beyond that if necessary (i.e., if Rob can't get the funds from home as part of his college money, as he's expecting to do and probably will do), but I deeply resent the snooty rectitudinous stance Barb's taking on this. And it's far from the first time she's done something along these lines during her stay here. who is she to be telling me over and over what's the right way to live, whom I should live with, how I should love and how bad and immoral I am for not following her program for me down to the very last codicil? why can't she realize what my upcoming "retirement" means to me -- that I've been struggling to save money for almost two years so I could have a chance to work full-time on my own stuff -- my life's work!

Saturday 4

Independence Day.

We're caught under the ragged streaming edge (like huge flickering gray horizontal flames) of today's fogbank. Rob and Don are peering out the two north-facing living-room windows, trying to spot American flags flapping in the wind down in the Judah gulch. So far they haven't espied a single one.

Over the din of the rock band Chicago (Don's choice) on the stereo I just told Valerie I'll be arriving in an hour -- and the taste of Nadine's lipstick is still lingering on my tongue. We got together last night after all. And before leaving here this noon she made herself up very carefully in case she'd find Byron waiting for her at home. We had a fine time over those sixteen hours or so, even though I conked out from exhaustion before midnight.

We sat in the last row of the balcony to see "The Landlord," a comedy about a young honky dude who gets a spade chick pregnant while her old man's in jail. When he gets out of jail he flies into a rage, nearly slices the honky in half with a hatchet, and then goes mad. Heavy, baby! -- And especially considering certain relevant facts in our own personal lives, Nadine's and mine. But we got through it all right. We were both a little ripped (strolling down Polk Street passing a joint back and forth, though mostly I passed and she toked), and Nadine was in a funny lighthearted mood.

"Is it all right to keep on seeing you," she asked, "even though I'm committed to someone else?"

"Sure it is," I answered. "God only knows what will come of it, though."

We have such a good time together, completely laid-back. Our social speeds are just about the same. But now having met Valerie, the truth is I hope Byron comes on strong with Nadine when he's released (almost certainly this coming week). It would greatly simplify what threatens to develop into yet another embarrassing and painful and this time possibly dangerous emotional mess. For years I've told myself I could hack through the entanglements of the crazy kind of love life I've been caught up in for much of this period no matter how complicated they might become. This may turn out to be the moment of truth for that dubious notion. And if the moment doesn't come from one direction, it might well come from another.

*   *

Valerie's kitchen. She's getting Danny ready for bed. "Everyone says he looks like me, but I can't see it. Sometimes I can't even believe he's part of my life." I hear her murmuring to him in her captivating accent as light classical music plays. She's such a delight! Waiflike mama -- except she's way too physically robust to be described as waiflike. "Gamine" they called her in France, but that doesn't seem right either. Picture her in tight jeans and shaggy

secondhand mixed-furs jacket and shades, this kid's
riding her shoulders, she's rushing up and down hills,
block after block, firecrackers bursting all around; and
she's bouncing along, she's imperturbable, she's
ravishing and vivacious, she has hindquarter action it's
hard to rip your eyes from, she's like a hip version of
an Olympic teenybopper gymnast set loose in the City of
Love or -- more to the point -- Baghdad by the Bay. If
not for the kid's presence she could literally be doing
cartwheels and flips: and in fact she likes to do
exactly those things just to blow off energy: and last
night in her kitchen and hallway she showed me exactly
how she does this. Backward and forward flips! walking
all the way to the front door and back on her hands as
we casually talked! Incredible!

    And today I learned a few new things about her
family. For one, her French grandfather wasn't merely a
"high-ranking official" in Vietnam; he was in fact the
colonial governor there for several years and also,
earlier, the mayor of Saigon. Back in Orleans everybody
calls him "the Governor." For another, Valerie's mother
was a celebrated beauty who came from a very poor family
in Macau -- she was one of nine children -- and was
forced into prostitution at an early age. Only through
her smarts and some serious risk-taking that involved
smuggling money into Saigon for Belgian bankers from
Hong Kong did she manage to escape the brothel. "So you
can see," says the cross-cultural and cross-racial
daughter of parents from the most widely separated of
social classes imaginable, "why sometimes I might be a
little schizo myself."

    -- The immediate question, however, is this:
should Danny be laid down for the night in the bedroom
or the living room? Either way's fine with me, I say.
we confer. We mull. Finally we decide on the bedroom.
We'll move him to the living room later.

Sunday 5
    Sprawled on Valerie's maroon rug -- writing by the

light of a white orb the size of a fortune-teller's ball
encased in a floor-level transparent red plastic cube.
It must be a French kind of thing, would be my guess.

Danny and I are once again feeling each other out.
We play hide-and-seek behind his mother's high-backed,
colorfully upholstered (by her) dining-room chairs (her
favorite colors are purple and orange and so are these
chairs and so's the TV, a 21-incher which she hand-
painted). He giggles, Danny does, but not quite loudly
enough, for I doubt she can hear him in the next room.
I want her to know he and I are getting along quite well
now -- certainly a lot better than before when he burst
into tears at the sight of me. So how about a
stentorian giggle, Danny boy?

Suddenly, just now, he picks up the Fourth of July
card I made for him and his mom and throws it at me.
Hard. It hits me in the face, narrowly missing my left
eye. I'm tempted to admonish him, but instead I toss
the card high in the air and we both laugh as it
flutters crazily to the floor like a drunken butterfly.
Yee-hee! Lookie there! -- And I say that's the way to
do it: join in the kid's experience. Try to keep that
firmly in mind, Glen. (Danny himself forgot about the
card a moment later. My cheek still stings.)

Somehow after winding down today's tortuous path
(through lush valleys, over icy precipices) we've
arrived at the point where I'll be staying on here for a
while. Not moving in but sort of hanging out full-time.
Shacking up, let's say. We're both more than a bit
surprised, no question, and yet we're acting as if
little has changed. "Just how it is now." In fact she
doesn't care too much for the term "shacking up"
because, as she explained, it reminds her of "Of Mice
and Men" which was required reading in her English class
at Holton High School and she hated it. In any case we
agreed beforehand -- and I'm pleased to say she's the
one who brought this up and insisted on it -- we're both
to remain "free," meaning not just to come and go as we
wish, but to see others if we want and to end this new
living arrangement at any time. There are no

obligations; it's an "experiment"; we're both grown-up people well aware of the complexities of adult life. This nineteen-year-old and me, eight and a half years her senior -- i.e., I've been walking this earth almost half again as long (and almost always right side up), and she about thirteen inches shorter and roughly half my weight and the apple of a whole lot of eyes wherever she goes, as I've not failed to notice right from the start: this the shacked-up "we" now constituted.

God only knows what we're getting into. How about it, fortune-teller's ball, are good things in store for us?

This extraordinary young mother's achingly sweet smile could melt an iceberg but I do wish, I really do wish I could make it appear a little more often and didn't have to work quite so hard to coax it out.

2

Monday 6

Flux. Already, just one day in, I'm beginning to feel uneasy about the new life with Valerie. This has nothing to do with my relations with Jang or Nadine or Ciara or anyone else (certainly not Denise). It's Valerie herself. There's something missing in her way of shacking up with a man. In a word, it's...joy. Her face is so often a study in gloom, melancholy, despondency, despair. She smiles wondrously upon occasion, but those occasions don't arise anywhere near often enough for me. And when they do, I usually have little idea of why they do.

To a degree she's aware of all this. Her childhood was largely, as she says, melancholic. She was almost always locked away in a boarding school and never had a loving family around her. She never learned how to express "positive feelings": this is her excuse for how poorly she does at showing me she desires and/or enjoys my presence. And then this tendency was exacerbated by her marriage, which, after the first year, seems to have become a singularly joyless union. And, to make things worse, the joylessness spread to sex. She grew to hate having sex with her husband. She felt he treated her as the quintessential sex object. Among other things, he forced her to submit too soon to a "resumption of relations" after Danny's birth, and consequently it took the better part of a year for her stitches to heal, and each and every sexual act during that time -- and apparently there were a great many -- was painful for her (and so they often switched to anal).

This may help explain why she seems almost without passion in sex, why we can't find much of a groove or a rhythm. I offered an accommodation: I wouldn't press her on the matter of sex. Better, I suggested, not to push it too hard when she's not fully involved. Should we maybe try to hold back until she could be more into it? To my surprise -- shock almost -- she said she thought this might be a good idea.

For sure it's an attitude toward sex that's about as far as possible from those of most of the other women I've been with lately: Nadine, Winnie, Jill, Celeste, and most of all, as always, Jang. (Denise would again be the exception.)

Last night in bed Valerie put my good intentions to the test: on our first night of shacking up -- our wedding night in a shacking sense -- she showed absolutely no sexual interest. It was hard for me not to feel rejected, unloved, unattractive, despite what I knew about her and despite the fact that I was being hoist on my own petard (that sounds sort of sexual right there). I felt a bit...well...duped. Chumped. Out of sympathy and perhaps inchoate love I've permitted this marvelous but also perplexing young girl to maneuver me into gelding myself -- and before we've known each other five full days!

*　　　*

Still at my dungeon desk, it's now close to noon, and in a few minutes Nadine and I will be meeting for lunch. "You've been avoiding me," she complained on the phone. Saturday she twice came looking for me at

[Shacking Up with Valerie]

Funston and then once more yesterday, leaving a note I
found on my pillow after racing home through heavy fog
early this morning so I could change into work clothes.
"I love you," it said. Or rather, to be exact: "I still
love you." Also awaiting me to look over was another
stack of Byron's drawings she had picked up at San Bruno
that very afternoon. For some reason they're delaying
his release, it seems, despite all the silent pleas I've
recently been sending their way. Byron, pal, I've been
holding up your end too long here. I'm counting on you
to come roaring back onto the streets and to reassume
your accustomed role with Nadine.

I plan to tell her the truth, whole, nothing but,
and as gently as I can.

*   *

Saturday in Golden Gate Park Valerie and I watched
the Mime Troupe put on the "world premiere" of "The
Independent Female, or, A Man Has His Pride." The rest
of my own ever-changing Funston troupe was there as
well. Barb, who's now informed me she'll soon be moving
out into a place of her own, gave Valerie a particularly
acrimonious once-over. As a result I decided not to
take Valerie to Funston afterwards, even though it was
just five or six blocks away; instead we went to see
"Woodstock" at a theater on Market Street (joints were
being openly passed virtually everywhere as rent-a-cops
prowled the aisles; one of the cops drew a round of
cheers and raucous applause for accepting a toke and
blowing a huge plume of smoke ceilingward, causing a
cloudlike shadow to cross the screen just as Jimi
Hendrix's rendition of "The Star Spangled Banner" was
reaching its high note: "la-and of the free-e-EEE...").

Yesterday Valerie and I waited at Ocean Beach with
hundreds of others for the creaking and teetering Hare
Krishna juggernauts, several stories tall and colorfully
decorated, to roll up on their great wooden wheels as
the parade reached its endpoint. We underwent something
of a crisis in which she turned grim and glum and told
me -- she who all but tackled me and hauled me into her
bedroom on the first night -- "you've been going too

27

fast." I thought it might mean we were washed up almost
before we'd even gotten wet. But last night she flip-
flopped again and confirmed the "shacking-up experiment"
was still on. "I'm very spontaneous," she explained,
when I pointed out a few glaring contradictions.

Tuesday 7

> Ten or Twenty Things She Said to Me
> -- As recalled on the steps of
> The Bank of America, Montgomery and
> California, as rush-hour traffic roars by.

1. "I can't believe you exist."
2. "I've come three times already. You mean you
didn't know?"
3. "He said, 'I can't bear the thought of your
giving freely to someone else what you always withheld
from me'" -- quoting her husband.
4. "I love you too" (whispered just once).
5. "There's not much of the animal left in you,
is there" (my least favorite remark of hers so far).
6. "You say the same things my husband used to
say" (blubbered tearfully).
7. "I'm a woman. I'm submissive. I'm just the
opposite of what I pretend to be. As a man of
experience you should understand this!"
8. "We can never waste any of the precious time
we have together. That's why we never get any sleep."
9. "How could I be just a quarter Chinese if my
mother is full-blooded Chinese?" (I knew I'd screwed it
up somehow.)
10. "That was frightening!" (after we'd run into
her short, thin, movie-star-handsome, extremely arrogant
and asinine husband on the front steps of the old
Victorian house where they once lived together, and now
she's shacking up with me; this was as he, Jim,
delivered the monthly alimony check a week late).
11. "I wasn't exactly bored. I just didn't want
to be there. Except you were there" (reflecting on the
two hours she sat at a corner table in a Marin Civic

Center conference room as Jerry directed Bayer and Rose
in a reading of their "Measure for Measure" scenes).

    12. "I didn't get any work done. All I could do
was talk about you all day."

    13. "It's not true I never smile! I smile at
least three times an hour!" (said very seriously and
unsmilingly -- in fact grimly and accusingly).

    14. "That first night I waited for you to touch
me. You didn't, so I touched you. But that wasn't
really me. You see why I'm confused?"

    15. "I didn't know it would grow that much!" (said
while she was going down on me Saturday night -- and so
I ask: just where was her focus our first night?).

    16. "Yes, I've been married for three years and
have a child. But you're older and I've only had three
lovers before you, and that includes my husband!"

    17. "From my marriage I learned some things are
better left unsaid. Honesty isn't always best.
Sometimes it's worst."

    18. "At first I'd be the one who gave in. Then
when I wouldn't, he did, or at least he acted like it.
It was so easy for him to say he apologized. In the end
neither of us would give in" (this again speaking of her
marriage).

    19. "It's better not to try acrobatics in the dark
at four in the morning" (after our attempt at standing
her on my shoulders to replace a lightbulb left both of
us sprawling sore-assed on the kitchen floor) (her
apartment, which is on the second floor, has unusually
high ceilings -- twelve feet).

    20. "After Jim said we should have a three-way
with another woman, I had nightmares for a long time.
He said I was a square! I would not want to be gay!"
                    *   *

    I don't think I've said enough in these pages about
her splendid breasts. They're firm, quite large
(especially for a gymnast and by Asian standards), and
pleasingly shaped. They have only two slight flaws:
faint stretch marks on the underside, and an aversion to
being touched. One must be very, very careful with

them. They'll tolerate only an extremely light circular
touch on the areolas that barely brushes the nipples
themselves, which erect noticeably when she's aroused.
A welcome tipoff, that! But she often dabs Vaseline on
those nipples and places Band-Aids on them under her bra
during the day to avoid pain otherwise caused by simple
normal workplace friction. (She tells me if I like her
breasts now -- and I surely do -- I should've seen them
before Danny came along. "They were really, really firm
and high and perky, like this" -- and she cups them with
both hands and presses them upward quite forcefully to
demonstrate and then cries "Ow! Ow! Ow! Why did I do
that?" -- And they also hurt sometimes if she's not
wearing the right kind of bra and a trip in a vehicle or
on an animal of some sort gets too bumpy, and the pain
or discomfort can take a full day or more to go away.)
                    *   *
     It's past five, I know, because a VW beatle with
macho ex-Marine Bill Dean from the Emp machine shop
behind the wheel just roared by and we laughingly gave
each other the finger (nor am I ashamed to say I was the
initiator). Valerie will soon be coming -- no, Valerie
is here.

Wednesday 8
     Again I'm afraid it's not going to work. I can't
break through to her. No less than when we met, Valerie
is still able to look upon me with total dispassion. I
can think of no adjective which adequately describes her
way of relating to me. It's not cold exactly.
Passionless, unloving, unreceptive, uneager, unhappy,
unenthusiastic, distracted -- those don't cut it either.
     As I get to know her better I become more anxious
rather than less. She's a rare treasure: and despite
her many ways of being sweet and kind, I have no doubt a
cool gem's at her core. Or to put it another way, she
can be a very tough cookie -- and not just at the core,
but when you try to bite in just about anywhere.
     When she showed me her poem "Exorbitance" last

30

night I suddenly thought I saw what it is about her.
She's made herself into a saint! And I still think this
might be true. The love she offers in the poem (written
not for me but for one of her three previous lovers: Jon
Tremont of the Downtown Peace Coalition, whom I've
actually met and admire, and who she tells me, with no
apparent qualms, is married) -- this love she declares
for him, I say, is some strange variety of perfect
chaste Catholic love resembling that of the troubadours.
It's invulnerable. It accepts the other person whatever
he may do or feel. It asks nothing and cannot be hurt.

 I read and reread the poem, written in purple ink
in her surprisingly schoolgirlish hand with its large
circles for dots above the i's. She came into the
living room and we talked about it, long past the hour
we had vowed to get to bed. I was delivering my pitch
for lusty, joyous, all-stops-out loving, and she was
denying that the poem necessarily represented her true
feelings. "Only at the time I wrote it," she said.
That "philosophy" was a product, she explained, of
loving not just Jon Tremont but also, simultaneously,
Brandon Wexler (an Emp guy I've never met). But I was
vastly different from both of them, she went on. I was
ready to love; I found it easy to love. She said she
envied me that talent.

 Perhaps owing to my comments regarding
"Exorbitance" I didn't wind up with a copy of it. But
here's a much shorter poem she dashed off earlier
yesterday for me and me alone:

> I can't love you
> the way you do
> wish me
> expect me to
> It has to be
> my own to grow
> and it must come & go
> as I feel
> loved with real
> tears and cheers
> ups & downs

           for that is I
           who is me
           to be
           Valerie
                 *   *

Emp morning coffee break. Valerie wanted to avoid
sitting with Brandon, the aforementioned other man on
this earth she's slept with outside her marriage
(besides Tremont and me). I briefly ruffled her
composure by observing: "You know what? I don't think
we're going to make it."
     A frown and a fetching thick-lipped pout. "Why?"
     "I don't know. It's like a premonition."
     "When did it come to you? This morning?"
     "No. Last night at 'the shack.'"
     "From reading 'Exorbitance'?"
     "That might have been part of it."
     She looked away for a long moment and then said all
this is "very frustrating."
     "It's a shame uncouth guys like me," I replied, in
a bungled attempt at humor, "keep coming along to
destroy the perfect symmetry of your life."
     "That's not true!" she objected. "I resent your
saying that!"
     "Aha! I got a reaction from you!"
     On paper I suspect my lines in this dialogue look
bitter or worse -- if not just plain stupid -- but we
managed to say these things, and quite a number of
others not much different, without causing serious
injury so far as I know. But, as I told her, "Sometimes
I want to sting you a little to pay you back for all
your coolness and detachment and lack of response to
me." I'm already at the point where it's much easier to
see why her husband acted in the shockingly ugly ways he
did. At times I'm seized by an overwhelming urge to
take desperate measures of my own, just as I sometimes
was with Denise. Even at age nineteen, however, Valerie
is infinitely more sophisticated and composed --
"together" -- than Denise. Fortunately for myself and
no doubt for Valerie too, I haven't yet discovered a way

to take desperate measures regarding her without becoming a buffoon in her eyes as well as my own.

Talking with Ted Kent and Milt Garry has helped somewhat. Ted in his usual succinct way says, "She's a spitfire, man, be careful!" and lets it go at that. Milt's similar but more elaborate and nuanced view -- they both know her from the Imp, I should note, though neither has ever mentioned this to me before -- in Milt's view she's a kind of ravishing zealot, an exotic Joan of Arc in a miniskirt who's emphatically not to be messed with. "Every time I run into her she flashes thunderbolts from those radical eyes and says I must go to some meeting -- or else. I go to the meeting." At one such meeting where he spoke with her, he and Ted were doing their usual thing, he said, joshing, making harmless fun of everybody, and Valerie stomped off in a fury. To her they were, to quote what she shouted at them at the time, "childish" (and they're both a decade or so her senior). And Ted confirmed all this.

My current mission is to see whether this teenage hellion (when she's not gloomy, mournful, morose) can be provoked, finagled, or loved into wanting a better kind of personal life -- more easygoing, joyous, generous -- while still remaining the highly admirable political fighter for peace she unquestionably is.

You can't change people, pal.

Nonsense! Look at how Lisa changed me! And then look how Jang changed me again! And back then I was still considerably further along in almost-grownness (to resuscitate an old term) than Valerie is now: I was twenty-one in Lisa's case, twenty-two in Jang's.

Last night we did the laundry -- mostly hers and Danny's but a few token pieces of mine so I wouldn't feel left out. It took hours. I tried to be helpful and amiably tolerant of the kid's nonstop tantrums.

"Perhaps you're not ready to accept such responsibilities," she sniffed on our way home in the L.C., after I thought I'd done so well.

"What! How can you say that!"

So it goes.

[Have Mercy]

*   *

My opinion of her has again skyrocketed. There was
a period not so long ago -- actually just forty-five
minutes ago -- when I suspected she might turn out to be
disappointingly ordinary on the inside. I'd been drawn
to her, I thought, because I'd never before encountered
such political passion and social savvy and high energy
in combination with so much charm and sexiness and
beauty -- and in someone so young. But perhaps such
things could coexist with ordinariness in a world-
traveling Eurasian Frenchwoman educated in very good
schools, at least up to age fourteen.

I was wrong. Suddenly it dawned on me the long
"Exorbitance" poem all by itself had demonstrated once
and for all time how rare she is. It's undeniable:
she's a woman of exceptional intelligence, imposing
literary talent, superb aesthetic taste, unusual
imagination, remarkable independence, enviable
sophistication, phenomenal will, boundless vitality,
unquenchable curiosity, and boggling awareness and
sensitivity. She's also strikingly, stunningly,
unbelievably beautiful and has a superb body and is
extremely sexy (no doubt I'm condemned to repeat all of
these already well-worn terms endlessly).

-- But then again what a shame it is she's so
often so serious, so solemn, so severe, so bitter about
her failed marriage and her turbulent and abusive
upbringing, so tightly constricted by fear of being hurt
yet again. In another age a woman with such views at
age nineteen might have become a fanatical nun. What do
you do with a woman who has great vitality (to say it
once more!), frequently proclaims her love of life, and
yet shows so little zest in actual day-to-day intimate
living and rarely even smiles? It's almost as if the
only thing she truly enjoys is playing the sad-eyed
lady. Except, granted, there's no indication she's
merely "playing" it.

What do you do? Well, for starters maybe you show
as much as you can muster of your own zest for intimate
living and smile a lot and crack a few goofy bad jokes

and hope all this will sooner or later prove infectious
and make everything okay and just the way you both want
it to be. And in the meantime? You prepare yourself to
show patience as you've never shown it before. (Though
you did try like hell with Ciara and Jang.)

    Valerie, this morning I told you I
    thought we weren't going to make it as
    lovers. It's true I fear we won't, but I
    simply refuse to yield to that fear. If I
    really felt there was no hope for us I'd
    move out tonight. But last night you
    agreed with me when I pointed out that your
    very fine poem "Exorbitance" in effect had
    declared you couldn't love. Specifically,
    you didn't object when I said if you felt
    about me as the poem said you felt about
    loving in general, then you couldn't
    possibly love me. You had consigned our
    love to failure before it had even begun.

    This morning I was merely getting back
    at you for putting me in a position where
    I felt I had to make such pathetic pleas.

As we know because we saw the Mime Troupe's play, a
man has his foolish pride ---

           *   *

    Valerie's preoccupied me but Nadine's crept back
into the picture. Monday for lunch we hit the Confucian
Bar on Grant Avenue, where, in a back corner, between (I
blush to say) impassioned kisses of exactly the type
Valerie dislikes, I told her we'd have to cool things
down a bit. She said she couldn't do that: it was all
or nothing. It would "cheapen" her "to see you only
when you want to see me." She was so charming in her
refusal to accept my proposition that as our lunch came
to an end I liked her better than ever before. The
chemistry between us is superb. Nadine lives for the
moment. She ain't no uptight chick. We can relax
together completely. But I know all too well we'd soon
be back to disappointing each other.

           *   *

[Have Mercy]

Now dig this. At lunch in the park Valerie scrawls
out the last few lines of a new poem (between bites of
an expensive strawberry pastry which I'd made fun of;
"You're not much of a gourmet, are you," shot back the
haughty teenage Eurasian firebrand zealot spitfire) and
hands me this:

                How dare you say
                that I
                do not love you
                when you are so vital
                and essential to me
                that when you are
                not here with me
                all life around me
                loses meaning
                and separates from me --
                you make me want
                to scream or explode with
                despair
                for I do not succeed
                to show how
                you glow in me --
                How can you imply
                that something is maybe
                dead or asleep
                inside of me
                when I feel it
                so much alive
                grasping at me
                that I'm unable to
                concentrate it --
                It overflows and leaks
                all over me
                I cannot see
                ahead of me --
                It runs in directions
                all beyond my control --
                You can't measure
                my love for you --
                I love you so

[Shacking Up with Valerie]

without fear
for what have I got to lose
when I have everything to gain
Must I prove it to you?
Oh can't you see?
or is it that
my poetry
has gone too far
inside of you
and has taken over for
the real me ---
                    *

   Should be obvious now why I'm thoroughly off-
balance and lurching about desperately seeking walls to
cling to while I try to figure out to get through to
this truly perplexing Valerie M. Bando, provocateur
extraordinaire.

Thursday 9
   Let's see. It's Thursday. Three in the afternoon.
This is the first quiet moment I've had in a stormy day
marked by a romantic two hours with Valerie, a grim
attempt to rush out projects for the Roachman, a
complex, stubborn, and disheartening letter from Jang,
and a gut-tightening call from Nadine.
   Point-blank she asked, Nadine did: "Did you tell
that Frenchie about us?" I thought the game was up.
But it didn't turn out that way. Either Nadine didn't
deduce from "Frenchie's" words that we're seeing each
other, or she didn't care. Mainly she seemed concerned
that word of our brief affair might have reached,
through "Frenchie," "the street." By which I think she
probably meant the aisles of the Emp cafeteria. (And by
the way, she's assured me Byron, thank god, doesn't know
anyone besides her, Nadine, who works here.)
   Valerie aroused Nadine's suspicion by asking her,
"How do you show passionate love?" and a moment later
referred to me. (Valerie and I had a long talk about
sensuality/sensuousness this morning. We were late to

37

work and decided we might as well make a good thing of
it. We drank coffee and rapped intensely just the way
Parisians do at sidewalk cafes, or so she informed me,
and we contrived an excuse for her to give to her boss
(who isn't Khaki but rather a very similar woman one set
of offices to the west on the same floor), namely that
she'd been taking her divorce papers to her lawyer:
which we then did do to make the excuse a bit closer to
bona fide, first backtracking via J Church streetcar to
"the shack" to pick up the papers, finally arriving by
L.C. at work at quarter to eleven.)

Evidently Nadine feared I'd said something along
these lines to Valerie: "Man, like in the past couple of
weeks I've learned what real passion is. I met this
bitchin' woman named Nadine and...."

That Valerie would be curious as to how one goes
about expressing passionate love is surely a good sign,
all things considered. It bolsters my hope that her
sensuality is merely underdeveloped, not irretrievably
retarded or damaged by the way Jim treated her. As she
pointed out this morning, she does like to experiment
with her senses, to indulge in them. "I've always loved
to hold smooth rocks in my hand," she confided, "even
when I was a little girl." But this sensuality -- or
really sensuousness, I'd say (though I admit I'm forever
confusing the meanings of the two words) -- this
sensoriousness, perhaps I should call it, stops far
short of embracing sexuality, and thus it's not unlike
proclaiming you're an atheistic Catholic: a whole lot of
the fervor goes out of it. And nailing down the
relevance of this point, an atheistic Catholic is just
what Valerie proclaims herself to be. And needless to
say -- but maybe not wholly so -- she long ago shucked
the orthodox Catholic brand of reactionary politics.
(But perhaps not each and every last precept of Catholic
morality -- cf. Ciara, who like Valerie renounced all
such Catholic precepts (supposedly) in her early teens
but then at twenty-two -- holy moly, she rediscovered
some that proved to be quite useful for certain purposes
regarding fencing in the new husband, i.e., me.)

[Shacking Up with Valerie]

In all the times we've balled I've heard Valerie moan with pleasure just twice, and I had to strain to catch both of those and wasn't totally sure I was interpreting them correctly.

This asexuality in one who's naturally so sexy, or more accurately -- if I'm not wrong -- this fear of her own sexuality and its power to make her vulnerable, infects other areas, although not uniformly. She loves passionate colors (often a sign of sexual coldness, as everyone except Valerie seems to know and way too often express) but apparently she doesn't care much for social dancing or rock or soul or funk music. In the morning she prefers to listen to what I'd call sterile, for the most part, symphonies on the radio, although the sturm-und-drang Beethoven is her supreme favorite (she's also into Goethe and Hugo and many other classical thinkers and artists). She's never even heard of the Cool Jerk or the Funky Chicken. She's not thrilled at all with the idea of bougalooing down funky, funky Broadway. All this may be a result of her highly high-cultured and supremely Frenchified classical educational background -- no one who's been with her for more than two minutes could possibly miss this -- but I'd say said background also seems to serve as a handy screen against overly sense-stirring phenomena. (Nadine likes to wake up to funkified soul music and so do I.)

The only other possible explanation is I just don't turn her on that much, but this seems less likely as time passes. What she asked Nadine reassures me on this score -- but not nearly so much as the way she looked at me during break today. For the first time she gazed into my eyes for a long period, and I saw receptivity and a smoldering sexuality and maybe even a trace of "adoration" there. (I can just hear Nadine coaching her, "Well, the first thing you do is look into his eyes as if he were God himself.") (Hey, it can't hurt. And I'm willing to reciprocate!)

This morning at the sidewalk cafe on Powell we rapped like new lovers. Valerie said she saw my historical period as the nineteenth century: "I picture

you as a count or duke, maybe English, or maybe like the
poet Lamartine, you know him? You have a long feather
in your cap." She saw herself as a daughter of the
French revolution and she was proud to mention Joan of
Arc as well, that other Maid of Orleans -- who died for
her righteous cause at just the age Valerie is now.
When she was only five she chased after the white horse
carrying the actress playing Joan of Arc in the city's
annual parade and just as she was about to grab the
horse's tail her father caught up with her and snatched
her away and she's never forgotten the excitement of
that moment and never forgiven him for shattering it
(and doing lots of other very bad things to her over the
years, including beating her frequently and locking her
in closets and banishing her to a distant orphanage for
a couple of scarifying months -- all this as he and her
hot-tempered mother battled over custody of their three
kids, as well as the other two of her mother's from a
previous relationship in Vietnam and earlier banished
for good to another orphanage -- none of this, clearly,
being the kind of behavior one would expect of a widely
known French intellectual of aristocratic lineage).
     We also got into the subject of what we would do if
we had a full day to spend as we wished. She mentioned
such activities as hanging out in Berkeley or Sausalito,
hitting the beach in Half Moon Bay, sleeping ---
                              *
     That was Moran, come to pay a surprise visit from
upstairs with three new assignments in hand for me.
Tomorrow will be a busy one for sure. -- And just to
complete the thought above: Valerie loves to sleep under
the stars at The Pinnacles or Point Reyes or a certain
campground near Mendocino or (best of all to me) up in
Gold Rush Country, and we vowed to hit every one of
those spots and more in the weeks ahead.

Friday 10
     It's hard to believe, but I've made it in to work
on time four out of five days this week. Valerie and I

40

[Shacking Up with Valerie]

burst out of the house at seven-fifty or so and hurry
hand in hand four blocks down 21st Street to Van Ness.
Usually I'm singing or whistling or goofing around in
some other way and she's quiet and preoccupied. Along
our path we pass a florist's shop that plays loud
schmaltzy music. Each morning I forget about that music
until suddenly as we come within earshot of it I begin
to feel I'm singing out of tune and pretty soon I'm
singing whatever the shop's playing and in the same key.
Just goes to show, sez I, what mere modulation can do
and also how easily influenced I am -- and most of all,
to be sure, when I'm not even aware it's happening.

As Valerie pointed out while we were sitting on the
grass in Dolores Park on the way home from work tonight,
"This must be very hard for you. You've given up all
your habits." It's true my life's been much altered by
the crucial fact that I'm shacking up at her place. I'm
often at least partly aware of the changes, but not so
much worried as amused and challenged by them. It's
more like watching an enactment as played by myself of
Mom's fantasies of the Good Son and Husband. I make up
beds, shelve groceries, set tables, help fix meals, wash
dishes, vacuum, perform repairs, fastidiously clean up
every mess in sight (only a few of which are of my own
making), and in general fall all over myself in eager
efforts to aid and support the beleaguered young mom.

Why? Well, I suppose it's partly because of subtle
pressures coming from Valerie herself. She expressed
this concern directly, in fact, in another new poem
complaining about the lot of a certain unidentified
"liberated" woman living in an unmarried state with a
certain unidentified "unliberated" man. The major
result of the woman's agreeing to such a liaison, the
poem implies, is that the man doesn't even make the
trivial efforts at helping out that he would be expected
to contribute if they were married.

Another reason for my sudden upwelling of domestic
conscience is awareness that Valerie, from her troubled
relationship with her father and her own disastrous
marriage and the subsequent engagement with feminism,

41

seems to have developed a highly rigid stereotypical
notion of what men are like and what they want; and I
hate to be seen as conforming to any kind of stereotype,
and most of all to such a simplistic and rather
revolting one wielded by a teenage know-it-all with a
huge storage shed full of axes to grind against men.

But the most important reason is simply it seems
unfair and inconsistent with my own principles and
beliefs to be any other way with her. Valerie is
terribly overworked, trying to hold a job, run a
household, raise a toddler son, and deal with an angry
and resentful husband to whom she's given the boot. At
the same time she's working to engineer an official
divorce, maintain a high level of political activity,
and stay on good terms with two former lovers (recent!)
both of whom are still pursuing her (though she says she
regards them as just friends now). My unexpected
arrival on the scene has obviously complicated her life
a whole lot more. Suddenly she has a "guest" in the
house whose comfort she feels she must cater to. (I try
to discourage her from viewing me as a "guest." As I
told her: "One who shacks up with someone is not a
guest; he's a shackee. And that would be equally true
if you were shacking at my place" (where, as she well
knows, some half a dozen other "guests" are already
present, although at least two will soon be leaving) --
and it would also be equally true if we were at some
neutral place such as, for instance, a real shack.)

As an outgrowth of this attempt to lend a hand to
Valerie as her fellow shackee, however, I haven't gotten
any of my own personal stuff done this week, except
during working hours at Emp, and not very much then.
Last night Valerie and Danny and I launched an
expedition to Whitefront (where I pushed the kid around
in a shopping cart). The previous night she and I
attended a Downtown Peace Coalition meeting (and I
canceled B-ball to do it, thereby irking Manny Lehrman,
whom I was supposed to meet at the JCC and wasn't able
to reach by phone in time to let him know I couldn't
make it). The night before that, as noted earlier, I

hit the laundromat with her and Danny (for three hours
plus!). All week long I've read a grand total of ten
pages in "Pluche" and nothing in anything else. I've
even pretty much given up reading newspapers in
Valerie's presence (because of several grumpy remarks
she's made about the way her husband hid behind the
paper "all the time," ignoring her; it even got to the
point where she would bash the paper out of his hands
and demand he pay attention to her: to my mind truly a
spine-chilling avenger-like act if ever there was one).
    In a way I congratulate myself for all this -- my
boggling success, so far, by and large, at maintaining a
tolerant, easygoing, uncompulsive demeanor in the face
of countless daunting provocations -- but at the same
time I worry about my penchant for finding excuses not
to get those things done which I most seriously want to
get done. At first I reluctantly concluded that getting
laid must be more important to me than anything else in
life. But it's worse than that, because what I'm doing
now can no longer be classified as mere philandering or
Don Juanism (if it ever could) (although it's true my
own sister has charged me -- outrageously! -- with both
of those sins and many others equally bad or worse).
Rather it appears my main thrust is a purely negative
one: I'll do anything just so long as it prevents me
from getting truly serious about my own personal
projects.
    My feelings about Valerie fluctuate wildly, just as
hers do about me, or at least appear to. After work
yesterday we were both hostile. Chalk up a good portion
of that to Nadine. What a phenomenal woman she is! She
spent forty minutes with me at the end of the day (after
talking with "Frenchie" for thirty minutes). She'd
dropped acid just before that, and she was marvelously
warm, understanding, and forgiving. Rather than being
angry at me for dialing things back with her while
Byron's still doing what I presume will turn out to be
the very last sliver of his time, she showed she had
accepted everything and still wanted to be my pal.
    "I dig you, Glen, I really do. I want to learn

43

from you."

   And I want to learn from her! Her "street"
knowledge is stunning. She appears to be one of those
rare people who really do accept others as they are.
And also, as she said, our balling is "too outasight to
just throw away." As for her "loving" me, well, that
she now admits was "a lie." She was telling me "what I
thought you wanted to hear." (Perhaps she overdoes it a
bit, though, in also saying she told me that lie "on
purpose because I knew it would drive you away.")

   In any case, Nadine and I have now become intimate
buddies, and Valerie, sensing this, doesn't like it one
bit. When I told her Nadine is one of the most
together people I've known, Valerie snapped back she
doesn't think Nadine has it together at all. I said the
three of us are starting to sound like a scene from a
bad movie about a high-school triangle ---

Saturday 11
   There just isn't time to keep up. I'm snatching a
few moments now, at noon, lying naked across stained
blue sheets, as Valerie prepares breakfast. Today she's
saying she doesn't want me out there getting in her
hair. And I'll be the first to admit it: I'm glad she's
saying that.

   It was a fine night and yet somehow we're both back
to suspecting we're incompatible. She can't stand my
"critical side" and I can't bear her cool moodiness and
blase' funks. We're both grudgingly trying to suppress
all offending traits but this seems only to worsen
matters. ---
                        *   *
   Whew. Now I've escaped to a concrete front stoop
across Dolores from "the shack." It got to be way too
oppressive in there. Even on an afternoon as bright as
this one, very little light gets into those heavily
draperied rooms -- and today that darkness turned out to
be infested with dismal resentments. While I was in the
shower she called Jim, as she explained, "to tell him to

44

come get his damn mail." Then for maybe the fifth or
sixth time in my presence she permitted him to upset her
and soon she was screaming at him in tones that made my
backbone fibrillate. It turned out one of his "spies"
had seen her with a "strange man" at the bus stop in the
morning. (Apparently he, Jim, didn't even notice me
lurking in the dark entrance hallway behind Valerie
during his alimony delivery the other day.) Now he was
letting her know he was thinking about splitting from
California so as to avoid making childcare payments.
    "He's so full of bitterness," she grumped
afterwards, her teeth grinding.
    Soon her own bitterness segued to despondency.
I tried to coax and then, that failing, wrench her out
of this, as I so often have to do or rather feel
compelled to do; and as usual I was only partly, and
sporadically, successful. Her efforts to relate to me
are rarely strong and deep during everyday life.
Consequently they seem, often, cool and distracted and
mechanical, as if she's just going through the motions
because she's got other things on her mind, much more
important things. And I'm pretty much convinced this is
exactly the case.
    I don't know what I'm going to do. Did I say that
already? If yes, I'm repeating it because frustration
is building rapidly. Last night it seemed quite clear I
should pull back from this shacking-up "experiment" and
do it soon, perhaps this weekend. Her feeble sense of
humor: that all by itself would justify it. How could
anyone possibly get along with someone who could sit
stony-faced, for the most part, through the movie "Hi,
Mom," which is wildly funny and had the full house
rocking with laughter all the way to the end? Of
reassuring signs I detected only two, and these were but
slight: (1) she was as engaged as I was by the highly
political movie "Z," which we also saw; and (2) for most
of the evening she was making an effort, not
continuously but from time to time, to show she at least
recalled I was present, e.g., by taking hold of my hand,
putting an arm around me for a moment, pecking me on the

cheek (yesterday afternoon I wrote her a long, impassioned, demanding letter focused on such matters -- i.e., "simple expressions of affection and caring"). But she still had the look of a wary, cornered animal whenever I swooped down to embrace her. Most of the time she seemed aloof and indifferent.

Then early this morning I awoke on my back with her straddling me, her hand reaching down between her thighs to grasp my maximally engorged cock and hold it upright just as she was about to settle down onto it. How lovely she looked with her face and torso veiled in that fabulous thick black hair, her luscious lips glistening in a shy little smile, her tender pinkish-brown nipples peeking boldly sort of like a matched pair of chipmunks through the swirling and swaying hair. For a while I thought I was seeing a sudden surge in her of what at least seemed to be loving erotic passion. Afterwards she was quite affectionate for maybe ten or fifteen minutes before getting up to face the day. And this encouraging spell in the sheets caused me to reverse immediately my earlier impulsive notion that I'd better get out while the getting's still good.

But the truth is this: I'd prefer to see Nadine tomorrow. Under the shacking-up protocols with Valerie I'm allowed to do that. And I told her, told Nadine, I would. Behind a cover of drugginess she's been coming on strong the past few days. She spends long periods in the dungeon with me during her breaks. She talks a lot about Byron, who still hasn't been sprung from the joint. She insists her interest in me is something other than love -- that same desire to "learn" from me, which she's attested to several more times -- but, whatever the reason, the mutual attraction is too strong to be ignored.

Twice yesterday Valerie saw me with Nadine, and she was obviously not pleased about it, but by the time we talked it over after work she'd overcome her displeasure sufficiently to deflect the subject of our inevitable showdown from the nature of my relationship with Nadine to my "hypercriticism" as putatively expressed in that

[Shacking Up with Valerie]

long letter I wrote her about affection and caring. But the key moment, for me and I suspect for both Valerie and Nadine as well, came when I stood outside the third-floor Pine women's restroom at four-fifty, talking intensely with Nadine, who had pleaded with me to meet her on the back stairs so we could "kiss goodbye forever" (in case Byron were to show up over the weekend, as she expected he would). Suddenly there was a sharp whack on my rear. I turned around just in time to see Valerie scoot into the restroom.

When she came out a moment later she hurried past us. Nadine said something to her to ease the tension, but Valerie's answer, as she paused at the stairwell door, was delivered in a strained voice and sounded hostile, although I couldn't actually make out the words. Then Nadine told her, very gently but with consummate one-upsmanship, she, Valerie, was being needlessly uptight. Valerie hotly denied this was the case and stomped off in her noisy high-heeled sandals, I'd call them: the ones she almost always wears at work. Nadine, it seemed to me, came out on top. Except, that is, for how smashing Valerie looked in her short silver velveteen dress with the long waist ties flying sassily about like furry little hip pigtails.

-- But now I've been gone from "the shack" long enough. Supposedly I'm "taking a walk" while Valerie showers and tends to some chores of the personal kind such as sewing a patch on her jeans and filling in more court forms for her divorce lawyer. (Every now and then my glance is drawn to the Land Cruiser parked in the shadows across the street. If I can just afford its upkeep, that gorgeous contraption could make a spectacular difference in my quality of life for years to come. It glows with possibility. If I didn't have it I think Valerie would've given up on me long ago -- though of course she'd hotly deny this too.)

I feel better about today. Danny's at the babysitter's for another twenty-four hours, and I'm fairly bursting with what seems to be a good kind of energy. ---

Sunday 12

Just crept out of the bedroom, leaving Valerie
asleep there, the sheet pulled down to the small of her
smoothly sculpted gymnast's back, her beautiful long
black hair cascading in wild profusion over the side of
the bed, her face smooshed into the pillow and only
partly visible, looking impossibly young and innocent
and yet also heartbreakingly sad even in sleep. For I
don't know how long I knelt by the bed gazing at her,
and then, to get the wide-angle perspective, did the
same thing again while standing by the door. It may be
a long while -- two, three, many lifetimes -- before I
see a sight as beautiful or as touching. And I'm not
just saying this!

Now I'm lying on her maroon living-room rug wearing
only my ancient blue bathrobe with the Old Glory patch
sewn on above my heart (by me -- no lie!). The floor
throbs faintly in time with Van Morrison's "Moondance,"
which is playing on the powerful stereo in one of the
downstairs apartments. Otherwise it's a quiet Sunday
morning. Distant pealing of church bells, whisper of
traffic, gurgling of pipes -- all these sounds trickling
in during the brief intervals between tracks on the
downstairs stereo. Through one of the uncovered windows
here I can make out a small quadrant of cold gray sky.

The vividly colored drapes have been pulled aside
from two of the five bay windows and tied in place. Two
of five, forty percent: not bad. Valerie did that when
I complained about the apartment's extreme gloominess
and darkness. She prefers it dark, she said, because to
her the apartment is a "refuge against the world."

This drape-pullback concession -- compromise really
-- was one of several I wrung from her yesterday. The
most important came over dinner at Tivoli in North Beach
when she reluctantly and even resentfully insisted she
loves me. This grim avowal, moreover, was further
tainted by the duress under which she produced it.
Since I pressured it out of her by belaboring my strong
view that no one who seemed as miserable and distracted
as she did could possibly be in love, or even "in like,"

it meant virtually nothing.

For the rest of the night I too was doing some resenting, definitely of her but also of myself for becoming so vulnerable to her. At Ted Kent's house, as we joined a party of some two dozen mostly Emp employees, many of them Imp contributors, watching a much-hyped quadraphonic experiment on color TV, I sank into a trance of disturbingly delicious melancholy of my own. At this point Valerie was being more attentive and loving than I'd ever known her to be out in the social realm, but it still wasn't anywhere near enough: it seemed willful and forced and more than a shade hokey. Nor did she know how to join me in the excruciating solitude to which I'd retreated. If nothing else I wanted her to realize I too could experience "tristesse": that outcome seemed extremely important to me at the time. I stood just a few inches from the speakers, trying to feel to the core, to the marrow of the marrow, groaning along to the music with painful intensity, though not loud enough for anyone to hear except when Valerie came near, when without exactly intending to I think I probably twisted my personal volume knob a half-spin higher just for her benefit.

She couldn't understand where I was coming from. "You've turned into a madman!" she cried, bewildered, perplexed, unprecedentedly anxious to get through to me. It was just what I'd hoped for.

I responded ardently but with intentional (and no doubt also some unintentional) weirdness to her loving gestures, and when she broke them off I immediately sank back into the same flagrantly stuporous trip. This frustrated her greatly, and when we got back home she suddenly lashed out at me as I lay naked on the living-room rug. As she saw it, I'd merely been feeling sorry for myself all evening. "And it's not the first time either." Then she surprised me by attributing my puzzling behavior at the party to my failure to get more writing done.

"You must feel a need to create fictions. If you can't be doing it on paper, then you have to be doing it in life."

I went along partway with this analysis, which
secretly flattered me. She thought I was "wasting my
talents"! But this brought us no closer together,
because, as before, I craved her genuine loving
solicitude, I needed her to show she wanted this
relationship to work as much as I did -- desperately! --
and of course she wasn't doing that.

When it became obvious our talk wasn't taking us
anywhere good, I proposed we go to bed. She refused, so
I went ahead by myself. A few minutes later she
followed me, throwing herself onto the bed (almost as if
it were a trampoline) in an angry bantamweight tantrum
which quickly dissolved into tears. "You aren't giving
me a chance!" she wailed. Soon enough what started as a
mutual consoling session turned into a balling session,
but her initial ardor diminished quickly and then
disappeared entirely -- she went inexplicably dead on
me, like a blank-faced open-eyed corpse -- and not very
long after this dismaying demise of hers my cock slowly
deflated and everything came to a halt before we'd even
really gotten going. It was obvious we were finally
coming up against it.

In our long talk at Tivoli I learned much more
about her life. What interested me most was the period
of her courtship with Jim. Valerie's mother didn't pay
much attention to her at the time -- they were living in
a tiny apartment above the restaurant in Holton -- so it
was possible for Valerie to slip out at eight a.m. and
return at one or two the following night or even later,
day after day, over a period of some six or seven
months. "We were both terribly lonely," she said,
meaning herself and Jim. "We thought we made a
beautiful couple. And really those were the only things
that seemed to matter at that point."

Her mother disapproved of Jim, finding him too much
like her former husband, Valerie's father, high-strung
and intense and demanding and volatile and at times
violent. On the other hand Jim's mother thought
Valerie, despite her jailbait age, was the best thing

50

that had ever happened to her feckless son. One day Jim
suggested they elope, and they did -- it was actually
the eve of her sixteenth birthday -- but they were
stopped by suspicious cops in Arizona and ---

                              *

(Right there she appeared on the sun-drenched steps
above me -- long ago I had moved out here to the back
staircase -- and wheedled me into reading this entire
entry to her. "Maybe I'll start keeping a diary intime'
of my own," she groused. Already she looks at this
journal with deep distrust. And then, after she went
back inside to throw together some breakfast, a whiff of
weed drifted up from the courtyard below. The
longhaired dude who lives in the back apartment came
into view -- this is the big Van Morrison fan -- and
passed up a glowing roach on a clip. "I guess you know
Valerie," I said. "I'm glad to see the change, man," he
said. "I always dug Valerie, but brother Jim, whew, he
was something else. Glad to see the change, man.")

     -- Best to finish up real quick with the girl's
sweet-sixteen story. A short while after being returned
to Holton by the cops as runaways they tied the knot.
Valerie was several months pregnant at the time, "but
we'd been planning to get married anyway." Astoundingly
to me, her mother demanded, and received, a $1600
"dowry" from Jim's family -- a hundred bucks for each
of the bride's years on earth -- before she would let
the marriage of her officially underage daughter
proceed. (A cultural thing there? Not one I've ever
heard of before last night, but Valerie said it probably
was, yes, and that her mother is very cunning and a
crackerjack bargainer.)

     In any event the newlyweds set up living in San
Francisco and this was right at the start of the Summer
of Love; in fact, it was just a month or two before
Ciara and I rolled into town and took up living some
five miles west of where Valerie and Jim did.

     About her three years with Jim she's said any
number of wildly conflicting things (but here she is
again: breakfast, sire, is ready) ---

3

Monday 13

Well, I snuck out of the house early this morning
"to avoid ruffling Jim" when he arrives to pick up
Danny. Now I'm leaning against a patriotic mailbox
(painted red white and blue) across the street from
Judell's Cigar Store, waiting for Valerie. It's a fine,
warm morning, but strange too, for me anyway, because
the fog hangs to the east here rather than the west,
diminishing somewhat the power of the sun, which is
casting an eerie throbbing silver glow everywhere -- it
has something like an underwater feel to it -- but of
course no one seems to notice. Most of the folks I'm
seeing here have probably lived in this area for years
if not decades. And it's a business day, a new week --
so let's have at it!

Valerie's hold on me is tightening. Yesterday may
have been the crucial day for us, and we survived it.
If only just barely. A series of petty hassles erupted
in the afternoon -- I don't even remember now what they
were about (I'm sure I could retrieve most of them if I
tried hard but time's too short) -- and finally
something she said provoked me into retaliating with a
threat to pick up my marbles and go home. "If having me
around makes things so tough for you," I said quite
seriously, "maybe it would be better if I moved my
things out like right now, you know, while we have some
free time before another week starts up. I mean, we
could keep seeing each other but it wouldn't be so
demanding on, you know, both of us."

After that her tone changed sharply. She said I
was free to do whatever I wanted, of course -- as we had
initially agreed, and as we've both been reminding each
other more or less ritualistically all along -- but she
wanted badly for me to stay. She needed me. She loved
me! In a way it's true she was saying all this, again,
under duress, but even so I'd never before heard such

52

things coming from her when they didn't seem merely a
reluctant echo of something I'd said myself. And I
loved it! I couldn't possibly leave her now -- even if
staying meant I couldn't see Nadine. So I stayed.

Later in the afternoon we took a stroll up to
Dolores Park and goofed around in the grass, running,
jumping, teaching each other exercises and tricks. I
was impressed by her superb body control. The girl can
do all sorts of things I can't do and will never be able
to do. She runs like a deer (that's a phrase I lifted
out of my own past, actually, but at this point it's
probably more applicable to her), she does perfect
cartwheels and headstands and flips, she broad-jumps
from a standing start almost as far as I do, she walks
about insouciantly upside down on her hands even on
bumpy inclines and talks volubly at the same time (could
even chew gum while doing all these things and still not
break a sweat, I'm sure). She's an acrobat and has the
ideal body for it -- puts me in mind of Elvira Madigan,
that shapely nubile tightrope walker in the Swedish
movie, except Valerie's far more attractive.

(And she can be an acrobat as a lovemaker too when
she wants to be. After returning from the park we went
at it Blazes/Molly style, standing, with her clinging to
my chest and stomach like a monkey on a tree trunk, her
legs wrapped around my waist and hips. Eventually she
leaned back and grasped an exercise bar mounted across a
closet doorway -- she often works out on it, and also
with twenty-pound hand barbells -- and began raising and
lowering herself by means of that bar until I came:
which for me was a first for sure.)

Her description of our romp in the park surpasses
anything I could say about it:

> In the cool green meadows
> dazzling with sun
> & there are no shadows
> I went with you to roll
> down the hills
> as little children do
> brushing branches down

[Have Mercy]

screaming loud our existence
and exhilarating our love
into its most
delighted forms of laughter
rolling down
the world with us
the sky spinning
rolling still
until
we reach the bottom of
the hill
and crush our roses in the grass
one purple little daisy stuck
between your teeth
our eyes leaking
our drunken souls
always ready
to start it all
over again
to discover
many new thrills --
falling down the hills.

      *   *

I wrote one for her too, earlier, on the back
steps, when she asked me to:

Sunday Breakfast Poem
   For VMB

Perhaps today as
bacon sizzles
and I bask
on your steps
sun-drenched & steep
leading up to
the cracked-open door
of your dark refuge
and you call
from inside
in the special way

54

[Shacking Up with Valerie]

of new lovers
"Breakfast!"
it's just another
in a long cascade
of loving
days.

*

So she's the poet. That's obvious -- and it's also
good. I hold in awe this special power she has to toss
off flowing lyrical poems. "Exhilarating our love"!
Lisa had it, Ciara had it, Jang had it, and now Valerie.
This may be the only quality all four of them have in
common. Well, no: they all look real good too. And
they all know how to keep me in line most of the time.
Anyway: with Valerie my own poems serve a purely
provocative purpose: I want to provoke her into
composing more poems for me. (I have very little sense
for the rhythms of poetry. Prose is it for me, sink or
swim. If I can work a little lyricism into it here and
there I consider myself to be having a very good day.)

*   *

All that was some twenty-five hours ago. There was
the one glorious moment, when I told Valerie I thought I
should leave, and she suddenly became so radiantly
loving that I could, and did, luxuriate in its glow for
the rest of the day.

Today, sorry to say, is a whole different story.
She's been grimly uptight since the moment her bedside
alarm went off, at least in part because of Jim's visit
scheduled for a short time later (but he didn't show
up). And I'm again battling strong doubts about staying
on with her. At such times it seems I unintentionally
heighten my demands on her, she becomes stubborn and
resistant and even more anxious, and the disputes spiral
up in intensity even as we repeat the same dull pleas
and arguments over and over. Before long I'm feeling
it's pointless to go on doing this.

To spare both of us further pain I think it's
probably necessary that I abandon certain elements of my
outmoded idealistic stance regarding love. This old way

of thinking requires me to believe, for example, that if
I love Valerie patiently, purely, and passionately,
she'll eventually break free of her own inhibitions and
compulsions. But given my current circumstances, given
my character, given my habits of intimacy and longing
for emotional closeness -- not to mention my own
inhibitions and compulsions -- I don't believe I can
maintain such a lofty stance toward her. I can't
continue going at such cross-purposes to my own deepest
needs, however crazed they may be. Apparently I can't
do it even for a single day, to say nothing of the weeks
or months or maybe years that would be required to win
or inspire what I would consider Valerie's authentic
reciprocative soul-deep intimate erotic/romantic love.

In other words: time to get real, Mr. G.

And there's this. I haven't been successful in my
efforts to purge Nadine from my life. I'd like to see
her again. She offers an excellent antidote to the
heavy tensions with Valerie. And when Jang comes back,
if indeed she does come back, matters will be even more
fraught. I'm more and more concerned it may be cruel
for me to go on frustrating Valerie so much. Even if
she did succeed in battling her way through to an open
and confident readiness to love, that would only succeed
in raising her onto the platform where she'd be
competing with Jang.

Is it unfair for me to go on with her? Yes, it
probably is. I can see that now. It's not so hard when
I'm lying on the grass in Dolores Park (still wearing my
suit) after a J Church streetcar ride during which she
and I wrangled the whole way -- standing up! -- arguing
around and through other strap-hangers as they gave us
the stink eye! -- and while she's waiting at home for
her estranged and probably enraged and without question
highly volatile husband to drop off their kid (this is
the rescheduled transfer; somehow he blames her for the
screwup this morning). It will be much harder when
she's in front of me and I see the need and the pain and
the tragedy and the freshness and the bewilderment all
reflected in her beautiful face, which nonetheless will

likely remain expressionless if not downright gloomy or
twisted with anger or fury -- in fact she's coming down
the hill right now, cutting across the grass, she's
moving fast and she does not look happy ---

*   *

It wasn't just much harder. It was quite
impossible.

One time last week she told me she's not sure what
love is. "I think I've always gotten love mixed up with
admiration and compassion." Whether that's true of her
feelings for me I don't know, but I do know love to her
is radically different from what it is to me.

In the park I pleaded fervently for her to overcome
her fears: I whispered "I love you" in her ear about a
dozen times straight, with as much quiet intensity and
heartfulness as I could summon. It didn't do the trick.
She's become so frightened and defensive she can reply
to my entreaties -- my begging really -- only by
remarking I'm "not seeing" her love -- and then
following up with voluminous criticism of my "demands."
From time to time she insists she does love me. But she
rarely shows it, rarely expresses it in words or
otherwise, rarely even appears to be pleased to have me
around, except at intervals much, much, much too far
apart. She becomes most ardent -- and still it's weak
and highly changeable -- when I suggest I've just about
had it with her.

That's what happened again tonight. "Will you
please become uninvolved in your feelings!" she shrieked
as we walked toward the house. I mean literally
shrieked -- it stopped people in their tracks on the
other side of the very wide Dolores Street. And that
shriek decided me. In the living room I told her I'd be
ending the "shacking-up experiment" and moving out. She
immediately became distraught and desperate.

"You can't do that! You're so cruel! I need you!"

My needs are mere feelings; her needs are real
needs. What could say it more clearly than that?

"You gotta love her with a feeling." So advises
the old R&B tune. And in my opinion the tune's got it

right. And the same goes as well for how she's gotta
love you.

And then another switcheroo. While Danny played
with the balloons I'd bought for him, his besieged
mother quickly won me back with a show of wholly
unexpected passion.

"I can't bear to live without you. You're
everything to me!" She hugged me ferociously and
addressed me with fervor. I couldn't, she declared,
reject her. "I won't let you go," she announced with
impressive defiance -- and I loved her again. "I want
to make love with you right now," she moaned. "I need
it really, really bad."

If her everyday dealings with me were invested with
even a tenth as much emotion we'd have no problems at
all. (She's just nineteen years and three months old --
as of tomorrow.) She even pulled my pants down in front
of Danny ("Peepee!" he shouted over and over, pointing
at my arc of erecting cock) but the notion of getting
it on in front of him in broad daylight discomfited both
of us. I suggested she could sit atop me, keeping her
skirt on, and Danny would never know what was happening,
but, no, she vetoed that. I could scarcely blame her
for doing so. But then she didn't want to let me leave
the house either. She knew I was expected soon at "M4M"
rehearsal.

"I still want to go with you," she kept saying,
even though Danny's presence plainly made it impossible.
Her instincts were good, however, because I fully
intended to visit Nadine as well, if possible, in hopes
she'd help me get my floundering vessel, I'll call it --
just for kicks! -- on a more even keel. But by the time
I finally split it was too late to squeeze in a visit to
Nadine.

*

Rob -- I'm back at 1616 Funston now -- Rob tells me
an ugly story from his last month at our Gatewood
homestead before he left for Arizona and eventually
here. It's midnight and brother Jeff's playing his
guitar on the upstairs porch. Dad gets up from bed and

58

storms over to the porch doorway half-naked in his
nightshirt and stands there shouting at him, "Parasite!
Parasite! Parasite!" -- repeating the word dozens of
times.

It's hard to believe Dad would be that cruel. How
could he have lost it to such a degree? Indeed Rob says
that in some ways Dad's actually much "looser" now than
he's been for many months: he's even considering sending
Rob some advance money from his education trust. (At
the moment Rob and Don and four of their friends from
Gatewood who are touring the Wild West in a VW microbus
this summer are staying here with Barb. I'm a stranger
in my own home.)

-- Barb, by the way, is barely making an effort to
be civil with me. She's apparently come to see me as
some sort of disgusting reprobate because I've taken up
with yet another woman, and this time it's a girl barely
out of puberty. I expect it will be a long time before
we can hope to regain the kind of closeness we both were
feeling only a few months ago. Perhaps I shouldn't've
told her back then she'd been too hard on Jang. But the
truth is she gave me little choice with her constant
harping on Jang's flaws as she saw them at that point
(and hasn't changed her mind about since).

Speaking of whom: another postcard and two short
letters came in from Hawaii. Scarcely a warm word can
be found in any of them. All the hopeful talk's gone
and so's the erotic lovingness. Essentially they offer
a string of her drearily familiar complaints about me
softened slightly by praise for Hawaii and an occasional
dutiful allusion to our potential future. She does
mention that the first of her Korean dance performances
in Honolulu drew "many people" and went quite well but
she gives no further details.

As for writing Jang, I don't know what I'll do.
Long ago I abandoned my ambitious plan to scrawl out a
paragraph or two for her every day. I came up with four
installments in the first two weeks and that was it. As
of this moment I'm putting off any further such
scrawling because I have no idea what to say. I guess

I'm waiting to see how things work out with Valerie.
(Jang's latest letter hints in a typically mysterious
way I may be seeing her "soon." In context it appears
she's not referring to her previously announced "early
or middle September" return date. My alarmed reaction
to this hint must mean the thought of seeing her at this
point is less exciting than disturbing. It must mean
that and therefore, yes, I'll just say it: it does.)

Tuesday 14
    Dragonburger.
    I'm in the midst of a shopping spree. This morning
it dawned on me that I can finally cash checks in San
Francisco shops and markets. Only now -- roughly three
months after the fact -- am I discovering this happy
ramification of scoring my California driver's license,
however belatedly. Having a checking account suddenly
becomes almost as dangerous as possessing a credit card!
And so, for the sheer joy of it, I'm about to buy
several items which for me are, as an economist might
say, of strictly marginal utility.
    At ten to one I'll be meeting Valerie at Grodin's.
If she wants to see me badly enough to be willing to
hike all the way down from Emp -- on a thirty-minute
lunch break -- well, I'm honored.
    Yesterday Walt Roach and I had a talk about my
future. As he sees it, I should spend the next two or
three years "getting to know different parts of the
organization." I should put in three months in the
Claims Department, three months in Loan Auth, three
months in Records, and so forth, all the way down to
Dupe (a total of eleven departments). Then when we move
into the new building on Market Street in 1973 I'd be
ready to assume a "position of importance."
    What a farce! The truth is, the man doesn't know
what to do with me. He realizes he doesn't have enough
to keep me busy (which is, I'll be so bold as to say,
the fault of his own arid imagination). Furthermore,
he'd like to maneuver me into a position where he could

more reasonably demand my conformance with conservative dress codes and thought patterns.

I objected, of course, quietly, hesitantly, and yet firmly. My talents, I told him (and this was truthful as far as it went), lie in speechwriting and advertising and A-V-related sales-promotion tasks like whipping up training videos and Honor Club films. Working in Claims would bore me to death and would probably screw up a lot of claims too. In addition, I'd learn little of value because I'd doubtless be looked upon as a spy from "the Roach"'s office.

So now I'm supposed to be thinking about it. My next meeting with him, or maybe the one after that, would be the perfect time for me to give notice. I'd say I've been thinking it over and I just don't see any way my career can move ahead at Emp. I'd say my decision's irrevocable and I'll be quitting as of late August -- the 26th to be exact (in fact I've already circled the date on my dungeon wall calendar but I haven't told anyone what this means except Jerry and Valerie and Nadine and they're all sworn to secrecy).

Or say I stay on with Valerie, either at her place or (far better) at mine. I could lay out a couple of hundred bucks a month for two years or slightly longer to meet most of our living costs. I'm sure the kind of life those bucks, when combined with her salary, would pay for would fall far short of her wildest fantasy. But might she still be okay with it? For sure she'd be quite a bit better off financially than she is now.

Or say I get back with Jang. Then I'd be able to put something down on a piece of land with a cabin in the Sierras and we could live there most of the year, depending on how many others, if any, wanted to get in on it. Unk Erik has already expressed an interest in the idea -- in fact he's the one who first proposed it. Brother Jeff's another possibility, though not a very live one (and I have my own doubts about sharing a place with Jeff right now: he's just too freaked out from the aftereffects of his battles with the Army, and no one's expecting any quick changes in that). And sister Barb is almost surely out by her own choice.

Well, enough pie-in-the-sky back-to-the-country speculation; it's time for part two of today's shopping spree to begin.

(I feel good. This morning I pounded out two articles for the Imp and did it on company time. Nadine doesn't hate me, yet. Valerie banged one of her fabulous eyes on the bus coming down this morning and had to lie down in Medical for an hour. Last night our late balling again fizzled out quickly once I was in the saddle. Neither of us has said a word about it or our notion of "holding back" on sex, now apparently abandoned. Danny crawled under the sheets with me this morning and fell asleep pressed against my right flank sort of like a hairless (almost) puppy.)

*   *

On the floor. The carpet rather. By the light of the glowing white fortune-teller's ball. Valerie is changing Danny's diaper on the couch. A moment ago I ventured to proclaim I enjoy the rhythms of her doing her mother-things here and there in the house as I read my book. I was prepared for a querulous doctrinaire feminist response, but she came back with a pleased and almost blushing "It's the feeling of a home."

I never know quite what to expect from her -- never know when she'll turn on me. Because she's capable at the slightest provocation of frightening attacks and also of long spells of moody indifference verging on catatonia, I always try to be prepared for both. In the same way she often seems terrified of what I might say or do next. Like others before her, she fears -- and she's mentioned this more than once -- I'll criticize anything and everything she says or does. Yet I don't believe I'm being overly critical -- in fact I think in general she's far more critical than I am. Then again, since we both have fathers with law degrees, maybe in reality we're not so far apart when it comes to lawyerly attributes: criticism, arguments, logic-twisting, playing devil's advocate, etc.

Enough of that.

[Shacking Up with Valerie]

"Will you please become uninvolved in your feelings!"

A demand which not only seems counterproductive in a love relationship, but quite impossible to realize and in any case directly contrary to Valerie's own -- and my own too -- celebration of spontaneity and self-acceptance. And yet it's still a demand I'm hearing often enough from her that it seems to be constantly ringing in my ears.

You got to, you just got to love her with -- yeah. Many of those damn things! And from the deepest chambers of the human heart! And may it ever be so!

I could write about the enormous differences between us stemming from her being French/Chinese-Vietnamese-American and me Anglo/Scots-Irish/Teutonic/Scandinavian-American. But the truth is I think about these differences probably a lot less often than I should. (Today I bought a French phrase book, and I was disappointed to discover French is not easy. After my wretched struggles with Korean I'd somehow expected French to be a snap, not much different from a tricky variant of English, like Pig Latin.)

Perhaps our cultural differences have largely escaped my scrutiny because, again after Jang -- that is, after the clash of East and West in much more extreme form -- they seem more like mere regional differences, say resembling those between California and Illinois. I must adjust my fine tuning, calibrate it in such a way it can pick up on these lesser, but undoubtedly even more complex, differences that really do exist between us at the sociocultural level -- not to mention the ones that dwell in Valerie all by herself (including those she picked up as a child in her most formative years from her Senegalese nanny, to whom she was very close, during the family's stay in Africa).

Or I could write about the equally startling fact that our answers to a standard newspaper computer quiz for prospective mates show us to be "highly compatible." Aside from two questions we interpreted differently, we answered them all the same way, although, again

surprisingly to me, in a third of the instances my
feelings and opinions were more emphatic than hers. If
she agreed "somewhat," I tended to agree "strongly."
"That's because you've had much longer to test your
opinions," she opined with just a barely perceivable
impish smile (she does like to tease me about what an
ancient I am -- two years older than the already ancient
Jim! Almost as old as her mother's current boyfriend!).

Wednesday 15
     What a bummer. It's become insanely manic. The
ups and downs hit in ever-shortening cycles. Valerie
kneeling by my chair here in the dungeon, glancing
anxiously at my pocket watch as we hassle gloomily. Ah,
fuck. The problem of the moment is once again a sexual
one, at least on the surface. We just can't get the
rutting right. When I'm turned on to her she rebuffs me
with indifference or gross insensitivity. She turns on
to me when I'm so tired I'm pure mellow or (especially)
when I get riled up because of her earlier rebuffs, and
by then I'm likely to be so upset I can do nothing but
withdraw into my fury and ignore her. We haven't had
real sex since Sunday morning, though I've wanted it
constantly and she says (now) she has too.
     The problem's a subtle one, because I find her
extremely attractive -- as I think by now I've made
plenty clear in here -- and I believe she sees me in at
least somewhat the same way. Yet when the opportunity
finally presents itself for our making something
carnally juicy of all this attraction, it's usually not
long before I'm put off by her sudden seeming lack of
interest not to mention enthusiasm and responsiveness.
When it really counts, getting it on with me appears to
mean little or nothing to her. This stings, but it's
how things are. The only times she's shown desire in a
way truly gratifying to me have come when -- to repeat
myself on this also just because it matters so damn much
to me -- the only times she's really seemed to want me,
I say, have come when I've gotten upset and thrown up a

wall against her and refused to let myself be seduced:
it's become a matter of pride not to give in. In other
words, when we're fighting.

It's a terrible bind to be in, because she doesn't
understand the dynamics of it, as far as I can tell, and
if I try to explain what I think she's missing she gets
uptight because she thinks I'm criticizing her for not
being servile and mindlessly adoring. That's not what I
want at all! Other than the fact that sexual desire is
involved, I'd say, the man-woman thing is actually
pretty much irrelevant here. It's a question of two
human beings expressing with their bodies the pleasure
they take in each other.

I can't find adequate words for it. So I'll try
again later. Or not.

At the moment it all seems hopelessly complicated
and devoid of workable answers.

I'm really down.

I need a warm, expansive woman in whose presence I
can relax and let things happen naturally and
spontaneously. Each day with Valerie I feel more
uptight, more frustrated, more desperate to find a way
either to break through to her or to break away from
her.

The other day she said something about wishing I'd
make her apartment my place too. It was a sharp
observation. I haven't yet felt comfortable enough with
her to adopt her place as my own. Because she's such a
neatness and cleanliness freak -- as I'm realizing more
and more -- I make every conceivable effort to keep the
place exactly as it was the moment I arrived on the
scene, or better to say the moment just before I
arrived. I feel uneasy if the slightest trace of the
debris of daily living kicked up by me remains
detectable. I conscientiously pick up and discard in
the trash not just the evening paper itself but every
last one of the tiny paper shreds that fall off the
ragged edges of the pages as I turn them (I scarcely
even noticed their existence until she pointed out a
scattered infestation of these shreds, much like

flattened inchworms from apples, on the kitchen floor).

Truth is, in our "shack" I feel I've become more an intruder than a beloved shackee. And this is at least in part because I'm trying to be sensitive to what she's told me was bad about life with Jim and what's hard for her now as, I'll say again, she tries to raise a kid by herself while holding down a full-time job and staying politically active. She disliked Jim's reading the paper when he got home -- so I read the paper surreptitiously and when she approaches I hastily lay it aside as if caught in a shameful act.

The girl -- the teenager -- has me thoroughly cowed. And feeling cowed is a state I prefer to avoid if at all possible.

How is it, then, that last night we could lie on the bed gazing into each other's eyes and I could feel, however fleetingly, that, yes, here was the love of a lifetime?

*   *

You are a formidable adversary, Valerie Mailloux. (For just a moment I'll try to ignore the Bando part.) To attempt to broach your ramparts, Mlle. Mailloux, is fearsome indeed. Where your walls are weakest you've garrisoned the most firepower under instructions to destroy anything that moves. You're well-nigh impregnable. The one man who's managed to breach your innermost conventional defenses (you know who I mean) was eventually demolished by your irregular guerrilla forces engaged in underground resistance.

What's the use?

Valerie Mailloux, how do you do?

The latest installment was a furious lunch-hour shouting match at St. Mary's Square and on the sidewalks of Chinatown. Luckily it's a cold, foggy day and the streets are relatively uncrowded, or we might have incited a riot (she is, after all, half Chinese: I've finally gotten that much straight).

No, it wasn't really that bad, or at least not that obvious to others, though plenty of people stared. We were still wrangling about last night, but the

proximate issue had switched to a poem she wrote this
morning and my reply to it. Her poem is a bilious flow
of four-letter words including such scatological verses
as "it doesn't sell/rot in hell/& eat shit" and "if you
shoot/mean to hit" and "life's itch/is a bitch." I
replied with appropriate outrage; but she dismissed this
by offhandedly remarking she really hadn't intended the
poem to mean anything. In fact she'd just slightly
rewritten a list of "dirty words and phrases" another
girl in Claims had drawn up for her to help expand her
English vocabulary in a crucial area.

The fighting between us is bitter, angry, intense,
fiery. The few lulls occur when I momentarily sigh and
give up and stare off into the distance. She always has
a bristling defense ready, whatever I may say. She's
never open to reason while fighting, never amenable to
compromise, never one to call for a truce or to suggest
ways to improve things. In short, she's a spitfire!
(And thanks for the attempt to warn me, Ted.)

An example:

It was past the time when she was due back at work.
We were standing at the corner of Grant and California.
She had stormed off charging steeply uphill toward the
Emp north-side entrance but then after about thirty feet
spun around and stormed right back down in truly
frightening fashion, "radical eyes" flashing and
nostrils flaring and tears streaming and those
magnificent lips of hers pouting as only such freaky
Mick Jagger-like smackers can do. Now, after taking her
in my arms and reassuring her ("Damn it, we'll beat this
thing!"), I was telling her I thought she'd better be
getting back to the office.

"Why? This is more important!"

"Well sure, but if you don't show up soon you might
be fired. We'll be okay. We can fight later. Come on,
be sensible."

"I don't care about the fucking job! What's that
compared to this?"

"But don't you want to be the one to decide when
you'll quit, rather than get booted out because we fell

into some stupid quarrel?"

And she, all but violently pushing down my arms and breaking away, again with eyes flashing, nostrils flaring, jaw jutting, etc., and in a cold, suspicious, disdainful tone: "You'd just feel guilty if I were fired!"

She calls this being "nasty." "I have a talent for it," she breezily admits. "People have told me that ever since I was little." It's also quite clear she enjoys using that talent.

So. The rages of "Frenchie" Mailloux. This was the third -- and actually the shortest -- in less than forty minutes.

*   *

A final stab at describing today's dismaying doings.

Valerie came by the dungeon at three o'clock during her afternoon break. This time she was more composed at the start but soon she pushed her objections further than ever before. First she told me things such as, "My girlfriend Jenny says I'm just the way I was when Jim and I were separating. For a while I was getting better, I was doing things, I was regaining my balance, and then I met you. Ever since then I've been regressing." Then, when I responded by suggesting maybe we'd better cool it tonight -- I would hit the JCC for B-ball and a swim while she was at her DPC meeting and then I'd meet her at "the shack" -- she began bawling loudly.

It's hopeless to continue this way. As she leveled her latest round of accusations I decided I'd had it: I would unilaterally declare the "experiment" to be at an end for real and return to living at Funston. I refrained from telling her this only because she'd take it as a threat and all hell would break loose right there in the A-V room.

Now that I've simmered down I'm toying with another approach. It's a fact that her coolness renders me all but impotent (sometimes literally and totally so). I become a bumbling fool trying desperately to win her approval. She'll deign to grant it to me only rarely. She believes if she gives in to me on anything -- even just tentatively -- she'll become too vulnerable and have nothing left to "hold" me with (or so she says).

So: I'll try something different. I'll become the self-serving tyrant she often accuses me of being. I'll no longer attempt to please her. I will indeed "become uninvolved in my feelings." My feelings for her and about her have become "too intense," she says. All right, I'll cut them off before they surface.

I'll try, anyway. Might as well. See what happens.

Probably I won't be able to pull it off. The sparkling give-and-take between man and woman often seems to be a big part of what I live for. I'm childishly martyring myself -- but what have I got to lose?

Valerie, that's what. But I've already lost her -- I've lost the Valerie I thought I could love. She's vanished!

It seems sooner or later I go through this stage in every serious relationship. I begin playing dangerous games, suppressing my own feelings, giving in to the volatile imperatives of desperation and resentment. This stage always precedes the death of my feeling for a woman I'd previously thought I was deeply into. For sure it was the case with the Big Three of my loves: with Lisa, with Ciara, with Jang (several times). And with others. When it's over, when my anger has purged itself, little will be left of the original super-powerful feeling but sympathy, pity, and an occasional upwelling of something that might be called instant nostalgia tinged lightly with regret.

I hope it doesn't turn out that way this time. But I fear it will.

The main difference with Valerie is it's happening sooner. The whole thing's been compressed into two weeks (as of today, starting from the "Human Chain") and thus become just that much more intense. As I get older it seems the cycles are becoming shorter and shorter and more and more intense.

And so what? So now for my role with Valerie I
turn totally selfish. I transmute into the stereotype
of the domineering male she loves to spout off about.
Marlboro Man updated. Mr. Macho. Mr. Swagger. The
hard line. Hud. Stanley Kowalsky. Maybe even Warren
Beatty in "Promise Leslie Caron Anything."

He was a great hit with Denise, Mr. Macho was. Why
not with Valerie too?

Thursday 16

I'm mystified as to what prompted it, but somehow
we reconciled 'round about midnight and balled twice in
the early-morning hours. -- Balled, in fact, as we
never have before. Valerie didn't even blink at my
tough-guy neo-Marlboro Man role, except to say, as we
returned home from the DPC meeting -- which we wound up
attending together, yes -- she felt "almost good again."
She liked Mr. Macho! Just as Denise did! And Valerie
is supposedly a feminist! -- So then I redoubled my
efforts, and after a while she did mention she thought I
was being "a little rude." Otherwise she seemed pleased
and rather relieved, I thought. I had become exactly
what she believes all men already are by nature.

I sparked the argument that began later by blowing
my cover in a letter to her. In the argument she gave
no ground at all -- not a single pinch of soil -- but
she impressed me with her ferocity and the cleverness of
her logic, she made me feel pity for her because of her
deadly and almost hysterical seriousness ("Jim and I
argued like this almost every night for two years; how
can I help but be 'defensive'?"), and she pounded away
at me relentlessly until my own case collapsed from its
seeming irrelevance. If she needed me this desperately,
what was the point of quibbling over her pose of disdain
and indifference? -- Such unconscious reasoning, I
think, caused my resentment to evaporate, at least for
the moment. I just hope it's true, as she says it is,
that although she may appear intransigent and uncaring

on the surface, underneath she's carefully considering
what I say and...she loves me.

Here's an example of her reasoning. In her own
words it lays out some of her major dissatisfactions
with me.

> When I said to you to get uninvolved
> from your emotions, I meant long enough
> for you to see and comprehend my own or at
> least acknowledge that I have some and as
> vivid as yours may be to you or me. I
> know you have been playing games, more
> obviously this evening -- don't you think
> I'm aware at all? This is beside the
> point. You did not get yourself
> uninvolved from your emotions, for you
> don't seem to be any more aware. All you
> have done is what could be called putting
> a leash on them.
>
> While you were typing, I was writing to
> you and at the same time discovering ways
> to improve our relationship. I was also
> trying to get out all the suffering that's
> going on inside of me because by your
> adopted attitude you are hurting yourself
> more than you're doing any good for anyone.
>
> I said to you earlier this evening that
> you were rude. The basis of my saying so
> is that you showed little concern about me.
> You had established plans and displayed
> them -- didn't care for my approval or
> consent -- maybe I had plans of my own? I
> do not resent you for having diverse
> interests -- I think it's great -- but if
> you love me as you say why don't you make
> an effort to get me interested too or
> somewhat involved so that I will feel I'm
> contributing and consequently not left out
> or rejected or dragged along ---

These concerns of hers perplex and dishearten me.
Ever since meeting her I've devoted nearly all my waking

hours to trying to please her. Can she possibly think I
do the laundry with her, shop with her, help her clean
up, etc., etc., etc., and try to do all these right
alongside her and to her standards and not mine, for
sheer love of such drudgery? Matters like these she
scarcely notices. Did I not join her at the DPC meeting
last night when I had intended to do my own thing at the
JCC? The truth is I'm much too considerate of her needs
and desires, to the point now where I think it's
probably become cloying to her in a way she doesn't even
recognize. And I know it's becoming more disturbing by
the day to me.

     She charges me with being so engrossed in my own
emotions I'm "unaware" of hers, I don't "comprehend"
hers, I don't "acknowledge" them. Again, the real
problem is I'm super-aware of her emotions -- the few
she shows. Because I sometimes object to them she feels
I fail to "comprehend" them. But her chief complaint is
that I'm unaware of her "real" emotions -- that is, the
ones she fails to express or intentionally keeps hidden.
I can't read her mind: that's her real gripe with me.
Well, actually I believe I can read her mind and I do
read her mind. I do sense her real emotions -- and my
pleas that she acknowledge and express them
straightforwardly and in detail make her uptight. These
"demands" of mine cause her to feel vulnerable. The
truth can hurt: especially when similar truths,
similarly expressed by her in the past to Jim, have
backfired on her and helped to cause a seemingly endless
series of terrible fights with him.

*   *

     Surprise: a fine, sunny, relaxed and yet very
moving and inspiring lunch with Valerie in the park.
And now I'm back in the mausoleum.

     "We're immune to life in this place," she declared,
before trudging off to Claims for the afternoon shift.

     First thing in the park -- right under the steely
eyes of Benny Bufano's Sun Yat-sen statue -- I gave her
a card imploring "Don't be so pigheaded!" in French. It
was meant as a joke, and for once she took it as one.

[Shacking Up with Valerie]

And then moments later came a wrenching revelation.
It was sparked by my joking reference to the ferocious
way she came storming down the California Street hill at
me yesterday. When she was a small girl, she said, her
father used to call her "Valkyrie" for the way she flew
at him in similar but even wilder and more desperate
fashion with her fists churning. She did this in an
attempt to stop him when he was beating her mother -- "I
wanted to kill him!" -- and then he would simply expand
the beating to include her -- and this was when she was
just five or six years old. "I always felt very proud,"
she said, "to be called a Valkyrie by him." "Sometimes
I even called myself that to my friends, like at school.
I played the role. It was all mixed up with my Joan of
Arc thing. I rescued my mother over and over, dozens of
times. My father's beatings would always leave her and
me bloody and bruised. I was very proud of that too,
like they were war wounds. My mother and I would salve
each other's wounds."

By now tears were leaking out. But she wiped them
away with a tissue and then -- those "radical eyes"
suddenly flashing and thunderbolting in a way I'd never
seen before -- she launched into a fiery rant on
"Indochine": how she'd like to be a "real" Valkyrie and
fly straight over there and do what Valkyries famously
do. "I'm serious! The American soldiers, I want to
strangle them all with my bare hands! They're like the
French before except all the bombs and napalm make them
a hundred times worse!" -- and continued in that vein
for a truly righteous and intense minute or two (about
halfway through this outburst the couple occupying the
rest of our bench departed with sandwiches in mid bite
for another bench on the far side of the park).

And this revelation of the roots of Valerie's
fighting spirit -- and simultaneous demonstration of
that spirit -- totally blew me away. Remind me: what
had our petty little personal quarrels been about again?

*   *

Ah yes, it's turned into a very good day, even
though I'm so tired and Dr. Walcott's waiting room is so

73

hot I dozed off and then lurched out of it a few minutes
ago, seeing an apparition of Ciara as Ophelia (she
called excitedly from Los Gatos to tell me of a Paine
Knickerbocker review in today's Chronicle which calls
her performance excellent: "Ciara Sandefjord...
vulnerable, eager, beautiful, sensitive, and does a fine
job with the difficult mad scene"). A very good day,
yes, but from my perspective only minorly because of
this review. It's majorly because Valerie seems happy
all of a sudden and again at least appears to be loving
me. At times she even lapses into bursts of outright
gaiety. They're short-lived and sometimes awkward or
even harsh in a strange sort of way, these bursts, as if
she were staggering around on raw new turf, but I have
no doubt they're real. When she visited me in the
morgue at afternoon break to pick up my copy of Kate
Millett's "Sexual Politics" the attraction between us
was so strong she could scarcely work up the will to
leave.

This sudden change, I think, can be traced to our
righteous talk in the park, yes, but at the same time,
and maybe even more so, to our balling last night. It's
the first time it's been really good. And good balling
can reduce lots of overblown tense domestic arguments to
the trivial and almost unnoticeable mere tongue-waggings
they should be seen as.

Actually the first round in bed last night wasn't
so great, but after four days of going without who
cared. I was on top, she was pretty much motionless
below. Too often she offers her body in a lackluster
sort of defensive posture that makes getting myself more
than about halfway in awkward, and so I put most of my
effort into finding a rhythm pleasing to her, hoping
she'll eventually relax and loosen up. She gives no
signals as to what she's liking or disliking, however,
or precious few, even if I ask or plead or demand, nor
does she show any sign of relaxing, and so after a while
my frustration leads to intensified attempts to break
down her defenses and/or go deeper, which as a rule she
doesn't seem to dig too much. On this occasion I pushed

her halfway off the bed three or four times and for each
of those we had to stop to rearrange ourselves.

   Even so, she seemed to like it...at least a
little...for a while. Probably I went on with it too
long. But when I asked about this in medias coitus she
insisted I keep going. Eventually she said (again only
when I asked) she'd like me to get her off with my hand;
and while keeping my cock partway in her, I finally
succeeded in doing this. Shortly afterwards I came in
great gushy spasms myself. (Even when climaxing she
usually moves very little -- a sudden, tightening arch,
a brief whimper that's barely audible, and that's it.
The kind of touch she likes on her clit is extremely
light, just as with her nipples but even more so.) ---

                 *   *

   In a field of flowers raised above the city, thin
sunlight, good air, only half a block down from 1616
(the house atop its huge rock up there dominates the
scene down here like a deteriorating watchtower that was
once part of a now-crumbled fort whose lower parts have
been replaced by standard city housing). And I'm
chuckling with delight. The doc, somewhat to my
surprise, says my health is excellent. The beat-up van
Jeff and I bought for a song seven or eight months ago
is finally repaired and ready for new adventures, the
novel ("Pluche" -- translated from the French) is a
wonderfully good read, even if it does frequently tweak
my conscience a bit painfully. And finally, ultimately,
things seem to be going much better with Valerie.

   It's good to get away from her for an hour or two
-- more would be too much under current conditions --
because suddenly, aided by the vista and the breeze and
the trembling purple flowers high as my waist in places,
I've gained the perspective to see what a large and
indispensable part she's already playing in my life.
One might almost say she's become my life.

   From here I can more easily see back over the days
we've been together. It's startling to realize I've
spent only one night at Funston since the hour we first
really met, and that one night was at the very beginning

75

and unavoidable, since she had to go to Tahoe for a day
with her brother and mother and her mother's boyfriend
(they're all big gamblers, which thank the gods she's
not). All of this fills me with wonder and awe -- and
fear. How could I so quickly love a woman so much?

    A moment ago when I felt the urge to write this as
I was rambling along Lawton Street, I heedlessly plopped
myself down on the ground next to a large rock and
immediately began scribbling. Only when I was well into
it did I notice that if I'd landed a few inches to the
left I'd've mutilated myself on the jagged edges of a
broken beer bottle half buried in the sandy soil like
some sort of Vietcong booby trap. That sent a shudder
coursing down to my toes. Who knows what dangers may
lurk in the abysses into which I hurl myself? And yet,
though one must maintain a cautious guard against the
perils of impetuosity and romantic illusion, among more
than a few others, there can be no better path than the
one marked out by sudden soul-stirring inspiration:
    Valerie it is.

Friday 17
    Dream fragments.
    Four famous movie actresses. Valerie and I watched
as they squirmed on the floor. Then four naked men
appeared. The eight balled in a neat row and in uncanny
synchrony, like robots. Valerie was fascinated, I was
embarrassed. This was in Lahontan; I was showing her
the city of my birth. I had parked the L.C. on a
rooftop. V and I somehow got separated. When we
returned to the parking garage we found it closed.
After breaking in and scrambling up to the roof we
discovered the L.C. had been upended with Danny inside.
His face was pressed flat against the window and he was
crying but we couldn't get the door open.
              *   *

    Valerie brings me English muffins and a glass of
orange juice. It's been a hectic night. Danny's
growing resentment of me is reaching new heights. He

made frequent trips into the bedroom, and at six he
moved in here permanently, crawling all over and around
us as we tried to grab a few last winks. Valerie easily
loses her patience with him, screams at him, is
alarmingly harsh at times, but she doesn't punish or
discipline or distract him effectively. So Danny can
act spoiled and be demanding and get away with both.
"He learns it all from Jim," has been her main comment
on this situation, usually offered with a grim nostril-
flaring effort at self-control. This topic is obviously
at or near the top on their current fight card.

I try to cool her off and also to restrain my own
impulses to make Danny mind his Ps and Qs. I yield to
them only when he hits or kicks me especially viciously;
then I lightly slap his hand or foot -- so lightly I
scarcely even touch him -- and even then I feel I have
no right to be doing such a thing, and regardless of
that I shouldn't be doing it. "I just wish we could
have a little privacy!" Valerie cried as Danny,
diaperless, crawled over us while she was fondling my
grossly elongated morning-wood cock under the covers. I
try to ease her mind a bit by voicing feel-good bromides
along the lines of, "Well, at least this will make us
value more highly the time we do have free together, am
I right?" She seems touched but not convinced.

"KCBS news time: 7:28."

Usually by now I'd be up, brushing my teeth in the
small bathroom with her at my back. Three of the walls
in there bear large mirrors, making for some fascinating
double- and triple-image infinite regressions that
nicely symbolize the complexities of coupledom. I'd be
secretly watching her put on eye makeup or brush her
gorgeous hair as her back muscles rippled above her
sweet little uptilted tush partially encased in purple
bikini briefs with the glutes swelling up out of them
making for deliciously curvaceous "butt cleavage" (I do
gaze a lot at her body when I think she's not looking).
Ordinarily I'd be up doing all that, I say, but last
night I brought over the Honda. This means we can leave
for work a little later, at five after eight or so.

"Details in a moment."

Most of yesterday was very good for us but it ended
miserably. The balling we'd been looking forward to all
day -- or at least I thought so -- fizzled badly. I
couldn't find her magic button this time, and when I
accidentally scratched her vulva slightly with a
fingernail her ardor quickly faded, to put it mildly,
and then so did mine. For me her cry of pain over the
scratch provoked too many images of her traumatic sex
with Jim after Danny's birth and her acerbic comments
to me about how much she hated it.

Two honks: the babysitter's here.

                    *   *

** I'm becoming more and more daring in the way I
dress for work. I'm in a suit today, true, but my shirt
is unironed, wrinkled by two days' wear. My hair hasn't
been cut in months, since well before New York. My tie
(the green-and-blue-striped one) has several greasy
stains on it in back and a faint one in front that may
be jizz-related, though I have no memory of how it got
there. -- Or oops, yes I do. Jang at the pornoflick
(our very first one together in a theater) during our
most recent comeback attempt.

** I was supposed to have the script for a new
Loan Auth training video ready for Friday. I haven't
even begun work on it. The Roachman could call at any
moment. What's more, a rumor's going around about a new
Phase II Emp crackdown on freaks like Jerry and me. The
crew down in the computer room (all Imp supporters, Milt
and Ted included) would be decimated.

** As I feared, a letter from Jang was awaiting me
at home. I put off reading it until this morning
because I knew my spirits would be dampened (and not in
the pornoflick sense) if I opened it last night. But
they were dampened anyway.

** I'll make no decisions about Jang until next
month. At this moment if I had to choose between
Valerie and Jang, I'd probably lean toward Valerie,
though the choice is far from clear-cut. It's just I
can't get images of Jang out of my head. My latest take

[Shacking Up with Valerie]

on Valerie is that she's permitted the world to defeat
her; she's rancorous and dispirited and full of her
goddamn unending "ressentiment"; she says so herself. I
don't know: the emotional differences between Jang and
Valerie are so great they seem to elude all my attempts
to pin them down. And, as I say, I don't want to make
any premature decisions. Then again it wasn't my idea
for Jang to go off to Hawaii for three months just when
it seemed we might be finding our way back together
again. Why she did that I will never, ever understand.
On the other hand it might turn out to be the best thing
that's ever happened to me. Or among the top ten, let's
say. And the same might be true for Jang, no question.
For her it may even rise to the top two or three.

Yes, it's depressing to me that I'm still
permitting my life to be buffeted by such "love crises."
Time after time after time. A line in "Pluche" hits the
mark: if you're not already happy, no lover can make you
so. (It could even be a few other writers beat the
estimable Jean Dutourd, author of "Pluche," in getting
that same profound thought into print.)

*   *

I don't believe it: I may have gained something of
value from a project I did for "the Roach"!

This week I've been working on, among other things,
a film strip called "Let's Be Human." In 1940s
trappings and I hope with a fair amount of humor --
relatively, for Promo Department filmstrips -- it
presents several fundamental notions which I too often
lose sight of.

Start with this basic principle: criticizing people
rarely if ever leads to any change in their behavior.
Looking back, I have to wonder if all the criticism I've
dished out over the years has ever produced a single
instance of real change of a positive kind. My
conclusion is that I criticize mainly because I need to,
because I derive personal satisfaction from it. To get
results one should take just the opposite approach: it's
praise that makes people want to do better. If it's
absolutely necessary to criticize, one should, first,

find something to praise; second, criticize gently in
the shadow of that praise, as it were; and third,
criticize as one sinner would another, i.e. with a big
dose of humility. Because all criticism, even the most
"constructive" kind, is fundamentally hubristic.

Arguing, that is, trying to persuade someone to
change an opinion, is actually just another form of
criticism. Forcefulness is useless, and logic is no
better. Argument is worthwhile, really, only between
people who understand and respect each other's opinions;
they engage in it to entertain each other and to sharpen
their own thoughts or help the other sharpen his -- or
hers, yes. Unfortunately, though, in my experience it's
rare to encounter an attractive woman who likes to do
this in the way just cited.

Bottom line: I should try to cut down on the amount
of criticism I dish out, including the argumentative
type. And then I should recommend to Valerie in
particular, and in a spirit of humility and
entertainment and as a complement to my own self-
improvement efforts, and gently and very cautiously too,
that she do the same.

To all of which I'll now retort: good luck, fella!

                    *   *

I never did write anything about the second time
Valerie and I got it on the other night. It was short
but it was by far the best it's been for us, and I
wouldn't be surprised if it turns out to be the best
it'll ever be for us. We were both startled, I think,
that it happened at all. Never before, so far as I can
recall, had we balled twice in a night (will we ever
again?). It happened, to my mind, because we were both
so relieved to have the fight over with.

After the first round we lay together on our backs
in the partially darkened bedroom, savoring our glowing
bodies and the air that we'd finally managed to clear.
I put her hand on my "fire eggs" (Jang's term), mostly
just for the comfort of it; she began absentmindedly
playing a little with my "membre viril" (she does call
it that sometimes). It almost immediately began to

stiffen again, first thickening and stretching out
navelward and then lifting slowly and creakily like a
beat-up old wooden drawbridge (to wheel out a wobbly
trope), eventually locking in place at about a thirty-
degree angle above my belly with her hand still lightly
riding it. Because she didn't seem to be responding or
even taking notice of this wondrous phenomenon I waited
a long time before making a move. I suspected she'd
been exhausted by the first go-round -- the one in which
I pushed her off the bed three or four times -- and
might reject me if I pursued a second round; and if she
didn't do that, she'd probably just be tolerating me as
she's told me she often used to tolerate Jim, hating him
the whole time (did I not mention this before?). Also,
despite what was happening in that one isolated part of
my body, I was tired myself and knew we had to get up
early for work and recalled, again, her comments about
Jim making her go through sleepless nights of rutting
before she went off to her job in the morning and the
daylong agonies this caused her. But in the end I
couldn't give up without even making an attempt, however
meek and mild-mannered it might turn out to be.

Fumbly-mouthed I asked, "You up for an encore?" I
said this so quietly she couldn't hear and I had to
repeat it.

"Yes, of course," she replied in an annoyingly
offhand manner, which confirmed to me she hadn't even
noticed the hyper-engorged state (veins protruding, head
torqued) my "membre" was in. It was as if I'd asked for
a second helping from a dish located near her at dinner
while her head was turned away because she was engaged
in conversation with someone much more interesting.
"Yes of course I'll pass you the broccoli," grump grump.

What happened then happened quickly, and probably
by accident: I rolled over and "mounted" her and entered
from a certain previously untried angle, lifting her
little gymnast's ass with one hand so that it tilted a
bit to the side, going deep almost immediately since she
was still juiced up from the first round, and then
pumping away; and it was obviously good for her, she

81

gave out with a series of delicious moans like nothing
I've ever heard from her before (or since), and within
just two or three minutes her body arched and she came
powerfully, shouting almost -- "Ah! Ah! Ah! Ah!" --
and taking me right along with her just seconds later.

*   *

James Kunen writes in "The Strawberry Statement":
"I can't be too close to the radicals sometimes. I just
don't feel as sure about myself as they seem to feel
about themselves." I often feel this way myself.
Radical leaders frequently repel me because of their
arrogance and seeming self-certainty. Of course that
doesn't necessarily mean I disagree with their views.
Like Kunen, probably, I just need periods of detachment
during which I can sort out my feelings about what these
people are saying or doing, and by the time I've done
this events have probably moved on. Which is to say:
Kunen and I are both basically writers, not politicians.

*   *

For a creative man the inability to
create is the supreme humiliation.
Personally, it makes me humble on every
level, fearful, timid, cowed. Ugh!
                    -- Pluche

Every day I live with this supreme humiliation.
What makes it even more agonizing is I'm not even sure
I'm "a creative man" to start with. (But then, who
really can be sure of such a thing? You may be sure
about something you did in the past -- if you're lucky
-- but you can never be sure about who you'll be or
what you'll do in the future. And so if you are sure
about such things, you're a fool. -- But I'll make an
exception here for Pluche.)

Saturday 18
      Sitting on a high-backed stone bench at the head of
the California Street stairs. Behind me the Palace of
the Legion of Honor looms like a Roman ruin.
      "What a ruthless thing it is," entones the pompous

fellow in tights standing a few steps below me, "for the
rebellion of a codpiece to take away the life of a man."
   "Cut!" cries Jerry Borden.
   The crew shivers in a tight huddle behind the
cameraman on this dead-end street. A few curious
onlookers peer out the upstairs windows of their
apartment houses. What? Elizabethan drama? Here?
Today? On a chilly overcast Saturday morning when they,
the onlookers, could be sleeping in? And yet also a
morning rattled incessantly by bellowing foghorns? (For
some odd acoustical reason the foghorns are so loud
here, well away from the bay or ocean, that one wouldn't
be surprised to see an overloaded cruise ship come
plowing around the corner and up one's block.)
                    *   *
   In the L.C. now. A hundred feet to the west the
cast is devouring egg-salad sandwiches. I'm still
perplexed, as I have been from day one, as to just what
my role is supposed to be as "co-producer." So far,
except for adapting a few lines from the play --
"rewriting Shakespeare," as I like to say -- I've been
totally superfluous, as indeed I am again today. But
out of curiosity, not to mention the good fortune of
being paid (maybe) for doing a little close study of one
of the darker and lesser but still undeniably mind-
boggling Bardian efforts, and of course out of the
simple materialism already noted, I'll stay on for the
time being. The production, however, is entirely
Borden's. (Don't know why I never thought before of
calling Jerry "the Bord" but I think I'll start now.)
   Perhaps I'm intending to stick with this gig solely
from awe of the Bord's creative energy. Regardless of
how the film turns out, at least he'll have accomplished
something. From where I sit I can see twenty people
who've been pulled along in the wake of his raucous
drive and not-to-be-denied vision, however cockamamie it
may be at times (meaning often). The twenty-first sits
here nonsensically jabbering in ink about it all. ---
                    *   *
   -- Pam Wineberry joined me there for a few minutes.

                         83

Together we burned through a marijuana-laced Park Lane
cigarette (filter tip) shipped here by a friend of hers
who "cleans up" on the Saigon black market.

Pam doesn't know quite what to make of me.
Aggressive woman that she is, it's not too hard to tell
she'd like us to get it on. For one thing, not only
does she openly stare at my codpiece, so to speak, but
she practically licks her lips while doing so. She's
also busty and knows how to flaunt the fact as well as
the glands themselves. Yet I fail to take advantage of
the opportunities she generously displays and all but
bundles out before me. I just make a more or less
polite feint toward them and then pull back. She enjoys
the game, it appears, but at the same time she's probing
to find out why I won't go further.

"You're shy, aren't you," she ventured.

When I confessed this could be so, yeah, she
observed I'm twenty-seven, I've "got it together,"
therefore I must know what I want.

Why do I hold back? She's attractive to me.
But...Valerie and Jang and Nadine as current interests;
Denise and Celeste and Ciara as fairly recent object
lessons; Pam's age (though it's probably not much more
than Jang's); the hassles which failing to keep things
tamped down could cause with the film company; her overt
aggressiveness, which is a bit much, to my mind,
especially given the other factors. Beyond that...well,
maybe I really am shy. Or on the other hand -- and I'll
admit this is a long shot -- maybe I'm finally starting
to wise up about how to deal with such temptations.

                        *   *

Valerie is gradually loosening up, but what she's
revealing in the process neither comes quickly enough
nor will it, I fear, be enough. Things have never been
better between us, but my inner doubts are again on the
rise. I can't say exactly why this is. My admiration
for her hasn't decreased at all; if anything it's grown.
Surely in part it's a matter of her still being numbed
by the breakup of her marriage and the nasty divorce
process she's currently going through and the ways that

nastiness spills over into so much else that's happening (not least, I'll note again, her endless shrieking and raging phone battles with Jim). Beyond this it seems to be largely a matter of our vastly different temperaments and emotional styles. And it could be she's unconsciously or even consciously (though she denies it) withholding something of herself because she realizes the depth of my attachment to Jang, which we've talked about a fair amount -- and she openly admits to envying Jang, and Ciara as well, for their professional successes and sometimes seems to act defiantly toward me as a kind of retaliation -- for my supposedly expecting her to live up to them or simply "expecting too much" from her considering she's such a tenderfoot).

Whatever it is, I'm again feeling gloomy today. It's not simply that I recoil at the prospect of making a choice between Jang and Valerie in the next month or two, although the anticipatory guilt is already bothering me no matter which way things may wind up going. Nor is it simply the near-terminal state of my hopes that Valerie will ever love me in the way I need and want. No, the malaise goes deeper. I think maybe my soul's fallen sick from inhaling corporate fumes for the past eighteen months, much as a native of tropical jungles will soon expire from sheer exposure in a smoggy northern city. And under these conditions -- and possibly, I might as well say, under many other kinds of conditions -- I may not be capable of making deeply informed ("solid") emotional decisions.

*   *

Back to Valerie. After zipping home last night we argued about letters to the editor in yesterday's Chronicle on the subject of feminism/women's lib. Each time something like this happens I'm forcefully reminded of how chillingly close to implacable is Valerie's hostility toward men. After the way her father treated her I wonder whether any of the rest of us ever had or will have a chance, and that includes even the despicable Jim Bando.

At this point she and I are so turned around that

every time I do something "considerate" for her I'm
tempted to announce I'm doing it and how thoughtful it
is just in case she hasn't noticed. More than once I've
succumbed to this temptation.

A magnificent sight as we left the house at eight
p.m. A massive fogbank rising to several thousand feet,
part of it an ominous black, was swallowing the upper
reaches of the taller downtown skyscrapers as it rolled
in from an unusual direction, the northwest, with the
obliquely sunward side glowing the same reddish gold as
the sunset far to, yes, the west. ---
                    *   *

Valerie seemed to be enjoying the Pitschel Players.
As we watched, however, resentment built up in me
because in a number of small but annoying ways she was
slighting me. When I whispered in her ear, "They're
pretty good, don't you think?", she replied way too
loudly rather than in a reciprocal ear-warming whisper,
"They're not bad." -- The real message seeming to be
this: "Stop with the idiotic questions, asshole!"

Things didn't get any better after the show.
Complaining of a headache, she disdained my suggestion
that we look for a place where we could dance, i.e., one
which would let her in without an ID. We limped home
(on my 90 with the flickery malfunctioning headlight)
and then lay on the carpet in the gloomy moonlit living
room. Now she didn't like my quietness.

"I feel you're very distant," she grumped.

Eventually I gave in and tried to explain: "I'm
mystified because it seems you're not able to get into
this relationship the way you've told me you want to."

She professed not to know what I was talking about.
She even offered a rare "voluntary" proclamation of
love. And I demonstrated the burning fervor for her
which I had earlier told her lay just beneath the
surface of my silence. Then we balled (first decorously
adjourning to the bedroom). It wasn't different from
most other times: I felt she wasn't really into it, she
mostly just wanted me out of her and off of her, I had
disappointed her again, etc. And this time, for the

record, the new one-handed sideways tilting of her ass
followed by the oblique plunge was a dismal flop.

Afterwards, in a roundabout, relatively inoffensive
way -- I think -- I gave her my views on this latest
failed fuck of ours. And she acknowledged it could have
been better for her. It also emerged that (A) Jim had
intensely disliked having his balls fondled or even
touched, (B) even though I was trying to be careful and
gentle with her I was probing painful vaginal depths
he'd never reached with his smallish cock (why hadn't
she mentioned this important fact before now?), (C) she
felt "less of a participant" because for the same cock-
size reason she couldn't "clamp down" on me vaginally as
she did with Jim, and (D) she prefers being on top (even
if the man's sitting on a chair) because she can control
the depth and tempo better, and this is doubly true with
me for that same size reason (how absurdly ironic this
is!) and because she's built quite small herself. And
when I told her I thought all this would work itself out
in time as we learn to read each other's responses
better, she could only say coolly, "Yes, I hope so."

The rest of my questions got a similar noncommittal
response (far more vexing than an out-and-out negative).

"Do you like it from behind?"

"Well, yes, sometimes."

This morning was a different kind of story. The
babysitter delivered Danny unexpectedly early. Valerie
was so tired she rejoined me in bed, letting Danny roam
at will. Before long he was clambering all over us. I
finally got up and played with him in the living room,
closing her in the bedroom, where she was lying on her
back, still wearing an open blue workshirt (her usual
bed gear), mouth also open, snoring just barely audibly.

When she awoke an hour later I heard her cry my
name in a panicky way. I returned to bed. She became
unexpectedly aggressive, taking my balls in her hand (an
act for which she says Jim might've slugged her),
snuggling up, pressing her lips and tongue against my
chest and nipples and suckling away (I liked it!); and
so, with Danny always playing nearby, sometimes climbing

87

on our legs or hitting our backs or in some other way
demanding attention -- he possesses a limitless stock of
them -- we got it on again as inconspicuously as
possible beneath the covers. So far as I can recall
it's the first time I've ever been witnessed in the act
that way by a "third party" in broad daylight.

It was quite a turnabout for Valerie to permit --
even initiate -- even choreograph and orchestrate --
this second round. I suppose it could show a growing
willingness to trust me. She does appear at times to be
developing a stronger attachment to me. Its motivating
force seems to be lonely neediness, I'd call it, not
erotic/romantic love, but that makes it no less strong.
This must be why, for instance, she goes to such lengths
to keep me from getting out of the house.

"I don't want to spend any time away from you," she
declares. "Not even one minute."

This declaration doesn't flatter me because she
voices it coolly, almost petulantly, more as if she were
simply saying, "I don't want to be alone and you're
always trying to make me be alone." Part of the price
of her kind of love is that the beloved bestow his total
attention upon her; therefore I can't very well insist
on my love for her and then say I need to go away and
get some work done for a change. But attending to her
has become something of a chore, and not always an easy
one -- in fact an increasingly difficult one.

Sunday 19

On Valerie's steep gray wooden back staircase with
sections of the Sunday paper strewn on higher and lower
steps and the sun beating down, a faint trace of shit
stink in the air and crusted blood on my fingers.

Last night she cried, "I hate myself!" At that
point a new dimension opened up. I learned she's
feeling deeply troubled -- much more so than I had
realized before now -- by the way her life is going.
She believes she's trapped and there's no way out.
She's chained to her job at Emp, where the chances of

advancement are virtually nil and the pay is too low for
her even to think about saving money. She's locked in
an unending series of fierce battles with Jim and these
always bring her down and make it all but impossible for
her to focus on anything else. She can't even permit
herself to think about the notion of giving up Danny,
and yet now she suddenly says she's seriously
considering letting him go.

"He's already ruined. He's so violent because he
saw Jim and me fighting all the time, and now Jim's
teaching him that being a fighter is the only way to be
a real man."

And as if all that weren't enough, even if she
succeeds in overcoming these formidable obstacles, she
has no idea where to go from there. Paris? College?
Design school? An "artistic" job? Start a restaurant
like her mother did (in Orleans as well as the one in
Holton)? Open a dress shop or boutique selling clothes
she'd make herself? And how would she finance any of
these? She sank deep into tearful despair. I tried to
console her, suggesting it was time for her to overcome
her wholly justified anger and resentment against her
abusive father and accept the financial help he's long
offered so she can go back to school, even if it's
conditional on her returning to France. She found my
concern about all this "noble" but my suggestions
"unhelpful." (Could her brother Armand and his wife
assist her? She says no, they've got their hands full
with Elise, their daughter. And her mother -- who's now
studying to become a restaurant inspector for the state
-- is worse than useless because the much-younger guy
she's living with, Rex, is an ex-military right-wing gun
nut who jealously shadows her every move and sometimes
tries to do the same with Valerie. "He wants to fuck me
really, really bad," she observed matter-of-factly,
while talking about their Tahoe trip two weeks ago.
"You can see it in his eyes. He's like eight or nine
years closer to my age than to my mother's."
                    *   *
It's ten p.m. A fire's going (a Presto log) and my

89

stereo set, transferred here this evening, is set to
play a stack of my favorite albums for Valerie, who at
the moment is lying on her back by one of the speakers,
her jeans unbuckled and unzipped, her head out of my
line of sight behind the speaker. She's sulking, quite
clearly, I think because in her view I'm once again not
paying enough attention to her, though for the moment
she's too proud to demand more and thus sound like a
broken, yes, record (which we could then play on her own
hopelessly broken record player over by the door).

If not for the vicissitudes of fate, I'm thinking,
at this stage of her life Valerie'd probably be a fiery-
eyed dean's-list college sophomore, one who's also
occupying the college president's office in protest of
this or that outrage -- the "Indochine War" for just one
rather obvious instance. And I'm recalling how my
finding her working in Claims at Emp seemed downright
miraculous -- still does -- on the order of, say,
stumbling upon a Vietcong guerrilla leader at a Gatewood
cocktail party.

(Or maybe she's not sulking, because between cuts I
can hear her snoring now, slightly, as she tends to do
after drinking too much wine. Or she could be sulking
in her sleep. For sure she's wasted because it's been
quite a day for her -- and me. And I'm turning off the
stereo.)

Meanwhile new complications have arisen concerning
my sexual frustrations and feelings of "inadequacy" with
her (here comes the irony again and even a new twist on
it). These feelings were already bad enough before
today. Now I'm nearly paralyzed. It turns out her
sexual life with Jim wasn't so terrible after all. In
fact, her major complaint was simply that there was too
much of it. Earlier tonight at the Trident in Sausalito
-- we zipped over there in the L.C. for dinner -- she
made an offhand remark that's still reverberating.

"All he cared about was how many orgasms I had,"
she grumped. "Each one was like a little merit badge
for him to wear. Whether it was two or four or five, he
always had to know exactly."

[Shacking Up with Valerie]

Four or five! For me it's an exhausting task to
wheedle a single one out of her! She also remarked she
couldn't fall asleep at night during her time with him
unless she'd gotten off (though she did reassuringly add
that usually once or twice would be enough). "It really
burned me up when he crashed out on me." But, as she
blithely let me know, he didn't do that very often.
"Sex was all he cared about. Sex and drugs." In bed
(where they spent a great deal of time) he loved every
position known to the Kama Sutra except basic
missionary. His hard-ons popped up in rapid succession
and could unfailingly be inspired to full mast by the
mere sight, or even just the mere thought, of her naked
or lingerie'd body, according to her anyway. (And I do
believe her on this, although sexual arousal doesn't
usually work that way for me, with her or with anyone.
Once in a while at best. What turns me on genitally, as
opposed to mentally, is in most instances touch and
responsiveness, not mere sight or thought.)
Perhaps dimly aware these revelations might be
troubling to me, she again tried to reassure me by
saying Jim had "no appreciation of beauty -- except in
bodies." But then she went on to say they balled in
every conceivable way (including lots of anal) and did
it frequently, often all night, especially in the
beginning. By the end, because of their ever-worsening
quarrels, they had cooled off to "five or six times a
week" (and it's sobering to remind myself "the end"
referred to here didn't come until a little over two
months ago). It wasn't so much that she failed to like
or appreciate this sex; rather the marital combat made
it more and more difficult for her to participate
enthusiastically. That's when she began to feel she was
being treated as "nothing but a sex object." (And being
treated as such an object, she and I have agreed before,
can also be natural and good at times, especially if
it's not overdone and one's feeling at least minimally
receptive to it, i.e., sexy; and by and large, she told
me, that's exactly how she felt with Jim all the way
through. Sometimes she actually liked being mistreated

91

and roughed up! In other words, the version of their
story she'd given me before had left out a hugely
significant part of her experience with him. And I
can't deny it: what I'm learning now about all this
strikes some deep notes of unease for me.)

    -- which brings me to the wrenching story (another
one!) of her climactic night with Jim. It came toward
the end of this past February, she said, when their
battles had become so hopeless she decided to take her
new "work friend" Brandon up on his "standing offer" to
sleep with her (Jim had already been boasting about
sleeping around over the previous couple of months). On
this night of her first infidelity she returned home at
one a.m. She found Jim lying naked on the bed with his
drug-deal gun in his hands, and he pointed it at her as
she entered the bedroom.

    "Who've you been fucking?" he screamed.

    She denied everything, indirectly, although she did
this by insisting he had no right to know what she'd
been doing. Meanwhile she was trying to avoid looking
at his angry red erection as it quivered before her.
Suddenly he leapt up, grabbed her, and shoved a finger
up her vagina. This didn't yield the evidence he was
seeking, apparently, because he picked up the gun again,
pressed it against her belly and then her head,
demanding she tell him the exact truth.

    "Go ahead and shoot," she dared him. "I don't even
care."

    So he ripped off her clothes, threw her on the bed,
and raped her. (That was the word she used for it with
me and I'd say it's exactly right, even though they were
married.)

    "I realized he was getting his kicks because I was
fighting him, so I stopped struggling."

    At some point before starting into the rape he
switched from the gun to a carving knife, which he'd
stashed behind some books on the headboard, and held it
to her throat. He kept it there the entire time of the
rape, which went on, she said, for hours. "I think he
came three or four times." In the morning, after an

utterly sleepless night, she persuaded him to go to work.

Poor Danny, just two years old, witnessed the whole scene -- about as primal as they get, I'd say -- from his crib right next to their bed.

(She revealed much else to me at the Trident -- including details on the affairs with Brandon and Jon Tremont, both of which continued up to within a week or two of the time we met -- but I can't go on with this account right now. She woke up and moved over next to me, and now her head's resting on my shoulder and her hand's in my crotch and it's moving ever so slightly and lightly, almost as if she's tapping her fingers impatiently....)

*

-- Forget the finger action. Now she's abruptly decided to do some writing herself. We're going to go at it tandem. See how long we can hold up (it's already past eleven).

If she can, I can.

Just some random thoughts about her:

** She likes me to kiss her closed eyes and go on and on with it. It's as if I'm blessing blindness.

** I begin to feel monstrous. This may be because I also see the beginnings of trust and devotion in her eyes -- when they're open, yes -- and this is happening just as I'm losing mine toward her.

** The way she plays frisbee (we did that for an hour in the park this afternoon) is the way she loves and also the way she balls: she's good at catching it but not so hot at tossing it back. And Jim evidently thought much the same. He even liked to call her a "bum fuck," which hurt her deeply and still does.

** Today, peering at her luscious pussy close-up from a certain angle in good light, I noticed for the first time that the hair (which is glossy black, straight, and quite abundant for a Eurasian woman; which is to say, just like her nose and breasts, the pubic hair comes from her father; "My mother," she tells me, "is completely bald down there") -- Valerie's own

93

handsome and abundant snatch, I say, conceals a field of
stretch marks much like the ones on the underside of her
breasts. In both instances they come from her pregnancy
with Danny, of course, and then his birth, and so they
could also be said to be scars left by Jim (as a kind of
Eliotic "objective correlative," say, of the emotional
ones). These scars are all very faint, though, nearly
invisible, because she gave birth at such a young age.
  ** Last night I remarked "it would be good if we
could get you a false ID so we wouldn't be so limited in
what we can do at night." She blew her stack. Accused
me of trying to make her feel like everything was her
fault! -- She's nineteen years old. When I was
nineteen, she was eleven. In fact, for the first seven
months I was nineteen, she was ten. -- But it's true
also that in some ways she seems quite a bit older and
more worldly wise than I am or just about anyone I know
is. This is something she herself has noticed and
remarked upon. (She also thinks it has something to do
with her being French and just about all the rest of us
around here being -- surprise! -- American. "Americans
can be so childish sometimes! It's maddening! I feel
I'm more the adult one than most of the so-called adults
I meet here." -- And by the way, speaking of French,
all this time she's been writing in French. So we won't
be exchanging journals to read each other's accounts.
Probably a good thing too. That may even be why she
decided to do hers in a language I can't read. -- She
says no (I just asked), she's writing in French because
she's afraid she's losing her command of the language.
In nearly every letter her father sends -- not that
there are very many of them -- he tells her exactly this
is happening. Once he returned a letter of hers to him
all marked up with red-ink corrections. And she added
this nasty little kicker: "Sometimes when I'm talking in
English I feel half the words I'm saying have little red
marks on them just like his. Even when I'm talking with
you. No, most of all when I'm talking with you!")

94

4

Monday 20

On the phone with me Valerie often, in fact almost always, sounds completely different from the way I know her to be. Her tone is a blend of fear (the foreigner speaking to a government official in a strange language), distrust (the outlander using electrical machinery for the first time), and shyness. In sum it comes across as an expressionless monotone suggesting she has no interest whatsoever in talking with you. Its main redeeming feature -- and it can be considerable -- is her unfailingly charming and sexy accent.

-- Or at least this is my immediate reaction to talking with her just moments ago. After a fairly good night with her (which itself caused me a certain anguish because it was neither better nor worse than it was) we overslept this morning, and I persuaded her that the best course for her, since she has so many tardies on her record at Emp, was to phone in sick. She wanted me to stay home with her, but the high likelihood of a call for me from "upstairs" -- Roach, Varden, Moran -- made that seem unwise. ---

*   *

Small puffs of fog roll by like gunpowder smoke from mysteriously silent battlefield fusillades occurring just the other side of Nob Hill, some of them briefly dimming the sun down here as in a series of rapid-fire eclipses. I'm glad to have a chance to spend lunch hour alone in the park -- it's been several weeks since the last time -- just as Valerie is no doubt pleased to have a few hours away from me to get her head together.

She's on the offensive now, clearly afraid I'm about to sprint for the exit. This is causing some real changes in her. Nor is she even slightly comfortable with them. She's showing a new warmth, yes, but a veiled threat lurks unmistakably within it (as if to

say, "You asked for this and now you'd better respond to
it exactly the way I want or else you're never going to
see it again"). And a decidedly contrived flavor clings
to her acts of "spontaneous" joy (in which, for
instance, she jumps up on me in greeting and while
hanging on does a little dance in midair with her feet
fluttering). And also a self-conscious or ironic tone
inflects her commentary during or regarding such acts,
as if she were inquiring, "Are you sure this is the kind
of silliness you're wanting me to engage in?" And such
warm and spontaneous acts are still rare, and overall
she still emanates an aura of subdued desperation that's
accompanied by frequent flashing scowls. At times I can
see her visibly convert one of these scowls by a willful
act into a phony little half-ass smile which makes not
just my eyes but hers as well widen in disbelief.

And yet...it's still a big improvement. I can't
help but respond to it. She touches my heart more and
more even as, by supreme paradox, my heart builds bigger
and stronger defenses against her. What at first seemed
to be wild love for her now seems to be transmuting
gradually into an all-too-familiar blend of admiration,
compassion, and strong physical attraction mixed with
ever-expanding portions of caution, wariness, and doubt
-- cf. my life and times with Denise Purcell.

This obvious cooling of my ardor of course makes
Valerie still more desperate. Nothing has gone right
for her in years -- in her whole life, as she sometimes
comes right out and says. Is this romance also to fail
-- to go the way of all summer romances (it is July!) --
and just as she's beginning to believe there's some real
hope for it?

I try to hide as much as possible my deepening
concerns about her and the way we interact, but at the
same time I know it would be foolish to let her think my
feelings remain what they were. Therefore my words and
actions reek with inconsistencies. I fall into long
periods of moody silence which almost match her own as
I've known them over the past two weeks plus. I change
subjects capriciously. I bluntly challenge the most

inconsequential things she says. I tease her more than
I should. I become restless and out of sorts. I say
outrageous things and then retract them. To her I've
become a complete enigma.

And yet she dares not make too much of this new
weirdness of mine -- which I should say retains a few of
the more absurd traits of the "rude" Mr. Marlboro Man --
dares not do so especially after the relative
indifference she's shown me all along. Also, I think
she fears I'll respond to any new criticism of hers with
new charges of insensitivity. But she can't entirely
prevent herself from expressing her fears -- "I want to
be honest," she avows with a winsomely grave seriousness
-- and neither can I prevent myself from giving my own
deeper truth some voice, however hedged or oblique. And
so we live right now in an uneasy state of confusion and
disharmony, unwilling to let it break fully into the
open, and yet we're still exquisitely sensitive to each
other. And once in a while, quite often in fact, we
declare a truce and exchange tender consolations.

*   *

So...after our tandem journal session came to an
end last night, balling again kept us up very late, past
three, and left menstrual bloodstains all over the
sheets. She blew me to ejac for the first time when I
asked her to. She insisted she'd always wanted to but
was "afraid you didn't like the way I did it" (and
unfortunately there is some truth to that). Not too
much later, while working on getting her off by hand, I
stiffened up again, and this time I suggested she take
out her tampon. "You could pull it out yourself, you
know," she pointed out, "if you want to." But I didn't
want to, so she casually yanked it and flipped it on the
floor (reminding me of the way Ciara used to do the same
thing -- but I wouldn't've expected such an untidy act
from neatnik Valerie, who's pretty much Ciara's opposite
on that score).

This balling was good enough to dissipate some of
the sexual strain we've both been under. (She too, it
now becomes known, was relieved by "the second time"

last week. When I pasted a big shiny green star on the
wall next to my desk here in the dungeon the next day
she thought it must refer to that. Not so -- I just did
it on a lark, sort of to garnish the three green flags
from the People's Park demo rising from a spare
wastebasket down below -- but she thought it was "like
the gold stars at American schools but with some twist
to it." And then when the sexual strain returned the
next night she was very disappointed.) -- But last
night we were even able to talk about all this in a
fairly relaxed way. Our balling's been mostly
"conservative" so far, we agreed, not "liberal" or
"radical." She reassured me (after a bit of fishing by
me) I'm indeed physically attractive to her. "I turned
on to you the very first time we met! How could you not
know that?"

    At the same time she continues to dwell on what it
was like for her with Jim. If she's doing this in an
attempt to please me -- because I do ask her about it --
she's at the very least going at it too often and in too
many ways at once and frequently with too much relish.
One moment she'll tell me how turned off she felt during
sex with him, how much like "an object," and the next --
to affirm to me, perhaps, she indeed likes sex -- she'll
say she used to get so horny for him (especially when
she was pregnant, when it was "just like terrific hunger
pangs only lower in my body") -- so horny, she says with
gleaming eyes, that "I grabbed him when he came in the
door and stripped him on the spot!" -- eyes gleaming, in
fact, just as they did yesterday at the Trident when she
was spinning out the rape story, among others. And
yet...she's also said several times she'd like to have a
kid with me -- "to have your life growing inside of me"
-- and this despite her fears concerning another
pregnancy and what it might do to her future prospects.
"I have nightmares whenever I forget to take my Pill."

    In the sexual aftermath last night she did to me
"something Jim used to like me to do -- especially when
I was in my period like now." To wit: she created a
phallic "butterfly" by tying a loop of twisted white

98

toilet paper around my "membre" and fashioning the loose
ends -- of the paper, that is -- into a kind of fluffed-
out origami swallowtail of sorts, mostly white but
smeared with red bloodstains.

I'll say this: at least I no longer have anything
like the level of doubt I used to have regarding the
strength of her libido (as she likes to call her sexual
drive, pronouncing the word "leebeeDOH").

*

One other thing that's bothering me: my
relationship with my sister. After brunch yesterday I
bought a bunch of marigolds for her and made a quick
trip over to Funston to say goodbye and to wish her the
best in her new apartment. She'd closed herself in her
room and didn't come out, even though in exchanging
greetings with Rob I intentionally raised my voice to
make my presence obvious.

In the end I knocked on her door. No response. I
knocked again, louder, and finally she opened the door
after a long delay, saying, "I can never tell whether
it's the bathroom door or mine when there's a knock." I
looked into her eyes, searching for any last trace of
that sense of happy complicity, of shared understanding,
we enjoyed for a month or two after her arrival in S.F.
in December. I could see none. She looked at me as if
I were a faintly menacing stranger -- a look that was
clear-eyed but chillingly detached. It took me a long
moment to gather my thoughts and put them into words:

"Barbara, I'm sorry things haven't been so good
between us the past few weeks or months or, you know,
however long it's been -- which is too long. And I hope
you realize I've never wanted them to be that way and I
still don't. I love you, and the main reason I came
over here today is to wish you well in your new place
and give you these as an apartment-warmer or apartment-
brightener, I guess." And I handed her the marigolds.

These weren't easy things to say, but she offered
no help, and when I was finished she came up with no
reply. She offered an almost mute "Thanks" for the
flowers and made no mention at all of my having provided

for the past six months a large part of her financial
support in the form of highly subsidized room and board.
I made some fumbling jokes to get myself out of there.
                    *   *
    (8:20 p.m.)
    Tonight I arrived at "the shack" in fairly good
spirits all things considered. That didn't last long.
Valerie was immersed in the exigencies of motherhood --
Jim had just dropped off Danny -- and offered a
lackluster greeting. Even the gifts I bought for her
during my lunch-hour North Beach prowl -- an anthology
in English translation of contemporary French poetry and
a cheapo six-panel kaleidoscope "for two triple schizos
like us" (as I wrote on the package) -- despite all
this, I say, I couldn't pry her out of her subdued state
(which of course is strictly her normal state at most
times at home) and neither did the impassioned kiss I
laid on her do a whole lot to liven her up. My good
intentions gradually drained as I struggled to keep
Danny away from the stereo and winced at his mother's
brusque treatment of him. Finally, by the time I left
for the laundromat, where I'm writing now, I was reduced
to a reluctant, exasperated despondency of my own, which
I fought hard not to let her see.
    "Cheer up," I said to her as I left. "Things can't
be that bad" -- the very thing I'd been saying to myself
sotto voce for much of the evening.
    As soon as I got outside, however, my downer
dispersed like heavy fog in a warm breeze. Now I was
shaking my head at my penchant for creating problems for
myself. Nature has a way, I told myself, of dealing
with species whose major energies are expended on
activities serving no useful purpose. Nor was it
Valerie I had in mind: her problems are real and
serious. No, I'm the one who's in danger of going
extinct. I saw clearly what a fool I am for letting
myself become so mired in her troubles, and a complete
idiot for allowing myself to be even slightly bothered
by whatever moral factors may be involved in choosing
between her and Jang. No matter what I do, two people

will eventually be hurt and I'll be one of them. It's
inevitable. And it's sad. But it's also life in the
love-and-romance bazaar -- yes it is. And for the three
of us taken together the positive aspects of our being
part of this bazaar far outweigh the negative, if I can
but keep my focus on the bigger picture.

The mere fact that there exists a woman with Jang's
many gifts, including the supreme one of her sexuality
(or call it our supreme compatibility in that regard),
who still says she loves me and despite everything wants
to make her life with me -- this all by itself should
make me ecstatic. So too should the fact that I've been
fortunate enough to know intimately someone as fine and
rare and complex and exacting and perplexing as Valerie.
And finally -- how could I forget! -- I'm still young,
I'm at least moderately talented and desirable, I'm free
and full of energy in this delightful city of San
Francisco; I have a few bucks in the bank; I'm about to
embark on the personal writing project for which I've
been preparing myself for years. In short, my life
stretches out before me, aburst with promise and
opportunity, and I couldn't be much more fortunate.

Tuesday 21
This addendum to what I wrote last night at the
laundromat:

It's horrible that life should deal Valerie
Mailloux such an unending series of setbacks. And it's
a personal shame for me that before much longer I might
wind up -- and all too willingly -- being another of
life's agents in this respect. Yet I can't help but
think I'd be crazy to martyr myself for love of this
woman. How foolish it would be to risk sacrificing my
own dreams and plans and emotional well-being on the off
chance that with time her temperament and overall
feelings about men, not to mention her highly specific
ambiguous feelings toward me and her extreme and endless
criticism of and demands on me, will change -- will
improve in the first case or diminish in the second. I

insist this is not a matter of selfishness; it's self-preservation pure and simple.

I might more justifiably upbraid myself for becoming as involved with her as I have considering that I knew almost from the start what sort of person she is and the massive obstacles I'd face with her. But I didn't really know then; I shouldn't say that. I only suspected. I saw superficial signs of her coolness, her lack of joy, her simmering anger at men, her abject failures with loving on a day-to-day basis, but I also thought these traits were probably, for the most part, only temporary manifestations of the tensions caused by the recent breakup with her husband and the painful process of divorcing, and perhaps to a lesser degree a kind of delayed culture shock and/or motherhood shock.

What's more, she took the lead in making our relationship more intimate. If anyone rushed things, it was her, not me. My crime, if there was one, lay in going along with her: and who can criticize a man for consenting to sleep with and spend extended hours and days and weeks in the company of a lovely and sexy and poetic and politically passionate and charming woman who appears to know quite well just what she's doing, even if she is only nineteen years old. After all, she'd been married for three years before we met -- and that was three times as long as I'd been married myself (although technically I'm fairly sure I'm still married right now and I know she is, though probably just for a couple of weeks longer).

I've done everything I can to make the relationship work, and I believe she has also: but for us to succeed as lovers I'm afraid we'd both have to be much more patient and accepting than we can be at this point in our lives. And yet...I still can't help but feel very tentative about any such conclusion. Which is to say: I'm not concluding it. Yet.

*   *

Today I'm trying to be colorful. The Roachman, it turns out, is off on a weeklong trip to Emp's New York home office and I'm taking advantage of his absence to

[Shacking Up with Valerie]

wear my new tight blue "feelie" bells and the
psychedelic six-inch-wide Peter Max tie Valerie gave me
as a surprise at the Trident on Sunday. What's more, I
have nothing to do all day -- nothing too urgent, that
is -- but to journalize, read, socialize, and -- mull.
And a good thing on that last item, because quite
clearly I've got a lot to mull about.

Liana, the temp clerk in Promo, dropped by an hour
ago to deliver our mail and we got to talking. Looking
luscious in a short, tight white lace dress which nicely
set off her new Hawaiian tan, she praised Oahu and Maui
so much I'm now thinking I might visit Jang after all if
things fall apart with Valerie -- and as noted already
(more than once!) I think just that could happen any day
now, though I'm still hoping it won't.

Taking off for a week would cost plenty, of course.
Is a short stay in Honolulu really worth several hundred
bucks to me -- or to Jang for that matter, if we did get
back together? (Actually more like five or six hundred,
since I'd also lose a week's salary here, because I've
already used up all my vacation time.) But if ---

*   *

Brandon Wetzel joined Valerie and me in the
cafeteria at morning break today. He's one of the two
men she balled shortly before leaving Jim and then
again, it turns out, over the course of some six or
seven weeks after leaving Jim but before meeting me. So
maybe half a dozen times in all, she thinks, as she
confessed during the aforementioned Trident purge --
which means fuckwise he and I are pretty much in the
same ballpark with Valerie -- so to speak. Ha ha.

He's a short, black-haired, damnably good-looking
guy -- quite pretty really -- with sparkling eyes and
snazzy hip clothes much like hers except he doesn't
design or make them himself. He also has a disarming
and somewhat peculiar manner in which he always seems to
be chuckling at himself. And I thought Valerie handled
the unexpected meet-up very well. She showed no sign of
being upset or embarrassed, except, perhaps, a slight
heightening of her normal social nervousness.

I did less well. What's worse, immediately
afterwards I took it upon myself to mention to Valerie
I'd be having lunch with Nadine today (we arranged it
yesterday when she dropped by the dungeon at break).
     "She's just trying to steal you away from me,"
Valerie said.
     "Actually," I replied, "she's already committed to
someone else. Didn't she tell you that?"
     She cocked her head and then said in a leveling
kind of tone, "Okay, Glen. I need to tell you Brandon's
birthday is this week and we were supposed to have
dinner together tomorrow night to celebrate it. I was
going to cancel that, but now I'm wondering if I should
go ahead with it, just to keep things even between you
and me. What do you think?"
     Long pause. "I think you should do," I finally
said, also leveling, "what you need to do. If you want
to see Brandon, you should. That's our deal."
     "Thank you. That's exactly what I thought you'd
say."
     She did not sound pleased. And yet she still
insisted she would bear no grudges about my seeing
Nadine and even suggested we meet in the park right
after I did that. She said she would switch lunch hours
with a friend to be able to show up at that unusual
time. I agreed to meet her there even though it meant I
would have to take two lunch hours -- which of course I
always try to do anyway if I think I can get away with
it, and with the Roachman out of town through Friday it
shouldn't be too big a problem.
     And then she did a one-eighty. Just as she was
about to leave for 2 Pine, she paused and said, "You
know what? I think I'll cancel the birthday dinner
anyway. In fact...I should be honest with you. I'd
forgotten all about his birthday until we saw him just
now. Then I decided to call him afterwards and cancel
the dinner, because I didn't want to embarrass him in
front of you, or you either. But...he's really a very
cool guy, don't you think? Eh? Were you jealous?"
     "Well...."

[Shacking Up with Valerie]

"You were, Glen. I know you were. I could see it.
You can't fool me -- your real feelings always show
through. You just wind up embarrassing yourself if you
deny it."

Then she gave me a quick kiss -- murmured "I love
you" and added one of her signature crooked little
closed-mouth impish grins, head tipped to one side, eyes
rolling up so winsomely -- and proudly strode off.

*

Going back, then, last night, after my return from
the laundromat, brought no great surprises. We shackees
sparred good-humoredly, for the most part, in the living
room for a couple of hours. After putting Danny to bed
Valerie indicated it was time for us to ball. Her way
of saying it -- I've spaced out the actual words --
sounded more than a bit mercenary, I thought, but we
headed straight to the bedroom and, yes, we did ball.

It took me a while to turn on, and the truth is I
was a little surprised I did. I'd been thinking I'd eat
her into "tension release" if that was all she was
really after (as her flat tone had seemed to imply).
But then while she was lying atop me, her back pressing
against my stomach and chest, I went further than
intended and got her off with a lightly teasing middle
finger -- ultra-lightly really -- while reaching around
and spreading her nether lips with my other hand.

It was actually her hard breathing as she lay atop
me, her skin warm and her impressive back muscles
rippling rhythmically, that first turned me on, although
she took no notice of this fact. But I got my own a bit
later after unsuccessfully trying some elementary Phys
Ed 101 acrobatics and quickly giving up on them owing to
her total lack of response. So then it was back to
basic missionary, the one position "brother Jim" never
deigned to engage in (she swears this is true). Out of
frustration I launched into a more energetic climactic
stage than she's seen me attempt before -- a mildly
rough sideways motion, closer to horizontal flagellation
of my "membre" inside her than standard in-and-out
thrusting (this new move, founded in something close to

105

desperation, she seemed to like at least a little) --
and then, following a series of my own gasping,
shuddering "after-tremors," I moved down to administer
the coup de grace by eating her out, as I'd been aiming
to do from the start. Unfortunately she soon fell
asleep without having shown the slightest response to my
complex orchestrations of tongue, teeth, lips, fingers,
palms, etc.

After a while I retreated to the kitchen and, still
naked, skimmed through the paper, listening to her faint
snore in the distance and, from the living room, Danny's
deep breathing. At one point I became fascinated by
mysteriously shifting patterns of light, glowing and
ghostly, on the wall out in the hall. For a freaky
moment I wondered if they might possibly be caused by
the flashlight of someone trying to break into the house
-- a certain Jim Bando being to my mind the prime
suspect. Eventually I realized a car had pulled into
the driveway of the house behind ours and its headlights
were shining in through the half-curtained kitchen
window behind me and casting shadows of my own head and
hand and a fluttery newspaper page on the hall wall.

Oops, here she is again.   ---
                    *   *
So what that was about, she snuck over supposedly
while on a bathroom break and harangued me for twenty
minutes on the subject of my upcoming lunch with Nadine.
She said she'd thought it over and now considered it
"completely unfair." She demanded I call it off. "You
have no right to use ten minutes of the time I usually
have with you to see someone else!" (Valerie's and
Nadine's lunch hours are staggered with a ten-minute
overlap.) So great was the uproar that Roy exited the
dungeon in a hurry and thoughtfully closed the door
behind him and stood guard outside to make sure no one
entered. I managed to maintain an even temper while
trying to calm her down. Meanwhile, unbeknownst to her
-- despite what she said upstairs about my transparent
emotions -- my determination to hang on with her was
collapsing right before her eyes.

Then wholly on my own -- after refusing her demand
and sending her off angry and in tears -- I called
Nadine and canceled our lunch ten minutes before I was
supposed to meet her at the St. Mary's lunch wagon.

In the park at one when Valerie and I met as agreed
-- the point at which my lunch with Nadine was supposed
to be over -- I surprised her. I told her I'd canceled
Nadine's entire thirty minutes, Valerie's ten included,
and I handed her a small purple plastic box containing a
tightly folded handwritten message: "Rumors of the death
of GPS's love for VMB have been greatly exaggerated."
Flushed with triumph, she suddenly deluged me with
tender proclamations of love, questions about why I was
now the one who was so "moody" all the time and demands
that I smile -- all these just like my similar questions
and demands of her at earlier times.

She might not have been so triumphant, however, had
she known I was already trying to decide which day would
be best for breaking up with her. My love for VMB may
not have died -- in fact I'm sure it hasn't -- but my
desire to live with her definitely has. Move-out day
should be Sunday, I think. If things go as currently
planned, Danny will be at the sitter's.

(Actually I decided this at least tentatively last
night when I was sitting naked in her kitchen flipping
through the newspaper. Then in the bathroom this
morning I caught an unobserved glimpse of her face in
one of the mirrors and her expression was so severe and
cruel-looking (this was after another phone fight with
Jim over divorce matters) it chilled me to the bone.
And of course the business with Brandon this morning
also played a role. And then her yelling at me for
twenty minutes in the dungeon, potentially putting my
job in jeopardy -- and saying "I don't give a fuck!"
when I pointed this out -- pretty much clinched it.)

                    *   *

So then she dropped by the morgue again during
break -- causing Roy's jaw to drop and his eyes to widen
in alarm as he looked over at me -- but this time she
was all sweetness and light, and she presented me with a

gift of her own, prefabricated with an adhesive back for
affixing it to this journal page right here. A labor-
saving gift. And without further ado, here it is (on a
white label, with purple-ink writing, lots of fancy
capital letters and curlicues):

> I LOVE YOU, GLENN SANDEFJORD.
> AND FOR EVER MAY IT LAST.
> I'll love you all the while
> and as full as my heart will hold
> and if our path diverge apart a mile
> must our love constantly be told.
>   -- Valerie

It's almost enough to revive my badly faded hopes for
us. The trouble is, the line "as full as my heart will
hold" is actually, as I see it, a kind of excuse for
failing to love me well -- me or anyone else. This is
an inescapable aspect of Valerie. Her heart, as far as
I can tell, will not hold anywhere near enough love, and
especially not under current conditions. The warmth and
innocence which formed those frilly Valentine's Day
letters comes from a deep, barricaded part of her soul
that can find few other means of expression. In my view
she's not ready to love in the way I want and need and
she probably won't be ready for anything like that for a
long time, if ever. And it's also likely that by
shacking up with her I'm just complicating her life and
pushing her to the breaking point. Or from a different
perspective, and to put the matter still more bluntly:
it's almost certainly too late for us. -- And this is
not even to mention the knack she has, beyond anyone
else's I've ever known, for putting me on truly colossal
bummers like today's.)

Wednesday 22
     Three years ago today Ciara and I tied the knot.
-- Is that all, just three? Same as Valerie and Jim?
Could it be? -- As I molder away here in the Emp Life
lower depths for what feels like the twentieth year,
it's hard to believe my own marital fiasco took place so

recently. To me it's history that seems even
more ancient than what came before it with Jang in
Mentoka Falls. And yet: other than family I have only
five live human links left to that earlier era: Jang
herself, Ken and Jo Deunoro, Jill Roberson, Ciara.
Before too much longer Ken and Jo may be the last ones
standing. Jang? I don't know, this morning I've been
revisiting old journals and chronbooks and my doubts
about our having a future together have flared up again
and this time even higher.

Thinking about what Jang wrote in her latest
letter, I began to feel so much life had gone out of her
love, and out of mine as well -- except for the
deathless sexual part of it -- that now it's just a
matter of our breaking away from each other for good.
The incomparable sex makes this much more difficult if
we're actually together. And I guess I'd have to say
the delusions of grandeur we share also play a central
role. For so long have we been telling each other we're
a "great love," "meant for each other," that admitting
final defeat will be like admitting we're worthless.

I just don't know. Right now, actually, I think
I'm testing myself. How does it feel to say it's over
for good and for always with Jang? It doesn't shake me.
Yet I have to admit I still feel strongly for her: love
her down deep and physically desire her to the max just
as always. Yet I also know what's gone wrong between us
again and again in the past and I'm all too well aware
of our long-running inability to find a way to live
with, much less resolve, our severe conflicts. What I'd
like to do over the six weeks or so before her scheduled
return (which of course might not happen at all) is
investigate the question much more thoroughly -- how
does it feel to say it's truly over for us? -- and then
submit it to the ultimate court of my unconscious for a
verdict.

Were Jang suddenly to appear today I'd drop Valerie
instantly -- but probably only because Jang has much
greater guilt leverage on me. Or...is that really true?
Could it instead be because Jang has a tighter grip on

my heart? How terrific it would be to come up with a
definitive answer to this question. In the meantime,
however, I'm taking a certain masochistic pleasure in
stretching myself out on the rack of the dilemma.

*

    Last night with Valerie started out well. At Jet's
on Mission, where we chomped on burgers and fries while
sitting on the curb in the late sun, she said the sort
of thing I always wished Jang would say: "I want to
learn how I can love you better." Then at her place,
with Danny pouring root beer on us and engaging in other
seditious acts, she supplied detailed answers to my
further questions about the "climactic" night of her
marriage which I was trying to describe in these pages
yesterday. Most of it was unsurprising, but one fact
twisted like a knife in my heart: Jim twice on that
night turned her over and for long periods fucked her in
the ass. Her dulled, distant, matter-of-fact tone in
talking about this saddened me greatly -- somehow it was
even worse than the gleaming eyes of Sunday's Trident
tales -- and so too did the notion that if I intended to
stay on with her I'd have to overcome the shattering
effects of a lost intimacy as extreme and nasty and
violent as theirs -- and as of right now I can't even
say it's in the past. Verbally they're still going at
each other on many if not most days. In fact I can say
their relationship exists emphatically in the present
even though technically it's not sexual. So how long is
it going to take her, I ask myself, to get over all this
and be able to feel in anything like a normal way? And
then: is she even capable of feeling in anything like a
normal way? Or better to ask: what is her normal way,
however strange it might be? Or: does she have even a
passing acquaintance with normality? As things stand I
have absolutely no way myself to determine any of this.
    In bed, after some good moments, with slow loving,
eyes open, her face soft and achingly lovely in the
flickering candlelight, everything fell apart. Once
again she inexplicably went dead and my hard-on faded.
We sixty-nined, she came, then I stuffed myself back

110

inside her while only partially erect and eventually
stiffened up and came, but it was still anticlimactic,
as it were, and disappointing. Even she said so: "I had
hoped it would be more fully satisfying."

*   *

A twenty-minute gig (that's tops) in the sunny and
warm and friendly confines of St. Mary's Square.

I don't know why I bought Valerie "The Sensuous
Woman." Am I mad? If she reads it, which is doubtful,
she'll find it contemptible -- and me contemptible for
giving it to her. Moreover it's a used copy with
hilarious little penciled checkmarks and exclamation
points scattered here and there in the margins.

For you, Valerie Mailloux, because you are sui
generis and your potential is unlimited! (Scratch that,
she'd hate it even more.)   ---

*   *

The new Downtown Peace Coalition offices on Third
Street. Valerie's roaming around in search of political
conversation but I've had my fill of that for a while.
Meanwhile I'll note three of her total of four lifetime
lovers are present in this room at this moment: Brandon
and Jon and me.

Attendance at the weekly meetings has gradually
dwindled since its highs during the U.S. invasion of
Cambodia and the Kent State/Jackson State killings some
nine or ten weeks ago, during which period, she tells me
(I was in New York then), it several times exceeded two
hundred. Tonight near the height of summer-vacation
season it's only about fifty, and for the most part
they're a strange mix of hardcore protesters and equally
hardcore lonelies and urban isolatos -- and then there's
the six percent or so, if I'm figuring right, who are
current or former lovers of Valerie Bando.

Meanwhile the business portion of the meeting has
begun. An eighty-two-year-old World War I conscientious
objector is introduced. Various protest marches are
announced, along with a women's-lib picnic Sunday
afternoon "open to all." The fund-raising party is
declared a social and aesthetic success but a financial

111

flop, having netted just $48.13. Plans for the street
fair, street dance, and ACT benefit are developing, if
not rapidly, at least at an orderly pace.

Hm. Hm. I'm impressed, actually: all this
bubbling activity. The downside is that the talk about
it will probably go on for another hour at least.

Valerie's now sitting next to me on my left. She's
even more colorfully dressed than usual tonight: nasty
vermilion mini, shiny purple jacket, glossy yellow
blouse with very large wing collars emerging from the
jacket, a bright orange scarf around her neck. With her
signature humped nose standing out in profile she looks
like a rare parrot -- a macaw, perhaps, whose mother
parrot (I've seen photos!) happens to come from Macau.

Her former lover, Jon Tremont, the electric-haired,
wild-eyed, impressively articulate lawyer, at this
moment is discoursing at the mic on the legality of
setting up a DPC booth in Crocker Plaza, and she watches
and listens attentively. Not raptly, exactly, but
seeing how she looks at him I ward off a stab of
jealousy and also envy because he speaks so well -- and
so rapidly, much as she also does when excited or angry.
A twist or two more tightly wound than your ordinary
peacenik, I'd say, and I'm talking about both of them.
And just as with Brandon -- who's sitting a few rows in
front of us to the left in what looks to me like a
custom-made Edwardian suit of black velvet with a red
tie -- and on the night of his canceled birthday dinner!
-- it's easy to understand the mutual attraction.

*

-- Now more reality shoulders in. As talk about
the street fair drones on, I lean left to show Valerie
some pictures. She ignores them, muttering something
with an intense look in her eyes. I ask her to repeat
what she said. "My husband's here!" she whispers. I
recoil in mock alarm because of the trepidation in her
voice, but underneath I'm genuinely shook.

"Where?" I ask, after cautiously looking around and
failing to spot him.

"To your right, last row. Black leather jacket."

112

[Shacking Up with Valerie]

I edge a peripheral look in that direction while
pretending to be glancing at the wall clock and there he
unmistakably is: a small but impressive-looking fellow,
truly Hollywood handsome, with a Zapata mustache, brown
cord bells, narrow, expressionless eyes. Not at all the
sort of man I'd expect to see at a meeting of a peace
group. Lover No. 4, this is, though of course really
No. 1 (and in several respects), thus completing the
convocation of Valerie's full lifetime set -- so far --
right here in a single room.

-- And no sooner do I write these words than I hear
a chair scraping loudly back there and turn to see Jim
heading for the exit at the far left with another, much
larger hombre wearing a brown bomber jacket and carrying
a motorcycle helmet. He walks on the balls of his feet,
Jim does, energetically, as high-school jocks of small
physical stature often do in trying to look tough, and
there's more than a hint of anger in it: I think, yeah,
definitely this guy could be a dope dealer brandishing
knives and guns, a sexual madman and rapist. Actually
the first thing I think when I see him is: fierceness.
Fury. Volatility. Vengeance.

Earlier when I ducked out to the head Jim came over
to say hello to Valerie, she informs me; and he told her
then, "It looks like I won't be staying around long,"
referring, she believes, to her being here with me
tonight and to his threat to leave the state and cut off
support payments if she takes up with someone else. She
seems unflustered by this, but who can really tell?

Ah, fuck, fuck, who cares.

(She leans over: "Why do you keep sighing like
that? Everyone's looking!" And I didn't even know I
was sighing! -- And since when, I might ask, is she
bothered by people looking?)

(I'm not sure she even realizes how remarkable this
scene is. She's entirely accustomed to being the center
of male attention -- consider my own obsessive
fascination with her. And consider the setting here.
The DPC is living up to its mission: peace is reigning
despite all the tensions. But that's only so far.

Because who knows what might be lurking just outside the door back there, which appears to be the only way out.)

-- And so now we've decided to leave. Actually we were supposed to leave -- agreed to -- before seven so we could get to the JCC for the second stage of our planned "double date" (in the doubleheader sense), and all this time I've been waiting impatiently for her to give the word.

*   *

Ooooeee. This is one ol' lady who knows how to stick it to a guy. Twice in one night! The way she perched on the edge of the stage in the gym upstairs -- we're at the JCC now and I'm hunched over in a corner of the men's locker room for a quickie entry -- she perched there, I say, in her skimpy yellow terrycloth bikini, the only female in sight, animatedly spinning out her life story to panting between-games players while I labored before her eyes on the basketball court in the five-on-fives: that was torture enough. Then she had the killer instinct to say to me, "You did very well until the guy in the blue trunks went in." That was the main guy she'd been rapping with! Tall, dark, blue-eyed, Greekish -- possibly the best-looking guy in the state of California, Jim and Brandon not excepted.

And this note: turns out she actually hit the quintofecta at the DPC meeting earlier. The dude in the bomber jacket who was with Jim was, as I suspected he might be, George, Jim's friend for whom she once had an extreme case of the hots in a sleeping bag in which Jim and George's wife were also enwrapped. Strapping brute in motorcycle gear -- leather pants, heavy boots. A bigger, meaner Marlon Bando -- no, make that Brandon -- no no no, make that Brando! -- as "The Wild One," yes, but this guy's much more believable in the role. "The only man who's ever made me feel that way," as she once tauntingly told me. "I got really, really wet."

Thursday 23
    Crisis. Valerie was furious at me when I emerged

from the locker room last night. To her way of thinking
I'd been "ignoring" her ever since we left Emp for the
DPC meeting. In a sense this was true, I suppose,
although I've been just as withdrawn at other times and
it hasn't fazed her at all. In another sense it was
totally false: I was obsessing on her the entire night.
It's just that in front of the various other men in her
life I was apparently less raptly open about this
obsession than she wanted -- sort of the way she is
toward me, i.e. unrapt, most of the time.

Once back at "the shack" she felt I was "rejecting"
her when she said she wanted to talk -- this was as I
was getting out of my work clothes -- and I said,
"Before we do that, can we rustle up some grub first?"
I'd eaten nothing since noon except a couple of DPC
vanilla wafers and the JCC workout had left me exhausted
and famished. So then I went ahead to the kitchen.
When she came in a moment later she treated me with a
sudden fierce coolness. I was glancing at the new issue
of Ramparts as we made our sandwiches. When I asked
what was the matter now, she didn't answer. So I
continued glancing. Suddenly she exploded. She
snatched the Ramparts out of my hands and threw it hard
on the floor and then stomped it to shreds.

I managed to remain calm but I was shocked. No one
has ever done anything like that to me before. It's
close to the absolute no-no -- didn't I already say?
And given her bashings of Jim's newspapers -- which she
loves to boast about -- it seems to be a well-
established character trait of hers.

"I don't know why you're doing this," I said
finally, drilling my eyes into her, "but it looks to me
like you're trying to finish us off for good."

When she continued her fulminations I got up and
left the kitchen. She followed me to the living room.
I told her I had nothing more to say and to please get
herself elsewhere for a while. She screamed at me.
Then she went out, and I could hear her weeping in the
bedroom. I'd already decided I wouldn't give in. This
time she was just too fucking much.

[Have Mercy]

Actually, though, the Ramparts incident was more in
the nature of a final straw. Even beforehand I'd
already pretty much decided the time had come to begin
planning my getaway. Now there was no point in waiting
any longer. With each day our ties strengthen, and yet
there appears to be no more love than before. In fact,
to me it appears more and more I'm being grossly
exploited. I suspect my real role in her life is to be
a stopgap provider, companion, and personal bodyguard,
more or less, someone to lend security and a kind of
minimal temporary excitement to her life until she can
find a more violent kind of man who'll know just how to
light her fire. I feel this way a hundred times a day.

At other times, it's true, I'm sure I've got it
wrong. Then I can see quite clearly she simply doesn't
know how to love. She wants to, but she doesn't know
how. She's nineteen fucking years old! Yet the kindest
thing I can do at this point, if I really care about
her, is to minimize the damage my departure would do to
her. And I do care about her! And regardless of that,
it's still a kind of obligation anyway, if for no other
reason than I'm eight years older and at least seemingly
a lot more emotionally stable. Right now she's in no
condition to survive another major heartbreak without
permanent scars. And the longer I stay, the worse the
scars will be when I go.

I've also been appalled by the degree of her
dependence on me, or rather perhaps just on whomever she
happens to be with, and for the moment it seems pretty
clear that's me. She insists her needs must come first
at virtually all times -- and her needs are insatiable,
leaving her little mental or emotional energy to devote
to filling or even detecting the needs of anyone else.
At first glance this may not seem so unusual, but
Valerie doesn't fit the stereotype of someone badly
needing love. Most such people, I'd say, are much more
loving themselves or at least ready to compromise or
yield. Despite the occasional flares of intense warmth,
on the inside Valerie's as cold, meaning also cruel, a
woman as I've ever known.

[Shacking Up with Valerie]

I often think we never would've come to this pass
had she not so quickly suggested, and I not almost as
quickly accepted, what we agreed to call our "shacking-
up experiment." Otherwise I would've broken things off
sooner or later -- probably sooner -- because I would've
taken offence at her insensitivity toward me and
interpreted it as lack of serious interest. And the
mostly bad balling would've clinched it.

The rest of the night was a disaster. From time to
time she came into the living room aiming to wrench me
out of my funk. She tried every trick in the book:
pleas, apologies, a poem, a declaration of love,
shrieks, tantrums, pails of tears, a banshee sprint up
the hallway one time -- or Valkyrie flight I could say
-- when I was heading for the bathroom with a burning
need to piss. I told her she was making matters worse:
I wanted to be left alone, and I couldn't possibly
respond to her after what had just happened (the
Ramparts snatch-and-stomp). When all else failed I
threatened to take my things and move out immediately,
i.e., in the middle of the night. That worked.

Eventually I stretched out on the couch and fell
asleep. She awoke me several times, and the last time,
at close to four a.m., her desperation seemed so great I
yielded and joined her in bed -- where I soon drifted
off again, lying on my side with her arm around me from
behind and her nakedness pressed against my back (her
workshirt open) and her lips and face, still wet from
her tears, against my neck.

This morning we overslept. I had to persuade her
to go in to work regardless, and I did this by softening
my stance slightly -- and temporarily.

This is her extemporaneous poem from last night:
> Glenn I love you precious lover
> always & I miss you more than ever
> > There is so little time
> > to let it go to waste --
> I am sorry I have been demanding
> to the point I caused you unhappiness
> > for now I can clearly see

[Have Mercy]

             I did far from using
             the best or right approach --
     I shall be more of your interest respectful
     & of your needs careful.
             Promises, promises, I know...
     Why is it that I always accomplish
     the exact opposite of what I mean?
     O please don't even try to understand
     I do not want any longer myself to defend.
             If only you would just
             open your arms to me
     as difficult or painful it may be
     it still might ease you to forget
             my ugly reactions
             & give me my chance to
     make it all up to you at least --
     I cannot bear to watch someone as delightful
     as you are, sink abjectly into silence --
             Must we both be punished
             for what we could erase?
     Glenn, I love you more than my pride.
     May I take my lover for a joyly ride?
                     -- Valerie
It's a touching creation. So were many of the other
poems and notes, the ones earlier in our time together
which I've eagerly responded to in every case. This
time I can't do it -- and won't do it. I've got to
extricate myself from this excruciatingly frustrating
relationship before it becomes inevitable something will
go really badly and perhaps tragically wrong.
                 *   *

     I've come up with a plan for rapid withdrawal.
This morning I avoided Valerie at coffee break. (I
wrote some of the preceding in a locked stall in the
men's room, with a procession of shiny-shoed insurance
men grunting and farting and plopping out splashy turds
in the stalls to either side and one guy who seemed to
be jerking off.) She left a donut and a note on my
desk: "I love you." I gobbled down the donut and
crumpled up the note. It's too late.

[Shacking Up with Valerie]

I'll also avoid her this noon. I'll be somewhere
else writing her a farewell letter. Then I'll take off
from work an hour or two early -- let's say ninety
minutes early -- and move my things out of "the shack,"
leaving behind only the letter.

What do I say if she manages to hunt me down before
I take off this afternoon? I'll try to be distant, as
if my thoughts were preoccupied elsewhere, but not so
unresponsive as to provoke her into throwing another big
scene like the one she hit me with in the dungeon
yesterday or the one at "the shack" last night -- and so
many others over the past three weeks. In fact it would
be best to be kind and loving with her, but in a
regretful sort of way. Later she'll realize I was
saying goodbye. She'll see my behavior as evidence of
what the letter she finds on her bed will say: in
effect, that I love her but believe this isn't the time
for us, and the longer I stay on with her the more I
doubt such a time will ever come.

I hate to be so calculating about this, laying it
all out step by step. But I can't see I have any other
choice.

*   *

I must be ready to withstand a deluge of regrets
and second thoughts (and perhaps, from her, pleas, wild
scenes -- god only knows what).

Flashbacks to last night. Valerie perched on the
edge of the stage watching us play ball. How terrific
she looked in that bikini and how proud I was -- despite
everything -- she was there with me. Her poise and
physical beauty and grace as she did a few routines on
the parallel bars and pommel horse set up on the stage,
with players in the ongoing game, myself included,
colliding head-on in our efforts to get a good look.
(Which recalls Cedric the Promo lawyer shaking his head
in tongue-hanging lust a couple of weeks ago and
exclaiming, as she walked away from our Emp cafeteria
table, "That girl is built like a brick shithouse! Who
is that?")

And how lovely she looked last night at "the shack"

119

when wracked by tears. Her anguished pleas voiced in
what seemed an unusually heavy accent (the greater the
anguish, the stronger the accent?). Her saying with
precocious or maybe just call it mature wisdom, "You
must remember I'm only nineteen and I have many things
to learn!" Her proud, gentle maternal look (especially
touching in a mother so young) as Danny lay in bed next
to me this morning, the covers pulled up to our necks
and his face wreathed with smiles. Her two boys.

I hate to give up all that's so marvelous about
her. But I must do it.

*   *

Yes, I think I did the right thing. I'm back home
now, in the fog-shrouded Inner Sunset, the greasy heart
thereof, waiting for a club sandwich at Mac's Grill, and
through the slot between buildings across the street I
can see a patch of blue sky still prevailing over
Valerie's part of town. I left there -- and I'm not
going back anytime soon -- at five-fifteen, hastily,
suddenly fearing that upon reading the brief and bland
note I left for her on my desk in the dungeon she
might've suspected something was up and left work early.

In fact, a strange force impelled me to linger in
her place longer than I should've -- a perverse kind of
cold-feet hope she'd arrive and somehow persuade me not
to take this drastic step.

The fact that I did take the step surprises me.
I'd expect someone like myself to remain with her until
something external forced me to leave, either her affair
with another man -- I'd put my money on George, the
strapping motorcycle dude -- or possibly, but not really
all that possibly, Jang's return to San Francisco. So
maybe I'm finally wising up a little in my old age.
Maybe a primitive form of standard straight-arrow
morality tinctured with a bit of foresight has begun to
take hold of me.

In any case I left work at quarter past three --
indifferent to the potential consequences should my
absence be noticed -- and rode the J Church streetcar to
the Dolores place. With fierce single-minded

determination I changed out of my suit, gathered my
things (emptying my one drawer, the far right end of the
closet, the headboard niche above my side of the bed),
and took it all, along with my radio, stereo, records,
typewriter, and toilet kit, down to the L.C., drawing a
few stares while doing so as if I might be one of the
"move-out" burglars so prominent in the news lately.

I wrote a brief supplement to the earlier letter,
which was already sealed, telling her she should go back
to the better life she was carving out for herself
before the "retrogression" allegedly caused by meeting
me set in. "Fly, baby," it ended.

When the going gets tough, the tough get banal and
corny and smarmy and insufferable.

I tried to restore everything in "the shack" to the
state it had been in before I arrived on the scene, even
going so far as to put her clock radio back on the
headboard (along with the candles atop the painted egg
cartons) (and was stopped for a moment by a detail: tiny
bits of maroon wax clinging to the wall above the
headboard, spattered there the other night when I raised
myself above her to blow out the candles after we'd
balled).

As a last-minute symbolic protest against the way
she's barricaded herself against life, I tied back all
the living-room curtains -- yes, all five -- flooding
that dark and mournful room with late-afternoon sunlight
slanting in over the backyard of the next-door house,
and I was almost shocked by how vividly bright the
colors Valerie had filled that room with suddenly
became. Then as an utterly ridiculous final gesture I
made the bed to the best of my ability. I placed the
note and letter on the bedspread next to the frisbee
which she'd left in the L.C. And on top of the letter I
set the keys to "the shack" which I'd finally accepted
from her only a few days ago.

Driving away I congratulated myself for at least
having the courage to break things off with her.
Everything had gotten much, much, much too heavy. I
kept thinking of something she said last night. In the

process of castigating me for "ignoring" her, she'd
tried to drive the point home by reminding me she'd
given up her dinner date for that same night with
Brandon "so I could be with you." At the time I was
stunned she could see things this way. (It's true I'd
failed to recognize the significance of the Brandon
date. They'd agreed to it several weeks ago for the
occasion of his birthday, which is actually today.
She'd broken that date, just as she'd told me she would,
on Tuesday afternoon after we made our own plans for the
"double date" on Wednesday night.)

"If having dinner with Brandon means that much to
you," I growled at her last night, once again furious --
this was not long after she'd torn the Ramparts out of
my hands -- "then please have dinner with him every
fucking night!"

She wouldn't know what to do next when she got home
and found my things gone and my note and letter and the
keys on the bed. Danny would be arriving soon. She
would feel, again, trapped. She might write me a letter
in reply -- or she and Danny might take a taxi to
Funston. Perhaps she would think some hope still
remained. But I'm pretty sure she doesn't even know my
address or home phone number.

*   *

A change of scene. And theme. I'm at The Chamber
-- one of those dens of iniquity I've been returning to
from time to time for almost three years now, especially
during periods of love-relationship change and rebirth.
Sam and Dave on the box, already some folks dancing.
Live music later, the Irving Street Soul Band.

I'd say I'm feeling fairly good about what lies
ahead. When I stopped by Funston briefly after leaving
Valerie's place I found the house clean, orderly, and
bright. My room hasn't been so presentable in months.
I want to go back to living there but in a more settled-
in way. And I want to get some of my own goddamn work
done there.

I thank you, Pluche, for reminding me that making
art is my life.

[Shacking Up with Valerie]

Two letters from Jang were awaiting me at Funston, one marginally more loving than the others she's sent, the other angry and disillusioned because I haven't written in so long, and also hinting she's been meeting other men. Figuring out what to do about Jang will certainly be a major project for the weeks and perhaps months ahead. I have to say I'm more pessimistic than ever about our prospects. But we've been together -- in a manner of speaking -- much too long, or better to say we've known each other much too long, for me to drop her cold, as I've just done with Valerie.

I may or may not see Nadine this weekend (depending on whether Byron's in or out). But in the future there will be no more entanglements of that kind with other women no matter how likable and attractive. Nothing will be allowed to interfere with the projects that will soon be moving to the fore. I intend to stay at least minimally active politically -- and certainly to keep track of what's happening in the world -- but I know that starting now my main focus will be on what matters most to me.

*

I can't stop. The beat in here is strong -- James Brown right now: Papa back in action with his brand-new bag even if it be a bit frayed and raggedy by now. The pool players are laughing, the miniskirted waitresses are sashaying by and one even remembers me. I pretty much stopped coming here when I met Denise. The place wasn't her style at all. She disliked being hit on or looked at with outright hostility by the black guys who fumed over seeing her with a cracker like me.

In all this confusion I've neglected to mention (I think) today's note from Valerie. She wrote it at noon, some four hours before I bowed out of her life, and left it on my desk in the Emp dungeon along with a small bag of snacks for me. Here are a few outtakes:

I understand how hard circumstances can be for you.

123

[Have Mercy]

I don't understand fully how you feel
since I am not in your position and I
can't feel it for you.... I wish I were
able to replace you [did she mean "to get
inside your head"?] long enough to
understand explicitly how you feel in
order to relieve some of the torments
that are stirring inside of you....

What can I do to bring you back to
normal? I am willing to do the impossible
for you whether it will help or not...I
want to help and I am determined to....
Whatever it is, don't let it get to you so
deeply.

I think I can make you happy if you'd
let me.

I am ready to fulfill your needs badly
enough [sic?!] to overcome any hang-ups.

I don't know what but something has
occurred that's new to me and makes my
love for you stronger than life itself and
beyond death.

And please don't think I'm pouring all
this on you because I feel rejected.

[Remember,] some people are never able
to express any kind of love or affection
at any time.

You see, when you're happy I often feel
we are on the same level and that we don't
need to pamper each other. I think that
my feelings are understood and that every
one of my actions is to you an
interpretation of love. This is really

insensitive and selfish of me...I should
always make sure it is obvious to you.
*   *

What's really wrong with us? It's most obvious to
me in her phrase "I don't understand fully how you feel
since I am not in your position and can't feel for you."
To which I say: well of course she's not in my
"position"! Therein lies the fundamental basis of
loving! To me this phrase of hers demonstrates -- in
fact the whole note does -- how lethally serious and
severe she can be. In the end I think this is what's
killed us.

-- And then she says "we don't need to pamper each
other." Like hell we don't! What else is loving about?
(In addition to what I just said in the paragraph
immediately above, right.)

No, I don't want to be writing this way.

I just dread what's to come tomorrow (perhaps even
later tonight). I don't deny I feel something for
Valerie that's perilously close to love. At this point
I refuse to regard it as love simply because I don't see
how, if I love her, I could leave her, which I'll
confirm again I've just done. This feeling for her,
whatever it is, is powerful. It will be extremely
difficult to control if she puts up a fight. I'll be
able to prevent myself from giving in only by fighting
back, by turning cold, cruel, hard. In a word (one of
her favorites), nasty. That's what I dread the most.
Because I can't give in to her, period.
*   *

In bed. My bed. 1616 Funston, third and top
floor, "blue room" in the northeast corner of the flat.
Alone.

I can't help noticing the sheets haven't been
changed since the last time I was here. And of course
before that they weren't changed for many weeks if not
months. Who all's been sleeping in this bed lately I
don't even know or want to know. In other words,
everything's perfectly normal around here. I must also
say it's a pleasure, although a distinctly uneasy one,

to be able to go to bed without worrying about whether
Valerie will respond to my way of loving or I to hers.

I was right in thinking she might drop by tonight.
That's the main reason I went straight from Mac's to The
Chamber: to stay away from 1616. She called here
shortly after I left her place and several other times
later -- at some point she must've noted my number in
her address book -- and finally, because no one ever
answered, she came over, leaving this poem/message for
me shoved under the door:

> I love you Glenn
> & please believe me --
> It hurts very much
> to be apart from you
> but I'll try to be
> strong and may be
> then you will give
> the chance I appeal
> for. I have faith
> in you that you will.
> I respect your decision
> although I hope for
> reconciliation. I would
> like to see you briefly
> tomorrow if you could
> (at coffee time in your
> office). I bought you
> a present today
> thinking we would
> celebrate our 3rd anniversary
> tonight. I'd like to
> give it to you hand
> in hand.
> I love you more each
> minute. I love you.
> I love you. Please don't
> stop loving me.
>   Valerie

*

I'm tired, tired, tired....

126

Friday 24
    "Did you think I was just going to give you up?"
    That's how Valerie opened our first meeting (which
ended only moments ago) of this latest new era. She
gave me the present mentioned in her poem/note -- a
blue-and-green psychedelic T-shirt, because she knows I
like that color combo -- and another letter which is a
point-by-point reply to my farewell letter and the
last-minute note I added to it at her place. The key
lines in this new letter of hers propose as follows:
        Maybe we could see each other on occasions
        which would allow us time for ourselves
        such as time to heal for me. I would be
        so happy if you would still enjoy me as I
        will always enjoy you whether it costs me
        a little pain on the side or not.
This is the direction we'll take, I hope. I won't
resume the "shacking-up experiment" with her unless my
feelings change drastically and certain important
conclusions I've already arrived at prove to be wrong or
outdated. It's the best of all possible resolutions for
me at this time. For her it will most likely be more
difficult and, finally, I'm afraid, cruel. But it may
work out. I doubt it. But perhaps. A slim chance.
Very slim.
    This letter -- which starts out "Glenn, darling
Glenn" -- asserts she "now" loves me. "I realized today
how much you mean to me." It makes me wonder how she
was really feeling during the first three weeks when she
was telling me the same sort of thing. "It is so sad,"
she writes, "that I had to restrain myself all along
except for those rare moments in order to protect myself
against what would have been nothing if I had not."
    To me the question is, will she always have to
protect herself "against...nothing" this way? What's
she so afraid of? Rejection? If that's so, now that
I've rejected her, what will her new fear be? Or will
the fact of having been rejected paradoxically free her

up to love? But then what kind of love would that be?
How would it differ from a wound?

　　This isn't fair, I know. But then we're talking
about love.

　　What we need, she writes, is more time. "Are you
refusing me time to give you what you want and cherish
the most?" She says she "realize[s] all the changes I
need to make...not only for you but for myself." But
she insists I shouldn't've expected so much from her so
quickly. This is what "nourished our failure (but not
wholly a failure)." Our love needs "not to be revived
but rather explored." And if her main problem is, as I
suggest in my farewell letter, that she's still
recovering from the breakup of her marriage and is
likely to need much more time for that, she asks, "How
can I heal a wound with another wound?" (That's exactly
why I got out when I did. To stay longer, I believed,
and still believe, would have all but guaranteed the
infliction on her of a truly damaging second wound.)

　　She feels I won't refuse her "because you're not
selfish enough"(!). Then she offers a curious bit of
reassurance: "Glenn, if someone is my man you are it &
that much I know." This kind of oddly qualified
utterance (that initial "if") certainly isn't how you go
about convincing a man of his importance to you -- not
this man anyway.

　　She easily spots the flaws and weaknesses in my
letter, however. To soften her feeling of rejection the
letter says I still love her; but in a different
paragraph, angling to keep her from protesting too much,
it pompously calls our love "memory and history now."
She nails me on that. "How can you say 'a love that's
memory and history now' when you say you love me still
and still have hope?" Yes, I still have hope, of course
I do, but I'd still prefer she not press too hard for a
serious answer to that question. My first line of
defense would be the old standby, "It's possible to love
someone and still not be able to live with that person."
If pushed really hard, however, I'd have no choice but
to say I no longer love her.

She also charges me with being "too idealistic":
>   'Separate futures'? Have you made a
>   definite final decision? I want to live
>   for now, not for tomorrow only. If you
>   remain so idealistic you might end up with
>   nothing.

Well yes, I feel this danger myself, and probably a lot
more strongly than she'd ever suspect. The problem for
me is that, while she often proclaims her "love" for
"reality," and indeed exhibits an admirable sense of
wonder about the real world, she seems to exclude me
from that very same "reality." I feel almost constantly
taken for granted, unappreciated by her. Loving cannot
be separated from living! Least of all when we've known
each other such a short time!

In another passage about separation she writes,
>   It may be necessary for a while for us
>   to be apart from each other to give us time
>   to breathe and straighten out and then if
>   we still want it [underscored "if" through
>   "it"] we shall begin an all fresh new
>   start.

I hope she can sustain that outlook. But I'll also say
it sounds queasily like what Jang said right before she
announced she'd be going to Hawaii for three months.

Elsewhere she states,
>   Not that I want to depend on you -- but
>   that I wish to share good feelings with
>   you -- I know it would do good for me --
>   it would give me courage and strength. I
>   adore you.

*

I don't know quite what to make of all this. Love
for me has always been a more mysterious and impassioned
thing and I'm quite sure it's even more that way for
her. "Sharing good feelings" (as well as bad) is just a
byproduct of love, is it not? Not a negligible one, to
be sure, but also nowhere near as important as some of
the darker dependencies and needs.

Nor do I know why I engage in all this

pontificating. In the realm of emotion it's always easy
enough to prove whatever you want to prove. The simple
fact is this: my feelings for Valerie seem to have
changed. While she was sitting here in the dungeon
earlier this morning I experienced neither desire nor
joy nor hope, but rather sorrow and uneasiness and
regret that the dissolution of our relationship now
looked as if it would be drawn-out and difficult. A
hidden voice kept warning me, "Don't let yourself get
sucked back into this."

When we meet in the park at lunch -- I proposed it
myself -- I'll have to take a hard-line stance.
Specifically, this means I'll see her no more than once
this weekend, and perhaps not at all. But I melt when I
see tears in her eyes and she throws her arms around me.
It's terrifically hard not to yield. I feel like a man
who's voluntarily waded into quicksand, and what's more
he's promised to love doing so. I'm sinking, sinking,
and it feels so good!

After reading my note at work yesterday she feared
I was about to do exactly what I did do later in the
afternoon.

When I got home and saw the letter on the
bed I screamed and then melted in tears.
I called a cab right away to go to Jenny's.
As you know I attempted to see you but I
soon realized you did not want to see me and
therefore I did not want to intrude on your
privacy so I left and went back to Jenny's.
I can't bear the sight of home so deserted
but still so full of your presence. It
hurts so much I don't know if I'll ever go
back home.

Why does she love me -- or think she loves me? She
rarely says what it is about me that attracts her. I
can't recall a single time when she suggested it has any
kind of physical basis. (She did say I was "beautiful"
once but only after I'd more or less begged her to.)
The letter isn't much help either. These are the only
positive statements: "I have faith in you." "Your

unique love." "You are inspiring to my life." "Your
love is my support, your trust my strength." She
asserts I'm "hypersensitive" but then says she likes
this quality. "I have always looked for that in
someone, rarely found it." And: "You are over-romantic
to an extent, but never too much for me." (In the back
of my mind I hear "the Bord" crying, "Sandefjord, you're
an emotion freak!")

What does it all mean? She says she loves me, but
she has no idea who I am.

*   *

(After seeing her in the park.)

Things are at least temporarily looking up. We've
reconciled to an extent, but with a "new relationship."
We'll live separately. We'll lay no constraints
whatsoever on each other. She'll see anyone she wants,
I'll see anyone I want. We'll also see each other, but
only as we want to and only as we feel we can do so in
the proper spirit. "Let's see what happens."

Kneeling on the rubber chair mat in the lights-out
dark down here in the dungeon, in the corner, Valerie,
tranquilized, lay her head on my knee as three men in
suits, not realizing she was there a few feet away
hidden behind the cabinets, gathered around the 16-
millimeter viewer (with the audio on), their dark
shadows looming over us. I had no idea who they were.
She was trapped with me. We were trapped together in
the dungeon (or as she likes to call it, the
"oubliette," which apparently means something like a
dungeon with a steep staircase leading down to it and
collapsing walls, which in fact sounds more like the Emp
computer room). -- But after a few minutes the men left
and soon after she rushed back to her workplace, all but
certain to be hit with another demerit or two.

*   *

Far freaking out! The Family Farmacy is just what
I've been looking for. It's an old Rexall drugstore --
the sign still hangs above the door -- converted into a
hip restaurant and gathering spot. Wait, scratch the
"hip." This place is far too laid-back and simple for

that word to apply. I'd guess about a hundred bucks
(and lots of devoted hard work) went into fixing it up.
Everything here could be found in any self-respecting
junkyard. The tables are large wooden telephone-wire
reels cut in half and laid on their sides. You sit on a
worn rug or beat-up cushions. The old drugstore display
cases, shunted off to one side, now offer for sale
simple items made by local craftspeople of the
destitute-hippie kind. At night various musical and
dramatic and hortatory groups of countercultural
persuasion do their thing here on a small stage in the
southwest corner of the room.

For dinner I ordered two organic peanut-butter
sandwiches.

A prediction: I'll be visiting this place often.
It's only a block off the usual route I take home on the
90, at California and Divisadero, and just a few blocks
down the hill from the JCC. And the prices won't break
you.

My plans for the weekend are a mix of the old and
the new:

1) Hit the JCC tonight, by myself.

2) March with Cesar Chavez to support the San
Anselmo newspaper strike -- peace freaks try to hook up
with organized labor -- tomorrow, with Valerie, who
suggested it.

4) Clean up 1616, shift my things from "blue room"
to "yellow room," pay bills, etc. -- all Sunday morning,
and by myself.

5) (Maybe) Attend DPC women's-lib picnic Sunday
afternoon, with Valerie, again at her suggestion.

6) (Maybe) Step out in Jack London Square in
Oakland, Sunday night, with Nadine.

7) As for the interstices, including later
tonight, improvise.

*

It's undeniable I'm anxious about seeing Valerie
again like this so soon. It might not be such a good
idea to arouse her "false hopes." But then she's the
one who explicitly (in print in the Imp!) disavowed the

necessity for any such concern. True, she meant those words for Brandon at the time (as she's informed me), but that doesn't mean I can't take them to heart as well.

Saturday 25
> Buzz a while.
> -- "King Bee"

"I've got to write in the damn journal at least once a day; it's my patriotic duty."

That's what I just told Valerie. We're at the new Family Farmacy -- same site as last night -- with an incomplete chess set resting on the tabletop between us, half a dozen bottlecaps bearing hand-inked labels -- "Black Knight," "White Rook" -- serving as stand-ins for real chess pieces. And if I had the right kind of marker with me I'd make one for her which might say "Dark Princess." Or maybe "Radical Eyes." Or "Valkyrie." Or "Sweetheart," why not?

When I went over to pick her up at nine this morning she came to the door wearing just my black scarf. She said she'd had it twisted around her neck all night while otherwise naked in bed. We returned there and balled immediately with my jeans pulled down to my knees and my shirt and boots still on. It wasn't the greatest reconciliation fuck ever, but -- it was a start. The first erotic action of our new era.

Because of that we were late for the march in San Anselmo. Trying to catch up to it, we got entangled in the traffic jam it created and fell ever farther behind. Finally, going only on a hunch that the parade's endpoint was nearby, we parked on a side street and set off in hot pursuit on foot, picking up the makings for a picnic lunch at a deli along the way. We caught up with the marchers just a couple of blocks short of the rally site, which was a sun-baked baseball field. We tramped in behind an ILWU "drill team" bearing sharpened loading hooks in place of rifles. Those hooks whistled through the air like scythes just a few feet away from us as the

133

drill team ran through a variety of scarifying precision
maneuvers and we peace freaks winced and shuddered.
Most of the marchers were union types, as straight as
they come, and that made the rally a triumph, even
though Valerie and I felt just a bit conspicuous in our
flashy/funky/far-out citified threads.

As a speaker Cesar Chavez was unimpressive. But my
first sight of him confirmed all the encomiums I've read
and heard. In a crowd of lacquered, besuited union
leaders with faces of cardboard, Chavez, dressed in a
cheap windbreaker and jeans, looked like another order
of being. (Sandy Koufax, it was said -- in strictly
gringo terms now -- "should pitch in some higher
league." Chavez too, sez I. His smile truly is
charismatic in its radiant openness and simplicity.)

At this moment Valerie is reading "Joy" by William
Schultz, given to her by "a friend at work" (Brandon?
"The Bord"? -- She's got him, meaning Jerry Borden,
salivating over her so much these days it's comical.
"The girl just oozes sex," he confided to me.)

Every now and then she asks me to define a word
from "Joy" for her. "Stamina," for example. "Ah, of
course, da-da-da," she says, rattling off the French
equivalent. She skips over a sheaf of pages and digs
into the crucial third chapter: "Personal Functioning."

Sunday 26
The bell rang just as Valerie was sponging my
weary vitals in her bathtub. She peeked down the
internal flight of stairs at the front door: it was her
mother! In extremely hasty whispered conference we
agreed -- she was very insistent about this -- that I
should beat it out the back way. She does not want her
mother to know she's being intimate with another man
even before her divorce comes through, and especially
not if this new man dresses a lot like Jim and has
longish hair like Jim and therefore in her eyes will
probably be considered another drug dealer and sex
maniac and not a real good prospect as a stepfather for

[Shacking Up with Valerie]

Danny, the grandson.

Like a character in a cartoon strip I emerged into the thin sunlight wearing only my jeans, carrying everything else. I crept pell-mell, if that's possible, down the creaky wooden staircase and dressed the rest of the way in the little alcove beneath it, thankful no neighbors were chortling nearby (to my knowledge anyway). And now, having made good my escape, I await breakfast at Zaki's, the 20th and Irving doughnut shop where Ciara and I used to hang out in an epoch long gone. And I'm feeling Valerie's soap (I never did have a chance to rinse it off) squeezing my genitals -- no lie! -- in a tightening love-grip as it dries.

Otherwise it was a very, very good twenty-four hours with Valerie. She was warmer and more relaxed than I've ever seen her before. Apparently my unshacking move (unshackling?) really did spark a reevaluation of her feelings for me, because now she's decided for the first time she's "in love" with me. It turns out she's one of those mysterious types who makes a big deal of the distinction between "loving" and being "in love" (if only she'd told me this before!). In my shirt pocket I have a bedraggled gum wrapper on which she confirms it in her trademark purple ink: "I'm in love with you." (I asked her to write it down so I could consult it for reassurance if I seem to be losing the faith again. This wrapper was her chosen medium.)

Four small items from yesterday:

1) On the roadside as we approached Golden Gate Bridge we saw a clown in an Uncle Sam hat gesticulating toward motorists. Planted in the soil behind him was a hand-lettered, flag-bedecked sign saying "Do It!"

2) Leaving the rally, we watched an impromptu show put on by a septuagenarian (at least) puppeteer who, reciting his own catchy doggerel, lambasted racism, war-mongering, pollution, and a host of other evils. Everyone was dazzled by his spry liveliness and charm. Valerie told me she thought of him as a "jongleur" and then, after saying reprovingly "With an 'o', Glen, not an 'a' like in 'Jang'," kindly wrote the word for me in

ink on my wrist.

    3) On the way back a van just like ours (Rob, by
the way, is out putting ours through its paces today)
passed us with a large plaster-of-Paris mouth and
protruding tongue attached to the front of its hood.

    4) Next to the parking lot on Larkin on our way to
the movie we came across a huge stack about six feet
high of twenty-foot lengths of four-inch pipe, something
like an overgrown calliope laid on its side. Valerie
stood at one end, I at the other, and we sweet-talked
each other through the pipes. Even the faintest whisper
carried all that distance with startling clarity. Her
voice sounded marvelously sensual and resonant, as if my
ear were resting on her chest. Also, switching rapidly
from pipe to pipe made for a nice symbolic
representation of the intricacies and perplexities of
multichannel love communication (but when you think of
it, is there any other kind that's truly loving?).

*   *

    My new room -- right here! I spent the whole day
moving, and now everything's all set except for a few
final details. The amount of labor required was
phenomenal considering the distance traversed:
approximately eleven feet (from door to door).

    So now I've pitched camp in the "yellow room"
(southwest corner of the flat) which served for six
months as Jang's studio, and then for another six, until
recently, as Barb's room. The only remaining trace of
Jang's occupancy is a sheaf of her calligraphy practice
papers hanging from a nail on one of the walls. Barb
left nothing at all behind in the room itself except for
a new coat of metallic blue paint on the gas heater, but
a long gray cloth coat of hers still hangs in the closet
(why she didn't want to take it with her I have no idea)
and an empty medicine box from Honeker's in Gatewood
rests on the shelf above the coat (a prescription in her
name written by Floyd Merritt -- my very own doctor for
fifteen years). Everything else in here now is mine.

    It seems I have a real knack for making a room look
instantly cluttered. The air of austerity which both

136

[Shacking Up with Valerie]

Jang and Barb brought to the room and which I at one
point yearned to duplicate has already been routed.
Chaos follows me wherever I go. So do innumerable
objects. I made an effort to sift out all unessential
items, and still the place is jammed: desk, typewriter,
record player, double-size bed, red armchair, a crammed
three-shelf bookcase, two hundred record albums, fifty-
odd hardbound notebooks and chronbooks and journals,
dozens of manuscripts, a big metal lockbox, a footlocker
(containing most of the journal and chronbook
typescripts), letter and photo boxes, etc. I don't want
my living quarters to have a moldy historical feeling.
I'd like them to be simple, bright, uncluttered, making
for a place where I can get things done.

This room is much brighter than my previous one --
meaning the "blue room" -- and much, much brighter than
any of Valerie's rooms. The walls are a light yellow
(thus the name, yes). It has four large drapeless
windows, all offering a mostly uphill view, one facing
the mounting terraces of homes and backyards to the
south and the fancier houses of Golden Gate Heights
hovering above them, the other three windows facing west
and southwest toward the meadowed steep upper slope and
the rocky bare summit of Mt. Moraga (a/k/a Grandview)
maybe two hundred feet above us here. Only an oblique
slice of the spectacular northern view of the Golden
Gate and Marin County on the far side is visible from
any of the latter three windows (if you're pressed
against them), but its absence in the rest of the room
should make the setting more conducive for serious work.

Because of the sink -- the "blue room" lacks one --
this room has more of the feeling of a self-contained
unit. It reminds me a little of the very first
student's room I rented, but never did live in, in a
very old house -- but probably not as old as this one --
in Mentoka Falls a few months before I met Jang. (Last
week Unk Erik talked with an Inner Sunset old-timer who
insists this 1616 house goes back to the 1870s and was
the first built in the area. Since Valerie's first
viewing of it the other night she's been calling it "the

Castle.")

In a few minutes I'll be picking her up, the V-
woman. She'll help with the dedication ceremony for my
new quarters here. Actually I would've preferred to
sleep alone tonight, but she deftly maneuvered me into
inviting her over. This was shortly after I'd decided
not to visit Nadine despite having told her I hoped to
(I did call to let her know I couldn't make it; she
didn't seem at all surprised or miffed, even though
Byron is, yes, still locked up). Valerie tells me she
wants to keep things going between us on "an intense
level." It's hard to discourage her after begging her
for weeks to be more loving and responsive.

Meanwhile the shadow of Jang's return looms a bit
larger, especially when I'm sitting in the very spot
where she used to set up her easel and practice her
calligraphy and dance. My sense of what the future
holds for her and me is highly uncertain. Why is it one
voice tells me I'm destined to live with Jang, another
tells me it will be Valerie, and a third insists I must
live alone? The artist in me pleads for relief from the
unending demands and confusions of love and romance.
And I ask myself once again: how is it I manage to
create one crisis after another for myself? Right now
the main characters in the drama are Valerie, Jang, and
Nadine, but with Ciara hanging just off-stage (because
she's on-stage in Los Gatos) and Jill and Winnie much
further off-stage (back east) and probably never to be
seen again. But no sooner does one cast member drop out
(cf. Denise) than an understudy or a hitherto unknown
phenom pops up and turns out to be the new star, and the
show goes on without dropping a beat.

Or maybe it will be different this time.

*   *

Got to get a grip, my man. Make a choice, commit
yourself wholeheartedly to it, and then set aside love/
romance as the matter of primary concern, even if it's
still of undeniably substantial importance. I.e.:

Get to work!

Part Two

[The War in Merino]

DECEMBER

1

Tuesday 1

Rain pelts against the windows. My pants are still damp. But...for transportation to a protest a scooter always beats a car, even in the rain.

Through no intention of my own I carried a Vietcong flag for the first time today. Someone shoved it into my hands and suddenly there I was trudging up the California Street hill with it. Moran, Bauer, and several others from the old Empyrean gang, standing outside near the Stockton intersection, watched in their suits and ties as our motley troupe straggled by. Moran: "We thought we might see you up here." Bauer: "Better not drop that thing or the KGB might shoot you." Me: fumbling and hemming. A block farther up the hill two beefy cops pushed me back using riot batons held horizontally with two hands when I tried to step through their line at Powell Street. "Ouch!" I said, though it didn't really hurt. But I did step back.

Valerie, meanwhile, radiates a new confidence after reading Karen Horney. She's trying not to be the "morbid dependent" and wonders whether I'm the "narcissist."

"You don't go quite as far as the book says."
"The hell I don't! You just wait!"

I've promised to reread the relevant chapters so we can discuss all this intelligently.

I mailed the final letter to Briana (and yearn for her regardless). Jang's locked out of her new apartment and upset because I won't come see her tonight (I have a game in Daly City). Friday I leave for Garnett. I closed my bank account today; hereafter I live on what's in my pocket and stashed under the mattress (if I'll even have a mattress in Garnett).

Though I'll do my best to keep this journal going,
the time for it will be much more limited and the
entries likely even sketchier than this one.

Wednesday 2

Mourning the loss of Briana. Tonight I gave in and
took her a number of items she'd left here -- a green
sweatshirt, a Nina Simone Live album, a design
sketchbook -- along with a manila envelope containing
all her letters and poems to me (but I'm keeping
photocopies). My real aim was to get her back in the
only way I thought might work at this stage -- by bowing
out -- hoping she wouldn't let me do it.

She let me do it.

Her soft heart only made things harder. Nervous
silences, horrible inane questions. "Have you thought
about me at all?" she asks with stunning obliviousness.
All this in the hall, right next to the door of her
apartment, which she, like Jang with hers, is still in
the process of moving into. I stayed too long -- long
enough she started feeling sorry for me.

Down on the street after saying what I thought was
the last farewell I leaned against a telephone pole to
beat back a wave of grief (yes I'm serious). Then I saw
she'd followed me down, shivering in the cold, her frail
shoulders hunched and her thin arms hugging her breasts.
She couldn't say what I needed to hear. She was also
too kind, too tenderhearted, to go back upstairs.

"Promise you'll see me again," she said.

I couldn't do that. Not, as I told her, because
the pain caused by my last such promise to her was too
great. No, it's because I love her and she doesn't love
me. Simple. In the end I resort to "pride": it's all I
know how to do.

Finally I had to walk her back up, make as if I
were going in, and then take off suddenly, hurry down to
the L.C., roar off in a blind daze.

She doesn't understand me at all. She doesn't love

me. She's being fucking nice to me and that's it. I
can't stand it. The pain really is too great: already
I'm beginning to construct excuses and rationalizations.
"I didn't love her anyway. It was just an infatuation
prolonged by her indifference." That's crap of course.
But before long (by tomorrow?) it'll be the gospel
truth. It'll have to be.

This note will stand as a sorry last reminder I was
once, if only fleetingly, crazy in love with Briana Tsu.

(Admittedly I'm insanely jealous and envious of
Terry. Terry the poet. I can't write a line without
thinking he'd write it better, just as he loves her
better. He must. Results are what count. And in his
own words, "the lady / the lady is leaving" -- but
leaving me, it turns out, not him.)

*

And by a bizarre jujitsu of the emotions, last
night with Val was very fine. A basketball game in
which I stunk up the joint (she watched), a stupid
argument later at home about why her ardent attempts to
seduce funkily were missing the mark, botched balling...
and then our surprising store of patience yielded a
quick slow-touching reconciliation, powerful fucking,
and throughout a blustery night (hail rattling the
windowpanes, garbage-can lids crashing to the ground far
below on Lawton, eaves moaning like an orchestra of
wigged-out kazoos) we held each other warm and close,
two lonely souls.

"Today you're a hero if you somehow manage to keep
your life your own."

Thursday 3

Another gray, cold, rainy day.

Brother Rob's been asleep almost fourteen hours
after pulling an all-nighter to do a term paper.

I slept alone last night, disappointing Val, with
whom my relations are indeed much like those described
in Karen Horney's chapter on "Morbid Dependency."
Instead of seeing Val I read about her in Horney.

[Have Mercy]

I had hoped Briana would call or come over. "I couldn't fool myself anymore," she'd say. "I'm wild about you and have been all along." I still nurse the same foolish hope today, despite myself, despite constant attempts to suppress it.

Today I have a list of chores to keep myself distracted. All the things I must do before leaving for Garnett. Laundry, letters, bills, reading....

The small brown male dog Chopper picked up during her heat, seemingly the least compatible among her pack of mangy pursuers -- he's maybe a quarter her size but also the most persistent -- has now moved in with us.

When Chopper and I go for walks she always waits for me at intersections, looking up to see which direction I'll take. Then she goes the other way.

Yesterday's hail ("a super mix of weather") decimated our sundeck flowers, some of which were several inches high but are now back to ground zero, so to speak. Then Brown Dog added to the damage while scrambling over the liberation flowerbox on his way out the bathroom window to join his loudly pining lady love locked out on the deck: he kicked black dirt all over the yellowy-white bottom of the bathtub. It was almost as if he thought the tub needed to be covered up -- like a pile of his own shit, say.

I'm counting on this stint in Garnett to help revive my spirits.

My tan is fading fast. Even my cock looks paler.

I've vowed to work myself back into top playing shape. Take long walks, maybe even long jogs, in Garnett. Will I be able to cope with the solitude?

The small Valerie plant in my room suddenly has seven leaves!

I still find an occasional Briana crab hunkered down in my pubic hair.

Friday 4
Last day in the depressingly gray city.
    1. Finish sundeck mural #6

2. Finish notebook entries
3. Write letter home
4. Do laundry
5. Pay bills
6. Read Horney's "Narcissism" chapter
7. Tell Jang I'm leaving
8. Take BC pills to Barbara
9. Pack

Last night another game, in San Leandro this time, exhausting, just six of our guys on hand. I was only slightly better than terrible (wearing unmatching kneesocks and a raggedy white headband torn from an old towel) with Valoshka again perched in the stands lovingly spectating and graciously abstaining from derisive laughter (as far as I could see anyway, or hear) as I clowned my way up and down the floor.

In bed I read late and then wanted to love her up as she slept, but as on other occasions last year with Jang the game had sapped my strength. All I could do in my heat was just lie there and wonder why my balls were aching more than any of my sore muscles (and no, I hadn't neglected to take a jockstrap to the game).

Earlier Val and I had met for lunch in North Beach, then picked out forty bucks' worth of tanned horsehide -- four "skins," as they're called -- from which she'll make a shirt for me (and she insisted on paying for them). Then she decided to take the afternoon off and we sped home to ball in the sun (but the fog forced us indoors). I dozed off atop her afterwards, cock still lodged inside (as has become almost routine -- because her groove grooves on it (as I lamely joked)).

When we awoke it was dusk. The pregame chowdown followed, greasy sliced potatoes and bacon rustled up by a mournfully and crookedly smiling dark-eyed French Eurasian teenage ex-gymnast mom looking terrific (and terrifically sexy) in tight patched jeans, scoopneck black leotard top, and powdery pink ballet slippers, her normally ass-length cloak of thick black hair braided into a tight "cooking bun" affixed atop her head.

-- These words going down at the wobbly kitchen

table. KCBS playing on the old Crest portable and
taking me right back to the Emp dungeon era. Rob's off
at school. Chopper's black snake of a tail, visible on
the floor to the left, starts thumping when I say out
loud, "Ooh, I like it, Cho-pair! Don't stop!" This in
response to a sudden spate of licking on my half-
moccasined left foot under the table. Then she stops.

Headline news, unchanged from thirty minutes ago:
six Weathermen members are arrested for trying to blow
up a bank in New York, Cesar Chavez is jailed in Salinas
for organizing the nationwide lettuce boycott. KCBS's
updated all-news slogan: "We've got you coming and
going!" And ain't that the truth though.

Ciara's Uncle Wayne calls. Roughly once a month
someone tries to reach her here even though she's never
lived here or even seen the place as far as I know.
Usually if put on the spot I'll explain I'm "related" to
Glen Sandefjord "but I'm not him" and let it go at that.

Barb (b. 1945) on Briana (b. 1944): "She's very
young." Also: "I think both of you have way too much
pride." She suspects Briana sees her mainly because
she's my sister (her old high-school gripe -- in fact
her lifelong gripe, and who can blame her? -- but it's
not as if I ever wanted her to suffer that way).

I kept my eye on the street all day, but Briana did
not appear. Nor did she call. Nor did she write.

-- "He was seeking for the unknown sources of the
stream of consciousness... Whence did it come, and
whither was it bound?" -- D.H. Lawrence.

Saturday 5
You can't go home again, but you can get painfully
close. Even if you're two thousand miles away.

Garnett is Gatewood all over again but roughly half
again as large at 42K versus roughly 27K. Both jumble
together an older small farm town, a newer medium-size
suburb, and a massive modern military base. Also in
both places the number of flapping Stars and Stripes far
exceeds the rapidly dwindling national average.

[The War in Merino]

    Among the most obvious differences: Garnett's a
county seat whereas Gatewood's officially just a
village -- whose county seat, however, is Chicago.
Also, lots of agricultural land still surrounds Garnett,
although probably not for long; Gatewood has none. And
Garnett has some residents who are not white, although
most appear to be confined to a satellite "other side of
the tracks" town called Tesuque; Gatewood to my
knowledge has, again, none, except on the base itself.
And: Garnett's about three times as far from the Bay
Area urban core as Gatewood is from Chicago's. But that
distance (Garnett's) is still much less than I thought.
The drive out this morning took only about an hour.
    Al and Sherry live in a newish three-bedroom tract
house in a huge subdivision on the east side of town.
Sherry, who's from small-town Indiana, feels the slight
Spanish flair of this house makes it "creative," but
even she admits not much else distinguishes it from a
million similar homes, including at least a dozen right
in the same block and a hundred in the same subdivision.
    Today the four of us, Val included, drove six hours
total, past Sacramento and Auburn and rolling Sierra
foothills laced with the rusty reds and yellows of late
autumn, to see the Ananda Ranch, a commune Sherry
intends to write about for her Marriage and Family
Living class at Merino Community College. Log cabins,
tepees, geodesic domes, a lovely peaceful woodland
setting. Most of the seventy or so communards remained
out of sight, but the prevailing spirit emerged
unmistakably: reverent blandness. I doubted any of the
four of us could be happy for long in such a place.
Certainly I couldn't.
    We did not, after all, pass through Holton. This
is the small farm town where Val first landed in the
USA and lived with her mother for just under two years
and nearly went mad from isolation and culture shock
before meeting Jim and eloping on the night before she
turned sixteen, thereby inaugurating three years of even
greater madness. My goof-up on Holton's location was
just the opposite of the one on Garnett's: it turned out

147

to be much farther out (and much farther north) than I'd
thought. We didn't come within seventy miles of it. In
fact, we came much closer to Sacramento, where her
mother lives now with her nasty right-wing boyfriend
who's around a quarter century her junior -- in fact
just two years older than me).

As I blaze away in my journal at one end of Al and
Sherry's proudly "sunken" living room, Val's blazing
away in hers (in English at the moment, she tells me) at
the other end. Halfway between us George Harrison's "My
Sweet Lord" lilts hypnotically from a Sacramento station
on the radio. (We also heard "My Sweet Lord" reverbing
through the trees at Ananda. Should this have been a
surprise? I can't quite decide.)

Al's nimble reply upon learning about Val's
illustrious grandfather and her mixed-race roots in
France and Vietnam/Macau: "Well, it's good to know
Western colonialism had at least one positive result
over there!"

Earlier this morning a good talk with Barb as I
delivered the BC pills she'll start taking to prepare
for her upcoming trip to Belgium to see Joey. She
accepts the contradictions in herself, she says, but
fears life. We both agree I'm pretty much the opposite.
She likes Briana and declares herself to be in awe of
her physical beauty but otherwise views her as somewhat
of a "blank." In Barb's view my infatuation (she calls
it that) stems in part from an irrepressible need "to
fill in such intriguing blanks" -- and in perhaps larger
part from Briana's refusal to let me do so. This sounds
at least as reasonable as anything I've come up with
myself but as consolation it's useless. Still, I've
convinced myself things would never work if I continued
to see Briana (Barb agrees), whereas they just might if
I disappeared for a while. Our "sacred vow" to meet on
Valentine's Day is the only remaining hope.

"You know what I'm writing?" Val asks. "I'm
writing that in this place I feel just like I did when I
was sick and put to bed by my mother: restricted and
nervous."

[The War in Merino]

Most Americans live this way, I might remind her.
I might even note that I myself grew up in a setting
quite a lot like this. But I just grunt. I've already
said more than enough such things today.

This afternoon at her behest I fucked a knothole in
a tree with a four-foot-long piece of fallen tree limb
which she "playfully" thrust between my legs from behind
(nearly "fixing" me in the process). Then, while I did
the dirty deed, she stood back to get a good look,
barking out instructions from time to time like a manic
movie director. After that she jumped on the trunk of a
fallen tree and, using it as a kind of pommel horse,
fully extended her left leg and caressed my crotch with
the toe of her high-heel sandal. Moments later she sat
on a smooth round beachball-sized rock, flapped her arms
a few times, stood, and declared she'd produced her
finest ovum ever. Then with a purple marker she
converted a foot-long cylindrical gray stone into a cock
complete with bunched-up foreskin and a vertical slit
dripping purple semen. "I'm a sex maniac today," she
announced. (All this as we took a walk by ourselves in
the sun-dappled Ananda pine forest. With her brightly
colored clothes and "Mayan" nose she looked like -- as
she so often does -- an exotic parrot, this time
anomalously flitting about in the North Woods.)

Al gives horsie rides to Danny and Tyler, his
thirty-month-old. Val is puzzled when I ask if she
agrees Al is the spitting image of Clark Kent. "Who?
Is he that doctor on TV?"

Politically Al and I still seem to be pretty much
in sync, yet our lifestyles could scarcely differ more.

Would I be willing, he asked, to cut off some hair
for the paper's sake? Said I: "Not a chance."

A vaseful of incandescent red plastic roses --
complete with white plastic thorns -- blooms perpetually
atop the coffee table near Val. Her comment: "At least
my own thorns are real."

I've been forewarned that emergency calls for Dr.
E. come in at all hours of the night.

Freeway traffic whines by incessantly just the

other side of the high wooden backyard fence. Virtually
all of it's headed to or from Fleming Air Force Base a
mile or so east of town. In this respect too I'm almost
home again: military planes roaring overhead at all
hours, military voices roaring on the ground, just as in
Gatewood.

Val deserves an Oscar for performing her "Gigi act"
-- being cordial, friendly, charming -- for so many
hours in a row today with only that single ribald break
in the woods. But it's still true, even after five
months of stern advisements from me: when she's anxious
or excited she speaks so fast that people who don't know
her can't understand half of what she says. Even when
she slows down and repeats, many listeners have trouble.
At times I have to translate as if she really were
speaking French (and as if I understood it). (I'm
thinking of one time especially when she launched into
an impish little rant about the staggeringly laid-back
Ananda guru and Al and Sherry looked at each other wide-
eyed and both silently mouthed the words in unison,
"What'd she say?")

Enough.

Sunday 6
Haven't seen my room looking so good in months.
This isn't because I just spent most of the afternoon
straightening it up -- though I did -- but because two
days' exposure to Al and Sherry's abode makes me
appreciate my own much more. The shabby eclectic
teeming cluttered richness and weatheredness and off-
plumbness of it. Color, warmth, excitement. Natural
light and lots of it. A great view of the city -- and
just as important, the feeling of perching above, yet
within, the city -- and not just any city, but a great
and beautiful city. Nothing pretentious about the room
itself, nothing conventional either.

Having seen Al and Sherry's place, I'm now planning
to take much more up there with me than I'd previously
thought I would -- just to keep everything real.

150

[The War in Merino]

I feel closer to Val. There are intimations of a
deepening attachment -- not to say love, but then: why
not say it? -- deepening love which has somehow managed
to coexist with and survive the Briana infatuation (why
not say that too?), perhaps in part as a kind of
harmonic counterpoint to it. In any case: the next
couple of months will surely make us or break us. Our
problems are the same as always (exacerbated by the
often ill-behaved Danny's more frequent presence) but
our mutual trust and need are growing.
How I'll miss my record collection.
Last night Val and I took an unedifying walk
through Al and Sherry's Garnett neighborhood. Sameness,
dullness, straightness. The high point of the evening
came half a mile or so farther down the main drag (North
Tahoe Street) toward the center of town when we were
booted from the bar at a sedate dinner club called
Mitchell's because Val is underage (a fact I often
forget -- though to her way of thinking nowhere near
often enough). North Tahoe Street, much like Winnebago
Road in Gatewood, features gas stations, motels,
hamburger stands, convenience stores, a big bowling
alley, and a few sanitized suburban-variety bars. No
sidewalks. Lots of mud. Few trees.
We made ourselves feel better by indulging in a
blistering attack on all this when no one else was
around to lynch us. But you must be able to find the
stuff of art and life, we agreed, wherever you are.
Amen!
At eighty miles an hour the trip back to the city
takes about fifty minutes. You want to make it even
faster.
Right now I'm waiting for the crowd from the 49ers
game to disperse. A few bundled-up fans are already
trudging by outside. Most carry cushions and blankets
and other kinds of spectator gear. It's amazing they'd
hike this far (fifteen blocks or so) and two-thirds of
the way up one of the steepest and highest hills in town
just to save a few bucks on parking.
I noodled around a bit on Al's piano. I can't

remember most of the structured stuff I used to play but
I can still improvise boogie and blues fairly well,
albeit within certain narrow limits. Hopefully I'll be
able to write a few tunes while I'm there.

The sundeck is finished. That is, our refurbishing
job is complete. The "Eagle '70" mural finally takes
wing just as '70 is about to take a permanent powder.

"We Shall Overthrow."

2

Monday 7

Lying on the floor in what's about to become my
Garnett bedroom. Gray day. In this entire house
there's no armchair, no comfortable place to sit. This
room here, which is ordinarily Al's study, offers a
Swedish-modern desk chair, a long fancy worktable with
nary a scratch on it, and a stiff-backed couch which
converts into a bed, though not without massive effort.
It also features a built-in bookcase containing many of
Al's, and my, college texts along with a spanking-new
set of the Encyclopedia Britannica. One could easily
lose golf balls -- possibly even slo-pitch softballs --
in the absurdly plush wall-to-wall carpeting.

The all-volunteer staff of the paper met last night
in Al's living room. Fine people, some two dozen or so,
mostly hip or semi-hip, I'd say, racially well mixed
(i.e., only about two-thirds white) considering this is
a suburb, but dismayingly short on journalistic
experience. It will be miraculous if we can survive the
first few issues. Sherry served sherbet punch. Not a
single joint was passed around all evening except maybe
in the backyard. I never did make it out there.

Much lively discussion about what the paper should
be, what it should seek to accomplish. I tried to nudge
the group beyond its notion that the Merino Mercury (the
excellent name decided on by near-unanimous vote) must
be a slightly more liberal version of the existing local
paper, the Daily Gazette (a reactionary rag positioned

well to Richard Nixon's right). But the group, with a
few exceptions, resisted my ideas. Suicidally, in my
view, we'll be attempting to compete with the Gazette --
which is indeed a daily, whereas we'll be a fortnightly
-- in such areas as sports, national news, birth
notices, club activities, etc. I yielded because I'm an
outsider and because the idea for the paper is theirs;
I'm just the hired help, as it were, sort of like an
out-of-town director brought in for a local drama
production whose run may turn out to be very short
indeed. But I haven't given up yet.

One pleasant surprise: the San Francisco FM
stations come in here. Better, in fact, than they do at
Funston.

Aunt Polly upon seeing my leather hat for the first
time: "You look like the hero of a grade C Western."
We, Rob and I, saw her briefly yesterday at Erik's
Stanyan Street "bachelor pad." She and Erik were
grumpily trying to work out the details on which kids
would be staying at which parent's abode and for how
long over the Christmas holidays, the first since their
separation. We split in a hurry.

Rob has instructions to give out my address to no
one -- and specifically not to Jang or Briana.

And the final word goes to Thomas Mann:
A man lives not only his own personal life
as an individual, but also, consciously
or unconsciously, the life of his epoch
and his contemporaries.

Tuesday 8
The Garnett Bowl is not the center of the world,
but it's not so bad either, all things considered. To
the loud clatter of pins I await my midafternoon BLT.

I've changed my mind about this gig. I like it.
It's just what I need. As I become immersed in the
problems of getting the first press run of ten thousand
copies of the Merino Mercury onto the streets eleven
days from now, I find little time to sink into the kind

of funks that characterized my months of obsession with
Briana. Or rather I should say the array of moods back
then was actually quite wide -- melancholy, despair,
joy, bewilderment, restlessness, frustration, etc. --
but they all had one other ingredient in common: self-
engrossment. I no longer have time for that.

      Already I've made more friends in Garnett than I
have in three years plus in San Francisco. Instead of
wallowing in self-pity I force myself to meet new
people, and I find I like doing so. Some lusty sparks
too: for Lisa, big-eyed, big-busted Italian wife of a
serviceman stationed in Okinawa; for Claire, our laid-
back, long-legged, longhaired, gently freaky advertising
editor; for a little black Lolita I just passed as she
hiked along the highway shoulder and will probably never
see again (but then in a small town you never know); for
the lead singer in the Vamps, an all-girl rock band a
group of us Mercurians grooved on here in the Bowl's
Paladin Room last night. Celibacy will not take root
(mine) here.

      Thoughts about the "sides" to every question.
Could I compose a list of categories? A people side
versus a progress side? Construct a tetrahedron of
typical political issues? Roll a set of them like dice
and be required to argue for whatever combination of
"sides" comes up? Peddle them as "The Family
Dinnertable Argument Bones"? -- Or would they work
better for law-school exercises? What's getting into me
here anyway? The unending explosions of the bowling
pins are having a strange effect -- it's like an
artillery barrage softening me up for reoccupation by
the suburban gremlins.

      I was conceived, as in sperm bashing into ovum, in
a moment of national hysteria twenty-nine years ago late
last night. (How do I know? My momma told me so.)

Wednesday 9
      Dazzling bright and cold. Freeway traffic rushes
by on its way to and from Fleming AFB. The huge old

wood-cabinet radio console which originally stood in
Al's father's office in Chicago blasts forth San
Francisco acid-rock oldies: first Quicksilver, then the
Starship (nee Airplane), now the Dead. Already I'm
homesick for the city. It seems a thousand miles away.

The sun -- first we've seen of it in twelve days or
so -- lured me into the dining room, where I'll unload
on these pages for twenty minutes tops. Then I have a
list of twenty-five things to do. Today I really get
rolling on the paper. Tomorrow it's back to the city
again for a couple of days.

Last night I began rereading Henry Miller. This
time around I think I'm going to like him a lot better.
His writing throbs with four qualities I can't get
enough of these days, especially in combination (as
synergy enhances their effect manyfold): high energy,
acute perception, wide-ranging joy, radical rage. As of
today I'm signing on as an apprentice in the studio of
HVM.

Valoshka called. At first she sounded warm and
cheerful, but after I said I'd be able to see her only
Thursday and Friday, not the weekend, when I'll be
needed here, she turned sorrowful and detached, her
voice went zombie, and I immediately began to feel we'd
both be better off if we gave it a rest for a while.

Thoreau: "Most of what my neighbors call good, I am
profoundly convinced is evil, and if I repent anything,
it is my good conduct that I repent."

Saint-Exupery: "It is always in the cellars of
oppression that new truths are born." (Granted he fails
to indicate whether suburban basements count as cellars
of oppression. But even discounting for the contents of
suburban wine cellars, why shouldn't they? -- And if my
point here is unclear, I'll just note fancy wine means
nothing to me anyway.)

Thursday 10
A redwood picnic table in Al and Sherry's backyard.
It's nearly noon but beads of dew still sparkle in the

lush, uncut grass. Arrayed around me: three lawn chairs
(also redwood), a lavish swing set, a matched pair of
aluminum-frame chaise longues set up in parallel about
eight feet apart, a rusting hand mower, a tiny plastic
tricycle, and two ping-pong paddles, all to a greater or
lesser extent buried in the grass. A six-foot-high
wooden fence encloses the yard on three sides (the house
occupies the fourth), but the spaces between slats in
the back portion reveal traffic flashing by on Air Base
Parkway (yes, that's its name; it connects I-80 with the
base, Fleming).

On the other side of the fence stand a few small
green bushes, a telephone pole, and a green freeway sign
which is obliquely readable: "San Francisco/Keep Left."
In a couple of hours I'll be obeying that sign (whose
message must raise a sardonic chuckle or two from
groundbound Air Force brass whizzing by). Several full-
size trees shimmer faintly in the breeze on the far side
of the parkway. Birds chatter. The lovely rolling
hills which surround Garnett -- velvety green this time
of year just as advertised, like a vision of Ireland --
unfortunately are not visible from here.

*

The underlying competitiveness between Al and me
came through clearly in a dream of mine last night. We
were the final two contestants vying for a single Rhodes
scholarship. His act was playing the piano, mine was
doing the tango (!). I was sure I would win, but at a
crucial moment the index finger of my left hand fell
off. I interpret this as a warning to come to terms
with the competitiveness. (I'm sometimes bothered that
Al's salary is so large he can buy fancy houses and
three-hundred-dollar stereos and underwrite newspapers
on a whim. Maybe it's just envy, but I think it's
something more like an atavistic urge to prove I too
could do such things if I wanted to. And how absurd --
how quintessentially suburban -- is that?)

Val's been down on me the past couple of days. She
complains I'm not loving enough with her on the phone.
It's true; but then I find it hard to be loving when

she's so moody and dependent and demanding and
insensitive to my needs and to, especially right now,
the madly proliferating requirements of this new job.
It's simply not in the cards that I'll be able to spend
as much time with her as before. How could anything be
more obvious? Yet she refuses to acknowledge this, much
less accept it.

   We'll have it out tonight, I suspect, after I get
back to the city.

   I continue to meet new volunteers for the paper, to
help them write news stories or find other ways they can
pitch in. I also continue to focus a special attention,
increasingly lusty as the week goes by, on the
attractive girls and women, whose numbers have been
growing almost alarmingly. The scene as a whole is like
an amped-up composite of a number of others I've been
involved with in the past: participating in sports at
all levels, editing the paper and performing with the
Nomads/Worried Men at Adams, "outside agitating" at
Tuscaloe, teaching at City College and counseling at LRY
in San Francisco.

   Next week will be a ballbreaker.

Friday 11
   It never fails: Caffe Trieste hits me with an
awkward surprise every time I walk in the door. This
time I ran into Briana. Six people present, and she was
one of them. Out of nearly three-quarters of a million
in San Francisco and five million or more in the Bay
Area. And I've never seen her there before, probably
never will again.

   Now I'm back at 1616 ("the Castle") and it's some
twenty hours later. Nothing seems to have changed here
so far. This, come to think of it, is a change in
itself, since normally by now the apartment, which we
straightened up Sunday, would have become a shambles
again. But it remains impeccably clean.

   Valerie stayed the night and got off to work a few
minutes late this morning, both of which behaviors are

also normal in recent months, at least for a day or two
a week. (Chopper right now scratches at the door,
skritch-skritch-skritch repeated again and again, the
same old pleading triplets. "Let's hit the street O
malingering master!")

In the pile of mail Rob set aside for me I find a
brief letter from Mother, an unexpected note from Jerry
Borden of Emp days, and a stack of bills. Nothing from
Briana. There is a phone message from Jang, however.
She's "sorry" to hear I've left town. The rest of the
mail (schlock excepted) consists of what appear to be
Christmas cards addressed to Jang. I'll probably avoid
calling her during this visit -- let it ride a while.

Christmas. That time of year again. Decorations
already up on many of the houses on the hillside.
Retailers, it's said, are unleashing exceptionally
obnoxious ad campaigns to scare up business in this
"tight money" year, but I've noticed very little of the
hoopla. For me the cards will be few this go-round and
the gifts fewer; I haven't the time or the money or,
unless I make more of the Garnett bunch than I probably
should this soon, the friends. Barb's going to Europe,
Rob to Chicago, Erik to Mexico City: San Francisco will
seem empty. "This will almost surely be our last
Christmas at 636," Mother writes. It's appropriate and
it's also very saddening. The family as we've known it
is breaking up. A phase is just about finished. I'd
like to attend one last family Christmas at Cedar Lane,
but this year it's out of the question.

*

At Trieste, then, Barb went over to say hello to
Briana and her friend Danielle, then returned to inform
me we'd been invited to join them. When we did so,
Briana and I scarcely spoke. Danielle picked up most of
the slack, nervously filling dead air. Lots of hollow
laughter and wry comments. Had I taken the lead I'm
sure Briana would've been more friendly, even if only in
a casual, noncommittal, "nice" way. But I couldn't do
it. So I said I thought my presence was making things
awkward for everyone and therefore I would step outside,

which I then did.

To my surprise it was Briana, not Barb, who
followed me out a short time later. For the next ten
minutes we stood together in the recessed doorway to
North Beach Leathers and exchanged perhaps a hundred
words. A contest of wills and pride. Briana looked
dazzlingly beautiful but she had adopted her superior,
I-can-have-whatever-I-want persona, annoying the hell
out of me. After long minutes of staring into each
other's eyes and tight hand-clasping, I finally asked,
"Well, what do you have to say, Briana Tsu?" (but the
tone was gentle).

"I miss you," she said. Not with particular
feeling, certainly not as a reciprocal plea, but more as
I'd expect she might say it to a strictly platonic
friend.

"I miss you too."

More silence. Then Briana said: "Why don't you
come over and see me sometime?" (That sounds like a Mae
West line but Briana's tone was still the same.)

I chortled miserably. "Why do you think I'm
leaving San Francisco?"

More silence.

Then I said: "Maybe I'm misunderstanding. Why do
you want me to come over?"

"I want to talk with you about something."

"Is there some reason we can't talk about it here,
right now?"

"I don't think what I say will be heard."

More silence, a double dose this time. (Tourist
cars nosing by on Vallejo; mom and dad and the kids
staring out at this bizarrely costumed, racially mixed,
quintessentially San Franciscan counterculture couple
(seemingly anyway) emoting in a doorway as if frozen on
a pedestal like a couple of mimes in Union Square: eyes
locked inches apart, hands joined at chest level, palms
facing, fingers interlaced.)

"It looks to me," I said finally, "like neither of
us has anything more to say."

"That may be your opinion."

A little later she came up with a few warmer words,
but they arrived too late and contained no hint of
compromise: "You know, I start thinking of you when I
wake up in the morning and I think of you all day long."

I waited for more -- I don't know what. Did I want
her to kiss my ass, as her friend Marty at Vitr once
suggested to Barb that I did? Beg? Plead? But that
was it; she offered nothing more.

"It's good to know you're thinking of me," I said,
"but that's not enough. It's not even close."

"If you want to see me, I'll be at home."

"All right, Briana. But it's not very likely I'll
be coming by."

She didn't ask why not. She disengaged her hands
and went back inside Trieste.

A few minutes later, as Barb and I were sitting in
the L.C., ready to drive off, Briana came trotting up
with my bag, which (showing just how shook I really was)
I'd left under the table inside and completely forgotten
about.

"I was tempted to keep this," she said, "so you
would have to come see me."

Barb was amazed by the change Briana underwent in
my presence. She reverted to the cool sophisticate Barb
had seen in her as an early impression, when Briana had
breezily announced (concerning a flap with me), "Don't
worry, I can handle this." Barb's observations were
incisive as usual. Briana had invited her over for
dinner a few nights earlier, and for the several hours
they were together that evening Barb felt Briana was
very warm and open and caring. She hadn't seen the
superior, more or less bulletproof side.

"Briana's one of those people who are too
confident," Barb said now. "Everything's too well
arranged. Like her apartment -- everything's painted
just perfect -- sort of arty colors. Her surfaces are
arranged in such a way she's always well protected. The
surfaces don't shatter. She's the same way with people
-- very understanding and compassionate, almost too much
so."

Barb had also noticed Briana's strange detachment, "something like a drug stupor" -- it reminded her of Joey. She also concluded that, contrary to Briana's strongly expressed views, she, Briana, doesn't understand me at all. "I just laughed when she told me you're 'ultra-cool.'" Barb agreed it had become a contest of wills and wounded pride -- and in her eyes this was a sad thing. She understood both of our positions, she said, and saw little possibility of a breakthrough on either side. She didn't think I should give in again ("She'll just continue to ride roughshod over you") and she didn't think Briana should, or would, give in either.

"She doesn't know what she wants, Glennar. She's in a state of utter confusion and guilt over Terry."

She told me Briana had complained to her about the difficulty of meeting new straight (i.e., non-gay) men in San Francisco. Though she does think Briana cares about me -- Briana had told her she missed me in much the way Barb had missed Laszlo, complete with "visions on the ceiling at night" (that is, like Barb's Sistine Chapel hallucinations at the hotel in Florence) -- she also believes it's a pretty hopeless situation.

As for Barb's own future, she doesn't know what to expect in Belgium. In her view the past year has been a complete loss, "paying the price for earlier failures to come to terms with things." She feels she belongs somewhere in the U.S. now -- maybe even in San Francisco -- and definitely not back in Europe; but she needs to get away for a while. She also senses an "incompleteness" in our relationship. "In every human relationship there's a point of fundamental disagreement. It seems we keep avoiding what ours is." So we probed into our childhood conflicts a bit, her belief, in high school especially, that I wanted her to be something she wasn't, mine that she was always acting morally superior. We seemed to reach a somewhat better accord. I came away from the talk feeling more positive about our relationship than I have since early last spring, before things started going bad over Denise.

161

[Have Mercy]

    -- The Val news will have to wait. I'm cutting it
too close on picking up Barb's radio at the repair shop
before it closes for the day -- at one p.m.! (Just like
the old machine shop at Emp!)

                    *   *

    You'll never find a more pleasant bar than this
one. Toulouse, it's called, in Berkeley on University
Avenue across from Mandrake's and Berkeley Publishing,
which I'm waiting to visit. Good jazz playing, a dozen
wine-lovers chattering away (old and young and middle-
aged, African and European and Asian as well as a few of
us USA honkies of the longhair subvariety), laughter
bursting forth, sun streaming in through sashed
storefront windows. Toulouse-Lautrec posters adorn the
walls: nubile little ballet dancers -- or acrobats? --
reminding me of pale blond Valeries. In an hour the
lady herself is coming over to Berkeley by bus, and I'll
certainly bring her here. To my strictly provincial
American taste the place has a delightful French flavor
which I think she'll probably like (which almost
guarantees she'll find it totally phony).

    Alas, things are not going so well with Val and me.
Last night when we met at Ted Kent's house before the
Warriors game I was still upset over the tone she took
in her two calls to Garnett this week (and also I was
vexed by the run-in with Briana), and she got angry in
return, and we scarcely spoke again until after the
game. Then I chewed her out in an intense hallway
showdown back at Ted's place, and she caved in. But I
could feel her resentment building to dangerous levels
underneath.

    Later the fight burst out again, in the L.C. at
Mel's Drive-in on Geary, and this time I came very close
to breaking it off with her. But for some reason the
final impetus wasn't there. Perhaps I need -- repeating
here, no question -- to be hooked in with another woman
before I can summon the strength to sever old ties. Had
things worked out differently with Briana yesterday I
probably would've done the nasty deed with Val. But
instead we reconciled (again), focusing on "constructive

                       162

change." She's vowed to be "more confident" (which is ridiculous). Inadvertently I sold her on the benefits of doing volunteer work for the Mercury and then I couldn't turn her down when she actually did volunteer. So she'll be coming to Garnett this weekend. She feels "excluded." If you feel excluded, try to get yourself involved! Gee, she hadn't thought of that before.

Balling at Funston was a chore, a misfire, no damn good at all. Why are our rhythms so often so completely out of whack? I've never encountered anything like it in my entire adult life -- entire fucking life, I should say.

Barb is happy about our talk (but here she is, Valoshka in her nasty white mini, whoo whoo! All is forgiven!) ---

Saturday 12
I'm already late in leaving for Garnett, but first this quickie. I saw Briana again this morning. I was sitting in the L.C. waiting for her outside Barb's place, and when she drove up (carrying Christmas gifts for Barb) I had a note ready for her. I'd written it earlier with the intention of dropping it in the mail before leaving town, but then when I called Barb to say I was on my way over with her repaired radio she mentioned that Briana would be coming by shortly and I decided to deliver the note in person. "This is an extraordinary beseechment disguised as a bitter farewell," it started out, and went on to reiterate my familiar complaint about how badly she's treated me and to say once again I'm outta this town and she'll have to come to me now and I certainly hope she will but I'm sure as hell not counting on it.

She sat in the L.C. and read the note while I went in and said goodbye to Barb, who gave me a bag of scrumptious Christmas cookies she'd baked herself and also some unsolicited advice: "Forget about Briana." I didn't have the heart to tell her Briana was at that moment sitting outside in the L.C. pondering another

tormented plea from me. (Briana slow-moving and
heartbreakingly frail and lovely in a thin brown wrap-
around maxiskirt on a crisp, bright morning, with every
miniscule strand of her miraculous peach-fuzz complexion
visible and radiant.)

And of course Briana disappointed me again. I took
her in my arms when I went back outside, held her
tightly, tried to make her feel by sheer force of will
and intense silent emotional projection what I could no
longer swallow enough pride to allow myself to say out
loud. Yet when we finally broke off this fierce clinch
she acted as if it had been nothing more than a
perfunctory goodbye hug. She had no comment to make
about my note, no comment about what had happened at
Trieste Thursday. Instead she wanted to know whether I
had an address in Garnett and when I'd be coming back
into the city. To me these questions clearly meant she
wouldn't be responding to my plea now or anytime soon.
She plainly preferred the status quo.

This time I put up no resistance. I refused to beg
any more. The final indignity. Outrageous! How could
she let me go like this? But she could. And she did.

Another triumph for Briana. At this point I yield
to her superior will. She disdainfully calls my most
desperate bluffs. She leaves me no ground to stand on.
We've killed our love. And I'm not even sure she'll
notice it's gone.

Sunday 13
Moving into a moldy motel in Garnett. In the
middle of a muddy field which moors dozens of mangy
mobile homes.

Sitting right now in the tiny downtown Garnett bus
station listening to the chuk-a-chuk-ba-ding of pinball
machines after seeing Valerie off.

Keep your options open and the course of your life
will never be predictable.

Klug's Motor Court it's called (pronounced
Kloog's). Near where North Tahoe runs into Air Base

Parkway. Mostly trailers, but out back stands a long
low white wooden building, old and thin-walled, and
that's where anyone who's looking can usually find me
these days. One room where I'll be living, another next
door serving as the Merino Mercury office. Wide, empty
fields, neon, cars rushing by -- the place is so much
like Shaw Street in Mentoka Falls I almost did a double-
take. One big difference, though, here the McDonald's
isn't next door, it's almost a full block away. But the
whiff's still pretty much the same if the wind's blowing
strongly enough and in the right direction, or wrong
direction I should say, as it was this afternoon and
probably will be most of the time I'm here. The
prevailing wind in Garnett, as in so many places, is Big
Macs and bagza grease -- no no I mean fries.

Al will be living with me in the same room at
Klug's. I don't know exactly why the change --
something about a "new working agreement" with Sherry
which he doesn't want to talk about just yet, but
clearly she's put her foot down about -- something.
Maybe it's even something having to do with my own brief
but raucous piano-bashing tenancy in their home -- but
then Al bashes the piano too. In any case, after eight
years, roughly, of going our separate ways, he and I are
roommates again. Starting tonight.

Val spent the weekend out here. I feel very tight
with her now (close to her, that is). She took my mind
off Briana. Balled like a goddess. Rustled up
breakfast. Churned out watercolors and sketches for the
barren walls of the motel room. Dashed off poems.
Deluged me with love. Made no unreasonable demands.
Nearly decapitated herself in squeezing her head out the
bus window for a goodbye kiss. She's a fine woman: I'd
better hang on to her. I've been a real bozo about her.

And now, chaos fans, back to the Merino Mercury.
"The Merc." ("The Murk"? "The Mer-Mer"? "The
Murmuration"?) At this moment we have just one
confirmed article for our inaugural edition and it's a
total mishmash. Can we possibly fill up twenty-four
pages by Friday morning?

3

Monday 14
      Less than four hours' sleep last night: a lot like
college days again. Most of today I haven't been too
wasted but, as now, my mind wanders easily, I can't
remember what I'm supposed to be doing, I repeat things,
drop things, don't know what the heck's going on.
      Tom Yost: a splendid fellow, a possible compadre.
      Al expounds on the messianic complex which he
believes lies at the root of his self-proclaimed
"inability to be warm." He accepts it, doesn't want to
be warm. Do-gooder projects like the Mercury are his
life. And a lot of people benefit from these projects
of his, I'm not denying. Why would I when I'm so
obviously one of them myself? (That is, I'm both a
beneficiary and an actual project of his, I do believe,
though mostly an incidental one in the latter case.)
      Right now at two minutes before midnight he's
catnapping in his street clothes and shoes a few feet
behind me on the rug near the door, exhausted from
staying up until all hours the past several nights
working on the paper. With his glasses off he looks
even more like Clark Kent -- just after he's stepped
into a phone booth and stripped to the wrong outfit and
come out as Mr. Magoo.
      He sees me as being "warmer as a human being" but
"less persistent" (as a robot?).
      It's true: his energy sustains the paper. But then
of course it's basically his paper.
      If it sounds like I'm complaining about Al, I'm
not. He and I work together easily and well and always
have. It's mostly just a matter of my getting used to
calling him "Boss," and really he's not making that hard
at all. Calling Sherry "Mrs. Boss," now that can be a
stickler. But I'm pretty sure I can handle it.
      Laughter and raucous banging sounds coming from
the office next door. Marcelle's due back any minute
with her dog-pound piece. So far she's my favorite of

166

the "Glen's Groupies" bunch. All day it's been, and
it's doubly so now with the full moon dangling out
there like a solid-glitter disco ball, CRAZY AROUND
HERE. Talking about our Merc mise en scene, a/k/a MES,
which is actually short for MESS, right. ---

Tuesday 15
        I see now why I didn't keep a diary or a journal or
even a serious notebook in high school or college
(except for the one brief spell in '62). When you're
caught up in a time-consuming, fascinating group venture
involving frequent contact with scores of people, little
inspirational energy remains for marginal pursuits like
writing things down about what you're doing. Back
before I got religion (i.e., the art religion) I was
almost always mixed up in such group or public ventures,
usually several at once -- just like Al. But spring of
my senior year in college I ruthlessly chopped them all
off and I've pretty much avoided them ever since. Until
now.
        Luckily, though, over the past two years putting in
a daily appearance in this journal has become mandatory,
habitual, a psychological need as strong as any physical
need. Once in a while my body might ward off for a day
its own need to sleep, to shit, to eat, even to ball,
but for me to skip writing in here for that long I think
I'd have to zonk out for the entire twenty-four hours.
        It's obvious this theory is about to be put to its
sternest test yet.
        Right now I'm perched warily on my rickety wooden
desk chair, Klug's Motor Court, the clock ticking, the
old Crest portable playing (the timelessly mournful "A
Whiter Shade Of Pale" at the moment), the heater
rumbling, my bowels aching...and nowhere do I find
inspiration. No doubt this is largely a matter of sleep
deprivation, but of course sleep deprivation comes with
the territory. So I'll just say I'm still something
less than fully acclimated to my new editorial niche.
        Ten more minutes and I begin the day's work. Russ

and Claire are waiting next door and Tom's due to arrive
any minute. I have three long pieces to copyedit, a
dozen calls to make, two stories of my own to crank out
along with columns on film, books, and music (which will
run under pseudonyms), and an entire paper to lay out --
as well as four people to see this evening in different
spots around town. That's a lot.

I'm enjoying it. There's nothing hard about it.
The easy life. Going face to face with the muse -- now
that's hard.

Val called an hour ago during her morning break at
Emp to cancel her planned trip here this weekend.
Armand and Adele will be joining Val's (and Armand's)
mother for another Lake Tahoe gambling expedition and
Val will be babysitting Elise. She "couldn't say no
after all they've done for me this year." And a good
thing, I'd say (though I didn't), since Friday and
Saturday will be our crunch days here. Unless something
else comes up I'll be seeing her in the city on Sunday.

And Briana? For the moment she's faded into the
mist. She's just a short dash down the pike but she
might as well be in Europe again (as presumably Barb is
by now). From time to time I think about her, and each
time I'm amazed, even feel a little guilty, that I've
been able to keep her out of my mind so long, even if
it's only been maybe twenty minutes. Unless she does
something totally unexpected, I'm sure we won't be
getting together again until Valentine's Day at the
earliest. I doubt she'll be making any more of her
classic halfhearted advances. After this week, with
both Barb and Rob out of town, she won't even have a way
to find out where I am.

Wednesday 16

Taking a break at last. I've been going for eleven
hours straight, again on about four hours' sleep. In
the office next door, Tom, Becky, Russ, and Roy are
working up their articles. In here the floor is
carpeted wall-to-wall with copy as Al and I take the

168

first faltering steps in laying out the paper. It's
ludicrous how little we know at this late date, about
efficient procedures for one thing but also about just
what additional copy, if any, we'll have to work with.
Lots of giddy laughter. A feeling of camaraderie and at
the same time growing conflicts over philosophies and
political views. It turns out we're not as close on
either of these, Al and I, as I'd thought. My views are
far too radical for him, and his in turn are far too
liberal for Russ, the paper's other main bankroller.

   I think often about the "messianic need to save the
world" which, by his own testimony, supplies Al's
energy. Does something like that also supply mine? I'd
like to believe so but in truth I don't. "A wildly
erratic urge to inspire the world" -- that might be
closer for me. (And might be sheer delusion, no
question. In fact, for me the urge could be more like
"have yourself as wacky a life as you can stand to have
in preparation for writing about it.")

   Talking with the admirably self-accepting Claire I
feel like a jerk for letting some critical remarks about
Al and Sherry and various others slip out. Claire
stretches out prone on the floor and doffs her glasses
to rest her eyes. This means she can't see you staring
at her long shapely limbs and terrific dancer's
hindquarters. She studied ballet for years. Her
husband's a likable guy, but if she showed an interest
in me I'd probably respond, especially since the word is
they have a "sort of open arrangement" (according to
Becky, Claire's sister, who in my view should know).

Friday 18 (X:17)
   Just took a look out the window and realized it's
dawn. For the first time this year -- I think -- I've
missed a day in here. And just two weeks from the
finish line!
   Another fine theory bites the dust.
   Cars screaming up University Avenue in Berkeley.
We're at the printer's. A change in their plans forced

us to begin layout at seven last night, twelve hours
ahead of our already impossibly compacted and rushed
schedule. It's been a madhouse ever since. Twenty-four
more hours without sleep lie ahead. (Sleep, lie,
scream, scram, I don't know what I'm saying or doing or
failing to do.) ---

Saturday 19
    Beyond tiredness now, into the limbo of numb and
dumb total exhaustion. Another sleepless night, the
second in a row, as we carted bundles of freshly printed
papers back to Garnett in a driving rainstorm and began,
a dozen of us or so, the tedious process of rolling,
rubber-banding, and distributing all ten thousand
copies. Now, at dusk Saturday, eight thousand five
hundred of those rolled banded inky newsprint cylinders
have hit the lawns or driveways or apartment entrances
of Garnett/Tesuque/Merimont residents, and I've had
exactly one hour's sleep in the last fifty-eight,
roughly six in the last eighty-two. I just gotta get
back to dreaming. To slumber. Oh yeah, slumber,
slumber -- just to say the word aloud (which I can't
stop doing) is enough to nod me out....
    Distribution in area "Dark Blue" still remains to
be exed off on our map and when it is I'll crash. Or
probably I'm doing that already, right now, with eyes
more or less open, and who knows for how long this
might've been the case. Several days maybe.
    The paper seems to be going over well so far. Of
some dozen phone calls only one has been unfavorable:
"Fuck you!" All the rest ecstatic. For twenty-four
hours more or less I was deep in lust with Claire, our
easygoing yet strong-willed and steady yet also amusing
and heavily toking ad editor. She crashed in my bed for
an hour and said afterwards, "All that male scent kept
me awake -- for about twenty seconds." Brother Rob said
Briana had called but didn't ask for my address.

4

Monday 21 (X:20)

Back home in the city, Rob's room (he's in Chicago by now), new albums playing. The ordeal of getting out the first issue is over. I loved every minute of it, every aspect, except the sleeplessness, and maybe even that in some ways. Where before there was nothing, now there's -- something, yeah. Thirty-five thousand people reading what we have to say or at least exposed to it (10,000 copies times 3.5 potential readers per household). Not bad: the average first novel sells 5,000 copies in this country. That's speaking only of the ones actually published, of course.

Printer's ink still stains my fingernails and even the wax I scoop from my ears (with the J-shaped hook on a stretched-out paper clip -- my harmless little grooming habit, I'll call it, which has been driven underground because it shocks and disgusts everyone and for the life of me I can't see why -- or is it possibly because it's isomorphic with nose-picking?).

It's four days before Christmas and so far I've done nothing for anyone in the way of gifts or cards, and at this point I doubt I'll be able to remedy the situation.

A word about the weather: in the past month S.F. has had only two rain-free days. Today may be the third, hard to say. Looking past the tiny crooked plants on Rob's windowsill (they tilt hungrily at a forty-five-degree angle toward a shaft of sunlight suddenly thrusting in) (and right next to them the ramshackle stovepipe rising from Rob's very likable handcrafted cinderbrick fireplace thrusts out) -- right there, I say, I see black clouds and patches of blue sky vying for control of the hours ahead. And at 9:36 tonight comes the solstice, as I know because Rob the meteorology freak has its exact time written in by hand on his wall calendar pushpinned up two feet to my right.

171

[Have Mercy]

Val's convinced she's seriously neurotic -- "a lot more than you think." This after reading Horney and some other wizards of the psyche. She also conceives of herself as both a "queen" and a "natural rebel," "proud like Joan of Arc," but hates (she says) every foxy/funky girl who crosses her path. She surprised me with her long and loud laughter at the Buster Keaton festival last night. Dripped menstrual blood on the sheets as she got up this morning, her beautiful breasts jutting so proudly out between the panels of her unbuttoned blue workshirt (yes, she often wore that very same shirt to bed during her marriage, she fessed up tonight) (she'd been needling me at the movie because I was wearing a shirt Ciara made for me long ago, so I struck back).

A merry afternoon at the Zaleskys' before I left for the city yesterday. Some three dozen of us, Mercurians all, gobbling pancakes and congratulating ourselves for beating immensely long odds to actually get the damn paper out. We picked oranges right off the tree next to the kitchen window (by leaning out!) and squeezed them into juice. An impromptu jam session started up in Kurt's study and I joined in, messing around on an electric piano and (for the first time in at least six years) a full-size string bass. I even croaked out the vocal for a chaotic version of our old Nomads/Worried Men crowd-pleaser "Alley Oop."

Kurt (Claire's husband): quiet, steady, he supports the whole lot on a meager musical-instrument repairman's salary augmented by a few bucks from the occasional party dance-band gig. Frightened eyes and understandably so.

Tom Y. (husband of Becky, Claire's sister): the archetypal easygoing political activist, adopted a black kid with Becky, worked with Cesar Chavez, braved shotguns to get our farm-labor story, wants to do something on the ongoing Indian occupation of Alcatraz. I still think he and I could become good friends.

Claire: steady, warm, hard-working, harbors secret tragedies, downs all sorts of pills both legal and not, does an ungodly amount of weed, sometimes looks very

172

good to me and feels close -- reminds me a little of Ciara, a little of Barb, a little of Jang.

One of the main reasons I'm enjoying this Mercury trip so much is that, as noted before, for the first time since college I'm working closely with a large group of people on a mission we all truly believe in. This is partly a function of the job itself, partly a matter of antiwar and counterculture folks being forced to hang together for survival in an uptight military burg such as Garnett. No doubt I also like it that the locals seem to look upon me as either a hero or a degenerate, depending solely upon their point of view: antiwar or pro. To Merc staff and contributors I can also be the mojo man kindly dispensing advice and help, even if I don't really know what I'm talking about (and all too often I don't) and maybe I'm not always as tenderhearted in my editorial dealings with a group of volunteers as I should be. But then under such frenzied working conditions brusque is quite often unavoidable.

Whatever the reasons, I dig it. Most of the time I'm trying to come up with ways to improve the Merc, and that includes in my sleep here at 1616: jolting awake at three a.m. to scribble batches of crazed "Eureka!" notes which I can't read in the morning.

When I think about it, it's not a bad "almost grown" life I've been leading so far. Al and I were talking about this. "What you been up to since you left college?" Well, in my case, teaching, speechwriting, making films and videos, working up ads, counseling high-school kids, scribbling four and a half (admittedly very bad) novels and maybe two dozen (mostly even worse) short stories, churning out thousands of pages of chronbooks and journals and just plain notes, contributing to an underground newspaper (the Emp Imp), now editing a quasi-above-ground newspaper. -- And what would our "professional men" fathers have given, we wondered, to have the amount of freedom we've had? Or more to the point, what would they have done with it?

Apartments in two cities fifty miles apart!

San Francisco is where Briana is. "The Land of

Briana Tsu." In Garnett she seems to fade, but as soon
as I come back here I find she's constantly on my mind.
The big ache returns. It's not very different from a
caffeine fit after you've gone cold turkey for a few
days, but with the fit originating in the heart or the
place where the heart used to be (aww...).

By now Terry's back in town. Most likely Briana's
playing nurse for him (he has "walking pneumonia," Barb
told me). I'm weighing the idea of dropping off a copy
of the Merc for Briana. We can't get back together now,
I know that much. Our Valentine's Day "sacred vow" is
lodged in my mind like -- like what? Like the hopes of
an overgrown kid, I'll say, for a roll in the hay with
the Tooth Fairy.

Dozens of errands to run today. Might see Jang,
Briana, god knows who. Write a long-overdue letter
home. Pick up some Doc Bronner's miracle soap. Check
out used layout tables. Drop by Barb's apartment to
water the plants and make sure she hasn't been robbed or
see what's left if she has been. Try to come up with a
decent Christmas present for Valoshka.

Dash madly about the city!

*

Buster Keaton: "What you have to do is create a
character. Then the character just does his best, and
there's your comedy." -- From the program notes.

Tuesday 22

Sprawled on the nauseating-green and utterly
napless rug in my room at Klug's. Midnight. A few free
hours open up for the first time in a week. I try to
read Harper's and I yawn every other sentence. The
paper is doing fine -- why, we have eight subscription
orders already! The next goal is to tighten up the
organization so that during production of issue No. 2 Al
and I won't have to operate for so long on so little
sleep. But I bought a new loose-leaf three-ring binder
today to do the organizing in, so what's to fret about?

Here's the real scoop. I may be about to switch

horses, from Val to Briana. What, again? Yup.
Yesterday I left a Christmas note for Briana, she
called, and I wound up spending the night with her. At
first we had the usual problem: her lack of overt
interest and receptivity annoyed me, I retaliated with
coolness of my own, she made no effort to win me back.
That's why we were clinging to the far sides of a bed no
more than three feet wide, both of us tossing about
restlessly and yet rarely making physical contact (and
when we did, recoiling as if bee-stung) -- and this on
literally the longest night of the year.
    Finally, as seemed inevitable all along, came the
showdown. I just couldn't go on with this charade, I
said. "Either let's talk it out right now or I'll
split, whichever you want." We turned on a lamp,
gathered blankets around our naked bodies, and sat
cross-legged facing each other on the bed. Eventually
she blurted out what she felt the problem was: she loves
me, but "something" makes her act "differently" in my
presence. So I demanded she show this love right then
and there, and to my utter surprise she did just that as
we threw aside the blankets and balled magnificently if
I do say so -- and I do! -- me whispering wild
impassioned words that came from I know not where and
even wringing a few of same from her.
    In the morning, though, little seemed different
from earlier times. She said "I love you" again --
twice -- but now in the same old juiceless way. Just
not ready to love deeply, her journal excerpts she gave
me last month said (I've reread them all yet again).
Maybe so. Still, there is a change. We'll be seeing
each other. If she survives Terry's return -- tomorrow!
-- without falling back under his spell and into his
clutches, we may be seeing a good deal of each other.
    Lovemaking in the afternoon: my eyes, she said,
were "like little animals" in the sun.

Wednesday 23
    As Tower of Power might put it, I'm back...back...

175

back on the streets again! Well -- almost. The day has
slipped away somehow. Now Sherry clears the table in
the dining room as "Sympathy for the Devil" congas and
whoo-whoos from the new four-hundred-dollar stereo (not
three hundred; what, did I think they went for the cheap
stuff?). Al bought it for her as a Christmas gift in
hopes she would ride him less mercilessly about the
immense amount of time he devotes to the paper -- or so
he seemed to be implying to me.

Let's see: where did today go? I read a few more
sentences in Harper's, helped with the installation of a
new IBM typesetter/justifier ("the Composer"), took
gentle-eyed Lisa out for lunch in Artesia, the sleepy
old river town that for a few months 120 years ago was
the capital of the state of California (and then at her
house met the notably ungentle-eyed husband she's
divorcing, who is suddenly no longer in Okinawa -- it
appears things can change fast when you're playing
footsie with an Air Force wife), filled in a few pages
in my "The Merc -- Top Secret!" organizational binder,
and then...hmm. Not an altogether inspiring day. Just
couldn't get off today! But I'm feeling good anyway.

The archetypal experience: editor with long hair
and "shabby-elegant" clothes (Val's term) and leather
hat invades local business establishment. Draws stares,
provokes shock, makes little children weep or once in a
while cry out with delight ("Look, Mom, a real
hippie!"). But all business deals are marked by extreme
courtesy on both sides, and editor exits wondering if
things in Garnett aren't quite as bad as he'd thought.

In fact, after two weeks' acclimation I'm beginning
to like this town. More peace here than in the city.
Easier to forget about the world. If that's what you
want to do. And in my case it clearly is. Or at least
sometimes anyway.

*

Might just as well keep going. About what, I don't
know. Cranberry stains on the white tablecloth: heads
could soon roll over this. Sherry laughing uneasily on
the phone as she tries to commiserate with Al's mother,

who's about to be divorced by his father to clear the
way for a twenty-two-year-old dental researcher (Al's
father is a dentist -- and also he's an (ex?) big shot
with the morally impeccable American Albert Schweitzer
Society, so what's going on here?). Or about the cars
endlessly zipping by on Air Base Parkway (how many
bearing fully occupied body bags from Vietnam?). Or how
about the odd luminosity in the early night sky: shaped
something like a huge ball of cotton candy complete with
inverted-cone cardboard holder, this phenomenon stumped
Russ Danner and me: could it be, we wondered, a
lingering radioactive blast cloud from an atomic test on
the other side of the Sierras in Nevada? Could this in
turn mean Nixon is gearing up to nuke Hanoi?

Well well well! (John Lennon on the new stereo
right now.)

Good music can make many outrages seem sufferable,
even forgettable. For that matter so can good painting,
good writing, good art of any kind. This is but one
of the many paradoxes to be faced by an artist with a
social conscience. (But can such paradoxes be
reconciled? Paradoxically, perhaps, this uppity ill-
paid newly minted editor of a small-town scandal sheet
says they can, yes.)

Sounds like Lisa arriving. How easily that name
still flows from my pen almost six years after the
breakup with that other Lisa. And could that other Lisa
relate to me in my present incarnation? I think not.
I'm quite sure not.

Thursday 24
Christmas Eve 1970, San Francisco.
Nostalgic and lonely night.
A bath. Reading the Examiner in the tub, racing
against the water soaking up blotterlike graph by graph
from the bottom. Two weeks ago Rob broke the lower pane
of the window next to the tub and stapled a red bandanna
where the glass used to be. My most Christmasy moment
of the season so far came as I lay back mindlessly in

177

the tub maybe half an hour ago and found myself becoming
fascinated by the way the lights farther up the hill
were filtering through this faintly billowing piece of
cloth. They were red and blurred and owing to the
cloth's slow undulations they seemed to be moving, sort
of like the running lights of sailboats gently rocking
on night swells in a misty bay -- except in this case
the sailboats were holding steady and the earth itself
was rocking. Far freakin' out, man!

Otherwise tonight felt more like Halloween. Cool,
clear air, empty streets.

God knows I shouldn't feel alone -- I'll explain
why in a moment. But I do feel alone, even when Val's
here. No family around this Christmas. No tree. No
obnoxious party to attend like the annual Christmas Eve
shindig at the Kendrickses' in Gatewood. No gifts to
wrap. No corny gift cards to write. Nothing. Even
memories seem pallid. KMPX, turned up loud so I could
hear it in the bathroom (and it's even louder now that
I'm sitting next to the speakers in the living room) --
the excellent KMPX, I say, offers an eclectic mix of
rock and traditional and not-so-traditional Christmas
music (Chuck Berry with the irresistible "Run Run
Rudolph" at this very moment). Propped on the coffee
table in front of me, two watercolor cards from Val,
hand-painted and hand-delivered and very lovely.

Not a single Christmas card for me in the mail this
year.

Then I think of Jang and how lonely she must be. I
told her I'd try to call this week, but I haven't done
it. The phone has rung a few times; I haven't answered.

It's Val for the weekend. Most likely we'll stay
here and paint by day, hit movie theaters by night.

Her note on neurosis bothers me. She's even more
troubled than I'd thought. "I'm going through one of
the most painful experiences of disillusionment and
frightening confusion as I become more aware of myself."
She pleads for my help and understanding. I'm doing
everything I can -- but I'll be very surprised if it
turns out to be anywhere near enough. I consider myself

lucky if I can come up with an occasional quip that
penetrates her mournfulness deeply enough to raise a
little smile. But then it's an undeniable fact (which
in turn can sometimes complicate matters a great deal):
she has one of the most stunningly beautiful mournful
smiles I've ever seen.

Separate letters from Mother and Dad. She sounds
much better; he sounds miserable. "'Tis the season to
be jolly," he starts out misleadingly, "and I'm trying
my best." He sends subscriptions to three political
periodicals, one left, one right, one center, thinking
that "for a reincarnated editor...some viewpoint other
than that of 'The Greening of America' would be both
practical and useful, satisfying your inherent
willingness to at least look at different points of
view." He closes sadly: "Merry Xmas -- and we'll miss
having both you and Barb here while we dream of earlier
and gayer Yuletide days."

Nothing much happened with Lisa last night. What's
been occupying my mind all evening, though, is the
afternoon with Claire. She brewed us a pot of hot
chocolate as I lay naked beneath the sheets. I painted
"Ript Wrapture -- Christmas Eve 1970," my first serious
attempt at a watercolor in maybe six years, while lying
on the floor in the office. When Skip and Stephanie
left, Claire had a joint lit up before the door was
fully closed. Not much longer and we were in each
other's arms. The weed high only made easier and
mellower what probably would've happened anyway. Both
of us were nervous at first -- cars pulling up outside
or cruising slowly by a few feet away, any of them could
be the cops or the FBI or her husband. Even so the urge
was irresistible and we wound up naked in my bed. An
embarrassing disappointment there -- my body wouldn't
function -- but maybe even this was for the best. A few
days to think it over. As of now a fling with her seems
inevitable. "It's going to be good!" she cried as we
ventured out for burgers at Mitchell's.

Going to be? It already is. Her exquisite touch.
We both like to think (or at least say) we've known this

179

was inevitable from the beginning. A fine handsome sexy woman. Stoic, proud face with strong-boned, almost Indianlike features. Warm smile. Those long shapely limbs and graceful movements. Reminds me less of Ciara or Barb now but more of a stretched-out Jang with her dancerly moves and similar exquisite touch -- and also, in her seductive sensuality, she brings to mind cousin Gwen, my favorite cousin of them all -- and I have fifteen of them and that's just the females.

Late. Time to pick up Val. We're taking in the Unitarian Church's candlelight service tonight, maybe. If I can stay awake. So tired. Too much weed this afternoon. Too much voluptuizing. Too much rotgut wine tonight. I'm numbed by it all. Just want to sleep and then...sleep some more.

Friday 25

Christmas morning. Bright and cold and still. On the way to pick up Val last night I happened upon a startling sight, a throwback to Scrooge's London. A woman probably around age seventy was standing in the middle of the deserted Ninth and Irving intersection at eleven-thirty; I had to stop for a red light about twenty feet away from her. No other cars or pedestrians were around. She was motionless, hunched over, her threadbare coat offering little protection against the cold. One foot was encased in a heavy plaster cast and the other was wearing a ragged blue slipper. Her face was scarred, white as death; her glare -- for a long moment directed straight at me -- baleful.

I wonder: if I hadn't been in such a hurry, would I have tried to help her? Did anyone else? Or maybe Christmas Eve is just a bad time to be expecting anyone to be a good Samaritan?

The Unitarian Church appears to be dying a slow death. The candlelight service last night filled perhaps a quarter of the pews. Singing carols was fun (especially with Val at my side shamefacedly struggling to carry a tune). Pieces of hardened wax from the

hundreds of flickering candles clattered to the floor
from time to time as the service droned on, reminding me
of falling icicles on calm cold days back in the
province of true winter. I kept an eye out for faces
familiar from my counseling days with LRY but saw none.

At home we made our own candlelight service in the
corner of the living room where brother Jeff used to
crash during his AWOL period. The devotional ritual was
the one you might expect. (Afterwards a proud Val
declared this was the first time in her entire life
she'd really gotten her whole body into it.) Instead of
retiring to the bedroom we stayed on in that same spot,
wanting to do something different just because it was
Christmas. Surely that justified keeping the candles
going all night, we agreed, even at the risk of burning
the house down, but shortly after dozing off I lurched
awake at the smell of smoke and wound up snuffing them
all out (the culprit was a single guttering wick).
Sometime later I fetched up a raucous and absurdly
apropos dream in which Val, Jang, Briana, Claire, Kurt
(Claire's husband), and Terry (Briana's ol' man) all
demanded I choose which woman would be my official ol'
lady.

Saturday 26
        I glance up from my armchair and see one, two,
three, four pale rectangles on the living-room walls
where Jang's calligraphy practice papers used to hang.
She showed up yesterday -- Christmas Day -- about noon
as Val and I were touching up the murals on the sundeck
flowerboxes. Confrontation! The Terpsi-K at her prima-
donnaish and petty-vindictive ugliest. She and I had it
out in the living room while Dwight, the dude she was
with, rapped cheerily with Val on the deck. Jang had
the gall to rip to shreds two of Val's watercolors and
while doing that to cry out, by sheer coincidence, "This
looks like wrapping paper!", thereby transforming them
into exactly what my own Garnett watercolor was
depicting: "Ript Wrapture" (far far out but true).

[Have Mercy]

After that she stomped around tearing down her own
works. When Val came in with a propitiatory offering,
Jang imperiously ordered her from the room. "A
secretary!" she hissed at me. "False teeth!" (She's
convinced Val's excellent teeth must be phonies because
one incisor is slightly discolored.) Nothing but scorn
and derision. Pleas to her pride finally persuaded her
to leave, but not before she extracted a promise from me
to see her before returning to Garnett.

Dwight told Val that Jang "wants to be hurt." In
his view she won't go back to Korea until she believes
there's absolutely no chance of our getting back
together. So now I'm mulling whether I should tell her
my love for her is totally dead and gone. It isn't --
probably never will be -- but I see no possibility of
our reconciling, no way we could live together again.
This, however, I've told her any number of times before.

That scene shot the day at home. Val and I rode
off on the Honda and wound up seeing no fewer than four
movies. Joe Cocker in "Groupies" had her creaming in
her purple panties -- she slid my hand down in there to
prove it (or maybe more to prove she's no longer so
uptight about public raunch as long as it's "discreet").
"The Last Grenade" was a dud. "Brewster McCloud" never
got off the ground. "Burn" with Marlon Brando, however,
was smokin' good, much more so than the reviews had
decreed (it's staunchly anti-imperial and thus, of
course, anti-U.S.; it even has the nerve to hint that
certain parallels can be drawn between Touissant-
L'Ouverture's glorious uprising in the Caribbean in 1801
and Ho Chi Minh's in Vietnam in the current era -- fancy
that!). We rode home at one in the morning with eyes
glazed, stomachs upset from indulging in too much
theater candy and popcorn over the long day, our fingers
buttery and funky and icy all at once.

At a $1.29 steak joint downtown between films two
and three Val and I talked some more about funkiness.
What, she wanted to know, is it again now? It's
definitely not hospital corners on our bed every damn
day, I ventured, and then boldly went on: it's the idea

182

that what's a little sexy and dirty or even a lot sexy
and dirty is much better, much more exciting, much more
human and humane (no less) than what's clean and pure
and sterile and formal and fastidious. Val finds the
concept fascinating but also confusing and in some ways
alien. "It's not exactly a Catholic kind of idea," she
observed, "or a French or Vietnamese or Chinese kind
either, would you say?"

The notion of confidence is troubling enough to her
all by itself. I, as someone who seems confident to her
(i.e., she buys my sorry act), make her anxious for that
very reason. I intimidate her. She says this. It's
why she becomes so fumbly or clumsy or silent or passive
or just plain blank with me, in balling and dancing and
conversation and just about everything. She's hardly
ever that way with others, she says.

What can I do to help this exceptionally attractive
and intelligent and talented nineteen-year-old discover
herself and her strengths? What would Karen Horney
recommend? Abe Maslow? Ortega y Gasset? John Dewey?
Ho Chi Minh? Joan of Arc? We rapped about all these
luminaries and many others -- Chateaubriand! Rimbaud!
Victor Hugo! -- and at the end she seemed to "get it" a
bit more. Indeed I was the one who was becoming more
confused. (Could any two of my Top Forty Big Heroes
converse together for even sixty seconds without a huge
battle erupting? How about Dostoevsky and Baudelaire?
Tolstoy and Kerouac? I.F. Stone and the ideologically
repugnant but breathtakingly talented Celine?)

Sunday 27
Disease has struck me down. A massively oppressive
cold. Maybe it's "walking pneumonia" like Terry's? New
Lennon and Cold Blood and Champion Jack playing. I
stumble around "the Castle" -- as we all call it now --
watering flowers. Sun's out, warming the back of my
noggin. New leather headband holding my brain together.
Val (who made the headband for me and another for
herself) is hard at work on a series of new watercolors

to replace the ones Jang shredded. I lack the energy to undertake anything a tenth as ambitious.

Now she brings in the blackberry wine so I can guzzle away my misery. Today she's contrite after starting two fights yesterday as we toured the "Polk Street Gulch" and dined at Minerva's in the Tenderloin and then sat through an execrable so-called rock musical, "The Last Sweet Days of Isaac." Fights about Jang: I'm supposed to apologize again and again for what happened with her not just Christmas Day or during our showdown back in August but six years ago (when Val was thirteen years old and locked up in a French boarding school!). Well I'm not gonna do that, sorry. Why is it Val can't remember we're not sworn to each other and never have been and I'm not accountable to her for every bad or foolish thing I've done in my life? In this realm she's threatening to turn out even worse than Jang herself, which would be a boggling accomplishment as well as a great pity.

I do like the decorated Levi jacket I bought on Polk Street, with its bright red and green satin stars sewn on the shoulders and its multicolored satin map of the U.S. on the back. It's just right, I'd say, for an outside-agitating editor in U.S. Air Force country.

I think of Briana with her promised box of "very, very humble Christmas presents" awaiting me. The fervor seems to have drained from my need for her now that Terry's back and it's all but certain she's with him. And what about Claire struggling (perhaps) with the moral implications of the kind of infidelity (if that's the right word) that might happen between us while she's in a "sort of open marriage." Will that act of quasi-sanctioned fornication ever actually take place? Almost from day one Val's been predicting Claire and I will get it on but also that she'll "bore" me. As much as Val herself bores me, I wonder, with her extreme moodiness and her endless impenetrable teenage identity crises and her unendurable moral sermons about my past and present and likely future transgressions?

I am not responsible for what I write today.

It's taken me almost an hour to get this much on
paper. Now I probably should rip the page out of the
book. But I've never done that yet and I'm not going to
start now, so here it is. Sorry if I've made anyone
SUFFER -- and I especially mean you, Val.

5

Monday 28
Turmoil grows! Spreading yerself too thin, Mr.
Editor!
Take last night, for example. Claire and I are
lying on the floor at the office of the M.M., marveling
at the touches, and the phone rings. It's Jang -- and
she's calling from the Standard station just down the
street!
She spent the night in my low-rent motel room.
"The night of the slippery quilt." A couple of glorious
long-winded and mostly carrezza-type copulations of the
most powerful kind. Why not? She managed to keep her
bitterness under control most of the time, almost as if
her furylike Christmas Day visitation at Funston hadn't
happened. Lots of nostalgia, mostly focusing on our
Fell Street days, lots of pleas from her for future
togetherness. Such pleas unnerve me. In fact, I
unnerve me. I'm watching all this sex & love craziness
with a mixture of bewilderment, excitement, and disgust.
Trepidation too, yeah.
Oops -- the phone is ringing again ---
*
Briana! Says she'll be coming up here Wednesday
to drop off her Christmas box!
See what I mean? This was not a setup.
What's more I received a letter from Briana today
addressed to "Editor Sandefjord." It's a series of what
she calls "simple statements" interspersed with "I love
you"s. Nine such statements, among them "you left me
with the sun on my body" and "there is rapture in the
soft wetness between our bodies" and "there will be the

clarity of being" and "each will explore the rings around the other's essence."

What if all three want to see me New Year's Eve? Somebody will wind up getting hurt. Who? Jang, probably. Val, probably. Briana, probably not, because the real truth is she doesn't care enough and she'd probably prefer to be with Terry anyway. But me for sure. Most likely I'm gonna be totally wiped out. And will thoroughly deserve to be, absolutely. Who's denying? My year of the crazed rebound romances is about to come to a deservedly pandemoniacal end.

See, one can't run away from one's own dueling (trieling?) embroilments.

*   *

What prompts this encore I don't know. Three in the morning at a motel called Klug's in a town called Garnett, heavy rain thundering on the roof and splattering loudly on the sidewalk just outside, and I'm unwilling to crash just yet. Instead some random notes.

** After our Christmas Eve orgy of touch, Claire tells me, she was so turned on "my ovaries hurt all night." (Blue ovaries?)

** Val likes the way I tear into meat, especially lamb chops -- "savage and joyful." (She likes to watch me do this -- meaty voyeurism.)

** Tonight I again took a few turns on the string bass at the Zaleskys'. Now my fingers are torn and aching, especially the two trying to hang on to this pen. I'd say I managed to hit a suitable note on the bass about one thump out of every four. When it came time to tickle the electric-piano ivories and bumble out the vocal on "Hot Rod Lincoln" (big chunks of which I discovered I've forgotten) I quickly had them scrambling for the exits (earlier, though, "Too Much Monkey Business" went over well).

** New Year's resolutions -- the very idea now seems laughable.

** It's beginning to trouble me that at the same time I'm going through all this emotional turmoil I'm at the center of way too much attention up here in Garnett.

Adulation almost, and most of all from the high-school
girls. It's like an eighth-grader's wet dream. "Glen's
Groupies" -- it's for real! And yes, I'm losing all
sense of proportion. I don't doubt the way I'm relating
with Briana/Valerie/Jang is affected by this situation
here in ways all three must find puzzling if not
downright disgusting. And rightfully so!

** Sometime during the night Jang slipped out of
bed and wrapped her bete noir, the same loud-ticking
alarm clock of mine that's been tormenting her since
Mentoka Falls days -- or is it perhaps a new one I
bought to replace that old one? -- wrapped it in a quilt
and banished it to a far corner of the room. And then a
few minutes later said, "It's like a time bomb!" and
jumped up again and deposited the whole clock-cum-quilt
bundle in the bathroom and rather noisily shut the door.

** What this paper needs is a hard-nosed
investigative reporter. Could I galvanize myself into
playing that role? It's true I dislike being rejected
and put down in the way that serious investigative
reporters inevitably are, but really now: this is a
phobia which I must overcome. Going nose to nose with
the bad guys is what it's all about!

** The heater roars like a diesel engine.

** Sherry's flirtatious antagonism toward me
became more understandable tonight. It seems I'm the
only one besides Gary (her sociology teacher at Merino
C.C.) she's found "really neat" since she married Al.
She confessed this flat-out, almost causing me to drive
into a tree. This as I gave her a lift to the college
library. Then she made me promise I wouldn't tell Al
what she'd said. One thing I know for sure: nothing
will ever be happening between Sherry and me. Period.

** Al tried on my Bat Masterson hat, also known as
(to him) the "Bat hat," and pathetically showed off his
shiny new lace-up oxfords. At times he truly is
pathetic, yes, undeniably, but also, and often at the
very same time, he can be hilariously funny about his
own straight-arrow pateticness; and he realizes this
and plays off it so well and always has. When he gets

going he's better than Wally Cox (making him a meld,
therefore, of Clark Kent with Mr. Peepers as well as Mr.
Magoo). It's also undeniably true he and the
aggressively shrewd and flirtatious and gold-digging
Sherry make for one of the odder couples I've ever come
across. But I still think she ought to hang in there
with him -- she ought to appreciate what she's got.
...Of course I'm a fine one to talk, oh yes.

Tuesday 29
     They say you can't be a revolutionary if you
haven't been to jail. So now the way's clear for me to
be a revolutionary.
     I spent most of the afternoon and evening cooling
my heels in a cell at the Merino County Jail. Right
now, thanks to the belated efforts of a battery of high-
powered Mercury attorneys, I'm a free man -- out on my
own recognizance -- but I stand charged with a felony:
"possession of dangerous drugs."
     I am guilty, yes -- but only if you subscribe to a
nonstandard notion about which drugs are truly
dangerous. The ones I was caught with were two
Coricidin (cold pills), two Phillips Milk of Magnesia
(for acid stomach), one Bayer's aspirin, and seven
Sudafeds (another kind of cold pill). But, you know, I
have long hair and dress kinda scruffy and display
antiwar stickers on my vehicle, so the blue meanies
figured there had to be contraband in such a variegated
haul of pills no matter what I told them they were. So
they slapped the cuffs on me and dragged me off to the
hoosegow.
     Briefly -- it's past one a.m. now, I'm back in my
room at Klug's and exhausted -- here's what happened.
Claire and I were in the L.C. nosing down the narrow
side streets of Tesuque City ("the Reno of California" a
century ago). We were looking for a potential
advertiser's address which we never were able to locate.
Just after we'd given up and returned to the main drag,
a police car suddenly flashed its lights behind us. We

pulled over. The charge was running a stop sign (which
we didn't do as far as I know; but I'll admit it was
dark and confusing even in broad daylight back in that
Tesuque maze). In any event it was obvious from the
start the police had something more than a mere traffic
bust in mind.

As I rummaged through my glove compartment for the
L.C.'s registration, the pressure began to mount. One
of the cops, a relatively benign-seeming, somewhat
tentative man (a reserve officer as it turned out),
stood by my window while the other -- younger, stouter,
brusquer, much more "professional" -- edged up to
Claire's window. He soon announced he detected "a
definite smell of marijuana" and asked my permission to
search the L.C., adding that if I said no they'd impound
the vehicle and search it anyway.

Traumatic moment. Feeling sure there was nothing
illegal in there -- Claire had whispered "I'm clean" as
the cops approached -- I decided to let him go ahead,
figuring he'd come up empty-handed and we'd stand at
least a chance of being released with nothing more than
a moving violation. I was aware he might plant
something, but I also sensed that this cop, officious as
he was, wasn't crooked or fanatically anti-hip. I
envisaged long hours in jail for Claire as well as
myself if I didn't yield.

It was a mistake. At first I was enjoying the
sight of that by-the-book cop gingerly picking through
the mounds of refuse on the L.C. floor and finding
nothing. But then he fished in my bag and triumphantly
pulled out the vial of cold pills and a small aspirin
tin, and I knew we were in trouble. The prescription on
the vial was made out to Albert Edwards, and the other
pills looked subversive as hell because they weren't in
their original containers, except for the aspirin. In
any case we were under arrest.

A crowd of kids and shoppers which had gathered
across the street watched wide-eyed as I was led off to
the car of the Garnett police "narcotics expert," who
had arrived during the search. Now he gravely examined

the cold pills and advised the Tesuque officer to
proceed with the arrest. So I had to empty my pockets,
take off my boots, and submit to a meticulous pat-down
search with my hands braced against the hood of the cop
car and my legs spread as the by-the-book Garnett cop
watched my every move ("One boot at a time, buddy!").
Then, as ordered, I put my hands behind my back and they
slapped on the cuffs.

In truth I was more worried about Claire than
myself. I knew she often carried weed in her purse and
I was afraid that, despite what she'd just said, some
residue might be in there, and I could see the reserve
officer going through her belongings. Beyond that, I
was thinking of what damage the incident could do to Al,
to the paper ("DRUG-DEALING EDITOR ARRESTED"), and to
the people at Claire's house. Also troubling, at least
as far as my own personal fate was concerned, was the
thought of Claire's baggie of weed resting in its sadly
amateurish hiding place atop my kitchen cabinet back at
Klug's. It seemed quite possible the cops would use our
bust to justify follow-up raids there and perhaps at her
house as well and even possibly at Al's house, since his
name was on both the prescription vial and the Klug's
lease.

As the two cops went back to sifting through the
trash in the L.C., Claire used the ruse of sticking a
cigarette through the wire-mesh screen between the front
and back seat in the police cruiser so I could take a
drag -- almost like a scene from, yes, "Dragnet" -- to
whisper that she knew one of the guys watching the bust
from across the street and was sure he would call the
Mercury office. In response I managed to raise my
hands, still cuffed behind me, high enough to flash a V-
sign to the crowd.

Then things got worse. Claire was summoned for a
few minutes to talk with all three reserve officers.
"I'm in deep shit," she whispered to me through the
screen when she returned. "They found some bennies in
my purse. I'd completely forgotten I had them."

Shortly after that they whisked us off to the

county jail.

The guy Claire knew did indeed call the office (she'd had the presence of mind to flip one of her business cards into the gutter within his sight), so by the time I was ready to make my single permitted call from jail the whole Mercury gang already knew about the bust. Unfortunately our gung-ho "official" attorney was off somewhere playing handball according to his secretary and then he would be going out to dinner in Sheridan and unreachable until after nine p.m.

In general, Claire, who's been through similar incidents several times before, was much cooler about things than I was. She made small talk with the cops, dropped a few names of Garnett and Merino County power brokers she knows, mentioned our being reporters, and did all she could to get us out of the bind (futilely, of course; but she tried). Except for a few mildly spirited outbursts I adopted a pose -- or more likely it adopted me -- of resigned, disgusted silence, simultaneously playing the innocent martyr and the weary bust veteran.

Tomorrow's installment: "Letter from Merino County Jail."

Thursday 31 (X:30)

Last day of the year. Briana sleeps in my overheated room at Klug's and I sit at the Denny's counter trying to make some sense out of recent events (I never did get a chance to write yesterday).

The drug bust became a matter of public record when yesterday's Ghastly (as everyone calls the Daily Gazette) printed an error-packed three-paragraph story about it on page two. According to this story, a "roach" and an "opium pipe" were found in my vehicle -- but the police report mentioned neither. Our handball-playing lawyer showed us the report last night and then blithely announced he'd be unable to take the case. It seems his firm also represents the City of Tesuque City (yes, that's the town's redundant official name, or so

I'm told).

The good news is that the police -- assuming their
lab analysis doesn't find my cold pills to be something
other than what they are -- have no case against me.
The bad news is they have a strong case against Claire.
Her only plausible line of defense is illegal search and
seizure.

*

Jail. What can I say? I was locked up from three
in the afternoon until ten-thirty at night, but I never
did make it upstairs to the permanent cells. I split my
time between the drunk tank and, briefly, the phone
cell. The drunk tank: low ceiling, no heat, worn metal
benches, a stinking open toilet, graffiti-scrawled
pastel green walls, two small barred windows up high
through which one could (standing on tiptoes atop one of
the benches) gaze out upon the immaculately kept Garnett
town green (and yes, it is very, very green). I paced,
did isometrics, tried to snatch some zees while curled
up against a hot-water pipe. Occasionally I had to
laugh at the ludicrousness of the whole situation, but
for the most part I was subdued, in a trancelike state,
suffering a headache mixed in with pangs of exasperation
and sighs of resignation. I tried to arouse my sense of
journalistic or writerly duty to observe everything
closely, but the place was at once too featureless and
too oppressive for that.

I did my time with, at various points, what I'd
assume to be a fairly typical random sample of Merino
County lawbreakers, although their racial and cultural
diversity unsurprisingly far exceeded the town's: a
crew-cut glue-sniffer (white), a bad-check artist
(black with a serious Afro), a longhaired farmer
accused of assault (white), and a mop-haired weed bustee
(Chicano). ---

*   *

Later. The office. A man old enough to be my
grandfather -- maybe even my great-grandfather --
totters in and orders a subscription and totters back
out. "That was nice," says Briana.

[The War in Merino]

There really are fulfilling moments in this
business.
Yesterday, however, offered mostly infuriating
ones. Russ Danner heard about the bust and rushed over
to get my side of the story, his face twisted into a
mask of earnest horror. When I'd finished telling him
exactly what had happened, he said, "You can tell me the
truth, Glen. What really happened?"
I was afraid I'd be facing a lot more of this sort
of in-house interrogation at last night's staff meeting,
but -- remarkably -- nobody even mentioned the bust.
The meeting, consisting of forty-five people packed into
Al and Sherry's living room and raised dining area,
roughly a third of them new recruits, was a grand
success, by our standards anyway, with Garnett's goody-
goody "All-American Town" façade ripped to shreds (more
"Ript Wrapture"!) as one person after another testified
about the bad shit that goes down around here. The list
of story ideas they proposed or inspired covered four
pages in my binder; by the time the meeting had broken
up we'd already assigned a dozen of them.
Meanwhile Claire was meeting with her longtime
personal lawyer (who'd been out of town the day before),
and afterwards she, Al, and I talked over our
predicament. A split developed between Claire and me.
I thought she should fabricate a story to explain why
the pills were in her purse; she insisted she must tell
the truth no matter what. Radical politics versus hip
virtue. I feel (in such company) I'm practically a
hardened urban guerrilla. The irony of all this is I'm
also the one who plays the role of buffering middleman
between the straight and the hip factions of the paper,
whereas Claire can scarcely control her temper in the
presence of Russ Danner and his pusillanimous middle-of-
the-road realtor pals. ---
                     *   *
Heart pounding. Briana and I just attempted a
stand-up quickie in the bathroom. It wouldn't fly; too
many people talking right outside the door and sometimes
knocking on it or kicking it. Last night's two lying-

down "slowies" did fly, however. Fantastic. The first
one, we came together in gorgeous sync as I, stretched
out more or less horizontally above her, with my knees
planted between her widespread legs, lifted her ass
slowly, yes, up and down with one hand while propping my
upper body aloft with the other arm, our bodies touching
only where cock and vulva/vagina and tufts of soft damp
pubic hair met. The second, maybe twenty minutes later,
was even better, long and so deep (from behind, sort of,
as I knelt on the edge of the bed and she lay on her
side with her right foot on my left shoulder, presenting
a truly gorgeous picture) -- so deep and so tight that
cervix-strumming eventually drew blood. She screamed
with each gasping breath -- a sharp rhythmic high-
pitched whine I've never heard from her, or anyone,
before. I asked if it was too much and she screamed
again: "No! God, don't stop!"

Afterwards she declared, and I quote: "I'll never
be able to make love with anyone else." Also, "I feel
like I lost my virginity tonight." (It was the first
time she'd ever bled, she told me, including the night
in Italy some three or four years ago when she really
did lose, or cast off really, her virginity.)

But just as our glory remained the same, so did our
impasse. Her block against caring too much is as strong
as ever. She admitted this straight out. Terry, of
course, is the reason. Damn his eyes anyway! Not that
this comes as any great surprise or anything, but he's
the one she'll be seeing tonight for New Year's, not me.
Their series of long talks after his return last week
seems only to have confirmed their "deep attachment," as
she explained to me with exemplary tender concern for my
emotional well-being as well as his. At one point
during our high-flying period last night she even said,
"I think you and I could have a good life together"; but
then today -- (now as I scribble away she leans through
my spread knees and when I ask, "Should I put down here
that Briana says she loves gnarly ol' 'Editor
Sandefjord' passionately no matter what?" she says yes,
I should, and nods gravely). (Her frail, ancient,

194

deeply lined and infinitely lovable hands.) ---
                    *   *
    -- So now (several hours later) she stomps out.
Slams the door. What's up with her? At one point late
this morning she suggested we're not "emotionally
compatible." Her exact words: "I'm afraid to let myself
love you because I think we'd be emotionally
incompatible." I talked her into retracting that one
for the moment, but even then I was sure it would be
back before long and now here it is.
    Most of today she's been absorbed in reading de
Rougemont's book about love (one of Terry's Christmas
gifts to her) and, often, completely ignoring me. All
by itself this affront (her reading that particular book
in that particular way at that particular time) has been
enough to pump up my own "emotional incompatibility"
suspicions to the maximum.
    It looks as though we'll be splitting soon -- and
definitely not together, that is, not in the same
vehicle. I may be spending New Year's Eve with Val
after all. Or alone. Val wasn't home when I called at
five to let her know I'd be able to make it into the
city tonight after all. She had said she would be.
                    *   *
    Hey! It's barely two hours later and I'm hunkered
down at one of the tables with checkered red-and-white
tablecloths at Mike's Pool Hall on Broadway in San
Francisco with -- Val!
    What the hell's going on? Well, I suppose it's
obvious. And yet it all happened so fast I'm still
dumbfounded. I feel like an actor who's rushing back
and forth between theaters to perform in three or four
wildly different plays on the same night.
    The crowd outside is growing fast. Confetti's
flying already and it's only nine o'clock. But the big
action of the moment is right here in Mike's: six cops
are busting a longhair dude by the back wall of the main
room (to avoid provoking the crowds outside, they hauled
him in here). They're searching him as I write.
    Talk about deja vu. Two days ago that guy was me.

195

Gives me the willies, it does. The guy's even wearing a
leather lid much like my own (except now a cop is
holding it by the edge of the brim between his thumb and
index finger, queasily, as if it might be radioactive or
infested with bubonic plague).

What happened earlier tonight back in Garnett (my
left arm casually, I hope, shields this private passage
to make sure it stays private) was that I tracked Briana
down in the trailer park and had it out with her on the
Terry issue for an hour or more. The result was the
same as every other time we've gone to the mat on this
crucial matter: she gave not one inch. She even accused
me of being "too impatient" and "pushing too hard" --
after I've put up with her nonstop equivocations on him
for almost five months!

By the time we returned to the office we were
nearly at each other's throats. At that point Al handed
me a note (very discreetly, thank you Al) saying Val had
called and she'd be coming in on the 6:55 bus, i.e., in
about fifteen minutes. I was already in such a state, I
simply told Briana I was leaving immediately (we'd both
been about to take off anyway) and wished her a happy
new year and, oh yeah, said I was done with her forever.
Period. And in case that didn't put it strongly enough,
I reiterated that I saw no hope at all for us in the
future. And I couldn't resist inquiring: had I now
succeeded in helping her find, at last, "clarity of
being"? (This was something we'd wrangled over in the
trailer lot, from a "Simple Statement" in her "Editor
Sandefjord" letter of a few days ago.)

She didn't respond to my inquiry, which to be sure
was rhetorical anyway. She was already on her way
inside to pack up.

So then I roared off in the L.C. Like a high-
school punk, no question about it. Even splattered mud
on the building with the wheels. I caught a glimpse of
Al's startled face at the office window as the L.C. spun
around. To my surprise Briana did not reappear in the
doorway of my room to give me the finger.

As I hit North Tahoe Street it occurred to me this

was at least the third time I've staged a melodramatic
roaring-off finale with Briana. Even my best stuff
doesn't work on her! And yes, I don't deny that when I
say "best stuff" what I'm really talking about is last
night's balling. But not only that. The point is that
nothing I do on any level breaks through to her core;
nothing I do inspires her to make the bold life-changing
move. And that's just the way it is and has been from
the start and I have to accept it and I intend to do
just that. Move on. Boldly and life-changingly!

If ever there was a time for it, this is it. The
number-one night in all Christendom for turning over a
new leaf.

*

So now we're in the city, Val and I. Came straight
from the Garnett Greyhound station to Broadway,
retracing the route she'd just taken on the bus going
the other way. Today she submitted her "two weeks'
notice letter" at Empyrean -- passed out a hundred
copies of it too, mostly to our old "underground" Emp
Imp gang but also at the Downtown Peace Coalition office
-- and it's a gem. She's sparkling with newfound
confidence tonight. Lovely.

Of course I've told her nothing of what happened
with Briana. I'll save that for some more propitious
time, preferably far in the future.

When Val's bright and cheerful as she is tonight I
easily fall into speculation about the "good life"
(using Briana's term, and why the hell not?) which she
and I could have together. The erotic side may never be
as spectacular as it is with Briana, true, much less
with Jang, but holy shit, man, you can't have
everything! It's plenty good enough as it is and will
surely keep getting better! -- And from her I can draw
courage and strength. Without a doubt she understands
me much better and sees just about everything there is
to be seen on this planet much more sharply and deeply
than does Briana or anyone else I've been with. And
shouldn't that count for something?

Oh, is Valoshka a sight tonight. La Gamine in her

197

droopy black hat and itty-bitty black leather miniskirt,
peace pendant dangling, breasts perking, sweet little
ass perking too (and back muscles rippling) when she
struts off to the loo -- tonight she's slashing out the
sentences in her own sketchbook as furiously as I'm
slashing the ones in mine. My teenybopper journal
disciple, riding an exuberant surge of strength and
excitement just as I did on the day I quit Emp. My
lover. My lover that I've treated so badly and yet
she's still my lover. Her beautiful lips and eyes.
Lips so full and sensual (I'm staring), eyes so dark and
deep, so "sloe" and sultry not to mention penetrating
and radical. Such a fox and so vivacious and so
bursting with nervous energy right now you wouldn't be
surprised to see her spring up and do a full backward
twisting flip between tables -- and as a former
gymnastics prodigy of sorts she could probably do just
that if she wanted to.

So fuck you, Briana!

Val's eager to hear the whole story of my bust.

"You loved it!" she cries. "You love everything
that happens to you! You're so lucky!"

That's what I mean: she can refire my enthusiasm.
All I need is a reminder of this every now and then.
Only someone who shares my political perspective and my
word-slinger obsessiveness could do what she does for
me. And that's only a small part of what we share.

Keep it up, O Valiant One, and I'll soon be needing
you just the way you want -- and I want.

That's never happened before. A fresh quadrant of
possibility opens up!

-- On New Year's Eve, the last few hours of 1970.
And a very good year it's been, all in all, I'd say now,
no matter how crazed and painful at times (including
now, I'm not denying) (but no, not true, I am denying,
oh am I denying!): but in any case just a preparation
for 1971. Planting the seeds in '70, getting sky-high
from those beauties blooming in '71.

Write on! (But probably no more tonight.)

JANUARY

1

Friday 1

Wine-dark rug, living-room floor, gray New Year's
Day. Rose Bowl on the tube but the picture's garbled.
Val's blazing out watercolors in the kitchen. The Land
Cruiser's parked a block away, above Moraga Street, to
foil anyone who'd intrude upon our privacy. Soon I must
pack up and return to the front -- seven days to get out
the next issue, four days to quash the felony
"possession of dangerous drugs" charge. In 1971 life
will not be dull.

A few minutes before the magical hour last night we
perched on a high curb near the corner of Broadway and
Columbus to watch the annual pandemonium erupt. Crowds
were surging and churning, horns were blaring, confetti
was swirling, cops on horseback were definitely not
horsing around. There were maniacal grins, hand-passed
joints and bottles, indiscriminate V-E Day-type kisses
(including several between Val and me but strictly the
discriminate kind), gooses and shrieks and quiet
promises too -- all as a red rocket rose and burst above
the neon midnight and the new year lurched on in.

Afloat in mellow funk, homeward we drifted, to
inaugurate another annum of balling, or so I hope. In
the anus, eventually, at her insistence, that the act
this time might be aptly special (by her lights far more
than mine, but of course I like it that way too, at
least every now and then -- but mostly because she does
-- and even though it's physically painful for her and
must also remind her of the bad old days with hubby Jim,
so just why is it so special for her anyway?).

At Mike's earlier in the evening the folks holding
down the next table chuckled to see us madly scribbling

side by side more or less in unison. I thought of a
comment in a Graham Greene novel -- how a certain couple
had become so alike they no longer could be
distinguished from each other, by sex or any other
characteristic. But with us any such perception would
be preposterous.

Passing by the recessed doorway of North Beach
Leathers on the way back from Mike's to the L.C. I said
a silent last goodbye to the ghost of Briana Tsu. May
the lady's memories of 1970 and the love that never was
to be prove as indelible for her as I'm sure mine will
for me.

And where will we all be a year from now (when I'll
be entering the year of my thirtieth birthday)?

In this new year why not growth, health, inner
peace, outer peace, productivity, good times for all.
Why not a love that actually works. Maybe even one that
lasts, or rather, to be strictly accurate, one that
either begins or advances a bit further in the intricate
long-term process of lasting.

If resolving is too much, at least one can hope.
And if all this be just unforgivably corny, what better
day to get it out of one's system.

So here be my 1971 why-nots.

                    *   *

Back in Garnett, where I find a note from Briana.
"It's really finished," she writes. "The door is closed
forever." This note's resting atop V.22 of my journal
which she's placed on my bed. (When I left for the city
last night this volume and several others were stashed
on the highest shelf in the closet, about seven feet up,
out of sight from below, safe and secure -- or so I
thought.) V.22, as it happens, is the one that covers
the day we met and the following four or five weeks
before she left for Amsterdam.

She's indignant about what I wrote in V.22, which
of course I never intended for her eyes. "I feel
fortunate," she says, "in finding out the truth before
it was too late." "The truth"? I wonder just what
she's talking about here. Could it be the truth (no

200

quotes) that I had some unflattering things to say about
her after learning she'd misled me (and perhaps herself
too) and hadn't booted Terry out of her life after all?
That, again contrary to what she'd told me, he'd be
going along on her European trip previously billed as
"the trip to get over Terry"? That I'd twisted myself
into some truly torturous knots trying, and abjectly
failing, to get her to change those travel plans once
I'd finally learned, to my shock, they included Terry?

Another truth is that it's not at all surprising
she snooped on me. This is the woman who first learned
about Terry's infidelities by clandestinely reading his
single-use carbon typewriter ribbon! -- And ironically
enough, if she hadn't done that, and hadn't immediately
told Terry she was through with him forever (which we
all know now she emphatically was not), I'd never have
had a chance to meet her.

But never mind the ironies and the Monday-morning
quarterbacking. What matters is this: she states
unequivocally I'm to exclude her from my life
permanently. "I do not exist for you -- don't ever try
to see me -- it would be unbearable -- I am too ashamed
to have actually succumbed to your 'game playing and
false openness.'"

I have absolutely no idea what those last five
words are referring to, but I do know this: she'll get
her wish.

And I remind myself: best not to complain too much
about this kiss-off from Briana. After all, didn't I
deliver pretty much the same message to her -- we're
through forever -- maybe an hour or two before she
composed hers to me? And wasn't she writing hers in at
least a little pain -- or anyway I sure hope so -- and
thus wasn't her reading of my words from months earlier
a bit distorted, say, and thus isn't the rank hypocrisy
and inaccuracy of her remarks forgivable?

True, yes, all of this. But none of it means her
note fails to stab me in the heart.

And regardless of the note's effect on me, nothing
changes the underlying fundamental fact. Which is:

she's the one who refused to let things between us go
any further. She's the one who refused, despite what
she'd said earlier, to break off with Terry and get
serious with me. This was true late last summer before
they left for Europe, true again in late November after
her return from Europe, true once more in December after
his return from Europe, and especially and decisively
true during our time together the past two days. She
even confirmed it to my face yesterday afternoon -- when
she was sitting right where I'm sitting now -- shortly
before she went off to be with him last night.

    That's what hurts most. She prefers to be with
him. So how could it not be over?

Saturday 2
    Bright and cold out there. Al raps on the door
asking for a dozen blank ad contracts "just in case."
He and Claire will soon be heading out to assess the
impact of the drug bust on the Garnett business
community. The feedback they get should give a pretty
good idea of whether the Merino Mercury can survive the
month of January.
    Meanwhile Val's on her way up here with Danny.
This time, unlike during her previous visits, she'll
really help with the paper -- she promises. It's
probably fortunate I'll have to be away from the office
much of the day, because after what's gone down with
Briana I'm not ready to respond as I should (and would
like to) with Val or anyone else.
    I never mentioned the cornucopia of gifts Briana
brought me. A battered bowling pin, a dozen boxes of
Jello (Barb told her I love Jello), a box of Ghirardelli
chocolate, a kaleidoscope (just like one I gave Val last
summer), a small piece of metal sculpture, three
superballs painted as pool balls (their numbers totaling
my age), and eleven marbles hand-painted to spell out "I
love Glen!!" Surprisingly to me, when she left last
night she didn't take the gifts with her -- but she did
take back the woodblock print which I'd brought in from

202

her car because I liked it so much, and when I told her
this she said I could have it. (It's not as if she
doesn't have other copies of it -- in fact as many as
she wants. It's a print! She made it! She has the
original woodblock in her studio!)

I'm now about to toss her gifts in the trash.
Briana, I'd just like to say this to you: it was great
while it lasted (when was that?) but for sure it's stone
cold dead now.

*

A letter to the editor from my own father. His
comments about our first issue (I mailed home a copy)
are by far the nastiest we've received from anyone.

> I suspect...you may be skirting the
> edges of libel in your 'Up the Organization'
> approach. However, I may be unusually
> sensitive to innuendo and subliminal malice.

He calls my editorial "skilled muckraking" and suspects
the people of Garnett will find it "offensive, if not
insulting," and compares the "hubris" and "arrogance" of
my "We go down, the Tesuque Valley goes down too" with
that of Louis XIV ("Apres moi, le deluge"). To which I
say: So it's not America's drive to dominate the world
that's hubristic and arrogant, it's our tiny outcry
against it? (This is the same man, I remind myself, who
outrageously called brother Jeff a "parasite.") ---

*   *

And now a wrangle with Valerie. With exquisite
timing she wants to know the "real truth" about my
current relations with Briana. Yet when I tell her the
real truth -- that it's all over with Briana -- she
refuses to believe me (sort of reminds me of Russ Danner
inquiring about the drug bust). "Knowing you," she
says, "you'll just wait a while and you'll go right back
to her and make a fool of yourself again."

Well, Val, if you know me so well and you think I'm
so bad, why do you want to continue with me? And since
we're seeing each other on the basis of "no commitments
on either side" -- and that's how it's been the entire
time I've known you and for that matter known Briana --

203

and you've always said you accept this condition
completely and even gratefully -- how is it you suddenly
think you have the right to grill me so relentlessly?

In any event, Norman Mailer's maxim about
depression applies once again. How does it go? Seems
very important to remember. (But here comes Danny --
Val chases after him. "Is he bothering you?" And off
they march. I'm left to keep wrestling with my private
thoughts. And one of these, I have to say, concerns
whether I'm disgusted enough at this point to start
telling Val some "real truth" kind of things she won't
want to hear and which will hurt her.)

Depression is the result of failing to admit
defeat? Something like that. Well, I admit it: I've
lost the battle with Briana for good. And I'm probably
about to lose the battle with Valerie as well.

I also admit I'm still depressed after making both
of these admissions.

Possibly my emotional state stems as well from the
cumulative effect of the many other battles I've lost in
much the same way with other women I've cared about a
great deal: with Lisa, with Jang, with Ciara, just to
mention the most important. But even so I still want to
believe that one of these days I'll manage to jump the
gap with someone. And yes, I admit it: I still have at
least a faint hope -- very faint -- this someone will be
Valerie. If, that is, she can bear with me in my
current fractured and confused and wounded condition a
while longer.

She knows, of course, I'm not always as open with
her as she might prefer. She doesn't say my openness is
"false," as Briana does in her note; instead she says I
have a "phobia" about it (and supposedly to show me she
has no such phobia herself, she told me she dreamed last
night I was "cavorting with Briana"). And I say both of
these women are way off base: in fact I'm a big believer
in openness, and I mean the real kind not the false
kind. That's right! But I'm also a big believer in
privacy. To me the crunch comes in how one weighs and
balances these two beliefs. And while we're at it,

let's also throw truth-telling and compassion into the mix. And how about some kindness as well? How about a little tenderness?

To some extent the provisional and ever-recalibrating balance I've established for myself on these various conflicting values may (or may not) help prevent Val from developing the degree of confidence or trust in me that I'd like her to have. Then too, her own deeply suspicious nature, stemming from the horrible battles between her parents when she was growing up and also from the many "betrayals" Jim laid on her over three years of failed marriage and in the five months since then as well -- all this, I say, makes it harder yet -- a whole lot harder -- for me to be as candid with her as I truly would like to be. And of course so does the fact that in the past when I've been open with her in the way she wanted about things it turned out she didn't want to hear, she's reacted in nasty and vindictive and hypocritical and in a couple of cases shockingly double-cross-like ways.

And speaking of her marriage, isn't she the one who told me it taught her that honesty isn't always the best policy in a loving relaionship, in fact on occasion it can be the worst? She's said that to me two, three, many times! So...is there perhaps something I'm not understanding about the difference between openness and candor and honesty as she sees them?

Someday, Val, if we keep fighting ---

Sunday 3

We've kept fighting all right. It's just that at this point the spirit to defend myself has gone out of me. It appears Valoshka of the flashing eyes has the goods on me, for whatever they may be worth. And, although she may not see it this way, I'd say my attempts to explain what happened with Briana have now become pretty much irrelevant to our well-being and could easily turn out to be counterproductive and destructive. And so I think it's better for her, Val, to go ahead and think whatever she wants about all that.

In her view I'm the victim of, yes, a kind of "openness phobia." That's what she stated again today. And I wouldn't want to say she's entirely wrong about this; it's just that I'd like her to rephrase the charge along lines more like these: I'm a victim of my own excessive reluctance to say hurtful things. She, very much to the contrary, tells me I'm "incapable" -- strong word! -- of making myself "truly vulnerable and available" in a loving relationship. What's more I'm "promiscuous" and "a voluptuary."

I don't like it at all when the tables are turned like this: Valoshka the righteous one on the attack, Glennario the squirming denier. And then she lets slip -- as she's done more than a few times before -- that many men are chasing after her these days. Right now as I write these words they're probably howling outside her door back in the city like a pack of dogs in musth. And I don't like hearing about this either. But I have absolutely no right to complain and so I won't. (Can dogs be in musth? Is that maybe only elephants? No matter, to my mind it still works as a kind of metaphor. Applies quite well to me too, no question.)

All morning I've been ferrying Danny around while his mother writes furiously in her "diary intime'. " Bright, clear, gusty day. When we got up at eight we found the puddles outside the door iced over. The awnings above the outdoor tables here at McDonald's (I'm picking up our lunch) groan horribly in the wind: sound like very large nails being levered from a very thick, warped plank.

*

-- Well, I've decided. To set Val free. It's impossible for me to give her what she wants at this point, and her harangues make it clear she's built up so much resentment it's impossible for us to go on as before. I'll concede this is running away from our problems in a sense -- hers and mine, yes, such as they are, whatever they may really be -- but I can see no other course to take. I have to work things out for

myself in my own way and at my own pace. And I believe
it's become unfair to her that she should continue to
suffer from what I need to do regarding my own mistakes
and confusions and yearnings for various kinds of
remakes and upgrades in my life. And it's now become
inconceivable to me that we'd be able to work out these
sorts of things together.

She's right, or at least not totally wrong: I still
have what she calls a "Don Juan streak" (a phrase I
suspect she got straight from Barbara). That is, I
still follow my balls at times even while insisting my
heart is true (the latter part of which statement I'm
not sure Don Juan ever bothered with, but I could be
wrong). Val's intuitive awareness of this "truth" about
me and her consequent resentment, magnified by her own
abundant hang-ups, paralyze her around me but not around
others -- or so she tells me. She's young, lovely,
spectacularly sexy and just on the brink of truly
discovering herself. She should be free to do so.

*   *

An unexpected turn: in reading a letter Val left on
my pillow but later said I wasn't supposed to have read
until after she'd left, I learned she did indeed already
know much more than I used to think she did about what
happened between me and Briana. In a word: like any
good lawyer's daughter, this morning she was only asking
me questions to which she already knew the answers, if
not in all cases at least in a good many.

(Did she also, like Briana, read my journal? When
I asked her this very question she deftly dodged it --
refused to answer. So I'd say it's quite possible she
did, yes. Or...did she perhaps, as I was already
suspecting, talk with my notoriously indiscreet sister
about me and Briana before Barb left town for Belgium?)

-- As a consequence of all this I confirmed to Val
most of the more embarrassing Briana facts she asked me
about. And afterwards, I grudgingly admit, I felt much
better. (We talked about other things as well,
including the shaky state of my relations with Barb.)
And: I promptly reversed what I'd said to her earlier

about our calling it quits. She in turn backed off from
this morning's abrupt and very harshly stated demand
about my making "an immediate commitment or else we're
finished." We even agreed that, while we'll keep seeing
each other on weekends, as we've been doing ever since I
came up here, we'll both remain "free" during the rest
of the week to try to work things out for ourselves in
our separate ways and in our separate cities.

She also conceded she has "at least as many hang-
ups and confusions to worry about as you do -- probably
more." And she said she feels "no resentment" about my
"affair" with Briana -- to add to, that is, the
resentment (or she'd probably call it "ressentiment")
she already feels toward me and for that matter toward
the whole world starting from way back, like as the
nurse was scrubbing off her afterbirth -- or as she,
Val, was still marinating in the womb as she likes to
say -- but I suspect she told me this mostly from fear
we'd be quits for good if she told me otherwise.

I still have strong doubts about whether we'll be
able to overcome all the obstacles we face. Nonetheless
it appears we've kept alive -- maybe even slightly
enhanced -- the possibility of developing a truly tight
relationship. As she points out, in only one sense am I
not "jaded," and that's in wanting to have just such a
relationship. By which we both mean one that's fully
(to the extent "fully" is possible) open, vulnerable,
caring, supportive, trusting, committed, impassioned.
And I'll just say: I've never had one like that! I've
been fortunate enough to have experienced some outasight
balling and plenty of intense emotionality over the
years, but true tightness at a deep level has been rare
for me if not nonexistent, and therefore so have those
other qualities defining it, except maybe in widely
scattered and sporadic instances.

Supposing Val and I can provide each other with the
sexual and emotional elements of a tolerably happy day-
to-day life together -- which is no foregone conclusion
-- we just might make it after all. In any case it's
much more clear now what our situation is. I said

point-blank I don't know whether I "really" love her and don't think I'm ready to assure her of fidelity under current circumstances; I just hope I can do so someday when we've been able to work out more of our personal conflicts -- and of course I hope she'll want to do the same with me. She said she still wants to go forward with the relationship under these conditions.

If we stay together now it will be because we both truly want to and for no other reason.

2

Monday 4

Office of the Merino Mercury, ten at night, six of us still plugging away. Homemade oatmeal-raisin cookies -- still warm from the oven! -- and a big jug of apple cider. Sisters Becky and Claire just finished assembling a cheapo five-shelf particleboard bookcase. "Does it mean anything," Al calls out to Claire and me, "that the two of you and Angela Davis are going in for your arraignments on the same day?" Tomorrow, ten a.m., Municipal Court for Claire and me -- and neither of us has any idea what to expect. We don't even have a lawyer.

Becky, Judy, Sherry, and I have been learning how to use the IBM Composer.

Grover Basse calls -- he's the long-white-haired high-school teacher who looks like a skinnier Lee Marvin -- to let us know Schuyler Tomey is agreeable to doing a column for us but doesn't want to hassle deadlines. "Now there's a man," Al observes, "with a good feel for how the newspaper business works." He's just sliced his thumb with my Swiss Army knife, Al has, spilling blood onto the mock-up of a subscription postcard he's been working on all evening. Everyone agrees this gory new version of the card will grab a lot more attention.

When Sherry opens the door to leave, cold air instantly permeates the room. There's no storm door, no foyer or wind barrier -- no bad-weather protection of any kind.

I call Valerie a day ahead of schedule, "just because the urge hit me." She still feels no new resentment, she says -- woke up this morning "in love" and "feeling very close." I can't yet say I love her in the way she wants (or the way I want for that matter), but I too feel an unprecedented closeness between us.

Last night I decided I couldn't let the charges in Briana's note stand unanswered. I wrote her, by hand, a seven-page "final letter." Then I rewrote it, also by hand -- nine pages in this version -- trying to excise all traces of anger and bitterness and to adopt a more philosophical and less maudlin tone.

"Hey, any cookies left over there?" (That was me. With no conscious intent I know of -- and knowing of it would itself make it conscious, correct -- the words popped out of my mouth like tarts from a toaster.)

Tuesday 5

I loved it when we did it but now the doubts and self-recriminations are stalking about. Tumbled into bed with Claire tonight. Two days after vowing to be more open with Valerie about such things, two hours after talking with her on the phone. (But then she did rave to me about Tibalt, "the mystery man," the same eccentric German-accented dude who used to fascinate Ciara and Barbara: she, Val, had coffee with him tonight, she told me -- and she also received her acceptance from S.F. State. She'll be starting classes there next month. "I'm over my neurosis," she announced.)

And so the question arises: Do I tell Val about tonight with Claire? Even though this liaison did not occur during a weekend and thus does not fall under the terms of the agreement with Val? And I acknowledge: either I should tell her, or I should break off with her for good, or I should renounce further hanky-panky with Claire. But I'm still not totally sure any of those things will be happening. But then again tonight was

not a weekend for Val just as it was not one for me or
anyone else, and yet she still told me about her tete-a-
tete with Tibalt. But...did she tell me "everything"
about it? Of course she didn't; it's not even possible.
And I can't deny having a suspicion or two about the
content of what she did -- and what she didn't -- tell
me. She's admitted she's outright lied to me about her
relations with men several times before, as she also did
quite often to her husband. And yet none of this stops
her from demanding that I be "completely open" with her.
And just for the record, the truth regarding Val is the
same as it is regarding Briana: so far as I know I've
never lied to either one. And Val says she's never had
any reason to think otherwise. "I know your word is
good. I really believe that."
     -- Of course Claire's superlative in bed, just as
expected. Passionate and strong, sensual and lithe.
She came twice, and this despite the fact that I was a
bundle of nerves.
     Seven of us working in the office gradually
dwindled to two by one a.m. (we installed the new layout
table, handmade and nine feet long). My mind was
preoccupied most of the evening with stuff I didn't even
want to be thinking about -- mainly involving Briana and
Valerie and Claire -- and I accomplished little.
Squandered energy.
     In a way Claire and I couldn't help being close
tonight: we went to court together today. More like a
classroom in a suburban school, the judge an emaciated
Gothic American whose name seemed just right: Melvin
Middleton. Could it be he's a man of the U.S. version
of the Confucian Middle Way? But after keeping us
waiting two hours beyond the scheduled time he continued
our case until next Tuesday and without divulging any
further clues about where he stands or where we stand.
     If the truth be known, I didn't even particularly
want to get it on with Claire. Rather I needed to. I
don't know why. "Needed" in the Rolling Stones sense of
"You get what you need." And then append to that the
G. Sandefjord sense of you get what you need "if you

211

can, and if you're very lucky." Or possibly it had
something to do with a delayed reaction against Val's
pressure tactics or my own outright defiance of her
hypocritical self-righteous questions and accusations.
And even more possibly it was related to the fact that
she, Claire, wept in my arms three separate times (while
we were at the courthouse) and during the last time
whispered in my ear, "I really feel protected when you
hold me."

   And a note in the mail from Briana: "Thanks for the
parting gift: crabs." I doubt she got them from me (Val
hasn't gotten them), but if she did, it was a case of
her very own crabs coming home to pinch her, as it were
-- or literally rather -- since she's the one who gave
them to me in the first place last August. But of
course she doesn't mention that. Maybe by now she's
suppressed all memory of those anguished days. And to
me that's exactly what her bizarre remarks about my
journal from back then would indicate. In any case:
what a sordid ending. (Or we could both blame Terry,
from whom she originally got those same crabs, again if
what she told me in August was true. And: did he not
return this past week from a month of backpacking in
Europe? Could the crab lightning have struck Briana
twice from the same roving cloud? -- But really now,
why bother with this nonsense? Let's just drop the
topic of the goddamn crabs and the topic of Briana and
Terry right along with it, or them, the crabs.)

   -- Wrote a long glowing review of "The Greening of
America." Certainly the book's flawed in numerous ways
but it still offers the best analysis I've come across
so far (along with Theodore Roszak's "The Making of a
Counter Culture") of what's happening among young people
in this country and what will have to happen to the
country as a whole if it's not to self-destruct before
much longer and raze the rest of the world with it --
say by next Tuesday if not sooner.

   And Dad, I hope you won't take this new evidence of
editorial hubris and arrogance too seriously if you
happen to run into it somewhere. (I've bought him his

very own subscription to the Merc -- at the one-third
staff discount -- and I might well steal a line or two
of my own stuff here for a column or editorial.)

Wednesday 6
        It's 3:53 a.m. Heater creaking. Desolate room.
For four days now I haven't even had a sheet on the bed.
        Al and I just closed up shop. He scraped the frost
from the windshield of his Impala and bucked off with a
boxful of copy ready to be set in the morning. He'll
drop it off at the printer on his way to work.
        Ever since I staggered out of bed today at eight
a.m. it's been one crisis after another as the article
deadline for this week's issue approached. Tonight the
office was abustle and abulge with volunteers, most of
them admirably well-intentioned and enthusiastic but
unfortunately incapable of doing much that was truly
useful in a nitty-gritty newspapering sense. Even so it
was good having lots of folks around and of course that
was plenty helpful all by itself in its own way.
Delightful in fact (though not always).
        Claire continues to be affectionate; when alone we
touch hands or rub legs, once in a while exchange a
quick kiss or two. Already I can see my fling with her
has injected new poison into my relationship with
Valerie. I called her at one a.m. and fell into a
stupid despondency when she told me she'd had another
long talk with Tibalt.
        "I'm just curious," she says. "He appreciates
what's valuable in me."
        Is she making this up or exaggerating it to get me
jealous? Maybe. But it sounds to me more like she's
genuinely fascinated. I could swear I recognize the
symptoms. And I know where things are likely to end up,
if they haven't already, if she's truly into him.
But...I don't trust my intuitions about her. In fact,
I'm well aware my current suspicions about her stem at
least in part from my own liaison with Claire. But I'll
grant they might also arise from my apparent failure to

appreciate, as she so unsubtly implied, what's valuable
about her -- which isn't to say I haven't tried.

Talking with Val I felt very alone. At times I
could scarcely understand what she was saying. After a
while it was as if we were vying to out-zombie each
other. Bad, bad signs, whatever their cause.

Meanwhile the long countdown has begun again, the
second round. Probably we'll get no sleep at all
tomorrow night, which is actually tonight since it's now
after four a.m. on Thursday. And the same goes for
Friday night. First thing in the morning today I have
to pound out a music column under yet another pseudonym.
Before then I could definitely use an epiphany or two.
(As Al pointed out, today -- the day we're still early
in -- is Epiphany.)

Sunday 10 (X:7-9)

Oops, it's Sunday already, I'm briefly back in the
city again, and Chopper has delivered herself of nine
pups. Where in the world did they all come from? Or
rather: how is it possible she squeezed them all in
there? As Rob observed, we now have enough to start a
canine baseball team complete with coach. Or how about
a new Supreme Court with a spare Chief Justice? Or a
full set of canine muses complete with Mnemosyne?

Meanwhile up in Garnett we whelped another issue of
the Mercury. The delivery pains for this one were even
worse than those for the inaugural edition. For
starters, this time we had no unusually helpful printer
like the one in Berkeley to assist us with paste-up. By
three Friday morning all the volunteer help had departed
from Klug's, leaving Al and me to wrestle pretty much
the whole paper into its final shape. Sixteen pages,
and at four a.m. only seven were even close to being
ready. Those final hours were incredibly tense. And
then it was nine a.m. and I was in the shotgun seat
penciling in edits on the last straggler, page thirteen,
as Tom Yost barreled the L.C. toward Union City.

The result of all this labor, crawling with typos

and blunders of every imaginable sort, in my proud opinion "still manages to live."

My main contributions (besides editorial rewrites of just about everything): the long rave review of "Greening" and a short and hasty but equally rave review of the new John Lennon album.

Valerie came up with me Friday (we balled as the production crew stapled and rolled in the other room, then again later deep under the covers and almost motionlessly as Russ Danner snored a few feet away on Al's cot). She returned to the city with me last night. Along the way she told me she likes to "play the heroine of a sad story," of her current infatuation with Dadaism, of the deep history of her "natural solemnity." My feelings are still numbed. So much does this newspaper business take out of me that when we go into countdown-to-deadline mode I don't even have enough left to scribble a note in these pages.

Val wrote:

> Glenn is one of those rare people whose
> well-curved motions stretch out like a
> constant yarn. He emanates a voluptuous
> feeling of bien-etre and a sleepy
> consciousness of joie de vivre. This
> gentleness rings into an infinite
> repercussion of sensuous waves reaching
> unknown depths.

Right on, Val! But...how about you start exploring those "unknown depths" a bit more enthusiastically?

3

Monday 11

To think that as recently as five months ago I would long achingly for hours every day to be munching away in this joint. Dragonburger. Where East meets West in a constant spattering of grease. In the shadow of the new Chinatown gate, on a day of intermittent downpours. The wet stony heart of a San Francisco winter.

In less than an hour Valerie will be arriving from
the old Emp mausoleum for lunch, and after that I'll
make the sixty-minute dash at sixty-five m.p.h. to
Garnett (though first, perhaps, a browse at City Lights
and then -- for sure -- a stroll down funky, funky
Broadway to its foot by the Embarcadero, because that's
where the L.C.'s parked).

"Everything Gohn Be Funky from Now On" -- that's
Valoshka's new slogan (courtesy of Lee Dorsey).

Last night at a Berkeley drive-in I was served with
a vivid reminder of what it is in me -- lacking in the
women I tend to wind up with -- that drives me to my own
mediocre Casanova imitations. When I become feisty,
irreverent, inspired, mad, Val wilts. I frighten her or
baffle her or just plain overwhelm her and she can offer
no foil. No teasing, no contest of wits, no provocation
or seduction or exchange of insults: she becomes a
melancholy marshmallow. ("Sheriff Bill" with his
preposterous red dildo was excellent, though.) All this
reminded me of the many bad scenes when we were shacking
up at Val's place last summer which eventually led me to
turn to Briana at least partly out of exasperation.

This time Val saw what I was getting at when I
complained. She vowed to break through her inhibitions.
When? Now! "Fuck my stupid pride!" she scrawled on the
L.C. windshield with her white eyeliner, symbolic to her
of the quest for purity (she then tossed it into the
gutter). "Work it, Wild Thing!" I cried, impressed by
this wholly unexpected display of dramatic flair.
("Wild Thing" is what Jim used to call her, as she knew
I knew, so she protested my use of the term; but she
seemed pleased anyway. That smoldering little slant-
lipped smile of hers, head tilted, one eyebrow slightly
raised: she does know how to zing you with it.)

Then at home last night and again this morning she
decided she wanted to practice balling better. At my
suggestion she's reversing my earlier recommendation
that she try to relax more and instead she's trying to
tense up a little. How's that for mixed signals? And

216

yet it worked, at least at times. But I dislike being
in a position where I'm expected to deliver coaching
tips on how to ball. Far better to be out there on the
court mindlessly and joyously playing the game.

Speaking of self-discipline and Casanova
imitations, yesterday I was "unfaithful" to Valerie for
the second time in a week -- with the Terpsi-K. She
called, I yielded to her importuning, visited her in her
new room, where she's working mostly on calligraphy and
Korean inkbrush painting. A houseful of freaks again,
but this time a higher caliber of freak and a better
house too, structurally speaking. I'm always happy to
see her, astounded by her energy and brightness. She
stirs me in heart, guts, balls in ways no one else can.
Yes, I think -- amazed all over again each time -- this
is a woman I love and will never stop loving.

But at the same time a strong countercurrent is
always present. I know returning to her on a permanent
or even provisional basis is out of the question. It's
her own spic-and-span image of me she loves, not the
real person -- not the one who's been (and technically
still is) married to someone else, who fucks around,
who's irresistibly drawn to certain kinds of craziness
and melodrama, who can be reckless and unscrupulous in
the fashion of a Dostoevsky antihero (Raskolnikov, say).
Her image of me resembles my own self-image from early
high-school days or for that matter, worse yet, my
mother's image of me from that time. Jang is simply too
balanced, too wise, too high-minded, too well-behaved,
too eviscerated (in some elusive sense) -- too civilized
and cultured -- too good and too noble and too pure for
me. Still, the attraction is there and as always she
balls like a dream. Such a fine, delicate, lovely face.
Almost makes me wish I didn't like turmoil so much.

Tuesday 12
Office of the Merc -- where things are looking up.
In the mail today came 119 return-postage-paid cards
ordering subscriptions. Yesterday I predicted we'd get

no more than 150 returns total; Al guessed 500. Glad,
glad, glad to be wrong (if I turn out to be).

John Lennon's a genius. I'm finally convinced of
it. First his new album, then the interview I read last
night in Rolling Stone. "I don't want to be a swinger,"
he says. And neither do I -- but nonetheless in a
certain way I continue to be. Years ago I read
somewhere that every man has his price, his weakness.
For some it's power, for others money, for others fame
-- and for still others, sex. Romance. Love.
Evidently these last-named are mine, or at least they
have been for the past year. Or maybe I should bite the
bullet and acknowledge it's been more like the past ten
years, or twelve. Yes, and I'd say it's still true now:
it's a rare attractive woman I don't yearn to get it on
with. Simple fact is it's in the genes. (What happens
between the prompting of the genes and how one actually
behaves is of course something else again.)

Today, for example. It began with Claire creeping
into my room at eight-thirty a.m. (after seeing Kurt off
and delivering her kid to the special school he goes to)
and then beneath my covers for an hour of fine slow get-
down with eventual optimal get-off (then she skipped
away, lithely dodging puddles on a dazzlingly bright
morning as I peeked out at her from beneath the uplifted
lower corner of the window shade). Later I drove Sherry
downtown and found myself making jocular advances which
culminated in a brief kiss (though mainly just to get
her off my case). And then I gave a lift home to Holly
McGann, a foxy blond high-school student who's
volunteering with the paper (and who lives in a
spectacular house in the hills above Spring Valley), and
I had to restrain myself from going after her, although,
again, it wasn't the genes that reminded me about
certain apropos social taboos; it was the post-gene
learnings that did that.

So much for my New Year's non-resolutions -- or
whatever it was I called them. (New Year's why-nots --
just checked.)

(Lennon: "Like I said in the song, I've been

through it all, and nothing works better than to have
somebody you love hold you.")

Wednesday 13
     During the off week the office gradually empties
every day around five-thirty or six p.m. and I'm left
alone to gather my fractured thoughts. Usually by this
time I've had enough of playing the editor's role. I
enjoy the respect and deference accorded to such a high
honcho as myself -- to a degree I do -- but I'm less
fond of the care and feeding I must lavish upon everyone
since they're all volunteers with, to repeat, no
experience in journalism. This is a matter I ought to
explore in depth. If I don't, though, it's because of
the job itself and the enormous time demands it makes.
I'm unable to focus on any single question for more than
a few minutes at most, and usually it's just seconds.
There's always another phone ringing, another knock on
the door, another urgent inquiry about something or
other, and often all of these at once along with a whole
lot of other stuff and then some more of same and more
and more. The pace can leave my eyeballs pinwheeling.
     One thing for sure: my lust for exploration of the
self -- my own self in particular in recent times -- has
been diverted into other kinds of pursuits. No doubt
this experience in Garnett is affecting me strongly, but
right now I can't say much about just how. I have no
choice but to leave probing into that for later.
Meaning of course it may never happen. The preemptions,
the preemptions: they have a way of never stopping.
     Today's news:
     ** Another 35 subscription cards arrived. At this
rate of decline we should get 10 more cards tomorrow, 3
Friday, and 1 Saturday, for a total of 168. So my
prediction of 150 wasn't so bad after all. Better than
Al's by a ratio of about 15 to 1, I do believe. (But
we're not being competitive here, no we're not.)
     ** One of today's cards was scrawled with four-
letter words and the opinion that we should go to

219

Russia, America doesn't want us -- the first "letter to
the editor" that's out-nastied Dad's. (I'm hoping to
wring a column out of all these letters, Dad's included.
The column slot itself I'm dubbing "Mercky Notions.")

    ** The police department told us we don't need to
register our press cards with them. No doubt this is
because they'll ignore them anyway.

    ** Russ Danner phoned to say he wants "a word"
with Al and me. Most likely he'll be objecting to the
word "screw" appearing in a film review and also our
decision to run a Merimont inmate's feisty and lovesick
poem about Angela Davis. At the meeting last night,
twenty-five of us at Al's house, a dispute arose over
censorship. I favor a maximum of free expression but
agree a line must be drawn somewhere. Russ and a few
others worry frantically about offending people in the
paper's infancy and think the line should be drawn
exactly where the Daily Ghastly draws its own line. Al
and I agree the respect accorded to Russ's opinions
should be proportionate to the amount of time he puts in
on the paper, which is to say, not much. In the first
weeks we fell over backwards, sideways, every which way
trying to satisfy Russ's incessant objections, but now
we pretty much ignore them.

    ** In court today Claire and I waived our rights
concerning arraignment, and the date for a preliminary
hearing was set: January 22. I tried to make my voice
ring out loud and clear in the courtroom but I'm afraid
it came out mumbly and wimpish. And I completely
blanked out -- probably a good thing -- on several
choice remarks I'd cooked up for the judge while we were
sitting there waiting.

    ** Calls to Nina and Marcelle Aguilar, Cassandra
McKenna, Ray Lewis, and several others about stories
they're supposed to be working on. Maybe they'll get
them done and maybe they won't. If they do, or better
to say if any one or more of them does, that's when a
serious and no doubt protracted copyediting session
cranks up (mine).

    ** Evan and I worked on new designs for the front

and editorial pages.

 ** I read pieces by Tom Y., Greg Knox, and others.

 ** Twice Greg Knox came by and I labored mightily to decipher his slow, strange way of speaking with its elaborately tangled syntax. He walks with a cane and talks with a kind of hitch too -- I don't know exactly why on either score -- yet he always has interesting things to say if you can just keep the subject of his sentences in mind long enough while waiting for the verb to appear (sort of like waiting for the point to show up in this sentence right here). Unfortunately if he keeps dropping around as often as he has lately I'll have to stop trying to listen to him; the day just doesn't have enough hours.

 ** The sister of Alisha Stewart, the black girl murdered in Tesuque last month, called to express her thanks for our story, which broke the outrageous silence about the case in the local media.

 ** A letter to the editor complained about our hospital story; Al was so concerned about it he had me read the whole thing to him over the phone -- and then after a puzzled pause he asked me to read it to him a second time.

 ** Blueberry muffins and magnificent tomatoes at Al's for dinner.

 Still sprawled on my stomach. Strange green rug. It could almost be chopped up into little squares for use as sandpaper. In less than a month I think I've become about a quarter inch shorter just from walking on it barefoot.

 I detect no change in my feelings for Valerie. I still take her for granted. And Briana, well, Briana's slipping away and I know I can't do a damn thing about it, nor will I try to do a damn thing or any other kind of thing. About it, yes, insert that in there somewhere. (Once an editor, always an editor. -- Or at least in my case an editor for two or three more months here in Garnett. Because that's the deal with Al and I'm determined -- especially in light of his remark about "persistence" -- to uphold my end of it. -- which

must mean he's savvy at incentivizing, and I'd say
that's definitely true. And thank god he is.)

Thursday 14
     Office again. The dreaded despair has settled in.
It's the worst yet. Everything annoys me -- especially
Valerie. She arrived this morning wearing a sexy new
lavender velveteen minidress of her own creation, a
"free woman" at last after her final day at Emp. It's
taken her all afternoon to lay down a few routine border
tapes on two layout pages. She's such a perfectionist!
Her tone is so condescending and ugly sometimes! (None
of this is fair to her, of course.) She mumbles again
and again, trailing off into clouds of French-accented
abstractions at least as hard to decipher as anything
Greg Knox says. "I can't understand what you're
saying!" I cry -- again and again. So of course she
keeps it up, even intentionally exaggerates it, in a
campaign to drive me still further around the bend.
Then she accuses me of being hypercritical when I
complain that her unending interruptions are preventing
me from doing my job. "If you didn't spend so much time
trying to reform me," she retorts, "you'd have plenty of
time for your job."
     In the L.C. as we drove to Sheridan with copy to be
typeset she read aloud, at my request, a passage from
Henry Miller about his first fuck ever, with the woman
"with the hand-woven cunt." Val dug it, or so she said,
but she also said she doesn't want to be seen as a
"slut," and in her view only sluts would show open
interest in such things, even in private. This is the
same person who wants me to be more open with her!
Today I find her exasperating as hell.
     Maybe it's because of the scene with Claire last
night. She "put me to bed." Somehow, moaning "let me
have it" over and over, she squeezed a second come out
of me just minutes after the first. She actually is
part Indian, I learned -- as anyone might guess from her
looks -- and studied dance for fifteen years. So that's

where her Maria Tallchief-like grace comes from. Or
maybe it's the reverse: her grace is why she did all
that studying and training. Or most likely -- conk conk
conk upside the head -- it's both at once.

Perry Bracken brought in a lovely smoky-eyed black
high-school student this afternoon, Kit Gilliam. Was
there a spark? With Marcelle Aguilar there definitely
was. "Glen's Groupies," as Claire unfailingly calls
them (not that I don't get a secret -- maybe not so
secret -- charge from it). It's my very own flock of
some fifteen mostly female high-school and junior-
college volunteers. At your beck and call, Mr. Editor!
The amusing -- boggling -- thing is it's literally part
of my job description to do whatever it takes to keep
them coming back -- to inspire them to give their all
for the Merc.

I yawn, jiggle my knee, roll my eyes, sigh, wander
about aimlessly. Is it Valerie? Is it Briana? Is it
that I'm already tiring of the paper? Is it unconscious
guilt? If so, over exactly what? I do know this: I've
got to eat better, get more exercise, develop
friendships not to mention loves -- or much better, one
big, all-embracing love -- but at least a love that's
not so damn ephemeral.

Friday 15
Fingers still gluey from pasting up the first
article of the next issue. A gray, drizzly day
completely without a sense of time to it. Lots of
balling with Val last night, lots of hassles with her
today -- or rather one long running hassle. Suddenly
she again thinks I'm "too secretive." My journal, it's
like "My Secret Life" to her. All these things I write
in here: why, she wants to know, don't I just say them
out loud and save myself the manual labor?

Well, in a nutshell, Val, it's because you'd never
stand for it, that's why. You've demonstrated this
numerous times in extremely persuasive fashion. And
even if you would stand for it, and even under the most

relaxed of circumstances (i.e., the opposite of what
we've got here in Garnett), my saying them out loud to
you would still be extremely difficult and extremely
foolish. My "secret" thoughts and feelings are ill-
formed, complex, contradictory, and often recede quickly
or reverse themselves as others appear. And the last
thing I want is to be constantly wrangling with you over
the ones you dislike or disagree with or disapprove of,
and of these it's guaranteed there would be plenty.

What's more, Val, many of those same thoughts, as
you ought to realize from keeping an "intime'" journal
yourself, are just knee-jerk reflexes or rebellions
against self which are actually the opposite of what I
"really" think. Further, many of the things I write
express my views at the moment of writing rather than at
the moment I'm writing about, or vice versa. You should
understand this, Val; you once made the very same point
to me about contradictions and puzzling reversals in
your poetry. "I'm very spontaneous," you said then. So
you know what, Val? I am too!

Further still, Val, the whole point of keeping a
journal like mine, and I assume yours too, is to
maintain a private space in which one can freely
explore, among other things, one's most troubling and
taboo thoughts and feelings, and do so without fear of
exposure or censure or ridicule or any other kind of
real-world consequences. And of course right now my
mind's too distracted by all the duties of my job to
focus for long on any particular personal issue, so
what's to disclose anyway?

Granted all the above, then, Val, it still remains
true I'm not as open with you as I should be or would
like to be. As I've said to you before, this is partly
because of the way you react to my openness on those
occasions when I do try to go beyond our current norm.
Simply put, they're nothing special to you. You don't
treat them with kindness, generosity, or gratitude. You
actively discourage acts of openness by responding to
their content with hostility and outright attacks (even
when I'm telling you what I've written about the very

matters you've said you want to hear about), either at
once or after a short but totally graceless grace
period.

What remains, I'm ready to concede, is my own fear
of revealing the unvarnished truth about myself. It's
one thing to say I want to do it, even long to do it,
but it's much harder to pull it off in practice. Quite
possibly, just as you say, Val, I'm "afraid of staining
[my] image." In any case it's absolutely true I don't
trust you unconditionally as you seem to think I should.
How could I when, for example, you snoop and pry into my
life behind my back and then refuse even to own up to
it? And then you use what you've learned -- or think
you've learned -- against me! Aren't you just as bad as
you say I am, or worse? Even much worse? Whole powers
of magnitude worse?

When we talked about all this right after New
Year's, Val, some hope still seemed to remain that we
could salvage the situation. A breakthrough to a new
and deeper trust still seemed possible. Now, I have to
say, that hope seems all but totally lost. I'd be glad
to assume full responsibility for the failure -- but
don't you think you ought to take on at least a tiny
portion of it? Don't you have anything at all to do
with the nature of what's going down between us?

In any event it was a fleeting "true closeness" we
had. For some reason we just can't sustain it. Now --
I don't deny it -- I'm back to being locked up in the
solitary of refusing to be "fully open" with you. And
you know what? I'd say you're stuck in pretty much the
same kind of place yourself with regard to me. And it
could even be that being stuck this way is part of the
human condition in general. Which doesn't mean we can't
keep on trying to do something about it. For example,
deploying other parts of the human condition against it,
for the purpose of unsticking us from what we're stuck
in. For example, loving better.

(I'll admit big chunks of the preceding half-dozen
paragraphs are cribbed more or less directly from my
letter to Briana. I worked on it so hard the phrases

are still engraved in my mind.)
*

Right now Val's curled up in a chair on the other side of the room fiercely scribbling away, just like me. The scratching of her pen is much louder than the scratching of my pen. We haven't exchanged a word in something like two hours. From a single glare she sent this way a while back I have the strong impression she's not very happy with me this afternoon.

Suddenly I dread tonight's return trip to the city.

Saturday 16

Valerie and I are stretched out on the dusty, musty, sandpapery office rug. Kayo Hallinan (he seems like an old friend; I've seen him many times around the city; he's a radical lawyer just as, who knows, I might have become myself) -- Kayo's on the radio dissecting the charges against Angela (I'll admit it, I almost wrote "Briana" there). Journals and notes and books and poems are spread on the floor in all directions.

The night is slipping by. Saturday night. Things are so dismally dull around here we're actually considering attending a dance for teens which Roy Dixon says will be getting underway any minute now at the Civic Center. Val, after all, is a teen herself. Alas, because I'm not -- not by a long shot -- we'd probably be turned away at the door. No doubt she'd find this righteously amusing after herself causing us to be turned away from any number of doors leading into various cesspits of adult nightlife. I can hear her now: "So you finally see how it feels? Eh? Eh?"

Last night when we rolled off the Embarcadero onto Broadway in San Francisco, plunging into all the lights and excitement and crowds, then creeping along in heavy traffic while eyeballing the fleshy sidewalk promenades on both sides of the street -- hundreds of simultaneous "Bougaloos Down Broadway" -- I yearned to slip away on my own so I could relax for a while and maybe check out a few particularly promising exemplars of those same

226

adult cesspits mentioned above. For most of the drive
coming in Val and I had been screaming at each other
over the roaring wind-friction of the boxy L.C. cabin,
until finally my voice gave out (but she managed to
scream on). I was totally fed up with her preachy
teenage-prodigy condescension. And prior to that I'd
been embroiled for four hours in a three-way policy
donnybrook with Al and the hopelessly antediluvian Russ
Danner.

And then suddenly at home on Funston nine bloated
pups and new drains in the sinks and a perfunctory
reconciliation resulting later in a fuck in Val's ultra-
sexy and ultra-firm and undeniably exquisitely teenagey
gymnast's ass just as she'd been whimpering for all
night. (When stony fury renders me uninterested I can
always be aroused in my sleep, she likes to point out,
thereby "proving" I really do love her and desire her at
deep unconscious levels and thus that the barriers I've
thrown up against her are not as strong as I supposedly
like to think.) But my enthusiasm is draining for the
Mercury and also for Val even though the new poems she
showed me today are powerful (and right now she's
writing about my "methods" of fighting; "silence as a
weapon" is one, she announces, to give me a kind of
preview, and another is "emotional confiscations"; she's
planning to put all this and more, probably much, much
more, into another of her infamous screeds -- which
often read, in case I haven't mentioned this before,
like the ravings of a dyspeptic French philosopher-
priest).

Valerie Mailloux Bando. One of a kind. The
"antipodiste," which in French, she tells me, literally
means something like one who exists upside-down. This
afternoon she was doing just that on the sidewalk
outside the office -- walking on her hands Elvira
Madigan style as she does so easily and well, waving to
people inside with her feet -- and then she wound up
flipping herself straight into a huge mud puddle. And
then, after cleaning up, she decided to show her
interest in the paper by writing what turned out to be

227

an extremely serious and solemn essay on the subject of
-- of all things -- humor. I tried to help her lighten
it up a bit for the sake of the Merc's less masochistic
readers but failed miserably, finally enraging her with
my gently offered (and well-intended) editorial
suggestions. From an outsider's standpoint this scene
itself might've been at least slightly humorous, but for
sure neither of us saw it that way at the time.

Her ever-changing moods, her searching and almost
shockingly serious mind, her bizarre combinations of
dependence and defiance, skepticism and irascibility,
sweet and sour, solemn and manic -- they all ought to
fascinate me, and maybe they do somewhere down deep, but
right now I just can't feel much interest up on the
surface -- not in any parsing of her abundant
abstractions, for instance -- but just and only in the
flow of life (with her, without her) and some of its
enlivening details. Psychological complexity like hers
no longer seems as endlessly intriguing as it once did,
or for that matter as complex. ("Haven't really learned
anything new from a novel in thirty years," sniffed Dad,
tossing aside "Catch-22" after sampling a few
paragraphs.) Or is it merely that the spark's gone from
life because at the moment I'm not in love? -- But then
am I really sure I'm not? What's my unconscious really
up to? And when will it decide the time has come to let
me know? Could it be trying to break through with a
crucial message at this very moment and I'm too busy
scratching away in these pages to hear it?

Sunday 17
I suppose the big news of the day has to be
Valerie's confession that she herself has again been
less than "fully open and honest" with me. This came in
two installments.
The first was no surprise: she did indeed snoop in
my journal. The irony is that it was the very same
volume Briana invaded (that's V.22) and she, Val, did
her own invading less than forty-eight hours after

Briana did hers, when she and Danny came up to Garnett
the day after New Year's. What's more: she found it in
the very same spot on the closet shelf where I'd
blithely returned it after Briana read it. (I probably
did that unconsciously under advisement of the
"lightning never strikes twice" maxim.)
       So while I was talking with Evan in the office next
door, Val was avidly reading my journal in my bed as
Danny slept so innocently next to her. And when I came
in unexpectedly, she told me today, she simply slipped
it under the bed; the next morning she returned it to
its spot on the shelf while I was in the bathroom. To
do this she had to stand on a chair and move things
around in the closet, but I never suspected a thing.
And Briana must've done exactly what Val did. Great
minds think alike! (Will I ever learn? Well, yes, it's
dawned on me it's time to buy another lockbox. As of
tomorrow I'll have home and away versions to supplement
those hard-to-get-to lockable footlockers at Funston.)
-- And by the way, Val insists the dream about Briana
which she told me about the morning after reading the
journal was real. She offered to show me, as "proof,"
the passage she wrote about it in her own journal at the
time, even though she's told me she writes whatever she
feels like there and pays no attention at all to what
actually happens or to any irksome distinctions between
fantasy and reality. I took a pass.
       The second revelation was truly a surprise: she'd
been "unfaithful" to me. It wasn't exactly recent but
she still seemed to have it firmly in mind. As a matter
of fact -- just a coincidence? -- it happened during
that very same period covered by V.22, late last August,
during my brief showdown with Jang after her early
return from Hawaii. She and I were in the mountains for
the weekend, as Val knew. Her Emp friend and former
lover Brandon Wexler visited her at her brother's
apartment, where she was staying temporarily at the time
after moving out of her Dolores Street place, and the
urge overcame them as they sat on the floor -- they were
reading the ms. of Jerry Borden's "Purple Virus"

science-fiction novel out loud together, alternating
paragraphs -- this just after Val made a pot of tea. "I
saw the erection under his pants," she confided to me
now, not without a conspicuous flush of excitement. So
then she offered herself to him, viewing this as an "act
of charity," feeling she "owed it to him." They balled
right there on the red carpet in her brother's living
room (where she and I also went at it a time or two in
that same era). The very next night as she and I balled
away at Funston during our "reunion" after my return
from the mountains and the breakup with Jang she
silently wondered whether Brandon's sperm and mine were
"mixing together in there like schools of fish."

Did it sting to hear about this incident? Yes, it
did: it absolutely did. But do I have any right to
complain about it? No, I absolutely do not. And I told
her both of these things. We weren't committed to each
other then, I observed, just as we're not now. And yes,
I did make a point of emphasizing that last part. "I
won't blame you," she replied with a scowly little pout,
"if you feel you have to retaliate." And then tacked
on a moment later: "Really, Glen, you're just hurting
yourself if you make a big deal of this. We should be
thinking about what's really important for us before
it's too late."

*   *

Back from the "special dinner," served on the floor
of my motel room, the sandpaper rug (No. 3 sandpaper,
I'd say, and gradually getting finer). Three calls came
in as we ate, and then Roy Dixon dropped by looking
natty in vest and desert boots. Becky's pounding away
at the Composer. All the garbage has been cleaned out.
The heater is hissing.

So what does Val's "infidelity" (her word) with
Brandon really mean? Just as she says, probably not
much. At least now she can't be quite so overbearing in
her outraged martyrdom over my "secret life."
Definitely I feel a shade less guilty about my own
wanderings, both of that period and of the present, and
this despite the fact that I've never believed I should

be feeling even slightly guilty about any of them. Her confession may wind up binding us together more tightly and also make it easier for me to be open with her about certain things, including my own divagations. Or it might drive yet another wedge between us. Who the hell knows.

As for the journal invasion, I'm going to let it go. I'll tighten up my in-house security both here and at Funston and that's about it. What she knows, she knows. I thought about presenting her with a revised version of my letter to Briana on this same subject or maybe the jumbled paraphrase of it I wrote in these pages some forty-eight hours ago since that one was addressing her, Val, anyway -- or should I perhaps just work up a form letter with the names blank so I'll have any future incursions covered as well? -- but no, at this point none of these projects seem worth the effort.

It remains true that numbness is my current emotional state and boredom is my current response to the relationship with Valerie. This is so even when she writes me a poem called "Blue Sperm," which she did today. Supposedly these sperm have nothing to do with the commingled schools of same spawned by her serial rutting with Brandon and me within a few hours of each other. So then maybe they're the product of a pair of anonymous "blue balls"? Perhaps even of the fairly familiar "blue balls" hooked up to the "membre viril" (not sure on that spelling) of a certain hard-working editor isolated too long out in the Merino County sticks and now delighted to see his city lover at last? When I asked her, she said this last reading might be a fair one. But then I have to ask myself: does she have any real idea of why things are the way they are between us? (I strongly doubt she does. For that matter I'm not so sure I do either.)

I yearn to go on the prowl again -- and I mean with serious and wholly honorable long-term intentions. Find someone I can relate to at a deeper level and yet also in a more laid-back and fun-loving and pressure-free fashion.

4

Tuesday 19 (X:18)

In San Francisco right now an emergency ecological action is underway. Yesterday two Standard Oil tankers collided beneath the Golden Gate Bridge in "the thickest fog of the season," according to the Chronicle, which of course paints the rosiest possible picture of this disaster, i.e., presents it through their normal Standard Oil filter (check out the Standard display ads in the Chronicle sometime; one might say they're the pre-filter as well as source of the Chron's emolument). What's crucial is that in just minutes more oil poured into the bay than fouled the Santa Barbara Channel in six months during the Union Oil platform blowout two years ago. Today thousands of volunteers, including at least a dozen from the Merc, are patrolling the beaches near the Golden Gate in search of oil-smeared birds.

I wish I could be there. Holding a terrified bird in your hand and saving its life: that might beat grinding out any number of newspaper stories. Or then again, why should anyone help Standard Oil minimize the damage it's done? But then of course why should birds die that we might hoist Standard on its own petard? Save the birds, then hoist Standard: that's the only way to go. But figuring out how to hoist a company so evil on a petard so big won't be easy.

Well anyway (enough with the extracurricular editorializing!), back here in Garnett work proceeds on the publishing of our third issue at the end of this week. I'm reluctantly coming around to the view held by most of the in-house moderates that the paper's appeal must be broadened. Our image so far is that of a crusading, muckraking journal of dubious quality (uneven at best), uniformly "negative," "shrill," "super-liberal." Without cutting back on well-documented investigative pieces we must find space for a larger number of "positive" stories. Otherwise only a small

coterie of confirmed radic-libs and counterculturists
will read us.

Work proceeds, yes, but oh so fitfully. Last night
Claire and I returned from a hike over to Short Stop
(arm in arm, floating through the sticky wet fog) to
find the office interior taken over by a huge spider
web. Becky had spun it, using a spent carbon justifier
ribbon hundreds of feet long. A perfect expression of
our feelings about the place: once you stick a foot in
the door it's impossible to extricate yourself. At any
moment a giant CIA-planted mutant tarantula will rush in
from the kitchen to suck out all your blood.

We also pasted up a mock front page, mostly
Claire's work, headlined "MERC PUBLISHER BUSTED/Caught
Absconding/With Newsbunny."

Claire. Not twelve hours after Val's departure on
Greyhound we were at it again. Once more she "tucked me
in" as Becky Composed away in the next room. As she put
it, "Even the quiet afterwards is good with us." I was
surprised she could arouse me so easily, as I was coming
down from a nauseating weed high. A nice fit, though,
the two of us. A groovy tucking-in for sure. And then
off she skips to Kurt's bed. She says she has to read
for an hour or more before she can face climbing in with
him. And yes, they still ball regularly despite, or
perhaps because of (though she says not), their "sort of
open" arrangement. And this could well mean she too is
at certain times pondering "schools of fish" (which
personally I think of as more like albino tadpoles).

Four of us locked in my room, sitting in a tight
circle on the floor, incense burning at the center, and
we're jumping up to check out every car pulling into
Klug's parking lot...all for a lousy joint.

Two nights ago, further confessions for Valerie.
Gradually the last of my "secrets" are trickling out.
Since she's now begging to know "the whole truth no
matter how painful or ugly," I told her about the
"office affair" with Claire ("it's no threat to you"),
and also about various other incidents with women in
Garnett (Lisa) and elsewhere in earlier periods last

year before we met (Winnie and Jill during my month in
New York). Then a wild fuck on the office floor -- the
first time Valoshka has permitted herself a frenzy of
passion like that, with me or, she says, with anyone.
My own frenzy, I'm sorry to say, was more forced than
erotically induced.

Wednesday 20
    Some night it was. Just as I was shutting the
office down, or so I thought, at two a.m., Ronni
Tavaras's husband arrived with the farm-labor piece, and
I stayed up until five rewriting it, beset with eerie
trepidations as I attempted to inject a proper degree of
skepticism into the tone of golly-gee-whiz gullibility
in which Ronni had reported the ranchers' self-
aggrandizing comments. The power of the editor! I
didn't alter a single fact or quote but still turned the
overall import of the piece very nearly on its head.
    At five, in setting my alarm for eight to take copy
to Sheridan for typesetting, I twisted the wind-up
mechanism too hard and broke the clock. So I had to
wake up Al at home (he's staying there more lately) and
ask him to alert me at eight -- which he did, stopping
by to shake me awake and then hanging around for a few
minutes until I was verifiably up and functioning.
    I remember what I dreamt. It was about as seamy as
they come. Al, Claire, and I had been unjustly
condemned to prison. In an examination room Al grew a
preposterously huge hard-on much like the red dildo in
"Sheriff Bill" and fucked Claire in the ass from behind,
trying to slip it to her stealthily but failing
comically as I stood guard next to the surgeon's table
and kept cautioning him to hurry up while begging off on
his plea to help him shove the ungainly thing in.
    Back in real life, a groggy drive to Sheridan,
blurry proofing in a small restaurant near Herron's (the
printer), then the rushed return to Garnett, and now I
lie on the office floor rebelliously journalizing (for
about two more minutes) as the rug sands down what's

left of my elbows and new crises threaten from every
direction: who will proofread, how will we come up with
photos for this piece and that, what will replace the
Merino Fox ecology column if the Fox himself can't be
located in time, on and on and on.

I talked with Barbara yesterday, very happy to hear
her voice again despite my having some new issues to
raise with her at some point. (This of course is sister
Barb, not volunteer Barb on the M.M. staff.) The month
in Belgium shook her up, she told me. Joey's still
there, and she preferred not to talk just yet about what
happened between them. "I feel much older," she said.

*　　　*

This is insane! A momentarily empty office at
seven p.m., sixteen empty page dummies, a foot-high
stack of copy. I am the Merino Mercury! Take the
dispute between the ranchers and the migrant laborers --
essentially I wrote both articles! Both sides of the
issue! I'm also Ray Dixon explaining why he does not
want to be called a Negro, and I'm Kit Gilliam, who's
also black, bridling under Ray's macho explanation. I'm
G.S. Dodge extolling the new Derek and the Dominoes
album, I'm Howard Gilbert pleading for creation of a
County Housing Commission so no more friends of mine are
roasted alive in deathtrap fires, I'm Heidi Crouse
describing how to make jello without lumps (one of our
new line of "positive" features).

It's too much. Where is everybody? Where are "the
people"? I am the people? Help!

(Could procrastinate and play one more time the
searing "Have You Ever Loved A Woman" track from the
album just mentioned, Eric Clapton presiding. Will!)

Friday 22 (X:21)

This is the courtroom for Merino County. Judge
Melvin Middleton has just droned through his opening
statement of "clarification" (sic!) concerning the legal
rights of us small-fry traffic violators. (I'll be
returning in an hour as a big fry in the hoked-up drug

felony preliminaries.)

Today I look like a dangerous dopester for sure,
red-eyed and trembly after another all-night stand in
the Merc office. At quarter to eight this morning Evan
roared off with the paste-ups and an hour later I had to
be in court. Forty-five minutes after that the judge
wandered in thirty minutes late. And now one by one we
small fry go forward, most of us pleading "guilty with
explanation," then launching into sob stories of various
degrees of improbability. Me, I'm planning to be
different. My "Advice as to Rights" sheet informs me
I'm entitled to be represented by the public defender
"if you are destitute and so request." ---

Sunday 24 (X:23)
Out soaking up rays on the Funston sundeck again --
something I haven't done in months and months. In fact
when I first saw what a beautiful day it was, Briana
came immediately to mind. Yes, she's the perfect fleshy
correlative for a hot, clear day in San Francisco.
Briana: sunny, bright, beautiful, clear, slow-moving,
cool in the way heat itself is cool in San Francisco,
where she was born and raised (and whose doting father's
first name, by the way, is Brian). I'm still thinking I
might present myself for our fabled Valentine's Day
rendezvous, though mainly just for the principle of the
thing. Better a suicide leaper's chance of surviving a
plunge from the Golden Gate Bridge than my chance of
finding Briana at that rendezvous, "sacred vow" or none.
Since I dashed off those lines in the courtroom a
great deal has happened. Two days jam-packed with
elation, anger, despair, anomie, indifference, false
smiles, hilarious laughter, and hundreds or maybe even
thousands of snap editorial decisions. I'm alone right
now because I told Valerie I have to be. Solitude is
one thing (among many) I can't get in Garnett. With my
room adjoining the office, and essentially nowhere else
to go, I'm always susceptible to the crises of the
moment; and in an operation as amateurish as ours the

crises often outnumber the moments. When at last a
chance arises for me to slip away to the city for a day
or two of desperately needed relief, Val appears and --
no doubt with the best of intentions -- begins badgering
me about our relationship and my failure to pay her
enough attention. She especially likes to mutter about
what she might have to do, or might already be doing, as
a consequence of my "indifference."

So it's unspeakably pleasant to sit quietly in the
sun for an hour or two, reconnecting myself with the
great timeless wheel of the Tao (or with whatever cosmic
phenomenon it is I see arcing up there above the summit
of Mt. Moraga right now -- probably an unusually shaped
stray wisp from a low-lying fog formation parked out of
sight on the other side).

Friday, then, anger came first. Scott Ferris,
Claire's red-bearded lawyer, the one whose sumptuous
office is studded with Quixote figurines, who declares a
broad sympathy with the Movement -- this same fast-
talking shyster wants Claire to accept an absurd,
vicious "deal" proposed by the D.A. ("Lord Byron," Scott
calls him). Poor Claire doesn't know what to do; I feel
it's wrong to try to influence her decision; and Al is
incensed because now the D.A. is maneuvering to
implicate him in the case (because the pills found in
the vial in my bag are prescribed to Al, and also by Al,
as attested on the label; they were originally for a
cold of his own, which he passed along to me before
giving me the pills he'd taken himself to counter it).

Al and I want to fight it out in court, but we're
aware we'd be indulging our own quixotic impulses to do
so when it's Claire who'd stand to suffer the most.
Meanwhile Scott's bouncing between "Lord Byron" and the
three of us, reporting on the latest status of the
"deal." Much to my disgust Al pulls his punches because
Scott treats him as a "fellow professional" (i.e.,
Scott's a lawyer, Al's a physician). I tell Scott
exactly how I feel about his hypocrisy. Claire informs
me later I've "shook up his confidence." He's even
asked, "How can I get to know that guy better?"

[Have Mercy]

The dilemma is resolved, at least temporarily, by
postponement. On the grounds that an "independent"
analysis of the drugs is needed, Judge Middleton sets a
new preliminary date of February 19. Also, in my small-
fry traffic hearing this same judge reluctantly agrees I
can at least be permitted to request the services of a
public defender and postpones my trial until Monday. He
also says the public defender's office will refuse to
help me (owing to the petty nature of my offense). He
agrees the "Advice as to Rights" sheet issued by the
court itself is indeed "ambiguous" on such matters (by
which term -- "ambiguous" -- he fudges the fact that the
sheet clearly states the opposite of what he originally
said it did) and he suggests my remedy will lie in an
appeal. Pure sheepdip, I say (but not out loud). I
still intend to ask for a jury trial and then to conduct
the case myself, as best, or at least as comically, as I
can, to bring the whole story to light and also, for
what it's worth, to expose a few of the hypocrisies and
absurdities of this one tiny provincial sub-substructure
of the System.
    -- Last night: we missed the babysitter, took Danny
to see "Dynamite Chicken," couldn't make our planned
trip to Pepperland for dancing. We were both tearing
our hair out. I tried hard to demonstrate the requisite
compassion and tenderness ---
                    *   *
    Aha: another sundeck fuck. This time it's a Henry
Miller special, both of us fully dressed, performing for
the multitudes if they but knew (and especially for our
neighbor Mr. O'Connor, the snowy-haired elder who Val
tells me is a near double for her storied grandfather
who kept Vietnam under a very heavy thumb some thirty
years ago; he's weeding his garden in the next yard up
the hillside, his head at times probably no more than
a body length beyond and below my feet). I'm lying on
the blanket down by the fenced end of the deck; maybe
fifty or more uphill houses are fully visible to me
above the peace panels or through the gaps between them.
Valoshka, in her new blue boots and lavender minidress,

238

straddles and unzips me, brings forth the twistedly
engorged and beveined' plunger ("horny to the hilt!")
(and no doubt looking so veiny because of the bright
sun; I myself am startled and so's Val). So then we
shunt aside her purple panties and, lovely to feel, get
maximally tight and she rides a deliciously slow ride
(her back to the hillside and dress drawn down low on
that side for cover) and we even manage to come
together.

"So, you feel like a 'slut' now?" I ask her a
little later, gently but teasingly, referring to her
comment about the rowdy female copulators of "Tropic of
Cancer." "No!" she cries. And suddenly I'm thinking
maybe there's hope for us after all.

*   *

So Friday night at ten the papers finally arrived
from the printer's, some 18,500 of them this time, and
another rolling-and-rubber-banding ordeal began. It
didn't end until six p.m. Saturday when, in a blaze of
relief, Val, Danny, and I fled to the city.

In the midst of the ordeal Val sneakily seized
another opportunity to snoop in my journal -- the
current one this time; this one right here -- and
confirmed for herself that I've gotten it on with Claire
and various others (Briana, Jang) and not merely as a
matter of ancient history. Apparently she's come to
distrust me so much she couldn't even believe my
previous confessions of having done just that. And the
truth is also just as before: I've never lied to her.
Not once. I had told her I was seeing other women and
who they were; I simply held back the details on exactly
when or how often or how fulfillingly. What's more, if
I tell her I've balled someone, as I did vis-a-vis Jang,
Claire, and Briana, it's the truth for sure. (If she
tells me she's balled someone, that's not necessarily
the case -- or so she tells me. "I could just be trying
to make you jealous, you know." "But Val, isn't that,
you know, a lie? The very thing you were warning me
about?" "Yes it is, but it's different. It's
justified." "How so?" "Because you deserve to feel the

pain!")

   She disappeared for several hours after this latest
invasion of my privacy and when she returned claimed
amnesia had obliterated all memory of what she'd done
during the interim. Then she sat in the bathroom for an
hour, her head hanging between her knees. So wasted was
I from the battles in court and in producing the new
issue of the paper (which everyone agrees is a vast
improvement on the first two) that my "response" to her
maudlin enactment of the hurt brought on at least
proximately by her own immoral act (snooping) was one of
disgust and exasperated indifference: if it meant the
end was at hand for us, I said, then so be it.

   To my complete surprise she turned herself inside
out and all day Saturday lavished me with touchingly
conscientious cheeriness, contrition, and consideration.

   Words at the end of a poem she wrote:

                Trusting you
                means accepting
                you can't be trusted.

-- By which she really means, although she doesn't
appear to know it, I can't be trusted to do what she
wants me to do or thinks I ought to do. As noted in
here before, she knows very well, and has never
disputed, that when I give my word, I keep it; or on
those rare occasions when I can't keep it, I at least
let her know this and the reason for the changes; or if
I fail even at doing this (which I don't think has
actually happened so far), she can be sure I'll
carefully consider her interests and do the best I can
to protect her (and she continues to acknowledge -- but
oh so blithely, as if it means nothing at all to her --
that she believes I have done this and will keep on
doing it in the future).

   And yet she still comes after me as if I'm treating
her badly -- I'm a monster of cruelty and obliviousness
-- for failing to tell her every last thing there is to
know about my private life, even when we've explicitly
agreed we're both free to see others and we'll fully
respect each other's privacy.

And so it is I've decided if it's extreme openness
she wants -- and I doubt it really is, but she still
insists I'm wrong -- it's extreme openness she'll get.
Since she likes to read my journal so much, I've offered
her the rare opportunity to read it all, every single
word in every single volume, along with everything else
I've ever written: chrons, fiction, journalism, poetry,
notebooks, school papers, and even my correspondence
with others (to the limited extent I have copies) and
theirs with me. In short, the works. "Let it all hang
out." And she's assured me she wants to read it all and
can handle it and I'd better not hold her age against
her in the sense of assuming she's not mature enough to
do it. And she's promised she won't use what she
discovers against me -- "no matter how bad it is" -- and
that I'll never, ever, ever regret this decision.

5

Monday 25
And this, folks, is Crusty's Doughnut Shop, where
the nabobs of Garnett gather for morning coffee. Just a
moment ago, in fact, I summoned the courage to approach
the D.A. himself, the redoubtable "Lord Byron" -- so-
named because he's "mad, bad, and dangerous to know,"
according to Scott Ferris -- as he primly poured himself
a coffee refill (cream, no sugar) at the table one aisle
over. No point in speaking with him about my case, he
said, his tone approaching absolute zero in its
frigidity, because he's being transferred out of the
area. I should see "Keith" -- whoever that might be.
Earlier today my cause suffered its first legal
setback when Judge Middleton ruled I must represent
myself in the fraught matter of my alleged stop-sign
violation. It seems I'm too wealthy to warrant the
services of a public defender. I own a motor vehicle,
see, or more accurately a small fraction of one, the
bank being by far the majority shareholder. Thus in
order to obtain legal counsel to defend me against the

charge of running a stop sign -- so the judicial mind
reasons -- I should sell my interest in the vehicle on
which my job depends. Nor does it matter that my income
from said job amounts to forty dollars a week plus half
the cost of renting a bottom-tier motel room, or in sum
roughly a dollar an hour.

So it goes. When you take on the System, it's
perhaps unreasonable to expect the System to pay for
your defense, especially when your "crime" is, in
essence, taking on the System.

Meanwhile we're picking up steam for our fourth
issue, which has the look of a real winner. Front-page
story: Mercury uncovers widespread racial discrimination
in Garnett and Merimont! In a nutshell, we sent out
matching teams of ostensible renters, one a black couple
and one a white couple, to test the market in places
where we'd received reports of bias. To no one's
surprise, most of the apartments (at the Camelot West,
Pagoda Grove, and VillaMer, involving 177 units in all,
every single one currently occupied by whites and whites
only) turned out to have "just been rented" when our
black couple showed up, but were available again thirty
minutes later when our white couple (of a similar age,
similarly attired, supposedly similarly employed)
inquired.

On this particular topic we can bring to bear a
surprising amount of influence. Ironically enough this
is because the U.S. Air Force is our chief ally (again,
to repeat, just on this one issue). Federal law bars
discrimination in housing used by military personnel,
and a large percentage of the renters in town are
military personnel employed at Fleming. The very last
thing the Pentagon wants in these days of burgeoning
opposition to the war is an expose' about rampant racial
bias at its main airborne transshipment point for
Vietnam (and also for many other U.S. bases -- scores if
not hundreds -- scattered across Asia and the Pacific).
Therefore, the Air Force will quickly declare any
facilities here in Garnett shown to be practicing
discrimination to be off limits for military personnel.

One other hot tip: at half past noon six outraged
Merino County librarians will be coming in. Unlikely as
this may seem, they feel the hard-hitting investigative
report on hanky-panky involving the upper echelons of
the library administration which we ran in the last
issue was nowhere near critical enough.

Tuesday 26
By the dim light of the -- I want to call it the
Palaver Room, but no, it's the Paladin Room, an integral
part of the liveliest local night spot by far, the
Garnett Bowl. Most of the clientele are off-duty
service personnel from the minority out at Fleming who'd
rather drink beer than smoke dope or do harder stuff. I
come here for an hour or so in mid-evening when I get
the chance, not so much from desire as from habit -- the
old college and grad-school habit of taking a ten
o'clock break at the local saloon. I suppose I also
come here to get a look at all the dolled-up women and
maybe even, once in a while, to meet one (to dance with;
to ball; perhaps even to get something serious going
with) -- but today I hesitate to admit those latter two
aims. Valerie, it would appear, has me spooked. All of
a sudden it's hard to write freely.

But that doesn't mean I'll stop trying. No caving
in to below-the-belt tactics!

Last night Claire and I interviewed two more
disgruntled librarians. This took place in on-base
housing at Fleming where one of the librarians lives
(wife of a career pilot who's currently away carpet-
bombing Vietnam). Afterwards we, Claire and I, hoped to
do a little recreational rutting -- it was an unspoken
understanding -- but when we got back to the office we
found someone waiting for me. Val! On a Tuesday! She
leveled an almost comically dramatic knowing smirk at
the two of us when we came in. Claire quickly departed.
(Yeah, it's the unashamed truth, I'd been lusting for
her, this craving first awakened earlier in the evening
by the way she sprawled spread-legged in her tight jeans

with one leg crooked over the arm of the very chair
where Val was now so primly sitting.)

Val then informed me, as we drove to McDonald's,
that she'd stayed up all night at Funston reading back
volumes of my journal (as I'd invited her to do Sunday
night, telling her where to find the key to the
footlocker in which I store most of them) and now she
had me pegged for sure. Rather than risk misstating her
conclusions orally on the phone, she made a special trip
by bus all the way to Garnett to present to me in person
the handwritten version of those conclusions, which
she'd set forth in yet another long letter. She handed
this to me and then sat watching gravely as I read it
(in the L.C. in the parking lot, by the light of the
Golden Arches, no less).

The letter called me every name in the book,
focusing on my alleged callousness and lack of scruples
and my state of severely arrested emotional development.
Then as we nibbled at our matched sets of "Big Mac'na
bagga grease" she declared she still loves me anyway, in
spite of it all. In fact, she confessed, my alleged
decadence-cum-depravity deepens her enchantment with me
because of the challenge it presents; and as soon as we
got back to the room she proved it by sucking me until I
came "like the way milk squirts out of a cow, there was
so much." But then I was too worn out to get it up
again right away for actual balling, and an hour later
at bedtime when I failed her a second time she was
pissed off, discouraged, she wept, she raged, "why can't
I turn you on again!" -- but shortly thereafter, in fact
even before that last phrase had stopped echoing, she
did.

On second reading her letter evokes, I have to
admit, a big yawn. I just can't work up much interest
in the points she raises. Whether this is because I've
already hit on satisfactory answers for myself to these
familiar criticisms, or because I really have become
"callous" (repressing those concerns which still make
me uneasy) -- this is a question I don't even pretend to
know the answer to. No doubt the whole issue is one I

should try to look into more deeply. But that doesn't
mean it'll happen anytime soon.

*

A long talk with Scott Ferris this evening. His
office with the massive desk and the massed cavalry of
resplendent Quixotes and footsore Panzas, his earnest
attempts to defend his integrity -- it was not easy to
rap with the man. But for unknown reasons I found
myself accepting his strained rationalizations for
structuring "deals" with the D.A. (which is technically
illegal), making large sums on drug cases (i.e., often
from the profits of his clients' drug sales), living
such a ritzy life in a backwater town whose main order
of business is to support American military deployments
abroad which involve the massacre of countless innocent
people, all in order to keep Americans living high on
the hog as the collective capitalist king of the world-
domination hill. Oddly enough, I sort of liked him once
he relaxed a bit (the expensive wine he provided may've
helped us both on this). I did score a few points,
though, in arguing that if more "deals" were challenged,
the legal justice system might be forced to change at a
quicker pace. Amazingly enough, the thought appeared
never to have occurred to him before.

Wednesday 27

Today -- first day of the Year of the Porker --
which means the Woofer is out and the Crower is ancient
history -- today didn't go at all as I thought it would.

** Joe Dargan, the IBM salesman, rousted me from
bed at eleven-thirty. I slept late because Sherry kept
me up until four a.m. with her latest perfervid defenses
of the one-hundred-percent plastic lifestyle she's
adopted and her disingenuous complaints about Al's
overindulgence in the paper -- not to mention her
unsubtle come-ons to me.

** Claire arrived, the office cleared out, and we
dove into bed. Yes, we dig each other in bed. Sex with
her shouldn't be better than it is with Val, but it is.

245

Something to do with grace. Can Val develop grace? I
wish Claire could take her under her wing and teach her.
I wish I could do it myself but I already know I'd never
get anywhere. However, that doesn't mean I won't keep
trying to slip the message to her somehow.

    ** Downtown I met the one Aguilar sister I hadn't
yet encountered, Nina. She's the prettiest of a very
pretty lot (from a progressive and politically active
Chicano family, most of whom are helping out with the
paper in one way or another).

    ** After dinner tonight at Evan and Judy Kott's
place we got stoned and grooved on a huge orange candle
which up close looked amazingly like an erupting
volcano, as we all agreed, even to the point of checking
out the "lava" of dripping wax with a big Sherlock
Holmes magnifying glass. Good people and a good laid-
back time. I need more evenings like this.

    ** A sotto voce telephone call from Valerie, holed
up in her brother's bedroom during a break in their Tet/
Chinese New Year's family dinner: everything with her
seems okay, at least for the moment. She's been too
busy to continue with her reading of my oeuvre but she
still plans to do it, to pursue it all the way back to
the very first word or, as she'd no doubt say, the
original sin (she's basically going at it in reverse
chronological order: "peeling the onion"). I also
learned she was born in the Year of the Cat, which I'd
never heard of before, but it turns out that's what the
Rabbit year is called in Vietnam. Because Dog years,
one of which we're just reaching the end of, are never
good for Cat people, she's expecting her luck will be
much better this year, the Pig year.

    ** Late visit to Al's: the poor harried physician/
publisher was still working on subscriptions. I
collected my paycheck and we fantasized about revenge
and vindication at the trial. My favorite: first
subpoena the notorious Norm Gaston (eponymous editor of
the Ghastly), then twist him into knots on the stand.

    ** Still later, another stop at the Paladin Room.
The lonesome hippie at the corner table: me. Nothing

much happening there, so I relocated to the all-night Denny's and read the S.F. Examiner cover to cover. It carried a story about a lawsuit Barb's friend Steve Vaughn is filing against Standard Oil for $12 million regarding the recent oil spill. Then I nosed home at about five miles an hour through a thick and sticky Tule fog.

Ho-hum. Lord I'm wasted. Just one last task and I can crash: make up a rough schedule for tomorrow. Approximately fifty items to find slots for. Is there an efficient way to do this or should I just try a blind draw? Throw darts maybe? No, because it's too likely they, the darts, would land on some of the items I'd rather avoid if at all possible. Better to go by sheer instinct-at-the-moment, a/k/a "gut."

Friday 29 (X:28)

Another downtown pastry shop, a different one but not all that different. I'm sugaring up (an apple turnover for breakfast and then a chocolate mini-eclair for "breakfast dessert") before locking myself in solitary for a bout of hard-ass high-test writing.

Yesterday I did my big interview of Mrs. Richards, the tyrannical county librarian everyone loves to hate, especially her own staff. A few minutes into the questioning the phone rang and it was for me -- ex-librarian Kelly Pool warning the interview was secretly being taped by one of Richards's cronies hidden in the next room. Never did I dream this library story could turn into such cloak-and-dagger stuff.

Last night four of us went out to the Pagoda Corners Bar -- where many of the Tesuque Valley's ranchers and orchardists hang out, as does, it's said, the aforementioned Norm Gaston of the Ghastly -- but nothing much happened except Al hung one on. Or more like hung on two or three at once to make up for having so few hanging-one-on opportunities. In the end we had to carry him out to the car and then into his house as Sherry barked orders and fumed.

[Have Mercy]

While we were at the bar, Claire and I took a long
walk in the fog. "I'm getting to like you better than
I'd counted on," she said. Is it just the great sex?
Is it the long periods of physical proximity under
deadline pressure? Is it the court case hanging over
our heads? Whatever it is, I know this much for sure:
she can make each small touch exquisite just as Jang and
Briana can. And I swear I'll teach Valerie how to
develop the same kind of touch if it kills me (and it
just might).

(Oops, Nina Aguilar on her bicycle nearly runs me
over. To her I'm the guy who looks "just like Jim
Morrison" -- about which Claire's snappy comment was,
when I told her, "What the hell was she was on? I need
some of that." So then I borrow a quarter from Nina.
"See you at the big game tonight," I say. Garnett High
versus Socorro! Nina's a cheerleader -- riding a bike!)
(Garnett is not Gatewood. In Gatewood no cheerleader
would be caught dead riding a bike. Gatewood is a lot
more liberal than Garnett in social mores, I'd say, but
probably just as conservative politically if not more
so. By this measuring stick the effects of Fleming Air
Force Base and Gatewood Naval Air Station pretty much
balance each other out, but "Illinois headquarters of
the John Birch Society"? Hard to top that.)

-- Now Mrs. Richards -- the very same chief
librarian I went nose-to-nose with yesterday -- shuffles
past the table. Talk about small towns: she's been
chowing down by herself in a booth over against the wall
right here in Thompson's and I didn't know it. Of
course we both manufacture smiles like long-lost pals.
Yet she believes her barony is under assault. To her
I'm the enemy. I can ruin her career. Media power!
It's even more insidious than blues power!

-- Yes, the fire's definitely flickering out. More
and more I'm tired of Garnett, tired of small-town
vendettas, tired of criticizing the crazy ways other
people choose to live, tired of living on what amounts
to a military reservation in the section serving as its
main support area. I long to be back in the city. But

like it or not I'll probably be hanging on here at least
another month. The paper's beginning to feel the
economic pinch -- or rather economic strangulation, I
should say. Everything's becoming a headache,
especially subscriptions and distribution. What we need
is about a hundred grand to bankroll a sustained assault
on the deeply entrenched establishment in this town.
And of course we have no hope of enticing anyone to
invest even a hundredth that much.

Since the first of the year I've done no non-
newspaper-oriented writing of my own to speak of --
other than in these pages -- no reading, very little
note-taking. Soon I must get back to the real work.
Henry Miller, I'm counting on you for inspiration. Yes,
fiction for me is dead -- nonautobiographical fiction,
that is. Which is to say I favor dishing out the true
scoop and I can do that only about (1) the life I know
through introspection and (2) the life that I perceive
going on around me; and both of those categories are
basically autobiographical. If various names and a few
identifying details must be changed for legal reasons,
all right, I guess I'll go along with that, albeit
grudgingly. Though of course some of the old-time
fiction could still rise specter-like from the grave of
my dear departed imagination and probably will --
someday. Not, however, soon. Not as things look now.

A personal financial crisis looms. It's becoming
ever more difficult to squeeze the L.C. payments and my
share of the Funston rent ($210 total for both) from my
monthly wages minus expenses. If Jang hadn't sent
thirty bucks out of the blue -- proceeds she wanted to
share from the calligraphy class she's begun teaching --
I would've had to borrow money this month.

*

And now some navel-gazing.

Valerie spent the better part of a day and night
poring over my journals and chronbooks, focusing
understandably enough on the wild months around the time
she and I met. Then she wrote the long letter spelling
out her reactions and delivered it personally (all the

way to Garnett) after going without sleep for some
thirty hours. Here are a few of her comments from that
letter and my reactions to them.

   Please respond to me with open honesty.
   It is our only way out, your only way out
   into further development and
   enlightenment.

  Yes, fine, I agree, especially if she would replace
"open honesty" with the more expansive (and truly more
open and honest) "real closeness." The catch for me is
I'm not yet sure I want us to find "a way out," by which
I think she really means -- and I mean -- "a way in,"
i.e., to something deeper and stronger and better
between us than what we've got now. But that, finally,
seems to be beside the point she's trying to make here.

   Glenn [she still insists on spelling my
   name her way!], you have led a life of
   debaucherie, diffusing your superior
   qualities at random and collecting trash,
   treasurable trash, but trash always trash.
   What a wasteful extravagance of emotions,
   thinking you are giving people rare
   extraordinary precious unique experiences,
   a concentrate of living -- and then
   dropping them back to their sad morbid
   reality.

  "Trash always trash" -- would that include my
loving Lisa, the tragically cut-off affair with Karen
A., my marriage, my year and a half living with Jang and
six years of knowing her, my failed affair with Briana?
In short, is there anything in my relations with women
in my adult life that isn't "trash" to her? And if not,
why does she care about me at all? Why would she want
to get involved with such a jerk?

  The term "debaucherie," however, is not without
interest. I don't think I've ever applied that word to
myself before -- how did I overlook it? The dictionary
defines it (in the English spelling with a 'y' instead
of a French 'ie' at the end) -- defines it as "moral
corruption," and I wouldn't dream of denying that my

morals have in some sense been corrupted or somehow simply corrupted themselves without any outside forces disturbing them. The question is whether anyone in his or her right mind in an age like ours would want to live by traditional "uncorrupted" American morals. (As for so-called "universal" morals, forget it: those are just a reflection of a single culture's dream -- usually aggressive and well-armed -- of superiority.)

I'd say "debauchery" -- or at least the kind most interesting to me -- is likely to begin at the place where two conflicting sets of moral principles collide. It's inevitable that many gray areas will develop as individuals try to find a way to live with both systems simultaneously or to transition from one to the other (perhaps not realizing this is fully possible only in theory). From the point of view of both systems the individuals moving about in that gray area will appear largely or even entirely "debauched." Writ big, I'd say this is the condition America as a whole, along with many other countries in the West, is in right now (see "Greening").

I certainly don't exempt myself from this condition. I don't imagine Valerie would exempt herself either if she really thought about it. Married shortly after her sixteenth birthday, divorced at nineteen, her husband metamorphosing along the way from a computer programmer with the phone company to a pistol-packing drug dealer; being unfaithful to that husband in the final months of their marriage and then screwing around with other men and shacking up with the sorry likes of me well before their divorce became final, and after that giving it away to Brandon (and how many others?) as an "act of charity," and all along permitting her innocent infant son Danny to be subjected to all kinds of horrors during his formative first three years -- not to mention relatively minor matters such as the snooping and the flat-out lies and the outright cruelties she's laid on me -- how does she come off, I ask, acting so uncorrupted and morally superior?

Or there's another way to look at the matter.

[Have Mercy]

Absolute moral principles must sometimes give way to
more practical and/or heartful considerations, including
the imperative not to hurt unnecessarily. This latter
injunction may in some cases boil down to, for example,
the task of moving from lover A to lover B without
hurting either. In practice it's impossible to succeed
completely at this, but surely one should still try.
Therefore, obviously, again, I'm "debauched," since I do
try to do this and it's often gotten me into some
whopping tangles, including with Val herself. (But am I
apologizing for these efforts of mine? No, I'm not.
I'm very proud of them!)
    And yet I'll concede it's true, if you're incapable
of being "fully open and honest" in a relationship --
much less a series of relationships -- before too long
you may lose some of your innocence, your righteousness,
your enthusiasm. This surely is not good. But then
again since it's a major part of the process of growing
up, of accepting and learning to live with life's
difficulties and limitations and confusions, maybe it's
not so bad either. Maybe it's not quite the pure evil
Val's working so hard to paint it as. In any case just
about everyone goes through this process, possibly
excepting a few saints and priestesses of high purity
such as, say, Briana Tsu and my own sister Barbara and a
certain Valerie Mailloux Bando. And really now -- for
after all we must be "fully open and honest" here --
don't these estimable ladies go through it too? Aren't
they tested by life? Don't they experience soul-shaking
doubts and temptations to which they sometimes, if only
very rarely, yield? In short: isn't it the case that
perfection is unattainable for human beings, including
even saints and high priestesses, whether it be with
respect to "openness and honesty" or any other abstract
moral ideal (and especially the "universal" kind)?
    Nor do I think my problem has been, as Val says, a
"wasteful extravagance of emotions." To the extent that
sometimes I must force or exaggerate or simply "ride
with" emotions, I suppose I'm guilty of "extravagance."
And if this is so, again, I'm glad of it. I don't

252

believe it's been "wasteful" at all, unless life itself
is wasteful. In fact I'd say it's made for some of the
best moments -- days and weeks, months and even years --
of my life. (And regardless of all that, I do admire
the phrase "wasteful extravagance of emotions" and I
commend the little scamp VMB for coming up with it.)

Finally, yes, no doubt it's patronizing, just as
Val says, for me to say I'm giving people "rare
experiences." But regardless, again, I still believe
I'm doing just that at least once in a while. Others
I've loved have told me I've done so; does that count
for anything? And I've told them they've done the same
for me; does that count? In any event it's absolutely
true for me and I believe for them as well: we'd swear
to the beauty and "rarity" of those experiences all the
way to the grave. And if you can't have this kind of
experience in your life once in a while, really now, why
live at all? (Or maybe it's better to bestow one's
sexual favors as an "act of charity"? -- And I suppose
it's not patronizing or condescending for Val to have
done that?)

And then this from her letter:
        What's so pathetic and frightening
    about you? Your attraction to an
    imperturbable sensualist's style of living
    -- hedonistic intensity freak. Verlaine,
    Baudelaire -- why do people think it is
    art, the only true art? Ugliness combined
    with talent. It's ugly, ugly, poignant,
    fascinating, but ugly, ugly.

Whew. The mad pursuit of pleasure. That's me,
folks! An anti-Savonarola (Machiavelli?) of the senses!

Ugliness, I've just gotta say, is at least
sometimes in the eye of the -- yeah. Or actually I
think much of what Val calls "ugliness" here stems
largely from my simple desire to live as well as I can
without hurting people if it can be avoided -- and from
the attendant bobbing and weaving -- not from any kind
of "hedonism." What hedonist would spend even a moment
in Garnett? Or for that matter, with Valerie herself?

253

What, does she think I enjoy getting morally beat up
like this every few days?

That I have a pleasure-loving "sensualist" streak
is undeniable. That I yield to such a streak more than
some people might do is at least a strong possibility.
And so it is that, yes, I likely suffer more guilt
related to such matters than most people do, since this
yielding does sometimes lead to pain for others (and
myself). Still, pleasure-seeking in and of itself, in
my view, is not "ugly." Or if it is, nature and life
themselves are ugly. And if that's how Val sees things
(and I can't believe it really is), then she needs to do
some serious tinkering on herself at the soul level. Or
just call it growing up and learning to view her own
inevitably conflicted nature with greater equanimity.
And if she'd learn to see life around her as a whole
more expansively while she's at it, so much the better.

I do want to note I'm honored even to be mentioned
in the same breath as such luminaries as Verlaine and
Baudelaire. I just wish she'd thrown in Rimbaud.

"Oh my Valoshka, we both have so much more than
just words to play with."

(To be continued.)

Saturday 30
        The whole thing is to keep working and
    pretty soon they'll think you're good.
                    -- Bogie
        Yeah, but maybe not in an ethical sense.
                    -- Glennario
        Saturday evening at the office. I lean back
against the heater as Val scribbles furiously and Al
types diligently. Barb's hand-me-down Crest radio is
belting out the great oldie "Have Mercy," referring to a
quality we could certainly use a bit more of around here
right now. Meanwhile drafts of cold wet air are
coursing through the room like the tricky currents
currently carrying spilled oil to the farthest reaches
of S.F. Bay and beyond. In a few minutes we'll be

closing up shop and Val and I will be going to a movie
-- a double feature. Whoopee!

Last night I was with Holly cheering for Garnett
High when Val materialized unexpectedly on the rubber
mat in front of the bleachers, almost as if she were
about to lead a cheer herself (she'd be the one they
toss in the air to do an effortless full flip before
sticking the landing with triumphantly outstretched arms
-- and the crowd goes crazy!). Moments later, after
she joined us in the stands, our first squabble broke
out when I couldn't hear her Frenchified muttering over
the screams of three thousand kids and other fans and
asked her to wait to talk about our problems until after
the game. (It was all strangely disconcerting, this
return to the scene of one of my primary youthful
focuses, the high-school gym during a basketball game:
and how minor and insignificant and poignantly comical
high-school sports seem now! -- Though I'll admit, yes,
I got caught up in the Garnett-Merimont game to the
point my palms were sweating.)

Then later in bed, after sex, a long, exhausting,
exasperating talk about -- sex. What else?

In short, I begged her to quit straining to be
someone she's not. Rather she should do what she
enjoys, i.e., gets off on (hopefully). Then at least we
can feel we're giving each other something. Her
gratification is a key element for my own -- of course!
-- and as I see things (as she well knows and has from
the start) at least some degree of sexual fulfillment in
turn is a basic requirement for a committed, sexually
faithful ("monogamous") relationship. Right now our
degree of sexual fulfillment, though, while it's
probably not lower than that of many other couples, is
still nowhere near as high as it could and should be.

I'm bad, she says, fuming and thrashing; I'm evil
for telling it to her so straight. She who harasses me
constantly to reveal to her exactly what I think and to
stop being "openness phobic" -- she has the gumption to
say this.

Who's truly evil here I don't know, and I'm not so

255

sure it's really worth trying to pin this down, but in
any event I do feel closer to Val today. I still
believe it's possible and even likely her sensuality
will keep developing along with her many other talents
and traits. But as this is happening can I be patient
and caring enough? She's still only nineteen years old
and has a lot to overcome -- not even counting the
effects of her horrific early marriage -- and that's
just how it is. And she knows it. Usually she's the
one who makes this point to me.

So am I saying I truly believe we may yet become
glorious fuckers? Yes I am. And I told her so too.
And she told me I was damn right about that. (Finally I
hit on something she could agree with! Agree with, that
is, as tears rolled down her cheeks and splashed on our
tightly conjoined hands writhing in her avowedly
lubricious lap. -- And just moments after that she
reminded me yet again that for gymnastics, back in
Orleans as well as in Holton, she would stay in the gym
twice as long as anyone else, practicing her routines
until she got them down cold; and now, she vowed, she
would be just as dedicated about fucking.)

*

(And she's just shown me a torrid letter she's
written to my sister. How is it she, Val, develops such
strong feelings of love and attachment for women? I do
believe it's at least partly a sensual thing for her --
something she really does enjoy, though as far as I know
she hasn't indulged in the actual physical aspects of it
just yet. It's almost as if the combination of safety
(no men around to fuck her over) and danger (erotic love
between women is unconventional and risky and thus also
super-exciting) frees up her deepest feelings in a way
ordinary man/woman romance doesn't. This letter to Barb
basically amounts to a love letter, at least as I read
it.) (Val talks about my "emotional extravagance," but
I'd say in most respects, maybe even all respects, hers
dwarfs mine. Basically she thinks I'm excessive in this
regard -- which no doubt I am, at least for a man --
because previously she'd assumed men have no emotions at

all or at best are oblivious about the ones they do
have, not to mention anyone else's.)

*   *

    Later. Much later. Val's gone off to bed in my
room next door while I try to get done a few of the
things impossible to do around here during the day
because of the general hubbub and hullabaloo. She's not
at all happy with my staying up, but the only sign of
protest she allowed herself this time was a slight pouty
frown when I tucked her in.

    She's being good because the films we saw tonight
-- both mediocre and both about very straight playboy
types, I'd say, and one of those dealing with a nasty
job of retribution performed by three women who discover
they're all sleeping with the same man -- that is, the
playboy, of course. These films seem to have had the
utterly unexpected effect of chastening her a bit. She
now believes she's been "unintentionally persecuting" me
-- like one of the three women in the film -- and so
she's holding off on further criticism, at least for the
moment. She even made an effort to imitate -- or outdo
-- the seductiveness of the most seductive of the three
women. But her femme-fatale guile was so transparent
and self-conscious and overdone and untrue to herself --
in a word, fake -- that I couldn't possibly respond to
it. I tried not to make my uninterest apparent, but
rather deployed in the gentlest way possible the need to
get some work done (which to be sure is always available
as a handy excuse these days in the office of the Merino
Mercury).

Sunday 31
    Something big may've happened today. Maybe I fell
in love with Valerie. Maybe I -- or she -- or both of
us working in unlikely tandem -- broke through my apathy
and numbness.

    Actually I think it began last night. When I
finally got to bed at six a.m. I lay next to her,
staring at the ceiling, feeling we'd reached the end of

the line. Her uptightness, her glooms, her attacks, her
bizarre fits of propriety, her outright nastiness and
hostility were simply too much to take. Yet I'd also
been struck by rereading a sentence she wrote long ago:
"Your emotions [meaning mine] are deepest and purest but
restricted to their center -- they must evolve into a
universal revolution of the soul."

It was that word "revolution" -- the same one,
admittedly, used in shameless bad faith by Richard Nixon
to describe his new budget and also by half the
commercials on TV and radio these days -- without a
doubt the most misused and overused word of the age --
and suddenly I couldn't get it out of my head. If my
soul were to undergo a revolution, the thought went,
then Val ought to be part of it. And I turned on my
side and stared at her. In the faint post-dawn light I
soon found myself cradling her extraordinary face in my
hands, touching it here and there with unexpected
tenderness, gazing at it for what must've been many
minutes, seeing her exceptional "exotic" beauty as if
for the first time. Seeing it, too, I have to say, as
if from a great distance, across absolute space, feeling
all but totally separated from her, and yet also
marveling that in all this the possibility of some sort
of miraculous rebirth was unmistakable. (Like, say --
I'm now thinking back on the scene some sixteen hours
later -- like the psychological ploy by which marriage
partners are encouraged to scream their grievances at
each other, finding that at just the moment they reach
perfect hatred, it transforms magically into ecstatic
love.)

Val, however, when she awoke and her truly gorgeous
eyes opened and came into focus as I gazed into them
from inches away, failed to sense any of this. She
didn't respond right, somehow, even though she seemed to
groove on the tenderness of the moment. And then later
this morning she started in on the moral crusade again,
and we soon recommenced screaming at each other, and
before much longer we'd reached the brink yet another
time. Just like that. Her taunts eventually led me to

tell her it was over for us; I felt totally undermined,
immobilized, shunted aside, unable to feel anything at
all for her.

Her response shocked me. Tears, wailing, rage --
I'd seen this from her before -- and then more of same
but now with a depth and intensity which was new and
truly merited that word "shock," a piercing, terrifying
agony as she paced back and forth in my room, faster and
faster, all but literally bouncing off the walls, with
my tinny portable radio turned up full blast as sturm-
und-drang accompaniment. A sudden trance of trauma
followed -- she flash-froze into a statue of silent "the
Scream" rage in the middle of the floor -- and then she
darted into the kitchen and when she came out she was
racing toward me and wildly brandishing a paring knife.

It was the return of the Valkyrie, this time with
her sword. And I wasn't about to go where the Valkyrie
wanted to take me. (That would be Valhalla, right?)

So then I had to manhandle her. When she wouldn't
put down the knife or hand it over, I forced her to give
it up -- no matter how strong she is (and I never
realized before just how strong she is), it's still a
definite advantage that I'm roughly twice her weight and
have a much longer reach. And then we talked. I mean
we talked as we've never talked before. It was almost
time for her to catch the bus back to the city but she
refused to leave, and somehow we inched our way back
from the edge, agreeing to try to make a fresh start,
being cautious about this at first but soon, as we
chowed down at Mr. Steak and looked through notes she'd
scrawled while reading my old journals and talked about
writing and art and politics and love, becoming more and
more excited and exhilarated -- I mean truly excited and
exhilarated. So much so that it's already hard to get a
handle on exactly how it happened. (But what meant the
most to me? The simple fact that she'd cared enough to
read all those words of mine and to respond to them so
passionately -- even if negatively for the most part.
Although she did groove on the writing itself at times,
she said, and that's something I've not often heard from

her about any of my other writing she's seen. Up until now it had seemed she was incapable of separating the moral from the aesthetic -- or better to say, incapable of seeing that the beliefs and values of another person, no matter how different from and conflicting with her own, could still be well expressed and have an integrity and underlying ethical quality and purpose all their own.)

Not that our problems are licked. But I feel a new interest in looking into them and a new strength for grappling with them. The inner revolution resumes, perhaps, after a period of consolidation and ordeal in remote hill country. This tragic view that Valerie adopts, this fundamentally negative and destructive, including self-destructive, stance she so often takes -- can she grow out of it? Is she always to be the sad-eyed lady most of the time and the avenging Valkyrie (I'm not forgetting this was her father's sobriquet for her) at the worst possible times? And me -- can I break out of my pattern of failed love and consequent, as she sees it, "debaucherie"?

Big questions. And it's good to feel a new burst of optimism about the answers. But I also know I'm not yet done with Jang and Briana: the period they represent is ending, almost certainly, but isn't entirely over just yet. And until life with Val yields greater fulfillment of all kinds for both of us on a sustainable basis -- and equally important, some kind of comfort zone or shelter from our own self-created storms as well as from those raging outside -- I'll still be keeping an eye out for someone new, someone I can both love and live with.

And that's how it is. If you're reading this, Valoshka, are you reading it clearly? Do you see why things are shaking out as they are? You've just attacked me with a knife and you were serious about it. Are you willing to do what it will take to enable us to bridge -- in at least this one way now more screaming than ever -- to bridge the abyss that separates us?

[The War in Merino]

1

Monday 1

> All [our great American novels] are in
> some sense westerns -- accounts of an idyllic
> encounter between white man and nonwhite in
> some variety of wilderness setting.
> -- Leslie Fiedler

This is Mr. T's Coffee Shop on a dark and shivery
night. The Merino Valley Bank's time/temp flasher said
thirty-one degrees as I passed through the center of
town a few minutes ago: about as cold as it ever gets in
these parts. The shop's empty except for a grizzled old
ex-merchant-marine guy spinning dubious yarns for a
slick-haired young counterman (a razor cut and he's
blowing big pink bubbles!). The L.C. bucked and
juddered all the way over here. My U.S.A. shirt is too
thin for this weather and it stinks anyway (scattering
fans at the basketball game the other night -- or maybe
that was just my imagination).

And, surprise, I like this place. It's got an
elusive kind of funk, I do believe -- as the old dude
staggers out the door, causing waves of Arctic air to
crash around the room -- yeah, I'll go over and feed the
box a quarter. The selection's bound to be good because
the Socorro High kids hang out here in the afternoons
(Socorro being mostly minority and low income, Garnett
High mostly white and high income). -- And sniff that
Charburger! And dig those crispy brown fries looking
even better than the ones in the glossy menu pictures!
(who shoots those things anyway? Does every restaurant
in the country order its pix from the same catalog?)

(A chalet, that's what this place looks like.
Couldn't think of the word until now.)

261

[Have Mercy]

*

(The grub was just all right but the jukebox more
than compensates. In the wake of James Brown with
"Lickin' Stick" come now Otis and Carla with "Tramp"!)
(I sprang for four bits' worth.)
     So today, let's see, I again wrote no articles,
enjoyed maneuvering through the thousand and one small
office incidents, laid out and pasted up a page, ate
faintly green chicken at Al's, was boggled along with
everyone else when black militant Kit Gilliam's fiance
turned out to be meek and white (closer to the
counterman's bubble-gum pink actually), talked on the
phone for an hour with yet another in the seemingly
endless ranks of dissident librarians, and all along
thirsted for some loving. It could've been Valerie --
for the first time in a while lascivious images of her
were teasing me, almost as in the early days -- but it
also could've been hip stud Chris's luscious and sensual
ol' lady who's about seventeen (jutting a pointy breast
up real close as she leaned against the layout table to
watch the editor do his thing), it could've been plain,
sweet Connie (still at work on her revisions in bed in a
low-cut nightgown when the editor arrived at eight p.m.
to pick them up), it could've been the "sure lay" Chris
kindly offered to fix the editor up with (the editor
virtuously declined), it could've been Audrey who works
at a downtown dress shop (she and the editor rapped a
bit at Thompson's but then she had to get back to work),
it could've been Holly who's even younger than Chris's
O.L. -- just sixteen -- but precocious and smart and
flirtatious and easy to banter with and without whose
help the editor's job would be a whole lot harder (but
she and he agreed any hanky-panky between them could be
catastrophic because of her jailbait status and then
moments later she cracked lewd about her own pubic
hair): but now it appears it will have to be (and not
for the first time) a denizen of a spread in Al's
massive stack of Penthouses and Playboys. Oh the
ignominy, oh the hominy, oh the grits, oh the slits and
the clits and the mmm-it's-tight-like-that fits....

262

[The War in Merino]

*   *

(Later)
Valerie continues in her bombastic and moralistic
and yet no doubt lovingly intended letter:
> Impulses are not all good, Glenn. Some
> of them are even evil, destructive, even
> fatal. 'If there's feeling into it, then
> it's got to be good' -- only in the
> philosophy of the nihilist, in the self-
> justifications of a scrupulous, selfish
> coward.

What nonsense, Val. I'm no hedonist and neither am
I a nihilist. I'm no more impulsive than anyone else.
Nor do I think I avoid facing the truth about myself --
don't suppress it more than anyone else does theirs and
maybe less than at least a few. Nor do I think I'm
selfish in any way that goes beyond the standard
American brand (a/k/a "independence" and "autonomy") and
I sure as hell hope I'm not a coward. I ask you to
consider carefully: would I be choosing to wrangle with
the likes of you if I were? (I do wonder about that
"scrupulous," though. Did she mean to put an "un"
before it? Or is she saying I'm scrupulous about coming
up with philosophical rationalizations -- false ones, of
course, in her eyes -- for my bad behavior? If so, what
an odd thought that is!)
> You are getting older, Glenn...your
> blase' spirit reflects upon your suave
> little charms which (you must be aware)
> will become less and less effective.

What, compromise my principles out of fear of
aging? Sorry but it's not gonna happen. And just so
you'll know, Val, I intend to age gracefully, mature
like good wine, never lose my high goals even as my
drive and energy start to dwindle. I'll keep fighting
and keep producing and stay as healthy as I can. It's
true, however, that for better or worse I won't even
begin to think about how to accomplish any of these
virtuous tasks until I hit thirty. And as for the
"suave little charms," if they really do exist and they

263

gutter out before that dreaded day, well, I guess I'll
just have to face up to the consequences.

> I sometimes feel you're growing numb
> and corrupted by your knowledge, your
> wisdom, and your wickedness. The man who
> was too wise, who knew too much....

Yeah, I've noticed some numbness and some
corruption, true, but I've never even thought of
attributing it to knowledge or wisdom. "Wickedness,"
certainly. That is, wickedness as you define it, Val.
Personally I think of the qualities and traits you're
referring to as being the outgrowth of a long run of
very good mojo interspersed with occasional bouts of
very bad mojo (e.g., Karen Avalon's death in the
motorcycle accident you've probably read about by now in
the chronbooks).

> Your inner weariness prognosticates
> our relationship -- self-denying, fear-
> fulfilling prophesies -- break away from
> her! Break away! How long will you go on
> fooling yourself, Glenn? How many times
> have you written, 'I have met the woman of
> my life'? How long will you flee from the
> truth, from woman to woman, exploiting
> them, marking them, using them as a source
> of approval: Glenn! You know how to feel
> intensely, deeply, but you do not know how
> to give yourself!

It doesn't ring true, sorry, any of it -- either in
this passage or the letter as a whole -- except maybe
the parts about my getting older (which to be sure is
hard to dispute) and my not knowing how to give myself.
As before, I pause at that last one especially. Do I
actually give myself? I believe I do, but surely I can
give more. The question is, does anyone really want
whatever the "more" is that I may have to give? Does
Val? I've seen no sign of it. Or no, I've seen one.
She's read all those journals and chronbooks and other
writings and thought seriously about them. But then
Jang did the same. And much like Jang's, Val's

interpretation of them seems about as far off the mark
as it could possibly be. How much of Val's misreading
is cultural is an interesting question -- just as it was
with Jang's -- but ultimately irrelevant. Two people
understand each other sufficiently or they don't.

     And yet: Val really cares and she really tries and
she's smart and beautiful and sexy and multitalented
and -- not least! -- she's capable of change. I've seen
her go through plenty of changes in just the seven
months I've known her, with the process happily seeming
to quicken and intensify recently as she delves ever
more deeply into her own psychological underpinnings.
However, I believe she needs to stop rationalizing her
moral failures (by her own standards) and projecting
them onto me -- as in many of these comments in her
letter -- and should instead get to work on the loving.
If, that is, that's what she really wants ultimately and
not just some bland form of security dressed up for show
as high romance.

*

     Or the key question may be (this an afterthought
going down in the L.C.): Is she willing and able to be
"fully open" in a way which really matters to me? That
is, not necessarily the "let it all hang out" way but in
terms of open-mindedness, i.e., the opposite of closed-
mindedness? Open, that is, to modification of her own
uptight views about "wickedness," "evil," "ugliness,"
etc., as shown so unequivocally in her letter? My
biggest fear being she'll revert to -- bunker down in --
that rigid French Catholic boarding-school morality
which often seems to rule at her core. It could be
she's faced so much trauma in her life that traditional
moral certainties imposed from outside and above
Catholic-style will always hold great appeal for her.
In which case I don't see how she can continue to hold
great appeal for me, or I for her.

Tuesday 2
     Still shaky from my latest run-in with the cops.

[Have Mercy]

This time I drew their suspicion by "being in an area
where a burglary's been committed." Actually I was
dropping off Claire near her house after an orgy of the
senses -- ours -- in which I found I enjoyed the
touching even more than the balling. And oddly enough
the cops seemed to be on the up and up. They just took
my name and let me go. Neither of the two officers gave
any sign of having heard of the Merino Mercury.

A lovely special-delivery letter from Valerie
today. I do still feel somewhat hopeful about us, it
seems, although then again less so after tonight's call.
It disturbed me that this latter contact quickly felt
like an intrusion because of her undertone of hostility
and suspiciousness. I'd like to give myself to her --
that is, commit myself to some sort of future with her,
however provisional -- but it seems I can't. Why? What
holds me back? Or, the corollary, what keeps me trying
to hold on to her? It's all beyond comprehension.

So then should I make an effort to comprehend it
anyway? I observe that even in commenting on her long
letter about my journal, I focus mainly on myself, my
personal problems, my own well-being, not hers. Since
self-absorption is one of the major flaws she finds in
me, I wonder if I shouldn't just concede her point and
carry on with the status quo until one of us decides to
take off in a different direction. And that, I suspect,
will happen before much longer no matter what stance I
take toward things now.

An amateurish darting-tongue kiss from Holly this
afternoon. "Just once," she said, "so I can be sure I'm
not a weinie." And I swing her in the error (I meant
air! Freudian lingerie!) -- this bright and attractive
kid who if she were two years younger would be half my
age and if three years older would be Val's age -- and
it also seems worth noting that Val was already married
and five or six months pregnant at Holly's age now. But
no, I don't think Holly presents any real danger unless
I'm careless. Chris's Diane, now, or Tanya the poet,
due to make an appearance at the M.M. office tomorrow,
just might.

[The War in Merino]

I should mention the groundhog failed to see his
shadow today and therefore we'll have an early and very
good spring. I'm counting on it.

Saturday 6 (X:3-5)

Valerie's wailing her heart out in the other room
-- we're back at "the Castle" again -- and I,
coldhearted bastard that I am and sometimes in my own
jaded opinion have no choice but to be with her, refuse
to go in there and comfort her. Instead I sit here and
feel lousy about it. Close to two a.m. now, and she's
getting ready to go home. After three hours of nonstop
wrangling over the same tired set of "issues," I left
the room -- she was already in bed -- so I could try to
get something done, be alone, recuperate, I don't know
why. She then insisted on not "depriving" me of my own
room. Nonsense, I said, it wasn't like that at all.
Nope, she said, she'd rather go home than keep me from
using my own room to escape to. And she absolutely
refused to let me drive her to her brother's place
(that's been her home since last fall) even though it's
over a mile's hike from here on a very dark and squally
night. So go already then, Val! Be my guest! (Huh?)
                            *
And there she goes. After more hassles and more
tears. I'm so strung out, all I feel is weariness and a
thick despair and an urge to crash as soon as possible
on the bed she just abandoned. Maybe things will work
out after all with Val, but I'm now back to feeling
she's so negative, so demanding, so gloomy, so often
such an oppressive presence, so deeply bitter about men
in general and me in particular (but her father and Jim
almost as much -- or probably even more, but underneath)
that we need to be permanently away from each other.
The fourth issue of the paper came out yesterday.
Rob bused up to help, as did Barb the day before. To
Barb the whole scene up there, with the monster C-5
Galaxies roaring off to Vietnam packed with new legions
of Cong-fodder and the cop cars circling the Mercury

office like sharks, was not just Gatewood deja vu but
"like a mixture of 'Animal Farm' and '1984.'"
     -- Oops, she's still here, Val is. All this time
she was sitting outside the door on the interior stairs!
And she apologizes. "I was using weapons against you."
Leans in the living-room doorway and says: "Besides, you
knew it was all a fake." Really? No kidding? I knew?
I manage a weak smile to reflect (or should that be
deflect?) her own. She asks rhetorically, heading back
into the bedroom: "You didn't think you were going to
get rid of me that easily, did you?" Proving her point,
I guess, I remember her saying the exact same thing when
I tried to break it off with her last July.)

Sunday 7
     Past two in the morning on an exceptionally foggy
night. I just nosed home from the Paladin Room, where I
stepped out a few times with an Air Force mama, Jackie
Stahl, flashy-eyed brunette, very funky dancer, quick-
witted, a drama-grouper (likes to play accent games) --
but no sparks flew between us. This after I'd charged
out from the city with Chopper and all nine pups in the
backseat to attend the weekly Sunday-night staff meeting
at Al's place.
     We're tightening up ship now that co-publisher Russ
Danner has finally quit the paper ("for financial
reasons"). Cutting back to sixteen pages again. From
here on out, I expect, it will be all downhill for the
Merc. I hope I can hang on until the end, but I'll have
to be getting back to the city before much longer -- by
April 1st at the very latest -- to take advantage of my
optimal period of eligibility for unemployment
compensation (which depends in large part on my much
higher pay in earlier quarters at Emp). And before I go
I'd like to see to it that an organization's in place
capable of surviving in this hostile environment -- or
at least do what I can along those lines, which probably
won't be much and in any case nowhere near enough.
     Something's missing with Valerie, that's all there

is to it. Over the past seven months I've given this
something all sorts of different names. Today I'll call
it playfulness. So solemn and mournful, Val is, and
when she's not, she's usually either hyper or caustic or
indignant or overly attentive or, quite often, simply
numbed out. She's no entertainer. Not playful at all!
Tonight talking with Jackie Stahl I had to shake the
rust out of my own wit, such as it is. It hasn't been
challenged to this extent in the man/woman light-
badinage arena in what seems like months.

Nice balling this afternoon -- much of it anal (at
Val's request yet again) -- but even that wouldn't do
it. Afterwards I still couldn't feel close to her. One
of these days I'll run into someone I really dig and
want to make a serious effort with and very suddenly it
will all be over with Val. It might even happen with
someone I've already met -- might happen next Sunday,
for example, Valentine's Day, in the extremely unlikely
event Briana abides by our "sacred vow" and shows up for
the long-awaited liaison. And in any case I've decided
I'll be doing that myself -- showing up -- if only so I
can say afterwards I was true to my word and she wasn't
and so nah nah to you Briana Tsu!

A crisis at Funston. Mrs. Hilyer, the landlady,
pops up unannounced on her way to the airport (bound for
a two-week tour of Japan) and is horrified. A pigsty,
she calls it! Only by prostrating myself before her,
groveling, immediately starting in on the cleanup before
her skeptical eyes, and also commiserating at length
about the death of her son in Vietnam, do I gain a
reprieve and another chance. But Chopper and the pups
have to go; there's no compromising on that. That's why
I've brought them up here. Chopper was never cut out
for city life anyway. And in fact we already have
several prospective Garnett and Merimont takers on the
pups. Chopper herself may be a harder sell but I'm sure
we'll find someone eventually. This is dog country up
here, no question (and I mean that in a good way!).

Squeezing the ink out of this backup Rapidograph is
too exasperating. I quit.

2

Monday 8

Back in that gritty Kerouackian poolhall, Mike's,
on Broadway in S.F. It's a slow night, Monday, the
joint nearly empty. At nine p.m. the whole of Broadway
resembles a medium-size town's main drag after midnight,
the people gone but the neon still flashing as if
someone forgot to turn off the lights. Juicy burger in
a fresh French roll, just served, tastes real good (I'm
left-handing it). In fact all day I've been transported
by intimations of euphoria, warm flashes of puzzlingly
reborn joy -- the world's terrific and life couldn't be
better! I've been working so hard the past two months,
enjoying it so much (on the whole), and it suddenly
occurred to me I've neglected to feel good about it.

Zipping, zinging, yo-yoing back and forth between
Garnett and the city....

I come to that fork in the road near the Bay
Bridge, the one which splits the traffic between San
Francisco and Oakland/points south, and each time I
recall my elation on my very first approach to that fork
three and a half years ago with Ciara riding in the
passenger seat during the ill-named (as it turned out
for us) Summer of Love. But -- in any case -- why in
the world would anyone want to go to Oakland/points
south, then or anytime, when simply by bearing right you
could be crossing into that mecca of hope and beauty and
energy and magic, San Francisco!

Sounds hokey and rah-rah I know but I still see
things this way and this is how I am, amen.

Briana's coming back into these pages. I just
remembered she's the perfect representation of this city
for me, its very embodiment: grace, intelligence,
"exotic" beauty, sensuality, artistic sensibility,
optimism, innocence -- yoked with, alas, a strong
undercurrent of quirky moral puritanism, a tainted
sophistication, a vague and shifting center -- not to

mention a deep attachment to another man. Anyway, while
I slipped off to the men's room a moment ago, a rolled
copy of the Mercury marked my place in the journal.
It's stamped and addressed to Briana Tsu. "Feb. 14th?"
queries a line written in bright red marker in the white
space above the M.M. flag. Designed to jolt her memory
in hopes she'll keep the rendezvous Sunday. Hatching
schemes again!

*

    -- Now I've scribbled two more lines with the same
red marker: "Love & Peace, Editor Sandefjord," with the
"Editor" lightly lined out and "Arch-Fiend" written in
above. If she doesn't show up Sunday -- and, though I
still nurse a faint hope, I certainly doubt she will
(the true embodiment of San Francisco, more a romantic
adventurist and/or fatalist than a vindictive skeptic,
surely would) -- if, as I say, she doesn't show up, I'll
be reviewing the letters and journals (well, mine
anyway) of our months together as I wait for her and
I'll write her a new farewell letter on the spot --
updated, yes, and perhaps this time truly a bit calmer
and more philosophical -- as indeed I tried to be with
that last rewrite but almost certainly failed.
    (Though I didn't notice it until long after she
left, Valerie taped a small note on my wall at Klug's:
"Briana's Magical Corner / why not admit it / he loved
her...once." Below, gathered in a neat display put
together by Val herself, were the small Christmas gifts
Briana brought out for me during her disastrous last
visit to Garnett: the marbles spelling out "I love
Glen!!," the ad mat, the splintered bowling pin and so
on. Val had found them in the kitchen cabinet where I
stashed them to keep them out of my sight. -- I had
vowed to throw them away, yes, but could never quite
manage to do that.)
    Today, by the way, a romance seems to have ended.
Claire, who's been flashing reproachful looks at me for
days, accosted me in the office. She suspected I was
getting it on with Holly. Not true, I insisted
(truthfully). But for reasons of her own Claire wanted

to close down the sexual part of our relationship.
After overcoming my initial reaction of hurt pride
("what, I'm so easily dispensable to you?!"), I agreed
it would be for the best. My own disenchantment with
Claire had grown to the point I found talking with her
awkward and sometimes painful. The drug part all by
itself was, and is, almost more than I can bear.

Another good effect: Claire's warning redoubled my
determination not to cave in to Holly's high-spirited
come-ons. "Do you know how easily a seventeen-year-old
girl can be hurt?" Claire crossly upbraided me
(undermining her own case a bit by aging Holly almost a
full year).

Earlier, one of the proudest moments of my life.
At the college I passed out, personally, some twelve
hundred copies of the Merc (shrugging off the occasional
contemptuous rejection) and then looked on with greedy
pleasure in the cafeteria as hundreds of students read
the paper before my eyes. This is a reward which I
would think few writers ever experience -- observing
their readers, large numbers of them in a single
setting, as they dig into the writer's own work which
is, what's more, speaking directly to them about matters
relating to their own lives (for this issue I wrote
several big chunks of a long piece about the financial
chicanery and ecological outrages perpetrated in siting
the college where it now stands). And what was going
through the minds of the several dozen black students
as, for the first time in Merino County history (to my
knowledge anyway), they read in a local publication an
editorial blast against the nasty and often violent
discrimination they and their families have always faced
there?

While driving back to the city I flashed on this:
as a writer what I'm most interested in is not truth per
se (to the extent it can even be expressed in words) but
rather the revelation of new facts, evidence, beliefs,
ideas, plans. Radical political truths, for example,
seem old hat now. I no longer get the kick I once did
from reading, say, Ramparts. No doubt the great truths

or putative great truths are still just as great but,
alas, like anything that's repeated over and over
they're tiresome. what's fascinating to me right now is
the realm of emerging "news" that's revelatory of
changing times, whether for society as a whole or a
smaller community or even just in the swirling emotional
universe of an individual or a couple's (family's) life.

*

An unexpected letter from Susan Bergman, the very
first girl with whom I had an honest-to-god down-home
American suburban nighttime date (Dad drove us to some
sort of church youth-group meeting -- this was shortly
before I quit all that church stuff for good -- and Sue,
of course, though I hadn't yet realized this, and
wouldn't have known what to make of it if I had, was
Jewish). We were both barely fourteen years old. Now
she's married to her old college boyfriend Harvey, has
three kids, is into "love & peace" (just like me!),
lives in Phoenix. For old time's sake I'll write back.

Tuesday 9
A day of sex, fury, and frustration. The sex,
unfortunately, was all on paper at the Broadway
newsstand (such a torrent of jizz spurting from a long
slender white cock planted between beautiful dark-
nippled breasts that might almost have been Valerie's
and into such a ravishing full-lipped Mayan-looking face
also a lot like hers except for the big astonished
seemingly genuine blissed-out smile) -- the sex was all
on paper but also in my mind, which in turn was
basically hanging heavy between my legs as I gaped --
Valerie, why, why, why can't you get into it with a
little funk and fun like this lady here? ...But it
ain't hardly likely, no. And this lady here, I must
reluctantly concede, is probably just very good at
faking it. I hope she was at least paid well.
Before that, almost three hours standing in line to
fork over sixty bucks to gain society's permission to
drive the L.C. for another year. It was hard not to

think about those lurid stories running in the Examiner
lately excoriating Cuba for its "ration economy" (gee,
and does our de facto twelve-year blockade of that
stalwart little island have anything to do with the sad
state of the Cuban economy?).

Yes, this time when I come back to the city to do
some of my own writing of the "autobiographical fiction"
variety I'll actually be doing it. And there are so
many books, magazines, literary and political
quarterlies I'm itching to get into....

Today Barb moved back in at Funston (taking the
living room this time). I came home to find my big
"billboard" collage in that room dismantled and
everything else in there moved around or otherwise
changed. At first I was annoyed -- too much change in
my life! She could at least have asked! -- But what
the hell, if change is what life's all about, what
better place for it than my own living room?

"You look very sexy tonight," I say to Valoshka.
"You always look super-sexy when you're excited."

It's starting school she's excited about. I drove
her there after dinner, still unhappy with her for
hassling me again (can't I be allowed a single day of
freedom to try to put myself back together?), and then
fretted away an hour in the automat at the student
union. All those heads turning when she came gymnast-
strutting back across the main room after class -- or...
better to say she looked like a petite miniskirted
springy-stepped possibly transsexual Eurasian acrobat or
perhaps wrestler of extreme gorgeousness being pulled
forward at high speed by a cord attached to her forward-
thrust chin -- call it Valkyrie doing some warm-ups --
but anyway, the point, all those hungry eyes checking
her out. I could feel a new jealousy creeping up from
my murky, not to say Mercky, deep. I don't doubt whole
roomfuls of mad artists and poets and politicos will
soon be chasing after her -- even quite possibly some of
the same ones Briana hangs out with (most of whom either
came out of State, as did Briana herself, or have never
gotten out of State, either as students or as

274

instructors or in some cases simply as superannuating
hangers-on).

Says Val now, popping her head in the door of the
"yellow room" (we're back at 1616): "You can really see
it from the deck!" The eclipse, she's talking about:
the one I've neglected to mention so far even though it
started more than an hour ago. "You can write later!
Quick, before the fog gets it!" (A whole San Francisco
philosophy of life right there.) (Also neglected, I
should note, this morning's earthquake in L.A.: Richter
6.6, fifty-five dead. Aftershocks continue. Are we
next?) ---

Wednesday 10
A thin line of blood across the top of my hand,
smudged slightly, hints that, as with lunch, so with
exuberance: it's never free. I'm strolling along in the
Financial District, arms swinging gleefully, and my hand
scrapes the abrasive surface of a cement planter. Ouch,
that smarts! Smited for a display of rebellious high
spirits by the street-level facade of a looming
corporate monolith!

Now I'm camped out at the Sandwich Tree, an
enormous snack shop, basically, buried on the ground
floor of yet another boxy glass-and-steel highrise on
canyon-like Kearny Street. Lots of bright colors in
here, hundreds of canvas director chairs. Once last
summer Val and I, both late for work, frittered away a
nervous but happy hour here. And right around the
corner to the south, how luscious she looked when I
caught sight of her for the very first time: handing out
antiwar leaflets in her bright blue mini -- day of the
"Human Chain to Stop the War" -- more than seven months
ago already! ("Devil In The Bright Blue Mini" is
the tune that comes to mind now.)

A glorious day like that one, today, though
abundantly smoggy: just before veering in here on
impulse I was gawking at the Bank of America's titanic
shadow cast onto the air itself, which right now appears

275

to be closer to a solid than a gas. (It recalled Mt.
Moraga up above Funston, the way its shadow as seen from
our windows occasionally imprints on a low late-
afternoon fog down in the Judah Gulch.)

Meanwhile: here sit some forty or fifty mostly
short-haired men in suits and ties. A stochastic
scattering of stolid corporate faces and eyes and pupils
seeming to reflect each other in a hall-of-mirrors
effect. They pose, I'd say, a supreme test for
Schweitzerian (e.g., Al's father's) love of all humanity
without exception. In some ways they're more daunting
to me than any onslaught of Hell's Angels or U.S.
Marines shouting "Kill! Kill!"

Now suddenly the female office workers begin to
filter in. By a cascade of wary individual choices they
create a buffer zone, a circle of empty tables around
mine. Counterculture shock! Even in San Francisco!
And I wonder: is there some new rule in the Financial
District declaring the boys must be let out for recess
ten minutes earlier than the girls? Why are they
arriving in different shifts? (This is not how it was
in the days when I myself was wearing one of these
stolid corporate faces. Or one fitted up to pass as
such anyway.) (Nor am I failing to realize that some of
these break-takers -- maybe even most -- are themselves
fitted up to disguise pretty much the same kind of views
I had back then and still do now only more so. In this
city they say it's a hardcore twenty percent or so that
would like to feed the rest of us to the crocodiles --
or to the Cong.)

I sip on carbonated apple juice packaged in
something like a miniature beer bottle. Martinelli's.
And nibble with admirable restraint at a delightfully
flaky and tasty apple turnover. But only one this time.

Barb asides to me (as we're hauling in boxes of her
possessions) that Briana has called, arranging for the
two of them to meet tomorrow. "Just because of what
happened between your brother and me doesn't mean our
friendship has to be hurt," chirps Briana. Also, "I
want you to hear my side of it." It's almost enough to

make me cancel my plans for Sunday, Valentine's Day, in
Sausalito. Such shallowness, Briana! Barb, the
omniscient sister, snickers once again at the thought of
how poorly Briana understands me. "She really does
think you're the quintessence of cool, Glennar."

Valerie, Barb insists, understands me better than
any of my other women she's known, and that includes all
the majors. A real possibility of trust exists there,
she thinks. But she also agrees something's missing --
yes, perhaps it's playfulness. And again Barb insists
Val is "extraordinary" in a hard-to-pinpoint way which
she thinks I fail to appreciate enough, just as Val
herself says. Barb fears I'll "extinguish" this unique
quality, not intentionally, of course, but by sheer
power of example, my "intense persuasion," which she
believes is gradually creating a crisis in Val as she
"attempts to become a female imitation of you."

Barb also puts her finger on what it is that makes
her detest Jang. "She's able to manipulate me at will."

As for me, Barb wonders whether I might suffer from
a "deep schizoid split" -- picking up on my joking aside
that "maybe they never liked me for the reasons I wanted
in high school; maybe junior high was the only time I
ever really had it going in that way." My "weakness"
revealed itself to her last spring, purportedly for the
first time ever, when Jang invaded Funston to pick up
various items of hers -- Denise was staying there then
along with several others and we were throwing a party
that night -- and I "hid" on the sundeck rather than
intervene. And why, I ask, should I have intervened?
It would've sparked an even worse scene than Val and I
faced with Jang on Christmas Day two months ago! But
this "weakness," Barb now believes, is further
manifested in what she asserts is my inability to make
myself "truly vulnerable" (that phrase again!) to
people, while at the same time "charming" them.
"Everyone finds you so charming, but at the same time
most come away feeling you'd be hard to know."

During her one day in Garnett Barb saw me in an
entirely new milieu, using my alleged charms supposedly

to "manipulate" people to do good, and she was at once
impressed -- "You handle people so easily" -- and
disturbed. She insists she can tell now when I say
something complimentary or encouraging or just plain
pleasant "for a reason." To her mind a comment of any
of these types should appear only spontaneously and
naturally; it should "flow out" with all other aspects
of personality, the good with the bad, or else it's
fundamentally insincere and exploitative.

Yeah, well maybe. To me all this sounds just a
tad, shall we say, over-idealistic. If real people
acted the way Barb seems to think we all should, would
anything ever get done in the world? To her if you make
nice to anyone for even a moment you're worse than
Willie Loman. The simple truth here is that Barb,
worldly as she is in some respects, is also one of the
most naive people ever to come tripping down the pike.
My own sister. How could it be? And I'm not the only
one who says so; everyone says so.

Another truth about Barb, even sadder in a way, is
that whenever I let my real self "flow out" with her,
she's soon gasping or gagging or turning purple with
moral indignation. The self she wants me to show is the
one she thinks I should have, and that's probably one of
the few that doesn't exist in my shameful repertoire of
thousands. In this she and Jang seem to have a lot in
common (gasp!). And also, obviously, she and Briana and
she and Valerie. (I have no doubt now Val picked up
much of her critical spiel on me from Barb --
"manipulative," "disingenuous," "falsely vulnerable,"
and many more such aspersions. Which is not to say Val
lacks negative judgments about me entirely of her own
contrivance. She was flinging them at me by the score
well before she got to know Barb.)

*   *

So it's Wednesday. I'm intentionally absenting
myself from Garnett for a few days, trying to accustom
both them and myself to the idea that Editor Sandefjord
will soon drive off into the sunset for the last time
and they'll have to produce the goddamn newspaper on

their own. On the other hand I suspect our parting
won't be half as hard for them as it'll be for me.

   But yeah, no question, I love this city, meaning
San Francisco. Barb doesn't -- to her it lacks "a
certain 'culturedness,'" that "rich mixture of tradition
and sophistication" she's been awed by in the great
European cities (she can be such a snob sometimes!).
Rob doesn't like it here all that much either, but for a
different kind of reason: to him it's too aggressive and
too polarized, the hip on one side and the straight on
the other. But Barb and Rob both agree it's perfect for
me. Simple pleasures. Flower stands on street corners.
"Exotic" beauties. Cultures colliding. Countercultures
blooming. Innocence and experience. Boundless radical
energy. Marauding fogs. Beauty glorified. Poetry in
motion.

   I'll still show up at the dock on Sunday. Doesn't
matter what Briana says or does -- that romantic
rendezvous, the very absurdity of it, always meant a
great deal to me. The moment she suggested it last
summer, right before her European trip of several
months' planned duration (or would it be longer?), I
knew I'd be at that dock on February 14 come hell or
high water. Maybe that was the moment I fell into my
"appalling infatuation" (Barb's term) with Briana.
Doesn't hardly matter. I'll be there, I'll revel in the
exquisite pain of her rejection, and then, perhaps, I'll
have freed myself of her once and for all. (Or perhaps
not -- a raucous objection from the peanut gallery.)

   Getting on toward noon now. Feels good to be able
once again to write freely and at a little more length
in these pages. A new sticker attached to the L.C. back
bumper right between the peace decal and "Get with the
Merc!" demands "LEGALIZE FREEDOM." Intriguing phrase.
"Legalize" has too many bad connotations for me (a
lawyer's son!) to endorse the slogan wholeheartedly,
even though the almost oxymoronic juxtaposition of the
two clashing words is precisely the heart of its appeal.
For me it's much more than a paradox; it expresses a
personal dilemma of the most soul-shaking perplexity.

[Have Mercy]

Thursday 11

And now once again the view from Merino Community
College. We the moguls of the media have just completed
a tour of the new campus led by the president himself,
the infamous Dr. Furman (who, before my incredulous
eyes, agreed with Mr. Big in Merino County, Burke
Orwood, former state senator, longtime owner of the
county's largest newspaper, the Sheridan Herald --
agreed that Reader's Digest has become "too radical"!).
Students smirked and signaled secretly upon seeing me, a
disheveled longhair hippie in a leather hat and a denim
"U.S.A." jacket, straggling along with this group of
officious bureaucrats and waddling high muckety-mucks,
every last one suit-and-tied. And I finally met Norm
Gaston, editor of, yes, the Daily Ghastly, an innocuous,
balding little man whom I secretly felt sorry for. He
did not look as though he's been enjoying life a great
deal lately. I went over and introduced myself when I
heard him asking a Herald photographer who I was.

"Name's Norm Gaston," he blurted.

"Been wanting to meet you," I riposted.

But then our tour group went through a complicated
set of doorways and arches, and by the time we emerged
on the other side Editor Gaston had distanced himself
from me by about fifteen paces. He seemed determined to
maintain that separation the rest of the tour. So I
enabled him on that, meaning I reciprocated.

Now I sit in the Merino C.C. cafeteria, where the
mob has thinned out considerably after the lunch-hour
rush. Hundreds of small tables, most attended by four
pastel plastic chairs, all but about twenty unoccupied.
Out the two-story floor-to-ceiling windows lining one
entire side of the room (which is long and low) the
morning fog has finally burned off, although the nearby
hills are shrouded in haze. Hundreds, maybe thousands
of cars jam the parking lot. As yet the area around the
college is virtually undeveloped -- it's lovely vineyard
and orchard country -- but the new presence of the

college itself almost guarantees this bucolic setting
will soon transmute into a farrago of subdivisions and
schlocky sprawl. Unless, that is, the Merino Mercury
can rally public opinion to preserve it as open space.
Which is indeed one of the things we're trying to do.
The Garnett business community and the Ghastly, to no
one's surprise, fail to share our view on this. If Russ
Danner the moneybags realtor hadn't quit the paper
he'd've hit the roof for sure over our editorial stance
on this issue and maybe persuaded Al to soften it.

This time around I'll have to get my act together
quickly. Already it's Thursday and I haven't even begun
working on the next issue. Spent four of the past five
days in the city, mostly just relaxing (saw two fine
movies last night, "Investigation of a Citizen Above
Suspicion" and "Wild Child"). The vibes were good with
the Wild Child in my own life -- the one in the movie is
also French, but male -- probably because Barb was there
with us to divert most of her attention. Val has a very
obvious crush on Barb, and Barb likes her too. Very
good; I hope it develops into a lasting friendship. If
it turns sexual at some point I hope Val will still save
some for me once in a while -- keep it all in the
family.

Then, arriving home at Funston last night, we found
a note in heavy black marker in Rob's hand tacked to the
wall just inside the door: "GPS & GCHS flying in
Saturday noon!" What?!? Feverish speculation: could
they be coming out together to tell us they're getting
divorced? But no, apparently it's just a business trip.
Still, how curious they should want to see us after
railing so bitterly against us -- especially with
Mother's health in such a precarious state.

-- I have to admit the crowd here at M.C.C. holds
little appeal for me. By and large it's very young,
bland, high-schoolish. But still, what better public
place does the area offer a "citizen above suspicion"
(ha!) for sitting and writing? A few freaks, a few
sassy girls, a few radical faculty members. Earlier
today I sat around with two of those dissident profs,

Bill Okrent and Gary Gagliardi (he, Gary, is the one
Al's Sherry has long had a big crush on, nearly
torpedoing her marriage at one point), devising schemes
for dousing the college computers with trash and sewage
which the college currently dumps untreated into a
nearby creek. Just talk, of course. As they said
themselves, real radical action is still years or more
likely decades away at M.C.C.

Friday 12
    The waitress here at Mr. T's says her daughter
likes the Merc. Why, the whole family likes it! "At
least it tells it like it is!"
    Two in the morning and I just split from the
Paladin Room. There I agonized through an hour or more
of "celebrating" with Al and Sherry, never even getting
close to the blond beauty sitting two tables away (the
flyboys who dominate the room move fast and hang on
hard). What we were celebrating was never clear to me
-- was it that we've gotten this far with the paper or
was it that I'll soon be leaving? (But wait a minute,
they couldn't know that yet because I haven't told them.
Then again, at the start back in October-November we
talked about my enlisting for two to three months, four
at the most, and it's now been two and a half. And
regardless, I'm pretty sure they sense something.)
    Harking back to yesterday: I tried with Marcelle
and failed, then didn't try with Irene and wound up in
bed with her. On an unseasonably warm and sunny
afternoon I took Marcelle to the top of a mossy green
hill in Pagoda Rocks Park -- the powers that be in their
wisdom want to curl a golf course around the showpiece
rocks -- and revved up some light pressure. Not enough.
A few impassioned kisses and then, equally impassioned,
when I tried to take things to the next level, "Don't,
Glen!" To apply more pressure was unthinkable, so I
retreated awkwardly into what we eventually agreed will
be a "warm friendship." It turns out Marcelle's still
obsessed with Rodney, the black high-school counselor

and married playboy supremo. She's from the same
terrific Aguilar family, a nest of Chicano activists
humming and buzzing away in the middle of a staid white
suburban neighborhood that voted almost two to one,
Marcelle told me, for Richard Nixon. Triple bunk beds
in both of the tiny bedrooms for the kids (and the whole
house plastered with Chavez posters: right on!).

Then Irene and I interviewed Leonard Urmston, a
Gestalt therapist whose application to practice in his
own home was turned down by the reactionary county Board
of Supervisors. Fine people, the Urmstons. We sat by a
crackling fire in that same home (near Artesia) and
rapped for hours, mostly about (A) Gestalt therapy as
Urmston learned it from his mentor, Fritz Perls, and (B)
Gregory Bateson's "double bind" theory (damned if you
do, damned if you don't, as in the demand, "Say you love
me!"), which I decided on the spot explains basic
human interactions about as well as any other bare-bones
theory I know of. Then Irene and I stopped at a
roadhouse on the way back and happily "kicked up our
heels" (as Mother would say, and so did Irene) until it
closed, then drove on through a thick fog to her own
mother's house in Merimont (from which moments later
Irene emerged carrying a tiny infant bundled in a huge
white blanket), and then to her place a few blocks away
where we reached the moment of truth in her living room.

"I guess the question is," said I, "whether we make
a night of it or I try to find my way back to Garnett
through this killer fog."

"Which do you want to do?" she asked.

We had to sweep aside a week's accumulation of her
four-year-old daughter's dolls and toys from the extra
bed before undressing each other in the dark. Sleeping
together was memorable mainly for the narrowness of the
bed and the resultant ungainly vastness (seeming) of our
bodies. During neither the night round nor the morning
round could we get it together very well. But holding
each other was good, and so were the bacon and eggs she
insisted on rustling up for breakfast.

Irene's story closely resembles Valerie's in some

283

crucial respects: pregnant and then married at fifteen,
divorced at nineteen, and now she's twenty and trapped,
forever deprived of that late-teen exploratory period
which seems so important in forming a balanced adult
personality. In body and looks she somewhat resembles
Ciara. In other ways she...well, what can I say? She's
very pleasant, warm and receptive, but sadly dull.
Pinned down in a life she doesn't really want.

A talk with Al about the paper. We're both
discouraged. If it's to succeed over the long haul, I
suggested, he'll have to devote more of his energies to
building a human organization rather than trying to do
so many of the daily tasks on his own while also working
a highly stressful full-time job at the hospital.
Delegating, i.e., depending on others, frightens him,
and he's candid enough to admit it. I'm the only one he
feels he can trust with the editorial functions, and
I'll soon be gone, and of course he's aware of that. (I
did let him know I'll be spending more time in the city
in the weeks ahead and bowing out by the end of March.)

Saturday 13
A fine day. I slept until noon, rapped with Evan,
Sherry, Terry (not Briana's Terry!), and my little go-
getter sidekick Holly, brewed myself a mug of hot
chocolate, lay in the long grass outside Klug's front
office and ruminated about ways and means of rejoining
my head with my body. Holly gave me a framed pubic hair
(hers) as a joke to commemorate our talk the other day.
I chirped away while the woman at the Leather Boteek
worked on a couple of last-minute alterations on the
black leather cap I'd ordered -- "captain's cap," she
calls it, though I've never seen one on anybody but a
fellow hippie.

Sally Bond and her little sister Marcy, fresh from
viewing Walt Disney's "The Aristocrats," came up to my
table here at Thompson's and joined me for a while. I
made them both Valentines with the construction paper
I'd just bought at Office Supply. I did the expected

hippie thing and convinced seven-year-old Marcy that the
marigolds and geraniums bursting from the arcade
planters had pushed up through the foundation and soon
all the buildings in town and out at the Air Force base,
even the runways there, would begin to crumble as the
blooms took over and the world would be much better that
way. (It's called Flower Power, kid.)

"You can see," I said to Sally, "I'm really not at
all the way I pretend to be. It's just this job -- it's
getting to me." And she nodded in grave agreement.

Tomorrow is Valentine's Day. My old red alarm
clock died last month (did Jang sabotage it during her
visit up here?) and so I bought a nearly identical
replacement for four dollars -- except it's copper-
plated instead of red-painted -- and went to all this
trouble just to be sure I'd be able to get up in time
to make it to Sausalito by sunrise. I've gotten real:
after mulling what Briana said to Barb during their
little tete-a-tete the other day, I no longer have any
illusions about her showing up there. This is probably
just as well because if she did I'd have no idea what to
do. Maybe nothing more than declare an official end to
our romance which in actuality ended long ago anyway.

Does Briana still see visions of me on the ceiling?
Does she still believe she'll never be able to make love
with another man? Feel like she lost her virginity at
Klug's Motor Court in Garnett, California? Ha --
dubious on all counts. But instinct tells me I could
still work a spell on her -- even though wisdom says
she'd be too proud to give in to it all the way (i.e.,
the necessary degree) no matter what the circumstances.

*　　　　*

Why was it I wanted Briana so badly? And why, if I
wanted her so badly, didn't I make a greater effort to
win her over after her return from Amsterdam in
November? To my mind these are the key questions about
the debacle with her. I have no answer for them, except
to say it's obvious I never really loved her. I
predicted I'd say this someday and now I'm saying it and
what's more I'm meaning it. It truly was a mad

infatuation whose crucial elements were her supreme
beauty and sensuality (and sensuousness too), but also,
just as important, her remoteness and closedness and
apparent unattainability (and perhaps certain
resemblances she bears to Jang).

And yet: I'm not prepared to say I couldn't love
her or that I've stopped wanting her.

Barb had a "very heavy scene" with her Thursday (it
seems to have turned Barb against me once again, just
when her opinion of me appeared to be hitting a new high
for the post-Jang era at Funston). Briana told Barb I'm
"very fucked up." Barb said Briana "appears to be hung
up" over what happened between us. Both of these
statements, now that I think about them, make me believe
it's slightly possible after all that Briana will show
up in Sausalito tomorrow. As for Barb's uptight
rectitudinous interpretation of things, well, all I can
say is I'm back to feeling sorry for her -- now that the
smoke she had curling from my ears has finally drifted
away. Or most of it anyway.

Sunday 14
> Where Alph, the sacred river, ran
> Through caverns measureless to man
> > Down to Briana Tsu.
> > > -- Update on "Khubla Khan"

How I long to see that old yellow Citroen nosing up
through the fog! I'm parked in the L.C. within a few
yards of the spot where we vowed to meet, Briana and I,
on this Valentine's Day 1971. The rotting pier on which
we first sat together, shoulders electrically grazing,
on a sunny Saturday afternoon some six months ago --
that pier, of course, was demolished many months back.
The first time I returned here because of my ache for
her, in mid September, shortly after she'd left for
Amsterdam with Terry, even then our symbol of reunion
had already disappeared.

It's fitting, I suppose, that now the oily waters
which lapped around the pilings are also gone, replaced

by ugly mounds of landfill. I clambered across them a
few minutes ago, ultimately reaching the point where I
estimated the pier must've stood. The air was cold,
damp, and utterly still. The only sounds came from an
occasional gull flapping through the fog, banking,
quickly fading into the thick gray backdrop as in a film
dissolve, and from a sailboat rubbing against its pier
across the way, raising an occasional ghostly moan.

Because of the fog the scene out there was utterly
timeless. It was like something out of Robbe-Grillet.
I didn't even know whether it was sunrise yet -- the
time we were supposed to meet. For that matter I don't
know if it is now. Already, though, a stoical
bemusement is stealing over me. Each time I look up and
fail to spot her -- maybe once every twenty or thirty
seconds -- I shudder a little more at the absurdity of
it all.

When the alarm sounded at four-twenty, after I'd
slept for only two hours, I awoke with a glowing cock
that tightened to aching iron hardness as for a few
delicious moments I drove all coherent thought from my
mind and immersed myself in erotic images of Briana just
as I used to do for hours on end every single day last
fall. Then, unwilling to waste any vital juices just on
the ultra-slim chance she would show up at the dock, I
hopped out of bed, feeling fully awake the instant my
bare feet hit the very cold floor. Soon I was plunging
down an empty freeway headed for Sausalito, gripped at
times by the eerie illusion that the L.C. was standing
still and the road itself was moving (all I could see
was fog and a few lane-separation dashes zinging at me
like machine-gun tracers). Somewhere near San Quentin I
nearly plowed into an embankment at the side of the
road. It was as if my own unconscious were shouting,
"Someone lock this boy up before he does something truly
demented!"

A couple of early risers, both elderly men, have
materialized out of the gray and are now greeting each
other a few feet from my driver's-side window.

"Hi, Sid. Can you pick your way through it all

287

right?"

"How do I get to London, that's what I want to
know."

Either one of those guys might be me on a
Valentine's Day maybe forty or fifty years from now,
right here.

Come on, Briana!

But of course she won't be showing up. Already
I've lost what little hope I had somehow -- through
utterly irrational dream power, I suppose -- temporarily
regained.

We pledged to meet here "no matter what happens."
It's sad to realize that what did happen was so
injurious to Briana, so outrageous -- neither of which I
believe for one second -- or, much more likely, so
meaningless it could allow her to break that vow.

As for me, I'm now declaring the Briana ordeal to
be at an end, or at least the current phase of it. A
heavy drowsiness is washing over me -- so heavy it's
almost a taste of death. I'll let myself dissolve into
it for a while....

3

Monday 15

It was -- he writes from a lazy perspective, lying
on the Funston sundeck -- one of the longest days....

By the time I delivered the letter to Briana's
place -- her two cars parked outside, one with the
stereo in it, suggesting Terry's presence upstairs -- it
was close to one o'clock, so I hurried straight to the
Fairmont atop Nob Hill downtown, finding Mother and Aunt
Polly in the Crown Room, top floor, splendid view, just
a few feet from the spot where three years ago I saw
tears roll down Dad's cheeks as he talked Sandefjord
family history. (No compulsion urged me to race up the
stairs to see Briana. The letter said I still ache for
her; it said if you're going to read someone's private
journal without permission, you owe it to that person to

288

read it with a generous spirit; it said who knows, I'm
such a fool for love I might show up at the dock in
Sausalito again next year and for as many years
thereafter as it takes.)

-- And now Valoshka pops out. Swings back the
glass sundeck door and -- voila! It's as if she's
stepping off a movie screen, so great is the shock of
her sudden presence in the flesh. ...Through the
monocular I watched her stripping off her purple shirt
well up the slope of Mt. Moraga a little earlier, then
stretching languorously in a white T and jeans in the
sun in a big meadow of knee-deep wildflowers, then
warding off some dude who came panting over from the
access road no doubt in an attempt to hit on her. She'd
thoughtfully gone off for a while so Mother and I could
talk privately; but now I signaled the coast was clear
again and she came trotting down the hillside,
cavorting, the small brown dog Rob dubbed Little Dog and
I call Brown Dog racing circles around her, a lively and
lovely sight.

"Every time you look at me when I'm walking," she
tells me now, "I think, 'Gohn be funky.'"

She handled Mother and Dad with admirable poise and
aplomb, I thought, first in the hotel room and then at
dinner at Tivoli in North Beach. She spoke slowly and
for the most part decipherably -- rolled out her "Gigi
act," as she likes to say (but hates to do) -- and soon
had Dad babbling happily about "gay Paree" and "glum
Norway" and "even glummer Turtle Rapids" and being "just
a country boy" (groan). In talking about all this later
she was perceptive about our family dynamics, noticing
the "tension just below the surface" in our constant
teasing and joshing, and hypothesizing that the source
of my "need" for playfulness and drama in a lover lies
in Mother's histrionic character.

She looks very good, ol' Maw does -- no visible
sign of her traumatic sleepless months. Dad, as again
Val pointed out, was restraining himself most
commendably considering all the provocations from his
"Left Coast" offspring -- he was even sporting

289

daring new sideburns and an "I'm available" button.
Today he's in L.A. for the key presentation which will
likely decide the immediate future of pay-TV.

When they, the parental unit, arrive back home in
Gatewood they'll attend group-therapy sessions together.
Lately they've been poring over the contents of crates
of mementos and childhood detritus in the basement
storeroom. Dad stumbled across a chart in which I
"statistically analyzed" the charms of ten girls at
Gatewood Junior High; everybody -- Val perhaps even more
than the others -- got a large charge out of that one.
When Mother asked what should be done with my high-
school letter sweater and the box of my mementos, I told
her to toss them, but the decision wasn't as easy as I
pretended.

"You provide some real local color for the
tourists, don't you, boy," Dad observed as we paraded
through the sumptuous Fairmont lobby, drawing stares and
glares (me in my "Bat hat" and U.S.A. bluejean jacket
and white cords, boots, reminiscing aloud about the days
when the industrial moguls were meeting in that very
hotel and I was a protester in the crowd milling angrily
just outside, held back by a cordon of beefy cops with
riot sticks at the ready and sadism in their eyes).

*   *

Back in Garnett. New copper alarm clock ticking
loudly (but no more so than its predecessor) at half
past two in the morning. Sprawled on green-striped
sheets. Just drew up a mind-boggling list of things to
do in the next two days, including "Send resume' to Bay
Bulldog." If they'll have me, when I move permanently
back to the city I'll try writing for them (an idea
that's been tapping on my shoulder for years as the
Bulldog's become ever more fiercely antiwar).

Taped to the table next to me: a seriously crinkled
but then reflattened photo of the second-most-beautiful
"Oriental chick" anyone ever saw, clutching her right
breast with one hand and her snatch with the other (from
the cover of Evergreen, two years ago; it went into the
collage on our living-room wall during Jang's time --

290

she liked it even more than I did -- and was gradually
covered up by other items, was exposed again recently
when Barb ripped down the entire collage, was spotted in
the trash by Valerie who was reminded of Briana -- whom
she's never seen as far as I know -- and then Val
masochistically brought it up with her to Garnett last
week and taped it there on the table and told me she'd
read about it in my journal. I mean, and she calls me
strange?).

     Today was so good I stayed on at Funston until well
past midnight. Separate talks with Mother, Dad, and
Barb. I defended "the Movement" passably well, I
thought, and miraculously Dad did not get too vitriolic.
I too was for the most part admirably well behaved.
Barb and I did wrangle, however, over her refusal to
polish Stanley's apple a bit in order to improve our
chances of staying on at Funston. She did this as a
matter of principle, and I admired her righteousness
even as I deplored her intransigence (which, since
Stanley, who lives in the first-floor "garden
apartment," is the newly appointed house manager
reporting directly to Mrs. Hilyer, may well lead to our
eviction). Val sang in my ear (well, tried to; singing
is really not her thing at all) and looked utterly,
stunningly foxy as she practiced dancing funky before
the full-length mirror in the living room (unaware Jang
used to practice traditional Korean dance and Denise
super-advanced funky dance in the same spot using the
same mirror; and of course for me those memories were
merging with Val's touchingly earnest and shaky yet
extremely sexy new moves in a kind of instant dance-hall
review and also hall-of-mirrors exploration of images
arising from the past two years). -- And Rob again
passionately defended "Love Story" as a work of high art
(and once again I absolutely could not agree even though
I still haven't seen it).

     Then when the others were gone I had it out with
Barb about Briana. There must be something "basically
wrong" with me, Barb believes, because I've supposedly
made "so many" women distrustful of me, have gone

through "so many" relationships, have failed to be
"fully open" (that again!) at all times -- have even
told a fib or two to avert a disaster. Yes, I too have
been troubled at times by some of these things, but I
truly resent her meddling in my affairs and then
condemning me so absolutely and with such a broad brush
and such boggling self-righteousness, as if she's never
had to wiggle out of a tight spot herself (and I know of
at least half a dozen where she's done just that, and
for the most part quite deftly, I thought).

    "The trouble with you, Glennar, is you want
everything. You're going to have to learn to
sacrifice!"

    Barb pronouncing judgment from on high. It was
about as pure an example of it as I've ever seen. And
I've seen a few.

    She traces all these shameful alleged shortcomings
of mine back to the impossible expectations showered
upon me as a child. "Deception," she asserts, is my way
of being "defiant." (As when I stole a new baseball
from Wieboldt's in Evanston at age eleven even though I
already had several, however old and ratty, at home.) A
canny insight, I grudgingly must acknowledge. At times
I (and Jeff) did indeed try to fly beneath the radar of
Mother and Dad's overly strict fifties-type morality
rather than confront them directly on it, whereas Barb
herself preferred to have things out with them face to
face every single time and thus to cause all kinds of
unnecessary hassles for everybody, not least herself,
and certainly including Jeff and me and for that matter
Rob (even though -- or rather I should say precisely
because -- he, Rob, was still in grade school; but he
hasn't forgotten it, as he told me himself).

    In any case I still believe Barb's going way too
far in what she's saying now. Her love of seriousness
and austerity and certainty clashes with mine for
playfulness and complexity and flexibility as well as my
fascination with the games we all play (Barb, again,
very much included in the "all," though she huffily
denies it). Also, she has a deep fear of "manipulative"

men (which, once more, she blames at least partly on the
alleged bad behavior of my boyhood self, though she
won't quite admit this either), and as a result she
takes positions which just about everyone finds
unbearably extreme and rigid and severe, not to mention
pious and self-serving and hypocritical. Or I'll just
roll up my sleeves and say it: this twisted sister of
mine is downright pharisaical!

　　And one more point while I'm at it. As I observed
to Barb, all four of the "so many" women whose testimony
against me she cited (Ciara, Denise, Briana, Val) (for
some reason she left out Jang) -- all four based their
grievances on what they'd read while perusing my journal
and/or chronbooks (as did Jang also), and in most cases
without my permission. That is, they distrusted me
because my private thoughts failed to match up with what
they assumed they would be or thought they should be or
simply wanted them to be. That's a generalization, of
course, but I think it's a fair one and I could cite
an abundance of chapter and verse in support of it
in all five cases. Yet Barb doesn't apply the same
absolute moral standards to the snooping done by these
inamoratas of mine much less to their persons and "value
systems" (possibly excepting Jang's), nor does she allow
for complexities and imponderables with respect to my
interpersonal relationships as she does for those of the
other couples she refers to as contrasting positive
examples. -- And really now, is there anyone in the
world, man or woman, who could pass a test like the one
we were talking about, the Snoop In Your Journal test?
Even Tolstoy flunked it! -- And then paid for this
failure the rest of his life, no question.

Tuesday 16
　　From the lower depths of the Paladin Room, between
sets, tables only a third occupied (but the bowling
alley outside is packed). Right here at my left elbow a
bag of Fritos leans insouciantly against a sweaty bottle
of Bud almost as if to say, "I'd like to soak up to you,

293

Bud." (Okay, that's gooney.)

Optimism prevails today at the office of the Merino
Mercury. Even though we've scarcely begun work on the
new issue, Al now believes he'll be able to keep the
paper going on his own (i.e., in the absence of both
Russ Danner's financial stake and my bargain-basement
editorial services). It's also a pleasure to see his
ideas of what the paper ought to be swinging gradually
closer to mine as he bangs up against the intractability
of the local power structure. The radicalizing of
Albert Edwards! -- And yes, I'll admit some of my own
ideas have swung closer to his as I've watched our
counterculture "lifestyle" drive away support out here
in Reagan country (the re-mainstreaming of G.S.!).

(A glance to the right shows, through smoky haze,
the talented leader of the Bow Ree Boys -- what a
handle! -- sitting with that sassy Air Force groupie in
black net stockings and red micromini and low-cut silver
velvet blouse with lots of fleshy cleavage showing, the
one and only Jackie Stahl -- who does a mean Elmer Fudd
imitation, by the way, among others.)

So far I've squandered the day, procrastinating
again until the last moment on churning out my (self-)
assigned pieces for this issue. I did accept Marcelle's
invitation to a late lunch at Kip's Place after she got
off from school, I did tail her boyfriend Rodney's car
at a safe distance for a few miles at her request, I did
hound her a little about getting it on with me (she
would gradually yield, she admitted, if I kept the
pressure up, so I just might try to do that, time
permitting), and I did talk politics with her father, a
very sharp and humorous working man who's not fooled
one bit by what's going down in the gringo power sphere,
local, state, national, or universal. Marcelle,
meanwhile, snuck off to ball Rodney, "because he was
good" (i.e., didn't go to see his other girlfriend when
we tailed him). Says Marcelle, and quite fetchingly by
my lights: "The trouble with me is I'm completely honest
with him. Why am I so stupid?"

Which takes me back to Briana. I neglected to

294

mention yesterday how Briana rationalized making all
those (severely tilted in her own favor) disclosures to
Barb about our private affairs. She did it, she told
Barb, because she now believes I must be "saved" and
that Barb's the person to do it. "Habitual dishonesty"
dooms me to an unhappy life, Briana says. This is such
an absurd distortion of what was actually going down
with Briana and me last August -- or any other time --
that I can scarcely believe Barb would buy into it. But
she leaves little doubt she does.

"I think she's hung up over the whole thing,
Glennar. I don't know if she's even functioning well."

Is that why Terry's over there all the time, then,
to shore up her functioning? Just like last August?
And the months in between in Europe? And New Year's Eve
a few hours after she'd told me she'd never be able to
-- never mind. No need to keep tormenting myself about
that. Any of it!

Of course I have my own opinions about why Briana
might be hung up -- in a word, her acknowledged failure
all along to be straight with me and even more with
herself about the depth of her attachment to Terry --
and I didn't fail to pass this along to Barb. But
Barb's mind is already made up. Probably it has been
for about twenty years, I'd say, if not longer. "Mom,
Glen's being bad again! He won't let me have the whole
spotlight to myself! Therefore I'm going to have to
make even more trouble for everyone!" (Brothers and
sisters, aren't they a trip though?)

Saturday 20 (X:17-19)
                    Everything you do counts.
                              -- Joan Didion
            Well yeah, but maybe not all that much.
                              -- Editor Sandefjord
     In any case, what is it I really want to do right
now? Some possibilities:
     ** Read the controversial new Mailer piece "A
Prisoner of Sex"? But my mind is too fragmented, too

drained by the dramas of the past few days, to follow
complex sentences for more than a paragraph or two.
    ** Take a long, hot bath? But that option would
entail writing off the rest of the evening, a Saturday
night when I'm free in the city -- free and restless but
also constrained by a skeptical mood and exhausted
spirit.
    ** Read the letter from Paul to Barbara which lies
open and unguarded on the table in the living room
(Paul's her new local boyfriend to provide some balance
for the one or ones in Europe with whom things are not
going so well). But to do this would confirm I am
indeed the lost and evil soul my very own sister sees me
as being. Oh, and by the way, I might mention that she,
Barb, had a six-hour (yes, six!) talk with brother Rob
about the Briana affair and my alleged turpitude. I
have "sexual hang-ups," she informed him. At this point
I've had more than enough of this sister's insufferable
self-righteousness and meddling and I'm going to have to
put my foot down -- but not tonight. Please.
    ** Visit Briana? But forget that: I refuse to go
crawling back to Briana. It's true she's been more on
my mind lately, and every day this week I hoped for a
letter from her in response to my Valentine's Day
farewell note, which is to say the updated version of
the revised New Year's Day farewell note, and tonight
the city again seems to be primarily the place where she
is -- but I won't be the one who caves in. No way.
Even though I know she's given Barb a patchwork stuffed
dog and a book of Terry's gallant poetry, mostly written
about and dedicated to Briana herself (and titled "Body
Ballads"), both gifts now resting with conspicuous
casualness on that same living-room table as if Barb had
placed them there intentionally to taunt me -- this
being a room where up to a week ago I felt more
comfortable than in any other on earth.
    ** Visit a bar, cafe, tavern, saloon or some other
such establishment of the night? But why bother, I
mean, what's to be gained, I mean, any and all forms of
impersonal socializing or cruising for companionship or

simple lonely brooding while perched atop a barstool
right now look to be unbearably arduous and empty.
     ** Pick up Valerie? But no thanks, I'm glad to be
rid of her, and damn the guilt. It all stemmed from her
refusal to lighten up this afternoon, leading to
escalating skirmishes and disgust in my case; I
suspected Barb's baneful influence again -- in fact was
certain of it -- and when Val openly threatened to find
another man if I didn't sign on with her moral-uplift
program for me I wound up dropping her off at Caffe
Trieste (her choice of place) at eight on a Saturday
evening after our return from Garnett, telling her to do
what she had to do and not to bother coming over to
Funston for the rest of the weekend; and if she needed
to get more marching instructions from my meddling
sister, I added, she should do it by phone or by meeting
with her somewhere other than here at "the Castle."
     ** Go back to Garnett tonight? But I'm too tired,
I just got here, I hate to think I prefer Garnett over
San Francisco -- and yet this just might be the best
thing to do -- the main difference between the two burgs
at the moment being that in Garnett at least I have a
few friends I can hang out with.
     ** Crash? But it's only ten after nine!
     ** Take a long walk? But that would require too
much energy and resolve nothing.
     I wish I could think of something Hemingwayishly
moral to do, i.e., something about which after doing it
I'd be almost guaranteed to feel good.
     ** Or I could write about the extraordinary events
of the past three days. Which, yes, I will do. And
knew all along I would get around to doing sooner or
later. So why not now?
     But first I'll put on a stack of LPs and open the
bottle of blackberry wine I bought earlier. (When you
bring home a bottle of rotgut on a Saturday night you
suspect you'll be passing alone it's probably time to
start wondering about the direction your life is taking.
But then I was wondering about this already -- in fact
that's why I bought the stuff, just in case.)

[Have Mercy]

*

Saturday-night memo from Editor S.:
Hectic and exhilarating and overwhelming, these
past few days. Beyond that I scarcely know what to say.
Claire and I breaking into laughter as the D.A.
bored in on her in court with weirdly off-key Perry
Mason-like ferocity. My own shaky voice as I attempted
to sound like I knew what I was doing while "cross-
examining" Officer Pierce (who later, as we waited for
the jury's verdict, tried to convince me he's not at all
prejudiced against freaks like me and Claire and
revealed that Eric Burdon, ex of the Animals and now of
War, is his cousin). Rapping with the D.A. and the
judge in his chambers. Asking the jury incredulously,
"You mean you really believe I'm guilty?" They all
nodded vigorously. I was fined nineteen bills. Guilty
of running a stop sign in a speed-trap kind of town.
That took eight hours (and probably consumed over a
thousand dollars of County funds). Ever since I've
enjoyed telling whoever would listen the incredible tale
about the jury deliberating for almost two hours before
finding me guilty of such a trivial offense. "I'm a
convicted transgressor, so judged by a jury of twelve of
the straightest peers anyone could ever imagine."
Then I plunged into the frantic business of writing
the library story, the Mercky Notions column, half a
dozen miscellaneous short pieces, and eventually putting
the paper together, finishing finally at eight a.m. with
just Rob (brother) and me and Claire and Becky still
awake (Chris sprawled on the floor in the corner,
classically passed out, an empty Schlitz can still
clutched in his hand, a hard-on so conspicuously
outlined under his jeans that the normally unflappable
Becky felt constrained to throw a paper-towel "fig leaf"
over it -- which Claire immediately and gleefully
removed). Twenty-four hours in a row at full throttle,
and on only four hours' sleep the previous night: a
maniacal day of which I felt and still do feel extremely
proud. Without question one of my best days ever.
Rob and I collapsed into cot and bed respectively

298

at nine-thirty a.m. after a blurry breakfast; at ten-
thirty, just an hour later, I was roused for another
court session. Two drowsy hours in the dock and then
finally the County prosecutor shamefacedly admitted to
the judge that the independent lab chosen by the judge
had found all my "narcotics" to be legal drugs: aspirin,
Milk of Magnesia, and two types of over-the-counter cold
pills. Evil stuff for sure not to mention subversive!
When the judge asked if I had anything to say I probably
should've expressed my gratitude that they hadn't tried
to plant something on me or somehow falsified the report
to cover their own ineptitude. But I just said I was
glad it was over. He then officially dropped the case.

(The hallucinatory Vanilla Fudge version of "You
Keep Me Hangin' On" flops down. Brings back Russ "the
Moose" Syracuse's three a.m. spinnings of the entire
album on KYA during the era of the extended final
meltdown with Ciara.)

-- All this heavy drama reunited Claire and me.
We needed to touch one another after going through so
much together; and at her empty house, on the mattress
in the study, despite total exhaustion, with none other
than Eric Burdon and War's "Bare Back Ride" playing at
high volume just for ironic effect (but also because
it's so fine), we did touch yes we did ooh ooh did we
ever. And then Claire with her luscious verdant cooch
and exquisite sensuality reconfirmed for me that sex can
be miraculous. Two hours after arriving at her place I
strode back to the office on a blindingly bright and
windy afternoon feeling reborn, astonished at the length
of the hair on the shadow knifing along at my side.

Today the library staff exulted over the expose
("MCG LIBRARY CRITICIZED/Employees Allege Vindictive
Treatment") and I wondered what fraction of the effort
put into it this redeemed.

A good talk with brother Rob while driving back.
The loyal, the perceptive, the levelheadedly wise and
plain-spokenly articulate and quietly humorous Rob (in
all of which traits he seems more than ever to resemble
Unk Erik). He realizes full well that Barb fails to

299

understand the real basis of my relationship with Briana
or the complex struggle I'm caught up in with Valerie
and that she, Barb, has a hidden agenda of her own which
badly skews her interpretation of matters with me and
everyone else -- but especially with me, her one and
only older brother.

   -- As visions of insurrection incited by the Last
Poets fade away. Flip that stack and cue it up again
right now! -- Or maybe it's already time to crash.

Sunday 21
    Valerie straggles in at nine a.m., her shiny new
purple micromini conspicuously undone and askew, and
gradually unfolds the story of her "infidelity." Four
times between three and six a.m. she had balled some
dude whose name she supposedly couldn't remember, and
she had liked it a lot and she just wanted me to know
that. She'd come three times and had thrilled at her
ability to turn him on again and again. Not only that,
but while she was at it she also wanted to confess to
balling someone else Thursday night, a guy who'd picked
her up hitchhiking, a "bang-bang fuck" she didn't like
at all. The main point of bringing up this second guy
seemed to be that she'd gotten it on with him even
before I told her to do what she had to do last night.
Nobody tells Valerie Bando what to do, you got that
straight, smart-ass Americain?
    Yet she begged my forgiveness and I forgave her.
Why not? Hiding both my pain and my skepticism, I told
her I thought her adventures were probably good for us
-- which enraged her. At first I said we should stop
seeing each other for a while, but by late afternoon I'd
relented, agreeing to meet her again this coming Friday.
    Only tonight is it really starting to hurt. Not
that I have any right to expect her to be faithful, or
to complain when she isn't (or when she is but pretends
she isn't, whatever the case may be -- and I'm not
really sure which it is regarding these particular
incidents -- but for simplicity's sake I'll assume she's

not making anything up here). Impulses tug at me -- ax
Val for good, rev up for another idiotic try with Briana
-- but so far I've put off deciding. I do have to say,
though, I wonder why Val had to come over and rub my
face in it. This is truly what bothers me most about
the whole thing. If this fairly represents the kind of
"complete openness" she wants, then I think I'm probably
going to want out.

     An eventful night at Al's -- a meeting, Charlie
Eldridge appears at last, so does Stacy, the beautiful
but hard-bitten blond who's been married four times and
is a couple of years younger than me -- and then I play
counselor for an hour with Marcelle, poor lovely hung-up
Marcelle, hopelessly in love with a philandering married
man who can take her or leave her, and I fail to attend
a party Claire invites me to -- she's begun hanging out
pretty much full-time with swaggering Chris of the
impressive office-floor genital display -- and now I
linger in a restaurant whose name I don't even know
feeling ridiculously misunderstood and lonely and sorry
for myself.

     Jack Nicholson (uneasiest of the Easy Riders):
"I've lived out the myth of the Fifties. I've balled
everybody, taken all the drugs, gone everywhere. I'm
still looking for something valid."

                              4

Monday 22
     Wait a minute: the spectators' stands at the
bowling alley? The place teeming with Monday-night
league action? All thirty-seven lanes going strong?
Thuds, rumbles, crashes, cheers or groans; a raucous
undercurrent of excited chatter; live rock music
coursing in from the nearby Paladin Room? Yike!

     But I like it. Even though -- and perhaps because
-- when most of these bowlers look at me they see a
Martian. I like the noise, the laughter, the
pandemonium of excited people doing mainly harmless or

low-harm things they love to do. No matter if the scene
is also "lowbrow," not to mention reactionary, a kind of
impromptu free-enterprise morality play. Set 'em up so
you can knock 'em down! Instant obsolescence! Bread
and circuses! Capitalism gone amok uber alles! Seig
heil!

And on George Washington's birthday, no less. How
pleased the old Indian killer and slaveowner would be to
see everyone celebrating with such patriotic jubilation!

Still burning in my mind, meanwhile, are the images
Valerie painted for me (verbally) of her purported
"infidelities." Several times an hour my stomach turns,
my chest seems to absorb an elbowlike poke, my throat
constricts as I think of her telling me about fucking
away Saturday night, four times supposedly and three
comes (which I'm pretty sure I've never been able to
bring her to in a single night). And then she snatched
an hour's sleep and hitched out to Funston just so she
could let me in on the exciting news, with the belt of
her skirt still -- or perhaps recently, say when she
reached the staircase outside my door -- that belt
dramatically unbuckled, yes, and the zipper pulled down
and the skirt twisted a bit and the rest of her clothes
arranged in what to me was suspiciously artful disarray.

I think of her marveling about the North Beach
dude's supposedly irrepressible cock, no sooner done
spurting (she said) than it was up again and demanding
an encore. Set 'em up so you can knock 'em down!
("When I left," she gloated, "he still wanted to keep
going!") She especially emphasized how much she loved
being able to turn him on so easily ("I don't even know
what did it!") and also being seen by him as such a
"gift," a miracle from heaven picked up on a foggy
Saturday night in February in a dingy Upper Grant Avenue
bar just a block from Trieste. Didn't have to go far to
find what she was looking for, our teenybopper avenger
didn't. Supposedly she never even saw his body naked --
it was dark in his bedroom -- nor did she suck his cock
-- "That's sacred!" (oh sure) -- but he turned her on,
she came and she came and she came again, she loved

302

every minute of it, and she clearly loved every minute
of filling me in on it maybe even more.

I guess I should be happy for her, but really now.

What is it that holds me back from calling it quits
with this girl? That's simple: she suffered through my
own "infidelities," which I'm sure were every bit as
painful for her and probably a lot more so, even though
I never made a point of letting her know the particulars
about any of them (on the contrary -- until she demanded
that I do so) and certainly never flaunted them. Beyond
that, I fear "damaging" her (to use Barb's word).

Later Sunday, yesterday, after triumphantly
relating her escapades in such abundant detail, she
suddenly and shockingly fell apart before my eyes,
ostensibly hating herself for what she'd done -- the way
she'd undermined the promise of our previous weekend --
undermined it twice, on two different nights, with two
different guys! How, she wailed, could she have done
this to me? What's more she would kill herself if I
gave up on her now! Balling these other men, she
assured me with tears streaming, had served only to
remind her how special, how tender and gentle and
wonderful and supremely, even otherworldishly precious
our loving is to her.

So why then, I have to ask, does she so badly want
me to know, or at the very least to think, she needs
another man to fuck her, to handle her roughly and make
her feel dominated even as she believes she's the one
doing the real dominating through her own imagined
superiority over just one more dumb animalistic male of
the species she's effortlessly roused into a raging
beast?

No, I shouldn't let that kind of argument for
staying with her sway me. Nor do I want to reciprocate
merely for reciprocity's sake her grudging
"understanding" of similar wanderings of my own. The
only important question, ultimately, is this: should
Valerie and I be together? Is there any hope at all we
can work things out in a way that would hold long-term?

The answer is no on both counts.

[Have Mercy]

It's true I have some rather strongly mixed
feelings about all this. But for once I'll try to do
what's wise. Valerie may be more sexually attractive
and more gifted overall and may offer greater potential
in the long run in several other realms than anyone else
I've known, but she falls far short on meeting the most
basic "maintenance" needs of a loving relationship. She
always has. I have not a single doubt she always will.
If I were miraculously to overcome every last one of my
own shortcomings, and not just the real ones but even
the alleged ones, we'd still fail miserably. To me I'm
afraid she'll always be the beautiful sad-eyed lady with
the deep and wild nasty streak.

*

So that's it. I'm done with Valerie. And with
this decision made, it's best to go ahead with executing
(apt term) it quickly. Mail her a note tonight, promise
to explain these things as best I can in person this
weekend. After that, a period of retrenchment and major
head-straightening. Then, perhaps, if I can figure out
a way to do it without debasing myself too much, another
try to break through with Briana. Or a move in a new
direction. Or maybe nothing at all for a while. Could
be the time has come to test my luck with a period of
rigorously self-enforced sexual and romantic abstinence.
A cleansing! For me no new direction could be newer or
more radical than that.

*

Can't stop without mentioning this. Last night the
library staff presented me with a huge cake as thanks
for the expose'. "Glen for Librarian," proclaimed the
surprisingly patriotic red and blue cursive lettering
atop white icing itself studded with leftover Valentine
candy hearts bearing inscriptions like "Be mine" and
"You're sweet!"

Wednesday 24 (X:23)
Four in the morning and me and two cops are the
only customers at Denny's in Garnett. The cops and I

exchange nods; we recognize each other from the
courthouse. My head's still swimming from a dreamlike
plunge down country roads to take Stacy home.

Stacy? Who's Stacy again?

Well, Stacy's the one who's gobbled up big chunks
of the past two days, that's who. Monday night she
popped into the office with perfect timing: I was just
putting the final touches on the farewell letter to
Valerie. The letter remains unsent, I'm embarrassed to
say, but Stacy's been doing a good job of testing what
little remains of my feelings for Val. Or let's say
she's doing a good job at playing the Garnett equivalent
of Val's North Beach pickup. Not that there's any
vengeance involved; Stacy's plenty interesting on her
own merits.

Admittedly things are getting a bit surreal around
here. But sometimes it can be a good idea to ride with
the surreal. This may be one of those times. Or not.
Probably won't take too long to find out.

From a distance Stacy looks like a Las Vegas
showgirl or, more likely, because her body is so
emaciated, a strung-out Las Vegas hooker, with her huge
lion's mane of peroxided blond hair and her dazzling
cat's-eyed smile. Up close you can see how her three
(not four) demented marriages as well as lots and lots
of dope have ravaged her -- and also that somewhere
beneath all the makeup lurk the remnants of a sensitive
soul. She's one of the most outrageously provocative
women I've ever come across -- the bandleader at the
Paladin Room accused us over the mic of trying to
undress each other on the dancefloor, "this incredible
fox" -- and she's also one of the most sexually fucked
up.

Tonight we went at it twice on the office floor,
and what she wanted was a fast, hard, brutal bang, and
the more bestial the better: "That's the only way I can
get off." Her body tightens up like a steel spring, an
ultimate physical expression of the internal barricades
you can't help but sense in talking with her. And yet
she can also be responsive and intelligent in

conversation. Stretched out next to her on a sunbathed rock ledge above the lake in Pagoda Rocks Park -- as two fishermen shouted encouragement to each other far below and a high-tension wire buzzed like a thousand beehives not very far above -- I felt surprisingly close to her. We're both emotion freaks of a sort and we've both gone through a lot. Obviously, though, she's way ahead of me, to the point where the barriers between us appear impassable no matter how close we seem to get in talking about them. And the simple fact is I'm relatively content with my life on the whole and she's miserable with hers, the light and hope in her all but extinguished (she's ready to move in with an ex-con biker smackhead solely because she thinks it would beat living alone; she met him last week).

I like her. Luckily she doesn't turn me on all that much -- because of the overdone provocativeness, which, it soon becomes clear, is fraudulent and empty of any genuine feeling or desire -- but even so it wouldn't be that hard to tumble into some weird entanglement with her.

Which brings me back to Valerie. And Briana. I'm still only beginning to get over the sting of Val's "infidelities." To repeat: it's not so much the fact (I'm still assuming it's a fact) that she did it; it's the mean-spirited and vindictive way she tried to stab me with it. The damage is irreparable. I know now I'll never be able to feel the same toward her. The danger lies in idealizing how I did feel about her -- at times -- before this happened. In any event: this weekend I'll be telling her goodbye.

(I wish I could read her journal account of what really happened. But then I'd probably just wonder if the account itself were the straight goods. As noted before, she's told me, in fact several times, that in the journal she writes pretty much whatever comes into her head -- dreams up stories to make her life look wilder, more glamorous, etc., and writes them down as if they were factual -- and that if I ever do read any of these accounts I shouldn't take them too seriously.

-- And the two short excerpts she's shown me have
confirmed all this and then some.)
    Meanwhile I've just about decided to see if I can
persuade Briana to give me another chance.

Thursday 25
    Doing time. At Merimont. Where Eldridge Cleaver
and Huey Newton were once locked up, among a good many
other heroes of our crazed times. Right now the con
master of ceremonies is reading off names from a roster
of prison officials. The audience of sixty or seventy
responds with lackluster applause for each and every
name.
    The white dude sitting between me and Claire is
doing time here himself, and I do mean for real. I
bummed him out by responding to a long racist rant of
his with the comment that in my view to hate blacks is
playing the man's game. It's easy for me to talk that
way, he rebutted, but if I were busted tomorrow, before
two weeks had gone by I'd literally be fucked within an
inch of my life by "nigger animals." His whole body's
covered with scars "from when four spooks attacked me --
they were trying to kill me, man!" Of course this
belligerent creep with the huge chip on his shoulder
would never do anything to provoke any hostility,
nah....
    -- Now it's threatening to get out of hand. First
a brave academic visitor from UC-Santa Cruz took the
podium to publicly attack the prison system -- from
within! Now a con approximately the size and look of a
rhinoceros risen on his hind legs (in this case a white
rhino) is doing the same, but he's not using such pretty
multisyllable words. Nervous laughter, vigorous
applause, shifting eyes as some of us check to be sure
we know where the exits are. ---
                    *   *
    Heavy day. Valerie paid an unexpected visit to
Garnett. In the college cafeteria I told her we're
through. But an hour later between stops in Tesuque

307

(where I always drive very, very carefully now) I
recanted: told her I'd just been testing to find out
whether she really still loves me and cares about me in
light of her four-fuck, three-come fling and various
other recent escapades both confirmed and unconfirmed.
Oddly enough, in saying this I discovered I believed it
myself. Then back to my room at Klug's for ninety
minutes of nervous balling as knocks sounded frequently
on the door -- Glen trying to prove himself the equal of
last Saturday's shadowy rival, yet at the same time
disdaining competitiveness and invidious comparisons.
Uneasy limbo. Val is suddenly a changed woman,
infinitely more aggressive and confident both in bed and
out. Or at least seemingly so, which is what counts
anyway.

"I should have learned it from Jim," she declared;
"Nobody wants to be given to!" And: "Everything I
invested in you is lost. I have to start over from
scratch and I know it. But this time I'll find a better
way to go about doing it."

                      *

-- Some bizarro Okie country stuff is playing in
the office now, probably Claire's doing. She and I are
feuding. She's been balling Chris like crazy lately,
doing a number on me, cold shoulder and all that shit,
groping his infamous crotch right in front of me. She
refuses to be upfront about all this -- verbally, that
is -- or doesn't know how, and it pisses me off. "You
can't have everything, my lad." Yeah yeah, I know, but
permit me a moment's regret.

With Valerie there can be no promises -- not even
hints of future possibilities of promises. Everything's
wide open as never before. Nonetheless I have to admit
it: I feel the hope of a new beginning with her. Yes!
No doubt it's foolish as hell but that's just how it is.
To love is, among other things, to feel a stab of proud
warmth as you watch your lover talking with someone
else. I was so stabbed as I observed her out of the
corner of my eye charming befuddled Evan Kott and Tom
Yost as Ben Kiel and I thrashed out some matters

concerning his column. I'd like to be so stabbed
forever more. As I often was with Jang, for instance.
Not to mention with Briana. Or Lisa and Ciara and Aki
J. and Karen A. long ago.

Meanwhile in a nod to March Madness we've set up an
office pool, not on the upcoming NCAA basketball
tournament but on the likeliest date for the impending
planetary ecological and/or nuclear apocalypse. Ben
picked 1980, I went for 2000, Al (ever the optimist)
chose 2100, Claire (the pessimist) 1975. Everyone else
zeroed in on the 1980s or '90s. The prize, donated by
Ben, is an old World War II "grasshopper head" gas mask.
Just how we'll pick a winner is yet to be determined.
We might not know who that will be until 2050, at which
point we'll all have to cede the laurels to Al. For the
half century prior to that, should we be so fortunate,
I'll be his last remaining challenger.

*

(Evan says Val reminds him of the amorous French
skunk -- whose name no one can remember -- from the Pogo
comic strip. And I'm wondering: how is it I never
thought of this resemblance myself? Possibly because I
never liked or read the Pogo strip that much. True, I
did name my first dog Pogo, at age nine, although I
can't recall why -- perhaps just because I liked pogo
sticks and this dog liked to bounce around. Miss Quinn,
my fourth-grade teacher, had decided I was in dire need
of canine companionship and told Mother as much, so off
we drove to Orphans of the Storm and fetched us a lively
white beagle with brown and black spots. Sad to say,
Pogo was run over on Gatewood Road a few months later.
The trauma of that bloody event, which I witnessed from
a distance of ten or twelve feet, may've caused me to
lose any interest I had in the Pogo strip, amorous
French skunk included.)

*

[Margin note dated 3/26: "The skunk's name is
Ma'm'selle Hepzibah. Holly tracked it down."]

*   *

(Much later)

Why not write about it? Society contrives to make
me (and you and everyone) feel guilty for keeping alive
the "infantile" desire to be loved by everyone. So I
should feel bad about seeking, in one week, the love, or
at least something I might briefly be able to perceive
as the love, of Valerie, Claire, Stacy, and Briana. I
should also feel bad about writing self-justifying
passages like this one. And I admit it: I do. Guilty
and bad.

But also...delighted. So I say fuck all that
opprobrium.

Claire and I resolved our differences tonight.
"You want me to fall in love with you, don't you," she
said. And then, before I could come up with a reply to
such a loaded question (Batesonian almost, isn't it, in
its double binding?): "Well, it's too late to say you
don't, because I already have. I just had to be sure I
could stay balanced." It was beautiful; she was and I
was. Claire and I share a rhythm. We're natural mates
in a way far deeper than I can comprehend or that needs
or for that matter can stand comprehending; it just is.
In a roomful of ten thousand blindfolded people we could
easily, even if blindfolded ourselves, find each other
just by feel, meaning touch. It's physical and it's
emotional, undercutting any incompatibilities
conditioned into us by a society with more urgent things
on its mind. It's in the blood and in the heart. Many
people think we're brother and sister because our looks
and mannerisms are so similar, because we seem so
comfortable together even when we're fighting (in the
way two people who've grown up together might be, and
years or decades of separation wouldn't make this any
less true). It's a miracle, that's what. And we refuse
to let any mere petty clashes destroy it.

In fact, even though sex with her is so fine, I can
honestly say it's my hope we'll be able to transcend
that as well. Because I do need Claire's deeply
responsive kind of caring, yes, even if we must call the
basis for it simply a friendship. I want her to be near
me.

The cost of this could be high. Ma'm'selle
Valoshka will not understand. But I must pay the cost
and so must Ma'm'selle, especially after what happened
last week and the earlier paring-knife incident which
actually was far worse than any mere "infidelity."
Claire's love must be part of my life, period.

Saturday 27 (X:26)
   Family Farmacy, Saturday night, San Francisco. The
floor is crowded with longhair freaks sitting cross-
legged and sipping green tea while nibbling house-
specialty organic peanut-butter sandwiches as Gary X's
band "Squeeze" lilts out its unique brand of bluegrass
rock (with Tower of Power/Cold Blood-type funk riffs
oddly flaring here and there).
   I told Valerie the whole Pogo/Ma'm'selle Hepzibah
story. Her comment: "You're about the only one in the
state of California who hasn't called me that -- either
that or Frenchie or Brigitte. Valoshka's much better.
It makes me feel like a character in a Dostoevsky
novel."
   Valoshka Filippova -- I'm the one who gave her that
name, styled after Nastasya Filippova in "The Idiot"
(both have fathers named Filippe -- or Philippe in Val's
case). She says now she even likes the patronymic part.
"I'm a sucker for family-related stuff because I never
had a family when I was growing up. Nobody ever
expressed love to me. No one ever touched me lovingly.
No one was affectionate with me. That's why I'm so bad
at it."
   We're finally feeling a bit closer, the Gallic
polecat here and I, after a long disputatious day. "I
could never let you go," I whisper into her ear,
reversing the judgment of only a few hours back when the
vicious undertow of this morning's sexual debacle -- in
addition to all the other bad things that have gone down
lately between us -- seemed certain to rip us apart at
any moment. The polecat's devotion is complex and
consuming but, finally, life-giving. Restorative.

311

[Have Mercy]

We exchanged journals and did a couple of hours of
edgy "no retaliation" reading. Hers makes me highly
uneasy -- it shows flashes of brilliance and precocious
insight but what comes through most of all is her
shockingly vicious mean streak. It's also self-absorbed
to a degree that makes mine look downright
disinterested. Some of its judgments about me stir my
anger and resentment. According to her it's my "male
ego" that makes me do this and that; you'd almost think
that as a female she lacked an ego of her own. I
"ignore" her; I "refuse to help" her. Despite all the
compliments and assurances she's given me verbally --
part of a "Gigi act" customized especially for me? -- in
fifty pages she shows not the slightest appreciation or
even awareness of the work I'm doing for the Merc. I
come off as an arrogant unfeeling clod. Poor Val is
asked to put up with so much, and then her understanding
and acceptance of my outrageous actions are just taken
for granted by me. It's crap, most of it, but I suppose
I must pay attention to it if I want to succeed with
her, to find some loving comfort with her -- and I do.
But I have to force myself, because the physical
magic is missing. She and I are not natural mates. I
appreciate her, I admire her, I empathize with her, I
lust for her, but, sad truth, I don't love her. Maybe I
need her, maybe I love her and don't know it and don't
want to accept it -- no -- the simple truth is I don't
love her but I'd like to. I'll keep trying to do so.
Because, as noted numerous times before, it would be
difficult to find a woman who's better for me in so many
different respects, who's more likely to be able to love
me and comprehend me and accept me as I actually am (and
that means with all the masks and disguises included,
and not just when they're artificially set to one side
-- or truly set to one side, if that's even possible;
it means accepting me when they're firmly fixed in place
and seem unlikely ever to come off because they're not
really masks and disguises at all, rather they're
different selves which are at the same time facets of
the same self; and from there it only gets more complex

just as is true for everyone else on earth; and so
really what's the big deal here anyway?).

   After reading her own accounts of her
"infidelities" I feel somewhat relieved about them. I
don't know why. If they really did happen -- which I
still doubt, despite her insistence that they did and
her lengthy descriptions of them -- it appears they
didn't mean very much to her. The condescending
mercenary tone she adopts in putting them into written
words, along with the cold eagerness she shows when her
protagonist, meaning herself, is in action (let's get on
with the fuck) and the straight shit she deals about the
fucks themselves ("long slow kisses as he undressed me,"
"tender and insatiable lover") as well as the arrogant
attitude she takes toward the men -- well, if I were one
of those guys and I read her account I think I'd want to
chop her up into tiny pieces and feed them to the
roaches. Better, so much better she should love getting
it on with these guys. Which perhaps she did, since
that's what she said when she first told me about it (or
about the second guy anyway), but then later that same
day why did she write about it so differently? Maybe
she simply couldn't be honest with herself in
journalizing about it. Who knows. As I told her this
afternoon, finally rising out of my lethargic funk, "My
own thought is, if you're going to screw around like
that, at least you ought to be proud of it. All this
abject contrition is just like adding insult to injury."

   The talk about sex (culminating at Mac's Grill out
in the Inner Sunset, six or seven blocks from 1616, the
same table where Jang and I on several occasions tangled
bitterly during our end-times) -- this talk revealed
once again the depth of our sexual estrangement. She
now says she "can't get into it" because of straining to
please me and to reach climaxes with me, not realizing
and/or refusing to accept I'd be far more pleased if
she'd get into it emotionally no matter what she did
physically. Complicating matters is the fact that I
find it increasingly difficult to get into it with her
myself (whereas with Claire, say, it happens easily and

naturally). The sad truth is this: Val's clumsy,
bungling, misguided, and (worst of all) resentful
efforts to make lovemaking "superlative" for me only
turn me off. And in the final analysis -- mine, that is
-- this is mainly because they also turn her off. Or
rather they cause her to forget about letting herself be
turned on and, worse, about responding to my own
increasingly fraught and stupidly dogged efforts to rev
her up and transport her to -- paradise! Sure! What
else is it all about?

    She now proposes that we try to get back to basics:
pure feeling, little movement. I'm willing to go along
with her on this but afraid it won't be enough. I've
had it too good with others in the past to tolerate
patiently, with long-winded perseverance -- for month
after month after month -- what in overly idealistic
moments I call "mere sexual differences." What it
really amounts to, at least from my perspective, is the
sexual education of a strangely inhibited yet also
disastrously experienced and exorbitantly self-conscious
nineteen-year-old girl -- and let's not forget she's
also a fervent perfectionist -- and I fear I've already
exhausted whatever strength I can draw from my feelings
for her and my own physical desire and my "natural
reformist impulse" (Barb's dismissive term for my
wanting to make a lover's sex life and that same lover's
life as a whole better and even -- dare I say it? --
fabulous, if possible).

    Can love sustain me with Valerie? More to the
point, can the mere desire to love sustain me? I doubt
it, but I'll try to let it happen. Then I'll probably
go back to Claire for fulfillment. Of a sort. But it's
a sort I need. Must have.

Sunday 28
    Upon dropping Val at her brother Armand's place in
the Richmond at eight p.m. after a day bursting with
fresh hope for us (two gentle and good copulations last
night sandwiched around another blow-by-blow description

of her "infidelities" which finally convinced me they
were real but also pretty much meaningless to her; then
today puttying of the Funston windows) -- after all
this, as it happens, I was seized by an irresistible
impulse to call Briana. "Just to see how you're doing."
To my amazement she cheerfully accepted my proposal that
we talk things over at her place. Whereupon, after I
zipped right over, she proceeded to devastate me,
smiling all the while as she shoved in the shiv, and
even though we were under the spell of a strong mutual
attraction -- she too, very obviously -- and even though
she said she still loves me, and even though...but never
mind.

   As I left at two a.m., frustrated, exasperated, and
bewildered, I had a sense of deja vu so queasy I felt I
was dissolving into it and could never escape from it.

   As always she looked even more beautiful than I
remembered her to be, and of course I always remember
her as being the most beautiful there is or ever could
be. Long soulful gazing into each other's eyes, the
voltage every bit as strong as the time in the meadow
overlooking the Bayshore Freeway on a warm and sunny
late-summer afternoon -- yes, I'd even say as strong as
the most electrifying scene of them all, in the fuchsia
garden at Golden Gate Park a week or so earlier where I
could see her sexual juices soaking through the crotch
of her brown corduroys as she sat spread-legged before
me peering at my own spreading damp spot at the top of
my maximal hard-on angling up under the pocket of my own
brown cords that happened to be the same brand as hers
-- Lee -- (and the sun beating down on the hard-on,
just like her eyes peering at it, felt so deliciously
warm!) -- but on this occasion last night we never
really got much beyond the gazes. Didn't even ball. In
a word, she's decided she can no longer trust me at
all...we "move in different worlds"...what love and
desire she feels for me (and she does admit feeling
"some" of each) is "masochistic." As for me, she thinks
I've "stopped growing," I'll be unable to achieve
"fulfillment in life"; she implies my ideas and concerns

are shallow (mere politics so much of the time, don't
you know); she wonders why it is I seem to have no close
male friends "with your caliber of mind -- men you could
bare your soul to and have a spiritual relationship
with."

I accepted all this solemnly -- in fact she was
openly puzzled and even miffed by my "serenity" in doing
so -- but that doesn't mean it didn't hurt in ways I was
trying not to let her see. Perhaps she sensed this and
was consoling me, perhaps it was sheer attraction or
nostalgia or even a resurgence of her old feelings for
me, but she kissed me then as she used to. The kiss
went on for a long time; in fact I was the one who
finally broke it off. I don't doubt if I'd insisted on
balling she would've yielded. But I couldn't do it.
The "strong magic" that went beyond the sexual just
wasn't there for her anymore and she made that painfully
obvious. Her string of revelations about other men --
that she's having an affair with some writer, also still
seeing Terry ("whom I love very much"), also
experiencing a "mad crush" on "this beautiful gay dude"
-- these were the final blows.

Even so, she said she'd see me "if we could go very
slow." And in any case she'd like to be my pal so she
could help out with my moral rehabilitation. Why, she'd
even be willing to introduce me to some of the fabulous
women she's met lately: "I'm sure you'd be much more
compatible with one of them."

"Or maybe with the whole group at the same time --
who knows."

"That could be too."

"Or serially. Or permutes and combos."

"Sounds like fun!"

Somewhere along the line I did promise to call her
the next time I'm in town. But when I drove off into
the fog I suddenly found -- after finally extracting
myself from the deja-vu whirlpool -- I was in a barely
contained state of fury, just as so often has been the
case when leaving her, and soon I was muttering and
eventually shouting at the top of my lungs the familiar

litany of vows to myself about being finished with her forever.

Of course the truth is I don't want to stop seeing Briana. But it's undeniable: everything seems hopeless with her. She obviously hadn't missed me very much; she was in fine spirits and extremely pleased with the way her life was going. I didn't see any problem at all with her "functioning," as Barb described it. What I did see was the same old niceness -- "She's just being nice to me again!" -- mixed in with a new patronizing "concern" which is even worse.

My conclusion? It would clearly be far better to concentrate on Valerie and on making a better life for myself, for her, for us.

Which doesn't mean I'll be able to do it. Briana still has that "strong magic" for me even if I lack it for her. If she calls or writes or otherwise shows serious interest, I may throw everything aside and launch another all-out play for her. If she doesn't, it's simple: I won't. So take that, Briana Tsu!

Whatever happens, I'm glad I saw her. I'm glad I could hold her and touch my fingers to her lips and sniff her gorgeous hair and feel her desiring me again (in spite of herself). And I'll say I'm impressed by her strength, her staunch way of protecting her "fragile" heart. She's right: she's much like Barbara. A similar kind of obstinacy, a similar kind of naivete oddly mixed with worldliness, a similar kind of narrow, blinkered, rigid wisdom, a similar tendency to hide behind convenient moralisms, a similar tendency to invoke the "spiritual" at unexpected moments seemingly just in an attempt to throw you off balance, a similar fear of losing control, a similar kind of attraction to poets and painters and also to house plants. In addition I think she really does have some of that beautiful simplicity which Barb aspires to but is much too messily complex ever to achieve (and thus she, Barb, comes off as a flaming hypocrite when she tries to act beautifully simple). Briana, though, perhaps as a corollary, is far more superficial in everything she

does, often failing to be aware of the deeper
implications of the values she champions and what it
would take to live as they'd require if she ever got
truly serious about doing that -- which it's highly
unlikely she'll ever do.

I love her anyway. This is all just sorry
rationalization and I know it. It's just words. (You
reading me loud and clear, Briana? In case you happen
to be perusing these pages again? At some point perhaps
far, far off in the future? Say on a day when one of us
says to the other, "Hey, honey, let's check out some of
the absurd things we used to write about each other back
in the benighted era before we finally got together for
good"?)

Let's see: right now I love Valerie, Claire,
Briana, and, down deep, Jang. I don't use the word
"love" lightly either; I mean it. It's real. And I
know this fracturing of my emotions is crippling me.
Today I decided it's probably true that all of this --
and my so-called voluptuousness and perhaps even my
"sensualist's philosophy" as well -- stems from
Mother's "excessive love and devotion" (to use Barb's
term which Val now knowingly echoes with a sad shake of
her head), especially during those all-important
formative years when Dad was gone in the war and before
Barb had even come along and I was all poor Mother had.
For three years! Freud would gobble it up! -- Those
three years being, as a matter of fact, about twice as
long as I've ever lasted with any other woman.

But...so what. The truth is I'd still much prefer
to have a tight, loving, long-term relationship with one
woman. It's always been that way and so that's probably
old Mom's doing too. I mean, what isn't? The real
question is simply: what happens now? What can I do to
nudge my life a little closer to what I'd like it to be?
And how do I make the love part of it fit with all the
other parts I'd like to keep in place or simply wouldn't
know how to jettison?

MARCH

1

Monday 1

I think I may be approaching some sort of philosophical flashpoint. When you reach the stage where the people who care about you most see you as a criminal and a villain and a threat to the ethical structure of their lives, it's time for, at the very least, a serious reexamination of underlying values.

These people have things against me:

** Valerie, who thinks I'm "narcissistic," "debauched," and "unable to give" myself.

** Briana, who calls me "shallow" and "very fucked up."

** Claire, who asserts I'm "on an ego trip" and "unknowable."

** Jang, who charges me with being "unkind" and "stubborn."

** Barbara, who finds me "deceptive" and "deeply schizoid."

** Mother, who suggests I've become "callous" and "incorrigible."

** And of course Dad, who accuses me of being "arrogant" and "hubristic," among lots of other things.

Do I believe I'm as bad as they're all saying? No I don't. I'm well aware they have their own interests and perspectives, blindnesses and prejudices, ethical shortcomings and axes to grind. At best they're seeing just a part of the picture, and often it's a small and/ or superficial part. And I believe I could easily rebut (and have!) all their charges, whether taken individually or as a group.

Nonetheless. A strong voice in me cries that it's

time for some changes. It's time to stop following my
heart "wherever it may lead"; it's time to seek greater
depth and less breadth. If further "intellectual and
emotional growth" is indeed withholding itself from me,
as Briana/Barb/Val insist, it may be because I'm
fracturing my emotional focus and dissipating energy in
a dozen different directions at once in mad pursuit of
what usually turn out to be expedient and transitory
satisfactions.

In other words, I'm acknowledging it's true: in
some ways I've been playing around too much. It's been
a full year now (as of last week) since Jang and I broke
up; I've had plenty of time to go through whatever
ricochet romances might have been necessary, including
several relapses with Jang herself. It's also been
seven months since I quit Empyrean (and met Briana the
same week); that should've been long enough for me to
celebrate my liberation from the workaday world and to
adjust to living in an unstructured way outside the
mainstream of society for the first time in my life.

And: the sojourn in Merino is coming to an end. In
glancing through V.23 of this journal, completed three
months ago right before I left the city for Garnett, I
realized with renewed force that one of the main reasons
for going up there was to get away, to gain some
perspective on things. After doing this -- my stint in
the wilderness -- I was supposed to come back recharged,
in possession of a far better picture of what I wanted
to do next and how to go about doing it. Now the time's
just about here to see how well I've succeeded in
realizing those goals.

Of the women I love I think it's true, as Barb and
Rob both say, that Valerie understands me best and loves
me most deeply. She's also the smartest, the sexiest in
appearance, and the most political, not to mention the
most sophisticated and probably the most physically and
artistically talented (or would that be Jang?).
Therefore I think I should seek her companionship and
support as I try to move into a new kind of life in San
Francisco while also helping her with her own challenges

(starting school, dealing with her "neurosis," coming to
terms with her horrific past, figuring out better ways
to handle Jim and to mother Danny and to reconnect with
her parents -- her father especially -- and her siblings
in other cities and countries, etc.). If that doesn't
work out -- but I don't want to go into that. Already I
must resist the temptation to hedge.

Specifically what is it I'd be trying to do? These
things:

* ** Cutting the strings that keep me tied,
      however loosely, to Briana, Jang, Ciara,
      and others.
* ** Committing myself solely to Val and
      striving to know her more deeply --
      making myself "fully open and vulnerable"
      to her (to the extent this is possible
      and desirable!) and encouraging her to
      do the same with me.
* ** Forging friendships with others (men
      especially) based on affinities in
      interests, ideas, values; deepening the
      meaning of my own experience -- testing
      my ideas and values -- by listening to
      their (the friends') criticism and at
      times simply by trying harder to see
      life, my own included, through their
      eyes.
* ** Exploring the roots of my "sensualist
      philosophy" with an eye to making major
      adjustments if not wholesale changes.
* ** Reviving my sense of wonder and touch,
      hope, innocence (to the extent this is
      even remotely possible at age twenty-
      eight).
* ** Working much harder and more
      "persistently," as Al would advise, to
      express myself through various art forms
      -- stories, sketching, painting,
      songwriting, and most of all a new novel.
* ** Continuing to engage with society

           politically -- fighting the good fight
           -- through work for the Mercury and
           (eventually) the Bay Bulldog or some
           other "alternative" publication.
  ** Striving to improve my health: eat
           better, sleep better, exercise more,
           relax more, get away from the daily
           grind more.

Lots of conflicts here, lots of idealism. Lots of embarrassing earnestness too. In a sense it's all just a more detailed update of my New Year's "why-nots," and I'm not talking about just this year's: I mean every piece of New Year's pie-in-the-sky gibberish I've tried to rally myself around since I was in knee pants.

Unfortunately -- or perhaps fortunately -- a big impediment stands in the way of all this: I can't even begin to get serious about most of it until the Garnett gig is over; and the way things look now, that won't be until the very end of this month that's starting today.

But still. I can begin gearing up. And on a few items I can plunge in right now. In fact, if the dryer weren't about to spin to a stop -- this whole spiel has been going down in an Irving Street laundromat -- I'd launch a full-blown, no-holds-barred analysis of the "sensualist philosophy" and whatever may underlie it. Because coming to a better understanding of that may well be the key to all the rest.

Tuesday 2

A long day later. Blood still on my hands -- literally. Bonnie Wolverton, one of our Mercury volunteers, tried to kill herself today, and she chose me to call right before she did it. Stacy and I arrived at her place minutes later, just in time to prevent her from slashing her wrists a second time. The first cut was superficial; the doctors at the Fleming emergency room wouldn't even see her; and the shrinks at the base mental-health clinic had just received a new order requiring refusal of service to dependents of military

personnel living off-base such as Bonnie -- evidently
the number of dependents flipping out under Vietnam War-
related strains has become overwhelming here and just
about everywhere in the far-flung U.S. Armed Forces
archipelago -- so I soon found myself nervously standing
watch over a suicidal schizophrenic (that word again) in
her rental home near downtown Garnett. I wound up
alternating one-hour shifts for twelve straight hours,
first with Stacy and later with Tom Y.

That exhausting experience on top of last night's
all-night rap with Stacy has left my mind numb. Right
now, sprawled on the office cot, I'm struggling to keep
my eyes open. But there are still some things to say:

    ** So far I've found my vows of yesterday
       even harder to implement than I thought
       they'd be.
    ** "Honesty is not a privilege you accord
       to or withdraw from someone on the basis
       of that person's behavior." -- Briana.
    ** "So what you do, then, Briana, is you
       let that other person stomp all over you
       and then you crawl back for more? Okay,
       I understand now. Thank you very much."
       -- Glen.
    ** Claire is a delight; Stacy is
       dangerously fascinating.

Too tired to go on.

Wednesday 3

I'm prepared to accept that a man must achieve a
balance between action and contemplation in his life. I
wearily -- oh so marrow-deep wearily -- submit to the
proposition that my physical energy is not limitless.
Nor is my emotional energy. I think one of the main
reasons I like Claire so much is that with her, when
things are right between us, I can at least feel
comfortable and at peace.

Right now I'm taking a break from cleaning up the
dog shit in Al's garage. It's amazing what ten dogs,

even when nine of them are tiny pups, can do to a small enclosed space in two weeks. Also it's a pretty good image for what I'm letting this newspaper do to my head.

*   *

And it's doing it right now. Close to three a.m. and only Tom is still here at the office, though Stacy should be back shortly. I couldn't be more WASTED. ---

Saturday 6 (X:4-5)

The city again. Only a few shreds remain of that strong impulse to reform myself and redirect my energies. It's been a week in which the center threatened to give way again and again under enormous pressures from all sides, not to mention above and below.

Somehow we got a paper out, miraculously, because, as Murphy's nasty old chestnut of a law decrees, everything that could've gone wrong did. At three a.m. Thursday night, an hour before deadline, I was frantically pounding out my own Mercky Notions column on the Composer, afraid the ribbon -- our last one -- might run out at any moment. Stacy was assaulting me with continuous demands for exclusive attention (she's childlike in the way she shows what she wants and how much she hurts if she doesn't get it) and I was trying to come up with the most painless way possible to establish a safety zone between us. From time to time Bonnie was bursting through the door, upsetting tables, letting in a fierce March wind, loosing volumes of loud words, madness in her eyes, blood dripping from the bandage on her wrist. She thoroughly frightened everyone. Oh, it was a heavy, heavy scene.

Now back at Funston I find Valerie and I are unable to get it on the way we both want to. Danny is whimpering and tantrumming and demanding constant attention much as Stacy did. Sex is a dismaying failure. Even so I'm touched by the "graveyard of flowers" Val set up on my desk, a cupful gathered each day I was gone, and by her surprise and apparent delight

that I've chosen to "commit" myself to her, that is, to
focus intensively on working things out with her once I
return to the city for good. (If I didn't so choose, I
must say, I might need to be "committed" elsewhere -- at
Langley-Porter, for example, our local mental ward.)

It pains me that I can't bring myself to tell Val
about the role Briana played in my "bellwether decision"
or the story of the emergency with Stacy and Bonnie --
but I'm not ready for that yet, nor do I think she is.
Nonetheless she's the single person in the world I feel
closest to at the moment, and I want the closeness to
deepen and blossom into true wholehearted intimacy.
Should I throw all caution to the winds and disclose
everything I can to her? The trouble is that every time
I've tried to do this in the past she's lost it
completely for a day or two or three and thrown me even
further behind whatever eightball I was already bashing
my head against at the time.

All but forgotten amid the turmoil have been two
other sad developments:

** From home we learn Dad has suffered a personal
catastrophe, an "uncorrectible" loss of thirty percent
of his vision. Sitting at the kitchen table, he can see
only a blur where the row of framed family photos stands
on the ledge above the sink. Corrective lenses don't
help. The doctors (he's seen several specialists)
speculate that overburdened nerves and a "general
condition of toxicity in his system" -- caused primarily
by too much smoking -- triggered the condition. It all
happened with terrible suddenness, just like his brother
Kar's laryngeal cancer two years ago. Dad woke up one
morning and couldn't see -- that was it. The only
hopeful note in it is that he'll be forced to give up
cigarettes, thus probably prolonging his life. Of
course he'll be hell to live with while he's kicking the
habit. As Mother grimly reminds me, his whole lifestyle
is built around smoking. At his age (fifty-four now!)
can he develop a new one? After all the defeats of
recent years, will he have the strength to try?

** Meanwhile Rob has returned to Chicago. Many

factors entered into his decision: disenchantment with
his courses at City College, running arguments with
Barbara, loneliness, longing for the type of strongly
variable seasonal weather he's used to, need for relief
from the stormy emotional weather so often prevailing at
1616. Ironically, in recent months he and I have been
getting along better than ever, and our parting was sad
and regretful. Barb has moved into his room -- the
"blue room": the one where Jang and I used to sleep,
then later Denise and I, then I alone, then Rob alone.
The one where I stay now is, of course, the "yellow
room," which is a name I'm suddenly resisting. "Just
call it Glen's room, willya please, at least for now?"

*

(At that point I set the journal aside for a moment
to steal into the kitchen and sing in Valoshka's ear "I
want you, I need you, I-I lo-o-ove you" -- lift her high
in the air -- gaze out the door at Mt. Moraga
silhouetted against a splendid purple sunset.)

So all in all this has not been the best week to
launch a new offensive to regain my sanity. But I have
hopes I can do better next week. Al and Sherry are
fleeing to a cabin on the coast for a desperately needed
week's vacation, leaving me in charge -- I even get to
stay in their house. A good thing too, because if one
thing's become clear, it's that I need a place to
retreat to when the office becomes a madhouse and my own
room next door becomes in effect part of the office
(which is indeed why we rented adjacent rooms in the
first place, so that my room -- Al's and mine at the
time -- could serve a dual purpose).

This is also the week I'll be doing all I can to
help shift the Merc from its makeshift crisis-by-crisis
operational mode to something a little less frantic.
And as well to lay the basis for a twenty-four-page
issue next round. I relish the challenge. At the same
time I know the whole project can go up in flames if I
allow people to put the emotional screws to me. So I'll
also be making it yet another goal to keep them from
doing that.

326

[The War in Merino]

On the personal front, there's one thing I must do immediately: let Briana know I'm now acknowledging she won't be present at the resurrection (mine, that is, from the pit of perfidy in which I've been digging myself ever deeper right up to this very moment, as of course she'd be among the first to agree).

Sunday 7

Briana --

Our meeting last week was so sad. The 'strong magic' has indeed disappeared. A tragedy if you ask me.

I'm trying to take a deep look at all the unpretty things you said about me. Right now, though, my mental frame isn't right for it. So later. When the pain has gone the way of the magic, when I no longer need to take the loss as lightly as possible.

I'll admit it burns me up that you could be so happy in the midst of all this. But in another sense I'm happy myself to see it, since it means maybe I didn't cause you as much grief as you say. Which, alas, also means you didn't care very much about me either. But then it's time for me to stop refusing to accept that fact.

What happened between us may eventually work some big changes in me. For now, though, I'll continue as before -- writing for the Merino Mercury (and I hope for the Bay Bulldog soon), trying to launch the long-delayed new novel. I'll also see if I can make a go of it with Valerie, who deserves more than I've been able to give her thus far.

Best wishes, Briana. Your presence in the city still brightens the place for me.

[Have Mercy]

And so Briana Tsu in the end becomes a pastime for a languorous Sunday afternoon. But is it really the end with her? The very impulse behind my composing such a sappy epistle suggests it's not, although I'll try hard to make it so. In fact, I don't even need to try, for the flow of events is carrying me away from her. With my strength restored by a relatively restful weekend, today I feel a renewed confidence and determination; hopefully this will find its first expression in the twenty-four-page paper. I'm assigning myself a dozen articles to write and rewrite. I want to show myself what I can do. Domestic peace can offer marvelous dividends! Whether the current shaky and tentative peace can be extended and deepened -- that's another matter entirely. Because Briana threatens it, I'll struggle against any impulse to resume chasing after her.

With Valerie everything seems to be fine for the moment except the balling. She offers another grand challenge to the idealistic theory that the quality of the sexual union is basically a reflection of the emotional union. (Ciara provided the major prior test of it for me.) (But Val and I have several advantages Ciara and I didn't. I do find her highly attractive virtually all the time, and our balling is not always a total disaster. Once in a while it can even be glorious. As her confidence in my love and in her own grows there's at least a chance she'll relax into her true sensuality and sexuality. Or perhaps she'll just grow into it, period, since she's so young -- in fact, she's about the same age Aki J. was when something like that seemed to happen with her lo these many years ago -- almost five!)

The months and years race by. Directions change little by little, imperceptibly but unalterably. Youth becomes more and more a memory, a puzzle, a chuckle, as the deeper meanings of those much-maligned words "maturity" and "adulthood" begin ever so stealthily to reveal themselves.

328

2

Monday 8
     In the last thirty hours I
          ** said "What's happening?" to Jane Fonda,
             who replied, "Not much";
          ** shrank into a dread of the future while
             watching, with Val, a Bergman flick called
             "The Ritual";
          ** had another falling-out with that same
             Val over a familiar issue: sex;
          ** announced to Barb that barring some new
             disaster, Val and I will soon be "going
             steady or maybe even pinned";
          ** balled deliciously with Briana;
          ** realized again there's no hope with Briana;
          ** talked warmly with Claire on the phone,
             both of us agreeing we'll be "eternal pals";
          ** rebuffed Stacy when she tailed me from the
             office to the Paladin Room;
          ** told Stacy I didn't want to hurt her; and
          ** realized I can do no more for the suicidal
             Bonnie.
     Now I'm curled up on Al's couch after banging on
his piano for an hour or so and imbibing a fine
interview with Daniel Berrigan in the New York Review.
I also glanced through Al's newly arrived copy of the
Encyclopedia Britannica Yearbook for 1971, which leads
with a long paean to the Free World purportedly written
by Park Chung Hee, the iron-fisted dictator of South
Korea -- his wife is a longtime friend of Jang's --
followed by a lily-livered description of the current
American scene churned out in his sleep, it would
appear, by Theodore H. White. What horror to think this
book will someday be consulted as an authoritative
resource on our era.
     Jane Fonda's and my eyes kept meeting! I marveled
at the fineness of her bones -- but found Valerie more

329

attractive. All those rich Pacific Heights liberal
women in their pantsuits and thick makeup, yeek!
    Briana gave in. Yes, it was true, she confessed,
the essence of the past six months was her inability to
open up to me. I wanted one thing understood and
accepted: I loved her. No amount of righteous
rationalization on either side could destroy that. Yes,
she loved me too, she said -- but only "in a way." In
any event, something still had a hold on her. She was
torn between wanting and not wanting me. I could see it
in her eyes, in her tense movements, in everything she
said. For a moment her resistance dissolved and we
balled with the old miraculous passion...but then
afterwards her "allergy" (her word) to me broke out
again. I guess we both knew it was over for us when she
began talking so rationally about that "allergy." A
strong, unexpected wave of gratitude washed over me: at
least this time the ending was amicable.
    With Valerie the domestic peace disintegrated with
appalling suddenness. Of course most of it was my
fault. While watching "The Ritual," mentioned earlier,
a prickly dread crept over me: fear of boredom and
stagnation with Val, disenchantment because we lack that
same magic Briana and I have. Poor Val is confused and
crippled and anxious and I can do nothing to make her
feel better about it beyond voicing hollow words of
reassurance. Those words echo with my own sense of
estrangement. The only hopeful part of it is the fact
that we're able to talk about it.
    Val at this point is taking all the blame upon
herself, acknowledging again and again she's beset by
the same deep-rooted fears and inhibitions we talked
about so much last fall (based on her childhood-
instilled "low expectancy of men" and Jim's brutal
treatment of her for most of their three years
together). She's again begging me to be patient. Yet a
familiar bind is surfacing: I can't commit myself to her
until a "magic" develops, and she can't give in to the
"magic" until I commit myself. This morning we
struggled to repair the damage, and I was heartened by

her brave show of optimism. But then Briana drew me in like a magnet. Yes, I have loved her, and I'm glad of it, glad I no longer need to pretend otherwise.

Tonight I had to make a difficult choice. Help Bonnie, or help the Merc. The Merc won. An "institution" over a person. What a bad taste it leaves. Yet if I were to continue making myself available to Bonnie, I know I couldn't do anything close to what needs to be done to assure the Merc's publication. The simple truth is the paper would fail.

Good news: Dad won't be going blind after all. Specialist No. 4 discovered the culprit is some sort of infection, not toxicity of the entire system.

Bad news: the righteous antiwar Muhammad Ali just lost the heavyweight title to flag-waving Joe Frazier.

Tuesday 9

In the Merino Community College cafeteria, almost empty now at nine p.m. as closing hour nears. A vacuum cleaner drones. I set aside the S.F. Examiner and mull a few questions that have been plaguing me.

** A bomb exploded in the Capitol building in Washington, D.C., last week. What's my thinking about this? On the positive side, it bolsters the morale not only of revolutionary groups within the U.S. (assuming such a group planted it), but, much more important, of antiwar, anticolonial, and liberation movements around the world. On the negative side, it hardens anti-Movement attitudes among many Americans, making those people even less receptive to new thinking at a time when the Movement -- to the extent it still exists -- desperately needs new blood and support. So the bombing can be said to help foreign victims of U.S. neocolonial domination at the expense of domestic foes of the policies producing that domination.

But...is even this true? A strengthened repressive government at home would seemingly be better able than a divided, unsure government at home to maintain its oppressive "sphere of dominance" overseas. Defenders of

guerrilla actions such as this bombing must finally fall
back on the argument that polarization of American
society, leading ultimately to thorough repression at
home, would also lead more quickly to a second American
Revolution -- a preposterous idea, I think.

Provoking further oppression in the U.S. itself
will bring about a revolution only if homegrown
revolutionary groups are large, well-organized, and
fully prepared to lead the way. Otherwise such
provocations are counterrevolutionary because of their
prematurity; they cause the destruction of precisely
those same groups; they set back the timetable for
significant change by years or even decades. The
campaign of bombings in the past few years has done
exactly that, making a shambles of the Movement just as
it was scoring its first political successes (ouster of
Lyndon Johnson, reversal of public opinion on the war).
Therefore, while I sympathize in some ways with those
who did the bombing, and can well understand their
motivation, I condemn their action.

** Gossip. This afternoon by chance I learned a
local high-school counselor was about to be charged with
raping and impregnating a sixteen-year-old student as
she babysat for him. Suddenly it dawned on me this
counselor might be the married man Marcelle's been
unable to stop loving -- "Rodney." If it were, would it
be ethical for me to pass the story on to Marcelle?
Would it be ethical for me not to? (The question turned
out to be academic -- apparently the villain was someone
else -- but memories of a similar situation in Mentoka
Falls still haunt me. In essence, the question is this:
can I purge myself of personal interests in weighing
whether the information will help the innocent person
involved? I doubt it. Even if I could, is it right?
I'm not a believer in the reliability or better to say
the possibility of "disinterested judgment." -- And
even if, again, I were, how presumptuous of me to think
I could gauge with any accuracy what will "help" under
such circumstances.)

-- And that's it, no more time for mulling tonight

even if the cafeteria hadn't just now officially closed (and regardless of whether this sentence with all its negatives makes sense).

Wednesday 10

Valerie shrieking in the night, tearing long hysterical pleas from her guts. All through the night. A mounting chaos of the heart. For hours rapping intensely with herself in Al and Sherry's darkened hall, guzzling wine, utterly mad and utterly righteous -- but I was lying in bed in A&S's "master bedroom" and could make out only a small part of what she was saying. Our balling had failed, I had sunk into a familiar weary despair, withdrawing further as her demands increased. Then the boiling acid of her fury, the meanness oozing from the depths of her soul. Glen is debauched, selfish, secretive, cowardly, unable to give himself, afraid to love, hypocritical, monstrous.

I stabbed myself with remorse because I was barren of feeling. I could not respond to her desperate cries. I could not offer the "profound refinement of sentiment" she sought. Her wails and moans sounded like a trapped and dying animal. She starts pounding her head against the wall; I leap up and pull her into the bed, trying to calm her, at the same time restraining her forcibly for fear she might seriously hurt herself or once again go for a knife in the kitchen and come after me with it. Suddenly she shifts to a wild sexual passion and begs for fucking and before long it's happening, she's hotter than I've ever seen her and yet groaning horribly even while still in the act about having "degraded and debased and humiliated" herself with those other men almost two weeks ago now, about having "nothing to live for" and "wanting to die now" -- and I let everything go and fuck her as fiercely and intensely as I know how and then beyond anything I know, a fuck of blood and tears and shit and sweat; and yet underneath I'm torn with disgust, pity, fear, shock, regret.

In her extreme agony she's shown me the living core

of her love (unveiling the need, the dependence, the
hunger, the fear, the madness) and I've drawn back in
fascinated horror. I don't deserve such a desperate
passion and I can't possibly return it. With dismay I
watch my elaborate plans for the upcoming day crumble as
the hours pass and dawn finally arrives and with it an
hour's sleep. -- In Garnett, California, on a quiet
street of neat green lawns littered with tricycles and
swings, beneath a full moon, as military transports roar
overhead almost nonstop and dogs up and down the street
join in Valoshka's mad and hideous and very loud howls.

Friday 12 (X:11)
     At last a moment of peace. All week long my
involvements with women have been devouring huge chunks
of time. Valerie the primary offender. Twice she's
shown up in Garnett unexpectedly, consumed twenty-four
hours or more with savage outbursts, leaving a trail of
wreckage behind her. I don't resent Marcelle or Claire
-- our hours together were beautiful and revitalizing --
but Val, I could strangle her.
     It was another long talk with my own damnable
sister that fired her up this time and she came armed
for a showdown battle, demanding to "know the truth."
She attacked me viciously, and eventually I returned the
honor, my fury deepening hour by hour as she failed to
show any respect for my obligations to the paper, where
we were on the usual impossibly tight deadline schedule
and dozens of people were depending on me for help and
because of her frequent disruptions I had to let many of
them down. Even so, I admired her staunchness in
refusing to accept what I offered her -- namely,
something less than the fully committed, unconditional,
throttle-wide-open-right-now love she demanded.
     At one point -- at a sordid drive-in in the rain --
we were both ready to call it quits for good. But she
buckled, so did I, and we were soon right back where we
started. Her argument is still essentially the same:
until I'm able to be "completely open" with her, I'm

334

emotionally crippled, "growth" is foreclosed to me, and
I'm a kind of criminal of the heart. I don't say she
has no truth at all on her side; but our lack of "magic"
-- as well as her viciousness and violence and demented
demands and egomania, and my own growing fear of binding
myself to the kind of woman she's revealing herself to
be -- all this prevents me from taking the steps she
wants me to take in the way she demands I take them. I
tell her I'm still ready to try living together when I
return to San Francisco for good, but that's no longer
enough for her. So she should withdraw, right? But she
can't. And I won't. So our relationship somehow
lurches ahead, each day a fearful struggle.

*

     Meanwhile my happiness comes not from Valerie,
whose arrival here I've come to dread, whose departure
always relieves me greatly, but from Marcelle and
Claire. Wednesday afternoon I picked up Marcelle from
Orchard Hills Junior High where she teaches (only four-
eleven, she looks more student-like than many of the
students do) and thirty minutes later we were balling in
Al and Sherry's bed, where we stayed for five hours,
joking, laughing, having a marvelous time irrespective
of the fucking (at which she's a near novice -- as
Rodney's surrogate I'm only her second lover). "We're
using each other," she observed, and that's the truth.
My appointed function is to drive Rodney out of her
mind. Hers is to ease my loneliness and drive away some
of the tension caused by the paper and Valerie.
Afterwards she ate a full meal and jabbered happily for
the first time in days, she said, relaxing my fears that
our balling would only deepen her gloom.
     Then the next morning, Claire. A gorgeous time
with her, going at it on a workout mattress on the floor
of her study as the stereo played full volume ("Bare
Back Ride" again): incredibly together lovemaking.
Touching. Comforting. Dancer's body and rhythms.
World's finest cooch, lush brown fur-like hair from her
navel all the way around to her tailbone tip. Natural
mates, I tell you. It surpasseth all understanding how

335

I can live without her. Yet I pretty much forget her
unless we're together, and then I love her abundantly.
I'm always delighted to see her, can't keep my hands off
her. I'd like to be her lifelong friend and lover. It
won't happen, of course. The miracle will pass quickly.
Gracefully, I think. I hope. What happiness, what
relief she gives me -- and I give her, yes!

So, obviously, I have serious ethical problems to
wrestle with. I envy Chris, twenty-two-year-old assman
supreme whom Claire's still balling -- Chris who can
blithely assert he doesn't let "any of them get to me."
Despite all seeming evidence to the contrary, I don't
work that way. I want more than good fucking, more even
than simple happiness (which exactly because of its
simplicity soon fades for me). Valerie's closer to my
destiny because that's where a more complex and
potentially more fulfilling relationship lies. But how
do we get there? What do we have to give up? Are we --
am I -- prepared to do whatever's necessary? Because a
lot more will be called for than I was figuring on even
as recently as a few days ago: that's for sure.

Sunday 14 (X:13)
Taking a Paladin Room break from typesetting my own
"Foreign Policy" column, which this time around is
basically a condensed version, Reader's Digest style
almost (that alarmingly "radical" rag in the eyes of
Merino County authorities) -- condensed version, I say,
of an impressive New York Review critique of Nixon's
Indochina policy. Still trying hard to make up the
deficit created by Val's unexpected visits and the
demonic tantrums she threw. The next four days will be
a colossal pain. The twenty-four-page issue is still in
the works. One final all-out binge for the Merc with
Editor Sandefjord at the helm. A monument made of
newsprint -- a living, snorting, rip-roaring monument.
Then I'll begin refocusing my energies on the novel:
"Symphony No. 6" (in newspaper lingo that's my "slug"
title for it). Still keeping a hand in on the Merc,

however, and also trying to catch on with the Bay
Bulldog.

First time I've come here in a week -- didn't want
to risk running into Stacy. After leaving me several
notes -- none replied to -- she's disappeared. Got the
message at last. In over my head with her, was I ever.

If Barbara decides to move to Los Angeles -- she'll
live with Paul "if I feel I can learn from it" -- I'll
probably ask Val to come live with me at "the Castle."
I told her I was ready to try it, and I am. I think.
I'm not quite done with mulling it. In fact before I
make such a drastic change I want to give the compass
needle another flick, a good hard one, to make sure it
winds up pointing me in the same direction. Confirm
it's not just stuck on it.

Guess that's what I'm doing in seeing Claire: the
flick. Not with Briana, however. The attraction toward
her has abated. Not seeing Marcelle, who's too young,
unformed, not meant for me (though we're still buddies
and she says she feels "a new strength" with Rodney
now). Not seeing Jang, who one day became a memory,
inert, no driving need for her left. But Claire.
Sister of the soul. Lover extraordinaire: "Pour it into
me." Yet also evasive, not permitting herself to go
head-to-head with me. She's worked out a compromise for
herself, a way to deflect her needs and drives,
sublimate them into drugs and natural highs, a way to
protect herself from further pain, and I guess it's not
too much to say I'm fascinated by it. This may be
because the time in my life for making a similar
sublimation move of my own is near (though one involving
making art rather than doing drugs).

Last night she, Al, and I visited the annual Merino
County Democratic Party fund-raiser at the Tesuque
Valley Farm Center. All the local party hacks soaking
up liquor as a shabby three-piece combo wheezed out
waltzes and fox-trots. Enchiladas and ham on paper
plates. Russ Danner stiff and awkward in our first
encounter since he bailed from the paper. Al pounding
out the same old schmaltzy college-days numbers on the

337

out-of-tune upright piano during the combo's breaks --
"Moon River"! "Autumn Leaves"! -- as Grover, Millie,
and I formed a Rockettes kickline and high-stepped
around the room. Hilarious Polaroid pictures. An
argument about keeping ahead of the Russkies with a trio
of drunken ex-military men who still haven't heard that
the so-called "missile gap" was and is a sham. And
these guys call themselves Democrats?

Everyone has to try on my "Bat hat." The combo
playing "Tennessee Waltz" for the third or fourth time
as a few couples hobble about the floor. Two or three
young political hopefuls glad-handing their way around
the room, including one with a beard! The loquacious
black supervisorial candidate Elijah Barton rounding up
votes ("My campaign manager told me to keep my mouth
shut until after I'm elected"). A twinge of atavistic
jealousy as Claire raps with Lonnie Reed, who's also
black and funky and smashingly good-looking and has a
major case of the hots for her. (Once the Merc ran a
photo meant to show him and to our everlasting shame
accidentally cropped him right out of it.)

Then, with Al already 99.9 percent ripped, we
boldly decided the night was only beginning. Half an
hour later at the Azalea, having just paid a nine-dollar
after-hours door charge for the whole group, he passed
out before we'd all made it through the door. I carted
him home, then rushed back to Claire, who was in the
process at that odd hour of applying for an open Azalea
waitress job. Delicious delightful dancer, Claire,
agile, loose, sensual, so superbly constructed. I drove
in on her, urge too strong to resist, "giving you all I
can," wanting that full-blooded hunger from her, wanting
her to yield to me, to love me up good as maybe now only
she can. Succeeded only for moments, upended quickly by
some irreverent irrelevancy she slipped under my foot
like a banana peel. Even so it was her idea, against
her own grain, not easy, to ball on the office floor.
"Why are you so turned on tonight?" With only one other
man had it approached this, she said. Same for me,
except it's two: Briana, Jang. Well, and maybe a few

338

times with Nadine, but we were on some powerful weed for
them all and so it's hard to know for sure.
     In any event it's still this way for me only when
I'm with her, Claire, not away from her. I doubt I'll
ever know whether, focusing every power we could summon,
we could've become "unconditional" lovers. But I don't
think so. Too many things that matter greatly to me
would be left out. Probably the same's true for her.
For one thing I won't go anywhere near a "red."

                            3

Monday 15
     One hell of a long happy Ides of March, all of it
given over to the blockbuster twenty-four-page issue,
ten pages of which are now pasted up (Tom and I rubber-
cementing articles onto the flats as eco-freak Ben Kiel
labored away at "The Merino Fox" and his dog Lucille,
named after B.B. King's guitar, comically chased rabbits
in her sleep while lying on her side in the middle of
the floor). I make up a list of things to do tomorrow
-- which will have to begin only four hours from now, at
eight a.m. -- and run it out to thirty-seven items,
including nine pieces to be written by me.
     Today's most surprising moment came out at the
college when I lifted eighteen-year-old Gloria Maholinog
(sp?), Filipina-American beauty and self-declared
virgin, high in the air and nuzzled her nose-to-nose
(this in that same complex passageway between buildings
where Norm Gaston of, yup, the Ghastly once distanced
himself from me) and suddenly her lips were pressing
hard against mine and her tongue popped into my mouth.
Later in the office she drew up a chair near my table
and did a sketch she labeled "Editor Hard at Work."
It's now tacked on the wall above the layout table.
     Lucille shakes a leg in her sleep. Ben gently
moves the leg a little faster with his hand, then
faster, then faster still, and Lucille, still asleep,
begins to vibrate all over. By slight pressure at a key

point, a subtle change in rhythms, you can manipulate a
creature into madness. That's what I do too. Or at
least that's what Valoshka would say.
    She writes:
        I'm not so sure after all that I'm
        capable of producing a magical chemistry.
        I never have before. I love you, you love
        me, we don't have it. That's all I know.
        The only thing that can help me is
        closeness between you and me throughout
        the day, peaceful harmony and acceptance,
        sincere warmth born from happiness and
        togetherness. For you these things emerge
        from sexual magic. I feel trapped, so
        badly trapped.... But such it is for me,
        ability to trust someone leads to my own
        nakedness and to my own melting and it
        seems to me that this is the only road to
        magic for me.
        I'm tired of fighting for your interest
        and desire. You must take some
        responsibility in the persistence of your
        own feelings. I cannot take it all. Of
        course I want to be your source of
        inspiration -- but Jesus! Glenn, you've
        got to want me! If you don't, let's face
        it -- why force it? Your only obligation
        to me is the truth.
    She proposes our living together "with no
commitment" to "see where it leads us."
        Wherever, it will accelerate our speed
        of discovery...you won't have to be
        tortured too long by the gamble...I am
        myself willing to take the chance at my
        own cost and risk.
    Some thoughts about all this:
    (1) For me these things (harmony, etc.) "emerge
from" sexual magic? No, but it often seems they can't
last without at least occasional exposure to that kind
of magic. And I don't think I'd want them to.

340

(2)   She's tired of fighting for my interest and desire? But she must never tire of that. It should be a joy! If it's not...well, she should find someone with whom it is. And of course the same goes for me. Of course!

(3)   I can take "some responsibility" that my feelings will persist, yes, but I can't guarantee that they'll do so. Not if, as she's so often saying, she wants me to be "fully open and honest." All I can say is I'll try my best to give them a maximal chance to persist. To me that's what a "gamble" (her word!) like the one she says she wants us to take is all about.

(4)   I still insist: disclosure of the truth (and I'm talking about the truth that really matters, the truth of the innermost soul) is never an "obligation." To the limited extent it's even possible, it's a privilege, a miracle, a gift of love.

(5)   Living together would be risky, yes. It would accelerate the speed of discovery all right, as she says, but could it be we've already discovered enough? Or too much?

She's coming up here Wednesday and once again she's saying she'll "help." Her brand of help, sad to say, the Merc can easily do without. I also personally fear her emotional intrusion. No matter how deeply she understands me and loves me, it's still not deeply enough that I can count on her not to disrupt my life in disastrous ways at crucial moments. She's demonstrated this several times already. But there's no way I can stop her from coming. If I forbid her to, she'll still come but in an even worse mood.

And in three hours now Sherry (of the comedy lounge duo Al & Sherry) will be waking me up.

Sunday 21 (X:16-20)
Many days since I last wrote in here -- six! -- the longest abstention yet! -- and of course much has happened -- some of it marvelous and some of it horrifying -- and yet nothing is very different.

341

[Have Mercy]

Except: the twenty-four-page issue exists. It's a
thing of beauty, scratched and patched and lashed
together under conditions verging on total hysteria,
impressively heavy in the hand, something to be proud
of, a fine piece of work (de resistance!) upon which to
make my exit from Garnett.

Yes, my status changes now: I become the part-time
editor. Henceforth I'll be domiciled most of the time
in San Francisco, spending only three days of every two
weeks in Garnett. I'll be living on unemployment comp,
I hope, and, probably, with Valerie.

And so it's yes again: I've decided to take the
plunge with her. "The gamble." "Another experiment,
'like we did last summer.'" And this despite several
extremely ugly fights -- new ones. This afternoon she
disintegrated before my eyes, revealing any number of
horrific naked truths about herself: in chief, that
she's a prisoner of her own rampaging guilt, a tireless
and merciless saboteur of her own happiness, a very sick
kid desperately in need of help. I don't know whether I
can give her even a tiny part of what she wants or needs,
but I do think I'm ready to take my life in my hands
(this is no exaggeration) and try. The biggest barrier
is her vicious destructiveness, which goes far beyond
anything I previously suspected; I don't know whether I
can stand it and I don't know whether (to repeat,
because it's frightening) either of us can survive it.

Images of the week:
    ** Pressing the sides and bottom of my
    achingly distended cock against Valerie's
    cheeks and lips and eyes as she groaned with
    pleasure on the office floor (where we were
    sleeping because that colossal bitch Sherry,
    after hearing stories from the neighbors
    about a woman shrieking in the night [that
    would be Val, of course], doesn't want us in
    her house anymore) -- and suddenly the
    heater flared up, casting a gruesomely bent
    and awesomely obscene cock shadow into a
    shimmering yellow rhomboid of light on the

rug and wall that elicited an involuntary shudder from me as if I'd seen the monstrous shaft of death itself (no less!).

** Val and I arguing fiercely outside the office three hours before deadline (Mercky Notions still in the Composer, half done), she shivering violently from the cold and looking utterly ravishing and also utterly mad in her glossy green St. Patrick's bowler and four-leaf-clover-painted cheeks, loudly demanding I be more demonstratively loving with her in front of Claire (who soon left quietly).

** Val reminding me with nasty fatalistic eyes of her friend Jenny's warning last summer that she, Val, as a "bossy Aries" and I as a "hypercritical Virgo" would be "fighting all the time" if we ever tried to live together -- and that her Aries birth month is coming up, "which means I'll be an even bigger bitch than usual."

** A vengeful shopping spree at Office Supply (put it all on the bill).

** That mind-blowing "quintofecta moment" (cf. Val last summer and the "convocation of lovers" at the Downtown Peace Coalition) when I was alone with five women in the Merc office and I knew all five in the biblical sense (Irene, Stacy, Marcelle, Claire, Val): the gradual acceptance of the idea that whatever I am, I'm not naturally monogamous and maybe no longer even unnaturally monogamous, that is, not capable of being monogamous even if I work hard at it -- which however I'm indeed vowing right now (again) I will do.

> -- So attested this warm and
> breezy and earth-smelling first
> full day of spring 1971.

343

4

Tuesday 23 (X:22)
     In room 118 of the English Building at San
Francisco State the young poets snarl and nip at Zara
Lemke, who's reading her stuff. I shudder at the
memories this scene evokes of Mentoka Falls and its
rabid writers' workshops. How in the world did I ever
survive three years of those? Hold your head high, Zara
Lemke!
     Valerie keeps quiet. She's cowed by my presence,
no doubt, though I suspect she rarely says much in class
anyway. She flashes a tentative smile at me, a sort of
sickly one; I return the favor.
     We've just made up after another nasty battle.
(She charges across Irving in classic Valkyrie style and
tears open the L.C. door -- "You motherfucker!" -- and
starts beating on me with her ring-studded fists.) It
stemmed from a sad afternoon failure in bed. And that
coming after we'd both tried so hard all day -- our
first full day of living together, I guess one could
call it, although things won't be official until April
1st when we start sharing the rent -- but you can only
do so much by trying hard.
     April 1st: need I point out it's April Fool's Day?
     The fact is we're both nervous as hell about this
"gamble." Already she's warning me about tossing dirty
clothes on my own floor (and then apologizing for the
warning, even confessing to malicious intent: she'd
recalled reading how Jang's complaints about this same
regrettable habit of mine -- and of brother Jeff and
cousin Kar too -- involving that very same floor slowly
drove me mad). She's also washing walls. Scrubbing the
toilet. Casting disdainful glances at just about all
current furniture arrangements and most other matters of
decor, such as they are. Makes me extremely uptight.
                    *   *
     (State Student Union cafeteria now)

[The War in Merino]

Yes, undoubtedly it's true, it's undeniable -- I
confess! -- I have my share of hang-ups about living
with a woman. And this is doubly or triply true for
living with a neatnik woman with a kid -- even if it's a
joint-custody kind of kid, on hand only half the week,
as Danny is and presumably will continue to be.

Also I'm bothered by two aspects of my return to
the city that have little to do with Val. First, I'm
again face-to-face with my gargantuan ambitions as a
writer (reworking the old novels, finishing the one I
abandoned halfway through, coming up with a new one --
and that's just for starters). Second, after managing
to make myself at least somewhat politically useful in
Garnett, I'm afraid I'll slide back into outright apathy
in San Francisco. (This is why I'm so eager to visit
the Bay Bulldog office. But when I was talking about it
with Val last night, she was not encouraging. In no
uncertain terms she warned me about taking on too much,
spreading myself too thin. Of course I vigorously
defended my aims, citing my "need" to be politically
engaged and dredging up evidence for it going eight
years back to Tuscaloe days in Mississippi.)

Also, as a third worry, I should acknowledge I fear
falling back into the solitudinous ways of my former San
Francisco life. In Garnett I was continuously exposed
to all kinds of people -- and I could meet them and work
with them and enjoy being with them in the process of
accomplishing something meaningful, and for a cause the
whole group believed in. If I can't fill that void here
at the Bay Bulldog, I'll try to find some other way to
do it -- anything. Perhaps another try with the Good
Times, or teaching a class at the Free University, or...
god only knows what. But the Bulldog, from what I know
about it -- and I've admired it ever since my arrival in
S.F. in '67 -- would be ideal.

Valerie, make no mistake, poses a substantial
threat to my hopes. But I'm also well aware she offers
all too convenient a target for projecting my fears
onto. Just small things like the way she tacks her own
watercolors all over my walls, covers my armchair with

her patchwork quilt, props half a dozen decorator
pillows (hers) on the bed, places hordes of flowers on
my desk -- in moderation, lovely ideas every one and
certainly well intended -- but taken as a whole they can
be upsetting because I begin to feel alien in my own
room. And she's doing the same with all the other
rooms. She's even mounted her gymnast's exercise bar in
the "blue room" doorway! I nearly beheaded myself on
it! So I ask: Is it totally crazy that I wish she'd
let me reestablish some control over my personal life in
the city before rushing in with all her plans and
revisions and remodelings? Or at least couldn't she
have sought my opinion before charging ahead on them?
Yet it's extremely difficult to tell her this in a way
that's not hurtful or provocative. She thinks I'm
rejecting her. So I'll have to deal with the matter on
my own. And I'm afraid I won't succeed at that.

If only we could exalt ourselves in the sack, could
ball gloriously and lovingly and mellowly, could
establish a deep sexual-emotional bond, these other
concerns would surely fade away....
                    *   *
Late, after a long hot bath, well after Val's gone
to bed, I think about the great bursting of habits with
which I intend to celebrate my first week back in the
city. "You must change your life!" cried Rilke. (Hard
to believe no one thought up a simple line like that
before he did. But I guess that's genius, or at least
one prime aspect of it: you know how to be first in line
when they pass out the credit.) -- In any event, how
should I go about changing my life? How deep the purge?

A good first step would be to nudge my diet in a
healthful direction (fewer fried foods, less sugar and
salt, more fruits and vegetables). Beyond that, well,
let's just say I'm still in the conceptual stage. I
don't think I want to alter the way I dress, the length
of my hair, the kind of music I listen to, the
importance I confer upon good loving -- but maybe I
should. All of them. Things may have gotten so bad
that I need to consider a total identity makeover.

[The War in Merino]

But then again, maybe I'm still pretty much okay.
Maybe just a tweak here and there will do the trick.
How delightful were it so!

More on this tomorrow, as well as a reconsideration
of the concept of monogamy as applied, or misapplied, to
my own needs as manifested in the time of the big, the
almost Pascalian wager with Valoshka.

Wednesday 24

Back at Mac's Grill on a gray, cold day, rain
threatening. The city. All the talk is of Mayor
Alioto's indictment for bribery and fraud. On the box
here Janis Joplin's posthumously released "Ballad of
Bobby McGee" is playing for the fourth or fifth time in
an hour, seemingly a little scratchier and a little
sadder each time. It takes me back to Zaki's Cafe three
years ago and eleven blocks due west of here when "The
Dock of the Bay" was the posthumous release whose
grooves were being worn off (and in fact it's still on
the box here, and probably at Zaki's too).

Last night was another wild one with Val. She
refuses to fight by any rules I've ever heard of. In
fact, it's hard to imagine anyone accepting her rules,
which can be boiled down to "anything goes." When I'm
angry at her and thrashing things out isn't working, I
tend to withdraw into myself, to turn "cold," as she
says (I consider it more sad or numb or despairing or
resigned). It's temperamentally impossible for me to be
warm and cuddly with someone I'm actually furious at,
someone who's ferociously attacking me. Val counters
this kind of withdrawal with an ascending offensive of
pleas, threats, shrieks, desperate demands, even violent
physical attacks; and of course all these just make
matters worse. The circle it results in is vicious in
more ways than one.

Last night, deadened to the core by the afternoon's
battles, I could summon no desire whatsoever to ball, as
she demanded (and I do mean demanded). All I could do
was roll my eyes. "I can't fuck on command, you know.

347

And you say I'm the cold one?"

Her response, unsurprisingly, was to go right back
on the warpath. Within seconds she was unleashing a
whole new round of threats and provocations.

"I hate myself!" she cried. "I want to cut off my
breasts!"

For once I had her correctly figured: I knew she
would never do that. She likes her breasts way too much
(as well she should). But she found a different
riposte: instead she began tearing out her pubic hair.
(Of which she can always, after all, grow another crop.)

She finally cooled off, but this morning we went
through the whole thing again, only worse, in part
because of her fury that she'd slept through all her
classes and an important conference with a teacher. I
pay no attention to her real needs, she charged; she's
forced to "break through" to me with these violent
hysterical scenes. She has no choice! (And of course
she's smart to do so, from her angle, since they seem to
work, because of course I'm forced to pay attention to
her. But inside I'm seething at the methods she's
using. The resentment is building and at the same time
I'm becoming paralyzed and incapable of loving or even
caring. And in the long run it's best not to think
about what I might become capable of.)

*

Barbara came up from L.A. last night. As soon as
she can sell twenty or thirty dollars' worth of jewelry,
though, she'll be heading back down to set up
housekeeping with Paul on a more or less permanent
basis.

"I'm not too enthusiastic about it," she says, "but
I do like him."

Paul is a thirty-year-old drama teacher, tall,
cordial and quiet, with eyes that to me hint of some
barely suppressed madness of his own that might even
exceed Val's. Currently he's trying to dry out after a
five-year alcohol binge. Barb says nothing about loving
him; but she does talk glowingly about the organic
garden she's planning to start in his very large yard

(his place is up in the hills a few miles north of the city).

No doubt she's also considerably relieved to be putting three-hundred-plus miles between herself and her big brother. Relations between us have crumbled beyond all hope of repair. While we maintain a veneer of friendliness, the tension and hostility run deep. It's hard now for us to talk for more than a few minutes at a stretch. If I don't take the initiative, she says nothing at all to me -- doesn't even offer a greeting when we haven't seen each other for a week and a half.

It's the end of an era. For eighteen months straight one or more of my siblings has been living with me at Funston. Now Jeff's in Lahontan, Rob's in Gatewood, and Barb's in -- soon -- L.A. I rarely receive a letter from Mother and almost never one from Dad. Telephone calls from or to either or both of them are few and far between. Clearly the breakup of our family has reached a new stage.

(Rob writes that Dad's eye condition has been "exaggerated" but that he, Rob, is still worried about him. More and more those same patriarchal eyes, Rob says, glaze over with pain and distance as the three of them talk at dinner.)

*

And so it is I now find myself holed up at Mac's Grill preparing as best I can for the "new life" here in San Francisco. The main way this attempted preparation differs from numerous past attempts launched in this same spot -- at this very table even -- is that the woman I'm avoiding at home this time around is Valerie instead of Jang or Denise or Ciara.

My greatest fear these days is that, at twenty-eight, my fate is sealed, I've trapped myself in a life of mediocrity (just as Briana and others have predicted). The accomplishments in Garnett are real and not wholly without value, I believe, but I know very well I could be doing much more. I'm dissipating my talents, permitting them to languish, "ego-tripping," just as they all charge. Like Barb's Paul I've been on

349

my own kind of five-year bender -- starting, I'd say,
with Karen A.'s death almost five years ago -- five
years on May 21 (a date that will live in my mind
forever) -- if not even before that: the breakup with
Lisa (and her subsequent abortion) six years ago last
month.

I can't help wondering whether some monstrous self-
delusions might not be at the heart of my reprobacy.
Lately I've taken to focusing on the delusion of
monogamy as a prime candidate. "I think you'll always
need to have two or three women," Claire says.
Instinctively I shudder at the thought. In prior times
when I've tried to come to grips with this issue, I've
always resolved it in favor of the idealistic solution
-- that I want to find a single woman with whom I can be
happy or at least moderately content, enough so as to
want to stay right where I am. This is certainly the
solution I continue to prefer.

Underlying this preference, I think, is a deep fear
of loneliness. I hate to think of myself as an aging
bachelor; my preferred fantasy image of myself as a
middle-ager features a wife, a family, a cozy little
house in the city and a secluded mountain getaway (the
Experimental Gold Mine or the Tuolumne Hotel up in the
Sierras would do quite well). If I'm alone for more
than a few days that other image of desolate loneliness
soon begins to plague me, I become restless, I cast
about for a new female companion, and in the end the
results are always the same. After an initial period of
seemingly brilliant hope and promise -- when I suppress
the realization that I'm probably deluding myself -- I
decide to settle for the status quo with whatever woman
it is "until someone better for me comes along." Most
of the time I'm in a state of tepid and vapid semi-
happiness as far as the love relationship goes. Yet I
never stop to question the basic assumption, which is
that somewhere there exists a woman who could "make me
happy."

It seems much more likely, given the nature of love
and my obsession with it, that I'll be "happy" only with

a long string of new loves. For, with me, so far
anyway, love inevitably dissipates itself or burns
itself out after a relatively short time: a year or two
at most. Yet I'm reluctant to accept this apparent
reality. To do so would seem to imply I'm indeed
"shallow" (as Barb, Briana, Val have all said), that
love for me is largely a game of conquest, a way of
supplying my ego with the unending adulation it
apparently craves. As soon as someone comes to know me
well, to see my shortcomings, I prefer to move on --
even if the lover is ready to put up with the
shortcomings -- for I can't put up with them myself.

But to accept I'm not the monogamous type would
involve the same sort of difficult self-honesty that
monogamy itself does. So I go on pretending I am that
type even as my actions show clearly I'm not, so far at
least, and I blame the failures on the women I hook up
with, finding each of them in turn unsuitable for me
(usually for the same or similar reasons).

To be ruthlessly self-honest, it appears only two
courses are open to me: the "realistic" and the
"idealistic." The first demands acceptance of the
ephemerality of love; the second calls for suspension of
my critical faculties, to either accept or suppress
awareness of major inadequacies in myself and others.
I'm trying the second course (for the hundredth time)
(and the fourth or fifth, really, with Valerie). Should
this second course fail yet again, as seems more likely
with each passing day, perhaps I'll switch to the first
and give that a serious try.

Is all this mawkish beyond hope? No doubt. But
the only alternative right now is silence: to write
nothing at all.

Friday 26 (X:25)
     "I can't get away from the flowers," wailed Valerie
as she burrowed in next to me and almost through me in
bed at four a.m. last night. She was trembling and
shuddering like a feverish child. "They're everywhere!

351

I don't want them!"

She'd just returned from supposedly inducing herself to vomit in the bathroom. That was to get rid of the dozen or so tranquilizers which she told me she'd gulped down in a fit of vindictive rage (she'd gotten them from her mother). I was so furiously distrustful I demanded she let me see her vomiting. She'd successfully kept me from doing this, slamming the bathroom door in my face and locking it, describing me caustically as "like a little boy, following me everywhere I go." The vomiting sounds she then produced from behind the locked door were impressive but of doubtful authenticity (and I've heard some real ones from her in cases where I also witnessed the puking).

Earlier she'd been threatening to kill herself if I didn't stop being so "indifferent" to her. I scoffed at the threat. So of course she had to follow through on it. When she told me she'd done just that (I've never seen such hatred on anyone's face), I angrily tossed her on the bed and held her there. At that point I wasn't sure (and I'm not now) how many pills, if any, she'd actually taken. She refused to go to the hospital. All I could do was wait, either for her resistance to fade or for her to pass out. As I waited, she told me the same thing she'd used to justify all her other demented actions: she'd done it to "break through" to me. "If I can't have you all the way," she declared, "I don't want to live."

"Keep this up," I said, "and I won't want to get within a thousand miles of you. No one in his right mind would."

It was a showdown -- another one. As usual, neither of us would give an inch. I was infuriated by several things, but mainly by the way her demands were, and are, consuming all my time and energy. She won't let me alone, won't let me get away from her, won't give me a moment's peace. I'm also disgusted by her incessant references to the past. She's forever sinking to new depths of despair over things that happened long ago -- many of them months or years or even decades

before we met. Last night, amazing me, she wailed
angrily and wound up hurling a hunk of roast beef at me
because I used to be so "touched" -- this too came from
the journal volumes she's read -- by the dinners Jang
rustled up for us at Fell Street. And I'd never said a
word about them to her!

But most of all I'm climbing the walls over her
willingness to do anything at all, even play at suicide,
to blackmail me into doing what she wants. She knows no
limits, has no shame, no sense of proportion or
restraint.

But -- all right. Of course it's more complicated
than that. Let's admit she makes some good points. At
times I truly am "cold," withdrawn, indifferent. I do
sometimes use my withdrawals as a weapon. Her
accusations are often highly accurate at least in some
respects. But her method of delivering them almost
always paralyzes me. I'm not opposed to making, or at
least trying to make, some of the changes she's seeking
in me, but I can't do this so long as she's
intentionally turning my life into a living hell. The
effect of her hysterical, violent drama isn't to open me
up -- far from it. It may appear that way to her,
because eventually I'm forced to respond. I have no
choice when she's prepared to go to such lengths. But
inside I'm freezing over. My responses are fraudulent.
Often they're made up of purely immediate relief. And
secretly I become convinced I'm not fit to live with any
woman at present, least of all Val. She wants to
bludgeon me into "health," i.e., the ability, or more
accurately the imperative, to respond to her needs in
the way she deems appropriate.

Maybe, just maybe, we've hit bottom and can now
begin moving up again. Last night's scene was some sort
of ultimate degradation for both of us. Maybe the shock
of it will lead us both to dismantle some of our heavier
emotional weaponry.

But last night it looked hopeless. It was truly
pathetic. Wrenching. I'll never forget how, at four-
thirty a.m., after as deeply dispiriting a night as I've

ever been through (and there have been some lulus even
before Val came along, especially with Ciara) -- last
night we knelt next to each other on the couch in the
living room and stared out the window, silently watching
a cold rain fall on the blurry night city, our faces
twisted into scarcely recognizable side-by-side masks of
despair as reflected in the wavy window glass. A lurid
image for sure, like the cover of a cheapo noir
paperback.

Not the first such image for these pages, no. So
why's it such a grabber for me? -- A question I'd no
doubt be better off leaving for another time.

*   *

In the midst of all this struggle it's been
impossible for me to get anything done. "Self-
improvement," forget it. What a laugh. But I'm still
determined.

Tonight I'll propose a revolution to Val.

Because, despite it all -- and I don't know what it
is in me that keeps me coming back for more punishment
-- I still want us to make a success of our living
together.

Yes, even while deeply fearing the bitterness,
cruelty, volatility, vengefulness, destructiveness which
I now see are ineradicable parts of who she is. For I
also see more clearly -- am stunned and awed by -- her
bravery and courage and fighting spirit and the depth
and power and complexity of her passion. Of her soul --
yes. This is not the awkward girl who could not respond
to my "full power." This is someone else entirely.

Flowers everywhere in the house. She picks them
from the Mt. Moraga hillside meadow, some as expressions
of joy, others as offerings of peace, still others as
tokens of sorrow or mourning, and she presents them to
me, bunch after bunch after bunch, with a kind of fierce
innocence that even at the best moments can make me
shudder.

*

One positive step I did manage to take this week: I
visited the office of the Bay Bulldog on Bryant Street

354

downtown and left my created-on-the-spot "resume'"
there. Operations are currently "in hiatus" as Mike
Meyerhold, the paper's publisher and editor-in-chief and
driving force, seeks funding for the next issue. But
Peggy Riddell, his assistant, seemed excited about what
I might be able to do for them (Meyerhold was out of
town for a few days). The office is three or four times
the size of the Mercury's but has a very similar feel to
it; while taking a tour I noted several innovations
whose adoption would surely benefit the Merc and the
details of which I'll be passing along to Al and the
others during my next trip up to Garnett. (Peggy
Riddell is a no-nonsense young woman -- probably right
around my age or a little older -- with an impressive
knowledge of the paper's aims and inner workings and of
the world of newspapers in general.)

5

Monday 29 (X:27-28)
     I've crept off to the living room "to do the
scribble thing." Hopefully Val's asleep by now. I was
reading the Chronicle in my old room -- the "blue room,"
as she too calls it these days, that subdued chamber of
cool colors and extreme austerity, showing Barb's recent
influence after Rob's departure -- and Val was shaping a
micromini from a pair of my old worn-out Levis. Tonight
she was as subdued as the room itself, because, as she
explained, "I always am when you go away" (I dashed up
to Garnett for the day) and also because she'd been
chilled by the sight of a dog lying dead in a pool of
its own blood outside the deli where she'd been
intending to pick up dinner (she settled instead for
Mac's Grill, our usual table -- "I always feel your
presence so strongly there").
     Yet we've done much better the past thirty-six
hours or so and it now appears close to certain we'll
extend the "experiment" into and hopefully through the
month of April and maybe even into May and, who knows,

355

beyond -- although nothing is firmly agreed to just yet.

Last week was wholly lost to our desperate battle over whose version of the past and whose guidelines for family living, so to speak, would prevail for the duration, that is, to the extent we thought we might even have a duration. The result of it all was that we both gave up (not in) and by default we've wound up taking a perilous and ill-marked middle path -- I guess. At this stage it's impossible to be sure of anything.

I can pinpoint, however, the exact moment when I gave up my part of the fight. It came yesterday, Sunday, when she joined me on the sundeck in her luscious yellow terrycloth bikini and began silently reading, of all things, J.S. Mill on utilitarianism. Only William James on "The Varieties of Romantic Experience" would've been more apropos (but true, he never did get around to writing that). At any rate: after a while I welcomed her, smiled, and she smiled back, and all that hatred and bitterness of the previous days mercifully vanished.

The night before that, Saturday, was terrible. I sank into a miasma of despair unlike any I've ever known. Squeezed myself into a "tiger cage" (as she mockingly called it) against the wall behind the couch in the farthest corner of the living room -- at the back of the niche where brother Jeff crashed when he was on the lam from the Army after his Vietnam orders came down -- and agonized for hours over the way my life seemed to be collapsing around me. At that point I was seriously considering even the most radical moves, including splitting for good from the Bay Area: to San Diego, to Portland, to Seattle or Denver or Lahontan or Wachute -- to Turtle Rapids, even, if necessary, where I could at least put my cow-milking skills to good use.

Earlier that same evening Val had disdainfully revealed that "everything" she does is fraudulent. She just gives people what they want, and I'm no exception. There was only one sincere thing she could say to me, she asserted. All too typically (as she'd no doubt agree) I don't even remember what that one thing was. I

do remember what it was not: that she loves me. On that
crucial question she said she could no longer be sure
one way or the other. As far as I can recall -- and
again, it's not far -- this is the first time she's put
any qualifiers on her love since shortly after we met.
Since I've been qualifying my own love more or less
consistently all along I could scarcely object, as she
of course didn't fail to point out.

Last night I got zonked on some powerful weed.
Frightening and fascinating. Paranoid moments.
"Brilliant" insights popping up like methane bubbles
from the deepest part of the swamp as I mentally lunged
to grab them for later study. Clear, simple, fragile,
beautiful images of fantastically complicated molecular
structures -- or at least the illusion of same. I
battled to keep control, lying on the couch, then
switched tactics and went with the flow, beseeching the
gods to put this chaos to an end soon...and they did.

Tonight we're dutifully drawing up a monthly
"family budget" for April, trying to minimize the
frictions that, alas, are still never far from the
surface.

Tuesday 30
Trapped. In too deep now with Valerie -- can't get
out. Out is what I want and I want it now but I'm
powerless to move an inch. Any slight feint toward the
exit provokes more hysteria from her, a cascade of
vituperation, a rush for the kitchen and the knives or
the bathroom and the razor blades, a vicious knife-
waving or Gillette-wielding murder or suicide threat --
and death-shrieks, collapses, incoherent wild-eyed
mutterings, eerie horrific piercing wails that surely
can be heard a block away. I'm appalled, scared to
death, fascinated, shocked, miserable. I hold Danny's
hand and we both look on helplessly in a trance of fear.
It's sheer terror, naked, ugly, horrible, worse than any
nightmare, worse than anything.

Even in her saner moments she can talk only of her

"neurosis," which now looks to me to be something a lot
more serious than that. Most frustrating of all is the
diabolical skill with which she's figured out how to
manipulate me with it. She knows I won't beat her up or
hold a carving knife to her throat or a loaded gun to
her head or belly as Jim liked to do, so she figures she
can get away with pretty much anything, and she's
basically right. If I try to leave, she simply
threatens to kill herself or, if that's not enough, to
trash the apartment, including everything I value most
in the world. In this way she paralyzes all my
prospective actions, leaving me in a stony impotent
fury, seized up by hatred and confusion and self-pity.
Her tempestuous scenes jolt me out of some of this --
how can you hate someone so pathetic? -- but leave a
deepening residue of resentment and fear for the future.

No, I'm wrong, one thing bothers me even more than
her successful manipulations, and that's my own
inclination to admire her perseverance, her demented
refusal to give any ground, the sheer power of her
savage attacks and counterattacks. Have my pride and my
ideals lapsed so sadly I'll trade anything for a few
hours or days of peace? Have I become such a pushover
it can be safely predicted I'll fold before a measly
suicide threat?

What I fear most is that in Val as she's now
revealing herself to be I'm getting exactly what I
deserve. Is this the cosmic balance swinging back? Am
I now being made to pay for all the suffering which the
fickleness of my love has caused her and others? Am I
witnessing an immense cackling flock of vultures -- or
Valkyries -- coming home to roost?

In her suicidal delirium this afternoon she spilled
out the story of her strong attachment to her great
aunt, the elderly woman who served as a surrogate mother
to her after her parents divorced and her mother split
for America. "I killed her," she wailed. "I murdered
her!" Great Aunt Mathilde had raised Val's father as
well after his mother died ("We're both the same; he's
as crazy as I am") but "renounced" Val six months before

her death from cancer. The reason she gave was that Val
had shown signs of reconciling with her mother, whom
Mathilde saw as a "low-class, evil adventuress."
Mathilde insisted the pain from this "betrayal" had
caused her cancer. "She was the one who rescued my
brother and me from the orphanage where my father sent
us after my mother left. She made me dresses from her
old ones even though she had nothing herself. I meant
the world to her and then I killed her."

    -- "Glen!" she cries out from the bedroom in a
panicky voice. (This is right now, live.) "Glen!"

    I wait a moment and then reply grimly, "What!?"

    No reply.

    (In over a week I've been able to wrench myself
free of her for no more than four or five hours
altogether.)

    -- Now she stumbles into the living room -- naked
-- and buries her head into the space between my thigh
and the sofa arm. "I had a dream about you," she
mumbles.

                         *

    (She's back in bed now. But I might have to break
off again at any moment.)

    At another point this afternoon I stalked out to
the L.C., ready to take off for good. "If you leave
now," she shrieked, storming out after me, "you'll never
forgive yourself for what you'll find when you get
back." I realized she was serious and might well try to
kill herself, or trash the apartment, or destroy all my
manuscripts and journals and whatever else her eye
happened to fall on. I angrily kicked at some rocks for
a while and eventually returned to the house, vowing a
time would come when I'd make her regret this -- as the
pile of things for which I could never forgive her
mounted ever higher -- but accepting again that for the
moment I couldn't do a goddamn thing myself but go along
with her demands.

    For much of the afternoon I was fingering Danny's
Play-Doh, fashioning it into thin sheets at the kitchen
table. The thinner it got, the more color patterns

showed up, bringing back times when I'd done pretty much
the same thing as a kid, fantasizing that the streaks
were veins of rare ore, dreaming of the day I'd be
prospecting out west somewhere (and this memory in turn
opened up a forgotten dimension of my Experimental Gold
Mine fantasy of last year, which I must say at this
point is starting to look pretty damn good again: the
life of a hermit or a Melvillean isolato in the
mountains).

At the Judah Fish-N Chips tonight: "This is the
place where you and Briana had the famous long talk
about your childhoods." Nothing can be concealed from
her; she's read every word of every journal and
chronbook I've ever kept, except -- as far as I know --
the latter part of this one right here. And here's
another of those unforgivable things: she doesn't
hesitate to use anything I've ever written against me.
In my view she's betraying a sacred trust, not to
mention the explicit promise she made never to do such a
thing. Now my pleas for even the tiniest amount of
respect for my privacy drive her to the most desperate
extremes.

At one point I swallowed my qualms and asked:
"Can you think of any peaceful way we might bring this
little 'experiment,' this 'gamble' of ours, to an end?"
That triggered the worst scene of them all.

So long as the general atmosphere is relatively
tranquil I can tolerate our being together, though just
barely, and with frequent soul-deep pangs of regret as I
recall what I'm giving up to stay on with her. I find I
can't muster the resolve to make a break for it, and the
even stranger truth is at times I'm not even certain I
want to. Nor is this simply because if I did just drop
her flat I fear she might kill herself and/or Danny
(though I certainly do fear this and know well she's
exploiting this fear as a form of extortion and has no
shame whatsoever about doing so).

So why is it? I wish I knew. It's as if I'm
momentarily willing to accept being crushed. Sometimes
I fall back on the banal thought that as long as we've

come this far I might as well give it an all-out try.
Weirder yet, at times I can even feel this would be the
strong, the good, the loving thing to do. Maybe this is
what it means to really love someone, I tell myself: to
be willing to accept a catastrophe like this.

In any event, here's where we stand now. She's
agreed to suspend all argument for twenty-four hours
whenever she feels herself falling into the "neurotic
cycle," as she calls it (she doesn't hesitate for a
moment to agree these scenes she's throwing are deeply
sick). However, this is only a trial arrangement and
it's only temporary, to last until Friday, "so you can
get something done this week." I, in turn, have
promised I'll be faithful to her during the same period.
But Thursday -- April 1st -- is Jang's birthday, I just
realized (and by a bizarre coincidence it's Val's
husband Jim's too; and for that matter two weeks from
tomorrow is Val's): so Thursday I'll probably visit
Jang.

All agreements made under duress -- especially
duress this extreme -- are completely worthless, of
course. Not even the most "accepting" love imaginable
could change that. Hopefully in some relatively sane
corner of her soul Val understands this. But in the end
it doesn't matter whether she does or not.

Wednesday 31
Lying on the grass in Washington Square -- bright
gusty day, a film crew at work from a French (wouldn't
you know) TV station, kites dragging along their human
anchors -- and I'm still trying to puzzle out a solution
to the crisis with Valerie.

Today I'm seeing things in what I want to believe
is a larger perspective. My personal relations with
women, including Val, will improve not one iota until I
can succeed in straightening out my own head. That
probably won't happen until I can write a book about
which I'm truly proud (though I'll keep trying). So,
under the circumstances, why not stay on with Val?

[Have Mercy]

I'll do that, yes -- but only so long as she
permits me to get my work done (for how many years have
I been adding qualifiers like this one?). Nor will I
yield to her increasingly blatant efforts at
manipulation and coercion (which she demands I accept
precisely because they are, she asserts, uncontrollably
pathological: "I'm sick, so you must do what I say":
that's a verbatim quote). No more accepting such
assertions, in other words, merely because they're
obviously non compos mentis and thus deserving, in
theory, of compassion.

The best we can hope for now is a peaceful
accommodation, a truce, that will extend itself day by
day and thus give us a chance to gradually work our way
back to something akin to normalcy (whatever that might
mean for us). Today I don't even like Val -- much less
love her -- and I see we're bound together largely by
these very same "neurotic" or possibly even "psychotic"
-- or just call them "wacko" or "demento" -- needs I've
been talking about. In fact I've felt this way for a
long time. Yet I still nurse a faint hope something
marvelous can arise out of all this pain and
degradation.

-- Less than two hours after making her "deal" with
me (no more hysterical harangues until at least Friday)
she unleashed another one. This time it was supposedly
because she was unable to detect sufficient "passion" in
my dead-tired, emotionally washed-out manual
manipulation of her bone-dry pussy. She was right, of
course, there was little there -- but then how
preposterous of her to expect otherwise after a day like
yesterday. I was exhausted and full of resentment. I
made it very clear I didn't want to ball (too harshly, I
suppose; but then her way of demanding was equally harsh
or worse).

So for two hours she shrieked and raved and tore at
her cooch. I was ruining her for life. She wanted to
cut it off! She'd never ball me again! Her maniacal
howls split the night and tore my guts to shreds. It
seemed a sure bet the cops would arrive at any moment.

House manager Stanley would be on the phone to Mrs.
Hilyer first thing in the morning (if he hadn't been
already): "Get these crazies outta here! We can't even
sleep at night!" My efforts to placate her -- including
several new attempts at getting her off, one by tongue
-- were contemptuously and angrily swatted aside.

    Then she began ranting -- in the same hideous tone
-- about how I'd "forced" her to break the "deal." She
came up with a new justification for her bizarre
behavior: Jim had put her through precisely the same
thing innumerable times -- "He was always trying to
pacify me through my cunt."

    I'm sorry to say it but with each passing day I
understand better how the execrable Jim Bando could have
been reduced to treating her as he did. She's
relentless and merciless; while on one of her freak-out
binges she can think only of her own feelings and needs,
for which she demands instant fulfillment. She becomes
ugly beyond belief. There's no reasoning with her,
there's no compromise, there's no breathing space or
time-out or rain check. And each time the threats and
the cruelties and the violence escalate. They're
already far beyond the point where I can gently restrain
her physically. At times I have no choice but to
manhandle her: get rough. It's the only way I can shut
off her high-decibel shrieking or ward off her physical
attacks, which have become more or less constant during
the extreme phases. In fact I'm sure that forcing me to
get rough with her is precisely her aim. She's fully
aware of how uncomfortable and uptight it makes me. And
yet everything she does seems designed not just to
provoke a brutal physical response but to make such a
response unavoidable. Worsening matters still more,
she's unusually strong for her size -- as noted before!
-- and very quick, not easy to deal with even given my
big advantages in weight and reach. I'm afraid I might
seriously injure her one of these times.

    Meanwhile all the rest of my life goes dead. I'm
consumed by bitterness and sadness and resentment. I've
begun to hate being stuck inside "the Castle." Self-

disgust and despair wash over me as day after rotten day
passes and I get nothing done -- in fact get nothing
even started.

How did I ever let her maneuver me into this?

More important, how the hell do I get out?

All sorts of schemes tantalize me as the empty
hours drag by. Move out, split from the city, call in
her brother or her mother, find her a shrink, deliver
her to the Langley-Porter loony bin, disappear from the
house early every morning and don't come back until
dinnertime.... But I'm well aware none of them will
work -- mainly because, as I can't forget for a moment,
any might cause her to do real violence to herself and/
or Danny and/or me. Either it's sick or it's criminal
for her to act as she's acting, but regardless of which
it is I'm genuinely helpless to do anything about it.
Therefore I prefer to imagine I'll be content if we can
just find a way to live peacefully and productively.

How? Trickery won't work, psychological pressure
won't work -- she's too close to the edge for both of
those. Obviously I can't buckle to her outrageous and
humiliating demands, and I can't just pretend to buckle
to them either; she immediately sees through any attempt
to do that (just like the "cunt pacification"). No, all
I can do is continue my efforts to wise her up to my
needs (and my aversion to her demands) and hope she'll
eventually realize it's just a waste of her time and
energy to battle against such fundamentally
unthreatening things.

Here in her own words (measured and restrained for
once) are Val's views on all this, from a note she gave
me last night:

> Yes, you are unfair and no matter how
> good you can rationalize things against
> me, you damn well know your own stubborn
> neurotic vindictiveness which takes a
> subtle form of superiority....
>
> I feel I am not allowed to experience
> disappointment, insecurity, or anything
> that is inconvenient for your moods and

364

plans.... You've got a hang-up. You hold
grudges. You can't open your arms to
sincere regrets and promises or
resolutions. I have to beg you to accept
my apologies and by the time I'm through
with this process I don't mean the apology
anymore because of the resentment I've
built up....
   Coldness is your inevitable response to
hassles and you expect it to be accepted
as part of you. What's your reason for
not making an effort to change? It's a
weapon and you refuse to drop it. I have
to accept you as you are but I should
change!

No doubt all this is true as far as it goes. As
noted a few times before, yes, I do sometimes try to
protect myself against her assaults by withdrawing.
What she seems not to understand is that this amounts to
a kind of temporary emotional departure from the scene
while physically staying in place. I'd much prefer to
leave entirely -- that is, bodily -- to get away for a
while, cool off, think things over -- but her threats
prevent this. I stay, but not by free choice. I stay
under duress, by her coercion. And yes, I resent this
coercion greatly and find it impossible to react
"warmly" to it.
   Further, her attacks are so unbelievably vicious
I can't quickly open my arms afterwards to her regrets,
which, contrary to what she writes in her note, often
seem a lot less than fully sincere to me.
   Is this a hang-up on my part? What the hell am I
supposed to do -- spread my arms wide so she can knife
me in the heart? Sure it's a hang-up! -- and it's
becoming more of one every day. Her incessant attacks
won't make it go away any faster, that's for sure. And
if there's a better way of dealing with these attacks,
I'd like to know what it is.
   Okay, sometimes I use withdrawal as a weapon. Of
course! This may seem unfair, but when the words run

out it's basically the only weapon I've got. And the
truth is it ain't worth shit anyway when it comes to
persuading her of anything and I know this all too well.
In the end it serves only one useful purpose: it permits
me to keep the battle from turning truly vicious -- by
which I mean vicious on both sides, not just hers.

Why don't I change as her note asks? God only
knows I'd like to. Can she really believe I get a large
charge from enclosing myself in heavy armor against her?
What's more, I know very well that the more it happens,
the more difficult it is for me to react in any other
way. What starts out as a defense very quickly becomes
one of those hang-ups she's so aware of. You wear the
armor long enough and you begin to feel it's part of
you. You'd be naked and totally vulnerable if you took
it off, and because she's who she is and does what she
does and has been doing consistently over and over for
the past couple of months and more, naked and totally
vulnerable is the very last thing you'd want to be.

Or I could ask her: why doesn't she change? And I
know the answer to that one because she told me herself:
she doesn't want to work things out peacefully and
respectfully and lovingly. That's right! She likes
screaming and fighting much better! It's her preferred
way of dealing with conflict! Always has been and
always will be! Of course she says later she was
exaggerating to make a point when she said this (she's
said it several times). But I think there's probably a
lot more truth to it than she herself knows.

Given all this, is there anything I can do to make
the situation better? Practically speaking, I'd say the
best thing now is for me to find ways to get away from
her physically until the anger and resentment subside on
both sides. And I'll try to do just that. But it will
be very difficult, because if she has the slightest
suspicion I'm trying to take off as a way to escape her
or punish her, no matter how I try to justify and
explain it, she'll start in with the terrorizing again.

The worst part of this armor thing -- or self-
protective mechanism, I'll call it -- is that it's

gotten to the point now where it can be activated by
purely imaginary attacks or even by simple
disappointment. All I have to do is see a frown pass
across her face and I tighten up: she's about to go off
again! Sometimes I think this is a product of my own
flaws -- a subconscious perfectionism perhaps, a hidden
wish she'd always be cheerful and happy and life-loving.
But it's impossible to know under the present extreme
circumstances why it happens. It does happen, just as
she says, and that's a fact we both have to deal with
and do so in a way that works for both of us. But she's
not interested in trying anything as reasonable-sounding
as that. For her any sign of wariness or drawing back
on my part is cause for full-scale attack.

*   *

(News from the front)
    It's tough. For reasons unknown Valoshka can
effortlessly deflate my spirit. Tonight she's back to
playing the sad-eyed lady. Dull and distant, gloomy,
unresponsive, self-absorbed, not a laugh or a smile or a
kindness in sight. Worse, she insists on pulling me
down with her.
    Balling makes no difference. I gave it my all when
I came home this afternoon -- trying to ease her over
the psychological barrier she created for herself last
night -- and things were no better afterwards than
before. (I fell asleep with her atop me and woke up
shivering as she brusquely lifted herself off, a look of
horror on her face, almost as if I were a disgusting
naked stranger she'd accidentally fallen onto in a
rather compromising way; and then, again for reasons
unknown, she made me a cup of hot chocolate, presented
it like an automaton, and suddenly knelt down and
started sucking my cock, and continued with that until I
came again -- and she was no cheerier with a mouthful of
jizz than without.)
    There's a difference this time. I'm doing my
utmost to fight off the urge to retaliate through
withdrawal. If she wants to characterize such
withdrawal urges as sicko, fine, I'll play right along

with her. If John Wayne can go to the mat with the Big
C, I can take on the Big W. Looking at it this
ludicrous way seems to cheer me up and actually provides
an unexpected source of strength.

It felt like a great triumph this evening when our
first joint trip to the supermarket since last summer
resulted in no major disputes. Val in Barbara's floor-
length black cape, me in my Bat hat. When we caught a
glimpse of ourselves reflected in the Park N Shop
electric-eye door we both had the same profound thought
-- here was a great New Age commercial. (I was pushing
an empty wire cart with her on my arm. "Look, honey,
it's Americopia! Let's truck on in and fill her up!")
                           *
A sage piece of advice from Robert J. Lifton which
I'm trying to keep in mind at all times:
        Renewal on a large scale is impossible
        to achieve without forays into danger,
        negativity, and destruction.
                  *   *
A letter from Briana came in yesterday, or rather a
note, enigmatic and elusive as always. She comments
that it's "a small world" (for no ascertainable reason)
and then apologizes for "carelessly intruding upon our
[sic?] privacy several weeks ago" (I have no idea what
she's referring to unless it was my last visit to her
apartment). Then she hopes Val wasn't upset by it (by
what?). Did she mean to write "your" instead of "our"?
Did she come over while Val and I were fighting -- or
loving -- and for some reason think we'd seen her? In
closing she observes it's spring and the begonias are
blooming (a pressed one is included). I scribbled a
reply to her in the margins of the most recent issue of
the Merc -- reaffirming my love for her and also the
fact that I'm settling in with Val now -- and left it in
her mailbox. (I thought of adding something like, "Do
not open if your name is Terry and you're a pretty damn
good poet." But decided against it. Whether he's
living with her again I don't know for sure, but I
suspect he is.)

Part Three

[Living with Valerie]

[Have Mercy]

APRIL

1

Thursday 1

The laundromat: what a groovy spot to be hunkered down in as the sun dies to the west (but of course) in a big sploosh of purples and reds on a lovely spring day in San Francisco and...and... -- but that's enough right there all by itself.

It's a day to be in love, and I have been, all day, in spurts, now with Jang (it's her birthday, I should be permitted to feel something), now with Briana (I think of certain days with her last summer that were as beautiful as this one), now even with the terrible Valerie (today she's contrite and, yes, mildly affectionate and we lie on the sundeck broiling up reminiscences of the two seminal loves of our lives who also happen to share a birthday: Jang and Jim).

Jang, Briana, Valerie. All three are still alive in my heart. I'm very sorry but I refuse to (don't have the heart to) deny this, and especially not on April Fool's Day. But then neither will I (do I have the intention to) act on it -- on any part of it. That is, kick anyone out. Unless it turns out I have to. And even then I might not be able to.

I do like my life to be crowded. To a degree the woman I'm with can make it feel that way single-handedly through a strong and many-sided love -- but only to a degree. Friends, activities, community are also needed. Granted if any or all of these are missing now for me it's no one's fault but my own.

An Elizabeth Hardwick essay on Ibsen in the New York Review drives home the importance of psychological complexity (presented simply) in great art. This is an appealing thought right now when my life is teeming with

such complexity. For some reason I've feared trying to
develop it in my own work. In some peculiar way deep
down I seem to believe my personal experience could have
no "profound" value -- I must instead distort whatever
modest value it does have by seeking to add to it layers
of psychological complexity which I simply make up or
borrow from other lives, as in fictify, as in writing
novels and short stories. Maybe, though, by doing this
I'm actually diluting the meaning of my own experience.
Possibly I'd be better off thinking all the elements
already exist in my own life and my first task is to
learn how to recognize them and my second task is to
find words for them and my third task is to fit those
words together in such a way that other people might
actually want to read them.

Failure to recognize these elements before now may
have something to do with my infatuation with the
unexpected. Perhaps it's because my life is too
familiar to me (too much introspected) that I feel I
must alter it fictionally. I must surprise myself even
as I'm writing. That's acceptable -- it's indispensable
-- but why not be satisfied, at least sometimes, with
surprising myself through new insights on the existent
and not seek instead new experience which I don't really
know anything about? Chart the extraordinary patterns
of thought and emotion that must underlie somewhere,
including in myself, the ordinary behavior I do know
about. Don't have my protagonist do what, in
retrospect, I think I should have done myself; have him
do what I did. Make all my characters, in other words,
more human -- or as Val and Briana and the rest of them
would probably say, less human.

-- All this on the day we officially start living
together, Valoshka and I, and also, of course, the Day
of the Fool, I'll note one more time.

Saturday 3 (X:2)
In the heart of the heart of misery.
Throbbing temples, churning stomach, stinging

scratches, burning eyes, desolate tangled mind.

Another day of all-out struggle with Valerie.

Here we go again.

It began with a total sexual malfunction last night. Today, as the battle heated up, she spat out (among numerous other nasty items) the statement that she's never actually "enjoyed" sex with me and that the dude with whom she had the four-fuck, three-come one-nighter in North Beach a few weeks ago -- whose name she seems not to recall and perhaps never did know -- was a better lover to her than I've ever been.

The scenes become increasingly pathetic.

Then there's this. I'll say frankly I can no longer abide Danny's presence. I like the kid himself, but I can't be a good surrogate father to him or any kind of father at all while his mother and I are at each other's throats. Nor can I bear to see him exposed to and damaged by what's happening to us. Nor can I stand to spend hours every day trying to shield him from his mother's ugly behavior. Nor do I want to devote a big chunk of my life to raising some other man's kid if I don't have a deep rapport with the kid's mother and if I'm not deeply appreciated by her for taking on the task.

Therefore I guess I don't pass the kid test. "If you love me," Val has said, "you'll love him as being a part of me." All right then, the conclusion will have to be I don't love her.

After a while the "Big W" controlled me just as in days of yore. Catatonic "coldness." I could feel nothing but a dull self-pity as Val again flew off into madness before my eyes.

Then my own shrieks of rage as she raked her nails down my flanks.

Desperately I pore through Fritz Perls's "Verbatim" in the midst of all this, hoping to find an easy solution I can treat myself with -- Val too -- even though I know very well no such panacea exists. Perhaps, then, a little boost to my spirits? And to hers as well?

"Classic power struggle."

Right in the midst of our ongoing war Erik drops by
all innocence and friendliness. Val glares silently at
him at first and then turns bitchy and nasty. "Why hide
it?" she says smugly after he's gone away puzzled and
hurt. Why indeed. But I'm ashamed to the core to be
living with a woman who would treat a man as fine as
Erik this way when it's completely undeserved.

Last night she and I gazed at rock idols Joe
Cocker, Leon Russell, and Mick Jagger on the big silver
screen. More than ever Jagger's act looks to me like
juvenile prancing. The High Age of Rock appears to be
over -- or is that true only for me? (Regardless I'll
agree Val has "Jagger lips," just as her husband Jim
used to tell her and she likes to tell me. And in turn
she agrees with Nina Aguilar that I have "Jim Morrison
lips, like a line drawing of a bird flying right at you"
-- although she, Val, says otherwise he and I bear not
the slightest resemblance, physiological or you name it
-- thus agreeing with Claire, although I didn't mention
this. "It's because of your hat," Val says. "It makes
your lips stick out and puts the rest of your face in
the dark." Which of course is exactly where I prefer it
to be, especially for eyes as cruel as hers.)

I don't want to go home. I don't want to be
writing like this. I don't want Val in my life any
longer. But I'm paralyzed. Again. Still. Even more.

One of the lowest periods of my entire life. But
there have been others -- even before she came along,
yes, as noted before -- so I shouldn't be too surprised.
And yet I still am. Over and over. Why is this?

Sunday 4

Picking up the pieces. Last night I slept on the
mattress in the living room (Val raised only a minor
ruckus) and this afternoon I've been wandering in Golden
Gate Park. It's a gloriously beautiful spring Sunday --
Palm Sunday, in fact, and as it happens I'm pressing my
back up against the corrugated trunk of some strange

kind of palm tree -- more like, I'd say, a badly
constructed mock-up of a palm tree, such as some quite
similar real palm trees I saw about a year ago in Palm
Springs on an Emp reconnaissance trip -- and here in the
park the streets (blocked off to cars as always on
Sundays) and footpaths are crowded with lots and lots of
apparently very happy people. Not even a disastrous,
disintegrating love could prevent me from enjoying an
afternoon like this. On the grass behind the DeYoung
Museum I watched a lively Mime Troupe performance of "A
Midsummer Night's Dream." I took off my shirt and
sipped orange juice warmed by the sun and traced dagger
patterns imprinted by grass spears on, yes, my palms.

All day I've been juggling and toying and
essentially failing to come to grips with a key question
of these incendiary days: should I decide to be alone
now? More and more it bothers me that I've never been
able to be alone -- that is, without a woman I'm seeing
regularly if not living with -- for more than a few
weeks at most. Perhaps I need to test myself.

But it wouldn't be easy to do that. In a few
minutes I'll be heading back up the hill to face the
lady. She's already paid her half of the April rent, so
there's no decent way I can kick her out. I intend to
disinter a proposal she made herself -- and seriously,
but much earlier in this infinitely long week -- that we
live in separate rooms at 1616 and go our separate ways,
without obligation, until such time as we can either get
along together again or agree our "gamble" is lost. She
probably proposed this just to test me, aptly enough,
but I'm tentatively planning to suggest we really do
give it a try. In fact, I might even insist on it.
Gently, however, if possible.

Somehow I've got to free my mind to deal with my
real needs, starting with the determination of just what
those might be at this point. It's no use blaming the
debacle with Valerie for my own failures in other realms
or making her into a scapegoat for those failures. It's
not as if someone else chose for me to get involved with
her.

[Have Mercy]

We may yet be able to reach an accommodation
through the separate-rooms/separate-ways idea or
something like it. If not -- well, I wouldn't want to
wager that either of us could survive another month as
hellish as the one just past.

2

Monday 5
    It's a first. Never before have I pried myself out
of bed at dawn to drive sixty-five miles through rush-
hour traffic for a dentist appointment. And then:
triumphantly arriving at the office ten minutes early, I
learn the appointment isn't at nine, as I'd thought, but
eleven.
    I always screw up dentist appointments. Or I could
simply say this is the kind of thing that always happens
at the edges when the center isn't holding.
    Spring in Garnett. As far as general appearances
go, the main difference between spring and winter around
here seems to be that even in the very early days of
spring people start wearing hot-weather clothing --
shorts, loose white dresses, sleeveless shirts, straw
hats. Garnett, separated from the bay by a small
mountain range, is on the fringe of the Central Valley
sweat belt. Hundred-degree-plus days are common here
throughout the summer.
    As for me, I suspect I'll be making myself scarce
in Garnett long before summer arrives. After two weeks
in the city -- even two utterly miserable weeks -- I was
reluctant to head back up here. It's all but certain
that whatever desire I have left to lay my body on the
line for the Merino Mercury will be fading rapidly. And
that will be doubly true if people in the office don't
start showing a little more gratitude for my efforts,
which at this point are strictly voluntary, however
limited and distracted they might be. Sherry Edwards
especially. She's now the paid full-time "office
manager" for the paper. I don't want to spend another

376

minute in that office if the vibes from her are always
going to be so bad. And that's the way they've been
during my last several visits.

We'll see.

In the tumult of the past week I neglected to note
my acceptance for unemployment compensation. Much to my
amazement it went off without a hitch. Just a quick
glance and the clerk bought Al's letter confirming my
"layoff" as editor of the Merino Mercury. Our
subversive little business had its "official letter"
treated with as much respect as one from Standard Oil.
Beautiful! Astonishing!

So now I'll be entitled to sixty-five dollars a
week for up to twenty-six weeks, on the condition I
continue looking for work. But the employment situation
is so tight my chances of finding something are slim to
none (especially given how I dress and look). With an
expected tax refund of five hundred dollars and, later
on, proceeds of a thousand dollars or more from selling
the Land Cruiser, I should be set for at least fifteen
months. Or say roughly until my thirtieth birthday. As
planned way back when! So for the interim I can stop
worrying so much about money and get on with living.

My main concern right now remains, of course, what
to do about Val. Last night as I clambered uphill from
the laundromat I decided to go ahead and propose we try
chastity for a while. Celibacy. This just might be
the best way to convince her, I reasoned, of my
sincerity about the separate-rooms plan. She's afraid
-- and justifiably so -- I'll want to get it on with
some other woman if I'm not sleeping with her. If I
pledge complete sexual abstinence she'll have greater
reason to trust me. (She still has faith in my
promises. I've never broken a promise to her! I was
"unfaithful" to her, sure, but as she was well aware I'd
never vowed or even hinted I'd be "faithful"; on the
contrary, she knew I'd be seeing others because I'd told
her I would. In essence she just refused to believe it
could really be happening. Strange but true. But then
she read my journals and she believed.)

[Have Mercy]

Val, as it turned out, was highly skeptical of the
celibacy idea. In her view I was once again being
oblivious to the pain I've been causing her. I tried to
persuade her otherwise. But I also confessed I've now
reluctantly come to believe that in our case to act
merely to avoid pain -- or to follow the least painful
path -- is self-defeating and ultimately will lead to
much more pain for both of us. Or to put it another
way, I've reached the absolute limit of my ability to
absorb pain in order to avoid causing her pain. Not
that I haven't caused her plenty by my own actions over
the months; but then again it seems to me she'd already
gone a long way toward restoring the balance on that
particular matter even before we started this new
experiment in living together.

In the end nothing was decided. Again we slept in
separate beds. We're both supposed to be thinking on
it.

Tuesday 6

The Mucklestone Motel. What in god's name am I
doing here? A purely rhetorical question to be sure,
but before trying nonetheless to answer it I must
describe the joint. A small, meagerly furnished motel
room with a floor of worn brown linoleum squares. To be
able to sweep back the curtains on the single small
window I first had to detach four large metal paper
clips fastening them together. Now I gaze out at an
orchard long gone to seed, two gas stations (Shell and
Standard), and a stretch of Interstate 80 congested with
early-morning traffic. As if in open admission that the
place is a firetrap, a fire extinguisher stands on the
sidewalk right outside the door to my room, next to a
barren trellis that would make excellent kindling, and a
green garden hose lazily snakes across the driveway and
terminates just inches from the extinguisher, possibly
as a backup for it. The far end of the hose loops
around the L.C., which looks admirably solid parked
beneath a pleasant little tree. The bumper stickers

378

displayed on the rear door, visible from here, are still
the same three different ones but the number of peace
decals has quadrupled (Val's work, ironically enough).
Reading from the left it's now peace decal, "Legalize
Freedom," peace decal, peace decal, "Get with the
Merc!", peace decal. And yes, these peace decals are
all the same as the large "'v' for Val" poster that used
to be on her door at Dolores Street and is now on the
"blue room" door at 1616, right behind her exercise bar.

So what am I doing here? Simple. I was so annoyed
by Sherry's snide comments in the office -- which she
now regards as her domain -- that I told Al I'd take him
up on his offer to provide me with a motel room. This
is the cheapest one we could find, a couple of miles
from Klug's and on the other (northern) side of the
freeway.

My staying here represents, to me if to no one
else, another step in the disintegration of the paper.
More and more it's trying to become a commercial
operation rather than a political one -- and the chances
are minuscule it will ever make it into the black. If
it does, I know for damn sure I want no part of the kind
of things it'll have to do to stay there, or for that
matter just to get there.

A sad letter from Jang yesterday. She's leaving
San Francisco in "one-two-three months."

> I am not living in an illusion. I am
> going to accept the reality and I must to
> live with the time. I am too weak to live
> by myself, giving the meaning of living
> only for me alone.... I love you and will
> never cry or cling to you.

She says there "was and is" something we must talk
about, and adds to that in a further wrenching confusion
of tenses and persons -- I'm pretty sure it's a
confusion -- this phrase: "To you who had been and has
been my love."

In my head I'm composing an answer. Must I let her
go? Can I let her go? No doubt the answer in both
cases should be yes. But it will be no easy thing to

do, especially when we're face to face. And even more
so given the sorry state of things with Valerie.

Wednesday 7

In bed, having just finished jotting down some
notes for two columns that must be Composer-ready by
noon tomorrow. Hunched over next to the single dim lamp
in this dismal Mucklestone Motel room as freeway traffic
roars by (a whole lotta trucking going on around here).
Still feeling good after a frenzied day of writing and
pasting up and then a mellow hour in the office with
Holly, Tom Yost, and Sid Portola. The minute Sherry
left for the day Sid produced a joint which we all
proceeded to partake of, Holly included, yes, and we
turned the music up high. Such a fine string of funky
R&B and classic blues on KRMA, golden oldies, Ray
Charles's "Mess Around" and the Flamingos' "I Only Have
Eyes for You," Muddy Waters, Little Esther, Junior
Wells. Even with Claire, Becky, and Tom out of town (in
L.A. -- where, if we last that long, Valerie and I will
be visiting Barb and Paul this weekend) -- even with
most of the people I'm closest to either departed for
good or temporarily absent, it's still possible for me
to feel at home and among friends out here.
What sours all this sweetness is the need to focus
on my column about the abhorrent "Calleyism" phenomenon
sweeping the nation (American public lionizes convicted
mass killer of Vietnamese women and children) -- oops,
I'm ambushed by a glimpse in the mirror of the green
star shining on my left shoulder, four days' growth of
beard, a single fierce eye peering back from beneath the
down-turned brim of my black "captain's cap" -- and then
about Nixon's latest shuck-and-jive on Vietnam
withdrawals. "Do you believe me?" pleads the president
in a prime-time speech shown nationwide on all three
networks. A most extraordinary moment in American
history. Nobody does believe him, of course, and it's
screamingly obvious he doesn't even believe himself.
Listening to his heavily promoted speech through the

echo chamber in Evan's living room lined with antiwar
posters while peering at that burglar visage on the tube
we all kept flashing on Big Brother. "Do you believe
me?" Of course we do! We believe everything,
everything! You, Tricky Dick, you are the Living Truth
of America as we know it!

Well anyway, I'm pleased to say the radical slate
romped in the Berkeley election on this same uncommon
day.

And I'm displeased by the strange detachment Al has
shown lately. But more than that I'm just sad about it.
I can't give him the brutally direct letter I pounded
out about the staff's feud with Sherry. When I go back
down to the office I'll just try to make myself
inconspicuous.

Doubts about another unsent letter, this one to
Jang. It leaves the door open a tiny crack. Impulses
to call her, to suppress the whole matter, to see her
tomorrow night: yeek!

Saturday 10 (X:8-9)
Hot sun. Classical music. Gently stirring trees.
Darting hummingbirds. Fields of California poppies.
Rugged hills and mountains green with spring.

From where I sit I could pluck any of a dozen
varieties of wildflowers just by stretching out an arm.

Big droopy old tree like a willow though it's not a
willow -- the L.C. is parked in its shade, the expanse
of undulating meadow grass reaching to mid-door height
making the vehicle look more like a moored boat than the
knockoff of a Land Rover which it is.

A homely white vintage dressing table also grazes
in the high grass near the knockoff, bringing to mind
photos of white Great Plains "pioneer" families posed in
front of sod huts a century ago, their meager collection
of worldly goods moved outside and proudly displayed for
the shoot.

In a small sun-drenched valley in the mountains
some fifty miles north of L.A.: Paul's place and the new

abode of sister Barb. A single footfall, however
delicate, causes the entire army surplus quonset hut in
which they're residing to shudder and resound (reminding
me again and again of the similarly noisy quonsets in
which the Writers' Workshop was housed during my first
two years in Mentoka Falls). A steep rocky hill looming
just behind and maybe as much as two hundred feet above
the hut makes it seem even more fragile and vulnerable.

The natural setting here offers a genuine sense of
privacy and isolation but only if one first imposes a
robust suspension of disbelief. A few hundred yards
away traffic groans up Route 101 toward L.A. Massive
power lines pass over the adjacent hill, their humming
audible in the night when traffic is light. Worse yet,
work begins next week on a three-hundred-unit trailer
camp which will border the fence in Barb and Paul's
backyard, forever demolishing the picturesque orchard
that stands there now. "When I saw those men pounding
in the surveyor's stakes," Barb said with startling
vehemence, "I wanted to pick them off one by one with a
rifle."

Paul drives his '60 Ford twenty miles every day to
Moorpark College, where he teaches drama six hours per
week and earns so little he qualifies for food stamps.
He's tall, shambly, easygoing yet also extremely self-
conscious and jittery in the usual way of former
alcoholics on the wagon. In all these respects and even
in looks he reminds me almost uncannily of Lawrence
Jakes (perhaps in part because I often watched Jakes
holding forth in those same Mentoka Falls quonsets).
Paul's eagerness to please sometimes gets so out of hand
(again just like Jakes) you almost want to gag him. If
I stand up, he leaps up, but edgily, and yet at the same
time also lamely, as it were, as if hobbled by awareness
that to grant his guests a measure of privacy is also
the duty of a host.

No matter -- I like this Paul just as I liked
Jakes. And I sympathize with him. I like his soft-
spoken, bumbly discourses on scholarly subjects such as
Sophoclean tragedy and Chaucerian wit. I like the way

he hovers over his garden, the sprouting beans, not
necessarily from love of growing things but because he's
trying to do the right thing, the good thing, the
healthy thing, the recuperating thing, and most of all
the thing that Barb will admire him and maybe even love
him for doing. I also sympathize with him for the
frustrations he faces in trying to get along with my
notoriously difficult sister. But then I don't doubt
for a moment Barb is bringing a ray of sunshine into his
lonely life, and I can clearly see he flat-out worships
her for doing so. (Nor do I doubt Paul is also an
extremely difficult person to live with in his own way.
I'll even say if being easy to live with were a
requirement for someone to be physically present on this
piece of property today, all four of us currently in
attendance would have to leave at once.)

    -- Speaking of one of whom, Valerie, a moment ago
she folded a sheet of paper into an airplane and sailed
it over to me. In her bright yellow terrycloth bikini
she looks luscious as always -- compact shapely well-
muscled acrobat's body, glistening smooth honey-colored
skin -- but there's no rapport at all between us today.
At this stage in our ongoing standoff, exposure to her
damnable physical assets stirs more regret than lust.
We remain isolated and despairing, bitter and
recriminatory, but at least it appears she's going along
with my plea to suspend open hostilities while we're
here.

    Thursday night, after leaving Garnett before paste-
up was finished, I stole into the house at Funston at
three-thirty a.m. I found Val asleep, lying naked on
her belly beneath a halfway-pulled-down sheet on her
"virgin bed" in the blue room ("I forced myself to move
from your bed," she'd told me on the phone). I
undressed, straddled her, dragged my genitals this way
and that over her splendid back and perfect little
muscular ass until, surprised and gratified to find
myself so throbbingly turned on, I balled her as
lovingly as I know how -- and not in the asshole either
-- as she pretended to sleep through it all the way to

the end.

   So much for sexual abstinence.

   (Actually we'd agreed previously, during a phone
call while I was in Garnett, that the celibacy idea
would never fly and scrapped it.)

   Yesterday, Good Friday as it happened, we got up
late (after another fuck, this one regressing to our
norm of dismal failure as Val exhausted herself trying
to come while atop me) and left for L.A. in
midafternoon. As we drove down I soon found her chatter
irritating in its total self-absorption and gradually
lost all ability to tune in on it. Another tiring,
dispiriting discussion of our sex life followed.

   During this talk whatever temporary rapport we
still retained at this stage quickly wore away (except
for a brief period of "playfulness" in a Santa Barbara
restaurant, during which I found myself nourishing
preposterous hopes we could someday become mutually
tolerable travel companions). By the time we arrived at
Paul's place (after hurtling down night freeways through
the Coastal Range and along a moonlit seashore where
palm trees tossed angrily in the stormy wind) we were,
again, as is pretty much standard these days, at each
other's throats, barely suppressing the feud long enough
to drink a glass of wine with our uneasy hosts. Val
finally went for a walk by herself (after a series of
tense whispered tearful confrontations with me in the
narrow hallway of the cabin); and I, exhausted from the
long day and the even longer previous day and night in
Merino, nodded off before she returned. That she took
as an affront, and she's hardly spoken to me since,
except for a few angry words in bed (how selfish I was,
how like Jim).

                         *

   Here's the poem that was folded up inside the paper
airplane she tossed at me maybe half an hour ago. I
hadn't even realized it was there until she pointed it
out. It's about her first boyfriend, Kerin, when she
was about to leave for the States at age fourteen, "but
it's also about us." She's been working on it for weeks

                         384

[Living with Valerie]

for her creative-writing class. Seems to me it
impressively sounds the depths of her anguish.

        Black-eyed idol of my youth
        swaying shivering cocks
        in my virgin bed
        I am not a novice anymore
        but no less impotent.
        I ask for fault of deliverance
        that a choir come
        to launch my grief
        in the amorous loneliness of the night.

        To the inevitable failure
        he replied at a time
        when wisdom does not console:
        "If we are meant we will meet."
        With my grimaces
        of disillusioned child
        I reluctantly removed
        the dead leaves of our love
        to yield way to new experience....

        But the circling flight of memories
        stains the ceiling with shadows
        I hear his step
        emigrate to the infinite
        his smile
        which once seized my lips so vividly
        rings in exile
        and his bronze eyes
        inhabit my walls --
        I cannot forget.

        I cannot forget
        for I know
        that the reproduction of a dream
        long ago lost
        will never come,
        and I can only lunge

[Have Mercy]

```
          at this vagabond hour
          for the moment you promised me
          when our bodies
          will repose in the dark
          our love untormented
          our love simply loved
          knowing nor heat, nor cold
          in the underlight of silver fire ---
```

Sunday 11
     For imagery it's hard to beat. Barefoot,
shirtless, wearing just raggedy denim cutoffs and "Bat
hat," seated on an upright chunk of log, chewing on a
footlong green weed, I scribble away at the small white
dressing table bizarrely stationed in the middle of Paul
and Barb's meadowy front yard as butterflies flutter by
and the egg-yolk-yellow Easter afternoon sun drips down.
     But when it comes to writing about what happened
last night my guts are churning and my writing arm is
paralyzed.
     A few yards away Val sits glumly hunched over with
her foot soaking in a bucket of cold water. Actually we
seem to be getting along better today -- knock on
dressing-table wood -- but she's "kicking the bucket
from the inside," as she put it a moment ago, because
last night, in yanking her back from the edge of the
cliff she was seriously threatening to jump off of --
the one atop the far side of the big hill behind the
cabin -- I yanked so hard I badly sprained her ankle.
     It was the ugliest scene yet. Terrifying.
Performed at the top of the world beneath an eerie full
moon with traffic crawling by on the freeway far below,
the cars looking no bigger than beetles. Such venom she
spat at me that even now I shudder to think of the look
on her face as she dangled her feet out over the abyss
while warning me not to come one inch closer: truly the
glare of a demented killer or terrorist.
     It was an extortion scene. She'd decided she'd
rather throw herself off the cliff than face any more

"torture" from me (by which she was referring to my
"Big W" withdrawals from her malicious harangues). For
maybe as long as an hour I was pleading, begging,
cajoling in an attempt to get her to move back from the
edge. Intuition told me she really would jump if I
couldn't talk her out of it. But doing this was
extremely difficult because she was trapped in her own
vicious rhetoric, knowing it was only driving me further
from her no matter what I might be telling her. So
finally I had to lunge, grab her, wrestle her away from
the edge by all-out force, with her fighting like a
wildcat, scratching, spitting, kicking, kneeing,
slugging.

 For sure I'll never forget it. Val shrieking her
pain and hatred into the night. The terrible distant
echoes of her screams pounding home the extremity of the
situation. Those eerie power lines whining away like a
huge turbine just a few feet overhead. Her face smeared
with blood and mud and madness. And afterwards Val
maniacally hobbling down the rocky path on the injured
ankle, muttering, like a bad actress playing Medea at a
girls' academy.

 My own rampaging fear, anger, disgust. I can
almost touch the deadened remnants of my shattered love
for her. For allowing things to come to this pass I
hate myself as much as I hate her. I swing between
self-confessions -- yes, I'm as bad as she says, worse
even, I'm unimaginably cruel and unfeeling and self-
centered -- swing between this and a weird joy that at
last we've reached the end of the line. One moment I'm
vowing to myself to reform exactly as she'd have me be,
the next I'm embracing the certainty that I can survive
only by fleeing. I congratulate myself for at least
having stood up to her through all this, for having
exposed before it's too late the full measure of the
ugliness that abides in her heart and soul. Then I
thrash myself for forgetting even for a moment how sick
she is and in that sense how far beyond being
responsible for her actions.

 -- "Don't forget to put in the moon," she calls out

right now, mockingly, her eyes full of resentment and guilt.

"Don't you be telling me what to put in."

"Yah, you're writing about last night all right."

"You were a fucker. Such a fucker. I demand a total apology and reparations."

"Fuck you! No!"

And then...suddenly, in a small hollow between large rocks right after I yanked her back from the cliff edge, as I struggled to hold her down, she abruptly changed tacks, her hands were in my crotch, we were embracing fiercely, my pants were down around my knees, she was on her back on sharp rocks and briars (damn bent safety pin refusing to allow the fly of her jeans to unzip), then her jeans were down to her knees and her knees were pressed together up near her nose, and it was a fast furious fuck (not really all that fast at times; in fact for an infinite moment deliciously tantalizingly slow) on a California mountaintop beneath a leering full moon (there it is again, Val, just for you) -- as voices crying our names rang out from below, barely audible at first over the hum of the wires.

Paul and Barbara. A few minutes later their car pulled up on the steep dirt access road leading to the electrical substation just as we were hitching up our pants before nonchalantly stepping out from behind the rocks. "Hey you two, what's happening?" We'd been gone so long, Barb said, they'd started worrying. I tried to joke about our delinquency. Val remained silent. Later, as we roasted hot dogs over a small wood fire behind the cabin, Barb confided that Paul thought I'd emerged from the rocks looking "very shaken."

"Paul had it right," I said.

So what happened next? In bed in the cabin Val unleashed her sexuality in a way I'd never seen from her before. And it was gorgeous. Incredibly, she was doing all the very things whose absence I'd despaired over since our first days together: she was whispering in my ear, she was caressing me with strength and desire and dexterity, she was moving and moaning and reaching, she was responding to everything I did, she was ratcheting up with me and at the same time fully invested in the power and rhythm of her own need and begging for more. One token of this: after so many long months of being forced to tread cautiously in the area of her hypersensitive clit, suddenly she was demanding I scratch and all but maul it. (And I did.)

For me and I believe for her also it was our first real fuck. It more than canceled the effects of her outrageous performance on the cliff edge. She meant it to do exactly that, of course, but that's fine with me. Maybe now she'll start using her erotic passion and her marvelous body as her chief manipulating tools and drop the terror tactics which have had the upper hand ever since -- when? -- around the first of February, I'd guess, the paring-knife attack at Klug's. But...I have to say I think the odds of any such volte-face happening are slim. I'm afraid it was precisely the terror scene on the mountaintop that turned her on so much, just as the paring-knife scene did before, along with a number of others similar to that one in degree of violence. And if that's the case, I'm probably in for a lot more such scenes, until one of them kills us off for real -- her, me, maybe both of us at once.

For certain I'll never forget Val grimly tossing little wildflowers over the cliff edge, each one "another living piece of our flesh." And singing mad out-of-tune French songs a few inches from the calamitous fall, feet dangling, as I stood helplessly above her, prevented by her threats from getting any closer, pitiably pleading and demanding she stop.

"The only purpose of it all," she says today (oh so blithely), "was to make love on the mountaintop. That's all I wanted from the beginning. If you hadn't been so moody and withdrawn it never would've happened that way."

3

Monday 12

Life begins to course in the old veins again.
About time, too, after a three-week brawl with the
furies. A three-week bummer! Valoshka's unaccountably
surly today, reading Kant ("Would you say he's a moral
absolutist?") -- and doing so with liberated breasts as
the Stones' "Honky Tonk Woman" blasts from Barb's state-
of-the-art Crest radio (tuned to the Ventura station).
I guess Val's staggered by the load she'll be facing
when we get back home: school tests, taxes, papers and
stories and poetry due, Danny. But I'm happy because
hope flickers again for us. Light at the end of a deep
and dark tunnel! Who knows, I might even stir up enough
resolve to get some of these former muscles hanging so
slackly from my bones back into working condition.
    -- "Move your arm down a little so I can see what
you got there!"
    "I'm feeding them some sun."
    "Oooeee, now that's a sight to get the ink to
flowing."
    (She's still inordinately proud of her breasts, I'd
say, and also I'd say one more time I like them a lot
myself -- though I'd like them even more if they liked
me at least a little.)
    Ideas for sketches and stories and whole novels are
frolicking in my head. Why, I've even achieved a new
appreciation of L.A.! Not so much because of our visit
to Hollywood last night (grumped the disappointed Val:
"Seeing Hollywood on Easter Sunday is worse than seeing
Paris in August!") but from a close reading of the L.A.
Free Press, a/k/a "the Freep," which revealed to me the
existence of a surprisingly vibrant cultural and
countercultural scene in these parts. It seems my San
Francisco chauvinism may have blinded me to some good
things happening down here in the southland.
    Also the four of us drank beer at Barney's Beanery

390

[Living with Valerie]

near the Sunset Strip and I either loved or sparred with
Val, depending on the moment, but in all cases fiercely.
Because I'd "driven" her "to betrayals," she warned, our
love could "never again be pure." Nonsense, I retorted,
there had been no betrayals and our love had never been
pure anyway and in my view no love could ever be pure.
And besides, our love was in truth only just beginning.
It couldn't really get going until we both risked all-
out intimacy. So then, she asked, did I think maybe it
had begun the night before on the mountaintop? Well,
maybe it had, yes, I said. And certainly I'm hoping
that turns out to be the case -- but not if it means we
have to go through any more way-over-the-top-while-at-
the-mountaintop scenes like that one.

And I don't want to fail to report I chided her for
some pushy, arrogant treatment of me during our
Hollywood night out. "Take a picture of me!" She still
thinks bluntly ordering me around in front of others,
including my own sister and her, Barb's, new ol' man, is
attractively provocative. "I can get away with it," she
shoots back when I tell her this. "Men like it." Maybe
"men" do, but I don't; to me it's embarrassing and
degrading. Parisian street waif trying to act tough:
there's more than a hint of that in it. Self-appointed
avenging angel. Vietcong dragon-lady guerrilla. Lead
Valkyrie of Odin's international contingent of comely
messengers of heroic doom with their swords flashing and
slashing (talent scouts for Valhalla!). For Val all
discussions and encounters become contests to be won.
"Softness is weakness!" she cries. She's forever
painting herself into corners by turning our serious
heart-to-heart talks into win-or-lose propositions,
which means in romantic terms they're no-win
propositions. She's like a delinquent who imagines her
square yard of turf is under assault at every moment.

(The Bold One! Suddenly she turns over on her
back, breasts jutting up and fully exposed -- "my most
vulnerable spots," she says of her nipples -- in this
abrupt flip doing something my mother would never have
done -- she who used to lie prone for hours in the

391

[Have Mercy]

backyard at 636 on lazy summer days with her blouse off
and her bra unhooked while the neighborhood boys, myself
included more than once, jostled behind the bushes for
glimpses. True, she kept herself covered when supine,
as Val is not doing now. The New Age is upon us!
-- But prone, when old Mom propped her head and torso
up on her elbows to read, that was the jackpot view.)
      -- And I just want to say: Val's not always such a
fighter. I sense a gradual mellowing ahead, now that
we've survived the test by fire. "You were very noble
up there on the mountaintop," she conceded grudgingly.
Certainly nobility is far from anything I'd claim for
myself in that incident or any other I can think of.
The truth is I nearly flipped out -- nearly plummeted
off some kind of internal cliff of my own. But if
nobility's how she saw it, fine. Meanwhile my inchoate
plans for leaving her have evaporated. So long as the
sexual reversal continues I can put up with anything she
throws at me.
      "We have been to the over-the-top" -- I can dig it.
                    *   *
      Guess again. The girl simply can't stand
prosperity. All afternoon and evening she's been
spoiling for a fight and I've been trying just as hard
to avoid one, not only putting up with her inexplicable
moodiness but trying to coax and love and "understand"
her out of it. But for every forward step, two
maddeningly exasperating backward ones. In our little
curved-wall guest bedroom I made love to her as fiercely
while also as gently and lovingly as I know how: this
time drawing no response at all. In another doomed
attempt at restoring good relations I talked with her at
length about the things she said were bothering her: it
didn't help. (And this when I'd expect her to be
exultant at surviving the "test by fire" and overcoming
all those traumatic sexual hang-ups.)
      Finally she exploded over a pretext. Completely on
her own she decided to cook a fancy French dinner for
our hosts. She more or less ordered me to drive her to
the store to buy the makings for her celebrated gourmet

392

beef stew and various side dishes and dessert (but no
wine, of course, owing to Paul's A.A. struggles).   To
keep the peace I did as she ordered. After returning,
when I stepped into the kitchen a short time later to
see how she was doing, she sullenly asked me -- again
demanded is more like it -- to peel the potatoes. I
complied, resenting her ugly tone. Barb appeared,
saying, "Glennar! Let me do that; that's woman's work!"
I chuckled at the irony of my supposedly staunchly
feminist sister saying such a thing but kept on peeling
-- then stiffened when Valerie objected to Barb,
sounding autocratic, "Why? They do it in the army!" I
piped up something about not minding the peeling but I'd
sure like to know who promoted her to drill sergeant.
That mildly sarcastic remark set her off.

Three times thereafter I overcame my disgust and
made yet another conciliatory gesture. The first time,
touching her arm, I asked, "You still angry?" "Damn
right!" she snapped. The second time I forget now, but
the last time -- to which she replied, "Fuck you, Glen!"
-- my patience snapped. That was it: this sad, bitter,
immensely difficult and volatile woman two days short of
turning age twenty -- I wanted no more of her.

During dinner we basically didn't speak.
Afterwards we both worked on our own things and inwardly
seethed -- or at least I did. Only after about two
hours of this did she seem to notice. Then she offered
a blase' apology "for being such a bitch." And went on:
"I know I've been taking my frustrations out on you."
She didn't know why, she declared a moment later, she
couldn't "be happy the way other people are" -- why she
couldn't be like those fortunates who don't let their
"anxieties" prevent them from getting their work done.
When I told her I didn't think I could help her on this
-- because, as I pointed out, I'd tried plenty of times
before and she'd never shown the slightest interest in
what I had to offer -- she stormed off "to take a walk
and get my head together."   ---
                                       *

Valerie says the above account is "distorted."   She

read some of it -- maybe most or all of it -- through
the window, over my shoulder, as I suddenly realized she
was doing while I wrote that last paragraph. She didn't
ask my okay to do this; she was snooping again. I
didn't even know she was out there. So now I'm
reporting her views on what happened. It's not an order
that I do so, she says; it's merely a request.

She especially objects to the term "demanded" on
the previous page (about forty lines back -- which shows
she was at the snooping for at least that long). She
asserts her tone with me was not at all demanding or
harsh or condescending; it was simply "normal." She
also describes it as "busy." True, she concedes she's
often admitted it to be harsh, demanding, etc., in the
past, but she insists it wasn't in this instance. Then
what was it, I ask her, she was referring to earlier
tonight when she apologized for being such a bitch?
-- But the hell with this nonsense.

Tuesday 13
At last the ignominious horror-filled journey to
Lalaland has come to an end. And fittingly, too, with
another disgusting scene, this time in Ventura as we
parked outside a place called Curly's Market (where I'd
pulled over when Val suddenly demanded -- yes, that's
exactly the word I want -- demanded that I stop to buy
aspirin to ease her headache, which my "coldness" had
supposedly brought on). Twice she fled angrily from the
car, refusing to travel any farther with me, and I read
the paper until she returned. My "show of nonchalance"
in doing this enraged her so much that the second time
she smashed the paper into my face and then ripped it to
shreds.

"You'd better take off your shades or they'll be
shattered!" she shrieked. When the ruckus drew a clerk
outside to see what it was all about, I waved him off
with my hand below window level outside as if to say it
was nothing, just a little family squabble. And after a
moment (as Val glared intensely at him) he retreated

back inside.

    The customary pose I've learned to adopt over the past couple of months in response to her vicious tantrums is a "thoughtful" reticence, sharp, focused, wary, sometimes sarcastic, sometimes sliding into weary exasperation or numbness or despair. All of these infuriate her.

    I refuse to give in to her threats or to respond in kind to her vituperation, unless it gets to the point where she's completely lost control and is threatening or engaging in physical attacks or other kinds of truly dangerous behavior. Then I "give in" to whatever she asks, my intended message being that if she's going to fight so unfairly I'm simply not going to care anymore. Meanwhile I'm building up huge stores of hidden resentment. I feel sorry for her, but since she uses her own undisputed -- in fact, proudly proclaimed -- sickness as a weapon against me, I can't yield to her on that score either.

    "If you don't give in, I'll do it again, Glen."

    This she says not as a quiet warning, not as something she regrets, but as an hysterical, wild-eyed threat, balefully, hatefully, as if I were her worst enemy in the world. She's now fighting totally without scruple or constraint. In an instant she can switch from a pleading lover to an obscene fulminating bitch. ("I'm just a frustrated bitch," she muttered when last night's installment drew to a close as Paul snored loudly in the next room. -- Yes, by that point our fights had become such a normal part of quonset life that Barb and Paul could sleep through them as if they were merely a series of cabin-rattling thunderstorms.)

    Oh well. Somehow we managed to establish a truce and drove off from Curly's before she could throw another truly nasty scene (the closest she came was an unconsciously comical attempt at self-strangulation with a string around her neck: "Each time you say something like that I pull it a notch tighter!" -- "like that" referring to my attempts to explain calmly and reasonably, at least by my lights, why I was less than

thrilled to be the victim of her continuing abuse). The
rest of the way home -- three hundred and fifty miles,
six hours -- I said almost nothing and she resisted the
urge to start it all over again when I spurned her
sudden turnabout into remorseless "friendliness" laced
with veiled and sometimes direct threats.

"I need your warmth now, Glen. If I don't get it
I'll sink back into that mood again. I can't hold on
much longer."

Now back at home, rainy and chilly San Francisco,
I'm grinding my teeth into powder as I write this. I'm
still furious. She's off at her creative-writing class
at the moment, meaning at least I get a few hours'
respite for the first time in days.

I'm disgusted at my inability to extricate myself
from this mess, sick of writing about these nonstop
battles with Val, bitter, exhausted, feeling utterly
trapped. It seems there's no alternative to fighting
this one out to the finish.

These days there are two Valeries: one I love and
the other I can't stand. One a gentle loving girl-woman
finally beginning to free herself from adolescent
inhibitions and ignorance, the other a savage sneering
dirty-fighting street brawler on a revenge mission. (In
a revealing comment she said she thinks of herself as "a
lion in a cage" when she compromises or gives in or,
most horrifying of all, begins to enjoy herself in a
peaceful way.)

The street brawler in her is always sabotaging the
lover. I don't really know whether she'll ever be able
to escape the ravages of self-destruction. At heart she
sees the world as hostile and barbaric. Men are
untrustworthy brutes. Society is a dog-eat-dog sham.
Happiness itself is suspect and somehow wrong. (When
sick as a child she'd never permit anyone to take care
of her.) She's genuinely paranoid, frightened that any
show of weakness or conciliation on her part will lead
to her being exploited -- yet irony of ironies, it's
only exploitation of the brutal variety that turns her
on sexually (and in many other ways). So she's always

396

bristling with her own soul-deep brand of "ressentiment"
(to resurrect a familiar term), ready at a moment's
notice to strike back at the world and especially at
anyone she suspects of trying to manipulate her.
("Don't try to pacify me!" -- I've heard it over and
over when actually I'm trying to help lift her out of a
horrific funk before it goes vicious and violent.)

It's impossible to ignore her provocations, her
insults, and, especially, her wildly disproportionate
reactions to any critical or mildly angry remark I make.
I have a pretty good idea why she does it, "where she's
coming from," but that's no help when she's trying to
tear me to pieces. At some point it becomes impossible
not to take her attacks personally. It's not men in
general or some mere stand-in for a malevolent father or
husband or society itself she's going after; it's me.

The only hope, as I see it now, is our learning to
regard her demonic street-brawler alter ego as a kind of
third presence whose influence we both must accept and
yet also struggle against. I see no hope at all of her
prevailing by herself in this struggle. I once thought
otherwise, but now I'm realizing, by degrees, how her
perception of the world serves to feed her fears and
thus becomes self-fulfilling: how it activates the very
forces she's struggling against.

What gets lost in all this is the fact that I'm
exhausting myself. Days, weeks, months go by and I get
nothing done. In fact, I retrogress. I become
accustomed to this crazy way of living. I begin to need
it -- its rhythms, its adrenaline hits. And so I waste
what's best in me and I fail to live up to even my most
minimal hopes and ambitions. Instead of coming to grips
with my own problems, I'm satisfied merely to have
survived another day. I actually congratulate myself
for being slightly saner than she is. This is my new
standard of excellence.

*   *

Enough of this. It's all crap! Truth, yes, but
also crap!

I've decided the truth that really matters is this:

397

[Have Mercy]

Valerie is endlessly fascinating. I'm hooked on her.
Her madness combines with her other extraordinary
qualities to make her absolutely irresistible to me.
She's an inspiration, a mystery, a mind-boggler, a turn-
on -- the ultimate turn-on. And no, she's not holding a
gun to my head as I write this.

Single-handedly she's succeeded in keeping my
analytical mills working at full tilt for months -- and
today I stand no closer to "understanding" her than I
ever have. How blind I've been! I've buried myself in
self-induced avalanches of psychological rot!
Valoshka's not the one who needs "liberation" -- I am!
Just as she's been saying all along!

Honest to god, this is for real. I haven't flipped
out. Or if I have, it's about time.

Val is to be loved and adored and appreciated and
wondered at, not analyzed. Fiery, funky, feisty, far-
out Valoshka. Wild Child! Queen of the Streets -- Slum
Goddess! Jungle Brawler! A worthy adversary and just
the mate I need!

For how long have I been playing the role of Glen
the Knowing? For years! Miring myself in swamps of
easy self-reassurance. Taking no risks at all. Taking
comfort in mediocrity of mind. Fettering my zaniness
and deep-down weirdness for fear of raising a frown or
exposing lack of coolness or hipness. No more!

That's right, no more of this insane wallowing in
phony psychological explanations of the actions of
others that threaten my self-image. No more sedate,
smug orderings of the world that always manage to
strangle vitality. All power to the sense of wonder!
Trample premature senility! Laugh "civility" out of the
house! Glory in the fertile depths of a teenage girl's
(teenage, that is, for a few more hours) -- teenage
girl's, I say, brilliantly demented imagination! Fuck
the reformer in myself! There's no call to "help"
people become "better." Celebrate life! Unleash the
manacled imagination! Resurrect the spirit!

And one other thing. Hope like hell that it works.
That it's not too late.

[Living with Valerie]

Wednesday 14

A stroke of genius, a flash of enlightenment, a deliverance from lifelong soberness (and it first came to me completely without warning as I drove over to S.F. State and what surely would've been another dreary and/ or tempestuous night after picking up Val: turned my head around in an instant).

She knew no more than I what to make of it, this sudden boundless flow of exultant energy. She kept saying things like, "Oh, I get it now: you're turning everything I say completely around!" (When she didn't want the Dreamsicle I'd bought for her, I hooked it left-handed over the top of the L.C. from my open driver's-side window and it landed dead center in a trash can across the street. Damn! Master of space and time!)

Nothing she says can upset me anymore. Now I see her words not as simple emissaries of meaning but as the bastard children of a spectacular conjunction of forces in her: gatherings of the miraculous!

Last night when the clock hit twelve midnight we spread out on the bed -- the room was tropically hot -- and slowly got into a first birthday fuck. Val at that point was still more than a little distrusting of this zany "mood" of mine. But she let go a bit more than usual, and that convinced me all the more I'd found the way.

Then we fell asleep with her still atop me and my cock still twitchily half-engorged and stretched out inside her. I dreamt of shooting an ejac photo for the cover of the Merino Mercury -- yes! -- and awoke to find I'd fully stiffened up again and was balling her in my sleep. It didn't work out, though, I don't know why, except I remember thinking, "She's as heavy as a cadaver." I also remember seeing a look of distaste spread on her face as she awakened (the lights were still on). I quit my movements, withdrew the offending member, which now was strangely purplish and still elongated and bloated and veiny but far from fully hard

-- lunker state, I call it -- and laved thickly with
our commingled juices. I hit the bathroom and when I
came back she was in a naked huff, miffed by my
"dropping" her in mid-fuck, angry as an Amazon psyching
herself up for a war dance.

    I could only chuckle. Lovingly, of course,
although also to be sure a bit uneasily (one can't
liberate oneself fully in a few hours). But what really
took me aback was her reaction to this reaction of mine:
unable to provoke anger in me, hers soon dissipated.
What before might've wound up with her coming after me
in a razor-waving mania ended with her snuggled into my
arms and something like a little contented smile on her
lips.

    This morning a similar miracle took place. It had
been her idea to wake at six (the hour of her birth) but
when the alarm sounded she snapped it off and we both
dozed on. Maybe an hour later I was jolted from my
slumber as she grumpily clambered over me to get out of
bed. Shortly after that I heard her weeping and wailing
in the kitchen. When I called out -- "Hey, Valoshka,
something wrong?" -- she appeared at the bedroom door
and flung two pieces of burnt toast at me. It turned
out she'd decided I should've served her breakfast in
bed on her birthday! Nobody had given a shit about her
birthdays since the days of her great aunt!

    This was indeed an outrageous state of affairs.
Transformed in an instant, I bounded forth as her naked
"birthday genie." I scrubbed her in the shower and
toweled her off from head to toe (including between the
toes and of course between the labia majora and the
labia minora too) and deluged her with crazy affection.
At first she wasn't sure whether I was making fun of her
or what -- poor, confused, neglected urchin of the
orphanage -- and for that matter I wasn't totally sure
myself. But what counted was this: soon she was
laughing again.

    In short, it works! It works! Not only for her,
but for me -- because as I sit here in Mac's Grill right
now waiting for the bank to open (so I can cash in a

bagful of coins hoarded over the past year in order that
I might buy her a birthday present or two) I'm
optimistic and bubbling with enthusiasm.

True, an undercurrent of shocked bewilderment is
still coursing on her side and occasionally it surfaces.
But I can deal with that almost effortlessly. Flip the
Big W -- easy!

And not only is today her birthday, but it's a very
special birthday: today she's bidding farewell to
teendom. Turning twenty. She's almost grown! And so
I'll write her a poem, compose her a song, ink her a
sketch, all to memorialize the occasion. I'll collect
her some junk (I know this is what she wants most of
all), pluck her a particolored bouquet of Mt. Moraga
wildflowers, buy her a terrific spur-of-the-moment gift
or two or however many I can come up with given what
little I have to spend. I'll tie her a red bow around
my cock and present her with that too (because she likes
to see cocks dressed up that way, as she's attested
numerous times and used to do quite often herself with
Jim's and also has done with mine three or four times).
We'll spend the afternoon together charging around North
Beach, and after that I'll treat her to a splendiferous
night on the town. There's hardly a moment to lose!

Except to say: thank the stars for such an
epiphany!

And to note: she began the decade of her twenties
with a bang (last night's fuck) and a whimper (this
morning's tears); then she bawled her heart out for
several minutes because she'll never be a teenager
again. I've never seen her looking younger or more
adorable. All but shattered my stony heart, it did,
into a throbbing heap of gristle.

And to promise: one of these days a rambling,
raving probe of this most unlikely Rilkean change in me.

Thursday 15
So far the new vision's still holding. It survived
a potentially catastrophic occasion -- Val's special day

-- and today it's recharging to meet the new trials
which undoubtedly lie ahead.

Yesterday the birthday girl was incredibly trying.
She had me coming and going over sex to the point of
vertigo. First she's utterly unresponsive when I rub up
against her and mutter a few loving seductive
obscenities. I've got "Happy B-day!" written on both
sides of the shaft of my cock and a clown face drawn in
on the head, all in bright blue, red, and green marker,
and I pull out this wacky "membre viril" and lay it
across her palm in a slightly tumesced state and then
waggle the dangling clown head like an overgrown finger
puppet while crooning ventriloquistically -- i.e., as if
the appendage were singing -- "April in Frisco / Moraga
in blossom / Valoshka birthday twenty / pumps me so
high...." She barely manages a tiny smile. Then she
folds her hand around the shaft and listlessly holds it
that way for five, ten, fifteen minutes -- a long time!
-- while grumping on and on about school and other
irrelevancies. Sometime during that eternity I give up
my hopes for an exalted celebratory copulation, feeling
quite sure no good can come from further advances.

But this infuriates her. "You should've been more
aggressive!" she instructs me a little later. Huh? I
point out that I'd tackled her and carried her into the
bedroom on my shoulder and laid her out on the mattress
and stripped off her clothes. Well, yes, but she saw me
as being "very strange" today, meaning it took her a
little longer than usual to get turned on. "You
should've been more patient with the preliminaries," she
grouses (she who usually thinks I take way too long with
them).

Thus enlightened, I go at it again, this time
prolonging the rubbing and scratching and nipping and
tonguing forever. The result is -- the same. I even do
a bawdy "topless/bottomless" dance swinging my half-
aroused "pierro" (she's now calling it) around for her
delectation and amusement. Nothing. But at least she's
not totally dead -- she does smile wanly upon occasion
-- so I go ahead, lubing the now fully stiffened Bozo

[Living with Valerie]

(I'll call it) with saliva for the dry plunge.

Lamentable decision! We wrestle for maybe thirty
minutes and get nowhere. I try every position and angle
and motion and rhythm and pressure I know of and all
conceivable permutes and combos thereof and nothing
pleases her. She keeps thrashing about clumsily like a
bound and gagged prisoner desperate to escape. So,
finally, with sweat dripping from my brow, panting, I
stop and pull out. Another lamentable decision! It
spurs a bitter assault. Why, she spits at me, don't I
do it "stronger"? (Why? Because I don't want to kill
her!) And she sniffs haughtily: "I'm sorry, I'm not
Jang. I can't feel a thing right now -- except
friction." Rarely have I beheld such total, and at the
same time totally inexplicable, contempt on a woman's
face. Rarely have I felt so totally incompetent as a
lover or that a lover of mine was so cruel.

It could've been devastating, no question. I
could've easily spiraled down into a stony Big W funk.
But nothing can make me do that now -- nothing.

"Well, Val," I say, "don't you know I can't give
you anything but friction? The exaltation has to come
from you too, not just me. As a matter of fact, I
thought I was laying some pretty damn good friction on
you there!"

Yes, maybe so, she admits, but I hadn't been
looking into her eyes. It seems that all along what
really turns her on is impassioned mutual deep gazing
during the act and I never knew it.

But something was wrong here, I was well aware,
because in fact I had been peering into her eyes. I'd
been all but burning holes through them. She hadn't
noticed, however, because her own eyes were either
closed or glazed and distant, fixed on the ceiling.

I tell her this and she gets fed up. She storms
off to the bathroom with her usual magnificent runway
strut as if she's about to leap for a high trapeze.

A while later she pads back. I'm lying right where
I was on the mattress bemusedly dangling her purple-and-
white-striped bikini panties from my left index finger

403

raised above my vertical left forearm for contemplation,
meanwhile glancing down occasionally at my mostly
detumesced "membre" lying diagonally across my left hip
with one of the "Happy B-day!"s partially visible, now
upside down and reading right to left, sadly smeared and
crumpled and twitching a bit, altogether looking like a
malfunctioning neon beer sign, as I oddly thought at
that moment, and this sign was hanging aslant on a
single nail in one corner of an anonymous bar. How dare
I ruin her birthday! she cries. I pull her atop me.
No, I'm not letting you get me down for anything,
Valoshka!

So we go at it again. This time she stays on top
because we both know that's where the chances are best
she'll feel something. It's not surefire, and it does
get a bit monotonous for me because for the most part
she's in charge and she's not too likely, to put it
mildly, to push things out to the limit and stretch them
there, bend them, hold them on the edge, make the most
of them, tantalize, but -- what the hell!

And it works. She rocks back and forth, slides me
slowly in and out, then faster, then slower again and
then still slower as we get close, and eventually brings
us both to a splendidly timed booming mutual climax --
and the whole time she doesn't once look in my eyes!
Despite the fact that mine are again burning into hers!

But eyes or no eyes, that climax saved the day.
Sort of. Later, in bed for the night, past one a.m.,
birthday officially over, she rubbed herself against me
until I turned on, and we went yet another round. "It's
nice to desire you again," she whispered. Certainly it
took some courage for her to say that after her tirades
of the afternoon. But then such contradictions have
never bothered her very much, even though they often
leave me reeling.

This time the rutting was a bit more complex: legs
tightly tangled at odd angles, lots of pressure, lots of
"strength" in each slow thrust and churn. I guess she
dug it, although she didn't climax and afterwards I had
to get her off by hand (she hates to ask me to do this,

but she also sometimes jumps on me for attempting to "pacify" or "manipulate" her if I go ahead with it on my own). And I should acknowledge that for me in the end this round was a complete bust -- the come a pitiful aborted sneeze, a leak, a dribble.

Even under the glorious new dispensation it won't always be gangbusters.

In between we did her birthday dinner at the U.S. Restaurant in North Beach and saw two films. Truffaut's "Bed & Board" scraped too many raw nerves because it portrays a struggling young couple somewhat like us. Rawest nerve of all, the French white-guy husband, alienated by his uptight French white-gal wife's pretentions and prudery, gets involved with a ravishingly beautiful Japanese businesswoman who looks a bit like (who else, even though she's Chinese) Briana. But Val swallowed it all pretty well, and afterwards she contended the film supported her conviction that the French are "rude" and "aggressive" as a matter of culture. From the little I know I would not dispute this -- but what we saw on the screen was almost laughably mild stuff compared with what Val's been bombarding me with as many as twenty-four hours a day for months now. Nor did she take well to my observation that if she insisted on using culture as a defense, then shouldn't she accept my excuse that I'm just a stereotypical reserved and "stoic" and "withdrawal-prone" Norwegian? At this she just rolled her eyes. "If only it were so simple!"

She also complained, bizarrely, that I'm not affectionate enough with her at movies. "I'll bet you weren't like this with Jang or Briana." True -- but that's because she, Val, goes dead on me. Jang was usually excited, happy, delighted with the world. Val is just as often dull, listless, bored -- even entirely absent except for the corpse. She gets into moods where she expects adulation to be heaped at the foot of her royal throne as she sniffs disdainfully, and in the face of this I sink into my own thoughts. If there's to be excitement of the peaceful, non-antagonistic type when

405

she's in this morose kind of mood -- and she can be in
it for days on end -- it must come from me or it doesn't
come at all. Sometimes I just can't keep it up if
there's no feedback from her. And that goes for sex
too, even more.

Valoshka, you're such an incredible challenge!
*

Today's tax day. In a short time I'll be picking
her up at school, as I often do now. She doesn't ask me
to do it. I have to cajole an acceptance out of her.
Now really, Val, don't be treating me like I'm your
vassal, expected to beg for the chance to serve you.

There's one trouble, I must confess, with all this
exhilaration of mine over the past several days. I ask
myself, in secret moments, why I should lavish it on
her. I mean, she doesn't seem to appreciate it at all.
It's taken for granted. It's simply the way a woman of
her obvious exceptional quality should be treated, she
believes, but without her making any corresponding
commitment to treat her man that way, to say nothing of
the way he'd really like. And at times this absence of
reciprocity can be quite discouraging.

Friday 16
It took Jang a moment to recognize my voice on the
phone, but as soon as she did she said -- almost without
hesitation, almost as if the last time we'd seen each
other had been yesterday -- "I love you, Glen." Ever
since then I've been trying to come to grips with the
question of how to handle the situation when we meet
later today (honoring the request in her letter that we
have a talk about "something very important").

It's a splendid day. At eight a.m. I dropped Val
off at State and then I was supposed to hit the road for
Garnett, where today the Mercury will be moving to its
spiffy new quarters in the Marvel Plaza. But here I am
at Mac's in the Inner Sunset, wondering whether I really
care about what's the morally proper thing to do
regarding Jang. I guess I do, or otherwise why would I

be agonizing over it? The real problem is that I know
she and I will be balling this afternoon if that's what
she wants. I suspect I'm casting about for some
stainless way to justify letting it happen.

A streetsweeper washes by, its big rotary brushes
leaving a sparkling black swath in their wake. The cool
morning air feels good. Outside is better, but writing
there would be awkward if not impossible owing to a
gusty, page-flipping type of breeze blowing off the
ocean.

Here's a way of rationalizing it. Jang and I have
split up for good, right? Wrong. Because if I say
that, then I can justify balling her only by invoking
the most outlandish theories (e.g., it increases the
overall amount of life and good feeling in the world, as
defined and tallied up by me). But if I say there's
still hope for us, however meager, then, of course, it
makes sense to check out how we're responding to each
other these days. Right?

Do I really care whether it makes sense? No. I'll
feel guilty, but I'll do it. Technically I'm not
exploiting either Jang or Val, but actually, in a deeper
sense, I am -- and both simultaneously. That's
according to conventional traditional morality, whose
prisoner we all are though some of us at times like to
pretend we're not.

By an eerie coincidence, or maybe not, Val and I
talked about the Terpsi-K for hours last night. Val
thinks I idealize her. "Your eyes always shine when you
talk about her." She says she doesn't want to destroy
my fantasy. She wants me to discover on my own (like
the young Frenchman in "Bed and Board") that the woman
at home is the one I really love. She's struck by the
"strangeness, otherworldliness" of Jang's letters,
which she's been reading lately (as I told her she
could). She also detects in them "the presence of an
unbelievably poetic, artistic mind." Also, she notices
the sudden, almost bathetic shifts in tone -- from
divine abstractions and romantic idealizations to the
most absurd petty complaints. "It's like two different

people!" Also she's envious as always, and admits it,
of Jang's accomplishments in the arts -- especially in
dance, but painting and writing as well -- while she,
Val, sees herself as "just getting started in the
world."

So what do I do? The urge is probably too powerful
to resist. I'm writing all this merely so I can say
I've at least thought it over. Perhaps if Valerie
hadn't just put me through more than two months of
living hell this urge wouldn't've arisen. Perhaps if
she and I had a more pyrotechnical sex life -- under
normal circumstances, that is -- it wouldn't've happened
either. In any case, I'm recalling the agreement which
Val insisted on if we were to go ahead with our trial
run -- "the gamble" -- and that was: no commitments.
And I'm realizing that somehow Jang, even after I've
known her for six and a half years, even some fifteen
months after our breakup, still holds considerable power
over me.

*

As for the "celebrate life" epiphany of three days
ago, I want to say I'm aware a lot of it was inspired by
my most recent and ongoing exposure to Henry Miller --
maybe enough so that he could successfully sue for
plagiarism. Yet at the time it all seemed to come
bursting out of my own head and heart. -- The real
question about this epiphany being: can I sustain it?
And to what degree? And with whom?

*   *

(6 p.m. -- seven hours later)
Charles McCabe writes in his Chronicle column today
that American men don't like to admit their involvement
in affairs of the heart. I admit it! I'm involved!
Doubly so now, if not triply. I'm torn now because the
hours with Jang went exactly as I'd hoped (and feared).
We spent the entire afternoon together, balling three
times, taking a walk down to Castro Street, reminiscing,
laughing, playing, mostly avoiding painful topics. Jang
is so lovely, so delightful, so lively, so beautiful.
Advancing age (she's thirty-eight now!) (which means up

408

until three days ago she was twice Val's age) -- Jang's
advancing age, I say, only mellows and deepens
everything that's fine about her. We're each straining
to be the first to forgive the other for our many past
transgressions. Now we're enlightened and recognize to
a much greater extent how and why we've failed in the
past. When talk turns to what the future might hold for
us, we're both uneasy: she doesn't want to chance
rejection, I don't want to face the insoluble
contradictions (in essence, that I still love her in
some deep and abiding sense but know all too well we
couldn't live together again).

As her letter said, it seems likely she'll be
returning to Korea this summer, probably in late July or
August, and quite possibly for good. She hopes I'll
come visit her there and I say I'd very much like to do
that, and will try to do that, but I have to add the
all-purpose qualifier "unless life carries us off in
other directions" (I avert my eyes when I say this; she
winces). Also, nonsensical as it might seem, we talk
about having a child. It's idealistic, romantic musing,
but it arrives with a serious overtone it never had
before. Jang brings it up (it's the "something very
important" her letter mentioned) and says she might like
to do this even if we don't get back together -- she'd
raise the child on her own. This is a big change in her
thinking; it means, in essence, and among other things,
that she's given up any real hope of carrying on with
dance as a career.

Another startling change: she's had an affair!
He's a Cawk Korean War vet almost exactly her age, named
Lyle, now bearded and prematurely white-haired, and she
slept with him over a period of months -- mostly last
fall, she says, and almost always under the influence of
marijuana (she insists!). She still sees him
occasionally but they're no longer sexual; he's pretty
much given up on her now and found another girlfriend.
What most fascinates her about him, quite clearly, is
his war experience, which she wants to write about. He
tells her endless stories about the villages he burned,

the Korean prostitutes he extorted from, the seventeen
North Koreans he killed. He won the Silver Star but
lost part of his gut. He now disavows everything he did
in Korea. To me he sounds like one of those pathetic
men so alienated from themselves by the trauma of war
they can never again function in society.

The fucks with him were usually over quickly, she
says. He's almost impotent because of his wounds, and
he always hid his body from her when they undressed.
She didn't like that. The affair made her realize, she
says, how "selfish and foolish" she'd been while living
with me. Now she wishes we could get back together so
she could help me move into middle and old age as a
"beautiful human being."

For six and a half years I've struggled to capture
in words Jang's appeal for me. I'm doing no better at
it now than I ever did. Her unquenchable sense of
wonder and delight with life just can't be pinned down
verbally, or at least not by me. Not that I can't keep
trying.

** Her throaty chuckles and moans of deep sensual
pleasure as we ball. The way she hastily lifts her
blouse and draws my head to her breasts, laughs, groans,
begs me to kiss her nipples harder, cups her small
breasts with her hands so I'll take more of them into my
mouth, moves my head with her hands from one breast to
the other, sometimes very fast and pressing my head in
tightly, gasping when I nip too hard.

** The marvelously graceful way she hops, darts,
scurries about the room completely naked as she searches
for my missing shades. (We did find them eventually --
out in the L.C.)

** The way she stares unabashed at our reflection
in the mirror as we get it on, just as fascinated and
absorbed and delighted as back when we used to go at it
before Charles and Ernelle's mirror in Mentoka Falls.
She moans deeply and grips me even more tightly with her
splendid (and splendidly hairless) cunt when we alter
positions and she sees my glistening cock sliding in and
out. She reaches under her ass and cradles my balls

with her hands, hefting them, rolling them about.
"Glen, your balls...your balls!" As if she'd never felt
anything more wondrous, more magnificent. (Yes, I know
how sappy and pathetic all this sounds. But when it's
actually happening it's -- delightful. Just how it is.
Always was and still is.)

    ** Her many wide-eyed tales about her current life
as a part-time substitute teacher in the S.F. public
schools (she's also teaching private lessons and classes
in both dance and inkbrush painting/calligraphy). The
"little Negro boys" sticking their hands up between her
thighs. The time she taught a fourth grader how to
write her first words: "I am." The Korean dance
recitals she performs at high schools throughout the
city and beyond. The time she was told she'd be
substituting for a principal and she replied: "Mr. or
Mrs. Principal?" One reason she enjoys the children is
because she has such a movingly childlike side herself
and can indulge it with them (she says this herself)
(and she still calls herself a Taoist, among other
things, and then says she doesn't like the "-ist" part
-- just as she's always said).

    ** The way she suddenly raises her head, gazes
longingly at the hills and valleys of my flesh
stretching down toward the end of the bed, looks in my
eyes, drops her jaw, exclaims, "The lines of your body
are so beautiful!" (Yes!)

    ** Her inexhaustible fund of memories of our time
living together. All such small, domestic pleasures.
"How you used to take off your reading glasses, rub your
eyes with the back of your hand, yawn like a lion and
say, 'Well, I guess it's time for bed.' Yes, Glen, that
made me feel so warm and good, getting ready to sleep in
your arms."

    ** As we sit naked on the edge of the mattress,
exhausted from the hours of splendid loving, she
suddenly reaches out, picks up a sock, examines it,
smiles. "I remember this one!" The sewing, ironing,
cooking, waiting to meet me at the bus stop -- it seems
there's not a moment she's forgotten. It's downright

411

embarrassing. All I can do is nod and smile and
occasionally dredge up some memory of my own...and I'm
not really surprised to discover I have a rather
extensive supply of them myself.

She focuses her complete attention on you. She
invests herself totally in every word she speaks, in
every touch and movement. It's a diet so rich I begin
to swoon, to need relief. And the warmth, the comfort
of her!

And even so -- yes, the same hard truth -- even so
I feel nothing's really changed. I still know we'll
never live together again. My uneasiness on this matter
surpasseth all understanding.... And I know I'll pay a
high price for today. To get another taste of her I've
opened myself to new pressures, new conflicts with
Valerie, new doubts. And what will be the consequences
for Jang herself?

Val lacks many of Jang's charms. Despite all her
physical talents and smaller size (she's two and a half
inches shorter, a pound or two lighter) she seems in
comparison a much denser, rawer, cruder creature. I
think of Val as a tragic character, fascinating in her
complexity, bewildering and frightening -- whereas Jang
is simple, comforting, far from frightening. Yet Val
penetrates me emotionally in a way Jang never has and
never will. The forces of darkness lurk in Val; even at
age twenty (barely) she's uncovered things about me and
about life in general which Jang will never know and
probably wouldn't want to know. Jang remains innocent
in some sense, moral to the core in her own deeply
traditional Korean way, blind to the truths of the ugly
and the ravaged, the crippled and the seamy. Jang never
explores her darkest impulses; in fact, she
intentionally ignores them. (Like Briana.)

I'm attracted to complexity and depth of character
as much as to innocence. But I'm also afraid of it.
How crippled is Valerie? How strong are the forces of
hate and cruelty in her? Can she balance the truths of
the gutter with the truths of light and a healthy love?

(She would never forgive me if she read this entry.

[Living with Valerie]

Not that I intend to let her do that. But it doesn't
really matter anyway. We've both already stockpiled
dozens of things we can never forgive the other for.
Her treatment of me over the past several months has
been degrading to an extent that makes this outcome
inevitable -- that is, my seeing her this way, rebelling
against her this way.)

Sunday 18 (X:17)
     Forget the eyes of fire. Forget celebrating life.
The idiot is me.
     It's the bleakest and most agonizing of chores to
face the horrors of the past forty hours.
     Start with the conclusion: I can't stay with Val.
There's no way. I may love her, but to live this love
with her is out of the question. I must feel something
like a man who's just discovered he's possessed by the
desire to become a beetle. Yet as I write this she's
stapling pictures onto her bedroom wall and newly
arrived boxes of her belongings crowd the living room.
     Blast self-awareness! If I weren't so well
acquainted with my flaws and hang-ups, I don't think
Valerie could hold on to me. She possesses an evil
genius for stirring up my guilt, and she uses it
ruthlessly. Somehow I wind up feeling that everything
she does, however outrageous, pernicious, malignant, is
my fault. Even worse, I wind up supposing this means
she's just the right woman for me, she's the only one
who can understand how conflicted I really am, only she
can help liberate me from myself.
     The truth, I'm sure, is just the opposite. Her
survival with me depends on her ability to exploit my
hang-ups. But to know this truth is one thing, to feel
it is a second, and to act on it a third. I can't get
much beyond the first. And when I do, pain quickly
chases me back.
     Yesterday morning, in front of scores of people at
the S.F. Alliance meeting in the Bresker Company
warehouse South of Market, she vilified me, shrieked at

413

me, hurled epithets -- in short, created a hugely ugly
and humiliating public scene -- all because I'd
neglected to introduce her to Barbara's friend (and Ari
Bresker's lawyer), Steve Vaughn. A typical example of
her shockingly disproportionate reaction to things she
perceives as slights. Sure, I was wrong, although it
was a very minor matter in my view and I had a
reasonable excuse for my screwup. But from her actions
you'd've thought I'd just ruined her life.

Then this. Last night, when she and I along with
Erik and Consuela took in a pornoflick at the O'Farrell,
she acted so despicably I'm still furious about it. She
demanded, under open threat of throwing more scenes like
the one in the Bresker warehouse (or so many others
stretched out over the course of many months), that I
not watch the movie at all. She demanded that I "show
my love" by touching her in such-and-such a way -- and
then she literally slapped my hand away when I tried to
do it. She brutally rejected the plea in my eyes
("That's not love -- you're just desperate!"). This
went on for two hours plus, in and outside the theater,
and I was absolutely terrorized the entire time.

And then this, the worst of them all. Earlier,
after I'd spent most of the afternoon moving her things
here (stonily putting up with her extreme bitchiness),
she refused to go to Erik's, where we were expected for
dinner, unless I voiced my request in a certain abject
tone. To have her insist on this in the first place was
a humiliation. Then when I refused to act as she
demanded, she immediately unleashed her entire
hysterical repertory -- wailing, shrieking, reviling,
threatening suicide, physically attacking, and all the
while moaning bitterly about the pain I was supposedly
causing her by my failure to obey her commands. Finally
she rushed into the bathroom and began gathering up
razor blades -- and then I'd had enough. The specter of
another prolonged suicide scene was more than I could
bear. I grabbed her and shoved her up against a wall
(unintentionally bumping her head rather hard),
eventually forcing her to hand over the blades.

[Living with Valerie]

She responded by going catatonic for thirty minutes or so, her face frozen (trembling slightly) into a mask of pure hatred. She came out of it only to threaten me with further horrific scenes if I made so much as a move in any direction. Then she announced, murderously, she was now "completely hopeless and desperate." (A moment later she smiled bitterly and said, "I'm not the desperate one, Glen -- you are.")

Meanwhile we were an hour late for dinner at Erik's and Danny was in his own state of hysteria. His presence for the entire melee hadn't deterred her even slightly -- she shrieked at him too. He was bewildered, changing quickly from pathetic pleas ("Please don't cry, Mommy") to anguished wails, to mute astonishment, to angry attacks on me ("Don't hurt my mommy, fucker!" -- when I was trying to wrench the blades out of her hand).

This went on for a long time. She scoffed at my suggestions that we call the babysitter or at least call Erik and cancel our plans. When I said I'd call him anyway, she immediately threatened to repeat the earlier scene. "Don't you move one inch or believe me you'll wish you hadn't!" She demanded that I apologize, and not just apologize, but kiss her ass (literally). She spurned my gestures at conciliation -- they weren't good enough, or they weren't genuine, or I hadn't yet humbled myself enough. They were just attempts at, she hissed, "pacification -- you know, like in Vietnam."

And then suddenly a complete turnabout. She was ready to go. No more demands, no more threats, nothing. Just: "All right, let's go." We went. What else could I do? Along the way we dropped Danny off at the sitter's. At Erik's Val was arch and cold and I was shuddering the entire time, afraid even the slightest annoyance would set her off again. Consuela seized on my joking suggestion that we all go see a pornoflick -- it was just, she cried, what she'd always wanted to do! -- and so to my considerable surprise off we went. As soon as we got to the theater, Val started in again with the threatening behavior. Just the fact that we were watching that kind of movie was enough. I should be

415

looking at her, not at those idiots fucking on the
screen. Actually I was so numb I couldn't see anything
on the screen anyway.

*

     How do I get out of this? She accuses me of
holding grudges, but if I really did that I'd be in much
better shape now. The truth is just the reverse: I
forget her maniacal scenes too soon. Forget them, hell
-- I actively suppress them. They're too ugly to think
about. I quickly summon new hope, like a prisoner in an
isolation cell dreaming of grassy meadows and leggy
nymphs. I'm so relieved by the return to relative
tranquility that I actually believe it can continue and
deepen. Val, riddled with shame over what she's done,
becomes almost unbearably sweet and apologetic and
loving for a while.
     But all this quickly wears off. She takes offense
that I'm too numb to respond to her as enthusiastically
as she'd like, she begins making demands again, she
escalates her contempt and harshness and bitchery. Or I
yield to my own underlying despair and utter some small
criticism or sarcastic remark that sets her off again.
     She says I'm "cold" after these scenes of hers.
She expects maybe effusive thanks? It's no help at all
that I see how I trap myself into all this. And it's
true I'm getting worse all the time, like that same
prisoner mentioned above now further enclosed in a
sensory-deprivation tank inside his isolation cell yet
still dreaming the same stupid dreams. No doubt the
deadening process began long before I knew Val, but back
then, by partaking of regular exercise sessions in the
prison yard, as it were, I was able to survive fairly
well. Val's thrown it all out of whack. It's merely
one more part of my problem that I can actually believe
she could help me resolve this problem. But it's hard
to hang on to this insight, it keeps slipping away --
just like the "celebrate life" epiphany....

*   *

Dirty Linen
(babble from the laundromat)

416

[Living with Valerie]

Inflation means paying fifteen cents instead of a
dime for a tiny box of snowy-white bleach.

Today's Examiner carries an unblushing wire-service
story describing how being antiwar has become
"respectable." Even in Galesburg, Illinois! Next
weekend's peace march here is expected to draw up to
half a million people. Of course Nixon is now applauded
by the hard-liners for his nobility in resisting the
temptation to jump on the peace bandwagon. Oh the
ironies of being a veteran of the antiwar! How I'd love
to stuff the Examiner's pro-war editorials of the past
eight or nine years down William Randolph Hearst's
throat! As for the march -- who gives a shit anymore?
I have no more illusions about the effectiveness of
marches. It's hard to feel anything at all about the
war, it's gone on so long. But I do hate the smugness
of the many who've now reversed their stand on it but
refuse to admit they were wrong all along.

Happy news from home. In her first long letter in
months, Mother tells how Rob's presence in the house has
turned Dad around. Rob isn't hypercritical, he doesn't
"attack" Dad or engage in endless arguments over
politics, and now Dad's suddenly bright and cheerful.
He's even willingly attending group therapy sessions!

Group therapy...will I be submitting to that too
one day? I am my father's son! Shudder....

-- A lovely long-legged girl in tight red velvet
bells sashays by outside. I smile admiringly and she
smiles back, running her finger along the glass in a
mock-alluring way. I turn my head to gaze after her as
she strolls. She turns too, and we exchange smiles
again. Then she does a little snatch of bougaloo in
place on the sidewalk before continuing on again. And I
ask myself: if I weren't so fucked up, wouldn't I be
pursuing that girl rather than sitting here stewing?

I'll be picking Val up at the Park N Shop in half
an hour, and I dread seeing her. Lately I find myself
taking an obnoxiously ironic tone with her,
intentionally provoking her. It's my latest contorted
way of striking back for the horrors she's unleashed on

417

me. It's a harmless release, really, but of course she
doesn't see it that way. She contests every word, every
craven smirk. This tactic might work if she'd fight
fair, but of course she won't. She has a way of looking
at me, head cocked, eyes narrowed, that implies if I
don't watch my step she'll drop another terror scene on
me. I detest this attempted intimidation. In the end
it will destroy us. In fact it all but certainly
already has.

   Meanwhile...what else is happening?

   Half a dozen more flowers have bloomed on the
sundeck. I don't know what kind they are, but they make
me ridiculously happy. They're tiny, runts, the
blossoms no bigger than a kernel of popcorn (a popped
kernel, that is), but I couldn't be more jubilant if Val
were to announce she'd move out tomorrow. But of course
she won't be doing that. She's just moved in! This is
insanity.

   The L.C.'s odometer is about to hit five figures.

   Val nearly always wears her irresistibly sexy
patched jeans these days, along with a tight Alvin
Duskin sweater and the silver peace pendant she
appropriated from me last summer more or less by force.

   After seeing the fuck films last night (the first
ever for her) we went home and tried to make like fuck-
film stars. Val moaned a bit more after hearing two
hours of nothing but moans in the theater (well, and a
lot of gasps and grunts too). First, though, she stuck
out her tongue in what she later called a "seduction
attempt," and then she threw a fit when I didn't try to
ravish her on the spot. "You're putting me down again!"
she hissed. My own thought was that she'd been putting
down not just the films themselves but the whole idea of
seduction. Anyway, when we finally got to balling, our
performance fell far short, to say the least, of porn-
star standards. I wound up "pacifying" her three times
by hand, and afterwards she entirely ignored my rampant
and pleafully throbbing fuck appendage. Oh what an
ignominious night it was....

4

Monday 19

How about that: I've actually succeeded in putting
one over on Uncle Sam -- or the State of California
actually. This morning I 90'd down to Bryant Street and
picked up my first unemployment check. Sixty-five bucks
just as promised! For a moment it appeared a hitch had
arisen -- they shunted me off to a back office and left
me sitting there for half an hour with no explanation --
but then a freaky-looking bearded dude in a raggedy and
dandruff-flecked Beat-era black turtleneck -- a classic!
-- came in to say it was merely a matter of my forms
being misplaced and now everything was cool again.

The Bay Bulldog office was nearby and I stopped in
for a moment. Still no word there on when or how Mike
Meyerhold and his staff might make use of my free and
eager services. Peggy, his assistant, can't even say
when the next issue will be appearing. The limbo is
becoming awkward for both of us. I pop in -- "Sorry, no
news!" -- I pop out.

My unemployment comp has only twenty-five more
weeks to run. If the Bulldog can't use me fairly soon
-- say by the end of the month -- I'll start looking
around for someone else who can.

Last night, fed to the earlobes with Valerie's
tactics of the past however many months it is now, I
read her the riot act. If she expects appreciation and
enthusiasm and loving attention, she also has to give
them. Boiled down, that was my message. Nor can she go
on taking for granted the huge sacrifices she's asking
me to make, especially on Danny's behalf. Fine, I say
to her view that Danny's part of her and I have to
accept and love them both, but she should recognize --
and act accordingly -- that adding him into the equation
is no minor matter. Does she think I like having to
remind her I'm not Danny's father and I've not yet
agreed to become his stepfather? Does she forget this

is a trial run "without obligations of any kind"? That this was her own stipulation and she insisted on it as a way of showing her regret for the massive disruptions she caused in Garnett? The sad truth is she refuses to accept responsibility for her own kid -- even the idea of it. If our current "gamble" worked out I'd certainly be doing most of the things she'd like me to be doing with and for Danny, and absolutely I'd be willing to negotiate with her about the rest, but we're far from that stage now and seemingly getting further from it by the day.

Things deteriorated to the point where we were absurdly sparring over which of us does the most for the other. "I fix you hot chocolate in the morning!" "I get up early and drive you to school!" "I helped you with the Mercury!" "I helped you with your poems and papers for school!" A little later she trotted out a few of the old feminist arguments she'd already rejected as too simplistic a year ago; but she soon dropped that line of attack when it became obvious she had no ground to stand on. Exactly what male-chauvinist demands am I making? She couldn't cite even one.

But to out-argue her does no good. So I'm better at playing lawyer than she is -- so what? She feels unappreciated, and that's a fact, and it doesn't make a great deal of difference that she requires much more than your ordinary person -- man, woman, or child -- for her to feel otherwise. The best I can do is to say something like "Let's both try harder" and hope for the best. And of course when I corner her in an argument she only resents me more. As far as she's concerned I'm merely piling up debater's points, "twisting things." "The only way I can get back at you is with those nasty scenes." She's never heard of compromise, I guess. Never heard of finding the middle ground. Never heard of trade-offs or negotiations.

Last night, after much cajoling, she did give in, briefly, by conceding she might at least try to be more aware of how I look at things. But this morning she was back at the same old stand (after I'd twice gotten up

for long spells during the night to deal with a restless
and grumpy Danny while she dozed on), chewing me out in
advance for what she imagined I'd be doing today while
she was at school. "You'll go to North Beach to look at
the girls!" That disgusted me so much I almost set off
immediately for North Beach out of sheer spite. She
still can't see that to demand for me to take her places
and do things for her is self-defeating. At the very
least she could express her needs and wants and wishes
neutrally -- or even nicely once in a while? -- and then
work in good faith on reconciling them with mine.
Better, she might try acting in such a way that I'd
actually want to do for her and with her a reasonable
number of the things she brings up. Right now I don't,
and that's for sure. Look what happened Saturday when,
despite being highly dubious about doing so, I took her
with me to the S.F. Alliance meeting.

But so what. Life goes on -- this much is all but
indisputable -- and I'd better get back into it. I'm
like a famished mutt that's aching to escape from the
master's super-sanitized kennel and take my chances out
in the world of real sniffs.

Some possible sniffs of interest out there:
newspaper work, free universities, Project One
educational ventures, art classes, bicycling, camping
out, protest groups, music classes, JCC workouts,
playground hoops, exploring the city.

This afternoon G.S. Dodge of the Mercury -- my
favorite among the nom de plumes -- vents his
complicated views on the subject of peace marches.

Tuesday 20
Dawdling at Mac's. I'm trying to build my spirits
before making the fifty-mile sprint to Garnett, where a
stormy day awaits me. Al's decision to relocate the
Merc's office to the plastic confines of Marvel Plaza
has alienated many of the anti-plastic volunteers who do
most of the paper's grunt work. The Sherry faction has
gained ascendancy, largely owing to her massive leverage

421

with the Merc's chief investor and thus chief decision-
maker (that would be Al, of course). For all I know,
Sherry may be the only member of the Sherry faction
aside from Al himself, and even he's questionable.
Everybody else seems to be madder than hell about the
move and also about the way Sherry's been ordering
people around.

Here it's been a relatively peaceful twenty-four
hours. I pounded out a draft of the G.S. Dodge column
and spoke at length with Valerie. A good talk for a
change. Perhaps I began to understand better some of
the strains she faces in living with a man. Her past is
so painful to her that she can't easily make connections
between what happened long ago and what's happening now.
"I don't know which questions to ask myself," she says.
"I try, but the same images keep reappearing over and
over again. It practically drives me mad."

Some of the worst images:

** Her father smashes into the family apartment in
Orleans brandishing a gun, howling obscenities at her
mother, breaking up furniture. "White foam" clings to
his lips.

** Her father storms in on another occasion and
locks her mother in a closet, not realizing Val is
crouching under the dining-room table. He stalks off,
taking the key with him, leaving her mother ("the evil
adventuress") locked in there screaming for help.

** Her father smiles "evilly" as he beats her,
Val, the stinging red imprints of his hands on her ass
and legs lingering for hours or even days afterwards.
This happens many, many times. She usually fights back
as hard as she can -- "I wanted him to die! He deserved
to die!" -- and that makes him beat her even harder.
(He often calls her, as do others in their family, "la
petite sauvage" or "the Apache" along with "Valkyrie" or
"Kyrie" for short as a kind of pun referencing also
"Kyrie Eleison," which in the Catholic mass, she
explains to me, means "Lord, have mercy" -- as in "God
help us, you're too much!")

** Her father is choking and beating her mother

422

(this also happens often) and Val does her patented
Valkyrie flight across the huge living room at "the
Governor's" mansion and bites her father's leg so deeply
she hits bone. "I can still remember how good it
tasted. Every time I taste blood that memory comes
back. And semen reminds me of it sometimes too." (why
has she withheld these boggling details from me for so
long? Lord have mercy indeed!)

    ** Her mother laughs contemptuously at Val at the
boarding school as she, her mother, is about to take off
for the U.S. for good. Poor Val can't get the "bright
red lipstick in cruel curves" out of her mind for years.

    ** Her little brother is standing near her in the
outdoor yard of the orphanage they've been banished to,
his shoes and clothes raggedy and grossly overlarge like
a clown's, tears streaming down his cheeks. They both
remain there for two months. "We thought we would be
there forever, like we'd been sent to prison for a
crime. We thought it was our fault that our parents had
divorced and didn't want us anymore."

    She told me about these matters and many others
haltingly and sometimes with great difficulty. It's not
merely painful for her to ponder them; it's close to
impossible. She misses even some of the most obvious
ramifications and still has trouble grasping them after
we talk about them for hours. She can't see the many
strong similarities between her own story and her
mother's. She can't spot the roots of her antipathy
toward most things Chinese (she rarely refers to and
even more rarely celebrates that side of her ancestry).
She doesn't necessarily discourage our talking about
such matters, but she resists going beyond the standard
canned and bowderlized versions she's handed out for
years; she sinks into long reveries, her eyes water, she
takes on a numb and bewildered look.

    (And I still can't get over the irony of it: one of
her pet names since childhood means "have mercy." What
does this woman know about mercy? Kyrie Eleison of the
Val! Valkyrie Eleison! Can there ever be anything
farther fucking out?)

[Have Mercy]

*   *

I'd gotten only so far as the corner market when
confusion set in. Planning only to pick up a soda for
the drive to Garnett, I wound up sitting outside in the
L.C. for well over an hour. I skimmed through the
Examiner (doing this with the evening paper at noon
seems a coup of sorts; you can actually get excited
about encountering such a pack of lies as long as you
can do it slightly before everyone else does), gobbled
up the peanut-butter-and-jelly sandwiches Val had kindly
thrown together for me, and then just as I was about to
take off, a longhair antiwar Viet vet who was curious
about the L.C. came over to check it out and we wound up
rapping for twenty minutes or more.

Fritz Perls says that when confusion sets in you do
best to flow with it until it resolves itself.
Basically that's what I've been doing today ever since
leaving the house. (Val and I have again been studying
"Verbatim" together in hopes of finding a way out of
our terrible impasse.) To hell with Garnett! There's
certainly no urgency about getting there.

Right now I'm battened down at a round blue table
at the MDR (Minimum Daily Requirement) in North Beach,
sipping apple juice and "ogling the girls," as Val would
no doubt say. It's sunny and windy out there. Not much
life on the streets today, actually; the cafes are
nearly empty. For close to two hours I browsed at
downtown and North Beach bookstores, along the way
ravaging my finances for the next two weeks by
purchasing another volume of Dostoevsky's notebooks --
this time the one for "The Brothers Karamazov" -- and
William Gass's "Fiction and the Figures of Life" (the
first hardcover books I've bought in months). Then,
after pea soup and a ham-and-cheese sandwich here, I
took a shot at sketching the place. I'm trying to get
back to some of the practices I had to abandon when I
went to work for the Mercury; sketching is one of them.

With his long blond locks, Pete Wynne, the Viet
vet, looked a lot like General Custer of Little Big Horn
infamy. He also reminded me of brother Jeff, who's just

424

a year younger and mixes charm and anti-Army bitterness
similarly. A friend of Pete's, according to Pete
anyway, was likely one of the fraggers mentioned in the
report released by the military last week. (The
incidence of GI's trying to blow up their own officers
doubled last year, with thirty-some acknowledged deaths
and probably a lot more kept under wraps.) He also knew
someone who went to school with one of Charles Manson's
zombified female followers. (Manson's sentence for the
Tate murders came down yesterday: death.)

And back to Valerie, who incidentally I'm now
calling Kyrie at times -- it rhymes with cheery, weary,
leery -- and I'm doing this with her permission. "It's
good to hear you say it because it sort of reminds me of
who I really am. I was always really proud when my
father called me that. Kyrie is at the core of my
fighting spirit."

Anyway, apparently Val/Kyrie managed to learn a lot
more from the porn film we saw last week than from all
the months of suggestions, not to mention pleas, from
me. (A picture is worth a thousand gasps and moans.)
One of her comments on the film: "That's the first time
I've seen a black cock. They have a red tip -- I always
thought it would be black! And they have more skin on
theirs!" "The dude wasn't circumcised, Val." "Oh." A
real-life examination of how the foreskin (or rather the
remainder thereof) attaches to the pinkish-ivory
cockhead of a certain circumcised former newspaper
editor followed, leading to a righteous blowjob, this
climaxing, literally, and gushingly, just as Pam the
babysitter honked outside and the napping Danny began
bawling. I can't deny I love to peer at Val when her
luscious lips are ministering to my "membre viril." And
most of all I love the moments when she looks up into my
eyes and smiles gluttonously like a kid working on an
all-day sucker. -- And then later last night our
balling, begun so sluggishly, resulted for me in a root-
deep explosive ejac like the one on her birthday.

(A quick computation, undertaken on impulse and
riddled with dubious assumptions, tells me I've balled

some two thousand times in my life. This is assuming an
average of one every other day since the first one with
Kristi in Seattle. Well, or maybe fifteen hundred. I
may even have reached a milestone: it's possible I've
balled more times than I've jerked off. Celebration is
in order. Another name for the milestone might be
"maturity" -- of, granted, an undeniably limited kind.)
      I'm vamping until the traffic thins out a bit,
that's all.
      People become conservative because they grow tired
of liberal and radical failures, many if not most of
which are caused by conservative sabotage. It's natural
enough that when doing good fails a few times too many
(not to mention a few thousand too many), most people
are inclined to circle the wagons and protect their own.
      Yes, the confusion has resolved itself. I think
so. My spirits are reviving. Come to think of it, the
new regime may already have begun. I've blown a big
chunk of the day but I've also produced a pretty good
sketch here! Keep flowing with it, my man!

Wednesday 21
      "Seems like you don't have your usual bounce,"
observes Judy, Evan's wife, as we sprawl on the desks in
the sterile new Marvel Plaza office sorrowfully
discussing the plight of the Merino Mercury.
      I sure as hell don't. It's distressing to find
myself reduced to repeating the same old arguments in
favor of long hair and new lifestyles -- here! In our
own digs! Last night's meeting in this very room wound
up as a philosophical battle with Al and me the chief
antagonists. The outcome was a standoff, I'd say, as
far as debate points go, but Al's views will of course
prevail regardless because he's the Merc's founder and
chief, and close to sole, moneybags. As for me, I'd
rather not go on donating, in effect, a significant
portion of my time and energy to an organization whose
goals I can no longer wholeheartedly endorse. So I'll
be resigning soon, even from the unpaid part-time gig.

[Living with Valerie]

I've already drafted a letter explaining why.

In brief, Al's position is this. He puts up the money for the paper (fills the gap between income and expenses, actually, a matter of some five grand so far, according to Sherry), and to him the paper's purpose is to challenge racism and the war; yet he finds he must spend "half" his time defending the lifestyles of certain people working for the paper, myself, of course, included. He believes the paper will be more effective and also cost him less financially if its image in the community can be changed from "hippie/commie/ underground" to "respectable," and he also believes he'll gain more personal satisfaction from it (and again, the paper's quality will improve) if he can devote more time to writing and less time to defending "hippie lifestyles." This image makeover, he believes, can be accomplished by the expenditure of admittedly considerable sums to mount a conventional business operation, and by requiring the staff to dress and groom and behave before the public in proper conventional American business fashion.

I take issue with this argument every step of the way. Just putting up the money shouldn't mean Al's opinions outweigh everyone else's combined (but of course it does, especially with no other major investor in sight). In my view the paper's aims should be much broader -- the key issues of racism and the war can't be artificially isolated from "lifestyle" questions -- and thus one of its primary goals should be to help sustain a growing counterculture, not to persuade the conservative opposition to cross over to our side (most conservatives don't even read the Merc). I believe the paper will be more effective in achieving its purpose (whether as defined by him or me) if it can become an institution of sorts, a community within the community, and help the local counterculture to identify the important issues in Garnett and Merino County as well as in the larger world and to propose and advocate for alternative solutions to them.

I also assert that the paper's expenses could be

427

significantly reduced if it didn't strain to achieve
business respectability; and in any case to hope to gain
large-scale business backing for an array of mainly
left-wing political causes is ridiculously utopian.
Even if we toned down our political stance and shifted
centerward as far as possible, the Ghastly would still
be able to, and no doubt would, blackball us with the
vast majority of potential local advertisers.

Certainly the Merc would benefit if Al could do
more writing for it, but I fail to see why he should
spend so much of his time arguing with people (whether
it's to justify jettisoning countercultural lifestyles
or to defend his positions on the war and racism): the
paper itself should be his forum for stating his case.
He conceived the idea for it in the first place in order
to express his views to an audience much larger, he
hoped, than the one he could reach directly.

Finally, I'd say the horse is already out of the
barn and it's well-known all around town what breed it
is. At this late date it's unlikely the paper's
reputation can be changed, regardless of efforts to make
it appear "respectable." What's more, it has no chance
at all of being regarded that way so long as it takes
unpopular stands, and it's pretty much a given that in a
military town like Garnett an antiwar stance will remain
unpopular. Ignorant and/or malicious and/or
ideologically rabid right-wingers will continue to call
the paper names and spread false rumors about it and Al
will continue to feel the need to defend himself and the
paper against them. Alas, most "respectable" people
will believe the rumors anyway, or semi-believe them,
and relegate the paper pretty much to the same political
limbo into which our lifestyle differences have already
cast us, and it.

So, yes, under these circumstances it's best for me
to depart. No way can I operate at anything close to
peak capacity while constantly being subjected to
lifestyle scrutiny and attacks from within our own
fortress walls. Further, while I of course fully share
Al's primary aims (fighting racism and the war), I doubt

428

whether a paper produced under such a limited vision
without counterculture underpinning can contribute much
to the Movement as a whole over the long run, and I fear
its efforts could turn out to be counterproductive.

And then I can't deny it, I personally resent the
implications of the sanctimonious position Al takes.
He'd be willing to cut off all his hair (or even his
arms, he says) if he thought it would help end the war.
So is he unaware he seems to be implying his view is
more valid and his stance more virtuous and that anyone
who takes a position differing from his is less
admirable, i.e. morally inferior, and what's more in
effect causing the war to continue? Aware or not, he
clearly is implying this (the same sort of thing used to
rile me about his paternalistic Schweitzerian idealism,
of which his current views are essentially a somewhat
updated expression). And under the circumstances, in
which he's demanding conformity with his views, all or
nothing, I simply won't stand for it.

It comes to me as no surprise that the paper is
disintegrating. Given Al's attitude it's just about
inevitable. In large part the Merc has been held
together by the esprit de corps arising from the
"lifestyle differences" of the volunteer staff, an
embattled minority in the community. ("Merc Nation,"
Holly likes to call it.) Of course the paper might've
failed anyway simply because the support base for a
venture of this type in a town like Garnett is so small.
In any case my own departure has speeded up the process.
But Al knew all along I'd be staying here four months at
most (we're now three weeks beyond that). With any
foresight at all he would've realized the need for him
to step in to fill the vacuum that would soon be
appearing at the center of the staff. His failure to do
this pretty much guarantees the paper will either become
an isolated vehicle for his own thoughts, or will
collapse.

And as I say, it already is collapsing. Everyone's
angry at everyone else. Al tells Ben Kiel not to come
around anymore (Ben, a/k/a the Merino Fox, has been

pestering county health officials over ecological
concerns -- and accomplishing a lot by it -- but word of
this has gotten back to Al, who disapproves because
those same officials can make life harder for Al at the
hospital). Stacy and Claire squabble over
jurisdictional rights to certain men (both covet
several, of whom I'm one for both, though no longer Mr.
Big for either). ---

Thursday 22
        Today I'm a little calmer. More resigned to "the
flow of things." True, right now I'm bivouacked in the
L.C. behind the office to avoid Sherry's oppressive
presence -- she aims long accusatory looks at me and
refuses to answer my questions -- but Sherry doesn't
know I'm out here. My self-instigated banishment from
the office is not intended as a putdown of her or of
anyone. I simply can't get any work done in there.
        Last night Al convinced me it's no use trying to
deal with Sherry. It wasn't what he said -- he simply
reminded me she's motivated primarily by "extreme
defensiveness coming from an insecurity complex" -- but
the way he said it, or rather the way he looked when he
said it: exhausted, washed out, pallid, devastated by
these months of heavy strain, deeply hurt by my
judgments about his political views and where they're
taking the paper. Yet when it got down to it, both of
us were able to suppress our resentment, and perhaps to
accept the other's, and act in such a way that our
longtime friendship wasn't obliterated on the spot. We
were able to rise above the political grievances as well
as the petty ones. For this I'm grateful. It's a
pleasure to discover we both may retain a little more
good sense than either was beginning to think.
        During a debate over an article Al wrote about the
recent "ping-pong breakthrough" with China I conceived a
new angle on him. As a Schweitzerian what he really is
is a humanitarian conservative, missionary type, shot
through with notions of the timeless superiority of

430

traditional Western values, including those of so-called high (read elite, as opposed to counter) culture. In some areas his political naivete is astounding: he actually believes, for example, that great nations such as China act for the reasons they tell the world they act. Thus it's inconceivable to him that China might (A) contradict its longstanding hate-America rhetoric by seeking to improve relations with the West, and (B) make such a move for reasons having nothing to do with either loving or hating America or Western nations.

    -- But here comes Holly. On her back she's hauling a netted sack of beach-ball-like globes destined to become door prizes at tonight's Earth Day celebration -- makes Atlas himself look less like a shrugger than a shirker. A wave, a finger pointing at the office, lips forming the words "You coming?" "I'm coming!" ---

Saturday 24 (X:23)
    "We can build public support if...."
    Oceans of rhetoric.
    "Wars are too serious to be left to...."
    Hundreds of thousands of us peaceful antiwar types are gathered on the grass at the polo grounds in Golden Gate Park. What's happening here must be important because at times as many as half a dozen TV news and police or army or FBI or CIA choppers are buzzing overhead, including right now. It's said the crowd's roughly half the size of San Francisco's total population. All I can see from my current vantage point, though, is a severely truncated cross-section of maybe forty people, and all of these themselves appear to be partial, as in various isolated body parts, mostly feet and legs, most within three or four yards of me, several more or less under me, as my feet and legs are under several others (Val's, for instance, at the moment). It's a glorious fleshy tangle down here.

    Dick Gregory steps up to the podium maybe two-thirds of a football field distant from us. Standing ovation. Everybody up! (As if it were possible.)

Splendid, windy day.

But...for me -- best not to pretend otherwise --
there's little joy in it. Possibly this is because I've
attended too many demonstrations, or because there
simply have been too many, period, and the effectiveness
of any one has been diluted if not entirely washed away,
but finally I can't say why or even think seriously
about the matter. This is because I'm sunk into another
bog of despair diligently drawn for me (like a bath of
warm venom) by...the Kyrie lady. Valoshka.

Four hundred thousand here! (Someone just heard on
the radio.) -- So how is it, I ask, that this one
person now leaning back against my half-raised left
thigh and knee can exercise such malign control over me?

"We have the power to...."

As of this day, Dick Gregory announces, he's eaten
his last bite until all the troops come home. Another
standing O. So how many years until the poor man can
tear into an apple fritter? (I've given up on trying to
join the standing O's, by the way. When some around me
do manage to struggle up it gets a lot darker down here
but also temporarily more private and less tense.)

A similar demo, maybe even bigger, is taking place
in Washington, D.C., today. Yesterday, also in D.C.,
hundreds of highly decorated Viet Vets Against the War
returned their medals to the Army in disgust. Next week
a series of far more militant actions will unfold there
and elsewhere around the country in an attempt to keep
the pressure on.

My head's still aching from the effort to put the
Merc to bed. I'd planned to leave by eleven Thursday
night but couldn't -- the paper wouldn't've come out at
all if I had -- and I wound up staying through until
morning without a single minute's sleep, again finding
those frantic crunch hours as exhilarating as they were
exhausting. At nine a.m. the last paste-ups finally
went out the door and suddenly I was alone in the
temporarily desanitized, cyclone-struck Marvel Plaza
Merc office for what I was fairly sure, and now feel
even more sure, would be the last time ever, lying on my

432

back on the cold tile floor, enjoying a few moments of serenity and wondering what it was, if anything, all the sweat and sacrifice had accomplished.

In the midst of the looming-deadline turmoil, three a.m., Claire and I took a walk around the block and said goodbye to each other. Strange, beautiful woman: we've gone through a lot together and shared quite a few blissful moments, including several extended ones of the sexual variety, and I'm not disparaging those at all -- far from it! -- but mostly it's the other kinds which mean more to me now. "Your terrible ego" was a phrase she uttered at one point, and I won't soon be able to forget that either.

Newspapers do that to you -- breed monstrous egos. Especially when you're sitting in the editor's chair. No other way the million and one decisions can be made: you must armor yourself against your own conscience since virtually every one of those decisions causes pain to someone (or many), and sometimes lots of it.

But now things will be different. Are different, I should say. Oh are they ever.

Sunday 25
Where it stands at this moment: while we were parked along the road to Thornton State Beach she unexpectedly offered a "deal": for two days she'd make no demands. On the road back she expanded the contract to include "no reproachful or hateful looks" because "they're the same as a demand anyway."

I guess I must care for her a great deal: how else to explain the depth of my resentment toward her?

Such abject misery! We've both been immersed in it.

The party we threw at 1616 for the thirty-plus demo attendees from Garnett turned into a disaster. Even if Claire hadn't shown up -- she'd told me the night before she wouldn't be coming, but then she decided she wanted to apologize in person for that "terrible ego" remark and a few others -- even without her presence, I say,

the tensions deriving from my split with Al and Sherry
would've been tough to take. With Val detesting Claire
and casting viperous looks at her and me and everyone
else, fulminating under her breath, brusquely ordering
people around in a way that made Sherry look meek and
sweet, openly threatening nasty scenes, it was hell.

But it turned out to be a lesser hell. The greater
one came later: first from eight p.m. until two a.m.
last night, after everyone had left, and then a second
installment all day today. Val once again in proud
fierce mean "Kyrie" form and just about totally out of
control. No apology was good enough for her.
Persecutions as if she'd been appointed by God to
execute them. Only complete, humiliating surrender
would do, enacted again and again: and the humiliation
was the important part. When it finally got to the
point where I drew a line, she did the pill trip again
(belched hugely all night because of it), a kitchen-
knife trip, a razor trip. In the end I actually broke
down and wept -- and then she spat on that. Literally.

There's no way out this time, she says. Either I
"fill her needs" or she kills herself. But her needs
can't be filled. They can't be reached. They can't
even be determined.

All I've heard about is her pain. The woman truly
believes she has a monopoly on pain, and since I'm in
the area I must be the trigger for most of it. Any
other sources, present or past, are strictly secondary.

She's announced I'm going to pay for my
"betrayals." Making me do so is the only thing she
cares about now. Hell hath no fury like a Valerie
betrayed. She says this flat out.

I should've known her show of selflessness earlier
this week was too good to be true.

Fuck it: I hate myself for continuing to be part of
this.

It's an ugly, ugly impasse. What do you do? Ride
with it. Accept the pain no matter how intense it is.
Maybe something good will come of it.

But how long the trial?

5

Monday 26

Mac's Grill again. What's unusual this time is
Val's presence here at my side. She more or less
blackmailed me into bringing her along. It's another of
the steps I must take in "proving" I'm sorry.

Sorry for what?

Well, she's now focusing on my "affair" with
Claire. I foolishly succumbed to her demand that I tell
her all about it ("If you ever want us to get out of
this alive"). So now the pain she writhes in is
ascribed to that "betrayal," that "infidelity." (In my
view it was neither. I was surprised she even thought
there might be something about it she still didn't know.
Apparently she had suppressed big chunks of what she'd
read in this journal and/or I'd already told her.)

The Valiant One used to be a lot more valiant about
these things. That didn't prove effective, however, or
so she feels, and so now she wails and persecutes and
takes the ultra-hard avenger line.

By rejecting my attempts to patch it up, to consign
our disagreements to the past and begin anew and build a
life together day by day by day -- i.e., by rejecting my
attempts to atone for my so-called sins, not to mention
my real sins -- she makes it impossible for me to do
anything.

Instead she gains a measure of sadistic
satisfaction by making me lie. In truth I'm not even
slightly contrite about what happened with Claire. Why
should I be? I wasn't pledged to Val or anyone else at
the time. But she demands that I say I'm contrite and
then act that way. If I don't, she'll kill herself.
So, under duress, I say it and then I do the best I can
to act it out. I can honestly say I'm sorry if my
actions have wound up causing her pain. That's not even
to mention the pain they caused Claire or me, and they
certainly did that as well (though not just or even

435

primarily pain). Nor was any of this disputed behaviour
of mine intentionally pain-causing. Nor did Val fail to
cause plenty of pain herself, and in many instances
neither accidentally nor unintentionally. But of course
this sort of qualified contrition based on the messiness
of a reality in which we both bear a portion of the
blame for the things that have gone wrong between us is
unacceptable to her.

*

-- Lots to write about but I can only take a quick
swipe at what's most important. We're engaged in a
theoretical discussion about love. Her ideal love is
two people "merged." Mine is loving as your heart
actually moves you to, and if that means "merging" and
it's what the other person also wants, well and good.

Let's face it, the ways of loving are legion and
not all of them live up to high romantic ideals. It's
possible, and even likely, just as an example, for
someone to love more than one person in a lifetime.
This of course is widely accepted in today's world, or
at least the industrialized part of it, but it
drastically conflicts with high romantic ideals as well
as the traditional mores of many cultures (e.g., Korea)
and also of course with the notion of "merging" (which
in most versions that I'm familiar with doesn't allow
for unmerging -- i.e., the emergency that demands
emergence from the merging -- not even momentarily, not
even to sneak out to the bathroom to take a whiz).

It's also possible, though inherently unstable and
certainly impractical in most cases, for someone to love
two or more people simultaneously. Likewise one might
have a main love and one or more subsidiary or lesser
loves (e.g., "intimate friendships"), serially or
sometimes even simultaneously. Whole civilizations have
been built on such principles, including, at one time,
our own.

I can't agree that any one of these kinds of love
is more "ideal" than the others (because that would be
consigning all the others, even though they're based on
true heartfelt loving emotion, to the realm of

436

inferiority). So I say all are equally ideal if
sincerely felt. The fact that I can say this -- in
essence say different kinds of love may be equally
worthy -- makes Val cry and insist we're incompatible.
And this even though I also say I believe the kind of
love I seek is basically the same kind as she does, and
that I'd be willing to commit myself to an all-out
effort to make that kind of love work for us -- if, that
is, we could first agree on certain elementary ground
rules, such as no suicide scenes, no physical violence,
no brandishing kitchen knives or razor blades, no
throwing sharp-edged or breakable objects or heavy hand
barbells, no shrieking so loudly the neighbors will be
alarmed and call the cops, no attempts to destroy
property or the other's artwork or writing, no threats
to prevent the other from leaving the premises to keep
legitimate outside commitments.

And she, of course, is not willing to agree to any
of these. Her admirably frank retort: "And what are you
going to give up? I'd be giving up my power over you
and you'd be giving up nothing."

Tuesday 27
Never did the pen seem less adequate than during
the past four or five weeks -- our first weeks of living
together and Val's weeks of all-stops-out rage. Life
overwhelms art, or better to call it attempted and
failed art. To capture on paper one of her maniacal
three-hour outbursts would take a book by itself (and I
hope someday it will). Beyond that, the scenes
themselves are so intensely painful that to reexamine
them (reopen the still-raw wounds) is usually more than
I can bear. In the end I'm much more likely to settle
into a despondent, exhausted malaise in which writing
becomes impossible.

It goes on and on. The latest sharp bend in the
road has brought me face-to-face with the
incontrovertible fact that she's mad. I've used the
word for her actions a few times before -- probably more

than a few -- but last night for the first time I fully
accepted its accuracy.

Yesterday afternoon it seemed for a while we'd
found a way out of the maze. The discussion of
differing philosophies of love had brought her to the
point of acknowledging that her tactics of late have
constituted both a denial of reality and a betrayal of
her own beliefs. She suddenly saw that to demand
certain emotions from me effectively demolishes the
value and meaning of my acts. No act can be meaningful
if performed unwillingly or under duress -- only if one
has freedom to act otherwise. She's become a terrorist
of love! Therefore, after some hesitation (from fear on
her own part that she was acting merely out of
expedience) she proclaimed I was now "free." I could go
if I liked. My time was my own once again to do with as
I pleased. She swore not to retaliate if I used it in a
way she disapproved of.

Pretty basic stuff for a loving couple, you'd
think. Yet this breakthrough exhilarated both of us.
An enormous pressure lifted from our shoulders as well
as from certain other crucial parts. We wound up
balling away the afternoon. It seemed our life together
might be about to take a major turn for the better. In
no way did I threaten or hint I would use my "freedom"
against her.

Yet toward dinnertime when we awakened from a brief
nap she was profoundly depressed -- bitter, ugly, and
cold. So shocking was this transformation, so wildly
disproportionate and contradictory to her response to
the events preceding it, I knew for certain she'd lost
her grip on reality.

In a sense this realization relieved me. I'd begun
to wonder if I'd unknowingly become the monster she
accused me of being. You can't let yourself be the
target of so much daily abuse for so long (five weeks
plus the two earlier months in Garnett!) without the
ability to fight back (because this would almost
certainly provoke desperate acts) and not begin to
believe there must be some truth to the charges against

you. It's a kind of brainwashing which you feel you're
helpless to prevent at the time, especially if you're
deeply attached to the person who's treating you this
way. But now I was able to lift myself out of that
state and see what had happened to me. I could also see
she was acting in accordance with her own demented
logic, totally divorced from reality. She really was
sick. Why hadn't I realized this before? Well, maybe I
had -- I know I've written in here that I had -- but I'd
never completely believed it or succeeded in hanging on
to the belief. Perhaps I was immobilized as much by my
own pervasive guilt (if for nothing else, for failing to
prevent this situation from developing) as by the abuse
itself. In any event, by a sudden flash of intuition I
now saw with certainty what the "problem" was.

Later Val herself agreed with me. What's happened,
she says, is that ever since she first started to become
aware of her "neurotic problems" last fall she's been
rushing into a crisis. My own comments and criticism
and behavior have unintentionally accelerated the pace.
Her own awareness of her bind has come overwhelmingly
fast. "What's taken five or six months probably
would've taken a lifetime if I hadn't met you." Now
she's suffering in the depths of the crisis, uncertain
herself whether the resolution she chooses will be a
"healthy" or "unhealthy" one. Symptoms of the crisis
include deep inner torment, self-hate, vindictive rages,
suicidal impulses, wildly fluctuating moods -- all of
these interspersed with short-lived (up to a day or so
at this point) periods of calm and what she calls
"superficial sanity."

Last night she gradually brightened to the extent
she was able to reaffirm her earlier emancipation
proclamation. "Tomorrow," she said, "is your day to do
with as you want. You have to rebuild your strength."
That's what I'm supposed to be doing right now.

It's impossible, of course. Tending to Val's
insatiable needs over this long period has so
emotionally exhausted me I can scarcely move. When I do
manage to move, I'm still a zombie. Even worse, I'm

frightened by what she might do if I take her up on her
"offer." The sad truth is, I'm just as caught in this
trap as she is, if not more so. At least she can gain
some measure of relief by letting off steam (by raging);
I must remain a tower of strength. I want to be that
for her, in fact. I dream of helping her to fight her
way through the crisis and emerge from it with our
relationship strong, growing, healthy, satisfying. But
we're at a point now where the chances of this happening
appear to have fallen close to zero.

I feel responsible for some of what she's going
through, not wholly but partly responsible, and this at
least as much as love or simple emotional attachment or
sheer momentum is what's keeping me trying to hang on
with her. But for how long is it possible to continue
this way? The tension is more than I can bear --
especially when it's temporarily removed, as now (she's
at class): then I start slipping into depression. The
resolution of a "neurotic" crisis as deep as this one
may be more than two people can pull off by themselves.
I'm the focus of Val's rage and it falls upon me to play
the role of confessor, authority figure, father,
brother, lover, friend, enemy -- just as, say, a shrink
might. But unlike a shrink (in theory anyway), I'm
personally involved. There's no escape for me when the
fifty-five minutes are up. I must live with the patient
twenty-four hours a day and suffer with her through
every stage of her illness and hoped-for recovery. Nor
do I have the professional training or the knowledge
which might enable me to understand better and cope with
her extreme actions and moods and needs. So I'm afraid
I'll shatter.

Up until last week Garnett served as a place which
I could escape to for temporary relief, for rebuilding
strength; I had the Merc to take my mind off Val's
overwhelming troubles, and I had several friends there,
notably Claire and Evan, but also Jeff, Tom, Sid,
Marcelle, Holly, even Al at times, to reassure me I
wasn't losing my own grip on reality. Now with the Merc
a thing of the past for me -- partly owing, it must be

said, to Val's repeated attempts, whether fully
conscious and intentional or not, at subversion of my
involvement there, although of course I would've left
eventually regardless -- now, I say, matters will be
incomparably more difficult. In San Francisco I have no
friends at all to offer relief, possibly excepting Jang,
and being with her creates more problems than it solves.
I have no place to go, nothing to take my mind off the
morass.

There's one possibility -- the Bay Bulldog. I'm
excited about it because yesterday Peggy Riddell told me
Mike Meyerhold, the publisher/editor, would like me to
accompany him on a hell-raising expedition to City Hall
tomorrow. But I'm also afraid the energy I'll need to
do a good job for the Bulldog will be consumed by Val's
ravenous needs.

Well, I brought this on myself. As I've noted many
times before, my intense involvement with a woman -- my
attempts to know her as deeply as possible -- tends
quickly to bring to the surface whatever contradictions
and conflicts ("neuroses") might be in her, or for that
matter in either of us. The difference is that with
other women, when such things have surfaced, and when
it's become plain to me that the woman would be unable
to or didn't want to cope with them, whether they were
coming from her or me or both, either I've been able to
disengage myself or she has or we both have. Not only
has Val been unable to do this for herself but also
she's succeeded in preventing me from doing it for
myself. On the specific matter of my own breakaway,
whether she's able to prevent this because she's a woman
of exceptional emotional power (as I prefer to believe)
or merely exceedingly unscrupulous and vengeful and
merciless (as I also believe), I don't really know. Nor
do I know for sure whether it's good (as I hope) or bad
(as I strongly suspect) that things have worked out this
way.

                    *   *

Driving across the Golden Gate after finally
breaking away from Funston at three, I got to thinking:

441

would it have been easier, say, to blow up the White
House? "Bye, baby -- I'm off to my 'freedom,'" I joked
feebly while planting a final kiss on her worried lips.
This was after she'd climbed onto my lap, fresh from the
shower, wearing only a towel -- and immediately let that
fall away to reveal her indisputably luscious breasts
with nipples crinkling from the chill in my room and
seemingly begging for "succor," which of course I didn't
hesitate to lavish on them. But yes, she's making a
noble effort to "allow" me more "freedom." Ironically,
though, in lengthening my chains to put Sausalito within
reach she's also made me more aware of how strong they
are. For all the "freedom" I feel at this moment she
might as well be sitting at the next table impaling me
with a glare.

The important question is this: how deep is my
current impulse to cut the chains? And I ask myself
this knowing full well that the glaring Val whom my
fantasy seats next to me is largely a projection of my
own self-contempt. No matter how convincing the
justifications I offer, I'm actually disgusted with
myself for buckling to her emotional terrorism. It's
not a matter of right or wrong; it's simple revulsion
for letting her control me and degrade me as she's done.
And it's irrational revulsion too, because I know I
really had no choice but to let her get away with it, or
otherwise she'd be dead by now (and maybe Danny and I
would too). I also know at bottom I did this "for
love." But so long as I'm in the throes of revulsion
and self-contempt over it I'd be foolish to make a
decision about what to do about her in the future.

That fact, too, disgusts me, because in reality
it's not a fact at all, but another subterfuge, this
time concealing a different sort of unpalatable truth:
quite obviously something in Val's actions fascinates
me, draws me in, deepens my attachment to her. It
becomes a highly complex and tangled thing, this
relationship, probably deranged on both sides, and that
likelihood too appeals to me in a way, even while
revulsing me.

442

[Living with Valerie]

And so my life winds on, its vital energies drained
away on compulsions and revulsions and fears and
frenzied efforts to understand and combat them all --
resulting in depression and disgust.

*

Unlike the Sunset District, Sausalito is sunny this
afternoon. Yet it's no longer the same place for me.
From the glassed-in deck of the Trident -- which reeks
as always of hip capitalism and big-bucks tourism but
remains lively and attractive -- the skyline of the
city, jagged and distinct like flashing shark's teeth
across the bay, still arouses the same too easy sense of
superiority (all those people over there slaving away in
their offices in knowing or -- is this even possible? --
unknowing support of the American empire that built it
and the current American war machine that keeps it in
business). Yet raise your hand and hold it out flat and
there in your palm stands one of the great cities of the
world. The blue-and-white color scheme of the ferry
right now backing out from its dock a few feet to my
left still dazzles with its purity and simplicity. Over
here we've got the atmosphere of a timeless, quaint
town, a misleadingly secure haven where the rich and the
privileged can fiddle away while watching from afar as
the world burns. And yet, for me personally, just as
Sausalito once became a different place because Kristi
Karlson moved away from it, now it's no longer the place
where Denise Purcell lives. The town is empty, foreign,
alien, and at the same time it also lacks the thrill of
a truly new getaway refuge. Which is to say it's a kind
of limbo, one of those picturesque out-of-the-way spots
you return to in order to see where life has taken you
since your last visit. Inevitably you're likely to
discover little is really different in your life except
for one obvious fact: you're that much older, that much
closer to no longer being a part of any of this, whether
it's picturesque and out-of-the-way or not.
My own last visit here, to the Trident? Roughly
ten months ago, and it was with Valerie: the night she
revealed Jim's despicable armed rape of her and also how

443

she often enjoyed his brutal treatment of her -- and a
number of other similar horror stories of their life
together. Back then I certainly didn't think this would
ever be the case, but now I have more than a few such
stories of my own to tell about life with Val -- and
here I am once again telling them to this journal.

(And one more thing. It's safe to say no woman has
ever faded so quickly for me after I've thought I loved
her, however briefly, as Denise has. I think of her
mostly when I encounter a group of stewardesses
downtown, especially if one happens to be black, and I
think: wouldn't it be something if Denise suddenly took
it upon herself to repay that hundred and fifty bucks
she still owes me?)

Wednesday 28 (X:27)
From the front room of the Bay Bulldog offices on
Bryant Street. Out the windows a dreary vista of South
of Market warehouses and factories and the Bayshore
Freeway. Kay, who's young and hip and adores Gold Rush
country (and delights in discovering I do too), just
flipped on the radio to KRMA. Her dog wanders the
streets leashless. I'm working at the desk of the
absent advertising manager, Yvonne, and I'm supposedly
gathering facts by phone about the little-known free
vacations accorded to VIPs at the city's Hetch Hetchy
power station up in the Sierras near Yosemite. But I'm
too blissed out over the way my first day with the paper
is going to worry about such things just yet.

Almost immediately I found myself plunged into the
thick of the fracas. The Bulldog styles itself as a
muckraker (its slogan: "We print the news and raise
hell") and if you're going to do a good job of raking
muck, the cost in labor (and fracas) is high. Upon my
arrival the editor/publisher, Mike Meyerhold, tossed two
lengthy news stories my way to read. In thirty minutes
we'd be descending on the City Water Department, he
said, our aim there being to force them to cough up a
list of high-ranking city politicians and power brokers

who've wined and dined at Hetch Hetchy on the taxpayers'
tab. Once we'd secured the list -- the hard part -- he
wanted me to stay on and copy it and possibly research
the identities of the listees if time permitted.

How to describe Mike. A newsman to the core. Tall
(about six-five), husky like a football tackle (weighing
in at maybe 240), with a large squarish head and a shock
of unruly dark brown hair, small but piercing green
eyes, an aptly bulldoglike jaw, shabby slacks, tie, and
corduroy sports jacket, an ability to summon an
impressive expression of worldly-wise weariness (faintly
dissolute, red-eyed). All he needs to fit the archetype
of the cynical big-city reporter, jumbo model, is a
rakishly angled fedora with a press card stuck into the
hatband.

But then you start noticing differences. In the
way his attention sometimes drifts off while talking
(wandering or glazed eyes) he's more like an
absentminded professor, as he also is in his shuffling
gait (almost aimless at times) and personal slovenliness
(which he tries to keep under control when the public's
involved). Clearly he's a man who cares deeply about
only two things: his family and his newspaper. He wears
no rings, no buttons, nothing stylish; you suspect the
only reason his ordinary black laced oxfords aren't more
scuffed is that last night someone polished them for him
(it turns out he's married to Peggy Riddell, the
"assistant" I've been pestering for weeks, and they
have two small kids; I suspect she's the one who did the
shoe polishing). Wholly absorbed in his work, he
doesn't laugh much -- though his wry wit is entertaining
-- nor does he show much enthusiasm for topics unrelated
to journalism, the current concerns of the paper, or the
public welfare in general. He's a polite listener,
however -- yet likely to burst out with an idea
(eureka!) at the most discomfiting times, as if to
suggest he'd been doing his best to listen to you, but,
well, this idea just popped up from nowhere and demanded
to be heard and now he's dying to try it out on you
before it goes cold.

[Have Mercy]

In action out on a story he's completely different:
strong, blustering, insistent, demanding what he's
certain the public has a right to know. An extremely
impressive righteous indignation possesses him. At the
Water Department I saw this for myself as a group of
uneasy bureaucrats gave us the runaround on the VIP list
for Hetch Hetchy. While I took notes and tried not to
betray any reaction, Meyerhold stomped, ranted, pointed
a quivering finger, lavished sarcasm.
    "Public. That's p-u-b-l-i-c. At the Bay Bulldog
we can spell. You guys can't count a list of names; can
you spell 'public'?"
    All in all it was a first-class if slightly
hackneyed performance. Without doubt it made for a day
to remember for the personnel of the Water Department.
Meyerhold had green-visored number-crunchers scampering
for figures, pompous supervisors stammering, matching-
skirt-and-sweatered secretaries giggling nervously. But
it was all to no avail. The head honcho was out for the
day, and without his approval no one was about to hand
over a list of names that could turn out to be political
dynamite -- and damn the "public record."
    So we'll return tomorrow. "We'll make those
bastards cough up that list if we have to go to court to
do it!" cries Mike, and you know he means it. The
outraged indignation is real! It's not merely a matter
of "principle" -- nothing so abstract as that. He sees
himself as the representative for John Q. Public, as the
embodiment of the public interest and the public's right
to know; he feels it in his bones. It's as if he'd been
created by a guilty deity to compensate for unloosing on
the world the huge pack of conventional journalists
working for mainstream corporate newspapers in whom a
sense of civic conscience, a willingness and readiness
to struggle against the powers that be, had
inadvertently been left out.
    To play this role calls for an enormous investment
of energy, an ability to withstand frequent humiliation,
and an almost inhuman amount of patience. It also
requires a set of values, an angle of vision, far

446

different from the ordinary. How else can a man justify
to himself spending days and weeks haggling with
bureaucrats over procurement of a list of names which in
no way will touch his personal life? Even if obtained
and published, the list will almost certainly not cause
any significant change in public policy. The same VIPs
will be entertained at Hetch Hetchy next year, or if not
there, some other similar place. Meyerhold's long-term
goal -- to force the Public Utilities Commission to
comply with law by restoring to the city its right to
profit from its own power source -- i.e., his campaign
for "public power" -- is roughly as likely to be
accomplished as is a complete withdrawal by the end of
the month of all American troops not just from Vietnam
but from every other outpost of the American empire, and
of course those number in the many hundreds. Yet he
pushes on as if victory were within sight.

An extraordinary man. And maybe some of his
dedication, his selflessness, his aggressiveness, his
vision will rub off on me. At the moment I can't see
myself becoming such a fierce crusader, not even on the
issues I care about most: the war, the environment,
racism, sexism, poverty, runaway materialism, American
imperialism in general, and the care and nurturing of a
counterculture which might be able to do something about
all of the above. But I still believe I could help him
considerably. Already a number of my story ideas and
suggestions for cutting costs based on our experience
at the Merc have elicited Meyerholdian bravos. But
dress down a group of frightened bureaucrats? I doubt
it. I have too hard a time partitioning off the
knowledge that they're victims of the system just as
everyone else is -- and in a sense even more so.

*   *

An exciting day -- that is, until I arrived home at
six-thirty. Valoshka refrained from chastising me for
my lateness, but she was plainly perturbed by it.
Either that, or some sort of reaction against me has set
in (this is of course to be expected if what she's
experiencing is truly an extreme emotional or "neurotic"

447

crisis). In any case she radiated a barely suppressed
hostility as we plodded through the evening: first at
Park N Shop, then at a bookstore on Geary, and finally
at home during a long bath I took as she read philosophy
in preparation for writing several papers for school
(these too, along with poems and stories which must be
readied, are pressuring her).

My excitement over the developments of my first day
at the Bulldog was enough to carry me through all this.
I was able to ignore a long series of indifferent
responses from her and instead joked about Hobbes,
diets, and my own morbid state (a bad cold coming on).
Looking at me strangely, quizzically, dispassionately,
she expressed anxiety over having to, as she put it,
"witness your disintegration." She was referring
mainly, I think, to my thickening waist (I'm back up to
205) from lack of exercise, but also to some deepening
worry lines which she herself has all but chiseled into
my face. To overlook a sally like that I must be in a
good mood. (Is she merely envious of my obvious
happiness regarding the Bulldog? Disconcerted by the
relative tranquility of the past two days?)

The real topper for the evening came in reading
through (in the bathtub) the tenth-reunion booklet for
the massively undistinguished Gatefield High School
Class of 1960. It contains few surprises about the
general direction my classmates have taken (more than
half remain in the Chicago area, but most of the
brighter ones, at least as I would judge them, have
moved away, and many of those were unresponsive to the
inquiries of the booklet's compilers). Still, plenty of
the details were funny or poignant -- but only if you
knew the people as they once were in our high-school
days. I was amazed by how many names could still summon
faces and even voices from my memory as I read the short
bios (the booklet, alas, has no photos). By far the
larger part of the class appears to have settled into a
conventional suburban life. It would seem our class has
been only lightly touched by the antiwar and civil-
rights and countercultural whirlwinds. Though

harbingers of all of these were present even at
Gatefield High School in the late fifties, it appears
the Class of '60 came along slightly too early.
(Apparently Bob Rowley is still the only class member --
of 325 -- who's died in Vietnam.)

Thursday 29
     "It's very hard for me to accept that I can't
control everything."
     This is Val's succinct explanation for her current
gloomy state. It's also an implicit justification for
the unresponsiveness, morbidity, indifference she's been
showing lately (though hardly for the first time).
What's more, she's righteous about it. If I express
even the faintest dissatisfaction with her, I'm once
again making "demands." I simply must accept her as the
person she is. More than that, I should at all times
act in such a way as to reassure her. Yet in the actual
event no acts and no words exist which will succeed in
doing that, with the possible exception of a certain
highly contentious promise, to wit: that I'll be
faithful to her.
     As things stand I can't make that promise. Not
under duress. Knowing myself, it would be a difficult
promise to make under even the best of conditions. Two
months ago I was ready to make it. But the moment
slipped by, and since then conditions between us have
deteriorated to the point where fidelity to Val is one
of the least appealing things I can think of. I'm still
drawn by the idea of fidelity to a woman -- but to Val?
Her lack of faith in my steadfastness is equaled if not
exceeded by my lack of faith in her overall temperament.
I can't and won't bind myself to a woman who despises
simple happiness and experiences any sign of its
existence in the person she supposedly loves as an
affront.
     So our struggle will continue, both of us trying to
make the best of a bad situation, but neither willing to
yield and go along with the other on faith alone.

[Have Mercy]

"You're dooming me to solitude," she says. That
she might be doing the same to me is irrelevant as far
as she's concerned. In effect, she's claiming her self-
declared neurosis gives her rights I don't have, since
I'm "strong." But her attempts to exploit her emotional
condition this way show she's as "strong" as I am and
also at least a shade or two more unscrupulous.

Strength: bleah. How pathetic all this is. It
truly is heartrending. Each of us can scarcely abide
the other's presence, but can think of little else.
Everything, every action, carries undertones of
resentment. I have the ability to forget (or suppress)
things fairly quickly, and thus every so often I'm ready
to make a new attempt at being loving, amiable,
compassionate, cheerful. But she ignores these efforts,
intentionally subverts them -- blithely admits she's
doing just this -- and soon we're back to being silently
furious with each other.

It's simple enough. She still feels betrayed.
"You're to blame for the way I feel," she insists.
Therefore I should kiss her ass again and again. I
should offer constant "reassurance." In short, I should
act like someone who's guilty -- a remorseful criminal.
I feel bad enough about many of the things that have
happened between us, and for that matter between me and
others during the time I've known her, but I don't feel
like a criminal. So I refuse to act like one. What's
more, I resent her efforts to make me feel that way and
to punish me for my alleged immoral acts. This only
deepens her own resentment.

A way out? Lotsa luck.

*   *

-- All the more reason to praise the Bay Bulldog.
Last night I boldly told Val I'd been "paranoid" in
saying she should let me have the Bulldog as a place
where I could "get away a little bit" as she does at
S.F. State; I told her I wanted her to come down there
with me to check it out "sometime soon." Tonight she
tells me, mincing no words, she doesn't trust what I'm
doing there and demands I stay home! Well, there's no

450

way I'll do that. Nor will I let myself become
embroiled in any romantic intrigues at the Bulldog.
Catching on there is too important to me to let anything
like that happen. Not that I say this to her.

Friday 30
     In the thick of it. I'm in the Bulldog office,
Val's in the L.C. parked across the street. Mike M.
chats indifferently with a garrulous Tanzanian (well,
not indifferently; in fact I admire his ability to ply
the Tanzanian with the kind of questions which I'd
personally consider tiresome but which the Tanzanian
clearly doesn't). Anyway, I'm exhausted, angry, and
once again scared to death of Val's burgeoning demands.
With her threats of hysteria and suicide she's back to
controlling me like a marionette, barking orders and
insults and forcing me to swallow them in ways no mere
marionette could do. It's intolerable.
     Last night, after five hours of rabid attacks, she
demanded (and I do mean demanded) I take her to the
Bulldog office today. I gave in after she blew up
(again forcing me to wrestle her to the floor and gag
her with my hands to silence an outburst of ear-
shattering howls). "I want you to kiss my ass!" she
shrieked at one point (later). If I didn't, she'd
prevent me from going to the office or anywhere else.
So, boiling underneath, as I still am, I kissed it. It
beat the alternatives! Now I'm thinking seriously of
contacting her brother to let him know I can no longer
be responsible for her and recommending he help her find
psychiatric help. If things get any worse I may have to
take her straight to the psych ward. So terrifying has
this ordeal become that I'm no longer shocked at the
thought of having her committed.
     Now I have to go out to the L.C. and kiss her ass
some more (though probably not literally this time),
pretend I "understand," suppress my own fierce
resentment, and escort her into the office. Hopefully
Mike and the others will soon leave for lunch. I have

absolutely no doubt what Val will do (I've seen it too
many times before): in front of the others, if they're
still here, she'll make outrageous demands of me
designed to show I'm under her control -- to demonstrate
this to everyone. If I don't yield to them, she'll
throw one of her patented tantrums right on the spot,
embarrassing me further, probably dooming my attempt to
catch on at the Bulldog almost before it's begun. Most
likely that was her purpose in wanting to come down here
in the first place.

"It's a risk you'll have to take," she said.

To "understand" the psychology underlying her
actions is not to be able to tolerate the actions
themselves. There are times now when, rather than yield
to her persecution and blackmail, I'd actually prefer to
see her kill herself. Such feelings are a terrible
shock to me, and so far, rather than submit to them,
I've submitted to her, over and over; but my resentment
at being forced to do so has reached gargantuan
proportions and I'm afraid it will soon explode: that
is, I'll drop her flat no matter what the consequences
might be to her.

MAY

1

Saturday 1

The life-and-death struggle goes on. Yesterday
afternoon Val hung out at the Bulldog office for several
hours without causing any incidents. Her presence,
however, so unnerved me I got no work done. I felt
controlled, abused, manipulated. I was physically and
spiritually miserable. Headache, stomachache, earache,
sore throat, heavy chest cold. Every second was agony.
All I could do was hunker down at the front-room desk
I've staked out as a temporary work spot and pretend to
work. Other than make a few brief phone calls I did
nothing. My act wasn't fooling Mike M.; it was easy to
see he was judging me as someone who wasn't really
interested in the Bulldog or in journalism -- a two-day
flash in the pan. That hurt most of all.

Afterwards I once again read Val the riot act. I
told her point-blank, furiously, I would no longer stand
for her manipulation of me through threats of violence,
maniacal rage, suicide. I'd taken all I could take from
her on that score. The next time she tried it, I vowed,
I would leave her, relinquishing all responsibility -- I
didn't care what she did. She had become an out-and-out
monster. Her monstrous acts and demands had driven me
to the absolute limit of my tolerance.

What's more, I demanded she take a stand one way or
the other on whether it would be "honorable" and "right"
for two people to separate if they were driving each
other mad. She agreed it would; but later she insisted
she'd done so under duress. But it made no difference
to me how she answered. Either she has some sense of
honor or she doesn't. If she does, then she must agree
I'd be doing the right thing in declaring our

453

"experiment" to be at an end and our "gamble" a very
big loss and therefore asking her to move out. If she
doesn't agree, then I'd be correct in regarding her as a
monster and relinquishing whatever responsibility I may
have for her.

After delivering my harangue, I assured her I still
want to make our relationship work. I put the angry
tone behind me, lavished her with affection, even threw
together a delayed dinner for her. Her response was
absolute silence and hate-filled eyes. I did the best I
could to ignore this and continued to try to cheer her
up. To my surprise a bit later she permitted me --
reluctantly -- to make love to her on the living-room
couch, and then we fell asleep in each other's arms.
When we awoke it was past eleven and I felt ill
(physically); I suggested we go to bed.

She would have none of it. She didn't care how I
felt; her own pain at that moment was too great. She
demanded I withdraw my threat (in essence, to ask her to
move out if she pulled another suicide/blackmail/terror
episode). I refused. If she felt she couldn't live
under a threat, I said, then she knew exactly how I felt
living under her threats. If she would withdraw her
threats, then I would withdraw mine. No, she couldn't
accept that.

When I said I had to go to bed, and again invited
her to join me, she began edging back toward hysteria,
angrily demanding I stay up and withdraw my threat. I
went to bed anyway. She followed me, turning the lights
back on and ripping off the covers. When I refused to
react, she stormed off to the bathroom. When she came
back she said, "Well, I did it," meaning she'd again
consumed a handful of pills.

I was tempted to call it all off right there, but
her tone -- more controlled, not raging -- dissuaded me.
I soon realized she hadn't taken the pills. An hour or
so of bitter argument followed, during which I offered a
concession. Rather than holding the threat over her for
life, I would withdraw it after a certain period -- a
year, I suggested. That enraged her. Two weeks, she

said. Three months, I said. Again she launched into a
venomous attack. I offered a final figure: one month.
"It's too late," she said. More attacks -- and then she
abruptly walked out of the room and closed the door and
the house became quiet, and it stayed quiet.

Unprecedented. Could it mean I'd finally broken
through? Never before in our time together had she quit
a battle this way. I spent an agonizing night, nearly
sleepless, wondering what she was up to, powerful fears
coursing through me. Earlier she'd packed a suitcase
and threatened to leave immediately -- was she making
the final preparations to do that now? Was she quietly
pilling herself to death? Was that gas I smelled? (I
opened my bedroom window as wide as it would go.) Would
she come storming in with a knife and try to maim me or
do me in while I slept (as she'd several times
threatened to do over the extended period of our
struggles)? Anything was possible. I shook with
trepidation and stiffened at the slightest sound. But I
would not move. I had to let her ride this one out
alone and hope for the best.

She never did come back in. When I awoke with a
start at seven-fifteen this morning, the house was
silent. In a dream I'd found her floating open-mouthed
in the bathtub, a cadaver -- then the cadaver winked at
me and laughed bitterly, maniacally.

In the morning silence I dressed quickly and, full
of dread, explored the house. I actually hoped to find
her gone. But I knew she wouldn't be. She lacks the
strength to release me voluntarily from the hell she's
created for me; she lacks the strength to cope with her
own hell.

I found her in bed in the "blue room." Dead?
Alive? At first I didn't know. But then she stirred
and leveled an accusing eye at me. I made an enormous
effort to restrain the fury threatening to overwhelm me.
I came up with a few reassuring words, kissed her, made
her a cup of coffee. She accepted it grudgingly.

"It's a good morning," I said. "A new day."

She continued glaring at me. Finally, in the

gentlest tone I could manage, I told her that in a few
minutes I'd be walking down to the store to pick up the
paper and maybe write a little -- I'd be back in an hour
or so. Was there anything I could pick up for her?

She blew her stack. I was "abandoning" her. I
"never" did anything for her. The few small acts I
performed for her were merely a "means to an end" of
getting away from her. Why did she have to "earn"
everything? Why didn't I want to be with her always?
Why did I want her only when we were both "up"? All I
"ever" thought about was myself! "You've never done one
single thing for me!" Now I was trying to "provoke" her
into another rage. I was trying to ruin her day!

This went on for an hour. Still suppressing my own
rage, trying to ignore her unending string of vicious
remarks, I attributed my desire to go out to a simple
need to "get my head together." Whether she could
understand it or not, I said, I deeply resented her
manipulations and was trying to deal with this fact in a
nonconfrontational manner -- by getting away from the
turmoil for an hour. What's more, I needed to feel I
was coming to her on my own, not because she'd ordered
me to. Therefore: if she was smart she'd let me go.

She wasn't smart. Her contribution toward a
reconciliation, she said, had been "letting you kiss me
just now." Her demands and insults flowed as thickly
and biliously as ever, along with her tears. But I left
the house anyway.

Now I've been away for almost two hours, not at
Mac's or any other place she could easily find me but at
Zaki's, the 20th and Irving cafe whose whereabouts she's
unaware of (so far as I know). Ironically I do feel
somewhat more together now, ready to go back and try
again, just as I told her I hoped I would. But I expect
she'll be quite the opposite, trying to humiliate me in
every way possible, rejecting any suggestion that we
start anew, deepening my own resentment with outrageous
demands. Finally we'll battle furiously and the cycle
will repeat itself. She may be indifferent for a while:
but the shape of things will be the same.

[Living with Valerie]

Love and freedom. Can they ever be compatible?
How deep is this resentment that's building in me? Is
it destroying my chances of finding a measure of freedom
and happiness in love not just with her but with anyone?
I fear it is. I shudder at the loss, at what I'm
becoming in the effort to cope with this one woman's
utterly unfathomable and malignant kind of love.

Sunday 2
    For about five hours yesterday it looked as though
it was all over for us. When I got home from Zaki's I
found a note left on my bed. It was a noble
renunciation of our love: she was leaving. I was
impressed by the note and not at all unhappy with the
decision she'd made. But of course I was of two minds
about it, wanting to think her ability to make this
decision (like her ability to refrain from staging a
diabolical scene the night before) meant she'd "whipped
the monster."
    I'd brought her a single daisy, and she unlocked
the door to her room (the blue room) to let me hand it
to her. Then she closed the door and locked it again.
I set to work, as I'd previously told her I would, on
typing the second draft of her long short story "Madame
Dussault" for class, making myself a carbon copy which,
if she really was about to leave, I intended to keep as
a sort of final memento of our time together. As I
typed I found myself worrying about the details of her
departure -- the sooner the better, I felt, but I knew
she had no place to go and little money -- and I was
also wrestling with the approaching problems of freedom.
For example, should I see Jang? Briana? If so, how
long should I wait before doing it? In general I felt I
should isolate myself from any and all kinds of
emotional involvement for a while and instead focus on
my work for the Bulldog and in my free time try to get
the new novel started. For money, with Val no longer
sharing the rent, I'd seek a loan from home and then
later try to rent out a room at 1616 starting on June 1.

I would not insist on Val paying rent for May, no matter how long it might take for her to move out.

But it all fell apart. Gradually we came back together, at first for a grocery-shopping trip proposed by me, and a discussion began. I asked for the specifics of her leaving: when, how, what help she'd need. She found this unbearable, and an argument ensued, quickly revealing our positions were indeed irreconcilable -- but also that our spirits were now more conciliatory in the face of an actual breakup.

Cutting to the nub, we did reconcile. I don't know how it happened. I don't think I was much, if at all, different from the way I'd been all along. Rather I think she probably decided giving in temporarily was better than plunging into the unknown. To do this, she had to come to terms with her own observation about my allegedly being in a commanding position because she supposedly loves me more than I love her. This putative superior position she found to be "unfair." She'd counterposed her rages against this: if I would love her equally, she said now, she would give up the rages. Of course I could hardly agree to love-by-threat, even if I wanted to. Besides, her real argument -- the unspoken one -- was different. To her way of thinking, the "fact" of her love for me being greater than mine for her put her under my control. "She who is [or loves] the greater is the servant of the other." This made her feel not just inferior but terribly vulnerable. As a consequence she was ready to take any measure to regain control. And she refused to put herself in the "humiliating" position of having to "earn" love.

But she gave in. Somehow we got to the point where we were each "daring" the other. "I dare you, Val, to banish this absurd sloganistic notion that the extent of your love can put you into an inferior or superior position." Another of the dares concerned making love, and we did, very powerfully. A startling change came over her in just minutes as she let herself get into the balling seemingly without qualm or qualification. Then we set about devising plans for doing all the work

458

that's been piling up for both of us. I felt enormously
relieved. We even agreed we both needed a break and we
could squeeze in a movie. Most important, she accepted
plans which obviously meant we'd be spending relatively
little time "together" in her sense of the term, which
is to say, with me constantly in attendance upon her and
concentrating all my attention on her and her rampaging
needs.

   Now Danny's here and a long Sunday afternoon of
typing stretches ahead. (I volunteered to type up all
her papers since she's so slow at it, and while doing
this I'll also, at her request, be trying to defrankify
her English "where it's so bad it really sticks out.")

   ** Last night Valoshka was flashing on being a man
and fucking me. This was as we lay on our sides and
she, from my back, jerked me off, with one finger up my
asshole. She'd really like to try it with a dildo, she
said. It was no fantasy of mine, I let her know, but if
she wanted to give it a whirl, or a thrust, or even a
bunch of thrusts, fine. It would be interesting to see
whether I could get into the feeling of being fucked by
her (although I sure wasn't able to last night when it
was just a finger).

   ** Speaking of rectal functions: my writing like
my mind is constipated from the unrelenting torment and
turmoil of the past many weeks since Val started moving
in -- almost six now. Hopefully a compensatory period
of exuberant creative intensity looms not too far off in
the future. For that I'd give anything (except my
bedraggled "man's pride," of course).

                    *   *

   Here are some excerpts from Val's "farewell letter"
I found on my bed this morning:

          ...You are...a fine man, Glenn, the
          kind of man I dreamed about all my life,
          and yet: it's irrefutably apparent that
          you are incapable of loving me the way I
          need. I die a thousand times each
          thousandth of a second. The deaths become
          a bit more agonizing each day: and now I

459

can take them no more. It's also evident
that right now the last thing you need is
a hypersensitive, over-romantic, demanding
deprived child as a lover. Yet I can be
no other way than what I am.
    ...I can't control the way I feel
inside: dark, deprived, abandoned,
misunderstood, cheated.
    ...You need support, inspiration, and
strength of a kind I haven't got. You
need a woman with a peaceful insight and a
solid heart, wholly devoted to you.
    ...More than any woman, though, I think
you need self-fulfillment. You have too
many talents to let yourself be dispersed
and injured by those who have loved you
and failed. Do what you have to do. You
have the strength, the determination, and
all the means to be desired. Many things,
many people, I especially, have worked
against you. ...By society's standards
much of what you have done is held
immoral. You, and I even, know better.
You have done what you thought to be
right, followed your heart, your true
inner voice. I admire you and despise you
for it. Because it has worked against me.
    ...I can envision the rightness of your
actions, the honest intention in them. I
have forced you to much ugliness, yet you
keep on trying the best you can and know
of. But it's not enough. It's not your
fault. You're only human. ...I kept
hating myself, blaming myself for my
inability to face reality...I now realize
I have been raising over myself the same
demands I have upon you. I need time for
healing...making up for my past
deprivations. I need more than my share
right now. It is unfair to ask you to

460

diet when you need all the supply you can
get, to reimburse money you never
borrowed.

...I'm a bungler. Also an idealist, a
perfectionist. I sabotage everything. I
would rather treasure the memory of our
love than witness its slow torture and
inevitable death.

...I see that we are locked hopelessly
into a destructive cycle of madness, of
antagonistic needs. ...I know you would
never have the heart to leave me to my
nightly state. I'm afraid it's more than
a phase, but a destiny. I've seen you
suffer, shriek silently inside yourself,
I've driven you to tears, to unbearable
torment, to things, actions that are
absolute no's in your beliefs. I've
watched it all, at times with triumphant
pleasure. I have no respect but for what
I want. My heart is made of stone. I'm
cruel. Cruel. I don't deserve your
efforts and your pains. I could only go
on enslaving you to my caprices of a
spoiled brat.

...I thank you for your help, your
patience, your love. We have lived, lived
for hundreds of people...try to think of
it that way...with time one only remembers
the good, the beautiful. I simply love
you and want the best for you and myself.

*

Probably it's all true. But maybe, just maybe....
It's been so long since I've lived a normal life with
Valerie I'm no longer sure what it might be like and
whether I'd want it, much less whether she'd want it.

*   *

I'd almost forgotten how pleasant it can be to sit
quietly in the living room here in "the Castle" in the
late afternoon with the sun slanting through the

windows. It's been many, many months since I've done
it. It takes me back a year and a half or more, to the
era when I ensconced myself for hours on end in this
same red armchair, with Jang dancing in and out of the
room. How touchingly innocent that scene seems now in
light of all that's happened since.

While strolling down to pick up soft drinks I
glanced through the early pages of the previous volume
of this journal (V.24). December -- how long ago that
was! I was still madly infatuated with Briana. It
gives my heart a tug to read over those impassioned
passages. Such confusion! Such agony! Still, the
writing is strong at times, impressing me enough that I
actually had the thought of trying to imitate myself. I
like it best when every word is somehow outrageous or
irreverent. In comparison life isn't so eventful or
exciting these days -- it's just deadly.

After devoting most of the afternoon to typing
Val's short story I feel I know her much better. For
one thing, I know she's more a poet than a story writer.
Her prose is surprisingly precious, loaded with flowery
descriptions, ten-dollar words, a tortured self-
consciousness. Like her journal (and like mine also,
I'm afraid, but like hers even more), it reveals a mind
infatuated with itself. Yet it also shows how strong
and deep her feelings are as well as how sadly rooted in
distrust and fear. Astounding vanity and self-approval.
A complex, spoiled child with, as she says, a mixture of
romantic idealism (often crossing the border into the
maudlin and mawkish) and unfettered egotism. Her
cruelty truly frightens me. Under certain circumstances
she might well murder someone, and in our current
situation it's all too obvious I'd be the target.

*

Briana: looking back now I can see how blind I was
about her. She did care -- but our ways of loving and
just simply communicating were incompatible. When she
came to Garnett I should've made her feel more welcome.
It seems I expected her to be enthralled merely by the
chance to be with me. Talk about vanity. "Your

[Living with Valerie]

terrible ego!" The journal also brings back how
marvelous lovemaking was with her. What magic! A gift
from the gods! And yet how little it means now. "I'll
never be able to make love with anyone else": she
actually said that! A moment preserved in amber, as
useless as last year's headline. That she could say it
when she knew she'd be seeing Terry and doubtless
balling him the very next night still boggles my mind
(and this despite the fact that I in turn saw Val that
very same next night, New Year's Eve -- the important
difference being I didn't know in advance I would).

    I still think a lot about Briana. She's receding
only gradually. Mostly her image arises in conjunction
with thoughts of an uncomplicated, low-key life of
domestic tranquility, a sane, easy, fairly social life
with lots of friends in San Francisco arts circles -- a
life that sometimes appeals to me and sometimes doesn't.
I imagine I'd get lots of writing done -- probably of
very low quality (but that's better than none at all --
except of course it's not really). I usually try to
suppress any yearnings for Briana by arguing to myself
that life with her would quickly become dull and
predictable. But I'm not so sure about that. I wish
she and I had lived together if only for a short time so
that I might now have an idea what it would be like, as
I do about, say, Denise and Ciara. Such ideas matter!
But then I also lack the sure sense about Jang, when it
comes down to it, and god knows I've lived with her. I
also fear I'd be bored if Jang and I got back together,
though the boredom would be of a different sort, less
the exasperated kind engendered by superficiality.
That's what I fear most with Briana. Would we be able
to "go deep"? I never saw any real evidence of it....
(No doubt I wrote things much like this about her last
summer and fall. That's probably the real reason why
V.22 upset her so much when she read it New Year's Eve.
In searching through that volume I can't even find the
sentence she quoted about "game playing and false
openness." Did she just make that up? Was it something
one of us said at the time and I've forgotten it?

-- And I wonder how long she hung around in my room at
Klug's on New Year's Eve. I asked Al about that once
and he said he didn't know; he left Klug's half an hour
or so after I did and she was still there. But did she
stay long enough to cause Terry to worry about where she
was? Did she perhaps not even make it back to the city
by midnight to welcome in 1971 with him? Just how
fascinated -- horrified -- was she by my evil ways as
supposedly revealed in V.22? Enough to have a hard time
breaking off her reading? If so, maybe I could even
take a little consolation from that....)

2

Monday 3
     A renaissance with Valerie? Could be. When I
hurried in she was sprawled on the couch reading a Paris
Review story about adultery. Who knows why she decided
she wanted to suck my cock just then (or to report what
she said: she'd been thinking about doing so all day).
Even more than before, that pornoflick we saw with Erik
and Consuela appears to have worked wonders: now she
goes at the task much more confidently and aggressively,
using both hands as well as mouth and lips and tongue,
milking me almost like a veteran (e.g., Kristi K.),
pulling back to admire her handiwork, establishing eye
contact from time to time, squeezing out the last drop
and relishing it as if she could imagine no sweeter
nectar. A good thing, though, we had to rush off to
State. I wasn't in any mood to return the favor....
     Now we write side by side in the State library
reading room.
     We've gone more than two full days without a sturm-
und-drang battle or even a minor hassle. Is it just a
matter of mutual exhaustion? I'll admit I'm appalled by
what a quick riffle through her journal revealed. Her
vicious rages of the past three months, she writes, have
been a conscious, premeditated attempt to "shock" me
into changing my behavior. Even if she's deluding

herself about this -- as I believe she must be, from the
out-of-control quality of so many of the passages -- how
annoying it is to think that to her mind the strategy
has worked! This thought alone is enough to foment a
new rebellion in me.

But no, I'd rather channel my energies into some
meaningful work. There'll be no messing around with
women at the Bay Bulldog (even though blond, hip,
twenty-four-year-old Monica, the art editor, appeals to
me). No futile stirring of the Briana ashes. Maybe
even no farewell gesture with Jang, though I do believe
I owe her something on that score. Truth is, Valoshka's
strategy, however mad the execution of it, has indeed
worked.

Unfortunately it's also exhausted my feeling for
her. In other words, she's overdone it -- way, way, way
overdone it. Not for a very long time will I be able to
look at her without fearing her face will transform at
any instant -- if only by the projective work of my own
memory-obsessed imagination -- into that of a hate-
filled, vicious child. Shadows of the monster!

Brrr: she leans over to whisper dejectedly about
the "uselessness of knowledge." If she can't come up
with an idea on her own, the discovery of its expression
by someone else just burdens her, confuses her, stifles
her creativity. Her mind shrieks with resistance. This
is what she says. If I reflect too much on the
implications of such a notion I start feeling seriously
depressed. Out in the world of ideas she can be a
sinkhole of nihilism. For delight and wonder she
substitutes contempt and self-important weariness -- at
the age of twenty and two weeks!

Earlier I told her about a TV news report I saw in
the student union here, while she was in class, about
mass arrests in Washington, D.C., as the antiwar group
Mayday tried to shut down the city. Her curt comment:
"If you really cared about all that you'd be there
instead of here."

In the interest of avoiding further conflict -- or
at least postponing it -- I stop now.

465

[Have Mercy]

Tuesday 4

An emergency plea to Mom, shamelessly enclosed in a Mother's Day card: send money! Suddenly it's clear our combined welfare and unemployment checks, Val's and mine, are insufficient. The payments on the Land Cruiser are a heavy drain. Hopefully my tax refund will stave off the day when I have to sell the thing. But when will that refund arrive? Chances are dismayingly high the IRS will launch an "audit" of my claims, leading to a long, perhaps permanent, delay on the refund, and quite possibly even to some sort of penalty or fine which will sink me still deeper into the hole.

The euphoria of yesterday didn't last long. Val's sudden bouts of depression, coming, as they so often do, just when you'd expect her to be happiest, are like a series of slaps in the face. If I let her see how they get me down, she hits the hysteria button. Yesterday, WHAM, three hours lost in exasperating attempts to reassure her and help her drag herself out of the hole she'd dug for herself. Why can't she maintain a moderately cheerful state for more than a day or two? Or, at the very least, why can't she exclude me for that long -- if not longer! -- from her list of targets for venting her bitter despondency on?

This morning her condition is only slightly improved: it's now subdued, distant, sad. She sidesteps my efforts to lift her out of it, bluntly observing they're "phony."

One matter clearly working against us is our clashing interests of this period. To her my hours spent at the Bulldog constitute little more than a form of abandonment of her. To her each and every day is a lonely desert which I should shepherd her through. Even if her temperament were consistently brighter, this would be an impossible task, for me or, I truly believe, for anyone. And so we struggle on, our remaining chances of finding a way out of the impasse, if indeed there are any, slipping ever further away.

*   *

466

[Living with Valerie]

"Why don't you just throw her out?"

Kay offers that advice after reading a few passages from this volume.

"Looks to me like you're on some sort of masochistic 'tragic love affair' trip," she adds. "I think this woman's just waiting for you to call her bluff."

Kay also points out "no one can be saved who doesn't want to be saved" and "sometimes you have to hurt people."

Who's Kay? An ad-seller for the Bulldog, twenty-five, a free spirit fed up with reformers and radical politicians, determined to liberate herself, to banish all agitation and entanglement so she can live the simple good life.

"If I saw Nixon walking down the street and someone handed me a gun, I'd shoot him," she says, "but I refuse to waste my life politicking over matters that don't directly affect me. All politicians are out to save the world -- that's their trouble."

In two weeks she'll be taking off for Hawaii on a thirty-foot sailboat with someone she met a few days ago hitchhiking.

Damn it, she's right! I know it!

Merely to imagine doing what she prescribes immediately fires up my resolve. I've taken enough!

If Val's still on her despondency/persecution jag tonight when I pick her up, I'll tell her exactly what I think about it. If she persists, I'll throw her out. I don't give a fuck if she tears down the whole house, tries to slice her wrist or my throat, undermines me at the Bulldog or tries to blow it up -- I've had it. She's going out.

Before picking her up at school I'll take the precaution of removing all my personal papers, journals, notebooks, chronbooks, manuscripts, letters, etc., to a safe place. Everything else she can trash to her heart's content.

*   *

No, no, no, no, no. Scratch all that. Whatever

467

happens will happen all right, but I won't be dropping a
bomb on her. Which is not to say she deserves anything
less than a bomb, metaphorically speaking here, but just
that I'd be a fool to go about it in such a way. (How
tangled is that? What's "it"? A new standard in
dubious logic, repetition, double negatives, twisted
syntax. -- But thank you, Kay, for trying to talk some
sense into me. Despite all appearances, who knows,
maybe you succeeded at least a little.)

Wednesday 5
    For breakfast a stale blueberry sweet roll and a
carton of slightly sour chocolate milk. The two go
together surprisingly well.
    A long spell of foggy, dismal days drags on.
    Here at the Bulldog I have a list of thirty-odd
phone calls to make today. These concern stories on
"The Truth about the City's Financial Condition," "The
Case of the 400 Missing Meals," "Small Taxes Bleed the
City Dry," and "The Footbridge No One Wanted -- Except
Justin Herman" (he heads up the domestically
neocolonialistic S.F. Redevelopment Agency).
    For way too long now I've been postponing making
these calls, probably out of reluctance or fear to lock
horns with the poobahs. I wish I could purge all such
obstacles. They're irrational, foolish, crippling, a
residue of "good manners" and a high-schoolish desire to
be thought (A) "responsible" or (B) "a good guy."
    Yes, the time for the purge has come.
    Still no peace at home. Last night, after a
relaxing dinner at Erik's -- just him and me -- I was
met at the door at 1616 (she likes to keep it locked) by
a sullen Val who then proceeded to devour the night with
arguments. Somewhere along the way I trotted out what I
thought was our previous agreement that actions
performed out of dependence or duress rather than from
genuine desire were meaningless. At two a.m. she
announced she'd be sleeping by herself because to sleep
with me "wouldn't be meaningful to you," and that's what

she did: slept alone. This morning, however, she did at
least promise to greet me with a smile when I come home
tonight and then as I pulled down the driveway she waved
a glaringly reluctant au revoir from my bedroom window.
During the day she'll be working on "extricating"
herself from Karen Horney-type dependence. That's what
she told me. I'm not at all hopeful about the results.

Crab, capon, and asparagus at Erik's. And several
glasses of wine apiece. We commiserated over our
foundering love lives. Val makes him, he confessed,
"very uneasy." He admitted to being surprised it's
lasted as long as it has with her. Consuela, meanwhile,
has bought a one-way ticket for Chile. He certainly
won't be trying to stop her from going. An ample supply
of patience and self-discipline, we agreed, is a
prerequisite for any kind of human relationship, really,
but especially for the kind involving cross-cultural
love and romance. A good talk. Maybe we'll go camping
again to escape our sorrows for a few days.

*   *

"There's bombshells going off around here," Mike M.
exults to the aptly named Matt Sparks, drama critic, who
comes wandering in with his review for the next issue.
Dave Dikeakos, Mike, and I are excitedly discussing an
anonymous letter someone's shoved under the front door
just moments earlier. It alleges the Army's planning to
build a huge new germ-warfare center at the Presidio.
How could we authenticate this tip? It wouldn't be
easy. At the same time everyone's enthused about my
suggestion that we interview some of the eleven
chauffeurs whose salaries appear as line items on the
city budget. "Get a shot of one of them polishing up a
fender outside the On Broadway," Mike suggests.

I find myself loaded down with projects -- mainly
because there's no one else to handle them. Already
I've taken on far more than I'll have time to do real
justice to even under the best of circumstances. Mike's
"requests" are so damn hard to turn down! When he gets
that fiery gleam in his eye you just can't bear to
disappoint him. So now my temporary desk in the front

room is piled high with stacks of paper. A little more,
maybe about six inches, and it will reach the point of
no return. A few more years' worth and it might begin
to approach the phantasmagoric state of Mike's entire
office: a disaster area the size of an average suburban
living room awash with books, manuscripts, reports,
letters, papers, Bulldog back issues. A huge old vine
meanders up between stacks of such detritus piled
against one wall, a malignant eagle hovers atop another
wall's stacks, ready to swoop down on unverified quotes.
The room's always in semidarkness: lair of a voracious
and undoubtedly dangerous Baskervillean newshound.

*   *

It's just too damn bad I can't seem to write
fiction worth shit. Life offers up one subject after
another, each one juicier and more incredible than the
last, and thus far I've been able to do nothing more
with them (the ones accumulating since the breakup with
Ciara, say) than to pile up cockamamie journal entries
and scribble a couple of hundred pages of notes. The
Fell Street "Art Center," Jang, Jill, Empyrean, brother
Jeff's AWOL period, Denise, Winnie, Nadine, Valerie and
Briana and Claire and the Merino Mercury, now Valerie
and the Bay Bulldog: each more than worthy, in my view,
of its own separate fictional treatment. And at the
same time life in general -- i.e., at the national and
international level -- is teeming with events crying out
for adamant prose witness. Not too many years from now
people will look back on this turbulent and tumultuous
era and marvel at its richness and excitement.

Just today thousands of youth battled with police
all over downtown San Francisco in an heroic effort to
"bring the war home." What was I doing at the time?
Alas, twiddling my thumbs in the Bulldog office. Making
a few dozen trivial phone calls, almost all failing to
pan out, including every single one trying to track down
the city's eleven official chauffeurs. Cracking wise
with Monica, Mike, Peggy, and Barry Ketterling (he's a
hippie postman with a Ph.D. in economics from U of
Mentoka) about a society lady who submitted an

470

unbearably cutesy story on organic restaurants. Vicky
Carrington this was, Vassar graduate, tall, beautiful,
husband an ultra-respectable lawyer. "She's the kind
they turn out on lathes at those Eastern schools," Mike
cracked, forgetting for the moment (or was he?) that I
was turned out on such a lathe myself. Everybody had a
good laugh at poor Vicky Carrington's expense, including
me. How naive she is, how she hires a babysitter three
full days a week to watch the kids, how she's a
Republican "because the Republicans want less
government," how her husband warned her not to take any
job which wouldn't pay well: oh it went on and on,
maliciously good fun as the four of us lounged around in
the front office and the rush-hour traffic droned by on
Bryant, until finally no one could think of anything
more to say on that subject and Mike suddenly
interjected in a dismal tone, "Jesus, it's a pain to run
a business when you don't have any money."

-- This wandering account going down at the
laundromat on a night when I'm unexpectedly alone.
Val's gone off to the hospital with her brother to see
their mother, who underwent surgery last night at S.F
General (for what I don't know) and is reportedly in
lots of pain today. All of this came as a complete
surprise to Val and of course to me as well. She'd
already departed before I got home, leaving just a short
note vowing she'd be back "as soon as I can." Added to
all her other misfortunes and miseries and pressures,
this one may prove too much for poor Val. It comes at
precisely the wrong time, at the peak of her struggle
with herself, just when she's showing signs of making
some headway -- and just when my patience has been
stretched to the breaking point. I do know this: if she
sinks yet again into the manic cycle of despair and rage
I won't be offering any further consolations.

*

It's dog-eat-dog at the laundromat tonight.
Formidable matrons plunging toward other people's dryers
as they slowly spin to a stop, ready (the matrons, this
is) to toss the half-dried clothes into a box or even

471

onto the floor if the owner of those clothes doesn't
claim them immediately, within seconds of the spin's
actual stop. One asked if I could give her two nickels
for a dime. I couldn't, but I told her the change
machine could. Oh no, she said, there's a sign saying
it won't change dimes. No, I assured her, it does; that
sign's not to be believed. When she skeptically tried
the machine and it changed her dime, she grumpily
flashed the two nickels at me as she walked back by. I
leaned toward her and said, as if passing along the
secret of the century, "See, you never know when a
hippie's going to do you a good turn."

In appearance I've never been more a hippie than I
am now. My hair's well past my shoulders, so long I
have to rubber-band it into a ponytail if I want to get
any serious work done. My boots are so worn the color
of the leather has faded from brown to gray and the
heels have all but disappeared. And my financial status
would do credit, so to speak, to any hippie: broke,
living on unemployment, into the state for three hundred
bucks and various businesses for several hundred more
(though actually most of these debts are long-delinquent
bills Ciara ran up and promised to take care of and
never has). I fall short only in the weight category:
I'd have to lose fifteen or twenty pounds to appear
hippie-emaciated. Or maybe more. (I weighed in at 204
a few days ago and I've been pigging out since then.)

But a hippie I ain't. I lack the free spirit, the
unlimited tolerance, the hunger for hallucinogens, and
no doubt a good deal more. Nor do I fit very well into
any other current category I know of. Certainly
"hippie" as a catchall term to describe those whose
values and lifestyle are unconventional and laid-back is
sadly lacking, but "bohemian" is even more outdated, and
"artist" or "writer" or "journalist" don't really cut it
either. (G.B. Shaw warned writers not to work in
journalism beyond a certain age or they'd become trapped
in it: from time to time that warning pops into my mind
and I shudder (can't remember what the "certain age" was
or where I saw the quote). -- And while I'm on the

subject, it's become painfully clear to me how mutually
antagonistic journalism and fiction writing can be.
Fiction writers depend on a vital unconscious spirit
which I'd say most journalists must stifle. It may take
a Dostoevsky or a Mailer or a Mark Twain to bridge the
gap. That is, a writer whose vital unconscious spirit
is so powerful it becomes news of a kind in itself.)
    -- So what am I? Protean man, new man -- maybe.
But why must I be anything? I simply am who I am.
Which is a tautology with a kicker. Or maybe that
should be a kicker with a taut ology, ho ho. (Don't I
wish I had a taut anything right now.)
*   *
    Hard to believe, but before the past month or so
I'd never prepared a cup of coffee. Even instant coffee
was beyond me. Now I've just brewed a cup for Val,
along with a hot chocolate for myself, and served the
coffee to her as, at my old oak table from Fell Street,
she works on a poem about her mother's operation. "You
deserve some happy days," it starts out, which may sound
a bit Hallmarky but I certainly wouldn't mind if she
delivered a card bearing the same sentiment to me.
Meanwhile Julie Driscoll warbles "Season of the Witch"
here among the proliferatious plants, including one
Briana gave to Barbara, in the room that brings back so
many memories of Jang and Denise and also brother Jeff.
    Going on midnight now, Val's Kleelike color squares
shimmering on the wall, her six oddly shaped pillows
huddling like a brood of well-fed albino seal pups on
the bed, therms pouring in visible waves from the gas
heater (which Jang and I never used, preferring instead
to suffer the cold like Spartans): and I'll say the gulf
between Val and me is unbridgeably wide right now. She
says it's because I'm happy and inspired by the exciting
new world at the Bulldog from which she's "excluded,"
and at the same time her world's so drab, so full of
pain, she just wants to hold me. But she doesn't do
even that, just sits looking sad and distant,
occasionally forcing a pathetic mournful smile. Her
mother seemed so old, she says. She was reminded, Val

473

was, of the days when Great Aunt Mathilde was wasting
away with terminal cancer shortly before Val left France
for good. "She accused me of causing her cancer because
I was so wild and ill-behaved." And Val emits a
sepulchral sigh. Oh the pain and injustice and
inexorability of it all!

Long ago I ceased feeling loved by this bogglingly
difficult and complex woman. Just needed. Needed
desperately at times, yes, but that's sure as hell not
the same as being loved. Will her love ever return?
Will mine for her?

*   *

Looking back I see that this volume soon to be
coming to a close, if combined with the previous one,
could essentially be called the Merino Mercury Journal.
"A two-volume set." The fit is almost too neat.

When I last saw her, Jang loaned me fifteen bucks
so I might have the cracked lens in my shades repaired.
I told her then I'd call "next week." I've done
neither. I often think of those two facts, and imagine
her balling Kyle, the Korean War vet, the one who
displeased her by always dressing so hurriedly and
taking so little pride in his nakedness. "I thought I
loved him," she said. Then she turned around and told
me she thought she'd like to have my kid and raise it on
her own. So what's really going on with her?

I'd like to wrap up this volume with a single
succinct, stunning, insightful comment summing up the
meaning of all that's happened in the roughly two and a
half months it covers: the shocks, the joys, the
sorrows, the lessons, the massive changes, the new
directions.

Can't.

Have I ever been more eager to begin a new volume?
I'd like to believe the new beginning is a matter of
vast symbolic import. My life again becomes a blank
book to fill in. Mercifully blank, promisingly thick.
Focus on imagining what fine things will fill those
pages.

[Living with Valerie]

Thursday 6

    In the barren heart of "South of the Slot."
Industrial San Francisco. Cal's Cafe, occupying a
corner lot, at least has plenty of big picture windows
looking to the west and southwest. Through them what
you see is mostly shades and textures of brown and gray.
Factories, smokestacks, water towers, rows of semis,
massive concrete freeway supports, cracked sidewalks,
dirty streets -- not a vision of "everyone's favorite
city" as most people might conceive of it, I'd guess.

    But I like it a lot here.

    Otherwise life is miserable. This morning came the
latest showdown with Valerie. Not until three this
afternoon did I manage to break away, and then only by
yielding on my threat. She threw another raging
hysterical fit, but I again failed to throw her out as
Kay and Erik and everyone else has advised and as I'd
assured her last weekend I would do if she freaked out
on me again. Instead I wound up accepting a raft of new
promises from her. Essentially these boil down to a vow
to avoid subjecting me to excessive portions of her
misery, even if it means hanging a black flag on her
door when her "ressentiment" threatens to boil over. If
she finds she can't do it, she'll move out of her own
free will.

    I don't believe a word of it. I should have thrown
her out. But, as she says herself, I don't have the
heart to do it. I'm too weak, or I'm too attached, or
I'm too crazy myself, or I'm too "kind," or I'm too
"guilt-ridden" as a result of all the terrible things
I've supposedly done to her by caring too much about
other people (mainly women) -- and does it really matter
which is the case?

    Her tantrum was, of course, unbearable. Demented
howls, literally beating her head against the wall,
clawing at her own body. "I've lost everything!" "Look
at me -- I've aged ten years in the past month!" "You
don't love me anymore!" "You don't know the pain I
suffer! You'll never know!" "I love you! I want to

die if you stop loving me!" -- all repeated over and
over with such wrenching agony, such fierce bitterness,
such unspeakable viciousness and (worst) such horrific
loudness that finally, again, because she refused to
tone it down, I had to resort to force to subdue her.
Rough shakes, a wrestling hold with my knees pressing
down on her arms, my hand clapped over her mouth, a
choking squeeze.

Great way to launch the new era.

*   *

So how do you set the unconscious free? Is there a
method? And how do you know when it's free? Can you be
in control of anything else if your own deepest soul is
out of control? But then why assume what's cooped up
"down there" is rage? Why not peacefulness, kindness,
and joyfulness? Or is it perhaps a combination of
extremes? Take yourself at your wildest and tamest and
most and least socially acceptable and then exaggerate
-- is that it? Or could it on the contrary be the lair
of your self at its most ordinary, the model citizen
whose attempts to act decently in the real world have
been brutally rebuffed or despised? Or for that matter
does an "unconscious" really exist in any significant
sense? Suppose dreams are just the product of random
groups of brain cells seizing control of the projector
room while the projectionist is asleep -- i.e., suppose
they have no meaning at all. Suppose the same is true
of love.

Notes for a night of raging unease.

Only smashing the pen against the page until the
nib shattered could begin to express it.

Cookies arranged on a tray to spell out that same
word, "LOVE," in caps -- oh how poignant, how touching,
what a brilliant stroke, Val, fucking savage "sacre
monstre" of my life.

Emotional terrorism is what she's all about at the
core. No one else could terrorize with a mere tray of
cookies. Her Midas touch turns everything into
virulence and then violence. The venomous Valerie
touch.

[Living with Valerie]

Another day irrevocably lost!

Searing bitterness, disgust and loathing tearing at my guts. Now I know what it is to want to kill. A precious gift you've given me, my sweet Val.

I desperately need something to provide some perspective -- a break -- help -- wisdom -- inspiration.

I'm at the crumbling edge, I really am, and even so I'm ashamed to write down these words which I'll have to look at again someday.

Grinding agony. Suffocating. Like acid eating at my brain and spine.

Friday 7

Mike, Monica, Yvonne, Arnie, Peggy, Melissa, Rachel and several others whose names I don't know yet are making the Bulldog office hop this afternoon. The IBM Composer has just arrived -- and now a messenger appears with the ribbon. We begin! I don my train engineer's cap and lead the troops off to show them what this marvelous machine can do. I'm the one who talked them into trying it -- and then Peggy lined up a "free introductory trial" for us -- and now I must prove I know whereof I speak (ha).

*   *

Mike writes a tough, no-nonsense news story. Tonight in leafing through yellowing back issues of the Bulldog I'm finding what he says about the "durability" of its copy is mostly true. A surprisingly large portion of the stories still retain freshness and impact. Mike's style isn't so different from mine that I worry about his influence being too strong. Exposure to his work should help me strengthen and deepen my own.

For a while, however, and perhaps a long while, it appears I'll be little more than a legman for the B.B. (as apparently no one ever calls it -- nor is it dubbed "the Dog," because that conflicts with the Doggie Diner and the Family Dog, the rock venue out at the beach, and probably any number of other Dogs). Admittedly at times I already catch myself chafing at the bit. I can't deny

it: I'd much prefer that someone else be making the
calls, poring over the documents, verifying the quotes,
confirming the facts, chasing after the chauffeurs,
interviewing the bureaucrats. Far preferable to be
making decisions, doing rewrites, formulating policy,
churning out stories which depend on information others
have so kindly and diligently gathered. But for the
time being I can serve in these higher capacities only
occasionally, and then only by being ready to step in
when Mike is overwhelmed. Not that I have any delusions
about being able to walk in off the street one day and
become an editor the next. For the most part I'll be
playing the role of all-around boy-Friday apprentice.
     Despite my stints as editor of the Mercury and
(long, long ago) the Adams College Inquirer I actually
have little experience in journalism. I've never taken
a journalism class or written a practice story which
someone else has criticized. I've never learned the
proper way to conduct an interview, to say nothing of
the higher or lower tricks of the trade. All I know is
what common sense plus longtime close reading of
newspapers and magazines have taught me. That's not
nothing -- at least I know if I work at it I can write a
clear, concise, sparkly little news sentence -- but it
ain't hardly enough. So for the next five months while
on unemployment I'll be serving my apprenticeship.
After that I hope I'll have shown enough promise to
convince Mike to make me a salaried staff member. It
would be ideal: working on my own stuff at home in the
mornings, say, and working for the Bulldog in the
afternoons and early evenings.
     Will the paper be able to afford another salaried
staff member? That's something else again. This
evening, after the rush had subsided, Mike, Peggy,
Monica, and I relaxed in the back room discussing the
extreme financial difficulties involved in getting a
newspaper off the ground and publishing regularly and
profitably or at least breaking even -- the last-named
being something Mike has been unsuccessfully trying to
accomplish with the Bulldog for five years. Sipping on

[Living with Valerie]

instant coffee and resting his long legs on a paste-up
table, he discoursed cynically about the uselessness of
voluntary help. "It always winds up driving you nuts,"
he says. Intent on maintaining professional standards,
he therefore insists on paying all contributors. This
in turn pushes up operating costs far beyond the return
from subscriptions and advertising (currently some four
thousand dollars monthly). Consequently most of his
time goes to fund-raising, both through appeals to
wealthy liberals to buy stock in the paper and by his
own teaching jobs at various schools of journalism. He
sees no way to break free from this cycle.

I think there must be a way. Rigorous cost-paring
plus vigorous subscription campaigns could bring income
close to meeting costs. The current gap between the two
is on the order of twelve hundred bucks a month. A
change in printers could reduce that by three hundred.
Subscription drives mounted by volunteer labor -- which
I could coordinate, just as at the Merc -- could zap the
rest.

-- And so much for dreaming. It's past midnight.
Val creeps in to turn down the radio so Danny can sleep.
My eyes are burning from too much reading (and they
still smart from the stupid tears of frustration I shed
last night in the darkened living room, between kicks at
the same chair Val mangled during one of her more
violent freak-outs last week).

"Am I invited to sleep in your bed tonight?" she
asks.

"No," I say.

"What!"

"Just kidding."

Ha ha. Ha ha ha. So far today we're managing to
tolerate each other. This latest crisis seems to be
easing. But as the clouds clear what's revealed is the
same old incompatibility -- and now with a nasty new
edge honed on it by the events of the past two weeks.
Or so it seems to me. The next few days just might tell
the story.

Saturday 8

So now it's early Saturday evening and I'm sunk
into my battered red armchair and Val's down in the
front yard playing ball with Danny as the sun goes down.
A memorably bright full moon is perfectly centered above
the Mt. Moraga summit as seen through the upper pane of
the window above my bed. Because of a defective frame
that window has never been fully closed in my two years
-- almost -- in this house.

Life at home has become ominously tedious. Today
Danny is driving me up the wall with his nonstop
whimpering and repetitive questioning. Val has altered
her behavior from monstrous to cautiously neutral, and
on occasion hokily sweet and even "Gigi"-like, but the
only benefit of the changes thus far is a slight
reduction in the constrictedness I feel when we're
apart (meaning when we're together it remains the same).

Meanwhile other pressures are growing. In spite of
the hundred-dollar loan Mother just sent -- a bit
grudgingly, it seemed to me, but still quickly -- there
will be little in the way of paid entertainment for the
next month. For the foreseeable future, in fact. I've
reluctantly concluded it's foolish to go on hoping for
an income-tax refund. It could even be that (because of
money Ciara earned working for Erik, as I recently
learned from him, but she never informed me about) -- it
could be, I say, I'll wind up owing more rather than
receiving a refund, and that's without even considering
the strong possibility of a penalty or fine. So: no new
magazines, books, records, clothes; no eating out, no
movies, no plays. What makes all this especially
difficult is the vapid state of my relations with Val.
Lacking "outside entertainment" we must come face-to-
face with the fact that we can give each other little --
least of all right now a few rounds of "poor folks'
entertainment," i.e., sex -- without risking a new
outbreak of hostilities.

Things might be better if we were living apart. I
don't know whether I'd be leading an active social life

-- probably not -- but at least I'd be able to devote more of my free time to matters that mean something to me.

But what's the use of griping. Make the best of the situation as it is. True, the rest of the weekend is pretty well shot (I'll be helping her again with a new set of revisions on "Madame Dussault," which I'd say is starting to shape up quite well) but I see no reason why next week can't be better. The trick is to find a way to deflect her silent demands. Get her off my back by announcing a schedule in advance. Possibly restart workouts at the JCC. Slip off to North Beach or other such places in the early afternoons. Make the Bulldog office, rather than this apartment, my center of operations (just be sure to keep it insulated from romantic affairs).

What I most look forward to -- allowing myself now a few moments of shameless reverie -- is the time when I'll again be free to do as I wish right here in my own home. When my room is passably neat, passably organized, a workable sanctuary from the world. When I can run in or out without worrying about what new outrages the lady of the house will hit me with.

Is it too much to hope some small portion of this kind of freedom might miraculously materialize in the not-too-distant future?

*   *

(Later)
So it's over between us. I've just told her that. She believes I'm making a terrible mistake, yielding to my "mood" at the expense of a love we've both invested deeply in. She takes all the blame upon herself for our failure, but insists she's now on the brink of controlling her "neurosis" and freeing herself to love me as I "need to be loved." The more she insists, the more I resist. For me it's way too late for all that. It's dead. If there's any love left for her in me it's buried alive in the debris of the past three months plus, and especially the past seven weeks since we effectively began living together. Pain is all that

remains. Her presence forces me to confront the pain
again and again and again.

I agree to "think it over" for a week. I agree to
sleep with her "one more time." I agree to make that
one time tonight, even though I know it's the last thing
I should do. She brings in a new poem calling tonight
our "wedding night." We're to sleep together in her
room, i.e., the blue room, for what will be the first
time and also the last time, as I see it, for both that
room and "the Castle" and anywhere else, forever. She
also points out that today's the day of the big Joan of
Arc festival back in Orleans -- the one where her father
snatched her away (at age five) just as little Kyrie was
about to jump up and touch the tail of the horse
carrying Joan's surrogate. Tonight, she says, she's
finally going to grab that tail for real "and never let
go."

The one thing I know is, having gone this far,
there's little chance I'll let her do that (even if
she's in some sense serious and she's not getting me and
her father's leg and the horse's tail all mixed up --
along with Joan of Arc's heroic defense of the French
against the invading English and her death at the stake
at Val's age one month ago, Marie Antoinette's defense
of her "castle," Ho Chi Minh's command to the Viet Cong
to kill off the American butchers one by one by one,
Frantz Fanon and Malcolm X's revolutionary teachings,
Odin's ukase to the Valkyries to pick out which warriors
will die on the battlefield and to haul their spirits,
I guess, back to Valhalla -- the house of death).

Kyrie Eleison, Val! Love and peace! Have mercy!
The one thing I know, I was starting to say one
more time, is that for Val and me it's over, period, end
of story.

"Love of melodrama," she charges me with, and
rightfully so -- not that she's such a slouch at it
herself -- and then she explains: "You're just after
revenge." Ha! She, the queen of the genre, dares to
accuse me of seeking revenge!

At this point I don't care what labels she slaps on

me and my decisions; I just know what I must do. To
wit: I must be firm and hard. I must ignore any
internal voices counseling me otherwise. Foolish fears
of loneliness, of losing her to another man, of blindly
botching the love of my life, of advancing age, of
wildly proliferating regret, of yielding to mere pride
or my own stupid guilt: all these have held the podium
for too long.

 Cut off the mic. Douse the lights and leave the
room and lock it tight and don't look back. Move on.

Sunday 9

 Brief notes on a Sunday afternoon when for the
first time in months the sun's shining warmly enough for
me to sit outside and catch a few rays. But I can't do
that: a storm of typing is about to unleash itself.
Meanwhile Van Morrison's lacerating "T.B. Sheets" is
booming from the stereo as a kind of overture.

 Being with Valerie is still agony but of a
different kind now that it's settled (for me) we won't
be living together any longer. Our "wedding night"
brought a twin pair of sexual disasters, continuing the
new series of same which began two nights ago. To the
long list of causes of our erotic dysfunction we can now
add Danny's uncanny ability to pick the wrong moment to
start wailing.

 Val has the incredible notion I want to break off
with her because of Danny. It's true he's sometimes an
irritant, and sometimes worse or much worse -- a menace
even -- but the far greater truth is that the serious
problems lie elsewhere. After all the horrors we've
gone through together how could she doubt this even for
a single moment?

 She also persists in believing I'm not really
serious about separating. As evidence of this she cites
her interpretation, which also is incredible to me, of
some things I said yesterday (when I pointed out the
obvious truth that we lack both sexual compatibility and
a mutually supportive emotional closeness to fall back

on in times of high stress, but glumly agreed "something deeper than either of those" seems to be keeping us together). Meanwhile she goes around showily reading an erotic how-to manual she stumbled upon yesterday at the bookstore on Geary. I'm trying not to disturb this delusion of hers too much, since it seems to be getting her through the day, but my heart is set now. I realize there's no other way I can react to the ferocity of her attacks starting back in early February along with her essential refusal to show any real regret about them -- not to mention real effort at repentance or expiation or atonement, including sincere attempts to repair at least a token amount of the damage she's done.

I doubt I'll be spending much time at home this week. One of the first projects I'm facing is the search for a decent roommate to help bear the heavy cost of rent. Or another possibility is to sell the Land Cruiser. I don't want to do it, but it's close to certain I'll eventually be forced to.

*   *

** Late this morning I drove the grim young mother and her mopey son over to her brother's apartment in the Richmond District for a Mother's Day lunch with her own recuperating mother. I had to drop them off a block away "because Rex would probably shoot you." (Rex is her mother's current boyfriend, the much-younger right-wing gun nut who's in town for the weekend.) I read the paper for an hour at a coffee shop on Clement Street, browsed at the bookstore, and bought a bedraggled bunch of yellow daisies -- literally the last ones available -- which I presented to Val when I picked her up along with Danny.

** She now blames Barbara for the current state of affairs with us. "I should never have listened to her!" she cries. Barb, after hearing her complaints as well as Briana's, persuaded her I needed to be shaken out of my "complacent arrogance toward women." It was a long talk with Barb one afternoon early in March that induced her to make the unannounced trip to Garnett and throw the first no-holds-barred hysterical scene at Al's

house. "After the first one it got easier and easier to do that. I couldn't wrench myself out of it."
   ** Here's a bold attempt to predict the future. Tomorrow night I won't come home until late. Val will grudgingly accept this. When I do the same Tuesday night she'll precipitate a showdown. Wednesday I'll be late for work, and then also late returning home. Thursday, a repeat. Friday she'll decide she can't take it any longer. She'll begin moving out Saturday. Somewhere during this period she'll get herself laid and come back to throw it in my face. Next week she'll drop by at least twice "to pick up things" and we'll get into heated arguments. She'll be temporarily staying with her brother and his family while looking for an apartment. Not until three weeks from now will she decide I really mean business and move her things out.
   ** "If only I could make love to you the way I kiss you -- all of our problems would be solved." She tried. Down with my jeans, up with her purple satin pullover. She mounts me (we rarely even bother with other positions anymore) and this time we manage to find something of a groove and she comes, taking me along with her. But afterwards we both know all too well this wasn't the "fuck like a kiss," as she phrased it in a poem, that would supposedly resolve all our problems and send us skipping down a new primrose path.
   ** The sex how-to manual mentioned earlier (after suddenly deciding she needed such a book and then picking it out, she declared herself "too shy" to take it up to the counter and pay for it and asked me to do it for her) -- this chirpy little manual dwells on the phrase "sensual focus." That, I'm sorry to acknowledge, is exactly what I've lost myself. What's more: as long as I'm with Val I believe I'll have little or no hope of relocating it. As things stand, my "focus" in sex must be directed, as it was today, toward finding and working a groove. On the rare occasions when she and I do manage to find one together, I must then concentrate on guiding her, on keeping her within it, since she's simply incapable of doing so herself unless I stop

moving entirely.

    ** The sun's going down. I'm on page eight of
"Madame Dussault," which after Val's latest rewrite is
hinting more strongly at the heroine's background
reasons for venturing into lesbos (Val herself never has
-- but the story is based on her relationship with
Madame Rousseau, her longtime dance teacher and
"surrogate mother," as she describes her to me).
Meanwhile the lady's locked in her room to work on her
poetry. Danny, after a spanking administered by that
same fire-breathing lady, has been banished to the
living room. He sits in the doorway yearning for
companionship. Occasionally I see a brown ball roll
past my doorway. As he rushes to fetch it, he glances
hopefully into my room. "You stay in the living room
now, Danny," I warn gently but firmly (I hope). But I
know he won't stay there and I don't blame him one bit.
Considering all he's been through it's amazing the kid
hasn't long since totally flipped out.

    -- And here he is again. (Actually for the fourth
or fifth time.) So how about we go outside and work off
some frustrations, eh Danny? There's no question at all
we've both got a full load of those.

*   *

    (If Danny were my own kid, would I feel justified
in pressuring his mother to treat him better? Even if
this mother were barely twenty and beset with abundant
infantile needs of her own? Damn right I would! -- But
I don't doubt I'd still find the demands a kid can make
on one's time plenty exasperating. And this kid right
here makes a lot more demands than any other kid I've
ever known, sometimes in a way which rivals his mother's
in ugliness. -- Or rivals his father's nasty temper,
according to Val, though she admits she's been a less
than stellar influence herself. Even so he's still a
great kid in many ways, as everyone agrees. It's a kind
of miracle.)

3

Monday 10
     A malingerer in the offices of the Bay Bulldog.
Trouble is there's nothing much to do here right now. A
few phone calls to make, that's about it. Tomorrow I
embark on my first solo trip to City Hall, the mission a
multifaceted one: seeking details on several tax items,
new ideas for the "poor tax" list, and, again,
interviews with those same damn chauffeurs. At the
moment, however, I'm festering, feeling shut out and
extremely dispensable. Gazing out the window on a
lovely day. Thinking about taking off for North Beach.
Dreaming about "Symphony No. 6," my ever receding new
attempt at a whang-dang-doodle of a novel.
     In its latest hypothetical incarnation No. 6 will
embody everything previously envisioned but at the same
time employ as its basic plotting vehicle the birth,
life, and death of a newspaper a lot like the Merino
Mercury. It would be lusty, feisty, fiery, irreverent,
zany, comic, outrageous, exuberant, hard-hitting -- and
that's just for starters. Pretty soon I'll try to get
my thoughts together on it so I can launch into the
actual writing this summer -- beginning in a few weeks,
maybe a month.
     At home Val has taken a sudden turn toward
gallantry and the high road. All her celebrated hang-
ups have magically disappeared. She's transformed
herself into a fantasy vision from some long-lost
romance -- say ours of last summer and fall, the moments
when she was idealistic and enraptured and at her very
best. Last night when she emerged from her bout with
the muse she handed me this extract from her journal:
          It's late afternoon now -- the world is
          empty except that it means night comes
          next -- many slow agonizing hours ahead
          yet those will pass too fast...and soon I
          will be all alone, without him, empty but

487

with no vacancy, facing summer. I resent
the sun and the blue of the sky which bring
me no cheerfulness, only remind me of my
loss, my failure and the death. I laugh in
my tears. Ah Glenn! One only dies to
begin a new life!
She appended this note:
    ...I know, I am aware, I fear, I regret,
yet I can't help loving you as if the truth
were not...because...because now I am fully
vulnerable to you and I hope it is not only
from despair but from deep realization of
the destructiveness which misled me away
from you and which I am never to take
again. God forbid! I'll quit living
before I do....
    I am very, very sad, immensely sad
because I fear that I have lost you
forever. Yet I am happy because you will
no longer suffer my destructive
exploitations. And you have put me back on
the right path -- alas, at a cost too high
for what you got in exchange. My heart is
in debt to yours -- and that's not beside
the point -- of my love for you.
    As noted almost from the day we met, there are a
number of Valeries around. One is this thoughtful,
kind, almost selfless one, and she appeals to me
greatly. But then there's also the tearful and deeply
melancholy one, the shockingly intense and self-
engrossed one, the numb or indifferent one, and of
course the massively resentful, cruel, raging and
violent and destructive one. From day to day and even
moment to moment I never know which Valerie I'll be
dealing with. Sometimes, for as long as several hours,
she's the spirited, smiling, abundantly loving Valerie I
so often yearn for her to be, and it becomes quite
possible, becomes even easy and in fact far too easy to
forget we're in the process of breaking up. Then a
single misstep on my part -- a clumsy comment, an ill-

[Living with Valerie]

timed smile or frown, a glance at a magazine cover or a
newspaper headline at the wrong moment -- transforms
her, by a whirlwind process which instantly resculpts
her features before my eyes, into an entirely different
Valerie -- the one I've come to know far too well in the
past few months.

During the good periods doubts about our upcoming
separation nibble at me. But even then my battered will
mounts counterattacks: it refuses to let me be suckered
by her again. Then during the bad periods its stern
judgment is confirmed, again and again and again.

What's hardest is having to be with her so much
with the decision already made. Inside I'm a welter of
emotions. Though she doesn't know the extent of this,
she can easily exploit my doubts and fears. She does
this best by being selfless, philosophical, resigned to
our fate and yet somehow irrepressibly hopeful I'll
change my mind, and acting as if she's still deeply in
love. I shudder at the thought of her loving another
man in all those ways which, precisely because I'm the
one who opened her eyes to them or encouraged her to
develop them, she couldn't and can't and won't extend to
me. For so long I've been fantasizing about an
idealized Valerie, focusing my vision on her when the
real Val fell short, that now, given the slightest
encouragement from her, I can't stop. But that other
Valerie, the baddest of them all -- the proud
terrorizing Kyrie monster -- has also blasted a place
for herself in my mind and won't go away. Both are
there. I can't live with both. So I must insist she
leave.

*   *

Back at an old stand, the Jolly Friar on Clement
Street. In the many months since my last visit the
joint's changed a lot. So has the Old Library across
the street (it's now called Woodstock -- a change in
nomenclature from the merely dreary to the terminally
trendy). Even the JCC, I found out today, has repaneled
its sauna bath and replaced the damaged basketball
backboard which used to jangle like a gigantic utensil

drawer every time a long shot hit the rim. But
otherwise things are much the same on the old circuit.
Even I am. I sit alone here by the Friar's circular
fireplace and find myself more or less involuntarily, by
simple dumb male reflex, ogling the girls. Ogling
subtly I hope, but still ogling. And really now, what
else can you do in a place like this? Why else does it
exist? I keep thinking, "If only there were some better
place to go" -- just as I fantasized about one, two,
three...many years back. Friends and cronies, good
conversation, compatible politics, harmless or perhaps
even dangerous flirtations, dancing, terrific music on
the box or maybe even live. But as far as I know it's
still the case that no such place exists around here.
Steppenwolf in Berkeley was the closest approach to it I
know of and of course that's long gone.
     Tonight is agonizing for Valerie. "Madame
Dussault" is being read in her creative-writing class.
Right about now she'll be looking for me on 19th Avenue
-- a note on my bed this morning asked me to pick her
up. But I won't do it. I want to, but I won't. As
Erik observed maybe an hour ago (I dropped off the
twenty bucks I borrowed last week and joined him in a
quick glass of Paisano): "It's very hard to break it off
with someone and start all over again. You feel unhappy
with what you have, but you wonder what your chances are
of doing better. You can't help but feel they must be
pretty low. It takes courage. And of course you have
to be awfully lucky with the timing."
     I hadn't been thinking of it quite like that. "You
can't help but feel they must be pretty low." Somehow
this gives me a boost. Even so, I also can't help
thinking about Val. A lot. That achingly beautiful
tragic face, those imploring eyes. The way her smile
("Smile a little smile for me, Valerie...Valerie") --
the way that one-hit wonder of a smile of hers can break
my heart. How good she looks when I can afford to let
myself look at her at all. How she can light up my mind
-- my days -- with her imagination and curiosity and
insight. Already it's a strain to think of her as a

490

monster. Even in her worst moments now she's no longer
monstrous.

*

In his three-dot gossip column for the Chronicle
Herb Caen describes Mike Meyerhold as "hotly talented."
I relish the phrase. How I'd love to be able to think
of myself in the same way. "All of your good reporters
come from the lower middle class," Mike declares.
Reshaping myself into the aggressive, pushy reporter he
wants and the Bulldog needs is much more difficult than
writing ads or speeches for Empyrean ever was.

*   *

(after midnight)
Instead of being pissed off or indifferent when I
arrived home late, past eleven-thirty, Valerie was
jubilant. She'd written me a long letter bursting with
hope and optimism and gratitude. Her class tonight was
wondrously inspiring (in part perhaps because her story
wasn't read after all). She saw now that she must focus
all her energies on developing herself and engaging more
positively with the world. In a city teeming with
opportunity it would be downright criminal if she wasted
herself on self-indulgence and petty recrimination.

Later as I was reading the paper in her armchair
she dozed off. Getting up to leave, I noticed her
journal lying on the table next to her bed. Feeling she
still owes me for all the times she's snooped in mine,
and also for acting in ways which caused me to literally
question her sanity but which she now says were entirely
contrived, I again glanced through it for a few minutes,
all the while listening to be sure her breathing
remained deep and steady.

It's still a cesspool, that journal of hers. Such
incredible hatred and resentment! Such a vengeful
spirit! It turns out the "marvelous" letter of
renunciation she wrote me a week ago was simply a
paraphrase of the one I wrote her last summer! Her
purpose was "to manipulate Glenn with his own
manipulative words." She still sees me as a prime
example of the male chauvinist, exploiting the emotional

491

vulnerability of women in innumerable subtle, devious
ways. I'm "far gone" into Horneyan narcissistic
neurosis. My only hope is that her punishments of my
transgressions will "shock" me into an awakening. (Then
too there's the story of the day last week when a guy
named Joaquin kissed her. She's never mentioned him to
me. In her journal she's repulsed by him but also
fascinated. Looks to me like he could be her next man
or maybe already is.)

   She started waking up before I could absorb as much
as I might've liked. "Hold me, baby," she moaned,
seemingly taking no notice of what I'd been up to. I
did hold her, but even while doing so I was feeling more
certain than ever the course I've resolved on is the
right one. I also was thinking how ironic it is that
it's snooping in her journal that's clinched my feelings
about this. -- What's good for the goose is good for
the gander, what goes around comes around, etc. etc.
Morals of the story by the bushelful here, take your
pick, five cents each.

Tuesday 11
   Fog shrouds Sutro and I'm bundled in black Russian
hat and colorful Briana scarf for the long Honda ride to
City Hall. Stopped now, though, barely out of the gate,
to gather courage and ignite energies at Mac's Grill.
   Thinking about an emphatic letter from Mother.
Encouraged by the Gestalt group she and Dad have joined,
she "levels" with me about the situation at home. It's
not quite the "greening of the Sandefjords" I jokingly
referred to in my last letter to her. The first six
group sessions have had the paradoxical effect of
"freezing" Dad in his resentment against us. But at
least he's owned up to it. The essence of it is that he
feels he spent the best years of his life working his
tail off for his family, and that now his sacrifices not
only go unappreciated but are openly vilified, as he
sees it, by his children. And at the same time we have
the gall to be asking for loans! He also resents Mother

because she so often sides with us against him.

Dad is "substantially satisfied with himself" --
this is the judgment he arrived at during the Gestalt
sessions, which in the end he denounced as "crap." The
group leader's opinion is that Dad's become a "work
addict" and needs more therapy ("work addiction"
supposedly being every bit as disabling and hard to
shake as nicotine or alcohol addiction) -- but Dad is
instead dropping out of the group. After being stalled
by years and years of litigation, pay television is
finally launching its first large-scale trial -- in
Chicago -- and Dad will soon be jumping horses from
Crest to Seco, the pay-TV subsidiary Crest has set up.
He'll be vice-president, general counsel, and secretary
and will receive a big pay boost and stock options.
It's the great triumph of his career, and he and Mother
are justifiably proud. But at the same time his
alienation from his children (except, perhaps, Rob) is
virtually complete. Mother urges me to show Dad
personally my "understanding" and "appreciation" of his
sacrifices, and she warns me not to expect any
miraculous accommodations or reconciliations.

What do I do? I fear that any steps I might take
to persuade Dad of my gratitude and my admiration for
him would be futile. He'd look upon them as solicitous,
regard them as insincere, probably be infuriated by
them. And rightfully so, I think, because in truth my
admiration is less than wholehearted. My feelings are a
blend of respect and gratitude for his dedication and
sacrifices, compassion for his emotional limitations,
and scorn for his inability to appreciate or at least
tolerate the differing values and ideals of others, not
least his own children. I really do believe that over
the past decade or so he's betrayed many of the
principles he's long proclaimed; I really do think he's
increasingly become a raving hypocrite, especially
regarding civil rights and the war. Still, I'll do what
I can to patch it up. (My father! How remote he seems
now! How isolated! Yet I also see I'm not so different
from him in any number of ways. Chief among these, I'm

in danger of blinding myself just as he did, both
figuratively and literally (almost), i.e. through
single-minded devotion to, verging on unhealthy
obsession with, my work. These are the crucial years to
make sure this doesn't happen to me.)

             *   *

City Hall -- the Press Room. Right now (high noon)
KQED is filming an interview in here. Both participants
look vaguely familiar, but I can't identify either one
for certain. The room is so tiny its other occupants --
half a dozen of us ace reporters -- are unable to work
in the klieg-lit commotion and instead sit quietly
exchanging quizzical smiles.

The place surprises me; its walls are plastered
with political posters. "Mailer/Breslin for Mayor of
the 51st State!" A row of old Fillmore posters.
Abstract art. On the blackboard someone has chalked
"Free the Indianapolis 500" (big upward roll of mine
eyeballs). The two chief denizens of this room, Jerry
Burns of the Chronicle and Russ Cone of the Examiner,
are presently closed up in their adjoining private
cubbyholes pounding out what I can't help but assume is
their usual dreck on deadline. A flock of self-
important hip capitalists and TV production types are
flapping in and out through clouds of cigar and
cigarette smoke tinctured with patchouli (yes!). An
ancient brown leather chair, very comfortable-looking
and now momentarily unoccupied, is beckoning from the
far side of the room: "Come on over, tenderfoot, and
mellow out for a while." ---

             *   *

The City Hall venture didn't work out so well.
It's a madhouse over there, bureaucratic type, hundreds
of men and women scurrying about in a Kafkaesque maze.
Thousands of vacant faces hanging above cluttered desks
like last year's dried-out sunflowers, evoking an
instantaneous certitude that nothing will ever get done.
I'm still shaking. Spirit me away, O Frodo! (Huh?)

At the moment I'm in one of those restless,
dejected moods where I just itch to do something at

least mildly subversive. Call Jang maybe? Aw come on:
I know how it would be if I saw her now. I'd have to
wear myself out constructing sympathetic smiles and
before long would feel I was floating out in space
somewhere. Call Briana? More or less the same
objection but with lots of frustration added in. Bar-
hop? The thought evokes a heavy sigh. Well then, what?

 The sensible thing would be to attack the new stack
of Bulldog rewrites rising atop earlier accretions of
same in my in-basket. No fewer than seven of them await
me, and every last one will be a colossal pain in the
ass. Maybe I'll do one and then write a few letters.
Letters! The notion of blazing out a long letter is
much more appealing. A letter to Susan Bergman. To
Rob. To Barb. To Mother. To Briana? No. To Jang?
No. To Dad? I don't think I could face that right now.

 This is a bad time for me. It's absurd but I'm
almost ready to burst into tears for no reason at all.
Everything's just -- grim. It's easy to see how a man
could be driven to drink, to shoot up, to shoot himself.
Everything's going wrong! Fuck! Life can't be this
bad!

 Flow with it, the wise counselor says. Sure, why
not, let the anguish and anxiety wash over you, at least
you'll be feeling something.

 A sudden impulse to do the laundry. Feels sort of
kinky, as with compulsive hand-washers -- or, to be
sure, journalkeepers.

Wednesday 12
 At nine-thirty this morning a timid knock sounded
on the apartment door. Val and I had just gotten up
after uninspired balling; I was wearing my bathrobe and
she just her usual unbuttoned workshirt. We'd slept
together last night, not because I wanted to, ironically
enough, but because I simply lacked the strength or the
heart to boot her out of bed when she crept in sometime
well past midnight.

 The knock? It was Jang. I said I'd come out and

talk with her and asked her to wait downstairs. Val
immediately assumed I'd been seeing Jang behind her back
and flew into a rage. She grabbed my journal and locked
herself in her room. This infuriated me and I smashed
open the door -- splintering the frame -- and retrieved
it.

Then she refused to let me see Jang alone. Jumping
into her jeans and a tie-dyed T-shirt, she trailed me
down the stairs to the lower landing where Jang was
waiting (she had two gifts for me: special ginseng roots
from Korea "to heal your father's eyes" and a fifty-
dollar check). Val was weeping; Jang tried to raise her
spirits. It wound up with me driving the two of them to
the Board of Education. At this very moment they're out
together somewhere downtown talking heart-to-heart.

Far out! It was so heavy I broke through on the
other side. Val bawling, Jang comforting her as her,
Jang's, hand rested possessively on my shoulder; Val
smiling bewilderedly. Jang lively, Val near dead. My
two loves together: I flashed on the notion of our
living as a happy menage, then on the idea of all three
of us driving over to Briana's place to make it a
foursome (a group photo would be nice). Jang as the
wise older woman who's been through almost seven years,
off and on, of this sort of craziness with Glen,
sententiously telling Val how very young she is, how
very difficult a man can be. Our eyes catching but not
quite. I said I'd call later, Val said she'd call me
(and also threatened to jump off the Bay Bridge). My
guess is they're jawing away at Caffe Trieste as I write
these words. It's a natural because, as Val well knows,
it's been the site of so many previous melodramatic
moments in my San Francisco era (with Briana, Ciara,
Denise, as well as Jang and Val themselves -- though
never before Jang and Val at once -- or any other two at
once, come to think of it, at least that I know of).

"Be kind to each other," I pleaded when dropping
them off. "And be kind to me."

Fat chance! The potential for mischief is high
indeed. I trust Jang but not Val -- she could stir

fresh resentment in Jang, even inspire her permanent
alienation (she's about ready for that anyway). Well,
but then perhaps that would be for the best. Or say
whatever happens, perhaps that, yes, would be for the
best. Perhaps this accidental confrontation will
liberate both of them from me and me from both of them.
Or then again perhaps it will return me to Jang (who in
my eyes far outshone Val when the chips were down;
toward Val with all her hate-filled histrionics I felt
dull anger and fierce pity and not a whole lot else).

*   *

All afternoon, meanwhile, we Bulldoggers have been
thrashing over city budget figures -- Mike parrying
magnificently on the phone with the budget director
himself and then with a lawyer at the city attorney's
office as I listened in on an extension and took notes
-- and meanwhile those two women have presumably been
feeling each other out, saying god only knows what
appalling things about each other and of course about
the man they both love (or did, rather, and maybe one or
the other still does, or maybe both do, despite
everything or maybe precisely because of everything, who
knows -- and if that sounds glib, at this point I've
completely run out of the will and the means to remedy
it). ---

*

Just then the phone rang right on cue: it was Val
and she was calling from Union Square with Jang standing
outside the booth. From the first word she sounded not
furious but icily depressed, resigned, also resolute now
as if the things she'd heard from Jang had sealed the
case against me. She wanted to see me right away, she
declared, or as soon as possible, definitely before I'd
have a chance to speak with Jang, because, as Val said,
she didn't want her own -- Val's -- anger and strong
sense of purpose to "dissipate"; and she let slip the
phrase "since I'll be leaving now." She sounded totally
disillusioned, finished, lost. She wanted to speak with
me in person before the pain became overwhelming, and
she thought I owed her that much.

497

What for? What have I done? What has Jang told
her? At seven I'll be finding out, I guess, and before
that I'll definitely try to reach Jang to see where
she's at now and try to get a better line on what I'll
be up against with Val.

Heavy, heavy. I may be coming out of this all
alone, and if that's the case, so much the better, I
suppose, though I feel shitty about it -- but why should
I? why? why? -- well, that's a complicated story and
maybe I should feel shitty after all. At this point,
again, it's getting hard to keep everything straight.
Later on there will be lots of time to tally up the
gains and losses and mete out the blame, the medals, the
sorrows and regrets.

A period of isolated withdrawal. It's the only way
you learn from a failed love, Charles McCabe says in his
Chronicle column that so serendipitously ran in this
morning's paper. You don't learn a thing, he asserts,
from leaping into a new affair, as has been my usual
practice. In doing that you only deaden the pain, which
will return redoubled later on, just in time to sabotage
the new relationship you've worked so diligently in the
meantime to coax into being.

(Or you can go the other way, as Mick and Bianca
have done -- that's Mick Jagger and his jet-setter
Nicaraguan sweetheart whose family is friendly with the
family of Unk Erik's Consuela who's fled to Chile, yes,
but has now let him know she'll be returning in three
weeks. -- Even KRMA recognizing a kind of cultural duty
to keep us distracted with the occasional hit of
celebrity news, but in the case of Mick and Bianca the
countercultural variety to be sure. -- And I'm
especially grateful for that distraction as well as any
other that might come along right now.)

Thursday 13
Another in a long series of grueling nights. This
one began at Trieste where Valoshka, in studded jeans,
ratty rabbit-fur coat and floppy black felt hat, eyes

498

tragic like a lost child's but with an added tinge of
bitter wisdom, handed me a bouquet of daisies and
marigolds and then launched into a fierce attempt to
destroy Jang, me, herself, and our love, all in the name
of hopelessness and openly acknowledged madness.

Nothing meant anything anymore, she said, because I
was the great love of her life, the only real love she'd
ever have, and I was leaving her now. The only question
worth considering was whether she'd bother to continue
living at all. If she did, she'd be loyal to this love
always, she'd never again betray it with another man;
for if this love no longer existed, then nothing would
exist, nothing could exist.

Death, insanity, tragedy were in the air. Yet as
for the man she claimed to love, the real person as
opposed to the preposterous abstraction, that is, as for
me (surprise!), I was once again the subject of
outrageous accusations and bitter merciless
vilification. I'd betrayed the love. I was a
"prostitute of the heart," a "debaucher" who'd sold his
soul to a "neurotic idealism" that allegedly forces me
to jump from woman to woman because none can come close
to meeting my impossibly lofty standards. So high is my
opinion of myself that I never even bother to try to
make a love work, I just insist on "magic" and when
magic fades or fails I move on.

Hours and hours of this stuff, uttered with hateful
and vindictive vehemence, shrill, cold, inflamed,
deranged, vicious, slicing to shreds all my attempts to
answer the charges or just to reach out to her. What I
felt was mostly sorrow and pity but what I showed was
mostly anger and exasperation. Why, she would leave
this very night! Go out into the cold alone, helpless
-- "It's the only way I'll ever leave" -- but then she
began quietly pounding her head against the wall (we
were back at Funston by now, having made a stop on a
bench at Washington Square in between after shocking the
patrons at Trieste with our battling), hysteria was
near, she couldn't breathe, her stomach was in knots,
and I'd better not read my newspaper, I'd better comfort

her, I'd better tell her what she wanted to hear -- or
else! And why hadn't I ever cared enough to take her to
a shrink (although of course she's always refused even
to consider the idea the numerous times I've brought it
up; and when I've downright insisted on it, she's gone
into terrorist resistance mode in every instance) --
couldn't I see she needed help, she was alone, alone, in
all the world there was no one to help her? Yes she was
a child, a desperate child, she wanted to be taken care
of, she moaned "Someone take care of me" over and over,
"I'm a desperate child now because I never had a
childhood and like it or not you're responsible for me
now, Glen."

   She finally agreed to go to bed. I had to tuck her
in and kiss her goodnight, I had to hold her, to commend
the supreme beauty of her breasts and her ass and her
cooch and many of her other parts (lips, nose, eyes,
teeth, back, legs, neck, hair...), assure her everything
would be better tomorrow...and early this morning she
came in and slipped into my bed and before I was more
than half awake was sucking me off like a woman
possessed -- like a succubus, exactly -- and gave a
shrill witchlike cry when I came (it scared the hell out
of me) and smeared the come all over her face, using my
cock to rub it in until I thought she'd scrape the skin
off (and it's raw and stinging now, driving me half nuts
because of my own salty crotch sweat).

                    *   *

   Fresh out of the bath and with Valerie once again
safely tucked away in the blue-room bed it may be
possible to conduct a relatively detached review of the
day's activities and to draw some conclusions that, if I
really do come up with any, will no doubt remain valid
just about as long as my freshly toweled and bath-
powdered groin will stay dry.

   Back at the Bulldog -- it seems like a long, long
time ago -- I felt better today with respect to my work
there, probably because Mike said something about my
being a "lifesaver" with my extensive rewrites,
especially of the complicated Lou Rizzo budget stories,

[Living with Valerie]

and Peggy downplayed the idea of my going up to Hetch Hetchy this weekend to take pictures "because I'm sure Mike will want you here." Having not yet quite caught on to Mike's rhythms or to the newswriting style he expects I remain uneasy, but I have greater confidence now that those things will come (one thing I'd like to do when time permits is read the rest of Mike's stories and editorials in the Bulldog back issues).

Then there was tonight, and I'm wondering how Gass's "The Stylization of Desire" may apply, that is, to what extent my actions and feelings stemmed from real desire as compared to its ritualization. There was Jang on the phone describing me as a "bee" because I supposedly fly from woman to woman fertilizing more or less by accident as I carry off the nectar (something like that, though strangely enough even at the time I didn't think she intended it badly) and sure enough, she opened the door and just like "King Bee" on the album I said "Let's buzz a while" and we were in bed balling away before either of us got out another word; and afterwards because of her consistent cheeriness, perhaps, her apparent freedom from resentment, the seeming growth in her toleration of and compassion for my undeniably erratic ways -- who knows why -- I found myself thinking, even if not daring to say, we might just be able to get back together someday, maybe we've learned our lesson, maybe we've come to recognize pettiness better and appreciate unusual affinities better and know how to maintain a respectful, loving distance when that's called for (though the distance she was maintaining most of the evening was a shade too much and, shamefully, little signs of her aging bothered me more this time and so did her usual obliviousness about things political and I didn't really know what the hell I felt except when I left I was happy and she didn't want me to go and we agreed to meet again soon).

And then I was home and Valerie knew goddamn well I'd been with Jang but chose not to talk about it, just acted mildly amused, declaring herself to be "back on the right track" for reasons unknown to her, but

maybe because she'd made an appointment on her own to
see a Langley-Porter shrink tomorrow "and that takes
care of the dark side of me."

She was bright and hopeful and "very much in love,"
she saw me as an "eighteenth-century man, very
romantic," and while performing her dance at State
tonight she'd decided to become "the world's best
lovemaker" ("We all have breasts and cunts," she
observed even before reading the piece about "The Female
Eunuch" which I'd brought home for her), and the method
she'd use was to lie still in her vagina until her body
gained sensitivity and movement flowed from it rather
than being commanded by her mind. So we gave this a
trial run, a very slow and gentle one, and it was --
yes, a bummer all the way. She's just not an
"exquisite" kind of lovemaker, or not yet anyway. And
it depressed me greatly to see her so despondent about
it and I vowed to myself not to ball her anymore (but
I'm sure this is another vow I'll never be able to hold
to unless she refuses me). Meanwhile she somehow
managed to hang on to her good spirits, kept talking as
if we were to be together always, and I sure as hell
didn't contradict her (yes, she's ravishingly beautiful
and I love her too no matter what but then I think of
Danny and what's going down with him and it hits me a
whole lot harder than, say, Jang's aging). And I
wondered to what extent I was guilty of, as Gass puts it
(he puts everything so well!), "the high brutality of
good intention" -- of being a manipulator. But if I
were truly good at manipulation Val and I would be
having no problems at all. In fact Jang and I never
would've broken up in the first place. In short: what
I'm really guilty of is being nowhere near good enough
at manipulation, among a number of other very important
even though widely reviled skills.

Ha, I should also note word's going around -- it's
on the radio, on posters, in lunchtime chitchat -- that
a massive demonstration will take place tomorrow in, of
all places, Garnett, California. The occasion is Armed
Forces Day, open house at Fleming Air Force Base, and a

number of Movement heavies from around the country will
be gathering in West Utah Park: it's almost too much to
grasp. For the Merino Mercury it's a godsend; I only
wish it had happened when I was there.

The Mercury still lives, by the way. Jang's mail-
subscription copy came in the other day and she noticed
my name had completely disappeared from its pages,
including from the masthead. Paradoxically this enables
me to claim I've accomplished what I set out to do,
which was to stick around long enough to see the paper
launched on a course that would allow it to survive and
hopefully prosper with no outside help. Truth marches
on! (We all desire stylization. This upcoming massive
demonstration outside the Fleming gates could quickly
kill off the paper, however, if it turned violent -- and
it might.)

Saturday 15 (X:14)

In a perverse mood, drifting in North Beach.
Valoshka doesn't know how to react to a mood like this,
how to handle it, she's overwhelmed. All she can do is
"tease" me about my ill-concealed triumphant glee over
the way things are going at the Bulldog (where I've put
in three straight ten-hour days agonizing over rewrites
of the majority of the stories slated to run in the next
issue). To her it's amusing I'm amazed to be doing so
well. "I've always had complete confidence in you," she
says, meaning I should regard my triumphs as a matter of
course. But for me, to impress the one San Francisco
journalist I've idolized for years stacks up as no small
achievement. Next to this, whipping together the
Mercury was "birdseed" (a favorite Meyerholdism).

What triumph? Just a few scattered encouraging
comments from Mike. "This is shaping up very well,"
about the budget story. "You must have done some work
around City Hall before." And best of all, he yesterday
offhandedly revealed he'd be paying me for all this
work. "Have to give you a little capitalistic
incentive," he joked.

503

[Have Mercy]

Mike is a crackerjack editor. After a session with
him I feel my writing is loose and sloppy, bland, vague.
Exposure to his methods and standards is just what I
need. That he's also a superb writer ("hotly talented")
makes it all the better. I should have done something
like this years ago.

One major drawback of working for the Bulldog: I
can no longer look forward to reading it afresh with the
same startled pleasure when it hits the racks.

One great advantage: it consumes most of my
energies. I have little left to apply to ruminations
about Valerie.

She's here right now, reading on the bed a few feet
away, legs tucked beneath her. Her facial expression at
this moment recalls that of the sixteen-year-old Laura
in "Claire's Knee" (which we saw last night): at once
innocent and prematurely knowing. She's puzzling over
an article about Fitzgerald in Esquire, "Trying to get
into your world," by which she means, she explains, "the
world of the American writer." Oh. Well, okay, in that
case I guess I'll just come right out and say she should
keep pouring it on, the flattery, and we can worry about
its degree of accuracy some other time. Flattery is
definitely not something I'm used to hearing from her.

Though it shouldn't, the extent of her ignorance
about things American sometimes astounds me. "Who's Rod
McKuen?" she asks. "What's a huckster?" "What's
Peoria?" (She thought it must be a building where some
important government department was housed. -- "How
will it play in Peoria?" And I expanded on that with
the story I often trot out when the phrase comes up in
conversation: that I myself have played in Peoria.
Played basketball there, that is. And lost. But
played, as it happened, about as well as I ever have.)

For three days we haven't mentioned the matter of
her leaving.

I peer at her with raised eyebrows. She shifts
uneasily.

"You're so weird," she says. "There's something
diabolical about you tonight."

504

[Living with Valerie]

For the first time in months I'm not wearing my Chavez Thunderbird medallion. Left it at Jang's the other night -- the "buzz a while" night.

Time for a root beer. A chunk of homemade banana bread wrapped in cellophane. Seems to be making a horrific face, this chunk does, like a bank robber with a nylon stocking pulled over his -- or is it her? -- head. (A second look confirms it's probably a her. And Val agrees.)

The financial clouds are lifting. Mike's promise of remuneration for the copyediting gave me such a boost I opened a new account at the Ninth Avenue branch of Bank of America, breaking last December's vow never to do business with them again. Alas, I must have a place to cash checks. Or was it just a knee-jerk effect of Mike's "capitalistic incentive"?

Last night when I got home at eight-thirty Valerie was unexpectedly welcoming and I found myself actually happy to be with her. By ten, though, the glow had worn off. Her increasingly truculent responses to my attempts to answer her elementary questions about the politics of finance and the gold standard (for a school assignment) annoyed the hell out of me. Did her hostility possibly trace back to the fact that her despised father is, in addition to being a lawyer and a declasse' former aristocrat, a financial journalist? Did my replies remind her of him (she's said this before but not specifically this time). But then "Claire's Knee" put both of us in a good mood again (for Val a big part of it was the pleasure of hearing French) and when we came home we tumbled right into bed. After a lengthy series of caresses (Jesus it takes her a long time to get turned on these days!) I pushed into her from behind as we lay on our sides, held still for a while until she could "get used to it" as per a request of hers made the night before, and then fucked her "roughly" (again at her request which specifically used the words "fuck" and "rough"), winding up banging maniacally away while straddling her thighs as she raised her ass beneath me. "I liked it last night," she purred this morning.

505

[Have Mercy]

That I can still desire her so much even though I
only occasionally like the sex itself a proportionate
amount and almost always feel disheartened afterwards
(and too often even during) -- and all this was true
again last night even though she was liking it -- it's
puzzling to me. It's unprecedented. I can't see why it
doesn't shake out one way or the other. Cf., "Love it
or leave it."

4

Monday 17 (X:16)
    Just as in olden times at the Merc I'm too busy to
scribble more than a few words (as Val whose legs look
smashing tonight warms my bed within easy ejac distance
at a few minutes past midnight and I nearly nod out from
lack of sleep after a twelve-hour day at the Bulldog --
and on Norwegian Independence Day!):
    ** Mustering the full power of my mechanical
genius I came up with a way to repair my broken
typewriter with a piece of wrapping wire from a bag of
dinner rolls: and yes it works.
    ** For five hours last night I rampaged through
carbon copies of Val's poems, slashing roughly half the
lines with Ezra Pound-like glee, arriving in some cases
at new poems with new meanings, and some quite good I
think. She asked me to do it. Whether she'll make use
of any of them, I don't know. She still has all the
originals, of course; I was working with carbons.
Tomorrow she reads for her creative-writing class.
    ** Val's father likes her poetry too, I should
note, and always has. In another pun of his related to
the "Lord, have mercy" one she told me about before, he
sometimes called her (fondly!) Kyrielle, which is a
woman's name in France but also a poetry form based on
the same "Kyrie Eleison" ("Have Mercy") litany. He and
she also share a love of Beethoven, who used that
liturgical phrase in several of their favorite
symphonies. It seems she was widely seen as a poet from

506

a very young age. And she was thrilled that her poetry
instructor at State was, unlike me, familiar with the
Kirielle form. (This was the only time I've ever heard
her say anything positive about her father.)
    ** She sucked my cock at four a.m. last night and
again I watched fascinated as the spunk spurted onto her
lips and cheeks and eyes and up into her hair, her
expression afterward turning almost beatific. I believe
it's becoming her favorite kind of sex, at least with
me. (Yesterday she coaxed me into a lengthy talk about
ejac trajectories and distances and other arcane aspects
of male sexual plumbing.)
    ** I've now extensively revised and in effect
written half a dozen stories for the Bulldog, with
several still to go and Mike leaving for New York
tomorrow evening on a fund-raising jaunt. I'm still
mesmerized by his power as an editor, his ability to
grasp complex issues quickly and to state them
forcefully in simple, concise language. Terse. The man
knows terse! To watch him composing heads, beating on
his old manual typewriter almost like a bongo drum,
exulting over snappy edits: it's all a delight. Because
pencils are so scarce at the Bulldog -- and expensive!
-- we all wear one dangling on a string around our
necks. On everyone else this looks awkward and a bit
ridiculous, like grown-ups with their mittens still tied
on, but on 240-pound Mike it somehow seems completely
natural. As he makes his rounds in the office he wields
that pencil like a beat cop twirling his truncheon.
    ** The deadline for my "thinking it over" about
Val has slipped past with scarcely a word spoken on the
matter by either of us. I can't be disturbed by
anything until the paper's put to bed. Val's on her
very best behavior and also deeply involved with school.

Thursday 20 (X:18-19)
    In the cavernous bowels of the downtown "World
Headquarters" of the Bank of America, behind the wheel
of the Land Cruiser, waiting for the line to shorten up

so I can cash a check at the drive-in window.

In a highly excited state, punchy, as deadline nears for the Bulldog and I still have several pieces to write and many other things to do. Just a month ago I never would've guessed it possible I'd not only be writing for the Bulldog this soon, byline and all, but also serving as something like acting editor-in-chief. But that's where it's at.

Mike left for New York Tuesday night and provided me with a list of several dozen things to do, ranging from writing photo captions to walking the plates through at the printer. Now Monica, Peggy, and I are acting as a sort of collective, along with whoever else happens to be present (writers solicitous of their stories, proofreaders, paste-up people), charged with making sure the paper actually gets published. When it comes to decisions about written words everyone looks to me for the final say (especially for writing headlines, or "heds," which I've always enjoyed doing: "PUC'S HOOK INTO THE ROUGH: 'WREAKREATION' IN SF'S PENINSULA WATERSHED") (all right, all right, I'll try to find a better example -- but later). -- Though I'm trying to handle it all calmly and steadily, underneath I'm rather overwhelmed: Jeep Sandefjord at the center of things!

Ridiculous, I know, of course. But still that's the way it feels, exhilarating and trepidatious. I mean this is not the Merino Mercury where you can just toss in whatever thoughts cross your mind; this is a quality publication with thousands of discerning and highly intelligent readers, including several dozen or more I now know personally. (Still I'm well aware in some ways nothing else could approach working at the Mercury. There so much depended on me, and there I participated in every facet of the labor that made the paper, from conceiving story ideas to tossing papers onto lawns: and how often does anyone get to do something like that?)

An authentic exhilarating moment: I answered a phone call at noon and the voice on the line sounded oddly familiar because I'd just been listening to it on the radio: Alan Ramsay of KRMA news. In researching

Bulldog back issues he'd come across a Dave Dikeakos
evisceration of PG&E business practices and tied it in
with a PG&E rate-increase request reported in this
morning's Chronicle (the newscast had all of us frozen
in place and then shouting with glee as he mentioned our
stuff). Now he was proposing that KRMA and the Bulldog
join forces for a raft trip up to the mountain hideaway
of PG&E at Hetch Hetchy. Sure, definitely, delighted, I
said, since who else was there to say yea or nay? So
tomorrow I'll be dropping by the KRMA studio downtown
with a copy of the new issue to talk things over with
Ramsay. A few minutes later Mike, calling from New
York, guffawed over this tale and said he thought the
expedition would make a great story (actually everyone
misses the thunderous commands of the old autocrat).
     An authentically bad moment: I had to ask Monica
what the letters "tk" penciled in on one of Mike's
manuscripts meant. (It was "to come": he'd be filling
in a certain section of the story later, except of
course now he was gone and I'd have to do it.) And then
maybe two minutes later I was back to ask her about a
circled paragraph with "cbk" written next to it. "Can
be killed," of course. I knew that! (Way back when.)
     A tickling underthought: Valoshka in our talk about
writing the other night put the whole Bulldog trip in a
different kind of perspective by saying she thinks I
should undertake projects more hazardous to my
imagination -- I'm too good for the newspaper game, you
see. For her father, it's fine, it's what he deserves;
from me she expects more. She herself is exultant over
the reception accorded her poetry by the class and
especially the teacher, who took her aside to say her
work was several cuts above that of the others and she
should consider making a career of writing (I'm exultant
too because I'm the one who talked her into returning to
school and taking the class and even had a hand in
reshaping several of the poems she eventually chose to
read: so maybe every poet needs an editor just as every
editor needs a poet). -- But otherwise things between
me and "Kyrielle" are merely acceptable right now, we're

509

"like liberal friends who have sex sometimes," as she
quipped at one point, both of us waiting, when it comes
right down to it, for me to announce my final judgment
on whether she's to stay or leave.

Friday 21
     The sudden longing to see Briana seems to have
blown itself out at last, after sweeping up unexpectedly
last night and finally carrying me to within a few feet
of her door this morning. I sat there in the L.C. numb
from exhaustion and kept thinking that if she suddenly
walked up it would be a sign from the gods we were
destined for each other, celestial lovers about to be
reunited at last.
     What kept me from knocking on her door was sheer
vanity (can't go up there feeling and looking so washed
out), augmented by my recognition of the near certainty
she's found someone else by now, returned to Terry, or
both; and, regardless, she'd greet me coolly, wouldn't
really want to see me (oh my god, not him again, he's
not about to try to start it up again, is he?).
     Just a brief detour. Now I'm waiting in the
parking lot at Neill's -- the printer -- for the
pressmen to come back from lunch and start our run.
(The ground shudders and the L.C. with it as a Southern
Pacific switch engine bangs boxcars together about fifty
feet away.) Thinking back to the all-nighter at the
Bulldog, wondering what made it different from others.
I don't know, but it was an enormous mental strain,
especially knocking out in less than ten minutes the
sidebar-like word-blocks that would anchor the budget
blast and "Justin Herman's Dream" (a capsule critique of
the S.F. Redevelopment Agency). Sheer terror, me and
that recalcitrant typewriter, Monica in back meanwhile
wrestling with botched paste-ups, Valerie long since
passed out on Mike's couch (resting up for her
presentation in class today of her personal philosophy,
which she's assembled under the rubric of, of all
things, "Harmony" -- "expressing my Asian side"). And

[Living with Valerie]

me sweating blood -- that's the closest I can come to it
-- whew, my brain is fried -- and let's see, later on
four or five of us munching takeout fried editor brain
-- no no, fried chicken parts in Mike's office saying we
sure could use another proofreader and just then
footsteps sound in the hall and a strange face peers in,
like divine deliverance: "Could you use some help with
proofreading?" Monica's trembling hands. My hassles
with Valerie (all right, at times I was a bit short with
her, but she was being a bitch and the reason was the
previous morning, yesterday, I'd suggested she cite to
her new shrink as one reason for her psychic imbalance
"love alienation." "Have I alienated your love?" she
asked ever so innocently. "That was the point of the
whole three-month terror spree, wasn't it? Isn't that
what you told me yourself? That and sheer vengeance?
'Teaching you a lesson'? 'Punishing you for thinking
you're self-sufficient'? Have you forgotten all that
already?" Then we went off separately to school and
work, playing it down.)
     Pressmen back? I'll check.
*

    It may be a while yet. Seated inside now on a roll
of white paper the diameter of a whiskey barrel.
Nothing happening at this moment, still lunch hour, the
three-story-high Goss press which will soon be spitting
out Bulldogs at ten or eleven per second standing idle
against a backdrop of the downtown S.F. skyline broken
into an industrial-picture-window checkerboard of
varying degrees of smudged opacity (to wing it just a
bit); and, let's see, behind me dozens of even larger
rolls of paper the diameter of telephone-cable spools
(the type everybody's slicing in half and using as
coffee tables these days, as at Family Farmacy) are
stacked twenty feet high against the rear wall; and in
the air that omnipresent whiff of printer's ink you can
never forget (it's Sewell's in Adams here all over
again, just on a whole lot larger scale).
    Now they're back and readying the press, oiling and
tapping and inspecting like engineers in the pit with a

511

rumbling, trembling race car or maybe stoking up the
boiler on a World War II destroyer. ---

Saturday 22
    Whoopee: once again the laundromat!
    Sun nearing the horizon, its golden rays slanting
through the snowy upper reaches of a mostly gray fogbank
hugging the Outer Sunset. Irving looks like the
deserted main street of a small midwestern town in that
last idyllic moment before the cyclone hits.
    A bit calmer perspective on things from this
vantage point.
    So I stood by feeling conspicuously useless as four
pressmen crawled over the monster machine adjusting a
knob here, tightening a plate there, and then in no time
at all seventeen thousand five hundred picture-perfect
Bay Bulldogs spewed out. Another thousand or so, the
"spoiled" ones which Mike likes to hang on to anyway
(because on many the damage is scarcely detectable), are
still weighing down the back of the L.C. parked just
outside, lopsided and low-riding like an overloaded bus.
    Looking into those thirty-two pages (at least ten
of which I had a direct hand in) I'm less pleased than I
thought I'd be. In fact certain of my own contributions
are dismayingly sloppy. Maybe I'm the only one who'll
react to them this way (having been so close to the
makeup process, it's hard to see the pages freshly; my
eyes fasten on the aberrant details as if they'd been
printed in a different color ink) -- let's hope so.
    Last night I was exhausted, I didn't even want to
think about the Bulldog, but today new ideas are
bubbling up. Mostly they relate to ways to help wrestle
the paper out of the red. By changing back-of-the-book
emphasis so it will appeal more to countercultural
tastes, for example. The Bay Area needs a paper
resembling the L.A. Free Press and the Village Voice;
the Bulldog's the logical one to fill the void. To make
such a paper maximally appealing, the vendettas against
PG&E and Superchron had best be toned down a bit. I

doubt Mike would agree to this. What's more, he's a far cry from a street hippie or even a Consciousness III university instructor (though he is a university instructor). But there's no harm in trying to persuade him to let things evolve a bit in that direction.

A liaison with KRMA (pronounced "Karma"), for another example. My visit to their studios in the Argonaut Building, heart of corporate San Francisco in the Financial District, yielded little in the way of dramatic breakthroughs but did intimate good things for the future. "We'll whoop up the Bulldog," promised Alan Ramsay in the closet-sized headquarters of "KRMA Worldwide News." Over the air Ramsay sounds like the voice of respectability itself -- the timbre of his voice, I mean -- but in person he looks more like a dissolute bad guy in some two-bit Western, complete with demonic red-rimmed blue eyes and a wispy goatee.

I was awakened this morning by Sid Portola handing me the latest copy of the Merino Mercury, a sixteen-pager high on content but dismal in appearance. "Sid's Corner" has now replaced my "Mercky Notions." Ebullient and garrulous as ever, Sid plunked his three hundred pounds onto the edge of the bed at Funston and we rapped for an hour or more. I like him but feel a little uneasy in his presence, as if I'm overly admired, as if I'm expected to be sharper and wittier than I can ever possibly be. (He, by the way, just to be different, calls his Levis "Strausses.")

The main thing on my mind -- I wish this wasn't the case -- is Valerie, the crack-up of our relationship. After a particularly oppressive afternoon on the sundeck, Danny misbehaving, Val short-tempered because of approaching exams (among other reasons), I finally yielded to her demands and summoned the courage to break the news to her: I still feel the same. I remain "open" to finding a way we can start anew, but I still want her to move out first. As far as I'm concerned our "experiment" has been a failure, our "gamble" a huge loss. She took it well -- a single tear -- and we agreed to continue trying to spare each other from

unnecessary anguish. When I left for the laundromat I
glanced up and saw her in the window, head bowed, hands
raised above her head as if shackled to the wall in a
torture cell: an unforgettable image.

I think of what Kay at the Bulldog said: "Looks to
me like you're hung up on tragic love affairs."

Well, it's Saturday night, and I told Val I'd be
coming home "later," though "not too late." I'm trying
to think of ways I might pass the time. They reduce to
these: Sausalito, North Beach, good movie, bad movie,
Woodstock, or a search for a "groovy new bar" rumored to
be somewhere on Noe. Or maybe Berkeley or Union Street.
But tonight I don't feel very adventurous so I'll likely
wind up at the place easiest to get to from here, i.e.,
the Woodstock/Jolly Friar matched set in the Richmond
District, and I probably won't stay long because I'll
feel guilty about leaving Val alone with Danny. On the
other hand if I go home too early I'll castigate myself
for giving in to her pressure and also for putting
myself at her mercy.

A hopeless situation. Tragic, I might say, if I
hadn't already so overused the word. I know I'll regret
giving her up, for a while at least, but pride and anger
force me to. "Cold fire." I don't want to lose her,
but the thought of letting her stay on at "the Castle"
after what's happened repels me.

In short: we must separate for the same reason our
love failed. Merciless logic of "neurotic attachment."

Trying to transcend this, I seek substantial
reasons for staying with her. I can't think of any.
She doesn't make me happy, she doesn't make it easier
for me to work, she doesn't bring me all that much
sexual pleasure, she doesn't make a good companion
socially (and that's putting it mildly). Danny's being
part of the deal makes life with her doubly difficult
mainly because I can't abide her way of raising him.
Aside from my fear I'll find no one better for me,
there's simply no good reason not to break it off.

What is it that's kept me with her so long? Her
beauty, her body, her idealism, her passion, her

creativity, her many talents, her high energy level
(when it's switched on), her need for me, her bottomless
compassion (while it lasted), her "exotic" mind, her
radical politics and worldview which I share to a large
degree, and maybe most of all the very fighting spirit
which has now made it impossible for me to stay on with
her. That I should ever again find so much in a woman
is unlikely: I'm well aware of this. But to accept her
on her own terms after the epic of terror and coercion
she's put me through to punish me for my "debaucherie"
is simply not imaginable now. If she'd made more of an
effort to repair the damage she's done and to convince
me it wouldn't happen again, things might be different.
But she's done very little of that, and I see few signs
this will change. On the contrary: most of the time
she's just as righteous about her nasty behavior as she
was in the baddest of the bad old days (up until a week
or ten days ago I'm talking about).

Sunday 23
     At the Park N Shop lunch counter which I share with
fifteen or so seriously aging and yet still burger-
ravenous worshippers just released from St. Anne's
across the street. Val and Danny are prowling the
aisles in search of items buyable with food stamps.
Before coming in I did the best I could to spiff up the
ramshackle Bulldog newsrack outside and stuffed two
dozen copies of the new issue into it; now I'm nibbling
on an oatmeal-raisin cookie and shuddering at the
prospect of what lies ahead -- another day of virulence.
     Last night I didn't make it home until one a.m.
That overstepped the outer bounds of Val's tolerance by
about two hours, and she met me at the door in the same
blue mini (now micro'd) and wedge-heeled sandals she was
wearing the very first time I caught sight of her, ever,
in the "Human Chain." Her eyes overbrimmed with a
tearful indignant fury. My freedom ended where hers
began, she announced. Did I know what I'd put her
through? She'd very nearly "done it" -- in fact she had

"done it" and then undone it -- and it was all my fault,
my responsibility. I was the bastard, the supreme
chauvinist, the neurotic par excellance, I was capable
only of infatuations (not love), I was hung up on my own
excessive standards. Well, she wanted me to know I was
"getting to be less of a loss every day." There were,
she reminded me, "lots of other cocks in the world."
Then she handed me two photos of herself with crude
knife wounds to the chest drawn in with a red marker.

    So when did I want her to leave, she asked. When
did she want to leave, I replied. After her exams were
over, she said. She let me know she expected me to help
her find a good place. "I'm tired of all this moving
around." And once she was gone she'd be gone for good;
I should understand that clearly. There would be none
of those weekly visits with a fuck and a goodbye at the
end. "I'm not becoming part of your stable."

    After her exams: that's another two weeks.

    Don't know how I'll hold out that long.

5

Monday 24

    So anxious am I to monitor feedback (mainly Mike's)
on the new issue of the Bay Bulldog that I can't sit
still, can't stay home, so here it is only eight-thirty
in the morning and already I'm lodged in my customary
window seat at Mac's Grill, passing time until the
Bulldog office opens.

    Val cooled off along about dinnertime last night,
did an abrupt about-face, emerged from her suicidal funk
all loving and cheerful. "Why do I do that to you?" she
asked rhetorically over and over, serving up lamb
patties and sliced strawberries with cream. For the
rest of the evening I allowed myself to indulge the
Pollyannaish delusion that from here on out until she
splits she'll spare me and herself and Danny and the
folks downstairs and next door and elsewhere on the
block and beyond -- including the staff at the Bulldog,

516

the members of the S.F. Alliance, etc. -- any further
bitter harangues and wild scenes.

For her piece de resistance before the about-face
she closed herself in the living-room closet. I found
her huddled there with a towel over her head fingering
razor blades. At midnight she trimmed my hair,
intentionally restoring it to something like the way it
was when we met. (Deja-vu swept in as she went at it:
for a moment it was Jang snipping away in that identical
spot in the kitchen shortly before we broke up last
year.) In the morning I found scales of her dried shit
clinging to my cock. -- All of which brings to mind a
Walker Percy phrase about the malady of the times,
existential despair, despair so enshrouding you don't
even know you're trapped in it (the exact quote, I've
lost it).

One thing I do know: if I have any sense, I'll
impose a period of sexual/romantic abstention upon
myself after she leaves. I'll read, write, draw,
explore the city, see what I can learn from this latest
failure and loss, try to regain my balance and reset my
bearings, rather than paper over the pain of the breakup
with some new infatuation.

*

The Bulldog offers great possibilities. By
sheerest chance I've stumbled into a situation ripe with
potential, one where it might really be possible to make
a significant difference. As noted before, I'm
convinced this city hungers for a first-class
"alternative" paper on the order of the Freep and the
Voice. Now I'd add that the Bulldog already has the
framework in place to become that paper. All it needs
is a shove in the right direction and then a lot of hard
work. It could be the country's first "responsible"
alternative paper focusing on political news and
investigative reporting (the Voice and the Freep both
emphasize cultural news and as a rule eschew real
political and investigative reporting, i.e. muckraking).
And surely there's no American city -- no city anywhere
in the world -- that offers more fertile ground for such

517

a paper. The potential is truly awesome; I lapse into
gibbering incoherence just thinking about it.
                    *   *
     It's a terrible irony, things going so well for
both of us separately when we're further apart than ever
before. It's all "incomprehensible," Val says, still
flush from the triumph of her creative-writing class,
where the teacher described her short story "Madame
Dussault" as "the best I've seen this semester" and her
poetry again drew accolades: "It oughta be published."
     Likewise for me: I spent the day talking with radio
news people and brainstorming with Mike about ways to
improve the Bulldog. My work on the new issue impressed
him enough that he's authorized me to plunge ahead with,
first, making the most of whatever opportunities KRMA
offers, and, second, seeking out first-rate writers and
reviewers for an expanded "back of the book" section.
In other words, I have a golden opportunity to help
bring into existence the kind of newspaper I was writing
about in here earlier today.
     I'd be more enthused about the project, admittedly,
if Mike himself were. But over the years he's seen too
many grand hopes and plans fizzle to allow himself to
get majorly worked up over this one. Under the
circumstances I feel I did well to gain the somewhat
begrudging support he did offer. Now it's up to me to
produce. This is as it should be, wise leadership on
Mike's part -- and tomorrow I'll start zeroing in on the
task. (A third matter I'll be thinking about: how can
the Bulldog maximize its return from the current issue,
or, as a corollary, how can we come up with the thirty-
five hundred bucks necessary to finance the next issue?)
     But right now all of that has receded and Val and I
are struggling over my failure to respond as she'd like
to her classroom triumphs. I'm proud of her but under
the circumstances I feel I can't get too involved or let
myself celebrate with her too much, and she's tearing
her heart out over this.
     At the Bulldog I've been given my own key to the
office and my own cubbyhole in the big wooden mailbox in

518

the front lobby: significant steps.

Tuesday 25
     This morning I begin paying the price for
concentrating so fiercely on the Merc and now the
Bulldog -- tackling a thousand tiny tasks here at 1616 I
should've taken care of long ago. Patching the gas pipe
leading to my heater, for example. Packing still more
of Rob's things and sending them off. Repairing the
doorframe for the blue room (the one I splintered to
retrieve this journal at the time of Jang's surprise
visit -- two weeks ago now). Cleaning up. Reorienting.
Then this afternoon I'll polish up my "presentation" on
the Bulldog as best I can and try it out on KRMA.
     If nothing important comes up in the meantime I'll
visit Garnett on Thursday. The prodigal returns -- to a
chorus of jeers and catcalls, no doubt. What's my
thanks been for the months of virtually nonstop work?
Other than Sid's visit, nothing: not a single word. Not
the merest postcard. In all of Merino County I'd like
to see only a few people: Sid, Evan, Tom, Claire, Holly,
Marcelle and the other Aguilars. Actually my main
reason for going up there would be to pick up my
"captain's cap" (and maybe the leather pants that were
promised me) at Donna's.
     Val cried softly in bed this morning. Instead of
celebrating her school triumphs she's had to accept my
"indifference" to her. It's a sorry and sorrowful
scene, extremely trying for both of us, the sooner ended
the better.
     It's not such a good feeling to look back and see
you've not only made a mess of your own life but you've
helped several others do the same with theirs.
     Then again the perspective's not the best from
here, this point at this time.
     What must I do to be able to live right? Well, for
starters, cast off as many as possible of the bad habits
I've picked up over a period of twenty-eight years.
Change directions, change costumes, begin anew. And

519

this time try harder to disclose more of what others say
they want to know of the whole truth as I see it even
when it's inconvenient and/or painful to myself and/or
the others to reveal it -- see what kind of trouble a
major change like that gets me into and whether it's
worse (as I fear) or better than what I've reaped
lately.

*   *

Speaking of changes, here's something Mike M. told
Monica: "Give Glen lots of encouragement, but I don't
think we're going to change at all."

That's what I'm up against. Mike's feet aren't set
in concrete, but neither is he jumping for joy (if he
did, everyone would know because the building would
shake). As he says over and over, he's seen too many
"great opportunities" slip away. So long and hard has
he struggled to keep the Bulldog alive and to build it
to its present state that he tends to be overprotective
and overskeptical. Yet this isn't so bad for me,
because it's an attitude that goads me into coming up
with new ideas. It also makes me work harder.
Sometimes I need to be goaded, no doubt about it. With
the pressure off and my points made, I tend to slack off
too much or be distracted too easily -- and then start
looking for others to goad me, I guess -- as I suppose I
must've been doing when I found Val.

For me it's tough work serving as a talent scout
and PR man, a drum-beater, but that's essentially what
I'll have to do to bring off any major change at the
Bulldog. I firmly believe it can be done. But do I
have the motivation to do it? Now that Mike has stated
his view I'm certainly more motivated than before. But
the batteries are low. To pull this off I'll have to
become a whirling dervish. Coax KRMA to enter into a
mutual aid pact with us. Persuade other stations to
give us some regular play. Tie all this in with a
subscription drive, maybe a fund-raising drive. Beat
the bushes for foundation help. Seek out individuals
who might pitch in voluntarily -- time, money, services.
Plaster stickers and posters everywhere. Devise a few

outlandish publicity stunts. See to it everyone's "whooping up the Bulldog."

Shit: can I really do all this? Even a small fraction of it? I'm much more comfortable holed up in out-of-the-way cafes scribbling about my fantasies and my crazed love life. If I were so good at conjuring world-beating newspapers out of thin air surely I would've already come up with a few by now (not that I'm saying my self-published fifth-grade rag should count for nothing). For that matter if I were such a dynamite writer I'd surely have churned out some half-decent fiction by now. Of course I'm well aware approximately ninety-eight percent of all newspaper reporters and editors, whether counterculture or not, have a similar debilitating suspicion about their own churnings-out or the lack thereof.

Well, so anyway, here's my chance to help bring into being a great "alternative" newspaper. Probably I'll never have another opportunity like this. Time to see what I'm made of. I succeed and I've done something valuable. Who knows, maybe I've set myself up with a minimum-wage, maximum-hours job for life. I fail and I'm right where I was before, no worse off, except a year or two older and bereft of a few more illusions -- but so what. If I'm going to do this Bulldog trip at all, it should be with bells and whistles, all stops out.

Wednesday 26

After playing just two games of pickup three-on-three my vision's shaky and so's my writing hand. But my hair needs to dry and a kind of elation clamors to express itself, so: let it happen.

Take quick stock. I'm twenty-eight, short just three months and four days of turning twenty-nine (starting my thirtieth year), shoulder-length hair, several pounds over the top of my normal weight range (though the excess isn't all that visible, even to my own hypercritical eye), sporting somewhat dirty white

corduroy pants, cowboy boots with heels worn into the
shape of a collapsed upside-down Bucky Fuller dome,
ratty blue work shirt, red-and-black Chavez Thunderbird
medallion, miniature "Free the People" button, clean-
shaven, short of breath after a few trips up and down
the B-ball court, teeth full of hidden holes that may
soon become conspicuous and painful, but otherwise in
fairly good physical condition, aburst with energy,
ready.

    (One thing gnawing away at my self-respect these
days is my unchanging public image. It's no longer even
close to outrageous. It seems to be verging on
anachronism. Yet to push it any further is to cross the
border into true freakiness, which I'm loath to do,
being at heart a seeker of respect. What I really need
right now is the aforementioned pair of leather pants
from Donna.)

    Why elated? Two good things happened at the
Bulldog. First, I succeeded in prying a thirty-
thousand-name address list out of the Ari Bresker/S.F.
Alliance people and in convincing Mike we should send
out a subscription mailer to every single name on that
list, hang the expense, because this is precisely the
group that would go for the Bulldog and therefore the
mailing would surely pay for itself and then some (maybe
even pay for the moon). So Monica and I have now
designed a funky mailer for that very purpose.

    Better still, Mike asked me to write the big
earthquake story to which we'll devote four to six pages
in the next issue. In fact, I was the one who proposed
that we do the story. Good idea, Glen! Actually it's a
natural, as I knew the minute I saw the BBC's "The City
That Waits to Die" at an S.F. Alliance meeting last
night. So powerfully does this film document the ever-
increasing likelihood of another catastrophic S.F.
earthquake that it's been banned from the airwaves in
California (not officially, of course, but by a
consortium of realtors and big businesses that could be
hurt by wide exposure of the film -- they simply bought
all the rights to it; but then the Alliance somehow got

[Living with Valerie]

ahold of a copy of it).

Finally, I've lined up the first prospective reviewer for the revitalized back-of-the-book, Craig Owen, twenty-five-year-old artist, very freaky I'm told and what's more an outasight writer.

The KRMA deal is still simmering, but the successes with these other matters have boosted my confidence. Also, I'm excited by the prospect of helping to edit a Bulldog primer on politics in San Francisco. Mike has been wanting to do such a book for ages and much of the content is already in hand, but he simply hasn't had the time and energy to whip it into shape. I've suggested we retitle it "San Francisco Survival Kit."

Other things:

** Jang called and wanted to visit me at the Bulldog office and I had to put her off. "Yes, you're not my man anymore," she said.

** Mike praised my Hetch Hetchy story, calling it "a minor classic."

** In a dream I rode on the forty-knot ocean liner United States and slid down the trunk of a falling tree.

** Lousy, lousy balling last night with Val, who vacillates from acrimony to tears to resignation to last-ditch attempts to win me back: an exhausting melange to deal with. The one thing she does not do is say yes, she understands why we have to start over in establishing a basic trust between us and show some real enthusiasm about it while also working hard at it.

** Meanwhile another gigantic story breaks out in Merino County: race riots at Fleming AFB. They're grabbing headlines across the country. Unfortunately by the time the Bulldog's ready to go to press again they'll almost certainly be ancient history. I'm still hoping to do a story on them for the Bulldog, but with all the other responsibilities I've taken on it's unlikely I'll be able to squeeze it in.

** And in New Haven charges are dismissed against Black Panther Bobby Seale. If this keeps up I may experience a rebirth of faith in the Movement -- i.e., that there still is one.

Thursday 27
     Lassitude's built into today. The fog's so thick
it's condensing and making everything glisten. I'm
stiff from hoops at the JCC yesterday. Soon I leave for
Garnett.
     I've been weighing the question of whether to tell
Val I'm going up there. It's probably best not to. At
this point what difference could her knowing possibly
make? She's diligently boning up on G.E. Moore in
preparation for tomorrow's philosophy exam -- the table
here at Mac's is piled high with her books and papers.
"My brain itches," she says. A moment ago a spell of
vertigo struck her as she was walking to the restroom
and she was convinced an earthquake had struck -- it
reminded me of Aki J.'s similar spells four years ago
before her brain tumor was supposedly diagnosed (but
that turned out to be another little fib of hers aided
by a great acting job).
     What's really important, though, is that Val's exam
tomorrow is her last one (it's coming much earlier than
she'd expected and I'd dared to hope). After that
she'll be looking for an apartment and moving out,
hopefully before the end of this month -- five days from
now -- so I can find someone else to sublet to for the
full month of June. As soon as it seems safe to do so
I'll be putting up a "Room for Rent" sign on the Bulldog
bulletin board. It doesn't matter too much who
responds, male or female, young or old, so long as he or
she is relatively quiet. At first blush I'd prefer a
funky female, but, rethinking, perhaps a reclusive male
would be better, a Bulldog freelancer perhaps, someone
with not just a good head but a level one. (Suddenly I
flash on the possibility I'm doing this whole Bulldog
trip to please Briana, or rather to refute her
contention that I'm letting my mind go to waste. But
then Val has contended likewise and a great deal more
forcefully, and she thinks my working for the Bulldog is
proof my deterioration is accelerating.)

[Living with Valerie]

She leans over and offers up her lips. Her new
form-fitting green pants. At night when she undresses
she's taken to taunting me with her breasts, flashing
them stripper-like, those fine, firm, well-shaped
protuberances, looking especially good now with her tan
setting off their whiteness and this in turn setting off
the pinkish-brown of her ultra-tender nipples. From
poring over my journal she knows how much I like her
breasts (and also about Jang's and Briana's lesser
endowments in that area) and so she leans over me as I
sit in my chair and gently rubs them against my face.
She's looking exceptionally fine these days, her skin
dark and glowing, belly flat, thighs and ass and back
more magnificent than ever thanks to dance and gymnastic
workouts at State: the kind of woman you drool over, so
incredibly sexy, those full lips, those big "sloe" eyes,
that long black flowing hair, that shapely robust body,
those rippling muscles, those curves galore -- a body of
sensual substance, strength, you just know she'll fuck
like crazy and return the best you have -- and then you
go to bed with her and what massive disappointment!
    Valoshka's an exotic centerfold and then some, lush
and voluptuous to look at, perfection itself, but not to
be touched, or at least not by one who touches as I do.

*   *

The Garnett trip hasn't happened. Instead I'm
holed up at the MDR in North Beach staring out the
window at a car that may be Briana's. Same make, same
color, same everything as far as I can see, although
nothing positively identifies it as hers. In fact I
hope it isn't hers: two pairs of men's boots stand on
newspapers spread atop the backseat. Could be they're
Terry's (for want of recent news of other candidates).
    No doubt about it: Briana still occupies a corner
of my heart. She refuses to be dislodged. I see that
car and my blood starts pounding. I search madly for a
parking place, rush through several old haunts where I
hope to bump into her, scrutinize the car so closely I
arm myself with a story about being a prospective buyer
just in case anyone's suspicious. Now I wait. If she

525

comes up, and if she's alone, I'll hail her as if I just
happened to be passing by at that moment. Can't wait
too long, though, because I have ad copy to write.

All of a sudden Mike has taken up my volunteer
scheme with a vengeance. By Monday we're to have flyers
out to all the local colleges pushing a Bay Bulldog
Summer Project along the lines of Nader's Raiders -- a
task force of unpaid "citizen journalists" looking into
various local sloughs of corruption and malfeasance.
Mike, Dave, and I will each captain a team. Mike fears
sycophants, being overrun by do-nothing types, lawsuits
-- he's cynical as hell -- but the essential thing is
he's willing to move. The fire's lit: now it's a matter
of keeping it burning high.

My one regret is I let slip a quasi I-told-you-so
and became too bold in my joshing with him. I've got to
tone that down. I'm in danger of becoming perceived as
an obnoxious, overly ambitious and overly aggressive
type bent on taking over the paper. I think several
people already may have suspicions along these lines.

All this came up after I'd decided to postpone my
Garnett trip; it didn't cause the postponement. That
happened because I followed the dictates of my aching
cock. Val annoyed the hell out of me with an absurd
argument about G.E. Moore and -- my old college bete
noire -- "analytic philosophy," so-called, in general.
Later I apologized, I thought so she'd be able to study,
but I found myself with a gargantuan hard-on, she took
note and fondled it, and we wound up getting it on in
bed beneath speakers blasting Long John Baldry's "Don't
Lay No Boogie Woogie on the King of Rock'N Roll." The
balling was good too, relatively, for us, for a change,
so immediately we blew it by going a second round which
wound up disastrously with both of us failing to get off
("I just can't keep up," she groaned). All that took
hours and left me discouraged, listless, lacking the
energy to embark on the Garnett trip with so much still
to do here. Instead I dragged myself down to the
Bulldog office, where my spirits gradually revived.

Well, fuck, it's been two hours, darkness has

526

fallen, I can barely make out the car I suspect is
Briana's. But it's definitely still there. She shows
no sign of appearing, and I have other things to do, and
besides it's just as well, I shouldn't try to see her
until the next issue of the Bulldog is out and I'm free
of all taints involving other women (not forgetting,
though, the chances are good of eventually meeting
someone with compatible political and cultural views
through the Bulldog if I can only be patient enough).

Saturday 29 (X:28)
     All seems peaceful here as I sit in Mike's armchair
on a Saturday afternoon suddenly turned sunny. But it's
not peaceful. Valerie threw another nasty scene this
morning -- locking herself in the L.C., lighting stray
pages of the Bulldog on fire with matches, partially
shredding one volume of the journal (mine -- the
infamous V.22 from last summer), later dashing madly
after me as I drove away. My back and stomach are
covered with scratches, my left elbow is bruised and
bloodied, V.22's a mess -- but I'm hoping I'll be able
to patch it up with bookbinder tape.
     It all began after her last exam yesterday, built
up last night, exploded in bed. "Touch me in unsexual
ways only," she hissed. Of course my response was to
completely stop touching her. Result: two hours of
vicious attacks. This morning the fireworks started up
again when I caught her in the act of reading this
journal volume right here. Wrestling to get it back.
Blood (mine) on the sheets from where one of her rings
ripped into my left forearm.
     Where it stands now (after two calls): she's agreed
to leave by Tuesday, which is June 1, at the latest.
Meanwhile I've pledged to be "kind" to her. Right now
she's waiting to meet me at the MDR at eight o'clock. I
said I'd "do my best" to overcome my fury and be there.
     I don't know whether I can bear the prospect of
another horrific night. She's pulled out the final
stops now: she tears up my journals, mocks my

presumption to think I'm a writer, hints maliciously I'm
gay and that's why our sex is often so bad. To say
nothing of her run-of-the-mill charges: I'm a male
chauvinist, incapable of love, stuck in a "neurotic
narcissistic" cycle, shallow, uncaring, manipulative,
monstrous; everything I say and do is "in subtle ways"
an attempt to gain or maintain power over others; I'm a
control freak and actually feel nothing at all myself.

The easy thing to do is concede there's truth in
much of what she says. There is. Of course! What's
hard is, on the one hand, to prevent my awareness of
this from completely crippling me, and, on the other, to
keep in mind that these charges greatly exaggerate my
various failures with her and in many cases stem from
her own bitterness and grief and derangement, much of
which actually has little to do with me except that I
happen to be around. She needs help on an extended
basis, and this time I'm utterly incapable of doing the
noble thing and trying to supply it myself. She's
determined to lay bare the allegedly cruel inner
workings of my soul, as she sees things, and to do this
she's willing to take any necessary measure no matter
how shameless and cruel. Her basic strategy is to
refuse all face-saving gestures and compromises. Pride
means nothing to her right now.

Her main tactical aim is to trap me in such ways
that I must either act hideously or give in to her
demands. Either love her, accept her, and take her into
my complete confidence, or be a monster. No other
choices exist. (Except, of course, when she has
something she wants to do or must do, such as going off
to take her exams; then she's willing to strike
compromises and abide by a truce).

I simply can't live any longer with this state of
affairs. Either I hate myself for treating her badly or
I hate myself for caving in to her outrageous demands.
Consequently I try to flee, to banish the terrible
dilemma from my mind. But she also makes that
impossible by threatening -- just as before -- to do
horrible things if I take off. Suicide, burning down

528

the house -- we both know the drill so well by now all
she has to say is "You know what I mean." I must face
the dilemma. But I can't. Instead I'm gradually dying
inside, the inner light is extinguishing, I'm once again
becoming a zombie. She's crippling me. How many years
will it take to overcome the effects of these tumultuous
months with Val? To what lengths will I be driven now
to persuade myself I can love again? If I resist going
to those lengths (as of course I must try to do because
of the painful consequences for myself as well as others
if I don't) will I ever be able to drag myself from
behind the walls of stoicism I must build?

Or is all this merely self-indulgence -- Glen
wallowing in his love of melodrama?

I try to feel something for what Val's going
through now and I can't. This really frightens me. All
I can feel is my own misery. For all I care she can do
just as she threatened and stick her head in the oven
like Sylvia Plath (whom she's been reading lately -- the
very last poet she should be reading at this point --
and by the way, her best writing often reminds me and
her classmates and her instructor as well of "Ariel").

If it weren't for Val, meanwhile, I'd feel exultant
(the old story). Thursday after I left the house my tax
refund arrived in the mail. $392: I'm flabbergasted.
I'd persuaded myself they'd turn me down for sure.
"Something always happens to save you," Val grumped,
full of resentment, of course, when I showed her the
check yesterday. And then not thirty minutes later Mike
sheepishly handed me a check for twenty-five bucks.

"I know it's not much," he said, "but it's the best
we can do right now. There'll be another twenty-five
next week."

Well, I'd been hoping for a little more, and also
fearing I wouldn't be paid at all, and the truth is I
was absolutely delighted because this is the first time
in my entire life I've been paid specifically for
something I've written (the first twenty-five was for
the Hetch Hetchy article; the second will be for
editing). So now I'm a professional writer!

[Have Mercy]

    Yesterday afternoon this newly anointed highly
evolved being devoted four hours to scribbling by hand
the sentence "Please subscribe now and help us survive
and grow" on each and every one of two thousand direct-
mail pieces to be sent to contributors to good-guy
antiwar liberal Jack Morrison's mayoral campaign.
    Well, a trapezoid of sun climbs the far wall toward
the framed, yellowing Bay Bulldog front pages ("Draft
Boards -- A Bulldog Probe") and the time for deciding
whether to meet Val rapidly approaches. She'll be
moving out Tuesday. Maybe I can swallow a few more days
of humiliation and degradation. I recall how lovely she
looked in profile as she stood on a rock in the yard and
I glared at her from the L.C. -- such a beautifully
proportioned, shapely, perky-assed, athletic, robust
young beauty in her new green corduroy bells (tight as a
glove), white halter top, bare midriff, yellow jacket,
flowing waist-length black hair, boots with red and blue
stars sparkling. Then I shudder to think of her acid
tone as (earlier) I kissed her breasts and she coldly
directed me to touch her only in "unsexual ways."
    Yes, I'll go.

Sunday 30
    On a street bench outside Park N Shop. Another
deadly day. Pestilential. In bed late at night with
the lights out Val and I cling to each other, but the
rest of the time we can barely contain our fury. Last
night in the L.C. outside Caffe Trieste I rebuffed her
halfhearted and wholly inadequate attempts at apology
and then we squabbled furiously over the $275 she by her
own insistence blew on us and the skins for my jacket
this past winter (if it was really that much, which I
doubt) but now insists she "loaned" me and wants back.
Incensed by her sudden display of indignation, I lashed
out at her until she crumpled on the seat, "not feeling
well," and then we went home with tensions still high
and nothing really resolved.
    If I don't "repay" that money she won't move out,

she says, knowing perfectly well I can't afford to do it
(the tax refund will just barely catch me up on the L.C.
payments and repay the emergency loan from home). Then
she threatens to stay on indefinitely if I don't help
her find another place, by which she means do her exact
bidding, driving her around whenever she wants and
wherever she wants and for as long as she wants.
There's always another threat, another excuse. Nor does
she merely request or ask for these things; rather she
demands them as her right, lacing her fulminations with
vicious sophistries which, now, I tear into every bit as
viciously. Later she apologizes: "I'm not really all
that bad." Today I noticed my photo box occupying a new
spot in the closet and discovered she'd removed all the
many pictures of herself, including the ones in which I
or Barb or Rob or Al or someone else appears with her.
She sheepishly admitted doing it, but wouldn't say why.
I guess I really shouldn't need to ask.

    Time drags on. At best we manufacture artificial
smiles, quickly looking away. These past few months
have been so excruciatingly painful, so acrimonious, all
chances of a post-move-out reconciliation have died. "I
want to go back to France!" she wailed last night. Her
mother at age seventeen loved an older Vietnamese man
(the father of her first two kids) who wouldn't marry
her because of her lowly foreign origins and she "cried
for the next twenty years and then never cried again."
Now Val says grimly she's learned how men are, all men
-- they're just like her mama warned her -- and swears
she'll never again make the mistake of loving one.

6

Monday 31
    It's Memorial Day, the papers are ablaze with the
usual shameless displays of triumphalist nationalistic
"patriotism," and Valerie and I are about to go
apartment-hunting. Right now we're procrastinating at
Mac's Grill: she scribbles with, as always, fanatical

intensity while I read the Chronicle from the first
trivial piece to the last and then pull out my own pen.

At the next table a longhaired Cawk dude and his
foxy Japanese ol' lady ("Junko," I overhear), both
dressed hip style and carrying similar expensive
cameras, look warmly if also quizzically upon the two of
us (both now whaling away in our identical black
sketchbooks). Who knows: had the four of us somehow met
back in better days we might've become friends. We
might even have double-dated or something.

For Val and me there will be no more friendships as
a couple -- not even one between ourselves. It's now
become glaringly evident we'll be unable to part ways
gracefully or amicably. The end approaches inexorably,
but slowly, terribly, like the final stages of terminal
cancer (e.g., her great aunt's, allegedly caused by her,
Val's, bad behavior -- and from what I've seen, she just
might've been capable of the feat).

Two incidents are griping me at the moment, both of
the type that have alienated me from her almost from the
day we met. Last night, after either coldly ignoring me
or treating me contemptuously all evening, she suddenly
burst into tears in bed and demanded I hold her, at the
same time chewing me out for not doing it sooner. She
couldn't comprehend that her nightlong -- daylong really
-- or I could say yearlong, as of one month from now --
rejection of all conciliatory efforts, and now the
acrimonious demand, made it impossible for me to express
any remaining positive feelings toward her.

Then this morning she suddenly disinterred her old
grudge about my not bringing her breakfast in bed. Yet
when the alarm went off she'd leapt up, giving me no
opportunity whatsoever to minister to her whims even if
I'd wanted to or intended to. (It's almost always been
this way in the current era: she has to get up first to
go to class, and also to get Danny ready for the
babysitter if he's with us. Then I drive her to State,
arising an hour or two earlier than I otherwise
would've. She can't recognize a fair trade-off here.)

So now she's wearing her sexy red apartment-hunting

minidress -- which she made herself not long before we met -- and glancing perfunctorily through the rental classifieds (nothing there will be good enough for her, I guarantee it).

Earlier, just before coming in here, I stopped by the post office two doors up the street to mail an anniversary card to Mother and Dad. They'll be celebrating -- I presume celebrating -- their thirtieth wedding anniversary on the 3rd, which is Thursday, which means there's at least a chance the card will arrive in time. Whenever it appears, they'll find, in addition to a few predictable banalities from me, a message from Val scrawled in barely decipherable purple ink on the back flap of the envelope: "Congratulations on 30 years! -- Valerie." She was highly displeased -- or pretended to be -- that I hadn't asked her to write something on the card itself before sealing the flap.

-- The friendly mixed couple at the next table just took off, the guy leaning in to say, harmlessly enough, "Now don't work too hard, you two." Val glared silently and balefully back as if ready to bite his head off.

Why? Why does she find it necessary to make everyone else -- strangers even -- pay for her own suffering? Will it always be like this? For the rest of her life?

I think back to my dream of last night, something about a huge jetliner exploding upon takeoff. I was miraculously thrown clear, but Lyndon Johnson, who was also aboard, was incinerated. Don't know how to interpret it, what it might portend, if anything, but I'll say this much: I'm happy to think the gods will soon be granting me -- if my luck holds -- another chance to loll mindlessly in bed in the mornings and to ponder my dreams at length, if I want to, upon waking.

Time to pull the plug here. Might as well circle the whole entry and write a big CBK next to it. Might as well do that to myself also, to her, to us. (That's "can be killed," yeah.)

*   *

It's only appropriate that the last full day of our

stormy time together (well, she says it's the last full
day and I sure do want to believe her) -- appropriate
that this day, today, should also be the most harrowing,
most debilitating, most disgusting yet. What began as a
search for an apartment for her wound up with two cops
frisking me on suspicion of rape, with Valerie wailing
and shrieking and literally foaming at the mouth in the
L.C. (we were parked at the Mt. Moraga overlook maybe a
hundred and fifty feet uphill from 1616). Eventually
the cops backed off, advising me to take her to Langley-
Porter for a sedative and to "get yourself a new girl,
buddy." As Val shrieked (falsely) about my "beating"
her, one of the cops took me aside and suggested I
should beat her more. "Women are like dogs," he
observed. The pig.

     I hadn't been beating her. I did wrestle her down
in the seat and clamp a hand over her mouth when she
refused to stop her sudden outburst of piercingly loud
howling shrieks and screams. So I felt bad enough. Her
efforts to manipulate and degrade me were so flagrant,
so incendiary, so infuriating, that I vowed I wouldn't
yield this time. In the end, of course, I did yield,
rather than deliver her to the mental ward -- which I
consider the penultimate no-no, exceeded only by calling
in the cops (who summoned them in this case I'll
probably never know) -- and for the rest of the
afternoon and evening I therefore had to endure a
cascade of incredibly virulent verbal abuse from Val,
until unaccountably something I said touched her and she
shut it off in an instant (I told her I'd most likely be
going into isolation after she left, that I wanted
nothing more to do with women "because I know I can only
hurt them the way I am now").

     There's much more to be said, all of it ugly, but
at this moment she's kneeling on the floor next to me,
glaring accusatorily, tears streaming down her cheeks,
fingernails gouging into my thighs, and if I don't stop
writing she'll undoubtedly launch a new attack...which
she'll almost certainly do anyway.

534

[Living with Valerie]

JUNE

1

Tuesday 1

Telegraph Avenue, Berkeley, for my money still the liveliest and most interesting ten-block stretch west of just about anywhere. I'm stopping at every telephone pole to add my two cents' worth, the Bulldog's "Help Wanted" poster (which Monica designed and I wrote the copy for). Helluva lot of telephone poles along Telegraph, and each one's matted so thickly with handbills the Bulldog's staples sometimes pop right back out. It's almost as if a reactionary gremlin were stationed inside the pole to eject them. In Berkeley!

I'm feeling pretty good, pretty jaunty, striding along on my righteous mission. The Valerie fiasco I'm pushing as far from consciousness as possible. Yesterday, my god, I can hardly bear to think about it. Chauffeuring her up and down the streets of the Inner and Outer Sunset and even parts of the Richmond in search of a place for her to live. Barricading myself in a cafe bathroom to escape her for a few minutes. Eyes misting over from the anguish of trying to calm her rampaging fears ("Tell me one thing I can look forward to in my life!"). And then at bedtime self-reproachfully yielding to her pleas to "make love one last time," her atop but not in the usual way, her back pressing against my stomach and chest, her hair tenting my face as she leaned back on her elbows, and then both of us climaxing in a mighty explosion I didn't even want to happen because I figured if we could prolong the act indefinitely, all night if possible, or until she passed out from exhaustion (she's scarcely slept in a week), at least for that period I wouldn't be subject to more vicious harangues in which she knows all the buttons to push to maximize the pain.

For unknown reasons she let me get out of the house this morning -- with only a few muttered nasty remarks -- and now I can at least hope she'll be gone when I return home. Which will be after an Intersection poetry reading/reception that, who knows, Briana may attend, with Terry of course, which would be a trip -- face-to-face at last!   ---

Wednesday 2

Jolly Friar. I'm here not because I particularly want to be, but because I don't want to go home and I can't think of any other place to be except Woodstock right across the street. Last night Valoshka surprised me with a brave burst of compassion and enthusiasm (she even returned all the photos she stole from my box except for a few of herself alone which she found unflattering and ripped up) but today she called me at the office and opened the floodgates on a new deluge of self-pity and woe, followed by shrieking gales of bitter accusations, and the last anchor gave way on my tolerance. I can't face her.

That's not the only thing troubling me. Talking with Alan Ramsay of KRMA I felt vapid and tongue-tied, useless, stupid (even though the news is good: KRMA appears ready to go for the "Mutual Aid Pact" idea), and then later this evening, at the S.F. Alliance's "press screening" of "The City That Waits to Die," I felt equally punchless and dull. I'm also displeased that I let myself be overly impressed with the group of local media "celebrities" who were present for the screening -- Paul Jacobs, Herb Gold, John Wasserman -- in short, the usual suspects. Why do I find them intimidating? (The answer's obvious: in some dark chamber of my soul I must envy them. I must want to be a local media celebrity too.)

Come to think of it, it's pretty frightening that the enlightenment of San Francisco depends on this crew. A few I genuinely admire: Jacobs, Tom DeVries of KQED,

[Living with Valerie]

Ari Bresker of the SFA (S.F. Alliance) (and "hardware
merchant" as the Chron unfailingly calls him). As for
the rest, it's shameful that I should turn so meek in
their presence. But at the same time I shouldn't let my
self-reproach over this get out of hand, because that's
how I stampede myself into engaging in what Briana once
called my imbecilic role-playing games. That's one kind
of trap I'm not falling into anymore.

What else? I stapled more of the same posters,
scores of them, on telephone poles and bulletin boards
around the city itself, focusing on North Beach and the
Marina and Clement Street. Rassled with Mike about this
and that (very cautiously -- I still don't feel secure
enough at the Bulldog to rassle righteously). Struggled
to push forward my brash strategy for rescuing the
paper. At present I'm concentrating on three areas:

(1) Expanding media exposure. KRMA's the key
here, but I'm also going after other radio stations.
KPFA in Berkeley is already broadcasting our Summer
Project appeal, for example, and several others have
said they'll do so. KQED TV is the ultimate target --
as a public station it's a natural ally for the Bulldog,
just as the network TV stations are natural allies for
(and basically owned by the same giant corporations as)
the Chronicle and Examiner. But that's months off, even
years.

(2) Building a stronger base among the anti-
Manhattanization crowd. The SFA, Ari Bresker's outfit,
is central here. Over the past year or two Bresker has
tapped a huge number of people fed up with politics-as-
usual (it's his list of thirty thousand supporters
who've clipped and mailed in coupons from his full-page
ads in the San Francisco dailies that we'll be using for
our Bulldog subscription mailer if we can scrape up the
funds to do it). The SFA people have also had it with
the local corporate media -- which is to say, all the
major ones -- who oppose them editorially and promulgate
all sorts of distortions and half-truths about the
issues they're involved in (which include the war,
racism, sexism, inequality, ecology, and out-of-control

537

consumerism as well as Manhattanization -- in short, all
the right stuff). So as a result Bresker has no real
way to communicate with his own political base. Again,
it's a natural for the Bulldog; we've been raising hell
over the same issues for years.

(3) Revamping the back-of-the-book. Here it's a
matter of boosting the intellectual content and at the
same time broadening the cultural appeal of the reviews.
At present the film reviews are appallingly bad and the
book, music, media, and art reviews -- well, there are
none. In one of the international capitals of rock
music not a word on rock! I'm not pushing too hard on
this just yet, but the idea is to come up with a group
of high-powered writers who'll contribute regular
reviews to the Bulldog mostly because they share its
political stance (which also means they know they won't
be paid much). If we can sign up the reviewers, we can
attract the hip readers. With that kind of readership
we can land the lucrative music, book, and film ads --
and those ads are the keys to financial success (which
at the Bulldog means breaking even).

These are the three main thrusts. Sadly, it
appears Mike himself stands to some degree in the way of
all three. His native Iowa/Nebraska cultural
provincialism, his stubbornness (ideas are extremely
suspect unless he thinks of them first), and especially
his cynicism bred by years of struggle against
overwhelming odds -- all of these traits have made him
an obstacle to the change and growth of his own paper.
In fighting so hard to keep the paper afloat he's
trapped himself in a vision of what the public wants
that's in some ways sadly out of date and bristlingly
defensive. But: he's not a hopeless case. He does
move, even though slowly and, as it seems to me,
grudgingly. His mind isn't closed. He does listen.
One piece of evidence here is that he hasn't booted me
out.

"He'll never say anything to your face," Monica
tells me, "but I know through Peggy [her ex-sister-in-
law] that he's very impressed with what you're doing."

538

Compliments Mike passes out as rarely as kudos for Ex/Chron or PG&E. It would help a great deal if I knew I could count on his enthusiastic support for some of these projects I'm proposing. Unfortunately I'm not sure I can do that. But so long as he doesn't rope me in, I'll plunge ahead on my own. He hasn't objected too much to anything I've proposed so far.

What the paper really needs is an immediate financial shot in the arm. I wish I could think of something that would bring in a few thousand bucks right now. A KRMA appeal, maybe. Shrewd use of the Bresker mailing list.

Meanwhile I'll try to keep in mind at all times two quotes posted on the wall of Mike's office. One, from I.F. Stone, is a longtime favorite of mine:

> I felt that if one were able enough and
> had sufficient vision one could distill
> meaning, truth and even beauty from the
> swiftly flowing debris of the week's news.

The other is from a Kenneth Patchen picture-poem which was originally published in the Bulldog and I like it a lot too:

> Words gettin people crazier all the time.

Thursday 3

The outdoor deck at Zack's in Sausalito on a lazy evening. Sundown nears. The Stones' "Brown Sugar" just barely overrides the din of a hundred glass-clinking cocktail conversations, not a single one of which involves anyone brown -- or for that matter any color other than more or less pinkish white. Meanwhile metallic green seawater swells a fathom or so beneath my feet with a massive solemnity that makes the music and everything else seem trivial and out of sync (and the accuracy of this sentence depends entirely on whether a fathom is six feet, as I think is correct, or maybe it's twelve? -- which would mean I'm saying those powerful natural forces are at work twice as far away as they actually are).

[Have Mercy]

Tonight nobody I see looks very interesting. Nor
does any idea seem very appealing. Aside from taking a
stroll through a supermarket of paper products (at King
Paper) it's difficult to remember what I did in eight
hours at the Bulldog office. I just can't mobilize
myself the way I'd like with Val draining so much of my
energy.

Currently she's plugging for "another chance,"
fessing up to every crime and every fault she can think
of (whether she truly believes she committed them or
possesses them or not). She's proposing we go on living
together, this time as "soul friends." Last night she
presented me with a lengthy letter (composed in a
maniacal and arduous six hours of pecking at the
typewriter) announcing she'd seen the light and begging
for reconsideration and reconciliation. In one
extraordinary passage she attributes her demeaning
Theater of Cruelty hysterics of the past several months
to habits she fell into during the three brutal years of
her marriage, when she came to see herself as a
"motorcycle princess and dragon lady."

But the damage is already done. Her second
thoughts come too late -- by about two months, I'd say,
if not closer to three. The damage is too great.

Tonight at seven-fifteen when I didn't find her at
home I dashed off a note ("I'll be back 'not too late'")
and drove off, narrowly missing her. As I crossed
Lawton Street I glimpsed her a block to my right,
trudging home with a bag of groceries. She broke into a
trot, waving awkwardly, but I pretended not to see her
and drove on. That's how deeply I dread being around
her right now.

Earlier at the office I tried to call home in
Gatewood (collect of course) with an anniversary
greeting, but no one answered. Presumably they were out
celebrating and my card arrived on time and all's as
well as can be expected on that front.

Before that -- it's coming back now -- I found
myself placed in a godlike role. Peggy handed me a
foot-high stack of unsolicited freelance manuscripts and

540

job applications; my instructions were to select the best and send rejection slips to the rest. Suddenly I was composing brief regretful thank-yous to aspiring writers whose work reminded me painfully of my own from not so long ago -- like last week maybe. Overwritten, brash, amateurish, horribly strained: the familiar catalog of sins. One reason I felt bad about so coolly turning down all these efforts was that, if I'd been dealing face to face with the writers, I'd've been much more positive with them. If a Merino Mercury volunteer had submitted virtually any of these rejected stories we'd've run it on page one with a banner head.

And yet: I'm still not convinced the gulf between professional and talented amateur writing is all that great. I don't want to give up my cherished belief that this kind of talent is allotted to many or even most people -- that what most writers lack more than anything else is confidence, experience, connections, and, likely above all these, adequate time for development of that talent.

On the subject of women, love, romance: it's encouraging that over the past couple of days I've met two women I find attractive and well-spoken and fun to be with (one the British-born fashion designer Leslie McDevitt who's on the board at the SFA; the other Jack Simon's ol' lady Sachi Inglis who's a very fine painter -- Simon being one of Bresker's lieutenants at his hardware company, a former scholarship hoopster at UC-Berkeley and a potential friend for me, I think). At the same time I'm rattled to observe that just as I'm all but certainly headed back into the mate-hunting market I've crossed over some imaginary barrier -- namely, that I can no longer feel I have much hope of attracting a woman I'm strongly attracted to myself. At my age "promise" means less and less as accomplishment means more and more. My flop with Briana was, perhaps, the turning point in this regard. She hangs out with poets who've accomplished a lot (Robert Duncan, Michael McClure, Jack Gilbert, et al. -- not to mention the flashy rising star Terry Morton).

[Have Mercy]

Unless someone new turns up, I expect I'll again be
trying to break through to Briana. For sure she's still
got a hex on me. But I'll wait until the smoke clears
after Val moves out. Perhaps in the meantime I'll
sentence myself to a period of celibacy. A month, two
months, maybe even longer. Or maybe I should try to
show Jang a good time before she leaves in August -- but
then that might mean she wouldn't leave, which would be
unfortunate, I believe, for both of us. In any event
I'll be launching an intensive effort to break old
habits, chart new directions, accomplish new "miracles"
at the Bulldog. Get myself back into good physical
shape, become at last the person I've always wanted to
be. Why the heck not give it a shot?

Actually I'll consider myself fortunate to have
survived the Terror Spring in one piece with all major
parts and organs still in place and working properly to
my knowledge. In at least one of his works Rimbaud
shows he knows exactly what I'm talking about here: "A
Season in Hell." -- Which as it happens is a work the
Kyrielle woman herself knows quite well -- and dislikes!
"It's so childish!" (He was, after all, a full year
younger than she is now when he wrote it -- and a male!)

Friday 4
Work piles up at the Bulldog, so much of it I can
do little else late on a Friday afternoon but sit back
and gaze nervously at the teetering stacks of
manuscripts and documents. I lack the stamina to dig
into them right now. To cope with such a plethora of
widely varied chores and such huge masses of
information, not only a certain kind of mind is required
but also a certain kind of mood.

Instead I sneak over to Cal's Cafe, where the
white-haired old man washes dishes, the middle-aged lady
brooms chairs, and the young waitress, who is the old
man's granddaughter and the lady's daughter, flips
through today's Examiner while keeping an eye out for
her boyfriend who's due here any minute (all four,

542

boyfriend included, being very friendly and likable
Filipinos who speak Tagalog among themselves). Right
now I'm the only customer.

For lunch today Mike, Monica, and I hit Sam's
Sandwich Shop, a block down the Southern Pacific tracks
from the office. Mike was in top form, tossing off
ideas and commentary on a wide variety of topics as
Monica and I tried to keep our plates and cups from
blowing away in the gusts of his enthusiasm. At the
moment he's enthralled with my Summer Project proposal,
calling dozens of people around the country and mailing
them flyers, formulating a speaker program, seeking ways
to make the whole thing professional and effective. But
he lacks the time to coordinate all the details, so that
job falls to me.

Valerie, meanwhile, appears finally to have found a
way to cope with our breakup. The shrink recommended by
Langley-Porter has turned her on to Gestalt. She now
tries to identify, verbalize, demonstrate, and "take
responsibility for" her feelings. For two straight days
she's maintained a cheerful, optimistic facade; behind
it she may actually feel a bit less hopeless. Chances
are good she'll rent her new room today (on Noriega
about a mile and a half west of Funston).

Despite all this, however, being with her is still
excruciating much of the time. Instead of terror, she
now plies me with solemn inquiries about my feelings.
For instance: Exactly what was going through my mind
yesterday when I dropped her off at the shrink's office
(which is conveniently located in a private house just a
few blocks east of Mac's Grill)? Did I think about her
while I was at work? If so, precisely what were my
thoughts? She recommends, quite seriously, our
undergoing Gestalt therapy together (just as my father
and mother did, briefly). Maybe it wouldn't save us,
she concedes, but surely we could both benefit from
gaining new insights on what's gone wrong with us. For
example, therapy might equip me to cope more adroitly
with the bitterness she knows her outrageous behavior
has caused (this is what she tells me -- deadpan!).

[Have Mercy]

I'm sorry to say at times it's all I can do to keep
from laughing in her face at this last-minute burst of
well-meaning advice and lofty intentions. It's
certainly true I could use some help in dealing with the
smoldering debris Valoshka has left where my heart once
beat more or less normally, but -- go through therapy?
With her? I'd rather bed down in a pit of vipers.

What remains (assuming she doesn't relapse into
terror, which admittedly is a shaky assumption at best)
is to get her moved out. If I had my druthers I'd
gladly pay someone to do it for me, but even in her
newly hopeful and "responsible" state she's not likely
to allow this. All but certainly I'll have to go to the
mat with her at least one more time. This weekend
probably. Then, if the parting really does happen, the
nature of my problems will abruptly change. From
wartime survival to postwar mourning, grief,
reconstruction. From achieving separation to relieving
loneliness and regrets.

I don't relish confronting these "new" problems,
But just about anything would beat the old ones.

In bed, wouldn't you know it, one of our best
stints of lovemaking ever: gentle, deep, slow, swelling
to a gorgeous mutual climax whose spasms meshed
perfectly as in a Masters & Johnson demo film (not that
I've ever seen one). (And in Sausalito I was startled
to find a new Bulldog handbill affixed to the Tides
Bookstore's bulletin board with a note scrawled on it:
"I'm in Sausalito, meet you here at eight-thirty. V."
She'd spotted the L.C. parked nearby and cannily figured
I'd be checking the Tides' bulletin board to be sure a
Bulldog handbill was still up, as I do these days with
bulletin boards and high-traffic telephone poles
wherever I go. But we didn't meet until I got home.)

Saturday 5
Breakfast in the Inner Sunset: then off to the
Bulldog for a day of work, escape, maybe even adventure.
On the Honda this time. With Briana's multihued scarf

undulating in the breeze behind me and threatening to
get caught in the whirling 90 spokes whenever I slow
down (possibly perpetrating thereby a spectacular
Isadora Duncan-style public self-strangulation).

Exasperation last night finally forced me to inform
Valerie in no uncertain terms that I'll be going my own
way now. I would've spelled it out before, but the
chances of her hearing me through to the end were too
slim. This time she's listening and she's also
accepting. We slept in different rooms last night.

When I went in to say goodnight she was sitting
cross-legged on the bed staring down at a note she'd
written herself. "Be strong," said the part I could
see. I pray she will be. And I pray I will be also.
She still hasn't found an apartment (yesterday's
prospect having fallen through), but she's looking
diligently. Today -- five days after she promised to be
out of the Castle -- her luck may finally change.

It's a gorgeous Saturday. Lovely swirls of fog
like Christmas angel's hair cling to the bay as seen
from the Funston windows; everywhere else a deep clear
cerulean prevails. It's the perfect kind of day for
picnicking in the fuchsia garden at Golden Gate Park
with, say, a Briana. Or a Leslie McDevitt (to invoke
another fantasy). In reality, though, the only kind of
romance that's open to me is the cinematic kind. Cocks
and cunts at the O'Farrell, perhaps. Or maybe I'll just
become a vagrant on the what's-happening circuit. Peer
darkly from a secluded corner in a body shop. The
prospects arc virtually nil but the variant forms of
nullity numerous.

*   *

Home again. It's late, past two, Tony's coughing
downstairs, and it seems tonight will be the first in
quite some time I'll be sleeping alone in an otherwise
empty apartment. When I got here a short while ago I
found the place resoundingly empty -- not even a note.
Val's things are all still here as far as I can tell,
the dinner leftovers are still in the fridge (including
an uncooked pork chop apparently meant for me and a bowl

of sliced strawberries I've already pretty much
demolished). The inescapable inference is that she sent
Danny off to the babysitter and is out with someone else
tonight. I can think of no other possibility: she
didn't find a place today, all of her hangouts are
closed by now, and (lamentably) she no longer has any
friends.

Well, I can scarcely blame her -- but neither can I
pretend it doesn't hurt (though I'll do exactly this to
her face; I'll even try not to mention her absence). My
feelings for her are such a stew (especially right now)
of bitterness, jealousy, regret, disgust, and the usual
grudging admiration for her fierce fighting spirit. My
hope is I'll be able to get away in the morning without
having to endure a confrontation. She may straggle in
noisily at six a.m. in a state of sleazy fucked-out
dishabille as she did that other time (after her night
with the "gentle and insatiable North Beach lover") and
vent her self-disgust and despair in the form of an all-
out attack.

Today was slightly less a bummer than expected.
Here's what I did:
   ** Took some sun on the roof of the auto-repair
garage next to the Bulldog offices -- it's accessible
through a Bulldog window -- and read Kropotkin until Val
called at four (we tried to out-apathy each other and
were off the phone in under a minute).
   ** Savored a lamb-chop dinner alone at the U.S.
Restaurant (first time by myself there ever) while
reading moldy back issues of the Bulldog.
   ** Broke the leg of an ancient wooden chair while
flipping through a stack of books on San Francisco and
California history in the basement at City Lights,
leaning back too far to stretch and shake myself awake
after starting to nod out (the chair itself possibly
being of greater historical interest than the books --
for surely a Kerouac or Ginsberg or Burroughs sat on it
at some point, if only to pose for a spread on the Beats
in, say, Look Magazine).
   ** Paid a return visit to the Pierce Street Annex,

546

the one body shop in town that's actually yielded up a
body for me (the Henry Miller-loving stewardess Celeste
some sixteen months ago), but the band was lousy and the
women unappealing and/or uninterested.

Sunday 6
    Imprinted on the soft red fabric of my pants:
hundreds of small indentations like pebbles in reverse.
From lying on the gravelly roof of Wendt's Foreign Car
Repair Shop. Second day in a row. Hard by the remains
of a wind-ravaged Bay Bulldog sign that once stood
proudly on the roof of the ramshackle three-story
"Bulldog Building" next door which, on this splendid
Sunday afternoon, is empty save for me, except that, of
course, I'm now over here. And I'm thinking it must've
been quite a storm -- last November, Monica told me:
right at the peak of the Briana crisis for me -- quite a
storm, I say, to blow the sign this far.
    I'm gradually recovering from a session of pickup
hoops at the JCC. What deplorable physical shape I'm
in! Thirty minutes completely exhausted me. This can
be at least partly attributed, however, to my shortage
of sleep last night. I got four hours at most. Didn't
turn off the light until after four and then dozed
lightly, leaping up several times because I thought I
heard Val approaching the house (and I wanted to get a
look, if possible, at whoever'd brought her home).
    She never did show up. I left at nine o'clock,
ostensibly to avoid her, but I kept a sharp eye out for
her as I drove to Mac's Grill and then, while there,
slogged through the entire double-backed Sunday Ex/Chron
(in Bulldog lingo) with a strange premonition she would
soon appear. But no Val. I did think of several non-
sexual things she might have done last night (visited
her mother in Sacramento, stayed with her brother here,
rented a motel room somewhere alone) but balling someone
new still seemed, and seems, by far the likeliest. Nor
is it improbable she'll continue doing whatever it is
she really was up to, or things like it, until she

547

finally does move out. Who knows, maybe she's hit on
some dude who's helping her with the moving right now.
(It's not hard to imagine her picking up a guy more or
less at random and then asking him to let her crash with
him until she finds a place of her own.)

Enough of this evil, jealous speculation. If I
stop to think about it, I prefer having it this way to
the only possible realistic alternative -- her brooding
at home and taking it out on me.

One good thing about today: after two years of
trying to make it to the JCC on a Sunday morning I
finally succeeded, though just barely, popping in the
lobby door at 11:55. Perhaps this augurs well for some
of the other changes in daily regimen I hope to be
making soon, or maybe even for every last one of them --
why not?

*   *

It's even worse than I feared. Past midnight now,
I just tucked in an exhausted, confused, weepy Valerie,
and I'm still reeling from the story she told me. I rue
the day I met her, I rue the way I failed her, I dread
to think what lies ahead for her.

When I came in I found her mired in a miserable
state. "If you knew what I did last night you'd
understand why." She said it was her responsibility,
she wouldn't tell me, she was too ashamed to anyway, but
she obviously wanted to talk about it, and I was
powerless to prevent myself from playing the sucker and
dragging it out of her.

In short, she's gotten herself involved with a
twenty-two-year-old "spoiled brat" of a rock musician (a
drummer!) whose father's some sort of Mafia honcho. The
dude's crazy about her, says he wants to marry her, "has
always gotten what he's wanted" and vows to get her --
"the easy way" if he can, otherwise by doing "whatever
it takes." He offers her a life of luxury -- he'll buy
her a car, he'll be a father for Danny, he'll pay her
way through State. Possibly he'd even buy her the
Golden Gate Bridge if she wanted it -- though he didn't
mention this last item; I offered it as my own

548

speculation. She brushed it aside with a glower.

She met him yesterday hitchhiking and spent the
entire night with him, "wrapping him around my finger,"
balling the bejeebers out of him. She must have done
pretty well, she says (I shudder as I write this),
"because he's had lots of groupies" and he declares
she's "the best ever."

His imperious, rough-and-tumble bedroom style is
one of the things she likes best about him; she makes no
secret of that. But she says she could never love him,
doesn't even find him physically attractive. "He
wouldn't stimulate me mentally. It would be a boring,
plastic life." She says this, but at the same time it's
obvious he fascinates her. Her eyes glisten with awe as
she repeats some scary things he told her (his father,
in Cleveland, bombed the family home of a kid who'd
insulted his kid). She's also riddled with guilt and
shame over the way she so easily and mercilessly
exploited him, the complete amorality -- destructiveness
-- of this, and what it reveals about herself. But of
course she's also proud of her conquest, and regardless
she's thinking seriously of taking up with him: he
offers her affection, luxury, a glamorous aura (he's
currently trying to catch on with a supposedly up-and-
coming Bay Area band which I had to admit I've never
heard of). He also provides her with not just a handy
way to punish me and make me suffer for having given her
the boot but, maybe even better, a way out of the hole
and the desperate circumstances she sees ahead (she
can't face the prospect of living in isolation in some
tiny, windowless room). Yet she's also well aware she's
selling herself out and facing some real dangers with
this guy. Just as her ex-husband Jim used to do, he
packs a gun. And he likes to say things like "Once
you're in the Mafia you don't get out."

I tried to persuade her to drop him while she still
can (he's supposed to be calling her tomorrow afternoon
at two to find out what time she can see him later in
the day), I tried to refire her resolve to make it on
her own, I even "assured" her I love her as much as ever

549

despite everything and still believe we'd have a chance
of reuniting if she could get herself together living
alone and convince me she's dropped the terror stuff for
good. I held her, I consoled her, I chewed her out,
but...let's face it: she's almost certainly a lost
cause. Given what she's revealed about herself in the
past several months, I'd even say this guy may represent
her best possible life. If the violence and cruelty go
as deep in her as they often seem to, she won't be
experiencing major changes in herself anytime soon. And
if the things I've stood for with her don't mean
anything more to her than she's showing now, if the
self-proclaimed fact that I'm her "love of a lifetime"
can't prevent her from acting this way, then there's no
possibility of my being able to help her. I can only
make her life more difficult.

What really rankles is the fact that I'm consumed
with jealousy in spite of myself. As the blues wailer
moans, "Another mule been kickin' in my stall." (How
retrograde is that?) But the truth is: I don't know
what to do. And I'm frightened, for her, for myself.

2

Monday 7
Some days you have to be a machine. This is that
kind of day. No other way to get through the hours.
I'm at the Bulldog office now, but a few minutes ago I
left Valerie at Mac's and tears were streaming down both
of our faces. In the space of a few minutes she'd
contradicted herself several times on this matter of her
new "mule," first saying, "I don't think I'll be able to
cut it off with him," then reversing herself, back and
forth, also telling me she loves me, then declaring she
hates me.

My own best guess is she doesn't really want to end
it with him. This new hookup is the only ray of hope in
sight for her. Despite her shame, she'll stick with it:
I'd say it's almost a certainty.

550

[Living with Valerie]

"I just want to be happy," she murmured as I left.

"So be happy already," I said.

"Thanks a lot for caring about me so much."

"I really mean it, you know, whether you believe it or not. And I always have."

"And somehow I just didn't notice it, eh?"

"That's pretty much how I see it, yeah."

What triggered all this was a statement I made first thing this morning. In essence, I withdrew the warnings about him I'd laid on her last night. "If he turns you on as much as he seems to, he could be really good for you. Maybe you need someone who'll treat you the same way you treated me the last few months, but perhaps a little less viciously." She broke down over that one, and I immediately realized my words came less from selfless concern (as I'd truly thought they did when I said them) than from my own pain and resentment. I was messing with her mind again.

I spent the next hour trying to undo the effects of that comment -- bringing even more pain upon myself. "You don't know how much it hurts me to say these things," I told her, my eyes watering ridiculously (I'd just said that if it were a choice between burying herself in self-pitying isolation in a room somewhere, or going with him, then she should go with him).

Later when I joined her in bed, she held me tightly, crawled beneath the sleeping bag to lick my cock. But I couldn't return the favor with any of her sexual parts or respond even slightly: finally I told her I was grieving over the thought of his seed "paddling ferociously inward" (a line from her own "Blue Sperm" poem) at that very moment. No, she said, they weren't.

"Where are they then? In your throat?"

She didn't reply.

"Well, so I'll assume they're paddling ferociously inward there instead. 'That's sacred,' remember? Remember when you told me that up in Garnett? After the North Beach guy?"

She started weeping. "Please, Glen. Don't."

I went on: "So now I think I know, Val, what Jim
felt that night he held the gun to your head and raped
you like a maniac. I think I understand what really
happened and why it happened, or at least your part in
it. You know, after you revenge-fucked Brandon. And I
know it twice-over after what you did with the North
Beach guy and the other one right before him and now
this new one."

"You're the real fucker, Glen. You're ten times
worse than me. And you know it."

"Yeah, right. The truth is, Val, you're just
repeating the same course you took with Jim and you
don't even realize it. You and your crazed out-of-
control acts of revenge against people you supposedly
love. You can't stop! Nothing satisfies you! You're
incorrigible!"

"You're the one who can't stop, Glen. And you know
what? I can't take much more of this. I'm going to
lose it again. You'd better watch out."

But then we both did stop -- for the moment.

One of the most uncomfortable aspects of this whole
debacle (besides the fact it was to be expected -- I
even predicted something much like it to her face a
month ago) is it's forced me to acknowledge that,
underneath, I'm still hoping things will work out with
her. Yes! In short, I still love her, or am still
hooked on her, still caught firmly in her trap, still
unable to pull off an escape despite repeated attempts.
She still touches me powerfully where it matters most.
She's still beautiful, rare, and valuable -- despite
everything! -- and my own heart still bleeds, aches,
convulses over her. Valoshka. Scourge of my life!

But I can't accept her as she is (whatever the
reason: rigidity on my part, pride, it scarcely
matters), so I should let her go. But how? Perhaps the
thing to do, if she takes off with this guy again, is to
throw her out, bodily if necessary, move her things into
the downstairs hall or the yard. Or perhaps just ignore
whatever she does with him until she leaves for good by
herself. If ignoring that sort of thing is even

552

possible. And maybe it is.

I'd like to help her. But what can I do? I'm
hamstrung by my own bitterness and outrage and jealousy.

(How similar all of this is to my end-time with
Ciara. But then it was a meek plastic surgeon who
aroused my stupid jealousy, not a drum-whacking, pistol-
packing Mafioso. And I had Jang's approaching stopover
in San Francisco to keep me more or less preoccupied and
at least somewhat hopeful about the future.)

-- A temptation nibbling: drive home a little
before two and see whether I can catch a glimpse of this
guy. Or catch them in flagrante delicte. That I would
truly love to do. Not once in all my years of intrigues
have I hit the IFD jackpot.

And I certainly wouldn't put it past her to invite
him over and ball him in our bed even though Danny's
present. In fact that's just the kind of revenge move
I'd expect from her, and not least because it's exactly
what she did with me as the invitee in her and Jim's
marital bed the day after we first met -- I should be
grateful it's already been two days with the new guy.

*   *

Later, past two in the afternoon, and so far I've
resisted this confounded urge to post myself as a spy
outside my own home. But I've also decided I'll give in
to it tonight, between the crucial hours of six-thirty
(when the sitter normally comes by to pick up Danny) and
eight (when la Mafioso picked her up last time). I
figure my odds of success are a bit better in that
period because (as I'm now thinking) she'd probably see
an in-your-face revenge move on her part as a bit too
crude after the way she talked with me last night about
how our bed is "sacred" to her and she'd never bring
another man there -- "sacred," I reminded her, just like
she'd said about the blowjobs. But no, she said she
really meant it this time. Really, really.

I'm just afraid she'll already have gone off with
him if I wait until six to go out there.

Meanwhile I'm wandering aimlessly, barely able to
focus on the many things that need to be done, muttering

deploringly, "Val, Val, Val...." I just wish, rather
than subject me to this torture, she'd leave. Or
perhaps I should be the one to move out. I've thought
about it (on the lam from a Mafia hit man), I've even
lovingly dwelled on violent fantasies regarding the
"spoiled brat" (as she called him). Zeroing in with a
telescopic sight. Beating him over the head with a
length of two-by-four as he mounts the inside stairs at
Funston with gun drawn. Tailing him around the city,
learning his habits, arranging a little accident.
Really sick stuff right out of "The Godfather." Best of
all I'd like to catch Val in bed with him at Funston and
shower scorn on them both. Val, you're such a fucker!

But then she's only returning (in spades) what I
did to her, or at least this is how she sees it. The
main difference being that when I saw other women after
our earlier breakups, I always tried to spare her from
the gory details, whereas she flaunts them -- loves to
shove them in my face. Then again she hadn't rejected
me after those breakups as I have her now (again, to her
way of thinking). But on the other hand I hadn't
subjected her to months of nonstop terror prior to those
earlier breakups, or after them either, nor was I
breaking any vows or promises to her then or at any
time, whereas she's done that herself scores of times
with me (and Jim) and called it justified revenge.

Round and round it goes: who's to say where the
blame should fall and in what portions. In the end the
blame doesn't matter: just the failure. And now the
mutual grief. She won't let me off lightly, she
exploits my guilt and good intentions and what love is
left in every way she can, and I can do little to stop
her. It's playing out just the way she wants it to.

Funny: I think of this Mafioso guy as the "black-
eyed idol of my youth" in her poem, as Mr. Death, as the
embodiment of evil she's always been attracted to (just
as I'm attracted to her, I suppose). Kerin, the first
boy she loved, at age fourteen, was like that: an
outcast with flair, "brutal": he loved to shove her
around and threaten her with a switchblade and burning

cigarettes; and she loved all that too. It's her
sadomasochistic split showing up again. She was
"thrilled" when the shrink identified it. Her words:
"Beat me." To be a truly exciting and satisfying lover
to her I'd have to do that, and I'd also have to get a
lot more pleasure out of her sadistic side. She says
this flat-out. But I can't do either one and I won't do
either one. How disastrously incompatible we are
"psychosexually" -- i.e., in bed -- and in the final
analysis this is so not because of her hang-ups or mine
but because of the utterly failed dialectic between
them. Each of us is too proud to play the roles the
other asks for or demands, each is inhibited in his or
her own way.

Again: I remember my distaste Sunday night --
that's just last night! -- when she said, after sucking
my limp cock, "I really have to learn how to turn you
on." The implication was plain: turning on la Mafioso
had been simple. Duck soup, twisting him around her
finger (and tongue): and she'd loved doing it. It had
been as exciting for her as it had been for him. "There
are some things I like about him," she admitted. She
wouldn't say what, but when I suggested, "You like the
way he balls you, plays tough with you, rough, his
style," she blushed. There could be no clearer assent.

Another funny thing: she attributed the whole
episode with this guy to her "numbness." "I didn't even
cry," she said. And: "When I'm numb, I'll do anything
for kicks." The sheer desperation in her eyes as she
said this confirmed its truth. "I prefer the numbness,"
she added. "At least I don't feel any pain." But it
also frightens her because of the things she knows she's
capable of. "I'll do anything, Glen. I mean that.
Anything."

Again the implication was obvious: despite what
she'd been saying before, in other words, she could not
be held responsible for her acts. Therefore: I must be
held responsible for them. I'd brought her to this, she
was saying; now I'd have to sit back and watch the
devastation I'd wrought and know I'd caused it. I'd

ruined her. All her pain stemmed from me. As one small
example, she complained again and again about being
"sore all over," especially her back, until finally I
made some ironic comment linking it with her hours of
balling la Mafioso.

"It's not what you think," she said. "It's from
all that walking when I was looking for apartments."

Naturally I'm the one who "forced" her to do all
that walking.

And so it goes: she spouts occasional intrepid
shrink-inspired phrases such as, "I'm taking
responsibility for myself now," but she doesn't really
mean it or do it. She lays it on me by smothering
herself in self-pity and hurling accusations at me. Or
wistfully declaring her love, her martyrdom. "I hate
the whole world," she declared today. No way around it,
she'll be much better off without me. Many of these
things she says solely to make me feel bad, solely to
get back at me. I'm the source of the embedded shrapnel
preventing her wounds from healing.

And she's the same for me. It's completely beyond
our control. Jealousy and resentment will rage in me
until she leaves -- and the moment she's out the door
I'll begin suppressing all memory of that, and before
long I'll be experiencing powerful regrets, yearning for
her, obsessing on her, idealizing her. My sweet
Valoshka! Christ, what a beautiful fiery woman she was!
I mean, when she was around, life was never dull! And
I'll accuse myself of handling her all wrong; I'll think
just a slight adjustment in perspective would've enabled
us to eliminate our major problems. "I was so stupid!"

Yes, yes, I can feel it all coming already. And
then somewhere along the way I'll meet another woman and
Val will be temporarily shoved back a notch further into
abstraction, she'll become the ideal against whom I
measure the new woman and find her wanting, the new
woman will be made -- completely unintentionally -- to
feel inferior, a wall of resentment will rise between
her and me, I'll withdraw and retreat toward my ideal
Val who in reality is not so ideal and also now herself

is full of new resentment to add fuel to the deep-going
and long-running "ressentiment." The cycle is drearily
familiar, deadly dull, disgusting.

To break out of it I must...must what? Stop
burying my women beneath an intimidating barrage of
expectations (oh, it always starts out innocently
enough, not as criticism of the other but as intense
declarations of my own profound beliefs; only later do
these gradually transform into what are felt by the
women as, and in a sense are, demands). To put it
succinctly, I must do what I've never done before,
despite an agonizing and tragicomic series of attempts:
I must fully accept someone. And to do that I must
first fully accept myself, blah blah blah blah blah.

The point here is I'm struggling with mad impulses
to take Val back, to declare all is forgiven, even to
undergo some kind of therapy with her. To admit I'm
wrong, to swallow my pride, to kiss her ass and actually
mean it. But...but...I just can't see it! I can't see
us even getting along. I can't see us developing a
sturdy, long-term relationship. I can't see myself as
Danny's father. I can't see myself satisfying her or
her satisfying me. Physically I believe we could do it,
both of us, as well as aesthetically and mentally, but
emotionally there's no way. It will always be a power
struggle; my "two kindred souls heartfully negotiating"
will always be pitted against her "absolute natural
rights and duties." Pride against pride, conflicting
needs. We both crave devotion, brightness, hope,
strength in the other (cravings that can't possibly be
filled by a single person). But instead of strength she
offers instability, wracking insecurity, ferocious
demands, whereas I...oh shit.

I'm just running scared right now, that's all this
loopy analysis really means. Very scared. She doesn't
even realize how much at her mercy I am. If she keeps
this up she could absolutely paralyze me, crush me.

My impulse now is to beg for mercy: to implore her
to live up to her previous promise to forgo seeing other
men until after she leaves. But I have no reason to

expect her to abide by whatever new promises she might
make, and I have plenty of reason to expect her not to.
I'll just have to take what she dishes out. If only I
could control my raging, self-punishing curiosity. But
I know there's no hope of that either.

*   *

Intrepid investigative reporter at work. Staked
out on Funston Avenue several doors up from 1616.
Parked behind a large orange flatbed truck through whose
windshields (front and back of the cab) I have an
excellent view of the entrance to the 1616 driveway.
And the cab is tall enough and wide enough to hide the
L.C. from anyone's view down there.

Here's where things stand now. I crept up the
interior stairs and listened outside the apartment door.
At first, no sound, but then I heard Val in the
bathroom. No other sounds -- no Mafioso. And no Danny
either. Which makes me suspicious. Why did she take so
long in the bathroom? Two possibilities come to mind:
either she was grooming for la Mafioso or washing up
after him. Or maybe she was preparing to go apartment-
hunting. When I first saw her she was still wearing the
green bells she had on this morning (I recognized them
in the nearly amorphous blur visible through the opaque
corrugated yellow plastic wall separating the stairwell
from the apartment's interior), but shortly after that
she reappeared in the short-skirted red dress (devil's
dress!) which she uses for apartment-hunting. Which
means she probably didn't do any of that yet today. And
I still detected no sign of Danny's presence.

Did la Mafioso come by early, perhaps shortly after
calling her at two, and just recently leave? But then
she wouldn't be dressed at all -- and probably he
would've taken her wherever she's preparing to go.
Perhaps she saw him (this would explain Danny's absence)
at his place and he just dropped her off -- she refused
him? Possible, but unlikely. I tend to think she spent
the afternoon innocently and just wanted to be spared
Danny's presence tonight. It's equally possible she
really is planning to go apartment-hunting now. It's

also possible Danny's there but asleep. If the
babysitter were coming she'd be due in a few minutes --
her appearance or failure to appear will be telling.
Could be too la Mafioso's coming to pick her up at any
moment now, or she's planning to meet him somewhere. If
she leaves on foot I'll follow her. If she hitches or
hops on a bus, I'll follow her too. But if she boards
an inbound streetcar I'll be out of luck because of the
tunnels the streetcars pass through but the L.C. can't.

Weird business. I'm getting out of the L.C. now so
I'll have a better view of the driveway. The great hope
is that...oh shit. No great hopes exist. Just petty
vindictiveness and morbid self-abasement and sad but
intense and irresistible curiosity.

*   *

Second report. It's close to seven now and
nothing's happened so far -- which must mean...
something. But what?

For an hour or so I stretched out on top of a
grassy mound well up the Mt. Moraga slope overlooking
the lower part of our block. "Recon mission." I was
propped up on one elbow so I could peer over the big
rock hiding me from view from our driveway and the house
itself, and with my leather hat pulled down low on my
brow to shield my eyes from the fierce wind I must've
looked more like a refugee from a Hollywood western.
Sinister too: an older lady walking two huge, muzzled
dogs froze with fear when she caught sight of me, this
big strange longhaired man lying in the middle of what's
probably her dogs' favorite shitting field -- caught
sight of me seemingly staring at her. "Hi!" I called
out meekly, waving feebly, but she didn't respond and
made a wide detour around the area.

Finally the sun sank behind the hilltop and I began
to shiver. I decided I'd had enough outdoor
surveillance work. Before returning to the L.C. I took
my first prone piss since age six or so, using the hat
to shield the pitiful and yet urgent urinary act from
the row of picture-windowed houses across the meadow to
the north, careful to piss downhill to show I was smart

enough to pass the prone hillside version of the famous
LBJ piss-in-the-wind test ("Degenerate Arrested on Mt.
Moraga / Lab Test Confirms Urine Is His, Not Dog's As
Claimed").

So she still hasn't come outside -- or if she has,
I missed her. As it got later and the babysitter still
failed to show, I felt more and more certain la Mafioso
would arrive at any moment. Why else would Val begin to
get ready so early and take so long making herself up?
Probably she told him to fetch her "early" Monday
evening and right now she's up there sweating blood,
afraid I'll get home before he arrives. Where the hell
is he! "The bastard's just like Glen: always late. Men
are all the same!"

But then why is she wearing her apartment-hunting
outfit? Another possibility dawns on me: maybe she's
dressing that way to fool me! Maybe she wants me to
think when she comes home later -- when and if -- she's
been out looking for a place! But no, not very likely.
So maybe she has a later appointment to see a place (but
why would she dress for it so early?). Other scenarios
of the fringe variety offer themselves. Could be, for
example, the sitter forgot to come. Could be, too, la
Mafioso stood her up --

But there she is. Right now.
Hello, Valoshka.
She's standing in the street, one leg up on the
curb, still in the red dress, peering downhill. Waiting
for him: no doubt about it now. She must be worried as
hell he won't show up.

Here I go.

*   *

(about fifteen minutes later)
It's as I expected: he picked her up. But there's
an all-important difference of tone and meaning. As I
strode down the hill ("Just happened to be in the
neighborhood"), she unexpectedly turned and caught sight
of me. We walked toward each other, she with a sheepish
look. Embarrassed. No, not quite that: exasperated and
ashamed. We embraced. Looked into each other's eyes.

560

[Living with Valerie]

She looked away.

"Is he late?" I asked.

"No," she said, not fazed at all. But it wasn't as I thought. "I'm going to tell him I won't be seeing him anymore," she said. She'd already given him a hint of this on the phone earlier today, she said, while arranging tonight's meeting. "I love you," she said to me now. I said the same.

She was very calm, subdued, not obviously nervous or agitated. We began to walk into the house. "Maybe he won't come," she said. Then I remembered my bag was in the unlocked L.C. parked up the hill. We returned to the sidewalk and separated, I going up, she staying by the driveway entrance, and after I'd taken a few steps she said something I couldn't quite hear. I turned and saw three cars coming up the hill.

"Is that him?" I asked.

"Please don't make it any harder for me," she said.

That hadn't been my intention at all, and I began hiking up the hill again. The three cars then passed us uneventfully. But I'd gone only a few paces farther when I heard an engine gun and looked around to see a fourth car, a recent-model gray compact, maybe a Maverick, bearing down on Val, who was now standing in the street on the far side. The driver was pretending to make a run at her -- a little good clean American fun, heh heh -- then slamming on the brakes just in time, of course. After that he spun around her, gunning it again, tires squealing, and roared up past me, swung into a driveway, turned around, coasted back down.

At one point as he powered uphill past me he was no more than twenty feet away and we got a good look at each other. (I don't think he could've known I was with Val, but he might've guessed anyway.) What can I say? He's not too tall (at least while seated), he's big-headed, with shortish brown curly hair. His face to me looks stupid and cruel -- on the chubby side, with small eyes and large shapeless lips, slightly pursed. He immediately reminded me of the asinine younger brother of Mike in "Derby." His face spoke of ignorance,

vapidity, dumb cruelty, as well as the spoiledness Val
mentioned. The way he drove suggested the same things.
What's more, he wore a sports coat of some sort and a
foolish smile. Jesus Christ, I thought, is this the guy
I've been agonizing over? Is this the guy Val described
as "funky/punky"? Is this the guy she let fuck her
twice two nights ago (and whose cock she sucked to ejac
for a little variety in between)?

"In town only seven months and he already knows all
the gangs," she had said while explaining how he was
breaking free of the Mafia (he apparently being the one
exception who can do it). Well, he looks like the type
who'd know all the gangs, all right -- a big-shot
syndicate hood's typical pampered offspring trying
desperately to impress the denizens of the civilian
world (like two I knew slightly in Gatewood growing up).
One thing, though: I could see where he'd fuck the hell
out of her. Also how she could easily feel superior to
him. "Wrap him around my fingers and tongue." Criminy!

So he coasted down past me to the 1616 driveway and
I saw the final corroborating detail: a drum kit stuffed
into the backseat. (Should I break out my old electric
bass? Try to develop my fingering calluses again?
Perhaps join him in a band?) -- Then he swung open the
passenger door from inside, and Val climbed in. No wave
to me, of course. For a moment I thought she might not
go, might tell him the bad news on the spot, but they
zoomed away. "I'll be back in a couple of hours," she'd
said earlier, before his arrival.

I was left feeling strangely elated, at least at
first. Man, like if she wanted a dude like that, she
was welcome to him -- and he to her. But now I'm
beginning to worry, and she's been gone less than an
hour. I can see where she'd overwhelm such a man (a
man? He looked like a high-school kid) not only with
her "exotic" beauty and superb body but, more important,
with her intelligence and penetrating insight (and her
appearance of respectability, her classy side); I mean
the dude might do just about anything to hold on to her.

When I got inside I found a cup of flowers and this

[Living with Valerie]

note, written before she knew I was down there:

> I'll be back. And I'm not out to do it
> again. So don't worry. I won't betray my
> love for you. Please don't turn your back
> on me now as I have renounced to him and
> every other man. I love you.
>
> Valerie.

So I'll sweat it out. (Could she be out there lying on
the hill now spying on me?)

Tuesday 8

Some day that turned out to be. Val came home well
before the two hours were up, I completely relaxed my
guard against her, and today I'm much happier. I wish I
could say all our problems had resolved themselves in a
flash of blinding mutual insight -- that we balled
rapturously -- that all is well again -- but come on,
even in the worst daytime soaps things don't happen that
way. Though that fact has never yet stopped me from
hoping against hope they might happen that way this time
or some future time for me.

At any rate, from relief, gratitude, I don't know
what, I was able to warm up considerably, treat her
again more or less as a lover (racked still by
shuddering flashes of her nightlong cock-sucking and
other unspeakable acts performed on, by, and with le
Mafioso -- as I realized I should've been calling him
all along, not "la Mafioso"; "le" is the masculine in
French) (so together they're le Mafioso and la Mailloux,
right). We fell into bed, balled, but, though both of
us worked hard at it, though she openly vowed to be the
"best lover in the world to you" and I silently vowed to
myself I'd be a better lover to her than any asinine
Mafioso, it was a bust. Sometimes -- often -- we just
can't get it on, that's all there is to it.

But it was also an education. Yes, she affirmed,
she wants to be "beaten," to be "overpowered," to have
her favors "taken": she wants pain. "Mark me!" she
cried. "Scar me! I deserve it!" So I tried, but the

best I could do was to suck the skin of her breast right
above her heart until tiny droplets of blood appeared --
i.e., give her a hickey (and even this pathetic act made
her groan ecstatically). The trouble with my balling,
to her, is its "over-sophistication." It intimidates
her. It's also too gentle, too sensual, too controlled.
This is her view but I don't really disagree: balling
with her somehow almost always becomes eventually a
matter of form. And this happens for a simple reason
(granted this is only my view): she doesn't respond well
to my kind of loving, doesn't show her needs or desires,
and owing to our many bad experiences I become
disheartened after going at it with her and on her and
inside her without noticeable impact for a certain
rather lengthy period. I feel unwanted and rejected,
passion ebbs and I find myself just going through the
motions. And this even though no one has ever been more
sexually attractive to me in a strictly physical sense.

She makes the same sort of charges against me
generally, not just in the sexual realm: I'm "too
easygoing," "too self-controlled," "too reasonable,"
"too tolerant." Maybe all her terror was simply an
effort to force me to lose my temper ("Maybe I just
wanted to make you beat me": she said that quite
seriously). All very dispiriting, not so much because
of the criticism itself (which I accept as at least
partly true) but because neither of us sees any way out.

"I don't think," she says, "we'll ever be able to
make each other happy, sexually or otherwise."

She knows as well as I do that the "psychosexual
mismatch" (her term) is what's crucial for us.

And yet: for the moment we're at least partly
reconciled. She's still planning to move out, but the
talk now generally proceeds from the proposition "the
sooner we're living separately, the sooner we'll regain
our balance and be back together." Sometimes I believe
it myself, sometimes I don't, but at all times I realize
it's best to go along with it if we're to accomplish her
move-out with a minimum of damage wreaked on both of us.
So we're still sleeping separately and she's still

[Living with Valerie]

looking for a place -- though none too assiduously.
(We're now eight days past her promised move-out date.
My hope to find someone to share the June rent is dead.)

Regarding le Mafioso (and his real first name is
Dennis, by the way, and she doesn't even know his last
name, or claims not to): naturally we got to talking
about this new conquest of hers, and her defense of him
provoked me into leveling both barrels. I did the
unforgivable: I ridiculed him, laughed at him. When she
said she thought he was "funky," I howled. Disgusting.
"The funky punk." ("There is such a thing, you know,"
she reminded me.) She obviously thought more highly of
him than I did.

"I saw him as a little English boy," she said. (He
grew up in England, he told her, before moving to
Cleveland.) (A little unusual for a Mafioso, isn't it?
But perhaps not totally unbelievable.) -- In any case
he's very playful, always teasing. For me playing in a
rock'n'roll band was a passing phase in high school and
college; for him it's "his life." Even as I put him
down I regretted doing so, because I feared this would
only drive her back to him. Simple rebellion.
Defiance. And indeed, though she'd persuaded him to
take her home early, she admitted she hadn't been able
to break it off with him. She's already developed a
proprietary interest.

"I don't want to hurt him. He's a human being too,
you know."

In his view she's just "running scared." That's
what he told her. He'll come around again after she's
had time to think things over a bit. He asked her to
call today.

"If I don't," she told me, "he'll think you did
something to me."

He's a violent sort, see, a black belt in karate
(he says), a real fighter. Also a whirlwind in bed, I
gather (she kindly said I'm "better" but had to be
prodded considerably). For these reasons I worry: not
only does she feel a motherly solicitude toward him, but
also a masochistic attraction to his violent side. I

565

predict she'll continue to see him, perhaps not
immediately, but soon, after she moves out. This
"little English boy/funky punk" may well turn out to be
the man who takes her away from me, who defeats me even
as he saves me: what bittersweet irony. But for the
present, as she said, "You're back in control. You're
back into me." (By which latter phrase she meant to
convey she's back into me. That's just how she talks.
In these pages I usually translate it automatically into
something I judge to be closer to idiomatic English.)

*

    Meanwhile things are popping at the Bulldog. Mike
is tossing all kinds of story ideas my way, the phone's
ringing off the hook with "hot tips" and inquiries about
the Summer Project, and we're all excited about the
notion of the paper becoming the "nerve center" as well
as the voice of a new "popular front" in the city.
There's a groundswell of revolt and discontent in San
Francisco these days, mostly coming from young people
and the political left but also from the
antiestablishment right and even the alienated center,
and this includes age groups across the spectrum; and
the silence and/or editorial disapproval displayed by
S.F.'s daily papers (and the network TV stations) on
such matters leaves a vacuum which the Bulldog is well
positioned to fill. Cultural/political conditions in
the city in many ways resemble those which produced
hugely successful underground papers in college towns a
few years back (e.g., the Berkeley Barb). That is, the
city is chock-a-block with dissident residents -- tens
of thousands, even hundreds of thousands -- frustrated
not just by the war and runaway ecocide and entrenched
commercialism but also by lack of representation in
government and exposure of their point of view in the
media (excepting a few FM radio stations such as KRMA).
    Also good: Mike (whose skepticism appears to be
melting away as the full dimensions of the prospect
reveal themselves) -- Mike has taken up the idea, which
I proposed today, of giving Bresker's S.F. Alliance
regular column space in the paper, maybe even a whole

566

page. He hemmed and hawed until I floated the image of
a front-page box, sixty-point caps, reading "Ari Bresker
Column Starts This Issue." All by itself this might
sell twenty thousand papers (considering SFA's
membership is about thirty thousand).

Wednesday 9
     Why am I sitting on a cement loading platform right
now, leaning against the side panel of a huge Mack
truck?
     Two stories.
     First, it was six-thirty last night, Valerie and I
had just dropped off a packet of "Bay Bulldog
Biographies" at K101 on Nob Hill after I picked her up
at Foster's, and we were on our way to an S.F. Alliance
meeting in Pacific Heights when I finally got tired of
waiting for her to spill what had happened with le
Mafioso. So I asked if she'd seen him.
     "I told you I was going to call him," she said
glumly.
     "So did you call him?"
     "Yes," she said.
     Pressed for more, she said it had been "very hard,"
but she'd told him she'd never see him again. The poor
guy: he'd decided to stay on in San Francisco, he'd even
taken a job at a tire-recapping factory "for me," as she
said, meaning he took it to be able to afford seeing
her. Now she didn't want to talk about it anymore --
this guy she'd known three days had been "hurt very
badly," she "felt terrible" about it.
     Second story. This morning I was talking with
Monica at the Bulldog about my troubles with Val and she
said she'd seen her over on Harrison (a block northwest
of Bryant) when she, Monica, left work yesterday. She
was arguing with some guy "who looked like a mechanic
who'd just crawled out from under a car." And: "Neither
of them looked real happy."
     And so the loading platform and the Mack truck,
which is parked in the lot a few feet down from the

entrance to Grady Padrow's Tire Recapping Factory near
Eighth and Harrison. Inside the "factory" (more like a
large auto-repair garage) a crew of men with blackened
faces, most of them, and wearing mechanic overalls is
sitting around tables at the back, presumably for lunch.
None of the ones whose faces I could see when I checked
them out from the street a few minutes ago looked
familiar, but just thirty or forty feet away from me
here, next to a huge mound of old tires, sits the gray
vehicle (a Firebird, not a Maverick) belonging to
Dennis, the "funky punk" himself, le Mafioso; I know for
sure it's his because his drum kit still rides in the
backseat right where it was two days ago.

I also know this is where Val went yesterday
afternoon when, at the Bulldog office, she said she was
going out to write at Foster's and borrowed a dollar
from me -- maybe thirty minutes before Monica left work
for the day and saw her here -- and several hours after
she, Val, had supposedly told Dennis she'd never see him
again. By a weird coincidence -- one that would be
laughed out of every fiction-writing workshop in the
land -- in a city containing thousands of blocks Val's
two men happen to work exactly one block apart.

So I can no longer pretend she's not lying to me.
I don't know what she told Dennis when she saw him --
why they were arguing and "didn't look real happy" --
but I do know I'd be a damn fool to believe her
assurances that she won't be seeing him again or for
that matter anything else she has to say about him or
about, yes, anything. In fact it's quite possible she's
seeing him right now, or will tonight -- and she almost
certainly will sometime.

There's no way I can get around it: this hurts like
hell. (And I've known her for 345 days, not just three
as my new rival has -- in my case twenty days short of a
year!)

*

(2:30 p.m.)
Well, perhaps I have no right to be, perhaps I
should even be glad, but all the same I'm crushed. Even

[Living with Valerie]

before I put two and two together today (and checked
under "Tire Retread" in the Yellow Pages) I was
devastated. It's ludicrous, the way I've been trying to
throw up a brave and casual front, my attempts to "beat"
her, to "overpower" her, to be "punky" and tease her, to
fuck her "really, really hard" -- in short, to be like
Dennis as she's described him to me. Suddenly I find
myself ashamed of my "refinement," my "sophistication,"
my "reasonableness," my "reformist" political interests,
my "tolerance," my "gentleness," my alleged "rigidity"
(meaning with respect to certain beliefs I hold) when I
consider myself spontaneous and practical and open-
minded. So I try to be different for her sake and I
become a buffoon. And then I wince to think about it.

I'm too old anyway. No matter what I do I can't
become Dennis. I can't be twenty-two again. What's
more, I can't become a punk, I can't satisfy Val's
peculiar definition of "funky/punky." Just like her, I
was never a high-school punk (wasn't I always too old
for my age, or too young, and in any case too
straight?). And also as with her I suppose my failure
to have been or to be a punk helps account for a certain
delinquent/rebellious streak in me -- the one that's
found expression as Glen the delayed adolescent (as Dad
used to charge), Glen the ladies' man, Glen the emotion
freak. True, for the most part I've always been able to
keep that streak under control (except for the sexual
tripping at times), at least by my own lights. Who
knows, maybe by doing so I've snuffed out something
crucial in me. Right now I certainly fear it's so. I
feel cut off from my own roots, my own sources of
strength. (A vivid dream last night: Val is taken away
from me, she's lost, we're all searching for her.)

Worst of all, I can feel the difference in Val
herself. She no longer cares in the same way. Dennis
engages her vital thoughts, her imagination; for me it's
merely faded love, nostalgia, regrets, guilt, pity, and,
not least, the poorly concealed gloating over revenge
accomplished -- or am I just imagining this last part?
In any event she's suddenly no longer hung up on me. My

569

reactions don't really matter (unless I'm "trying" to
make her feel bad). I can't really touch her. She
effortlessly deflects my intensity. I don't excite her.
No longer a lover, I'm suddenly more like a father
figure and not even a beloved one.

Perhaps at bottom that's the way it was with us all
along and I just never realized it. It's incredible to
me when I think about it, but, with rare exceptions that
can easily be explained in light of what I now know
about her, I never did turn her on! Dennis, on the
other hand, does it the first night. (That I enabled
her to overcome certain of her inhibitions with others
-- and taught her most everything she knows about a good
number of things -- right now only deepens the pain,
though perhaps one day I'll be able to view it proudly.)

Once again: despite what she's told me more than a
few times, I never really did turn her on! The magic
was never there for her! Sure, I know why this was, I
know what hang-ups in her and in myself prevented it, I
know we both tried like hell to make it happen -- but we
failed. She failed and so did I. I failed with Val.
Admit it!

So that's the source of my envy for Dennis. That's
why for the time being at least my own "street prince"
side has seized control. At the moment it seems
everything I've done in life is a sham, I'm a sham, and
all I want is to turn Valoshka on.

Last night I tried. I poured it on for her. I
battered her with a sort of faux-brutal affection
(except when I forgot and drifted off into sorrowful
thoughts, acrimony). I issued "loving orders." At the
S.F. Alliance meeting (held at the palatial Pacific
Heights home of Ross and Jodi Morrow) I bored in on her,
I wrote her several imbecilic notes, I tried to amuse
her with crazed gestures (such as pulling a bouquet of
cut flowers out of an ornate vase and handing it to her
dripping wet: "For you!"). Then when we got home I took
her to bed, spread her beneath me (pinning her arms
above her head in much the same way that's required when
she flies into a violent howling rage) and fucked her as

[Living with Valerie]

"overpoweringly" as I could -- but it still didn't work.
It didn't turn her on. Instead she strained to prevent
me from knowing she wasn't turned on. But I knew, of
course, because her body simply wasn't into it. She
barely got wet. She didn't come. She deflected me as
indeed she'd been doing in numerous other ways all day.

And I knew it was ridiculous anyhow. It was all
pathetically self-conscious and false. There wasn't a
touch of punkiness or funkiness or swagger or erotic
power in it: it was shot through with fears and
inhibitions and pathetic implicit pleas. At the end,
still panting, collapsed on top of her, I knew it was
all over, there was no hope, I'd failed, we'd failed;
and I felt myself sliding down into a despair so total I
knew I'd need weeks or months to climb back out of it.

But some last shred of pride held me back, and I
think I managed to keep the worst of it from her. And
even so I'm sure she sensed something of my pain and
disappointment. "I admire you for going through all
this the way you are," she said. Admiration! I'm
afraid that's the best I can expect from her now. In
any event my replies were more bitter than I wanted them
to be, I guess, because an hour or so later she came
into my bedroom and, her face edged with panic, begged
me not to be too hard on her. "Please don't reject me
anymore" -- something like that. And I was able to be
loving enough, to smile enough, to reassure her, and we
managed to get through the night.

*

Now: what to do about today.

First, I'm powerless to prevent myself from spying
further on her and Dennis. Tonight at quarter to five
I'll return to the recapping factory -- just to get
another look at the "street prince." And after that?
It should be interesting. That is, if she shows up at
home at all.

*   *

All hell has broken loose -- inside me. Maybe
inside her. I'm afraid now of death: hers, mine. Death
of dreams, death of feeling, death of physical bodies.

571

[Have Mercy]

I'm dismembering "the Castle," taking down the pictures
in my room, making its walls the desolate shadowed blank
image of my mind. I'm preparing to abandon this place
and all it represents.

Valerie, stony-faced, separated the paintings she'd
done from the others.

"Why are you doing that?"

"Because they belong in the Castle."

"There is no more 'Castle.' The 'Castle' is a
smoking ruin."

With that she stomped out of the house. To Dennis?
To death? To madness? Great shrieks in me. My heart
thunders helplessly. She hasn't come back.

Yes, I'm afraid of what she'll do now. Not only to
herself but to me. Which will it be, self-destruction
or Glen-destruction? I destroy us (as she sees things),
I destroy the "Castle" in terms of its availability to
her. She destroys -- what? My journals? My other
writings? My wheels? Does she say tauntingly to her
Mafioso who packs a gun: if you're really as crazy about
me as you say, why don't you go kill the bastard I've
been living with who's been screwing me over so much? I
suspect she's down there right now breaking into the
L.C. with the key she stole from me: tossing a lit match
into the bundles of Bulldogs in back, releasing the hand
brake, setting the L.C. rolling down the hill ablaze.
I'm utterly paranoid, craven, furious, mad -- and
immobilized.

*

It happened when I walked back over to the tire-
recapping place a few minutes before five this
afternoon. I rounded a corner too fast and there she
was, pacing in between the huge piles of old tires near
the entrance in her favorite purple micro and a bright
orange top, her back turned to me. I scampered away,
sprinted down an alley, edged along Harrison to a point
where I could get a view of the scene. But evidently
she'd spotted me, for a moment later she approached me
from behind. I didn't see her until she was twenty or
thirty paces away. Then we slowly walked toward each

572

other. Her haughty, taunting smile: that was what
killed me. That smile! I couldn't bear it: a mad fury
seized me as I reached her. I hauled back and whacked
her -- a hard slap on her left cheek with my open right
hand. It didn't even wipe the smile off her face. "You
lying bitch! I can't believe you're doing this!" And a
moment later: "You happy now? You like being treated
this way? You want some more?" Then for thirty
minutes, in the recessed doorway to a bar, she laughed
and riposted coolly as I hurled my furious charges at
her -- but no more slaps or violence of any kind, if
only because she clearly would've relished that. And
finally, because she demanded to do so and I couldn't
deny her without causing myself great damage at the
paper, she accompanied Mike and me to our K101 interview
almost as if nothing had happened, both of us bloody and
shaken (more on that incident later). ---

Thursday 10
　　What a lurid night it was. Val reappeared as I was
writing the previous entry and announced she'd just
called Dennis and told him she would never see him
again. This morning, however, she admitted this was
just another lie: she'd merely gone down to the market
and gotten herself a popsicle. As for the real state of
affairs with Dennis, she says contradictory things: this
morning she volunteered not to see him "for a week." I
said she should do whatever she wants to do and it's
none of my business anymore what happens between her and
him. My own prophecy, though, is she'll return to him,
and soon, and I told her that. She didn't even bother
to deny it.
　　Back to last night: her disdainful treatment so
infuriated me I did something utterly mad. I ripped off
my shirt (popped two buttons), sliced an X into my chest
over my heart with a razor blade, rushed into her room
where she was lying in bed and rubbed the blood onto her
face and onto the hickey, still plainly visible almost
like a second nipple, I'd sucked into her breast the

other day. "Phony drama," she called it, snickering.
If I really loved her, she said, I'd stick with her,
"persist," no matter what she did. I attacked her for
expecting me -- indeed, requiring me -- to conform to
her "adolescent expectations" about love. Gradually my
fury subsided and, helplessly bound together in mutual
degradation, we descended into a long night of weary,
morbid self- and mutual punishment.

"I guess it really is dying in me," she announced.
She could now "understand" my side of the story -- for
the first time, she said -- but she couldn't "feel" it.
She could feel nothing. She rapped listlessly about
"going chaste" for a while, tried to pin me down about
how long I thought we might be apart after she moved
out, moaned about the gigantic hassle of moving itself
-- all this in a weary, cold, often bitter voice. At
times hints of hopefulness popped up on one side or the
other or even on both sides at once -- we talked of how
"tight" we could be, should be, of how frequently she
wishes she could be my sister so that a permanent
relationship would be guaranteed -- but even then the
tone was wistful, resigned.

She'd accepted it was over between us as of late
last week, she said, and that was why she'd agreed to
see Dennis the first time Saturday (he went through so
much money trying to impress her that night, she finally
had to loan him twenty bucks; but she won't say what
they spent any of it on, her money or his); now,
however, she supposedly doesn't know how she feels. She
can't really feel anything at this point. But to me it
was all quite plain: what real hopes and excitement she
had lay elsewhere. The shrink sessions have helped her,
but to work out the new ways of living they suggest and
promote, to "test" herself, she needs a fresh
environment and a new man, or more likely, men.

But most of the talk went to our sexual failure.
Her experience with Dennis was the touchstone for our
exchanges about this -- all of them painful, resentful,
bitter. We just couldn't stop ourselves from going on
and on about it (as we lay on her bed, my chest bare,

both of us still bloodied, the "X" wound aching). What
was best about her "righteous" fucking with Dennis, she
said, was the way he'd reacted, his gratefulness, his
bliss after each round, the way she'd been able to "keep
exciting him over and over." He was "hard, hard, hard,"
she said, and that's what turned her on. It wasn't so
much the way he handled her: in fact, he hadn't known
how to, she said; he'd left her "frustrated." Nor was
he particularly well hung; far from it. But he'd been
hard right from the start, and over and over again, and
this was what she missed in me. Why wasn't I like that?
Why couldn't she affect me that way? Why did I like to
do "foreplay stuff" so much and let things build up so
slowly? Why wasn't I hard and desperate for it from the
second I walked in the door? (As Jim was also, she's
told me before; not just Dennis.)

She compared her night with Dennis to one last
summer when Briana and I balled half a dozen times. Why
hadn't anything like that ever happened with us? She
assumed it was because in some crucial way she's not
attractive to me, or doesn't know how to turn me on, but
at the same time she recalled the way things went down
on our first night, when she'd been "incredibly wet" and
I was in a wilted state for hours, discombobled by how
strongly and nervously she'd come on to me right from
the start in the living room and then even more by the
fact that Danny was sleeping and sometimes wailing in
his crib within arm's reach of us when we hit her bed
(she also attributes some part of her excitement with
Dennis, and with the others she's balled since we met,
simply to their "newness"). And she mentioned with
chilling condescension how much it bothers her that at
times she "has to" stimulate me manually or orally, turn
me on, because before we've had some actual physical
contact I'm usually not in a rock-hard, fully erect
state. (And here I always thought she liked to do this
"foreplay stuff" and it meant as much to her when she
did it for me as it did for me when I did it for her --
which was virtually every time! And she herself often
takes a very long time to turn on! And just in general

the usual beef many women have with men is that we're
not enough into foreplay!)

It's incomprehensible to her, all this ambiguity in
bed, and makes her sexually very insecure with me
(exacerbating fears that already existed from the bad
old days with Jim, who always called her a "bum fuck"
even though he still loved to fuck her almost nonstop).
She feels "intimidated" by me in bed. I'm so much more
"sophisticated" and "refined" a lover, so much more
experienced, have known "so many exquisite lovers," that
as a consequence I have enormously high expectations
which she can't possibly meet. The fears resulting from
all this inhibit her tremendously, make her uptight, too
conscious of her performance, and feed her resentment of
me, lead to defiance, a proud refusal to respond,
anxiety which cripples her when she does make attempts,
physical and/or emotional paralysis that require violent
assaults if they're to be broken through ("beat me so I
can feel"), efforts to evade all physicality in sex ("I
can feel only if I'm completely motionless") or to avoid
all necessities for response (she can "let herself go"
most easily when she's on top, fully in control, and I'm
passive to the point of being motionless).

All of this leads finally to her sexual
disenchantment with me, her efforts to avoid sex, to
avoid being seductive and funky or even warm or
friendly, to reduce sex to a habit indulged in merely to
achieve physical release and placate my need. It robs
sexuality of all joy, curdles sensuality, makes the body
an enemy, places too great a stress on the abstractions
and consolations of love, produces a craving for
physical reassurances of a "safe" nature (constant
companionship, sterile embraces), deepens insecurity and
fear of abandonment, heightens dependence.

The upshot: she has to find another man who offers
her the reassurances she needs -- the touching, the
gratitude, the instantly and perpetually hard cock which
proves how desirable and what a good lover she is -- and
all the emotional aspects of love are suppressed.
Physicality and emotionality are walled off from each

other, love and sex become enemies, and the accompanying
guilt leads to self-alienation.

As for the despicable hard slap I gave her outside
the recapping place, her comment was this: "I deserved
it -- and a lot more. You should've been doing things
like that all along. You should've hit me much harder
than that. If you could've done that last summer, all
our problems might never've even come up. But it wasn't
in you then and it never will be. That slap tonight, it
was nothing. I didn't even feel it."

That she could say this with such contemptuous
directness and apparently believe every word of it is
all the explanation necessary for why we're doomed.

Friday 11
What do I know today I didn't know yesterday?
Well, I can still fuck good at least once in a while.
And Dennis has got a "really curved cock" -- it's not
particularly long or thick but it's shaped sort of like
a banana or a scimitar only more so; it actually pokes
into his lower belly when he's standing (and when it's
standing too, right -- and merely at the sight, of
course, of Valoshka). "Weird," said the lady herself.

Today I'm sucking on a bottle of orange juice in
the front office -- I've moved my base of operations
back up here after a spell at the side table in Mike's
office (the big time!) -- and waiting for Penn Gerhardt
to arrive for a talk about the Bulldog's long-planned
book on city politics and urban ecology (which could
easily be revised and expanded to appeal to the Bresker
crowd -- and I think I've convinced Mike we should drop
the "San Francisco Survival Kit" idea and do the book as
an anti-Manhattanization philippic instead); then after
lunch the shock troops from KRMA will be landing.

But the truly important matters for me again lie
elsewhere. Val's night with Dennis, for example. She
unloaded the details on me at Zim's last night, past two
in the morning, with surprisingly little hassle. She
kept calling herself "dirty," said she couldn't look me

in the eye, felt she'd "betrayed our love" -- but the
facts rolled out.

"I feel like you're making me stick a knife in your
back," she said.

"You already stuck it in," I replied. "I'm asking
you to pull it out."

She didn't really "plan" to sleep with him, she
insists. He took her to the Trident in Sausalito, where
they had a long wait for a table (she was more reluctant
to give up this detail about the Trident being their
destination on their first "date" than almost any other;
apparently our having gone there together several times
made it seem to her that this was a great betrayal);
then they drove around in Marin for a while, winding up
at a beach on the coast somewhere. He began kissing
her. "I don't like car scenes," she told him fairly
early on, the implication of course being it was time to
hit a bed somewhere. He drove her to his one-bedroom
apartment in the Richmond District.

She couldn't remember much about his place.
"Modern furniture, a stereo -- I don't know, Glen."
Immediately when they arrived he ordered her to take her
clothes off. (This she found highly exciting.) Then he
"checked me over" -- and took a shower.

"He's a cleanliness nut," she chuckled. "Each time
he went to the bathroom afterwards and washed himself
off." (Sounds to me like someone who's tangled with an
STD or two, but she didn't ask him about that.)

Surprisingly to me, they went only three rounds.
(I'd expected her to say eight, ten, a dozen.) The
first and third were fucks; the second she sucked him
until he came in her mouth. "Not in it -- sort of
around it." The fucks were "the usual length," she
said, and she found it difficult to describe how he went
about it. Toward the end of the final round she mounted
him, asked him not to move, and brought herself off.
One of the oddest details: he pulled out at the end of
both of the fucks and came on her pubic hair and belly.
She could offer no explanation for it -- she'd already
told him she was on the Pill. (Most likely, I'd say,

she was lying to me to maintain consistency with her
earlier solemn declaration that not a single sperm
of his was "paddling ferociously inward" -- that is, was
ejac'd by him inside her vagina.)

As for his body, she described it as "almost
hairless" and "not firmly muscled -- too soft." His
balls "weren't loose and dangly -- sort of compact and
small, like bird's eggs or something." And his cock:
she'd blurted right at the start, "Yours is a lot
bigger." It was almost diabolical, the way she said
that, implying at once she suspected this was the single
piece of information I most hankered after and also
scoffing at me for wanting to possess it ("Men are so
weird about their cocks"). Then she added: "It was a
puny little curved cock -- more like Jim's size really.
I don't know, Glen, what do you want me to say? I'll
say it." (But afterwards she swore everything she'd
told me was true -- even though she flatly contradicted
herself roughly every third sentence.)

One final detail: all this raunchy sexual activity
took place in a burst at the beginning ("with a little
rest in between"). Nothing more happened that night or
in the morning. After he fell asleep she cried. "Not
my usual kind of crying. I didn't have many tears
left."

One other matter interested me: she really does
seem to assign crucial importance to my lackluster
first-night performance in bed with her last summer. I
never took her seriously about this before now. But she
brought it up again last night, telling me that first
night at Dolores Street in her view determined
everything that followed with us sexually and in a
way even set the tone for our whole relationship. On
that night (one year ago as of July 2nd, three weeks
from today) -- on that night she was extremely
aggressive and turned on but also tense and wired, so
much so I worried she was on some sort of bad trip
(speeding?) and about to freak out. And when her
opening seduction gambit failed to draw the expected
response from me, she simply assumed I didn't find her

attractive. (She still can't believe my semi-inebriated
state from the post-play drinks with Pam Wineberry or
Danny's presence in the bedroom or her warnings about
Jim's attempted break-ins with a gun had anything to do
with my state of mind or body. She thinks all that, and
especially the break-in warning, should've sexually
excited me even more!) Worse: my poor performance led
her to assume I didn't respond to aggressiveness and
open expression of desire. She didn't want to fail
again (blaming this on what she called, last night, for
the first time ever to me, the "bum-fuck complex" Jim
gave her). As a result the "complex" only deepened, of
course, and she rarely was aggressive with me after that
-- and this despite my many requests that she be so and
our long talks about it.

A second interesting point. Despite the scores of
times over the past year she's told me she sees men as
the enemy and hates us all (and certainly has acted at
times as if it were true), she now said she never really
meant it -- but she did admit to feeling, when she turns
a man on, when she gets a man "really hard," he becomes
her "slave" and "I really groove on that." She also
denied that her treatment of men, her confounding of sex
and love (the hostility and violence arising from the
distortion), itself constitutes a kind of dehumanizing
of men. Yet she also insisted the "first thing" men
want is "to be regarded as a sexual object."

I found all this appallingly shallow and told her
so. In what almost seems a parody of the shameful old
male virgin/whore categorization of women, she seems to
think of men as belonging to one of three groups, or at
least so she told me. These groups are, first, the
"prince" (noble in sentiment and thought, refined, to be
admired and worshipped abstractly); second, the "punk"
(callous and brutal, gifted with swagger and street
smarts and -- in a relatively recent addition for her
this past winter -- American-style funk, to fuck and be
fucked by); and third, all the rest (not even worth
considering). The prince and the punk are "antipodal"
in her view and never found in combined form in a single

person: therefore Val can fuck freely or love freely,
but never both at the same time or with the same person.
In me, she said, she at first thought she'd found the
impossible "funky-punky street prince" (and by god she
had!), but she couldn't cope with me, "didn't know how
to deal with someone who might be both -- and who was so
much older [almost nine years!] and had been around so
much more." Thus her original confusion and eventual
hysteria and terror, in effect reducing me, finally, to
neither prince nor funky punk but to that lowly third
mass category: the one not even worth considering. And
she said: "I want all men to love me -- I mean, all men
who meet my standards." And I'd say only now am I
beginning to understand what her standards really are.

Last night, luckily -- and for a sadly predictable
reason which I'll get to in a moment -- I wasn't feeling
quite so meek and defeated as I usually have of late
with her, not so defensive, and I was able to override
all the invitations to despair or to provoking her into
the hysteria cycle. The most tempting of these came
when we returned from Zim's and the Dennis revelations.
Just inside the door I kissed her passionately and
immediately found myself grossly turned on. To me this
was a surprise, even a triumph, to swing out a big
bells-and-whistles hard-on when I pulled my pants down.
To her, feeling morbidly bad after detailing her
transgressions with Dennis, my arousal at such a time
was unbearable. She tried but she couldn't respond at
all, and gradually I cooled off (I didn't press her).
The temptation to walk out of her bedroom or subject her
to a scornful dressing-down was strong, but for once
mercy was stronger. Or was it just wariness? Or was it
just the fact that, all appearances to the contrary, I
actually wasn't feeling all that horny myself? In any
event she must've felt terribly bad about it, because
two hours later I awoke to find her atop me fucking
away. And then this morning we went at it again. A
triumphant night in a perverse and pathetic way.

*

Now for some background. In an important sense

581

this partial recovery of dignity with Valerie (call it
that anyway) was possible because of Jang. After two
weeks of silence she called, and we arranged a liaison
for last night.

The original plan was to do the town ("have some
fun") but we set this up on Wednesday afternoon, at a
point when it seemed Val and I would immediately be
going our separate ways. Then Thursday afternoon Val
called full of warmth, love, apology. I felt I couldn't
break the date with Jang but also couldn't stay out too
late -- for fear of starting another cycle of
recrimination with Val and further delaying the day of
her departure -- and I told Jang this when I met her.
She was surprisingly accommodating. We agreed to go out
for a quick dinner. But in the L.C. before pulling out
we began getting affectionate almost immediately and
this was such a turn-on she proposed we go back upstairs
right away, and we did.

What followed was one of the all-time most
delicious fucks, Jang wildly tossing her ass, coming
several times, finally carrying me to a blockbuster
climax with exquisite deep vaginal squeezes as I rode
her dog-fashion. It made a man of me again. Not that
all was light and joy: I had to keep the X-shaped scar
on my chest hidden from view, I had to contend with the
certainty I was again exploiting her, with the sure
sense we'd both have to pay for this splendid
indiscretion with future pain: but still, it was
unavoidable, necessary, and marvelous, for both of us,
and even in a way for Val -- because without it I
would've been absolutely incapable of treating her later
on with even the slightest compassion at a time when
she, by her own testimony, desperately needed it.

And so I justify my own "betrayal" in much the same
way Val did hers. The only difference is this: I
haven't flaunted it before her. And I won't. And I
suppose this is my damnable "nobility" acting up again.
Or call it narcissism. Or call it lack of candor. Or
call it deception. Or just call it compassion or mercy
or kindness or even loving kindness. Whatever it is,

582

that quality in me has caused her much grief, even
doomed us, but at least it will spare her, and perhaps
me even more, some pain in the parting moments.

Saturday 12
    Well, life goes on, offering up another day with
different coloration but suspiciously familiar shape.
Here I am back at the Bulldog office on a Saturday
afternoon. What's different this time is Val's here
with me and we just balled on Mike's couch.
    "I feel like one of those cartoons of naked
secretaries being chased around the office," she says,
returning from the head with a handful of kleenex to
wipe away our commingled juices and other telltale
evidence of nonjournalistic activities threatening to
stain the couch. She's wearing only her knee-high blue
boots, and semen trickles visibly down her inner thigh,
as she spunkily, as it were, not to say proudly, points
out to me.
    Another difference this time: my tooth is aching.
Although the worst of the pain has disappeared since I
stuffed cotton gauze into the hole created by the broken
filling, it's still bad enough.
    I feel slightly different about the Bulldog too,
somewhat more comfortable. Basically this is because
yesterday Peggy made a point of telling me she and Mike
appreciate what I'm doing for them. "It's one of those
things where we don't know how we ever got along without
you all these years!" Mike, she said, doesn't do too
well at expressing appreciation directly, but you can
tell how he feels by how much work and responsibility he
gives you. "If you're overwhelmed, you know!"
    So I knew. And that made me feel good. And so did
the talk with Penn Gerhardt, who seemed quite pleased
with our plan for redoing the "Survival Kit" book to
appeal more to the S.F. Alliance crowd; and so did the
staff meeting with KRMA, in which Wallace Tuttle (their
station manager) proposed we draw up an actual written
agreement spelling out our "Mutual Aid Pact." All ego

trips for me.

The disappointments have come from Valerie, who persists in trying to pin me down on a date when we'll get back together. I can't offer one, of course. I want things to work out for us, but my sense of whether they could actually do so vacillates wildly. How can I possibly say what my feelings will be a month or two from now when I don't know what they'll be in a day or an hour and maybe not even what they are right this moment? Yet she castigates me for "withholding certainty" from her.

Another good development: this morning garrulous Sid Portola again dropped by at Funston with a fresh issue of the Merino Mercury along with news that the paper seems to be prospering ("Al wants badly to come out every week"). My reaction was a mixture of pride, pleasure, surprise, and, I can't deny, disappointment (how dare they succeed without me?). (Of course the demos and riots at Fleming might've helped, and Sid thinks those in turn were sparked at least in part by our expose' on housing discrimination in Garnett.)

And then a startling coincidence: It turns out Bruce Nelson, the Bulldog's strangely diffident and almost courtly black poetry editor, knows Briana and Terry and saw them at a party just last week. He wasn't sure whether they were back together. "They were hugging," he said, "but from the way they were doing it I got the feeling things were either cooling off between them or an explosion was about to happen." To him Briana's beauty is such that "she seems practically untouched by human hands" -- which I'm pretty sure he did not mean in an entirely complimentary way (i.e., he certainly wasn't implying he sees Terry's hands as godly -- or beastly for that matter). He did promise to check into their current status a bit more and report back.

As I write, Val is using Mike's phone to call about apartments listed on the Bulldog's bulletin board. The final break between us still hasn't happened (we're now twelve days past our agreed date). Today we got into useless altercations about art and Mishima's suicide

(which she finds gloriously stylish -- despite his
blatant fascism -- and hopes to emulate in an equally
glorious style all her own before she's thirty -- or so
she says). At this point it's hard to come up with
anything we can talk about civilly.

How is it possible for a twenty-year-old to be so
riddled with hostilities and antagonisms? She assails
my "hang-ups" regarding work, yet derides hippies for
their lack of ambition and diligence. She adores
violent tensions, glamour, easy success. She openly
despises the Bulldog ("reformist") but wonders if she
might do some work with the Summer Project to keep
herself busy in the weeks ahead. She laughs derisively
at -- ah fuck it.

The truth is I can't think a coherent thought about
her. Right now the massive resentment on both sides is
distorting everything almost beyond recognition. Yet
this can't be true either, because it's easy to
recognize resentment has become (and not for the first
time) our normal state and the normal kind of normalcy
would itself be the shocking distortion. (Or
ressentiment is our current normal state, that's another
possibility. The distinction between those two words
starting with "res" and ending in "ment" is back to
being a useful one. For me our battles have been going
on so long and at such a pitch and depth of intensity
that the "ress" word applies just as much to me as to
her. Or so it often seems. -- But of course it's not
really so. What am I saying? She's got at least
nineteen years of it on me, stewing in it -- if not a
couple of centuries, if the anticolonialism she's
steeped in by birthright is included -- and as she's the
first to insist, it should be.)

Sunday 13
What a bummer it is when you can't turn on your ol'
lady. Last night on the way home from Project Artaud I
found myself suddenly possessed by the diabolical idea
of staging a "therapeutic car scene" with Valerie. I

pulled over on a residential street up in Corona
Heights, parked directly beneath a streetlight, and laid
some heavy necking on her. She knew I was up to
something bizarre but couldn't decipher exactly what it
was. I kept waiting for her to say "I don't like car
scenes" in a way that would imply we should hurry home
and jump in bed. She never did, though, and finally I
revealed the plot and enlisted her (crazy gleam in my
eye) in the game.

With a show of reluctance -- yet also with scarcely
hidden relish ("Glen, you're such a masochist!") -- she
provided the script, a step-by-step description of the
seduction scene with Dennis -- which took place exactly
one week ago last night -- and we acted it out
methodically, stepping in and out of character,
commenting on the action and the meaning, as two actors
might do when first reading aloud a play they're
thinking about trying out for.

The scene went something like this. Dennis's gray
Firebird -- with the drums in the backseat sometimes
"vibrating weirdly" and seemingly of their own volition
-- pulls up to an observation point overlooking a Marin
beach. Val, wearing tight satinlike black bells and a
scoopnecked purple jersey, is leaning against the far
door, and they're separated by a low-slung stereo tape
deck issuing "fairly loud" rock music (it would be
interesting to know who the band was, or bands, but she
doesn't recall -- and surely he would've told her, and
she'd remember, if it was his own band). So then Dennis
leans back, at the same time edging toward her, and
sighs: says he's feeling sorta wasted. Val too is
playing it cool, though she's as excited as he is by the
prospects ahead. He reaches over and takes her hand.
She thinks that's corny and after an interval long
enough to convey she's not rejecting him, she replaces
it on his lap, at the same time provoking him with the
celebrated line: "I don't go for car scenes." Her tone
is a mixture of disdain and come-on.

He temporizes for a while, tapping his fingers and
feet along with the music. Then he starts up the car

and drives down closer to the beach. All the time
they're joking lightly, he's teasing her about "not
liking car scenes," coming on cocky and confident, just
as she is. At their new, more secluded site he reaches
over and pulls her head down on his lap, so that she's
looking up at him, and then kisses her (has her back
been aching all week because it was jammed against that
console and not, despite what she told me, from the
apartment-hunting?). He goes for her breasts, sliding
his hand beneath her jersey -- she's not wearing a bra,
just as she wasn't on our first night together, and for
the same reason -- and he asks, as the hand goes in, "Do
you mind?" (She chuckles recalling this.) A few
minutes of fondling there and he goes for her cooch,
again directly, sticking his hand inside the waistband
of her pants. He finds her very wet.

"You sure are horny, aren't you," he says
triumphantly. "Don't like car scenes, huh?"

She tells him she'd prefer a setting where they
could get it on truly righteously. He starts driving
to his place back in the city. On the way he grabs her
hand and places it on his cock, which is hard under his
pants. After a moment she pulls her hand back, saying,
"I want to make you wait."

That's the script. Naturally as we went along I
commented on Dennis's techniques, describing what I'd do
instead, "the jaded older guy's way."

Yes, it would make a good story. Both levels
should be included: Dennis and Val parked at the beach
in Marin, Glen and Val parked on the street in Corona
Heights. Lots of unexpected twists. The key would be
to find a way to suggest, without saying directly, the
characters at the Glen-and-Val level were trapped in a
vindictive cycle, with each new twist ratcheting them
closer to a final blowup. ---

*

What colossal timing: real life preempts mere
storytelling. Ten minutes later and now I'm trembling
from the indignity and outrage of it.

As I stepped over to the stereo to lift the stack

of albums for a replay I happened to glimpse Dennis's
Firebird hovering in the street in front of the house.
I froze where I was, no shirt on, arms imperiously
folded across my chest, and glared down at him for most
of those ten minutes as he waited, pulled into the
driveway, gunned his motor several times, honked, backed
out, parked, waited, pulled out, hovered a few minutes
more, and finally roared off. No doubt I was highly
visible in the window, and probably Dennis and I
conducted a lengthy staredown, although his face was
obscured by his glary windshield and I couldn't be sure.

Meanwhile I kept up a running commentary for Val.

"Valoshka, guess who's here!"

She peeked out the window in the yellow room and
promptly flew into a panic, locking the apartment door,
tearing at her hair, closing herself in her room,
issuing instructions -- "If he knocks, say I'm not in!"
-- grimacing, rolling her eyes, rushing about the house
trying to look composed. Oh it was great melodrama all
right. Or was it farce? The old rooster squawking and
strutting as the young one scratches dirt onto his turf,
both roosters appearing ready to rumble. And meanwhile
the young hen flies into a tizzy and then retires to a
secluded corner of the coop to await the victor.

*   *

This time the old rooster prevailed. It would be
expected he'd then punish the young hen for her straying
and fuck the hell out of her just to show who's still
king of the coop. Both of which, in this case, he
actually did do, or anyway did as best he could.

But with several differences. For one thing, it
was the young hen who first attacked the old rooster.
Not sexually, however. Rather she lambasted him for
failing to lavish sufficient compassion upon her to
salve the torment she was going through. "After all,"
as she poutingly pointed out, she "had to worry about
hurting two of you." This assertion provoked a cry of
hypocrisy -- like maybe she was expecting the kind of
compassion she'd shown the old rooster at the Merino
Mercury office, for example, when that sexy old hen

[Living with Valerie]

Claire's fluttering about the coop was the issue? Now
at 1616 sexy young hen Val's feathers ruffled at this
suggestion, she stiffened, she fought back, but
eventually she collapsed in the old rooster's wings:
"Hide me," she cried.

So I (enough already with the third-person barnyard
fable) -- I stroked her hair and led her to the living-
room mattress. Although she'd previously announced, as
she put it, "I no longer want to do sex with anyone,"
she changed her mind, or pretended to, for after a
period of rubbing and caressing she whispered (with
unsure irony): "Take your clothes off." (Echoing of
course Dennis's punky command upon their arrival at his
apartment.) A fucking scene somewhat short of fabulous,
but still not all that shabby, followed.

For this fuck, as well as an attempt at a second
one which ensued, she assumed, at her own insistence,
the dominant position. The first round (during which we
eyed each other profoundly and begged each other to "get
tight") ended in a glorious eyes-locked mutual come
(unless, that is, she feigned hers, although, assuming
her acting hasn't improved a great deal, I'm pretty sure
she didn't). The second, initiated by her vigorous
handjob (as she squatted over me, ass raised
provocatively and lips pressed against the "X" scab on
my chest, arm extended down between her legs: surely not
the easiest way to execute a handjob) -- this second
round very nearly achieved that balance of tension and
movement known as "the erotic exquisite." But then at
the precise moment of my premonitory ejaco-tickle she
abruptly halted her movements, proclaiming fatigue, and
the entire effort collapsed. (Moments later Danny,
asleep in the next room this whole time, began
whimpering.)

Still, it was the closest we've come so far to
truly stupendous balling, at least by my own definition
of what such a triumph should entail. Naturally this
would happen after the pattern for the future has
already been set in steel -- a few days before I banish
her permanently from my turf.

3

Monday 14

The most gorgeous day of the year so far: waves of
dazzling golden sunlight, rivers of earth-sweetened air.
The Chronicle says we skipped spring -- I'd say it's all
been compressed into today. So strong is the magic it
even induced Val to wake up with a smile this morning
(alas, it soon vanished). Then around noon came the
good news: she phoned me here at the office to say she'd
put twenty dollars down on one of the apartments she'd
learned about from the Bulldog bulletin board. She'll
start living there -- at Fourth and Irving, just twelve
blocks or so from "the Castle" and a mere four blocks
from her shrink's office -- as soon as I can muster the
energy to haul her stuff over there.   ---
                         *
     She just called again, this time requesting we meet
at the JCC. But for some reason the prospect of
exposing my flabby three-fifths or four-fifths naked
(depending on whether I'm a shirt or a skin) hooping-it-
up self to her at a time like this is less than
appealing and I proposed taking her out somewhere
instead. Now with the breakup truly imminent, of
course, I find myself uneasy, plagued with doubts, far
from the image of bubbling relief I try to present to
others. But I think I can weather the transition.
     I should also note this: Monica here in the office
has invited me over for dinner sometime next week after
her newly remodeled kitchen is ready to go (she's said
to be a terrific cook). I've accepted, with the exact
day to be worked out later. I just hope I can be wise
enough to avoid getting sexual with her (which, if it
did happen and it didn't turn out too badly, or maybe
even more so if it did, would be sure to lead later to
work-hours awkwardness if not outright disaster).
     The main thing now is to keep calm, not rush off
into wild excesses of the flesh or the heart. Make the

parting as gracious and loving as possible. Last night
at two a.m. Val laid another damn good fuck on me.
She's trying hard to be cheerful. Her new homemade
crocheted pink hot pants: she vows, without my asking,
to wear those outrageously sexy things only for me: a
vow I have zero confidence in. New revelations from
her, too, about Dennis: she says he was "jealous" of me
that first night, asking whether she planned to sleep
with me and let me fuck her when she returned home. Her
answer to him, she says, was yes on both counts if I
would have her, but she told him she doubted I would.

     She described me to Dennis, she says, as a "tall
dude, wears a cowboy hat," "very intelligent," "a stud"
-- and she supposedly told him she loved me but I was
kicking her out. (This is her general line on the
Dennis fling: she did it out of desperation after being
rejected by me and emphatically not as a matter of
revenge. And her own heinous treatment of me over a
period of months up until very recently had nothing to
do with the fling either, or with anything else.) She
now says she'll never see Dennis again "because what
happened with him caused you so much pain." She really
did tell him goodbye last week, she insists, again with
zero credibility. And regardless of that, the sparkle
in her eyes as she says these things leads me to believe
she'll return to him shortly after we separate, if not
before, and if she hasn't already, and if she hasn't
kept seeing him all along, say while I've been at work.
And from what I saw of him the second time around, I
really do think he might be good for her -- not good for
the ideal Valerie I create in my head, but for the real
one. What he likes to dish out, she likes to receive,
and vice versa. And I'm certainly not one to deny that
that can matter a lot.

     At the Bulldog, meanwhile, we're plunging ahead on
several fronts, making slow but steady progress. KRMA,
S.F. Alliance, back-of-the-book, revised political book,
Summer Project. My main problem is that I spend too
much time rapping with Monica, Arnie, and the others,
including roly-poly red-bearded Carl in distribution who

posted the apartment listing Val found on our board and
will now be her housemate (one of six or seven) -- too
much time rapping with them, I say, and not enough time
on the phone pursuing stories, checking facts, hunting
down new writers, "closing the sale" on shaky Summer
Project volunteers.

(It's Flag Day. I'd forgotten all about it, but
Yvonne just pranced in waving two small Old Glories --
collector's items almost -- with peace signs
superimposed on the field of stars. "Hey, where's the
patriotic spirit around here?!?" -- And down in L.A.
another sleazy Mafia-linked musician name of Sinatra
gave his farewell concert last night. And I say to him:
good riddance! And please take Richard Nixon and his
whole hard-right Rat Pack with you when you go!)

Tuesday 15
     Another day every bit as spectacular as yesterday
-- weatherwise I mean, and only that, thank god. All
day long I've been longing to stretch out on that
sundeck gravel for an hour or two, but the jolting news
is I seem to have lost my Lamy pen, probably at "Love
Story" last night, and without that pen it's no
exaggeration to say I'm frequently "at a loss," i.e.,
panicky and bewildered. I mean, that pen has truly
become the mainspring of my world, and without it chaos
threatens on all sides.
     "Love Story," bad as it is, meant something to me,
largely because the romantic myths on which it's based
-- upward mobility is available to everyone, democracy
always works, athletics matters a lot, love is always
groovy, only blind chance can grind down a good man, a
good man is hard to find, a good man is proud, strong,
polite, earnest, noble, sincere, honorable and blah blah
blah -- these were also among the governing myths in the
world where I grew up. On the surface at least, my own
story is somewhat similar to that of Oliver Bartlett,
the all-Ivy hockey player and magna graduate, an All-
American boy in the old-fashioned sense of the term (a

major difference being that my parents were and are
merely upper-middle class at best, not upper-upper-
middle like his). To my displeasure I found the movie
tugging at emotions which I long ago learned to dismiss
or belittle. So naturally I turned right around and
dismissed and belittled the movie. That it could
squeeze a few tears from Val surprised me as well until
I realized she did indeed see elements in it not only of
our story but also, with the gender roles reversed, of
her and Dennis's story and also her and Jim's story and
maybe even her mother and father's story. It may be
schizophrenic but it can still be handy to play both
sides of the rich/poor divide at once the way Val can
and often does (her mother's family and upbringing being
desperately poor, her father's affluent and aristocratic
or close to it). (And I should note that "Love Story"'s
ability to be all things to all people explains why this
piece of pap is raking it in like nothing ever seen
before. Even brother Rob, I recall -- in fact have
never forgotten and still can't quite believe -- thought
it was terrific.)

*

Oh how I love to brainstorm about the Bulldog's
plans for the months ahead. All day today I've been
pacing these hot and humid corridors trying to come up
with ways to help nudge this paper over the hump into
regular publication. Meanwhile the usual kinds of
things keep happening, some good and some not, but in
sum imparting a sense of modest headway being made.
     ** I call Nick Kazan (Elia's thirty-year-old son,
a Berkeley playwright) and he agrees to write film
criticism for us.
     ** Carla Matchett from Chicago comes in for a
Summer Project interview and she turns out to be a gem,
widely experienced, sharp, yet still engagingly fresh
and enthusiastic. Mike immediately writes her off as
another of those brainless types they "turn out on
lathes at the Seven Sisters" -- but I think he's wrong.
     ** Matt Sparks, theater critic, wanders in, and I
rap with him, as I have with dozens of others, about the

593

changes going down around here. "Is the editorial
office moving up front?" Matt asks facetiously. At
almost the same moment Mike wanders by, casting a wary
eye upon us. I flash (not for the first time) on the
suspicion he must naturally be feeling, the fear that
decisions are being made behind his back, that the
younger generation (and in particular the ambitious
volunteer newcomer sitting in the front office) is
trying to put one over on him, maybe take his newspaper
away from him. But if he is feeling this he usually
keeps it well hidden, and I do all I can to avoid giving
such a false impression. The truth is, and I well know,
he can do much more for me than I could ever do for him.
    ** A bearded longhair drops in. I'm taken aback
to hear he's attending Stanford business school. Why
would any intelligent person want to waste himself in a
place like that and on the kind of life all but certain
to follow? But he volunteers to help us in the fall,
says he knows numerous people working on projects that
might fit in with our campaign to build a popular front.
    ** Monica, slim and blond and frizzy-haired,
wears a baggy dress and what Fred calls "Minnie Mouse"
or "Lana Turner Fuck-Me" shoes: she's my closest ally in
the effort to revitalize the paper with a transfusion of
counterculture spirit. Her cat died of distemper last
week, leaving her histrionically distraught (she visits
the vet daily to view the corpse in cold storage).
(Peggy, Monica's ex-sister-in-law -- both use the last
name Riddell on the Bulldog masthead -- Peggy's taking
a well-deserved day off.)
    ** And Jang calls. That marvelously warm and
energetic greeting. Her delight hits me like a dose of
adrenaline. Deeply felt: "I love you, Glen." It's been
one summer short of seven years since we met (which
means we've now known each other slightly longer than
her time with her cherry man Guamo the Italian
diplomat). I'd like to start seeing her again before
she goes, but holding off her demands for exclusive
attention would be agonizingly difficult. Already she's
insisting on giving me money to help pay the rent at

Funston, saying it's to begin making up for her failure to keep her promise to alternate years with me in paying the expenses when we were living there together. "Now I understand much better about how life is." For her it seems I actually am a young and virile "funky street prince" of the type Valerie says can't exist. (Age differences, I'm reluctantly noticing again, can mean a lot more than they should. Jang is now two years short of being twice Val's age, not exactly twice her age as she was for two weeks back in April, but the gap between them seems to be growing, not shrinking.)

   (And this note about Val: the words "raw" and "crude" best describe her these days. A blunt directness that often crosses over into tastelessness, vulgarity, rudeness, provocation, insults, even outright cruelty. I'm much more aware now how much she likes her man to be macho, to tell her what to do, to push her around more than a little (while perhaps maintaining a certain "virile refinement" and sense of humor) -- so she can push back. She likes and even needs the frictions and the ugliness: at the core of her psychosexual dynamic (and I'd say many other psychodynamics of hers) they're what turn her on. When I look back with this expanded awareness of her I realize the evidence for such motivation has been plentiful right from the start. Why did I play it down so much? In any case, if ever there was a time when I could be this kind of man for her, it's certainly not now. I'm too self-aware, trying too hard to hang on to my last shreds of dignity and self-respect. It's a shame. If it weren't for Danny, though, I think we still might have a shot at making it. I simply can't continue to be a party to what she and Jim -- but also she and I, yes, and our kind of life -- have been doing to him.)

Wednesday 16
   Back in action with the fourth Lamy pen I've bought in a little over two years (Jang has one, the other two

[Have Mercy]

I've lost). "Stately, plump Buck Mulligan..." -- and
now just as I'm ready to roll out an artsy-fartsy
Bloomsday intro, Val walks in and it's obvious I won't
be at this for long.

"Telescope?" she asks, noticing my spotter scope on
the desk. "What's that doing here?"

"I was going to spy on you."

"Really? Today?"

"No, not today. Before. There's no more need now,
is there?"

Bleah. No more need now, that's a laugh. I just
wish (to bleat out the thought yet again) she'd quit
prolonging the pain. Even though she has her new place
lined up, she's taking her own sweet time about leaving.
In fact she hasn't even begun preparing for the move.
Probably I'll have to get firm with her on this again,
or "hard," and then, of course, she'll have to get even
with me (meaning even firmer and harder) as payback.
She'd probably do it anyway. It's just about inevitable
we'll part in a storm of extreme animosity. So be it.

All the flowers on the sundeck are dead or dying
(yes, yet another blatant but irresistible symbolic
comment on our sorry time together).

Now she hands me a dried leaf to use as a bookmark.
An idea she picked up from Barbara, she tells me.

Today I accomplished only one thing: I finally
succeeded in dragging myself to the dentist.

Last night we saw a good film, Jack Nicholson's
"Drive, He Said" (from the Jeremy Larner novel, whose
title comes from the Robert Creeley poem whose extreme
popularity I used to find so puzzling back in Mentoka
Falls days). Val gains a little better understanding of
the American jock world and the mentalities it produces
in malleable teenage boys -- such as I once was, for
sure, and no doubt still am in some ways -- while
beefing them up for their likely future role as cannon
fodder in Vietnam or elsewhere.

And a deflating failure in bed, one last one for
the record. As soon as I take the "superior" position
(as in missionary) she grinds to a halt. Goes into a

trance with eyes focused on -- or rather unfocused on --
that same nondescript part of the ceiling they so often
seem to seek out under such circumstances. Awful.

*

On second thought I shouldn't call it "one last
one." A strong potential exists for many more last
ones, I'm sorry to say, and they may be even more awful.
"Like being hit in the gut with a gallon sack of
nickels." Over and over. Meanwhile I suspect she's
still seeing Dennis during the day (though she denies it
-- and does so in that subdued, glum, eyes-averted way
that's often a tip-off she's lying) (and besides, she
looks like she's been sleeping very little and balling a
lot). -- In any case I'm glad she's no longer trying to
flaunt it or torment me with it. And I've seen someone
else too (Jang) and have plans to see at least one other
(Monica), so to hell with her.

-- And so much for my special Bloomsday entry.
The Buck, stillborn, stops here.

Thursday 17

Spectacular weather continues: temperatures in the
high seventies, pure azure skies, just enough breeze to
keep the air fresh and sweet. It's so good I don't
really need to wear a jacket when I ride the Honda in to
work. On days like this I head down to the outdoor
picnic tables at Sam's Sandwich Shop for lunch, glancing
through the early edition of the Examiner while nibbling
away (my vision is still cloudy even now, ten or fifteen
minutes after returning to the office, from focusing too
long on newsprint in that glary sunlight).

This morning's rap with Ari Bresker's right-hand
man, Tim Sorrel, a personable bushy-haired young lawyer
whose eyes blaze with idealism, sparked some new ideas
about how the collaboration between the Bulldog and the
S.F. Alliance (SFA) could work synergistically. The
major problem is this: for the SFA's height-limit
petition to have a chance of winning at the ballot box
in November they must come up with a convincing factual

analysis showing that further highrise growth
("Manhattanization") would be economically detrimental
to the city. Yet the SFA has neither the expertise nor
the manpower to do this, hasn't conceived a program, and
may not even realize the need. In short, if it's to be
done this summer, the Bulldog Summer Project will have
to do it for them -- coordinate the effort, map its
direction, push it to completion, and then present it to
the SFA as a fait accompli. This is a staggering job,
of fundamental importance in my view, a rare opportunity
-- and how supremely ironic that leadership of it should
fall upon me. In just a few weeks I'll have to make
myself an expert on urban economics. Plunge in, see
what I can do. Well, why not? If it works maybe I'll
feel my life's been worthwhile.
     (Me too, ablaze with idealism!)
     This will probably become the focus of my summer
(who knows: perhaps my life) and if it does I hope I can
write intelligently about it for the paper and the
revised Bulldog political book. The enormous difficulty
of the task would stem primarily from the fact that, in
human terms, it's all so shallow and superficial. As a
general statement I think it's true to say I'll succeed
in this Bulldog job to the extent I'm able to organize
well -- not get to know people well. Close personal
relations will only muddy the waters. Or to put it
differently: I'll do this job well to the degree I can
succeed in suppressing the "emotion freak" in me.
     Speaking of which: last night almost became a full-
fledged disaster. It started with my failure to greet
Val with what she deemed the proper degree of enthusiasm
and warmth when she strolled into the Bulldog office at
six-thirty. A series of recriminations followed, the
nastiness gradually mounting to culminate in a scathing
tirade she delivered an hour later as, while sharing a
U.S. Restaurant booth with two students, we waited for
our orders to arrive. "You think you're doing me a big
fucking favor having dinner with me?" -- that sort of
thing. The two students snickered and cringed,
reddened, pretended not to notice us inches away from

them as they nearly choked on their pasta. Pretty much
the same was true of a lot of other people at nearby
booths and tables and probably also at some far-off
ones. I wolfed down my lamb chops as quickly as
possible, afraid Val was about to uncork another high-
decibel public rage like the doozer she let fly back in
April at the SFA meeting. All the signs were there.

As we got to the street, however, we had the good
fortune to see a car hit my Honda and knock it to the
ground. This definitely served to distract her (and me
too). The car, a shiny silver Mercedes maneuvering to
get out of a tight parallel parking space, backed into
the 90 and then zoomed away. Astoundingly, three people
volunteered their names as witnesses. I'm now mulling
the idea of tracing the car's license number, which one
of the witnesses gave us (along with a detailed
description of the driver). The Honda, however, doesn't
seem all that damaged: just a couple of new dents and
bent pieces to go with the many of same previously
existing. The driver "looked rich as hell" (said that
same witness), but I doubt I'll pursue a lawsuit. Val's
comment when I told her this: "You're just like some
stupid laid-back hippie!" But no, that's not really it;
I just don't want to waste lots of time on a court case
that probably wouldn't be worth much anyway. Not even
in San Francisco could a jury be impaneled that would
think my pain and suffering from witnessing such a scene
was worth more than a few bucks at most. They might
even suspect I enjoyed it. And in fact I did, though
only quite a bit ex post facto.

We managed to get all the way home -- the Honda
worked just fine -- before the fight burst into the open
again. This time it happened as she was separating her
kitchen utensils from mine and preparing to start
packing. She flung verbal acid at me, I ducked and
tried to restrain myself (afraid anything I might say
could provoke the ultimate explosion). Her basic charge
was that I had now become a "big phony." Most of her
words were bitter speculations about how I'd soon be
blithely fucking around after she left, still wearing

the clothes she'd made for me, beneath paintings she'd
painted for me, on sheets she'd washed for me, etc. etc.
(the last part isn't even true, though I'll concede she
may've helped fold them and definitely smoothed them out
a time or two while maniacally making the bed).

The whole evening she was angling for some sort of
promise or commitment, and of course I wasn't about to
give her any such thing. "It's not real wise of you to
be attacking me now," I finally said, "in the kind of
state I'm in," meaning that as a result of the Dennis
episode her nastiness was just driving me deeper into
the proud, bitter, resentful "withdrawal" which would
make any prospect of eventual reconciliation that much
more unlikely. At the same time I tried to make it
clear by tone and body language that she'd pushed me far
enough: I wasn't about to budge another inch. And as it
turned out, much to my surprise, she was ready to
compromise, to back down, perhaps as the result of a
late-arriving twinge of guilt over her actions with
Dennis and her lies about them or maybe because she now
had her own apartment lined up and was feeling less
stress; and so I tried to meet her halfway, and we wound
up reconciling (in a sense) in bed and vowing to "try
to stay tight" when we're living in our separate places.
But the hostilities preceding all this gave me even more
reason to doubt we'll be able to do that.

                    *   *

Val banishes me from her room while she removes
paintings and posters from the walls.

"I'd feel bad if you watched," she says. "I
remember how I felt last week when you took down your
things."

I could read the newspaper, she suggests. When I
tell her I don't have one, she retorts with mock
incredulity, "This would be the one night when you don't
have a newspaper to read!" And I sheepishly confess I
failed to bring home tonight's paper only because I'd
already read it -- did so way back at noon, in fact, in
the headache-inducing (as it later turned out) sunlight
at Sam's Sandwich Shop.

600

[Living with Valerie]

So now I sit and listen to the metallic clicks of
the staple remover as down come the Klee color squares,
the thunderous Goethe and Tolstoy quotes, the glaring
Hedy Lamarr and Beethoven posters as well as dozens of
her own watercolors and sketches. Already an empty
corner gapes in the living room where her bed from the
Dolores Street place used to stand on its end against
the wall -- one of her new housemates moved it for her
in his van this afternoon (I came home hoping all her
things would be gone, but no such luck). The apartment
here is in a shambles, of course, partly because of her
moving, but also because months ago when our battles
started escalating she dropped all efforts to keep the
place up and I lost interest in trying to do it on my
own while she was still here. One reason I'm eager for
her to go is so I can restore a little primitive order
to the premises. For far too long anarchy and chaos
have been the reigning domestic standards around here.
No, I'm not ashamed to hear myself uttering such
heresies. Maintaining my balance is what counts right
now. Anything of a loftier nature will just have to go
hang for a while.
As I wait I'm also mulling things we talked about
in the L.C. after dinner tonight. In passing I
mentioned I already know what I'll be doing with my
spare time this summer.
"what?"
"Trying to become an instant expert on urban
planning and economics."
To Val, as she didn't hesitate to let me know,
nothing could be drier, duller, more academic, more
boring, more reformist, more irrelevant and
contemptible. On the contrary, I replied, it's
extraordinarily interesting stuff and also might even
turn out to be important in Movement terms. Had she not
heard of Jane Jacobs? Lewis Mumford? This led to a
rhubarb about intellect in general, with me in the
somewhat unusual position of defending intellectuals
while she was putting them down. Her interests now lie
largely in emotional or "creative" subjects such as

601

style (clothes) and art (poetry, painting, design).
What's more, she insists they always have. To the
extent she's interested in intellect -- and politics and
philosophy too, she's adamant in saying -- it's really a
matter of emotions and nothing else.

My attempt to snare her on the obvious
contradictions between this new stance of hers and the
feminist rhetoric she sometimes spouts drew only hot
denials. She can't even admit the super-sexy way she
dresses has anything to do with making herself sexually
appealing (that is, a "sexual object"), claiming instead
it's all a matter of aesthetics (to which sex is
unrelated, incidentally, according to her in this
argument, although at other times she's championed the
opposite view and every bit as vehemently).

What all this is leading up to is a scathingly
critical comment she made about my own perception. In
essence, she said I'm not an "artistic" observer. In
this journal, for example, I rarely dwell lovingly on
setting, on describing a scene, on getting the feeling
of it just right with lots and lots of ambient detail;
rather I tend to plunge more or less directly into what
she scornfully calls "meaning." "You should sit back
and observe more," she said. Jang did this, for
example, she pointed out. From Jang's letters to me
(all of which Val has read -- a boggling undertaking)
one gains a sense of a unique vision, she said, of an
individual perspective rich with insight. Not so from
any writing of mine. The closest I ever come is when I
get "sort of humorous about meaning" -- and that, she
went on, "really has nothing to do with aesthetics or
art. Not to me anyway." -- And after filtering out the
spite and the extreme terms in which she couched these
remarks I think she's at least partly right. My efforts
at description, when I do venture them, tend to be quick
strokes in which I try to make a tiny part stand for the
whole. This way I may occasionally succeed in revealing
a hidden quality or two, but I'm rarely able to impart
the in-depth feeling of a place or event as "inflected
through the vision of a unique sensibility," as the

[Living with Valerie]

critics might say.

And maybe I never will be able to do that. But it's something to work on, and I thank her for bringing it up. At least it shows she cared enough to read and form an opinion about my stuff (even if it was mainly, as is so often the case with her, for the purpose of unearthing evidence with which she could later tear me to pieces).

*   *

Hours later. Stefan Mendes, one of my former students at City College, has come and gone, perching awkwardly on the edge of my bed in this massively disheveled room, talking earnestly about political and academic matters, glancing about uneasily as Val moved from room to room gathering her things, occasionally muttering obscenities. She and I have just decided to put off doing the rest of the move until Saturday. For the most part all evening here at Funston she's been operating in a sort of trance of resignation, subdued, weary, dazed, moving cautiously "because of the sunburn." (At one point she proudly displayed her almost rose-colored naked breasts for me, pulling up her jersey and jutting them forward by arching her spine and thrusting back her shoulders (and her chin up) and then squeezing the boobs out still farther with her hands -- and then abruptly yanking the jersey back down over them with a sneer as if to say, "Don't think you'll ever be seeing those again, Jack." Sort of the mammarian version of sticking out her tongue -- which she's also been doing quite frequently of late.)

But still: for the time being at least she's not making things as difficult as she might. Thank the gods for that -- and in particular thank Odin, dispatcher of the Valkyries. (And knock on wood!) (The fine funky Otis Redding/Carla Thomas version of which was knock-knock-knocking out of the radio a short while back.) She even cracks the occasional joke. "My toothpaste!" she cries from the darkened bathroom (a lightbulb burned out in there); "You've been using it again without rolling up the tube!" (Or maybe it isn't a joke. It

603

could even lead to a battle like the one we had last
fall over my failure to make my own bed with hospital
corners -- and back then she was sleeping here no more
than a night or two a week -- but nonetheless issuing
commands at every opportunity.)

Now she's going through the big stack of paintings
she did for me, deciding which ones she'll let me keep.

"You want this?" she asks, stepping into the
doorway, holding up a rice-paper watercolor showing five
blurry stars of different colors and, in white on white,
the words "I love you."

"Well, I don't know, it might be a little too much
to look at that every day."

"You just don't want to have 'I love you' on the
walls where other women can see it."

Is that true? Quite possibly. But of course I
deny it's the main reason. And one thing I do know for
sure: I don't want to have to look at those words myself
when she's loving someone else. -- And while I'm at it
being so truthful, I'll just note this is unquestionably
one of her worst paintings ever, however heartfelt its
message might've been at the time. And I'll also admit
I'm thinking I'll store it in my footlocker just in case
we, meaning Val and I, do manage to pull off a
miraculous comeback someday.

We dwell on each painting, the memories evoked, how
and where she painted it. "This was the first one I did
for you, one of my best." And then a complaint: "You
want to keep all the best ones!" -- And now she tells
me something I never realized: the green mug I've
favored for hot chocolate (until Danny broke the
handle), she's the one who gave it to me. This whole
time I've been thinking it was part of a wedding present
that went back all the way to Ciara days! ---

Friday 18

The cops are forcing me to write this (you could
say). Two of them are lounging out there on their huge
parked Kawasaki 10000s or whatever they are, the motors

idling, rumbling, making the blue meanies themselves
seem to vibrate slightly, something like rodeo cowboys
atop mechanical bulls except a lot more rapidly --
almost as if they might dematerialize at any moment
(thus signaling the start of the true Age of Aquarius or
at least reel two of "The Yellow Submarine") -- and
twenty feet away from them stands my inert little Honda
90 with its peace and "Get with the Merc!" decals. No
way could I pull out without those cops seeing my
expired license plates. So I have to pass the time
here, only a block from the Bulldog office, until they
leave. Might as well use it for stringing a few words
together.

Last night things did not go as expected. When the
final crunch came I was the one near collapse and Val
was smiling and strong. I found myself inundating her
with long lingering looks of infinite sadness or dumb
bewilderment. At one point outside the bay windows of
her new place (they're set right at eye level above the
sidewalk where any creep who came wandering along could
peer in) I nearly passed out.

The one great relief to me was that her rooms are
quite attractive. She has the former living room and
dining room of a large decaying semi-Victorian house on
the southeast corner of Fourth and Irving. The wood
trim in her rooms is dark and solid and the walls
recently painted a spiffy green and yellow. She has a
working fireplace, a fancy chandelier, several large
plants, and three sets of windows, including the ones
overlooking the street. The communal kitchen and
bathroom (both on her floor and very large) are
plastered with psychedelic Fillmore and Avalon and
Family Dog at the Beach posters. A cheery stained-glass
flower graces the window on the front door. The main
drawback, as she sees it, and I suppose as I see it too,
is the fact that most of the house residents (the number
jumps around between six and a dozen according to Carl
at the Bulldog) are heads of one sort or another, with
acid presumably the consciousness-expander of choice.

In short, this house is a whole lot like the 832

[Have Mercy]

Fell Street "Art Center" where Jang and I were living
together for the period between thirty-three and twenty-
four months ago, except the neighborhood here is without
doubt a good deal better -- cleaner, prettier (with
Golden Gate Park just a block away), and what matters
most, safer. And I even pointed all this out to her.

Then, surprise: after leaving her there at
midnight, I woke up at four a.m. at "the Castle" to find
her energetically balling me. She stayed the rest of
the night, and this morning delivered a series of
bracing encomiums to my "big red Viking cock" which she
suddenly swears she loves so much and she's not going to
let anyone else have a hunk of. On my way to work I
gave her a lift down to Union Street to buy her BC pills
(even though only an hour earlier she'd been announcing
she was about to embark on a period of chastity) and
now, well, I've told her I'll bring by the rest of her
things tomorrow morning. And tonight is Friday night.
No doubt I'd do well to keep myself maximally
distracted, if possible, on this night, perhaps more so
than on just about any other night in my entire life so
far.

*   *

Now the sedate chambers of Judge Maurice Garvey,
proceedings dragging along in State versus Emil Garza,
addict.

"Looks like we drew a lemon judge," says Dave
Dikeakos.

"He's a jerk," confirms Mike Meyerhold.

For the better part of an hour Judge Garvey has
been sermonizing on the weakness of Emil Garza's
character and the necessity for him to undertake
immediate moral uplift. Most of the people in the
courtroom, including two imposing teams of lawyers, are
awaiting the opening round of the Bay Bulldog's suit
against the S.F. Chronicle. A scholarly-looking KQED
reporter sits two rows up and to our right; an Examiner
man, I'm pretty sure, squats evilly a row back and to
our left. And a KRMA stringer, self-appointed, an
underground-rag type if ever there was one, holds forth

right here in the middle -- scribbles these very notes.

To Emil Garza this trial is deadly serious, but the high-powered corporate attorneys find it irritating and amusing. They stifle yawns and exchange wry smirks. To them it may be difficult to conceive how a great constitutional question can be raised in this courtroom and before this judge. Yet that's precisely what's about to happen.

The question concerns the Newspaper Preservation Act, passed by Congress last year, which permits daily metropolitan newspapers to merge certain crucial non-editorial functions and, in effect, to establish a monopoly. The Bulldog argues that such mergers work to stifle both freedom of the press and the normal competition among businesses. Someday, it's hoped, this suit will yield a large sum in treble damages to the Bulldog -- and, more important to be sure, liberate, and change the course of, the American "Fifth Estate" and thus American democracy. Nothing less!

*   *

Why not write? It's ten or so, Woodstock is filling up, the revolving mirror ball above the dancefloor is casting rapidly spinning galaxies of sparkle across the walls and tables and excited patrons -- small single-sex clusters and a few couples and one trio (a young married couple and the woman's mother, it would appear) and me, all of us waiting for the band to return from break.

On this night it's entirely fitting that I should be sitting alone at my own table, leaning back, sometimes emitting heavy and possibly quite loud sighs of the kind Val has often disparaged, other times drifting off into melancholy speculations, still other times frantically tapping my feet and fingers.

Flash: drum set "vibrating weirdly" entirely of its own accord in the back seat of a gray Firebird. Counterflash: who the hell cares?

It's the first night of the new dispensation. I remind myself to smile. I'm on display here! Even on the make it could be said. Yet I'm also feeling the

internal bumps and thrashings of a sort of compulsion to
reorder and revive my life. Bought myself a bouquet of
daisies today, I did -- and how long has it been since
I've done something like that? Leaving work this
afternoon I found myself drawn back to the U.S.
Restaurant (pandemonium reigned there -- and I had the
pleasure of watching out the window as a red-bearded
apparition in bib overalls and fantastic thigh-high sky-
blue lace-up boots jotted something down -- presumably a
phone number -- from the Bulldog Summer Project handbill
which I myself had stapled on that pole last week).
Then to the Family Farmacy (everything peaceful there as
I stretched out on a big floor pillow sniffing incense
and watching a muslin curtain incandesce as a shaft of
late sunlight angled in on it well past eight p.m. on
one of the longest days of the year). And now -- the
body shop.

Saturday 19
        I'm at the office getting nothing done. Leafing
through the latest issue of the Atlantic, the one whose
cover features plaster casts of Coach Lyndon Johnson
lecturing Waterboy Richard Nixon about the "game plan"
for Vietnam. Carol King's "I Feel the Earth Move" plays
humdrumly on the radio (think what Janis Joplin could've
done with those lyrics!). -- This on what in Texas is
known as Juneteenth, the anniversary of the joyous day
in 1865 when the slaves in that swaggeringly reactionary
state (is it any different today?) finally learned
they'd been freed at least technically by the issuance
of the Emancipation Proclamation two and a half years
earlier.
        It seems I'm suddenly reluctant to ensconce myself
down here when no one else is around. It's too dark,
too dingy, like a dungeon or a cave. Then there are all
the nut calls, which I have to answer myself. They
don't stop calling just because it's Saturday and the
office is supposed to be closed. Or I guess I should
say I don't really have to answer them, but for some

reason I'm doing it anyway.

The best call so far today, a guy asked me for a
loan. He's a former editor of a Spanish-language paper,
he said, just out of the joint, with only fifty-five
cents in his pocket. The guy sure does know how to sob
it out. I wound up agreeing to drop him off some money
for food (actually it'll just be food stamps) at a mom-
and-pop store near Eighth and Market.

Then there's this: Valerie came by this morning
while I was still in bed asleep. She couldn't reach
Jim, she explained, to tell him to deliver Danny to her
new place instead of 1616 as he's accustomed to doing.
Meanwhile she was climbing into bed with me after
brewing two cups of hot chocolate. My cock was soon at
full mast and she, still dressed, pushed aside the
crotch panels of her damnable pink hot pants and the red
bikini briefs clearly visible underneath through the
lacy knit and slowly worked me in. We'd just gotten
going pretty good when Jim arrived with Danny and beeped
his horn outside. She leapt off, closing the door to my
room behind her.

When she came back I was still in a half-aroused
state and she insisted on sucking me off. She did it as
Danny popped in and out, spraying us a couple of times
with his water pistol (unable to see what his mother was
up to beneath the comforter). I didn't think I was all
that interested at first but then I put my hand on her
sweet and very wet little ass inside those two layers of
provocative cloth and almost instantaneously sticky
white streamers were flinging themselves out onto my
chest and stomach under the tent and making for some
lacy webbing in Val's fingers, with a couple of stray
gobs suspended like tiny orchids in her hair. It was an
explosion. She wiped us both down with a washrag.

Later we drove over to West Portal to buy more
flowers to brighten up our respective rooms. Then we
loaded the L.C. with several more boxes of her things
for delivery to her place. "Your new house, Danny!"
One more trip remains for tomorrow morning.

*

[Have Mercy]

Last night, by the way, I couldn't prevent myself
from cruising slowly past Fourth and Irving at midnight
(she was there; she'd just returned from a W.C. Fields
flick at the Surf which she attended, she voluntarily
told me today, with a couple of her housemates -- "I
wanted to cheer myself up"). On the way home I sternly
advised myself not to do any more of that sort of spying
on her. "Let her go, Glen. It doesn't matter anymore
whether she's telling you the truth about what she's
doing at night. You have no right to know. And more to
the point, you'd be a fool to expose yourself to that
kind of knowledge." Then at home I found a note on my
bed, hastily scrawled, saying she loves me "very, very
much."

Today, after Danny joined us, her good cheer
quickly dissipated, and suddenly I knew in my bones
she'd be unable to abide living alone for long at her
new place (just like me, I've little doubt, at 1616).
Soon, probably within days if not hours, another man
will enter, or more likely re-enter, or simply continue
entering, her life. I'm even toying with the notion --
seriously -- of leaving a note on Dennis's windshield at
the tire-recapping place informing him of her new
address. But she's likely way ahead of me on that. She
hasn't volunteered anything about it, however, and I
haven't asked and won't. I'd chop off my tongue first.

*

No fewer than four letters arrived in today's mail.
Jerry Borden announces the birth of Jonathan Klee
Borden. Chad Arnold belatedly mourns my departure from
Garnett and the Mercury and says I'm missed up there
(and for this I'm very grateful). Mother grouses about
my "cussedness" in failing to box up and mail the last
batch of things Rob left behind. And Barb tells me she
and Paul will be coming up from L.A. in August.

"Sometimes I think of the fights we had over the
past year," Barb writes, "and especially in your absence
I regret them very much. I would regret them anyway.
In our various positions there was a lot of 'right and
wrong.' I don't think I was right. I only hope you

listened to me. (I listened to you.)"

To all of which I say: And just what is it, Barb, you think you were wrong about? Oh -- and do you think it had any consequences?

But I'm still pleased she wrote this and that she feels some regrets over something. Maybe our relationship can now start moving up from its nadir.

Sunday 20

Let it all hang out? All right. Valerie and I just parted ways, probably for the last time. Interesting that the first thing I do afterwards is stop in New Age for a large bottle of Dr. Bronner's 9-in-1 soap. Truly I feel like I've been needing to give myself a good scrub-down for months.

Cleansing is what it's all about now. In our time together a great deal of nastiness and filth has welled up on both sides. Perhaps this truth presages what will turn out to be my most lasting impression of Val: the lover who exposed me to so much ugliness, including that of my own worst self. I can't complain too much, though, because I've played the same role with others, many times, including of course with the very same Val. I know better now what Briana meant when she said I cast an "evil spell" on her. Val has done the same to me, and what's more in a violent, spiteful way even Briana might agree makes me look almost saintly by comparison.

I've been entranced, fascinated, hypnotized by the extraordinary qualities of this precocious teenager (until two months ago) -- she's a prodigy at once brilliant and ignorant, nimble and clumsy, compassionate and cruel, hip and straight, crude and sophisticated, destructive and creative, passionate and icy cold. She's also loving and indifferent, angelic and diabolical, melancholy and euphoric, gaspingly sexy and heartbreakingly beautiful and ugly, ugly, ugly.

The list of antitheses could go on forever. Of course she not only fascinates but repels me. It's obvious a moderately healthy, sane, sustainable kind of

love could never take root with us. My true feelings
for her have always had to struggle mightily to break
through the latest layers of self-protective armor I've
been forced to extrude -- like the exoskeleton of an
overgrown Kafkaesque insect -- out of revulsion and
fear. Today those feelings, even though exacerbated by
months of fighting, remain in much the same inchoate
state they were in shortly after our first meeting --
for example, some two weeks later when I caught a
glimpse of that hostile and deeply vengeful look on her
face reflected to infinity in her triptych bathroom
mirror at Dolores Street. "Mirror, mirror on the wall,
who's the most vengeful...."

Surprisingly little of a positive nature ever grew
or developed between us. Mainly we just became
increasingly adept at hurting each other. Now we go our
own ways robbed of the most essential certainties and
self-assurances. I feel I'm not much of a man
(especially to her) and she feels she's not much of a
woman (especially to me). The battle between us has
been a draw -- like, say, two tiny isolated nations
destroying each other in a fight to the death as the
world yawns and directs its attention elsewhere.

*

Today Val enjoyed having her breasts rubbed
(peeling sunburned skin had started to itch). We tried
valiantly to get something going in bed, with Danny
snoozing at her side, occasionally waking to blurt high-
pitched admonitions such as, "Don't put your nose in my
mommy's cunt!" (that language came courtesy of Jim, she
reminds me). But what began well enough ended in
despair. We're so used to this, however, we
recovered quickly.

We gathered the last of her belongings -- yet
another stack of paintings, a box of kitchen utensils
and food, a chair, a green plastic laundry tub -- and
drove over to her new place, where we lingered outside
in the L.C. as Danny sat on her lap and then on mine and
then hers again, neither of us eager to face this
ultimate parting moment. She declared she could bear

612

the looming loneliness, she wanted to make friends
instead of lovers ("I can make myself vulnerable only
with lovers"), she wanted to "get involved in things
again" and to "try expanding my mind." Did I have any
books to recommend? Would I let her know of things I
thought she ought to do? Would I be on the lookout for
any work she might be able to take on with the Bulldog
Summer Project? Yesterday, she said proudly, she'd
filched a Newsweek from Mac's Grill and she was
determined to catch up on all the political news; not
only that, she'd also salvaged the most recent New York
Review from my discard stack at the Castle and would be
reading that cover to cover, "every single word." She
felt very "clean" in her own head right now, she said,
but then admitted this was only because she'd "pushed
everything back into the closets." But that was all
right, she insisted, because soon she'd finally be able
to start dealing with all the suppressed things in her
life, including those.

And, yes, she could understand why we shouldn't see
each other for a while if that was still the way I
wanted it, as I'd already said was the case. But I
could come by her place any time I liked, she said; I
needn't worry about embarrassing myself or her by
finding her with someone else. I assured her I'd do no
more spying on her of the kind I did when I lay on the
slope of Mt. Moraga while awaiting Dennis's arrival (she
brightened: "Were you really up there spying on me? I
thought you were making that up!") and I'd call or leave
notes rather than disturb her privacy. "Then you'll let
me know," she asked, "when you don't need to be so
isolated anymore?" I said I'd let her know, yes. As I
left she was planning to take Danny for a walk in the
park. "Right now I don't feel like staying around all
those people at the house."

*   *

Last night I treated myself to dinner at The
Boarding House, a hip restaurant on Bush Street a few
blocks from the old Emp mausoleum where Val and I got
our start. The restaurant was almost empty when I

613

arrived -- very early -- and I ate slowly, reading
"Space for Survival" by candlelight, savoring each visit
by a sweet-faced honey-haired waitress with a glittery
silver star painted on her bare left shoulder.

Afterwards I drove over to Stefan's, where I was
among the first to arrive for the party he'd told me
about when he dropped by the other day. This turned out
to be one of those strangely awkward shindigs where
everyone is of a different nationality and people keep
trying corny new ways to break the ice that just drive
everyone further apart. Mostly I rapped with Stefan
about politics or with Solana about what had gone wrong
with me and Jang back in a whole different era, but also
about a friend of Solana's, another nutritionist, she
wants to fix me up with (maybe later, I said). Other
than that I hung out in the bookcase corner leafing
through Stefan's ever-growing library of arcane
socialist/anarchist tracts.

I left a little after midnight and went straight
home, picking up an early edition of the Sunday Ex/Chron
on the way. After brewing myself a mug of hot chocolate
I settled into my armchair, intending to read just a
short while, but I got hooked on an extraordinary story
reprinted from the New York Times, very long, describing
the contents of a "top secret" Pentagon study on the
origins of the Vietnam War. Item after item in this
study officially confirms what everyone who cared to
know already knew years ago, i.e., that the United
States has been the aggressor right from the start in
that shameful conflict and that the American public and
for that matter the whole world has been repeatedly and
egregiously lied to by this country's leaders over the
entire period. A lengthy sidebar, equally fascinating,
lays out the government's bungled attempts to prevent
the Times from running the story. Eventually I nodded
off in the chair with sections of the paper serving as a
makeshift blanket, waking with a start from a bad dream
at four-forty a.m.

*　　　　　*

For at least the past dozen years I've avoided

doing many things I should've done and sometimes even
wanted to do, by a most commonplace (but still
irresistible) form of procrastination. I simply tell
myself this: "I'll begin doing that when I get older."
All of these postponed actions, reforms, revisions,
etc., fall under the broad rubric of "the wise thing to
do." Wisdom, I've pretty much always believed, is
something to be admired but not embraced at too young an
age. On the contrary, it's mostly to be shunned. But
inherently so rational a fellow have I also pretty much
always been, especially up through the middle of my
college years, that I could justify this stance to
myself only by vowing to embrace wisdom at a later stage
in my life, and one not too preposterously distant.

Today, June 20, 1971 -- Father's Day, as it happens
-- I've decided this later stage has arrived. I'm now
"older." For no particular reason I'm quite sure I've
crossed a major divide in my life. Quite simply, I now
see myself differently. I'm no longer a "youth."
Though I hope I won't lose all the admirable qualities
of youth in one fell swoop -- e.g., energy, vision,
idealism, openness to new ideas and new experience -- I
know the time has come to get serious about developing
certain other important qualities. Among these:
physical self-preservation, focusing of energies,
writerly productivity.

Many of the specific reforms I'm about to undertake
-- I swear I am! -- are scarcely new to me. Some I've
been toying with for years. But the point is that now I
must begin living them on a consistent daily basis.
There's no excuse for more procrastination.

For example:

Getting in good shape and staying there. The old
standby. And it still means many things. Eating
healthfully, for one. (No more junk: no Cokes and such
crap.) Sleeping eight hours a night. Exercising, that
is, using my body fully. Walking, running, hooping,
dancing, perhaps bicycling.

And: living thriftily. Within my means, in other
words: spending money in such a way I won't be forced to

give up too many of the things that are truly important
to me. Taking a bag lunch to work instead of spending
two dollars daily at Cal's or Sam's or Harold's. Eating
out only when I have good reason to. No more throwing
away money on things I don't really need.

And: living a balanced life according to my own
values. That is, not being too rigid but also not
letting everything go. Potted plants, art on the walls,
an orderly house (but not too orderly). Hours for
working. Exploration. Discipline, developing latent
talents. Sketching, painting, cooking, even sewing when
something needs mending.

And: producing. Writing regular articles for
publication in the Bulldog or elsewhere; grinding out an
irrefutably reader-worthy "Symphony No. 6" (slug title)
-- the publishable novel which, yes, I still believe I
have in me somewhere.

Also: relaxing. Cultivating friendships with males
as well as females. Connecting better with my
unconscious through dreams. Reading more of the books I
should've read long ago -- maybe even a few, gasp,
classics. Writing letters. Composing a rock tune or
two. Getting out. Developing more moderate habits
while at the same time keeping myself open to change.
Indulging in fresh-cut flowers once in a while.

Somewhere in all this, or rather everywhere in it,
there ought to be a place for love. But just how I can
find this love and accommodate myself to it in a way
that's compatible with all or just a good portion of the
newfound wisdom adumbrated above, I don't know. All
previous bets are off, all former methods discarded.

And my final piece of advice to myself here at the
start of yet another new era (and tomorrow, by the way,
or rather today now since it's past midnight, is the
first day of an official new season as the long, long,
deranged "Season of Hell" spring of 1971 comes to an
end) -- my final piece of advice to myself, I say, also
regards love and it's this: at all times, and especially
in the next few days and weeks and perhaps even months,
PROCEED WITH EXTREME CARE.

Coda

[valedictory]

4

Monday 21

Eleven p.m. and I'm sitting alone at home feeling
overwhelmed by Bulldog work. The kitchen table groans
with it. Where to begin? It's hard just to stay a step
ahead of the avalanche. I enjoy the challenge, but
fears are mounting that this time it'll turn out to be
too much, especially over the next week or two.

Today alone more than a dozen applications for the
Summer Project arrived -- fourteen in fact (just
counted). A triumph! But now I have to read through
them all in preparation for upcoming interviews, which
start tomorrow and will continue all week. What's more,
I dread rejecting anyone. If I don't thin out the
ranks, though, I may soon have cause for regret, because
most likely it will be the clamor of summer volunteers
that more than anything else will keep me from working
on articles and the anti-highrise book. I could easily
become mired in the Summer Project and have to watch
helplessly as my more important aims go aglimmering.
Setting up a tight organization will be the key.

Meanwhile...personal life? The day began with
Valoshka and ended with Jang. Leaping from horse to
horse in midstream. I "ran into" Valoshka at Mac's
Grill. We were friendly but said little. For the
fourth straight day she was wearing her pink knit
hot pants and the multihued jersey with lots of purple
in it which her mother bought her. It looked as though
she'd slept in them. Very unlike Valoshka. Her face
was greasy. It was almost as if she'd been walking the
streets all night. Or, much more likely, been out
somewhere balling Dennis. She looked exhausted --
almost desolate. It worried me. But I said nothing

about any of this. We parted amicably enough despite
what I'll call a grudging resentful reticence in her
manner. The entire time we were together she seemed to
have other things on her mind. Or perhaps this was an
illusion and I'm spewing these words here in a
ridiculous effort to deflect guilt from myself.

What I'm saying: I don't know what she's doing, but
I do know what I'm doing.

Jang. Dashing back to her. She sat in the waiting
room at the Bulldog for more than an hour before I could
get away, and then we raced to her place and hopped into
bed (again I concealed the X scar on my chest). Balling
with her is incomparably good, joyous, miraculous. I
love it! I've always loved it! And every bit as
important, she loves it and has always loved it! From
the first touches her fervent expressions of pleasure
and excitement turn me on to the maximum and often to
what seem to be astounding new maximums. The way she
urges me to kiss her breasts, massage them, rough them
up just a little -- so different from Valerie. The way
she groans with pleasure, shakes her ass, grooves with
rhythms, bends the high notes, melts into the motionless
carrezza pulses, teases and tantalizes on the brink,
comes with cries that echo happily, exults afterwards:
oh what delightful mutual pleasure and oh what heady
mutual esteem pours from us afterward. And the
suppleness and liveliness of her body! The strong
squeeze and superb muscle control of her vagina! It's
all irresistible to me. Her delight and joy in life: an
elixir to me now. Jang's the perfect antidote to Val
just as she was three years ago (I wince to say) to
Ciara.

What's astounding is that she still permits me --
indeed, begs me -- to love her this way. I worry about
what lies ahead. I don't want to plunge back in with
her too quickly. Caution. See how things go. She's
willing to accept this but not happy about it, and of
course this leaves me feeling uneasy. I'm
hypersensitive about the subtle denigrations that come
my way as a result. What will happen? Will she still

be returning to Korea in August? God only knows. But
how lovely she was in her brightly patched jeans. How
touching the careful, neat austerity of her rooms, the
display of gorgeous new calligraphy "practice papers" on
the walls. How comfortable I felt with her on my arm
again. No doubt about my deep attachment to her. More
talk of having a kid someday. Sneaking fish-and-chips
into the Surf Interplayers and feeding it to each other
by hand as we watched an amusing Godard propaganda film
on the Chicago Seven trial: how much simple and
addictive fun it can be to be with her!

And then at her door her stomach began to act up
and I remembered in my own gut how she can use her pain
to manipulate. The implication (too subtly conveyed for
me to protest it) is that my "neglect" of her causes the
pain. Instead of rising to the bait, ignore it: this is
the only tactic possible. No more simmering fury and
despair as during our time living together: just move on
to the work, hers and mine, that must be done. That's
why I don't want to reinstall her at Funston. Could be
we're destined for a lifetime of on-again/off-again
romance spiced with splendid lovemaking and jibing
idealized self-images.

Tuesday 22
Today's leading characters were Judy and Monica.
Judy Jacobi. She's a Berkeley journalism student, New
York Jew, remarkably poised and knowledgeable. I
interviewed a dozen or more applicants today, but she
stands out. Some indescribable quality. She's not
physically beautiful in any conventional sense, but I
found her highly attractive: she turned me on. No doubt
her voice is a big part of it -- deep, sensual, musical,
throaty, husky, yet in no way self-conscious -- a voice
that surely belongs on the radio (I'll be trying to line
up something for her with the KRMA news department).
Also her lips: almost as full and sensual as Val's. But
it's more than the physical stuff. Clarity, composure,
intelligence, humor: I don't know. Just a fine woman.

[Have Mercy]

Or girl, I suppose I might dare to say of someone who's
the same age Val was when we met: just nineteen. But
under either description I found her both exciting and
inspiring to talk with (over a lingering lunch at Cal's)
and now hope I can persuade her to work closely with me.
Directness, candor and down-to-earth sophistication. I
usually get along well with East Coast Jewish folks.
Maybe it's the hint of Lisa I see in her.

Which is the tie-in with Monica. Tonight I finally
took her up on dinner. In fact I drove her to a buffet
at Zack's in Sausalito, and while we were dancing there
(slow sensual embraces even though the music was fast
rock) I flashed on how her hair resembles Lisa's, same
color, very light brown, and silky fine, gossamer. Also
like Lisa, she's round-faced ("Dutch girl") and very
young-looking for her age (she's twenty-five going on
seventeen) and has a similar slouchy sensuality. At
times she comes across as something of a snob
(supercilious, lots of name-dropping), but otherwise
she's likable, friendly, smart, cheerful, funny. She
laughs frequently. Her high-strung nature and
nervousness (her hand shaking as she refreshed my glass
of wine) are touching but also disconcertingly
infectious, and I find myself playing the buffoon to
disguise the real source of my klutziness, making fun of
myself until she says, "Aw, Glen, it's okay," and pats
my head. Lots of ludicrous awkward moments. More ahead
too, because tonight we established a certain intimacy
(we could easily have wound up in her bed, I think, but
I bade her adieu at the door and came home at midnight).

I'm holding back with her for two reasons, which in
fact we talked about: fear of creating hassles at the
office, and continuing emotional turmoil over Valerie.
Monica dismisses the first, resigns herself to the
second. "That's your call, Glen. What can I say?" But
also lets it be known she's been "going crazy" over me
the past two weeks. And so...well, whatever happens.

Or holding back for three reasons, I should say,
because I doubt I could ever love her. The first two
reasons just keep me from diving into bed with her (and

622

not for long, most likely); this third one makes me
wonder if I should risk any kind of outside-the-office
relationship with her at all given the likelihood of her
becoming attached (if she really is "going crazy") and
eventually hurt and possibly vindictive.

Yet...on the other hand...I'm "unattached," I'm
curious, I like her, I'm touched by her, and she's an
adult human being and evidently willing to try a little
fling with no strings attached. If she is, why
shouldn't I be? Like Val, she was married for three
years (although childless) and is now divorced, so she's
surely well acquainted with sex, love, and the ins and
outs of the mating game. Living alone in North Beach,
working hard (and well) for the Bulldog, nurturing the
hope "I'll be an artist when I grow up," avowedly lonely
and horny. Frizzy hair, fashionable baggy dresses one
day and leather hot pants the next, a nicely
proportioned body (shapely ass, long legs, small
breasts), tinkling bells when she walks.

But...whereas I want to talk with Judy Jacobi
forever just to listen to her marvelous voice, after a
certain period with Monica (at the office this is) I'm
nervously casting about for graceful ways to escape.
Also, she's undergoing analysis and has been for some
time. (Her weight blew up to two hundred pounds after
the divorce, although it's now, about a year later, back
to her normal one hundred ten.)

Well, I don't know what I'll do. Just be careful
to avoid early entanglement, I guess. Now Judy, she's
got an old man on the East Coast, it turns out, and
he'll soon be joining her here for the summer, and even
though that's regrettable it's also probably just as
well. In the meantime, and even after he gets here,
I hope she'll be spending lots of time around the
office. I'm scheming up ways to install her as my
"right-hand voice" (chauvinist pig!).

And: first aching for Valoshka. Thinking: how
bubbling with life I felt cutting through the park on
the 90 at night, in a light rain, to pick her up at her
brother's where I found her peering out the second-floor

window eagerly awaiting my arrival and then she came
running down and jumped into my drenched arms before I
could even dismount -- this eight, maybe nine months ago
-- and why does this particular scene come to mind so
strongly now? But Briana too helped to make those times
rich, I shouldn't forget and don't intend to (and in
fact can't).

Wednesday 23
     Here I am at Funston before sunset. Surprise!
Each day upon returning home I charge upstairs
expectantly, eagerly, with a tremor of trepidation, as
if something momentous might've happened while I was
away. I quickly check out each room, looking for signs
of change, possibly of an unapproved presence. And when
I find everything's exactly as I left it, I'm
disappointed and a bit deflated. What? Val hasn't come
by? Again? In four days not a single thing has changed
up here? No little vases of wildflowers? No imploring
notes? What's going on? I settle uneasily into my
armchair. The lack of disturbance, I must confess,
disconcerts me. It's almost as if I were sitting by a
campfire in the wilderness and the symphony of night
sounds suddenly ceased: something big's about to happen!
But here at 1616 nothing does.
     My only contacts with Val come at Mac's. It
appears we've tacitly adopted a policy of meeting there
most mornings. Nothing's ever said to confirm this; we
just "run into" each other. It seems natural enough
since we both used to go there on our own as well as
together and now it's centrally located for us at Ninth
and Irving, five blocks from her place and six from
mine.
     Today she looked less washed-out and she greeted me
cheerfully and we talked a little before I had to rush
off to do more Summer Project interviews at the office.
She said, unsolicited, she's had "nothing but good
thoughts" about me the past few days. "I don't feel any
resentment at all." Had I read McCabe's column

yesterday? She agrees with him: love is best when
neither party "needs" the other.

"I've decided," she announced with a flash of the
old provocative pride, "not to try to come back to you
until I don't need you."

Her major problem at the moment (she says) is,
again, finding something to "get involved in." And I
again assured her plenty of work would be available at
the Bulldog once the Summer Project starts up next week
but warned her she'd probably find it boring as hell and
politically retrograde (not -- from her standpoint --
"radical" much less "revolutionary" like the Vietcong,
as she prefers to see herself these days -- in her hot
pants!); and she said at this point she doesn't even
care what the work is.

I also recommended she scour the bulletin boards on
Union Street and Upper Grant, but she'd already done
that, she said, just yesterday, and found nothing
(adding quickly she was doing it in the afternoon, not
evening) -- well, not nothing, really, because some dude
at Malvina's had offered to see to it that her poetry
was published. I congratulated her on this but advised
skepticism about such offers -- I mean, was there to be
nothing in it for him? -- but then quickly, catching
myself, advised even greater skepticism about taking
this very advice, meaning my own, considering whom it
was coming from. "Of course!" she chirped. (Today I
fell prey to new shudders of disgust in thinking about
her with Dennis. I have little doubt she's still seeing
him. If she weren't I'm sure she would've been quick to
tell me. This is presumably how she's working toward
not needing me.)

One thing that surprises me a lot: right now I'm
utterly without desire for her. She's as spectacularly
attractive as ever -- even more so, because independence
becomes her (as it does any natural-born provocateur and
especially one of her caliber) -- and yet I can't see
her that way except indirectly, as it were, as if
through someone else's eyes. To me she's just Valoshka.
With others -- it's mostly Jang I have in mind here --

625

it's been far different after we've split up.

So: another lost day vis-a-vis the mating game.
Monica and I had little contact at the office and I put
off calling Jang. It was an authentic one-hundred-
percent-pure workday. Most interesting event: a noon
meeting Mike and I attended at the Milner Hotel, the
South of Market flophouse for single men. The agenda
was essentially to dream up new ways of harassing
Redevelopment, in particular through compiling a book.
Another book! I was invited along to assess whether
Summer Project volunteers might be able to lend a hand
with the research for it. And I believe they could and
probably will. Nonetheless I personally felt out of my
element, in over my head. Many of these people --
Chester Hartman being the best example -- are pros, on
top of the subject, trained political organizers and
activists thoroughly acquainted with the most arcane
subtleties of low-income housing issues and municipal
government. Not my bag, I thought. What the hell was I
doing there? I ought to be working on my own projects!
I felt slightly fraudulent, also a bit disdainful, I'm
ashamed to say, just as I did in similar ways at
meetings back in my college overachiever days aimed at
uplifting Springfield and Holyoke slum-dwellers. This
was drudgery. Dull do-gooders trying to score points.
Nothing truly new or exciting here. Playing urban
games. A waste of time.

Must nitty-gritty political engagement inevitably
come to this? And these were top-notch people! I
feared I wouldn't be able to take an entire summer of
being forced to sit around bearing witness as high-power
types revved their engines and spun their wheels.
Meetings droning on and on. God help me! I had to
stiffen my backbone to get through it. I applaud the
ideals and the good works of such people, but the sad
truth is that in person most of them bore me stiffer
than any South of the Slot drunk, including the ones
already passed out in the gutter.

Valoshka would fess up to this sort of conflict
immediately. I find it hard to do. But: how long can I

stand it? How much do I really care about the sins of
Redevelopment in San Francisco? How high does this
agency rank on my most-wanted list of evildoers? My
time seems too precious now to squander on interminable
meetings if they're not dealing with villains near the
top of my list.

     Well, for the nonce I'll keep on pushing.
Eventually I suspect I'll either fence off a different
corner for myself at the Bulldog or move on to something
else.

Thursday 24
     Today was much better (but also planted seeds of
new future dilemmas):
     ** While Mike, Peggy, and I thrashed out details
for the Summer Project, Monica slipped a note onto my
desk: could she lure me to her boudoir this weekend? (I
nodded to her across the lobby. Why not? We've already
agreed that if anything did spring up extracurricularly
between us we wouldn't let it disturb our work at the
Bulldog. And visiting Monica's boudoir -- it'll be
Sunday night -- certainly beats sitting at home alone
wondering whose boudoir Valerie's visiting. Not that
there's really any mystery about it. But of course I'm
only assuming she's with Dennis -- and yet assuming with
an intuitive sense that approaches absolute certainty.)
     ** The mail brought a check for a hundred and
sixty dollars from Jang, to be used for rent ("You paid
our rent for two years") (eighteen months actually), and
subliminal impassioned come-hither moans. Later I
called her with the news that our tentatively scheduled
trip up to Steve Vaughn's cabin in Marin would have to
be postponed a week at the very least, and she countered
with the news that I (or someone or something) had
afflicted her with urethritis; but the center held and
we're getting together tomorrow night.
     ** Last night I stayed home and moldered -- was
too wasted even to draw a bath -- but tonight I dropped
by the Family Farmacy and wound up making a comically

inept play -- more like a farcical Second City skit --
for a very pretty but stoical art student, Chris,
extremely cool and prosaic, blue-eyed, of Swedish
ancestry and divorced mother of a golden-haired three-
year-old son (oh god, not another one!).

    ** Another breakfast talk with Val at Mac's.
Nothing much new. She volunteers that she hasn't been
seeing anyone, but of course I don't believe it for a
second. Last night while she just happened to be
wandering around North Beach again some sleazo dude
offered her a job as a topless dancer on Broadway: "With
a body like yours you could clean up." (She just can't
resist trying to provoke me with such tales -- which of
course isn't to say they're not true or that she fails
to provoke me with them, but I do try not to let my real
reactions show too much -- do a lot of ain't-life-
strange shucking and jiving that I'm sure itself is
quite strange to her. Then at home tonight I found a
small label pasted on the outside of the upstairs door:
"'Declassify' the bed on July 1," it says, the purple
handwriting quite familiar. I'm not sure how to
decipher this, but July 1st is our "meet anniversary" (a
week from today) and I think maybe she's saying she
actually wants us to celebrate it together and to do
that in bed.

    ** Wade Crowley, a friend of Arnie's at the
Bulldog and a Summer Project volunteer, dropped by here
later tonight and arranged to rent a room -- the "blue
room" -- for the month of July for seventy-five bucks.
This suggests, if I can find someone to take his place
in August and thereafter keep the monthly rent checks
rolling in, I should be able to hang on to the L.C. well
into autumn (until unemployment runs out).

    ** During the day I raced from meeting to meeting
-- Thad Quigley at City Hall, Tim Sorrel at the Bresker
warehouse at Third and Bryant (SFA headquarters), Mel's
group at Legal Assistance -- and for some reason felt
much more competent and personally involved: by god all
these deranged Work Group projects just might add up to
something!

[valedictory]

** And for dinner I badly burned six slices of
bacon, causing an unbelievable amount of smoke to pour
out the kitchen window and the sundeck door. From up
the hill it must've seemed the house was on fire. (And
since no fire engines appeared, one could say it's been
confirmed our uphill neighbors would prefer to see the
place with all its antiwar and counterculturish murals
holding forth from our sundeck burn to the ground -- but
we already knew that.)

Friday 25
Valoshka's curled up in my bed within toe's reach
(if I stretched out my leg) wearing a proud and
mischievous smile. "I'm just glad to be back here," she
murmurs.
No, our anniversary hasn't been pushed up a week.
Nor is she here by invitation. Rather she's escaping
an alleged cockroach infestation at her new house (the
exterminator cometh tomorrow, she says) and I've agreed
to let her sleep here a second night in a row. At four
a.m. last night she burst in panting and trembling. She
blurted two sentences -- "There's a carload of men after
me!" and "My bed's full of bugs!" -- and then dived into
my bed -- i.e., our old bed -- and soon we were fucking
fiercely. And not long after dawn a gentler rerun.
(Now she lifts the quilt to scratch, revealing
breasts more blotched than ever by peeling swatches of
sunburned skin.)
But: I must report that the breeze wafting up from
my crotch carries an unmistakable whiff of Jang and
kimchi. Which means I'd be well advised to undertake a
thorough crotch-wash before climbing back into the sack
with Valoshka.
A fire crackled in the hearth when I arrived at
Jang's place tonight. A feast of favorite foods. She
insists I must "rest" while she prepares the meal. Then
her post-dessert creation: delicious, exquisite, superb
lovemaking. What delight! I pull out at the end after
a very long go and spurt on her stomach and breasts --

she's on the Pill but has said she wants to "see it
come" -- and then together we administer a thorough
massage to the area. And then rap naked in front of the
fire, her head resting on my chest. Marvelous ease and
comfort. The only hitch came when we discussed the
disease I supposedly gave her -- urethritis -- but she
spared me from massive recrimination.

What does it all mean? I'm going with the flow and
the flow is carrying me back toward Jang. Or at least
at certain points earlier tonight it seemed to be. But
misgivings still whisper -- clamor at times -- and the
matter is thus far by no means settled. In fact it's
only just barely being addressed, or rather re-
addressed. Among other things, there's the strong
possibility of her leaving for Korea in August or early
September -- regardless of what happens with us -- to
explore in depth.

Furious workday at the Bulldog, much of it given
over to defining group objectives for the Summer Project
with Mike (who regrettably often switches into his
negative "anticipating problems" mode). A rare tribute
from him: "You're doing a good job on this, Glen." Judy
Jacobi comes by, provoking more interest and even an
upsurge of lust (a fine figure she cuts to go with
everything else -- tight corduroy pants, tight T-shirt,
full breasts -- Tuesday she'd been wearing a baggy dress
and I hadn't realized this about her trim and toned
voluptuousness). Her lips fascinate me: much like
Valoshka's they're full, crooked, unsymmetrical,
wonderful, overwhelmingly sensual. But I felt less of a
natural bond between us today and I suspect this is
because -- though she hasn't come right out and said it
-- she's decided she doesn't want to risk damaging
relations with her boyfriend. And it just could be that
this kind of loyalty makes her even more impressive to
me.

Meanwhile back here in the suspiciously mellow
present I keep getting the signal bedtime is upon us.
But I have to hit the bathroom first for that cleanup.

[Valedictory]

Sunday 27 (X:26)

Earlier tonight Monica served the chicken and the candles flickered and beyond the fogged picture window the downtown San Francisco skyline loomed up close, just blocks away. I thought: how many people out there (and beyond) might think I'm fucking them over right now?

The measure for this: from which people would I withhold the information that I was there with Monica? (Unless, of course, they truly wanted to hear it.)

Valerie, for one. She's now asked me point-blank if I'm "seeing anyone." In reply I've said we should stick with our agreement not to talk about such things and I've reminded her I haven't asked her that same question, and for the time being anyway she's grumpily backed off with nothing more in the way of objection than almost violent nostril-flarings and threatening looks. Truth is, though, it's difficult enough, painful enough, just trying to maintain our separation without things flying out of control because of stoked jealousies. She spent Thursday, Friday, and Saturday night here at Funston -- contra that same agreement -- under the pretext that the cockroaches were driving her out of her own bed and she had nowhere else to go and now she was pleading for my mercy and understanding. When I came home Saturday evening at five-thirty and found her crocheting a new pair of hot pants -- the pink a bit more purplish this time -- in the living room, my tolerance cracked: she was not holding to her part of the deal. For the next hour I fenced with her, or I should say we played a grisly game in which we both said the worst things we could think of about the other, but this time pretending to be joking. Valoshka: top of the charts in nastiness. Finally I dropped her off, at her request, at the Family Farmacy. When I returned home at midnight she was back and she apologized again for coming around so often and imposing herself on me. "You're trying to deal with your resentment, and I'm just setting you back." However, the exterminator's visit had been rescheduled to Monday and she needed to stay over one more night. After that, she vowed, she

wouldn't darken my doorway "until our anniversary,"
which is this coming Thursday. But then, after I let
her stay again and then dropped her off at her place
this morning, she called late this afternoon, worried
about Jim's failure to appear with Danny. "I don't know
why I picked you, but I need help." So I wound up
driving her to his place in Noe Valley and then back to
the Inner Sunset with Danny in her lap.

And Jang? I saw her again Saturday night after
dropping off Val at seven -- arriving half an hour late
and in a sour mood. She soon lifted me out of it, and
we enjoyed watching the nostalgic tearjerker "Summer of
'42" at the Castro. Its interest was heightened for
both of us by the fact that '42 was the summer of my
birth and Korea was so different then compared with the
way it is today, and of course even more different from
America as it is today, as Jang well knows because she
was already nine years old that summer of '42 in Korea
(which had been under harsh Japanese occupation for
thirty-some years at that point). But then afterwards
she pressed me too hard to take her to Funston. Rather
than engage in the battle which suddenly seemed
inevitable, I headed straight to her place and left
quickly before the argument could escalate. Today she
called at the Bulldog (after failing to reach me at
Funston) with "one thousand apologies." She'd only
wanted to "drive by" our old place, she insisted. A
fib. But a diplomatic one. And last night was still
good enough that I want to go on seeing her. Once or
twice a week would be often enough for me at this point,
but I doubt she'll want to limit it to that given her
Korea plans. I've already promised to take her with me
to the JCC for swimming later this week.

My conclusion, then, to the question posed way back
at the start of this entry: both Valerie and Jang might
well think I'm doing them wrong by seeing Monica, but
neither would have any right to do so. And as far as I
know no one else would either.

A good thing too, because I'll now report that I
succumbed to Monica's blandishments and wound up in her

bed. Both of us were nervous wrecks: a spilled drink, a broken dish, clumsy Alphonse-Gaston bumpings, etc. But she moaned and moved well once we got going and when it was all over she said brightly: "I feel very thoroughly fucked." And: "I had a hunch Valerie was failing to appreciate the finer things in life." Actually all this had more than a trace of kindness in it: my balling was unfocused and awkward. But rising to get ready to leave, I began caressing her back as I knelt over her, my cock took to her round, soft ass, started growing again and swinging around and inviting her attention, and in lieu of a goodbye kiss I at least managed a decent goodbye schtup. (Monica greeting me at the door to start the evening in her black velvet V-necked antique dress, vintage 1938: I was stunned because she was the spitting image of Lisa in her very similar black dress, e.g., at her graduation dance at Morley in 1964.)

So there will be complications ahead at the office if nowhere else. How could there not be? As if I don't have enough already to consume all my energy! Today from ten a.m. until nine p.m. I worked on the Summer Project resource handbook, most of that time with Mike, and in just three hours, at seven a.m., I'll have to go back down to finish typing it up. Tomorrow will be another arduous day, culminating at seven p.m. with the Summer Project's first full meeting.

5

Tuesday 29 (X:28)

I thought I'd steeled myself against this, but when Valerie's housemate Carl inadvertently (I think) revealed she hadn't made it home last night, the news hit me hard. Since then I haven't been able to stop thinking about it. The Summer Project has begun rolling, there's a colossal amount of work to do, and my mind keeps returning to Valerie. The lover I asked to move out. It's sheer vanity: I can't bear the thought that one day she's promising an all-out effort to get us

back together and the next night she's out fucking
someone else. And the fact that I was out doing the
very same thing the previous night with Monica, not to
mention the two nights prior to that with Jang, doesn't
really change this at all -- unless it heightens it.

Thoughts of Val at the center. Around those swirl
great chaotic galaxies of vows, responsibilities,
projects, hopes, needs. Letters: Jesus, I've fallen
months behind. I promised Mother to pay her back by
July 1 and also (this too was months ago) that I'd mail
the rest of Rob's things. Debts: falling behind again
on car payments. Rent: Arnie's friend, Wade, has now
moved into the "blue room," but I never see him because
I don't get home until midnight after he's gone to bed
and in the mornings I leave before he's up. And now
another Summer Project volunteer, Ron Hilliard, will be
moving into the living room at Funston and I'll be
moving back into the other bedroom ("yellow room").

My whole life at this point is the Bulldog: other
than the loving, no time for anything else.

The big scene: Mike's office, seven p.m. last
night. His massive stacks of documents and papers have
been shoved into corners, the office is as presentable
as it will ever be, all the handouts ("Summer Project
Packet") are ready, we've decided what we want to say,
four gallons of wine are cooling. I walk in and a round
of applause erupts from the regular staff for "our
Summer Project leader." Mike in red shirt and
peppermint-striped coat betrays surprising nervousness
and excitement.

Then they start arriving (I'd been afraid no one
would show up) and finally the office is packed: thirty-
one volunteers, mostly freaky-looking young men
(including Valerie's housemate, the aforementioned Carl,
who's hoping to jump from distribution to the newsroom)
-- freaky-looking, I say, but still an obviously
competent bunch, many among them grad students in
journalism at Berkeley and Stanford, highly articulate
and curious as all-get-out. How will I ever keep them
interested? Mike delivers a forceful introductory

634

speech emphasizing the rigors of investigative reporting
and some of the Bulldog's triumphs in that realm. I
follow with a nuts-and-bolts rundown on how the Project
will work, and even to my own ears this sounds halting
and confused: for some reason I can't quite think
straight. I do better, though, during the questions and
answers. That one-on-one is my best way of relating is
confirmed yet again, in case I ever doubted it.

Afterwards, merry pandemonium as the wine flows and
people get to know each other. Great clouds of
impractical ideas are marauding about like lightning-
spitting thunderstorms in Nebraska in June (Mike would
like that simile but no doubt find it too cumbersome by
half -- and for newspaper purposes he'd be right!).
Peggy whispers to me: "That Judy looks exactly like
Valerie!" Far from "exactly," but the resemblance is
more than slight, especially in their lips but almost as
much in their carriage: athletic, proud, busty, sexy.
Nothing romantic will develop between me and Judy,
though. Awkwardnesses are proliferating. She's too --
what? -- too serious, I don't know. Or maybe just too
involved elsewhere -- or admirably loyal, didn't I say?

The hope was to revolutionize my life and
personalize my journal, but I have no time to effect
changes and too many people to deal with. Got to start
soon building a fence around my involvement with the
Bulldog, then apportion the time I spend both inside and
outside the fence. Strictly, I mean strictly enforce
those apportionments.

Wednesday 30

At last the office empties and I'm alone. Dusk.
Big trailer-trucks rumble by on Bryant Street. The room
still echoes with the deliberations of our "Power
Structure Work Group": seven young, naive, idealistic,
bewildered prospective journalists gathered together to
wrestle with the nefarious Establishment. I'm the
eighth for this one night and I pretty much fit the
description of the other seven, though I don't think

635

they've quite realized it yet.

Fortunately there's a ninth. This is Jim Beard,
the group leader, a community organizer for the Mission
Coalition, exhaustively knowledgeable about the city,
well educated, hip to computers and their uses, slave of
no illusions at all so far as I can see. He's totally
dedicated to his job, a "demon," as Mike says
admiringly, enormously energetic, tough-minded, yet
patient and easy to talk with. He looks something like
D.H. Lawrence with a paunch: reddish hair and beard,
cool and rational blue eyes, gaunt face, dressed in a
frayed plaid sport shirt from J.C. Penney's, baggy
jeans, bedraggled mountain boots, weathered sports
jacket with elbow patches that are completely worn
through, no tie. He's a spellbinding speaker simply
because he so obviously knows exactly what he's talking
about. I just sit back and drink it all in, brimming
with awe and incredulity, taking a few notes now and
then for appearance's sake. If I'm suspicious at all
it's not of Jim Beard but rather of my own cynical
streak (which is asking not only how could a man know so
much, but also how could he dedicate himself so
selflessly to this particular kind of knowledge?).

In the Anti-highrise Work Group, on the other hand,
I'm the authority, the leader, though I don't kid myself
that anyone sees me in anything like the same way I see
Jim Beard or that anyone should see me that way. The
fact is I'm an almost total ignoramus on the subject for
which I'm the go-to guy. (But then isn't that pretty
much the definition of a journalist: a person who can
write knowledgeably about a topic while knowing almost
nothing about it?)

*

And standing on the corner table: a vaseful of
brightly mixed flowers Valoshka brought in for me (I was
in a meeting with Mike at the time and she left before I
could see her). And tonight's when our anniversary
starts and tomorrow she herself begins work with the
Summer Project, the Consumer Work Group. But that's a
story for another volume. ---

636

[Valedictory]

JULY

1

Thursday 1
"You're not hooked on Coke, are you?" Judy Jacobi
asks incredulously.

Well, yes, as a matter of fact I think I am. In
the past eight months of struggling through so many
sleepless nights to meet newspaper deadlines and
detensify domestic emergencies the caffeine hits seem to
have become indispensable.

Right now I'm holding down my favorite corner table
at Cal's. Here the Coke is dispensed in the so-called
king-size bottle along with a glass of ice: the best way
to drink the stuff. When I'm finished with this other
obsessional task ("wording the day," as Monica describes
journalizing) I'll stroll over to the counter and order
five Cokes to go. I always take people's orders before
I leave the office. That's so I won't be disturbed at
Cal's, especially by Monica, who has the disconcerting
habit of showing up just as I begin to write and
barraging me with conversation, or rather with the
expectation of conversation. Usually I much prefer
being -- need to be -- alone for thirty minutes or so.
With the Summer Project underway I'm virtually never
alone in the office.

A note from Kay Boyle (in an elderly lady's shaky
hand): she's so busy she fears for her sanity. Which
means she can't do reviews for us.

Right now Valerie's down at the Bresker warehouse
performing volunteer work. And I'll note -- to start
catching up on another couple of crazy days -- that
Tuesday evening she burst into the Bulldog office at
seven (said she'd been waiting outside since five while
our meeting droned on and on) and her face looked just

637

as it did when I saw her at Mac's the morning after
she first moved out of Funston some ten days ago.
Desperate despair, I'll call it. The reason she gave me
for looking this way: "Everything seems so hopeless."

The bugs were so bad at her place Monday night, she
went on, that she'd had to stay with a friend (the
exterminator's visit, rescheduled from Saturday to
Tuesday, had itself driven her out of the house).

"And it wasn't who you're thinking, Glen. It was
this married guy -- "

"Val, please. You know, Carl let it slip -- "

"No, don't talk about Carl; I know what he told you
and I know he means well. I just want you to hear what
really happened from the horse's mouth, can I say?
So...it was this married guy I know from philosophy
class, Gavin, and his wife. They live down in San
Bruno. He's a weird optimist type who's sort of taken
me under his wing or something. He's only a friend,
Glen, I assure you. And I didn't want to impose on you
again by coming over to 'the Castle' just because the
bugs were eating me alive."

"Okay, fine, Val. I'm sorry about the bugs. But I
just think it's better if we don't -- "

"I think I can decide what I need to tell you!"

"Okay, I hear you, I hear you. Peace! Peace and
love!"

"Very funny."

"Well...so then, what else is making you feel
so -- "

"Everything!"

"Everything? That's a lot! But...can we talk
about it somewhere else? First maybe talk about whether
it's really something we want to talk about, but do that
somewhere else too?" (Several Summer Project folks were
still hanging around the office and their ears were
turning red.)

So we went out to the L.C. There I immediately
launched into a pep talk about fierce application to her
work, and within about three sentences she cut me off
and said we should forget about the talking, what she

really wanted to do was to suck my cock right there and then, and she did just that (as a switch engine rolled by a few yards away on the Southern Pacific tracks, trainmen whistling and hooting). So wholeheartedly did she get into it that at the exact moment of my ejac she barfed on my genitals. Ah yes! The timing was so perfect, the circumstances so grotesque, we both laughed for I don't know how long. (But I do know how hollow that laughter was for me: which is to say, very.)

So now she pronounced herself to be feeling much better. And since the exterminator gases had likely dissipated by then and the bugs were presumably all dead, she decided she wanted to go home and sleep in her own bed for a change. She asked me to drop her off at Reliable Drugs at Ninth and Irving and I did.

Yesterday she went to Berkeley, surveyed two stores for our Bulldog food-price survey, looked for summer diversions for herself. At midnight our "meet anniversary" began so we decided to start celebrating early (we'd arranged this the previous night). After a late dinner at Mel's we arrived at Funston a few minutes before twelve and there she laid on me what had to be one of the most zestful, energetic, and cacophonous fucks ever -- for me with her at the very least. It wasn't lovemaking, it was prizefighting, but it still managed to be delicious, oh yes it did.

Today, the big day, after a second round between the sheets by dawn's truly early light (near-solstitial) that was almost as pugilistic as the one the night before, we feasted on French toast and strawberries with cream and then put together the second box for Rob, a mere three months late, mailed it, picked up my new shades -- all almost as if we were living together again -- and then I dropped her off at her apartment because she had many things to do there before heading over to Berkeley and this was still a workday for me.

She says she continues to believe we'll get back together someday. I don't tell her this outright for fear of triggering another battle but I still believe if she keeps acting as she has been -- the wild vacillations, the sudden imposings, the interrogations, the threats and demands and outright lies and the dubious tales and unlikely alibis and refusals to deal with my own requests (carefully formulated, of course, so as not to come across as threats and demands like hers, but I'm sure she still sees them that way regardless) -- if she keeps this up, I say, there's not even a chance for us and I don't care how well things go in bed or anywhere else, whether for twelve hours in a row (as yesterday) or a thousand.

Saturday 3 (X:2)
It's beyond belief. My fragile emotional fabric is stretched to its uttermost limit. Clark Mayes, Tim Sorrel, and I were huddled in my office this morning, a Saturday morning no less (superb day: not the kind you'd ordinarily wish to spend indoors), excitedly discussing how we might apply the results of a highrise study undertaken in Charlotte, North Carolina, to downtown San Francisco, when Valoshka again burst dramatically into the lobby, this time with Danny in her arms. She stomped around out there and glared in at me for a while, then disappeared into the back office.
An hour or so later I learned what was up. Now we were sitting in the L.C. in the parking lot, Danny's breath rattling (turns out he has tonsillitis), Valerie burning with resentment. She grimly interrogated me:
"Where the hell were you last night?"
"Val...I thought we weren't going to ask that kind of question anymore."
"I already know you didn't come home, Glen."
"Maybe you've forgotten something? We said we weren't going to see each other last night, remember? It's what you said you wanted."
She glared at me with pure hatred.
"Well, Glen," she said finally, voice dramatically lowered now, "I just want you to know your failure to come home makes you responsible for what happened to me last night."

[valedictory]

At first she refused to tell me what this was --
just referred to it as something "horrible" which I
should feel guilty about. Then clues began to appear:
she'd been "looking for" me at Funston, then she'd
headed for the Bulldog office (where I've been known to
sleep on the couch at times) but something happened
along the way (tears streaked her cheeks as she scowled
at me).

Finally I asked: "You got raped?"

Silence. Glowering eyes.

Then she started castigating me for not coming
home. Never mind that she herself had not come home at
Fourth and Irving earlier this week (or that despite the
pain which knowing this caused me, whether she was
staying "at Gavin's" or wherever, I never said a word
about it to her). And never mind that this new attack
of hers was now bringing me to a slow boil.

But then she confirmed my guess.

"That's right, I got raped."

At first I thought she was making up a story to
knife me with, but over the course of the afternoon I
heard enough to convince me it was real. The memory was
too painful for her to dwell on (as she tearfully
reminded me several times as she spun it out). Here's
the story:

Friday night she'd been prowling outside "the
Castle" for hours, waiting for me to get home. One
thought obsessed her: I was out fucking somebody.
Finally she decided impetuously to check if I might've
crashed at the office. She walked down to Lincolnway
and stuck out her thumb. It was close to three in the
morning. A beautiful and outrageously sexy twenty-year-
old girl wearing pink hot pants. The two dudes who
picked her up ("Mexicans or something, I don't know")
forced her to go to Berkeley with them, to a quiet part
of town. There they raped her by turns in the backseat,
with the one who wasn't doing the fucking holding her
down. Her response to all this now in the L.C. was
disgust, revulsion, bitter anger not at them but at me.
"Men," she muttered over and over, lip curling.

[Have Mercy]

Adding insult to injury: she called Dennis from
Berkeley, she said, after the rapists let her go in the
industrial area near the water, and he drove over to
pick her up. At dawn they were drinking coffee at Zim's
and Dennis was scheming to get the bastards who did it.
(Valerie of course didn't bother to call the police:
"What good would it do? Besides, those guys said they'd
come back over here and cut me if I did. They have my
address and everything.") -- But Dennis, she let me
know, didn't hold her or touch her ("That's the last
thing I wanted") and she was quick to tell me without my
even asking that the incident hadn't gotten her involved
with him again (oh right Val). Supposedly he still
doesn't even know where she lives now after moving out
of Funston.
     "I said I'd call and tell him whether I'm okay.
That's it."
     All of this she imparted with her jaw set
defiantly. She muttered gravely, tears flowed, her tone
was bitterly resentful and accusatory toward me as if I
really were the actual cause of the whole thing.
     I'll admit my reaction to this rape revelation
wasn't always what it should've been. I tried to
console her, tried to show love and concern for her and
anger at the alleged perpetrators, but I also lashed out
at her at one point for being so stupid as to hitchhike
in pink hot pants at three a.m., and also for holding me
responsible for her own demented actions.
     And all along I was thinking: why do these
incidents keep happening with her? The volatile, wife-
raping husband, the brutal Mafioso hanging around, cops
descending on us and frisking me on suspicion of rape,
fist and knife and razor attacks on me by her in my own
home and workplace and elsewhere, a highly dangerous
threatened suicide attempt on a clifftop, magazines and
newspapers bashed out of my hands, a thousand other
outrages -- and now a rape by strangers. And eventually
I brought all this up. In response she rationalized and
justified her incessant attacks on me taken together
(the incidents with others she just ignored) as

constituting "irrefutable evidence" of her "love," and the more violent they were, the more such evidence they constituted. Under the circumstances I didn't say it, but I've told her plenty of times before: to me such horrific actions can't possibly signify love or even minimal caring. Hateful acts are hateful acts, period.

On the one hand she romanticizes all those acts; she declares them to be righteous, proper, loving, heroic, and fully deserved by me and what's more she states point-blank she's acting responsibly in unleashing them on me. On the other hand she insists she loses self-control; her nasty streak -- "the monster" -- takes over and she's not responsible for unleashing those very same acts. I'm responsible for her being raped by two men who are total strangers to both of us and also for her attempts to kill herself; "the monster" is responsible for her own attempts to set "the Castle" on fire or to kill me with a paring knife.

She can't see the flagrant contradiction here or that her defense of her horrific acts is every bit as mad as the individual acts themselves.

(She'd even written out a list, she told me, of all the things she wouldn't do -- such as staking out my house late at night or popping in unannounced -- but then she'd been powerless to stop herself from doing them.)

The awful thing is that I do harbor some guilt toward her -- I'd say it's inevitable on both sides when a love fails -- and she knows all too well how to exploit it. So today I wallowed in fumbling indecision, vacillating from tender care to tough questions and objections and protests, all the while seeing clearly what I must do: break things off completely with her, yes, but this time be truly hard-ass about it. "Set her free." "Don't let her keep on hanging on and destroy herself and maybe you too." But I can't act this way toward her in her moments of heartbreaking desperation any more than I can in her moments of euphoric hopefulness. And with her it often seems there are few moments of any other kind.

[Have Mercy]

An argument with her yesterday morning at Mac's
cemented my feeling about all this even before she
divulged the dismaying rape story. This argument seemed
to lay bare the heart of our increasingly demented
relationship. It began with her belittling my role at
the Bulldog (for all this trivial Summer Project stuff I
was spending more time on the Bulldog than Mike was --
he was exploiting me and I wasn't even on salary -- why,
I'd never devoted a tenth as much time to her -- not
even a hundredth as much). In return I denounced her
for savaging people like Mike who were accomplishing
things when she herself was doing so little. And I
complained yet again about her long-held belief that she
and I are a classic example of a Karen Horney morbid-
dependent/narcissist relationship. The underachiever
and the overachiever. Supposedly I'm just projecting --
bleah. Never mind. This will take us nowhere. Forget
the shrinkology!
Back to this particular incident today. Valerie
has no right to interfere with my private life but I
wouldn't deny for a moment she has good reason to think
I might be seeing others. At Mac's Friday morning, for
example, she told me she'd dreamed that night of a naked
Jang fixing up her "aging face" for me. Shudder: I had
plans to see Jang that same evening. And I did see her,
yes. That's the actual reason why I didn't make it home
last night (and "therefore" Val got raped). Another
fire at Jang's place, another restful meal, another
laid-back hike around the Noe neighborhood, another pair
of fine fucks. And Val, I'm sorry, but what happens
between me and Jang -- or anyone else -- is simply none
of your business. Not after what's gone down between us
and what you've agreed to as a condition for our staying
in contact. You don't like it but you have to swallow
whatever I may be doing with Jang (or whomever) just as
I have to swallow whatever you may be doing with Dennis
(or whomever). You think I should see such things
differently but in the end I don't care; I'll defend my
way of seeing these things to the death. And I realize
full well you think it might just come to that and you

think it's for you to determine if it will. And on that
I guess I have no choice but to say: you're correct. It
won't be me; it'll be you who makes that decision.

One more thing. It's a hard truth for you, Val,
but when I'm with Jang I desire her as I never have any
other woman. I think it could be like that with us too,
as I've told you, but it's not yet and it looks to me
less and less likely it ever will be. And I've told you
that too. Because you've insisted on my doing so. Over
and over you've insisted you want "full candor."
"Complete openness and honesty." Never mind that you
offer me an unending series of evasions and fabrications
and outright lies. I must be "open and honest" -- or
else!

(It remains equally true that when I'm away from
Jang, I remember how our life together, Jang's and mine,
taught me that blissful sexual fulfillment alone is
nowhere near enough to make a love work. And yet also
how easy it is to suppress this awareness! How easy to
con oneself into believing that this time by proceeding
lovingly and cautiously and applying new wisdom the
connubial pair will discover a way to build a fulfilling
life together around all that glorious fucking. -- But
one mistake I won't make: I won't move in with Jang
again unless I'm certain or at the very least close to
certain we can make it work this time.)

*

Footnote: as I was leaving Valoshka's place after
spending several hours trying to comfort her (and taking
Danny to the hospital for a checkup), she grimly
declared to me: "I feel worse now than I did before,"
meaning when we were living together at Funston, and
again implying it was all my fault. That is,
"everything" was my fault. She dared to say that! I
was carrying the flashlight and stapler she'd borrowed
from Funston (without asking), and, safely out of her
earshot, I smashed the flashlight on the concrete stoop.
Then stormed away.

Sunday 4

An exciting day. Almost by accident I found myself
seated at Ari Bresker's kitchen table when he decided to
enter the race for supervisor. This decision means more
than may appear at first glance, for he'll probably win,
and it's at least possible he'll be able to sweep into
office with him two or three other candidates on the
S.F. Alliance slate. The Alliance could become a highly
influential voice in city politics, not only this fall
but for years or even decades to come. This first
attempt in modern times by a "radical" political force
to "take over" a major American city via the ballet box
could generate reams of national publicity and foment
one of the most heated (and exciting) municipal election
campaigns in memory.

Five of us had just returned from hooping it up at
a playground atop Russian Hill and were rapping at the
kitchen table: Bresker, Steve Vaughn (his lawyer),
Mitchell Kern (director of the anti-highrise campaign),
Jack Simon (the Bresker veep who used to be a big wheel
at Levi Strauss), and me (ha!). Halfway through, Lanny
Zinn (owner of the hot new Salmagundi restaurant and
several other organic eateries) joined us.

We're all of that age group extending roughly from
twenty-five to forty who were born before the end of
World War II and passed through high school and college
in the fifties or early sixties but before the
counterculture had fully emerged. We joined up in
this new way of life relatively late in our own lives,
after many of our values and habits were formed, and
consequently we wear our hair long but not below-
shoulder length, we enjoy organized sports, we disown
violence as a means to achieve political ends in a
democracy, we're "responsible," we nurse a fundamental
belief in American society, a guarded optimism
concerning its possibilities for accepting nonviolent
radical change, we're not bitter and alienated in the
way so many people slightly younger than us are. We're
all, to a certain degree, converted liberals, "radic-
libs," first cousins to the liberals of the JFK era, not

the militant radicals whose values have been formed in
reaction to the wartime draft and the government's
clampdown on peaceful protest over the past five years.
(Of the group, I'm the youngest and undoubtedly the
closest to being a bona-fide counterculture radical,
both in appearance -- my hair's the longest -- and
beliefs, possibly because I'm the only one who had to
deal personally with the draft during wartime.)

Bresker appeared to be still suffering jet lag
related to his return last night from Israel (only Steve
and I in the group are not Jewish, by the way). But as
the conversation turned to political matters, he
brightened. He's immediately recognizable from his TV
ads for Bresker Hardware: probably in his late thirties,
soft-spoken, humorous, affable, a bit bumbling, even
harmless-appearing. His charm reminds me a little of
Ike's and a little of the singer Tony Bennett's (whom he
resembles quite a bit physically): he's the sort a
proverbial granny in tennis shoes would immediately
trust. A fine gentle smile. Very easygoing: no sense
at all of the conniving politician, the hardheaded
businessman. He's constantly chuckling at himself,
making light fun of pretentiousness, defusing tensions
with charming diplomacy. In short: a fine man and a
fine candidate.

First he asked me to give a quick rundown on the
anti-Manhattanization book, and in doing so I raised the
subject of political action this autumn by stressing the
need to show the impact of out-of-control highrise
development on major city neighborhoods, that is,
translating the appeal of the Bresker movement into
political power. Someone, I'm not sure who -- it may
even have been me -- suggested the Alliance put up a
slate of candidates for the supervisorial election this
fall. Everyone agreed this would not only be the best
way to gain wider exposure for the anti-highrise issue,
but also the next logical step for the Alliance to take
since the true objective of the group is to wrest
decision-making power from large corporate interests and
return it to city residents. But who would the

candidates be? Someone asked Bresker whether he'd be
interested. To everyone's surprise, I think, he said
yes. Lots of self-disparaging humor: "As a bankrupt
'hardware merchant,' I'm the perfect example of how to
stop growth."

Then the discussion turned to practical questions,
such as: who else would run? Where would the money come
from? What stands should they take? Suggestions flew
thick and fast, but most were intended at least half-
jokingly: no one there, after all, knew a great deal
about politics. But everyone agreed the campaign should
be highly unconventional, low-key (that is, not high-
pressure, which takes money, whereas "telling the truth
is always much cheaper than telling lies," as Bresker
observed), that no one would be required to toe a party
line, that the objective this first time around wouldn't
be winning but rather "making the unspeakable speakable"
and establishing a sort of "government in internal
exile," and that the whole thing "oughta be fun." "I
think politics are going to be fun again," Bresker said
with a goofy smile that immediately made them seem so.

There will, of course, be lots of headaches along
the way. For example, do you make up a slate of people
you know and trust, or do you try to put together a
broad-based coalition? How do you counter the influence
of the establishment media, all of which are sure to
ignore the Alliance and everything it stands for --
unless it becomes a real threat, in which case they'll
blast it relentlessly? And a million others.

But the machinery is in motion, if it can be called
machinery: Bresker will consult with Cedric Turner, the
antiwar minister with strong connections in minority
communities (he's black himself) and elsewhere, and
several others of like mind who might play a part or at
least advise him about political realities.

One of those advisors he'll consult will be Mike
Meyerhold -- at my suggestion. The first thing I did
after leaving was call Mike, who was so fascinated by
the news he questioned me about it for well over an
hour.

"This could be the best thing that's happened in this town in years," he said in that dramatically lowered tone he adopts while talking about "insider" matters. "It could change the whole ball game. It could even change some of the rules for the ball game."

Meyerhold himself was suggested as a possible candidate, but he scoffed at the idea when I told him about it, although he didn't hesitate to kick it around a bit just to see if it had any life in it. His conclusion was that his influence would be far greater -- potentially -- at the Bulldog. It wasn't necessary for either of us to say out loud that the entrance of the S.F. Alliance into the political arena should vastly enhance the Bulldog's significance as an oppositional voice and thus boost its circulation considerably and maybe even attract some new advertising and investment dollars from anti-corporate interests.

*   *

Also encouraging to me was the seemingly trivial fact that on a Sunday morning I was playing basketball out in the sun with half a dozen people whose company I truly enjoyed (at Alice Marble Park atop Russian Hill). Everyone there seemed like a potential, maybe even already an actual, friend. One month short of four years after arriving in San Francisco I was for the first time feeling I was not a stranger, an outsider.

2

Monday 5

> Love the art in yourself,
> not yourself in the art.
>   -- Stanislavsky

Today's an official holiday since the Fourth fell on a Sunday -- yesterday -- but I'm doing what I'd ordinarily be doing, working at the office, attending one meeting and conference after another (the whole Summer Project is hard at it, all six work groups), and already I'm beginning to feel trapped in the role of

administrator. Therefore to gain a little respite and
set down a few undisturbed thoughts I'm sitting outside
in the passenger seat of the L.C. -- Bryant Street's
empty at what's ordinarily the beginning of the
afternoon rush hour, a strong July sun is glaring down,
and I'm suddenly finding myself gripped (how else can I
say this?) -- gripped by a kind of rampaging nostalgia.

   Last night I opened up the lockbox in my closet and
brought forth two volumes from last summer, one, V.21,
describing my initial enchantment with Valerie (it was a
year ago today we began shacking up at her Dolores
Street place), the other, the infamous and still torn
and tattered V.22, intoxicated with Briana (I finally
officially met her on July 30, several months after the
first sighting while visiting Barb at Vitr). Both are
on my mind now.

   And I'm thinking I might make another play for
Briana. This is because Bruce Nelson tells me it
appears she and Larry are "sort of drifting back
together." If that's true, this would probably be my
last chance to get something going with her. On the
anniversary of our first meeting, I'm thinking, I could
contact her just as a friendly gesture and at the same
time feel her out about things. Probably nothing would
come of it. She might be tempted, but it's not likely
she'd want to jeopardize a reconciliation with Terry if
one's really in the works (for if that's the case, it
would probably lead to marriage). And really now,
jeopardize it for what? To shoot the rapids once again
with Editor Sandefjord? But deep down I want to try it
anyway. Better to be rejected definitively than to keep
nursing a faint hope we'll someday get back together.
(And regardless I still can't shake the gut-deep sense
she's Terry's woman, not mine, and always will be.)

   And Valoshka? Feeling for her creeps back in via
the back door. Also via the basement windows, the
chimney, the sewage pipes. I'm besieged by chilling
images of her "rape scene." I'm plagued by the notion
that she must be with Dennis simply because I keep
thinking she must be with Dennis. Impulses to see her

[valedictory]

rise up and must be swatted down. Her housemate Carl
from the Bulldog tells me she's "doing surprisingly
well." But when I half-kiddingly ask him to give her my
love, he takes me full-seriously and says (with a touch
of resentment), "I think maybe you'd better give her
your love yourself." Well, I can't blame him. Or her.
I just can't cope with her extreme recklessness with my
emotional well-being, that's all. So anyway I'll see
her in the morning at Mac's, if she chooses to be there.

*   *

Spin-dry notes:
A year ago I was confused, bewildered, perplexed...
and deliriously happy. Looking back now I suspect those
delicious summer months of 1970 will always rank among
the best I've known. What made them that way? For one
thing, freedom. It's one of the few times I've felt
myself entirely free of obligations to women. -- No,
shit no, it wasn't that, what am I saying? The truth is
I had "a whole series" (one of Meyerhold's pet phrases)
of obligations to women back then, though of varying
degrees of seriousness: with Nadine, Jang, Valerie,
Briana. So I don't know what it was. But I was nearing
the end of my stint at Empyrean and then I really was
free, as of early August as it turned out, and for the
first time in almost two years -- free of the burdens of
a nine-to-five job. And I was digging life to the
maximum. Prospects appeared extremely bright. In the
space of a single month I'd met two women who excited my
strongest possible interest. I had financial security
-- at least enough to spare me from the need to hunt
down another job for roughly eighteen months -- and I
was ready to get to work on the "Symphony No. 6" project
I'd been building toward for the previous three years,
i.e., the big novel which at that time seemed almost
destined to be publishable just because I was so intent
about it and had piled up so much material for it.
And what do I say about all this now? I say -- I
say -- I say what the fuck, why dwell on the past? Yes,
that's what I say. And why do I say it? Because things
are even better at this very moment! -- If, that is, I

651

can just find the right perspective and hold it firmly
in place for a while. And may the gods damn this as
hubris but -- I know I can do it!

And I mean now.

The writing of my own which I like best, I want to
say, is that which races ahead of itself unself-
consciously, infatuated with people and images and
details and ideas. The mad, delightful quest to get
everything down on paper. "Word the day." Everything I
can remember about Briana, for example. The tiny
details which can illuminate a soul. Far different
stuff, to say the least, from cost/revenue analysis of a
city business district. But the truth is I'm liking
this latter stuff a lot more -- "a whole series" of lot
mores -- than I should. Or: "should."

A paper I wrote for Economics 21 at Adams sustains
my belief I can put together, and write a big chunk of,
a lively book about such an inherently dull subject as
"Manhattanization." The professor who graded the paper
(and gave it an A-plus I've just gotta mention) took me
aside to say I should be a writer. The topic of the
paper was highly complex, but he said I'd made
everything about it clear and easily understandable.
Well, yes, I immodestly confessed, I did intend to be a
writer. But at that time I certainly wasn't thinking
I'd ever be writing about economics. Not seriously or
at length. That thought didn't come until the past few
weeks.

This Bulldog anti-highrise book will be my first
real test at writing an extended nonfiction piece for an
all-but-guaranteed audience of serious readers.

So clank on in there and do it!

How marvelous it would be if I could spend the rest
of my life engaged in volunteer labor. It endows you
with an undeniable sense of moral righteousness. Alas,
it also undermines you by triggering an ineradicable
doubt: would they still have you around if they had to
pay you? I'm sure the Bulldog would have me around if
they could pay me. But they can't, other than a tiny
dribble every now and then. Without an astonishing

reversal of fortune before October, when my unemployment
runs out, they won't be able to pay me then either.

Oh well, why worry, especially if you have so many
other things with regard to which you're also saying
"why worry." I mean, it's still only July and all
sorts of things are happening. Just about my only real
worry comes from my fear that I won't be able to live up
to my promises and vows -- to the Bulldog and to myself.
I'm plagued by the usual subterranean self-doubts, which
certainly preceded my becoming a volunteer at the
Bulldog and undoubtedly will linger long after I stop
being a volunteer there. And a good thing too, because
without self-doubts how would one ever learn, change,
grow, etc. etc. Right? Right. Or: Right!

(A pause to transfer two washerloads into the
dryer.)

So: what to scribble about that isn't dull?
Convoluted introspection regarding matters of financial
insecurity certainly is dull. Better I should wing it.
Let's see. Oops: Valoshka again. At six-thirty tonight
on the way home I overrode my own presumed (in this case
by me) good sense and stopped at her place. The reason
I concocted for myself and for her: I'd like to borrow
forty bucks to tide me over until the next unemployment
check arrives. (I suddenly felt bad about trying to
squeeze it out of Jang, who's already played sugar momma
for me to the tune of around two hundred and fifty bucks
over the past few months.) And it was early enough that
I presumed I wouldn't be interfering with any social
life Val had lined up for the evening. But: no one was
home. Monday night, Danny sick, no one home. So I
can't help but wonder what she's up to.

Tragic Valoshka.

Two guys taking turns raping Val in the backseat of
a car. Yes, I ought to feel guilty about this. I'm
absolutely not responsible for it but I ought to be
experiencing the guilt that inevitably arises regardless
from any love worth its beans. I also ought to be
experiencing upwellings of sympathy and pity and rage.
But that's not happening either, or at least not much

(because I won't let it happen?). Instead when I think
about the rapes at all I either wonder if they really
took place (my doubts are increasing entirely of their
own volition) or wonder what they were like for her, I
mean really -- considering, that is, how she often talks
about being turned on by her own rape fantasies and how
she's such a fan of rough sex and she makes no bones
about it, how she wants a man who will treat her
violently, how in fact when it comes right down to it
she glorifies rape and traditional forms of male
dominance under the patriarchy, and at the same time she
rejects them in the name of feminism and egalite' --
either I wonder about all this, I say, or I castigate
myself for thinking such raw thoughts and not worrying
enough about what she's gone through and must still be
going through at this very moment; or I do all these
things at once in a maelstrom of pain and confusion.

    Flash: I'd like to carve an X onto her chest to
match the one on mine. Mine isn't fading fast enough.
It really will be there for years, I'm afraid, just as I
said it would at the height of the crazed moment when I
sliced it in.

    Or I could mention this: Sid Portola calls from
Garnett, yaks about his disenchantment with the new
"Marvel Plaza Merino Mercury," as he calls it, says
Claire was disappointed when I didn't put in an
appearance for the big Fleming AFB demos (I'd told her I
hoped to) but she "understands." On the phone a while
ago Claire informed me she'd told Kurt everything about
us (he too "understands," she said) and suggested we
renew our affair. The idea doesn't repulse me, but
carumba, Garnett seems so far away now and time's so
limited and Claire's so opaque and so often stoned out
of her mind or flying high on who knows what (including
during that same call). I have to admit it: the main
reason I still want to go up there is to retrieve that
ridiculous "captain's cap" (because the leather pants
I've pretty much given up on).

    Or this: an offhand remark by Bruce Nelson led me
to a back issue of the Bulldog where I found a review of

[Valedictory]

Godard's "La Chinois" under the byline of none other
than Terry Morton, Briana's longtime ol' man and my
ghostly rival. Good piece too. Could that be at least
partly because Briana herself is of Chinese ancestry
(just as half of Val is, DNA-wise)? I love to play with
the idea of sending Terry a note asking whether he'd be
interested in doing more reviews for the Bulldog. Ho
ho. I'm pretty sure he'd recognize my name. I could
even legitimately sign the note "Editor Sandefjord." He
and I could sit around the Bulldog office swapping
stories guaranteed to keep each other in stitches.

Or I could get busy and finish reading Jane Jacobs.
Hie on home, immerse myself in a hot bath, sip on
blackberry wine (bought weeks ago, in unconscious hope,
perhaps, of reliving last summer), let the cool breeze
wash over me as the hours drain slowly while I'm
pondering ways I might help make a great city a measure
or two more livable and humane for all of its residents
-- not a single one excepted, damn it!

Tuesday 6
Nine a.m. I meet Valoshka at Mac's (I never did
try again at her place last night), we laugh, we
exchange impassioned kisses on the sidewalk and in a
long line at the bank. In the L.C. she says, "I want to
suck on it and make it shoot off like a fountain," and
by the time I find a shaded place along the road in the
park she's already got it out and then -- the fountain.
And a sticky steering wheel and a smeared speedometer.
Eleven-thirty a.m. Tim Sorrel at Bresker's
warehouse takes Valoshka upstairs to begin a
photocopying stint and I find myself confronted with her
journal sticking up out of her bag stashed on the floor
in front of the passenger seat in the L.C. For maybe
five minutes I wrestle with my conscience, thinking of
all the times she's snooped in my journal but also how I
chewed her out for doing so. I wonder if she's
intentionally left it where it is to entrap me somehow
-- perhaps she's even booby-trapped it. Finally I give

in and glance at two pages, just enough to let me know
I've been duped again. The rapes were indeed a hoax.
She slept with Dennis that night. It was hardly the
first time. And last night she wrote a journal passage
at his place as he sat with his arms around her. I left
seething with anger and also confused: certain lines had
even seemed to suggest she might be whoring for him.

Chump! Idiot!

Four p.m. I return to Bresker's to pick up the
photocopies and find her journal still available right
where it was before. A hurried rereading of the entry
in question confirms everything about Dennis but
disabuses me of the whoring notion.

Four-fifteen p.m. I find her at the photocopy
machine in Bresker's main office and immediately confess
I've read her journal. My tone isn't at all harsh; I
even suggest we move on and forget about the whole week
right up to last night. But her response -- cold,
aloof, reproachful -- soon has me feeling uneasy about
my lack of toughness with her. I feel she wants me to
treat her harshly. She insists she left the journal
there purposely for me to read it: "I wanted to see
whether you still felt you owned me." Later she revises
this: "I felt so badly about making up the rape story I
couldn't even sleep. I wanted you to know the truth so
you could act on it."

Five p.m. Back in the L.C., parked outside the
unemployment office just around the corner from
Bresker's warehouse, she hands me the journal rather
than answer any more of my skeptical questions. "Go
ahead, read it all. I read yours." "All right, I'll do
that." As she hides her face in her hands I quickly go
over the entries for the past seventeen days since she
moved out, details of her affair with Dennis, her
misery, her lies, her bitterness, her love/hate (mostly
hate) for me. For the entire period she was fucking him
practically nonstop. She fucked him at night on the
nights she didn't sleep with me; she fucked him during
the day before and/or after she did sleep with me.

After I've taken all this in (and I'm leaving out

656

most of it here) I tell her very calmly it's over for
us. Then I lose my calm and soon I'm raging at her,
mainly about the straight-faced lies and the despicable
rape hoax. She cries, berates me for taking advantage
of her "honesty" in showing me the journal (the
hypocrisy of which statement enrages me further after
all the times she's done precisely that to me -- taken
advantage of my openness -- with no qualms at all).
Then she leaves.

    Ten p.m. She calls at the office and puts in a
final plea. Will I meet her at Mac's tomorrow morning?
This time, she assures me, she's really reformed. She
has absolutely no desire to see Dennis again. Just last
night she'd come to grips with herself (sitting up all
night at Zim's, she says, but I don't believe her, and
she certainly doesn't sound like someone exhausted from
staying up all night). Why does everything "positive"
she does, she wants to know (referring to the "decision"
to leave her journal in the L.C. for me to read, which I
now suspect wasn't that, a "decision," at all, but a
simple matter of believing I'd never read it without her
consent because I'm such a virtuous, trusting, straight-
arrow imbecile) -- although it's true, I can't deny, I
did read a few snatches of it before under life-and-
death conditions during her terror regime -- why, she
wants to know, I say, does everything "positive" always
boomerang against her? She doesn't blame me for
reacting as I did to what I read, but she "knows" I'll
regret my decision to drop her flat and I'll soon want
to return to her. Therefore, she adds, from now on
she'll live in such a way as to draw me back to her.
Yes, I'm her true love, the one and only man for her in
the whole world, the one she'll love until the day she
dies. All the dreadful things she's written about me
are exaggerations, she insists, they're release,
catharsis, purgation, attempts at comforting herself.
She doesn't really feel any of that stuff. (Familiar
arguments all: as she points out, I made most of them to
her myself last winter when I was the one whose journal
had been invaded, who was begging for understanding.)

[Have Mercy]

I turn down everything. I don't hesitate to mouth
every cruel, petty, bitter feeling I have about her. I
want nothing more to do with her, not even the tersest
communication. I can no longer make myself vulnerable
to her in any way. I want not a single future contact
with a woman who's thought of me and treated me as she's
been doing over the past several months. This goes on
and on, back and forth, neither of us capable of
breaking it off...until finally I do it.
"I love you!" she cries at the end. "You're being
a fool!"

*   *

Maybe so. She's gotten to me in ways no one else
ever has. But I have no choice: I'm boxed in. Pride.
Fury. Rage. I still boil at the thought of some of the
things she wrote. That rape gambit was worst of all.
Dennis had wanted to fuck all night (as he often did),
but on this occasion she'd let him do it "only once."
They slept little, tightly curled together against the
cold, and that was when she dreamed up the story she
would tell me to explain why she hadn't made it home on
the night Carl indiscreetly told me about (and then told
her he'd let it slip to me). Oddly enough, the story
she came up with was inspired by an account she'd read
in one of my own chronbooks from Mezzu days about the
rape Deirdre Bond experienced in Ohio. I scribbled that
down five years ago and had pretty much forgotten about
it. But what if I hadn't forgotten? It enrages me
doubly that Val thought she could get away with using
one of my own passages against me this way (and disgusts
me that she easily pulled it off up until the moment I
read the page gloating about it in her journal).
Sunday night, shortly after telling me she'd never
see Dennis again (she'd just call to tell him how she
was doing after the rapes "and that's it"), she went
back to him and they quarreled and she had to coax him
to fuck her; then Monday evening she went back again and
found him still in bed, drunk, hung over. He'd picked
up a waitress at the Peppermint Tree ("I'm not jealous,"
Val wrote), he and Val squabbled some more, Val left (or

[valedictory]

so she informed me) at eight having told him (again)
she'd see him no more.

Ah, and that chaste night she supposedly crashed at
the home of the mild-mannered "optimistic" philosopher
Gavin? She was with Dennis then too, of course. That
night she wrote about being endlessly fascinated by his
self-impaling cock that curves up like a sickle. Again
he wanted to fuck all night. This time she seemed to
find him less appealing: no more raves about "righteous
fucking." In explaining the passage to me she said by
that point he no longer turned her on. Already she was
bored with him. "If only he had an education," she
wrote that same night. But even so he offered her more
than I do. "I'd prefer any slob," she wrote, "even a
rightist pig, to a liberal phony like Glen." She
couldn't get a word of truth from me, no real feelings,
no sincerity, just "hung-up politeness." Definitely I
wasn't the man for her, she concluded: I had the
qualifications, but just the bare minimum. "I've never
met a man who could handle me" -- the only sentence in
the whole sketchbook she underlined.

Her disillusionment with me is complete. She felt,
according to the journal, "nothing but pain and
indifference" when we fucked during the past few weeks.
No feelings toward me at all at any time, except
contempt. I'd "never make it as a fiction writer": "he
just doesn't have the imagination, the whimsy" -- in
fact she has more of both herself. I'm a great
disappointment to her. She despises my "softness," my
tears, my "coldness," my need for constant "reassurance"
and "pampering," my bourgeois background and family and
tastes, my inability to cut her free, everything.
Everything! Bitterness everywhere! She digs cute
curly-haired Tim Sorrel at Bresker's (those big blue
eyes of his) and vows to ball him just to cause me more
grief. She's consumed with vengeful schemes. She sees
herself as a righteous one-woman fifth column
representing the oppressed victims of Western
colonialism worldwide and this justifies any and all of
her acts of terror against me including a ludicrous

659

fantasy plan to burn down the Bay Bulldog Building. She
also wants to catch me in the act of fucking someone
else (just as I hoped to catch her with Dennis, yes, and
wrote as much in here). Supposedly I can't fuck all
night because I'm "no longer young" (in truth I've been
fucking practically nonstop myself over these two weeks,
maybe even matching Val and Dennis's production). I'll
always be fucking other women, she writes, always
messing with women's minds. And then vast swatches of
morbid self-pity and misery, real misery, desperate
loneliness, pathetic secret visits to "the Castle." Her
obsession with me. Not love, although she calls it that
at times, but rather obsession, fear, fury at being
criticized and rejected, rampaging guilt for all her
many, many, many "transgressions."

*   *

    As for me: I throw all this back in her face (she
disavows it all) and righteously, sternly, furiously put
her down, leave no openings, act strong. Underneath,
though, I'm severely shaken. Again! I fear many of her
observations are true. I can't shake loose of my pride.
She really is the right woman for me if only....
    The truth is I'm badly split. I yearn for her, but
I don't want her. Danny, sex: these are the two big
problems, as we both know, the specific ones, and
reflections of the elemental emotional one: the barriers
we can't overcome. She never did learn how to
"understand" me, how to make me feel good, how to avoid
hurting my pride too much. Funny thing is, pride drives
me toward her as well as away from her. I'm too
attached to her and too proud to accept failure. If I
were strong enough I could take her endless abuse and
outrageous misbehavior and we could make it as a loving
couple, highly eccentric, perhaps, but truly righteous:
therefore I must become stronger. Well, horse manure.
My strength and energies are needed elsewhere. Save
yourself, my son!
    Enough.

[Valedictory]

Wednesday 7

"When your girlfriend comes in," says the waitress
here at Mac's, "tell her we're out of orange juice. We
do have grapefruit juice if she'd like that."

Well, it just could be my girlfriend won't be
coming in today. Who knows what she did after I hung up
last night. I said I didn't want to see her here today
-- or have any contact with her at all at any time --
and so perhaps she'll scratch Mac's from her list of
hangouts.

Anyway: the weather did a quick change last night.
Stormy winds, now a thick fog. Before going to bed I
took a two a.m. stroll out to the street because I felt
certain Val was hiding out there (as she described
herself doing several times over the past three weeks in
her journal), but the street was empty beneath the
bright full moon. I whistled once -- calling for my
dog, Val would probably say -- and of course there was
no response. The only sound came from pennants flapping
in the breeze on the new house across the street, the
big "luxury" home, now standing empty and for sale. Its
lights burn without pause day and night.

Back in bed I once thought I heard Val come in, and
I bounded up to check: it was just the wind. I left the
apartment door unlocked. It took me forever to slide
down the bumpy hillside into sleep. My mind was
obsessed with images of her fucking Dennis, rolling in
the sand with him at the beach (as her journal described
at length), lying tightly cuddled in his arms at his
place, sucking his cock an hour or two before she sucked
mine and then an hour or two after she sucked mine
(playing out that same gagging scenario twice, almost
identically, BOOM-BOOM-BOOM, BOOM-BOOM-BOOM). I deserve
to suffer this way, no doubt, after putting others
through much the same sort of thing, and Val more so
than anyone. It's almost a relief to feel the pangs and
to know the arc of justice is finally bending down right
where it ought to bend down.

*   *

Chaos: here it is. A new peak in ugliness,

661

melodrama, tragedy, martyrdom. For all I know Valerie
may be dead by now. She promised she would be.

The last I saw of her she was sprinting along
California Street, cutting through the gas station
across from the JCC (which must be near Dennis's place).
Before that she'd dashed out into the street, stopping
traffic, just standing there glaring at me in the bright
theater-stage-like glow created by dozens of vehicle
headlights. People on the sidewalk all stopped and
stared at the madwoman. Then she accosted an older
woman getting into her car, begged for a ride home with
her (most likely claiming a madman or rapist was lurking
across the street fixing to grab her).

She did get into the car, but then Jang (I'd taken
her earlier to the JCC, where Valerie encountered me) --
Jang ran across the street with Valerie's bag, which
she'd left lying on the road next to the L.C. Jang said
something to the older woman about the police coming and
Valerie split from the car. Her reason for dashing away
from me: Jang had just returned from the phone booth
where she called the cops. I'd asked her to do it.

All this came after a series of agonizing
hysterical scenes both inside and outside the JCC. I'd
been dressing in the locker room when a note from Jang
arrived saying, "Valerie is here -- what should I do?"
I found Val outside by the locker-room entrance.

"Do you know Jang's here?" she asked.

"Yes. I brought her."

She smiled. Said: "I really blew it, didn't I."

I mumbled something about how nobody blew anything,
whatever happened happened, but in any case for us it
was over. She told me excitedly and incoherently about
a disgusting racist scene involving white cops and a
black customer she'd witnessed less than an hour earlier
at the nearby Fillmore Safeway where she'd been
conducting a Bulldog shopping survey for the Summer
Project. Finally I said I had to go.

"This is the last time you'll ever see me," she
said.

"Yes, I'm sure it is."

662

[Valedictory]

Triumphantly: "I just took fifteen Libriums and two sleeping pills."

"That's wonderful."

I spun on my heel and walked into the men's locker room -- and she followed right behind me, howling and cursing all the way as the naked men scurried for cover. So I walked back outside, to the street.

"I'm taking you to the hospital," I said.

"No you're not." And then: "Take a good look at me. I'll be dead in two hours."

"I think you're lying."

"Call my mother if you don't believe me! Ask her whether her Libriums are there."

"Okay, then I really will take you to the hospital. You wait here while I tell Jang."

She refused, again following me inside. "You're going to fuck her, aren't you." (I had just done that, in fact, at her temporary apartment on 28th Street, on sheets spread on the floor where she sleeps because the bed's "too dirty" -- as did the previous occupant, who was a man, she concluded, on the basis of several raunchy paperbacks she found under the bed and showed me. And a very fine fuck it was, even though my mind was simultaneously obsessed with Valerie.)

Upstairs at the JCC I asked Jang to wait for me in the lobby there while I took Valerie to the hospital. At that point Valerie split out the front door. When we reached the sidewalk she dashed off to the corner and leaned against a telephone pole, glaring at us.

"Let her go, Glen," Jang advised me. "She didn't take any pills."

"I think she may have," I said, and took her, Jang, with me to the corner.

Jang asked: "Do you want to go to the hospital, Valerie?"

She glared at Jang. "Have you been fucking him behind my back?" But she spat the words out so quickly Jang seemingly didn't comprehend what she was asking.

"Don't listen to her," I said to Jang (who later just laughed when I asked about the seeming implication

in Val's "behind my back" that they'd made some sort of
compact regarding me).

Jang put her hand on Valerie's shoulder and tried
to talk some sense into her, though she sounded almost
as incoherent as Valerie did: "No, you don't need to
die. Why? Individuals die. You die, I die, Glen
dies...."

This went on a while and Valerie just glared,
alternating between Jang and me.

"No, she didn't take pills, Glen. Her eyes do not
show it."

"Fifteen Libriums and two sleeping pills," Valerie
insisted again (she repeated it several more times, like
a magical incantation).

This crazed dialogue sputtered on until finally
I said, "Come on, Valerie, I'm taking you to the
hospital." Then an aside to Jang: "She's sick, you've
got to realize that. She may actually have done it."

I put my hand on Val's arm to guide her to the L.C.
She pulled away as if stabbed -- "Don't touch me,
fucker!" -- dropping her scarf as she did so and leaving
it behind as she retreated into the street again. My
scarf, actually: the brightly colored one Briana knitted
for me back in our brief high period. Now Val stood in
the middle of Masonic, still glaring. Cars screeched to
a halt and detoured into oncoming lanes to avoid her,
horns blaring. Then she sat down in the street, the
inner southbound lane. Then she lay on her back in the
same spot with her arms spread wide on the pavement and
slowly moving horizontally up and down, like someone
making a snow angel, her face twisted into a lunatic
wrathful smile.

"Let's go, Glen," Jang said. "She'll keep doing
bad things if we stay. She'll stop if we go."

"All right. You're right."

The two of us began walking back toward the L.C.
Valerie leapt up and ran after us in her familiar fierce
Valkyrie way, shrieking, fists churning, "Give me my
scarf!"

"It's not yours," I said, like a total idiot. "You

gave it back to me, don't you remember? You said you
wanted nothing to do with it."

"Bullshit!" She grabbed it and tried to pull it
away with her left hand, simultaneously pounding her
right fist with its several large menacing rings against
my upper left arm, looking utterly vicious and demented.
A brief tussle.

Jang was totally shocked. "Valerie, you don't be
this way, no!"

I let her have the scarf. We continued walking
toward the L.C., Val right at our side, taunting us
every step of the way.

"We'll take her to the hospital," I said to Jang.

"I'm not going to the hospital," said Val.

"If you come with us," I said, "you're going to the
hospital."

I tried to let just Jang into the L.C., but
Valerie, after stalking off in the opposite direction
for a few yards, again came sprinting up and bulled
through, clinging to the doorway, refusing to get in or
get out. That was the point at which I asked Jang to
call the cops from the phone booth.

When she'd left to do that -- now Val and I were
standing alone on the edge of the street -- I suddenly
feared Val would throw herself beneath one of the trucks
or buses roaring by a few feet away. I clamped a grip
on her arm.

"Don't you dare touch me! You have no right!"

"You're a fine one to talk about respecting
rights!"

Another skirmish: knots of people gathered at a
distance --

(Is this her coming now? Many fast-moving
footsteps on the Funston stairs, loud noise. I fear for
our lives) ---

Thursday 8

Betrayal or altruistic act? Self-preservation or
self-destruction? Today I took the ultimate step and

handed Valerie over to the Langley-Porter shrinks. In
front of a team of three "psychiatric aides" (all women)
in the third-floor "center" (a bland, surrealistic world
of dreamy head-cases gliding about soundlessly in blue
hospital gowns) Val and I told our separate stories, and
then the aides huddled by themselves in another room for
a few minutes as an armed guard stood between Val and
me, and then the aides returned to inform us of their
decision. On the basis of what we'd told them, they
said, they would hold Val for observation for several
hours and then release her to the care of her mother and
daily sessions with her shrink.

    "You betrayed me!" Val had hissed as the "team"
filed out to make their decision. She was referring to
my statement to them that, for me, a clean break would
be best. Earlier at Funston I'd told her I still had
some hope for us if she could "get herself together."
The aides properly noted the "ambiguity" here and
requested a clarification. Did I want a clean break or
did I want a reconciliation? Clean break, I said.

    When the conference was declared to be over, Val
clung to me tearfully rather than let the aides usher
her into that dreadful locked ward. (None of the aides
struck me as the type who'd have a prayer of
understanding our kind of conflict.) Several times
she'd told them that if I didn't want her, she preferred
to die. Now she reaffirmed she'd done it all in an
effort to win me back -- the hysterical scenes of the
previous twenty-four hours, the several weeks of the
vengeful escapade with Dennis, the spring terrors at
Funston, the Merino rampages, all of it -- and asked me
to wait for a call at the Bulldog. Then the guard
walked her to the door and closed it behind her.

    It shook me to the core. I've always dreaded the
time when we'd each try to justify our actions before
some third party, a "neutral" judge. I came out of the
experience feeling I'd indeed been a bastard to Valerie
all along. She was the one who'd loved and her crimes
were the crimes of passion; I was the shallow, arrogant,
condescending manipulator. How weak I was! I knew what

[Valedictory]

I'd've thought of myself had I been sitting in judgment
on us: "The girl clearly has problems, but her love goes
deep. The man has her mesmerized. He never did care
that much about her -- he just exploited her while
keeping her at arm's length. He deserves everything
he's gotten and more -- a lot more. Underneath his
facade of strength and self-control he must be wishy-
washy and totally self-centered or he'd've set her free
long ago and never let her come back onto the scene for
another round of desperate and wildly misconceived
attempts to win him back. All he had to do was tell her
to get out of his life and then insist she do it. But
he's incapable of that kind of selfless kindness. He's
a prisoner of his own guilt. His emotional troubles are
far more serious than hers."

That's the kind of martyr trip I'm on right now. I
ache for Valerie, what she's gone through, but even more
for myself. How could I turn her over to those
heartless robots? It's disgusting, what I've done. My
whole relationship with her. Glen, when are you going
to learn: you can't treat people that way! You can't
lead them on and then withhold yourself from them!

Well fuck that. I can't let myself be trapped in
the martyr's role. Can't! I know very well what the
mistakes I made were. I also know we've irreparably
damaged our relationship. There's no way back. The
best thing I can do now is let her go her own way, force
her to if necessary, coldly and cruelly, and try to let
the lessons of our failed love sink in. If I don't I'll
be crippled, closed off in my own world more than ever
before.

Now's the time to make the clean break the aides
asked about. I must do it. But it's extraordinarily
hard. I must wrestle with powerful impulses to return
to her. It's all sadly demented. I know that; I must
be strong and do what needs to be done. I've never been
able to do it before. I don't want to give up her love,
her spirit, her energy, her beauty. If she comes around
I must treat her with friendly coolness, even though
that's not what I'll feel. I'll ache for her, yearn to

reach out to her. Another great temptation will be to
plunge immediately into an all-out affair with someone
else -- Briana, maybe, or Jang, or (god forbid) Monica.
I mustn't do that. This time, for once, I'll act
wisely.

I haven't up until now. Last night, for example, I
couldn't bear to turn Valerie out. Carl, at his wit's
end, brought her over -- that was them making all that
noise when I stopped writing as she dashed up the steps
with him in hot pursuit -- and he told me he couldn't
look after her anymore. She was in desperately bad
shape, unable to walk or stand, incoherent at times,
ashen, her left knee and elbow scraped from a fall, her
eyes sometimes rolling up so far only the whites showed,
makeup smeared, clothes disheveled and stained with
vomit. She'd really taken the pills, she insisted, but
then she'd thrown up most of them. Carl had driven her
around for two hours looking for the L.C. parked outside
Jang's house on Potrero Hill (where she no longer
lives). He'd also tried to take Val to the emergency
room at U.C. Med Center, but she had refused to go in.

She repeated over and over that she'd been so
optimistic this afternoon, so excited about turning in a
report on the outrageous racist scene she'd witnessed at
the Fillmore Safeway where she was conducting the
Bulldog food-price survey; and then some "magnetic
force" had drawn her to the JCC (I'd told her I'd be
working out), she couldn't resist it, and then I was so
cold, so negative -- and when I said Jang had come with
me, it "blew my mind," she said, and she swallowed the
pills right there in front of me -- removing them from
the watch pocket of her jeans -- and she was enraged
that I didn't even notice her doing it: it was typical
of my negligence and inattention. She'd stolen the
pills from her mother earlier in the day. Her mother
had dissuaded her from her plan of killing herself
immediately; in fact her mother had given her new hope
by advising her to "leave him alone, get strong by
yourself, wait for him to come back to you." Valerie
came to the JCC nursing the wildly unrealistic hope she

and I could now become "intellectual friends."

By this time I was so exhausted, so desperate myself, so guilt-ridden, so helpless to think of anything else to do, I asked her to stay the night -- in the morning I'd take her to her usual shrink appointment at quarter to nine -- and when she came to bed we collapsed into each other's arms, both of us pitifully shaken. I made love to her then, trying desperately to express physically the tragic sorrow and pity for her I truly felt. She could scarcely move, but her face was transformed the whole time into an almost Madonna-like smile.

"I can feel, I can feel!" she kept crying out (her words blurred, barely decipherable), and, I remember vividly, "Let it all come out, baby, the hatred, the fears, the love: fuck me, baby, fuck me, fuck me, fuck me," and I wanted to, I wanted it all to come out, but it couldn't, of course, my body couldn't resolve in a moment all the terrible dilemmas of the past year and the hang-ups of a lifetime.

Thirty seconds after I came she was snoring.

In the morning I couldn't wake her. The time for her appointment neared and then passed. Despite numerous promptings she didn't stir. Suspecting she was faking it, I got up and dressed; suddenly she came alive and wouldn't let me leave the house.

"I thought I would die," she moaned. "Why didn't I die?"

Not only had she not thrown up the pills as she'd told me, she said now, but she'd gobbled another handful of aspirin and other assorted medications she'd found in the bathroom before coming to bed. I had to help her down the stairs to the L.C., her knees buckling several times. We went to her shrink's office, but he didn't have time to see us after we'd missed the appointment earlier and coolly suggested Langley-Porter. All along Valerie was refusing to move unless I promised not to "betray" her. I had to convince her over and over I believed there was still hope for us, and of course to me each repetition was simply one more demonstration of why there could be no more hope for us.

And then to Langley-Porter for the final scenes.
These I'll no doubt be reliving in my mind (like the
rest of these past couple of horrifying days -- these
several horrifying months) for the rest of my life.

*

From the hospital as we waited for the interviews
to begin I called Peggy at the Bulldog and explained why
I was late for work: Valerie and I had gotten into it
again. When I finally arrived at the office at two I
found myself facing a mountain of urgent tasks (built up
over the past several days because of my inability to
focus on anything as the Valerie crisis deepened). Half
a dozen people were waiting in the lobby to see me and
more were on the way. I tried to joke about it all,
shrug it off, but I was barely able to comprehend what
people were saying.

Making matters even worse, Monica was angry and
disappointed with me because yesterday I'd told her --
she'd come right out and asked where she stood with me
because I'd been noncommittal for so long after our
promising evening at her place -- told her I wouldn't be
able to see her again on a romantic basis because of the
new troubles I was going through with Val. And then
Judy Jacobi picked today to tell me her own troubles --
she's beginning to act much less guardedly toward me --
and Madel Roth, the Radcliffe Summer Project volunteer,
stepped up another notch or two her already outrageous
flirting. It was the Merino Mercury at its worst all
over again. I'd done it again! And then I had to call
Jang and tell her how everything had come out and
reassure her. God: I don't know how I got through it
all.

In addition, Mike is acting much more abrupt toward
me as it becomes evident I'm not exactly keeping the
Summer Project under the tight rein he and I would both
prefer. I thought the moment when I could leave --
eight o'clock -- would never come. Then I sped home
half-expecting Val to be waiting there for me: dreading
it, hoping for it. But she wasn't here, and then she

wasn't at her place when I drove back to check there,
and I had no way to reach her mother or her brother.

Forgotten in all this: my talk with Val at noon
yesterday at the S.F. Alliance offices at Bresker's
warehouse. If she broke our "no-contact" agreement at
the JCC last night, I had already done the same earlier,
at noon, so I didn't have much right to complain when
she did it later (technically, legalistically). Morbid
talk, for an hour as the SFA staff and volunteers
pretended to ignore us wrangling away over in the
corner. My bitterness poured out -- so pathetically sad
-- and she kept referring to passages in her journal in
an effort to show my interpretation had been wrong, she
had "never written that" (almost always she had, as I
showed her, reading her own words aloud numerous times;
at the most I may've misinterpreted her once or twice,
and I doubt even those instances). After having me read
aloud the passage she'd written after I first read her
journal in the L.C., she admitted it was untrue -- just
as I suspected, she'd never really planned for me to
read the journal. She'd been shocked when I came up and
said I had.

I questioned her closely about her relationship
with Dennis. (Hadn't she done just what she'd so
deplored me for doing, fucking us one right after the
other? Yes, she had, and in spades, but she wouldn't
admit it until I showed her the actual passages
describing it. Here she was fucking him in "a bloody
mess," here she was vomiting on my cock two hours later;
here she was begging him to manhandle her and fuck her
in the ass, here she was sucking me off in the L.C. in
the park barely an hour later; here she was fucking him
"righteously" all night long, here she was fucking me
"unable to feel a thing" in my bed at "the Castle" less
than two hours later.) It was completely over with him,
she said. Oh sure: I've heard that one before, Val.
No, this time it really was. Why this time as opposed
to the others? At first she said it was because she no
longer thought he was "a good man." Then I dragged
another version from her, and it seems a lot more likely

to be true.

For one thing, they'd been squabbling and fighting
a great deal -- she'd been "imposing my values on him,"
as she put it to me. And he was pissed because all she
ever talked about was me (or so she says to me). The
last couple of times she saw him they didn't even fuck.
(Doubtful.) No, all that was part of it but the main
reason was -- and this admission set her to weeping --
he'd fucked her over too, "just like you." And just
like Jim, I wondered? Just like her father? Just like
all the men in her life all the time -- all the men in
the world all the time? "That's exactly right! I'm
glad you can finally see it!"

Monday night, it turns out -- this was the night of
our big Bulldog Summer Project opening-night blowout --
she'd stayed much later with Dennis than the seven
o'clock which she'd told me before. His former old lady
had ripped him off for his car, stereo, money, and even
his drum set -- sounds intriguing, all this, but I
didn't learn anything more about it -- and he'd picked
up a waitress the previous night, Sunday, at the
Peppermint Tree (a block from the JCC) and she'd
promised to give him money Monday night when her shift
ended at two a.m., and shortly before then he made ready
to go out and collect it. Valerie protested violently
against this -- yes, protested with her fists and
kicking him in the balls or trying to -- but he
overpowered her and pointed out that she, Valerie,
didn't love him anyway and demanded she grow up, quit
the fighting or if she didn't he'd beat her really bad
and ruin her face for life with a razor blade, and he
assured her he'd be back by two-thirty. Val furiously
lectured him about how you can't get money like that
without obligating yourself, but he said if the waitress
didn't give him the money right away he would split and
return home.

Val waited for him until four-thirty a.m. and he
still hadn't shown up. Then she went out to Zim's and
sat there for three hours and then returned to Dennis's
place "just out of curiosity," as she cavalierly told

me, and he still wasn't back. That was when she vowed
she'd never see him again. (And an hour later she was
sucking me off in the L.C. in the park after telling me
she'd sat up all night at Zim's and had "finally gotten
my head together.")

"I can't trust anybody!" she wailed after spilling
out this sordid story.

I predicted she'd be back with him soon.

"No," she said resolutely. "It's not going to
happen."

Shortly after that I left, and the way I left, my
disgust, my perfunctory final embrace, my contemptuous
dismissal of her, all indicated I wouldn't be seeing her
again.

And then some six hours later the mad showdown at
the JCC.

That's it. Now comes the acid test. The torture
chamber. I'm closed in my room as Ron and Wade come and
go, and each time I think it's Valerie. She'll be out
to haunt me now, I know it. In my own mind she'll be
tracking me down and rushing at me from behind every
tree and telephone pole with fists churning and a death
rage in her eyes. Damn, damn, damn: get off the martyr
trip! Your life -- and hers -- may depend on it!

Friday 9

Well: I can breathe again. Tentatively and
shallowly and temporarily, it's true, but still, once
more the future starts to brighten. Many reasons, but
the main one concerns Valerie. Naturally.

(Brush the dust off the stereo and Otis Spann
bursts into "Blazing Fire.")

As I was driving away from Mac's this morning I saw
her approaching, walking up Irving half a block away. I
honked and pulled over, but she pretended not to see me.
Then she turned around and glared at me. Finally she
came walking slowly back and joined me in the front
seat. Glaring still. Angry because I'd "put her down."

At that point all my vows crumbled. I would've

673

said or done anything to win a smile from her. And what
it took to do that was this: a promise to think things
over for the next three weeks (she'd do the same) and
then we'd make a "clear decision," go or no go.

Three weeks? That's how long she'll be in Quebec
with her brother and his wife and their daughter. He
and Jon Tremont -- she called them both from Langley-
Porter -- got her released from the ward, having brought
her mother with them to sign the papers, and her brother
then offered to take her along on the vacation camping
trip he and Adele have had planned for months; in fact
he had asked her once before if she wanted to join them
(this was back in our spring terror days) and she'd
turned him down.

They left this afternoon. By now she's probably in
Oregon (on the way they're stopping off in Vancouver,
B.C., to see some French-speaking friends of Adele's,
before driving straight east through the mountains and
across the plains to Quebec).

Another breath, a little deeper.

The shrink agreed: it would be good therapy for Val
to achieve a "geographical separation."

Funny thing: as soon as I knew she was leaving (now
back in the L.C. parked on Irving this morning), my old
feelings for her kicked up. A revival of optimism (her
philosopher friend Gavin would surely approve). "Let's
both go for a rebirth," I said. "Of idealism, realism,
optimism -- the whole schmear." Sparkle returned to our
eyes. We couldn't kiss each other enough. When we met
again at noon (so she could give me her food stamps, on
her way to buying a new pair of panties to replace the
red ones ravaged over the past couple of weeks) and
stopped for lunch at Doggie Diner on Van Ness (she was
nervously preoccupied with last-minute details regarding
the trip) -- during this time, my god, we were two kids
in love again. It all seemed crystal clear.

"The reason we get so jealous is the sexual thing,"
she declared. "We've both got to stop performing and
start enjoying."

Right on, Val.

[Valedictory]

"What we have to do is exorcise all this bitterness."

Most definitely.

And yes, for that moment at least it actually seemed possible. She would come back from the trip with her head all straightened out thanks to the weeks of solitude and family togetherness and immersion in nature and freedom from tension, she'd be determined then to live a constructive life by herself, maintain some independence, become again the compassionate and kind (but not the closed-down and inhibited and cheerless) Valoshka of last fall. She had to run back to the L.C. three times for one last kiss. A last suck? A quickie fuck up at Funston? Damn, not enough time....

Quixotic, uproarious, unmanageable hearts. Hearts of fools, yes, but still: hearts.

On a gorgeous, sweet, frisky day.

(Last night she stayed "on the couch in the living room" at Tremont's place (same couch where they'd gotten it on several times in the past). What he had to tell her made a lot of sense, she thought. "You make too many rules for everybody, Valerie, and most of all for yourself." Tremont and his ol' lady have been together on and off for seven years -- off for most of the period when he was sleeping with Val some thirteen to sixteen months ago but mostly on again when he was sleeping with Val last summer and fall (though I didn't know about it then; and of course I had a few conflicting interests of my own at the time) -- and they, Jon and his wife, according to Val, "still look at each other with the excitement of the first meeting." When she asked Jon how this could be, he said it was because they'd learned to control their jealousies. Hearing this awakened some of Val's old idealism, she told me in the L.C. this morning. And apparently that awakening played a big part in why she was suddenly able to talk with me so excitedly about the future. Pretty slender reed to erect a future on, I'd say, but...stranger things have happened (not that I can cite any specific examples).)

She didn't even say goodbye to Dennis. Or did

she? I don't really know. Maybe that's why she didn't
have time for a quickie with me back at Funston? But
no, I don't think so. Or maybe I'm just trying to
control my jealousy Tremont style. The role model
that's good for the goose is also good for the gander.

So, at least we both have a three-week breathing
space. Or should I say all three of us do, Dennis
included? All four, Jang included?

Attempt at a mildly deep breath -- lean way, way
back and gaze "apodiste" style, head hanging down, at
the upper reaches of Mt. Moraga and a sparkly night sky.

(I should note too she offered to leave her journal
with me so I could read it more closely, until I
understood it all and her with it. "You let me spend
all the time I wanted to with yours. It might help you
think things over." But I turned her down. "I got the
message I was hoping for," I proclaimed with maximum
schmaltz, "in that last kiss -- your valedictory kiss.")

In a few minutes Ron and I are going out somewhere
to "hoist a few" (the first time I've heard that term in
ages -- and used so innocently!).

Jang called this afternoon, her tone restrained and
saddened. I got her off the line quick -- I'll stand
for no more of that kind of manipulating pressure,
however well-founded and well-intentioned it may be --
but I'll be seeing her tomorrow around noon and taking
her up to Steve Vaughn's summer place near Inverness.
We've had it arranged (on and off and on again) for more
than two weeks.

Monica stomped out of my office when I couldn't
respond to her renewed come-ons. She's going out of
town next week (also to Vancouver, B.C., as it happens).
I'm glad of that. I'm pretty sure we'll be able to
resume working amicably together after a cooling-off
period.

Then at the end of the afternoon Mike suddenly took
a strong interest in my experience at Empyrean Life. He
thinks an account of my work for Walt Roach on the
Chamber of Commerce housing plan for San Francisco would
make a tremendous story. "A blockbuster!" He's been

looking for something along those lines for years: a
firsthand "insider" account of the way big downtown
business interests work together to control the city.
I'll be plunging into it next week.

I even got my desk cleared off!

Best of all: I now have a chance to put into
practice my "revolution of habits." Free! No more
terror! No more fear I may be hit at any moment with
another suicide scene!

Valoshka, I'll love you forever for sparing me from
yourself, even if it's only for a little while.

Sunday 11 (X:10)

A cabin in the woods near Inverness, perched on the
side of a thickly wooded hill overlooking Tomales Bay,
delicious aroma of lamb roast in the air -- good fresh
air -- Bob Dylan croaking out "Sad-Eyed Lady" (of all
things) on the stereo, sun going down over the top of
the hill, Steve Vaughn working on roughly the seventieth
minute of a "ten-minute nap" (his health kick's wearing
him out), Jang chopping vegetables in her nifty homemade
white canvas shorts and top (looking ooh ooh ooh so
fine), Ari Bresker out somewhere on a walk with his
lover Leslie, his two ten-year-old daughters from his
previous marriage and their friend frisking about nearby
like colts. Birds chattering outside the window,
dappled sunlight turning the wooden deck columns into
naturalistic barber poles, leaves gently undulating:
truly an idyllic Sunday afternoon.

When Steve and I first arranged to come up here
last weekend, the idea was to do some hiking in the
hills and get to know each other better. Since then
some serious talk about legal questions pertaining to
the anti-highrise initiative has been added to the
agenda. Earlier this afternoon he and I hit on the idea
of tacking a five-year limit onto the initiative measure
before it's resubmitted to the voters. "We ought to
call Ari right now," he said. At that instant the phone
rang and it was Ari himself saying he'd be coming up

with the kids and Leslie, the British woman he's been
living with since he and his wife separated two years
ago (the same Leslie McDevitt who caught my eye earlier
this spring at an SFA meeting and whose London contacts
tracked down a copy of "The City That Waits to Die").

Bresker doesn't know yet I'm here. All of a sudden
I'm his shadow. In the past week we've bumped into each
other half a dozen times, the latest incident yesterday
at a Henry George conference at the Holiday Inn near
Fisherman's Wharf where Bresker presented the keynote
address -- titled "Can the City Be Saved?" -- and I
attended with Mike. The "Georgeists" believe Bresker is
one of their own but doesn't know it yet (their ideology
is founded on the notion that land ownership is the
basis of all economics and that all funds necessary to
pay for governance should derive from a so-called
"single tax" on landowners).

During the past twenty-four hours I've mostly been
sleeping or lying in the sun. At first Jang and I were
warily feeling each other out as a result of Valerie's
flip-out at the JCC and we weren't able to respond to
each other very well -- no surprise there -- but we took
a long walk together on the beach after dinner last
night and were able to work things out and then we
sealed the deal in the best way possible in our little
fir-lined bedroom as Steve snored in the next room.
Today she casually but also carefully brought up Funston
again: she'd love to stay up there sometime "for a week
or two" before she leaves for Seoul. Of all the places
she's lived in or even visited during her years in S.F.
and for that matter the whole U.S. of A., Funston's her
favorite. We had so many good times there! And given
the events of the past few weeks I'm thinking: why not?
Surely Valerie would agree she owes us one, and I mean
both of us. Or even if she wouldn't, I say she does and
that's the basis on which I'll act.

But here they are, Bresker and entourage rolling in
from the woods....

END

www.ingramcontent.com/pod-product-compliance
Lightning Source LLC
Chambersburg PA
CBHW070708100726
47907CB00001B/95